GODS AND DRAGONS

GODS
AND
DRAGONS

WAKE THE DRAGON, BOOK 3

KEVIN J. ANDERSON

A TOM DOHERTY ASSOCIATES BOOK · NEW YORK

This is a work of fiction. All of the characters, organizations, and events portrayed
in this novel are either products of the author's imagination
or are used fictitiously.

GODS AND DRAGONS

Copyright © 2021 by WordFire, Inc.

Maps by Bryan G. McWhirter

A Tor Book
Published by Tom Doherty Associates
120 Broadway
New York, NY 10271

www.tor-forge.com

Tor® is a registered trademark of Macmillan Publishing Group, LLC.

Library of Congress Cataloging-in-Publication Data

Names: Anderson, Kevin J., 1962- author.
Title: Gods and dragons / Kevin J. Anderson.
Description: First edition. | New York : Tor, 2022. | Series: Wake the dragon ;
book 3 | "A Tom Doherty Associates book."
Identifiers: LCCN 2021034621 (print) | LCCN 2021034622 (ebook) |
ISBN 978-1-250-30220-5 (hardcover) | ISBN 978-1-250-30221-2 (ebook)
Subjects: GSAFD: Fantasy fiction.
Classification: LCC PS3551.N37442 G63 2022 (print) |
LCC PS3551.N37442 (ebook) | DDC 813'.54—dc23
LC record available at https://lccn.loc.gov/2021034621
LC ebook record available at https://lccn.loc.gov/2021034622

Our books may be purchased in bulk for promotional, educational, or business use.
Please contact your local bookseller or the Macmillan Corporate and Premium
Sales Department at 1-800-221-7945, extension 5442, or by email at
MacmillanSpecialMarkets@macmillan.com.

First Edition: January 2022

Printed in the United States of America

0 9 8 7 6 5 4 3 2 1

To Terry Goodkind

For showing me the scope and possibilities of epic fantasy,
for writing advice and elaborate brainstorming, for great conversations
about race cars and rugged wilderness, and for years of friendship.
I'll raise a sword high.

Ishara

Fulcor Island

Sérépol

Ishiki

Kassah

Salimbul

Mormosa

Tarizah

dhabban

Khosun

darkha

Prirari

Sistralta

Tamburdin

Janhari

hétthrén lands

BGM

BlueWater River

Crickyth River

Konac's Castle

Convera

BGM

Fulcor

I. Docks
II. Barracks
III. Cistern
IV. Armory
V. Cistern
VI. Keep

VII. Main Cistern
VIII. Dining Hall
IX. Barracks
X. Cistern
XI. Parade Grounds
XII. Review Stand

BGM

GODS AND DRAGONS

1

ᔕᐤ

"Y OU just declared war," Penda said. Her face was drawn and weary, but still beautiful to him under the stars on a night that had been filled with bloodshed and dragons.

"I had no choice." King Adan reached out to stroke her dark, sweat-streaked hair. The smell of smoke lingered in the air.

She cradled their newborn daughter in her arms, and Adan wrapped both of them in his embrace. He relished the intimacy, the peace, knowing it might be his last calm moment for a long time to come.

Pulling away, he turned to survey the devastated Utauk camp: fires from the ravages of the dragon and the sandwreths, torn tents, smashed wagons, mangled horses, scattered and broken bodies.

With businesslike determination, Utauks moved around in the firelight gathering the sandwreth weapons strewn on the ground. They would take the spears, swords, and pikes away, disposing of them where they would never be found. The enemy corpses had been burned in a hot pyre to leave no evidence. All human lives would be forfeit if the sandwreth queen ever guessed that King Adan Starfall had murdered her brother.

"This camp must scatter." He spoke mainly to his wife, but loud enough for others to hear. "We have to leave soon."

Hale Orr, Penda's father, stood with his wrist stump propped on his hip. "*Cra!* The Utauk tribes know how to pack up and disappear. That's what we do." He worked his jaw and spat on the ground, then looked at his son-in-law with new admiration. "I despise the sandwreths, Starfall, especially that vile one who wanted to take my baby granddaughter. But I never thought you'd kill him." He let out a booming laugh. "Skewered him right through the chest!"

Adan flinched at the loud statement. He wasn't a cold-blooded murderer, and his action had not been impulsive. He had hesitated long enough to be certain, and then he had thrust his sword through Quo's heart. "I'm the king of Suderra, and I need to protect my people. The wreths are the greatest danger we face."

Hale gestured to indicate the damaged camp. "Dragons notwithstanding."

"You protected me," Penda said, "and our child."

Quo's sandwreth war party had come north on the pretext of helping King

Kollanan fight the frostwreths, but his real purpose had been to find Penda, to seize her and the unborn child for Queen Voo. Adan had also learned that the sandwreths were hiding a secret human slave camp in the desert. So when Quo was badly injured by the dragon, Adan had been unable to control his anger. He'd more than enough reason to kill the vile man.

"Yes, I declared war," he said, "but the sandwreths don't know it yet. We will keep the secret for as long as we can and turn their own ways against them."

"Voo is treacherous enough," Hale said. "We can follow her example."

A loose auga, one of the wreths' sturdy and stupid reptilian mounts, wandered through the camp, lost and disoriented. Two Utauk teens chased the creature, but it snapped at them and bounded off into the forest. Several other augas lay on the ground, slain in the attack.

"Leave it," Adan called. Queen Voo would eventually realize that something had happened to her brother, but a few wandering augas would give her no further information.

Eventually, after the incredibly long night, dawn suffused the eastern hills. "It is a new day," Adan said, his thoughts still ricocheting around. "We are at war . . . and I am a father." He bent down to kiss Penda on the forehead, then the little girl they had named Oak. "Both things are terrifying in their own way."

Xar, Penda's green ska, circled overhead with an annoyed cry. The reptile bird mischievously harassed the young squire Hom, who flailed his hands to shoo him away.

Adan's few soldiers helped put out the last fires, wary in case some other attack appeared out of the forest. Two Utauk men fixed a broken wheel on a cart, and others mended damaged harnesses for the horses. Their efficient movements signaled an urgent desire to be gone as soon as possible.

The wreth funeral pyre had burned down to coals. Utauk men and women raked through the ashes with sticks, then used rocks to bash any lumps to powder. A second funeral pyre, enclosed within a perfect circle of stones, had cremated the Utauks killed in the night's battle; they were treated with much more honor and respect.

Two cookfires heated tea water and cooked a grain porridge. Several mothers rummaged in their packs, adding dried fruit and crushed honeycombs to sweeten the mash. Though Penda had just given birth the night before, she tried to help with the camp work, but Adan insisted that she rest.

Penda sat on a log beside the central campfire, joining old Shella din Orr, the matriarch of the Utauk tribes. The old woman's arm was bandaged from an injury she had suffered during the attack, but she did not look the least bit ruffled.

"It was a nice campsite," Shella said. "I might have stayed another week, but we will move out two hours after daybreak. I'll lead the heart camp far from here, maybe east over the Dragonspine Mountains. I haven't been to Convera in ten years."

"That's far," Penda said. "Are you sure you're up for the trip?"

The crone snorted. "I travel all the time. What difference does it make if I travel in a straight line or just wander in circles?"

With her finger Penda traced a ring around her heart. "The beginning is the end is the beginning."

Shella din Orr repeated the common phrase. When Adan delivered bowls of the porridge, the matriarch smacked her lips. "There aren't many things I can enjoy with so few teeth."

Taking a seat, Adan grew serious. "We will go in different directions." He looked to his wife. "It has been long enough. You need to go home, take our daughter, and be safe within the walls of Bannriya."

"I doubt any place is safe from dragons and wreths," she said, then picked up on his tone. "Are you not going with me?"

Captain Elcior stepped up to report, accompanied by the Banner guard Seenan, Hom's older brother. "We are ready to depart, Sire. The three of us can ride fast and hard all the way to Norterra."

When Penda gave him a questioning look, Adan explained, "I'm going north to Fellstaff. Kollanan has already struck against the frostwreths, and now I've killed sandwreths. From the start, Suderra and Norterra recognized the danger of the ancient race, and we have to prepare to fight together." His thoughts soured. "Even if my brother in Convera continues to be fixated on the Isharans."

Penda gave him a solemn look. "You and your uncle may think of grand wars, but do not forget about Glik and the slave camp. Another secret the sandwreths are keeping . . ." Her face hardened. "And another thing I want to take from Queen Voo."

Adan had been trying to find a way to liberate the isolated slave camp. Taking action would surely provoke a fierce retaliation, but if it was going to be open war, he had to consider his options differently. "I'll talk to Kollanan and discuss how we could do it. If it comes to direct battle, Voo just might slaughter all those poor captives out of spite, just so we can't free them." He stroked her cheek, lowered his voice. "I promise I'll think of a way."

She nodded, accepting his words.

Adan continued, "I don't want to leave you, especially not now. But I need you safe, and our baby needs shelter."

Shella din Orr made a rough sound in her throat. "You think the Utauks can't protect her? Did you not send your wife to travel with us, just so the wreths couldn't find her?"

"This is different," Adan said.

"Everything is different," Penda replied. "I believe our daughter would be safe enough among the Utauks, but in times like these Suderra must have its queen if the king is riding out to make war plans." The baby fussed in her arms, and she shifted position. "You and I will each do what we must, Starfall."

With a gnarled finger, Shella drew another circle around her heart.

Adan finished his porridge and stood. Seenan had saddled their horses. Hale Orr promised to accompany his daughter back to Bannriya. "We'll ride fast enough, Starfall. *Cra,* I haven't slept in my own bed in weeks."

Penda gave him a teasing laugh. "You are an Utauk, Father. You said the land itself serves as your bed."

"That was before I came to appreciate the comforts of a soft mattress, dear heart."

Hom presented himself to Adan. "I will ride with you, Sire, to take care of your needs on the rough journey."

Adan could see the worry in the young squire's face. He was eager—too eager—but not particularly hardened to the trail, and Adan was sure that he, Seenan, and Elcior could ride faster without him. He turned gravely to the boy. "It's more important for a squire to tend to the queen and our baby. She'll definitely need your help." Hom's face showed immediate relief.

Penda teased, "And you must also help keep Xar company."

From a branch nearby the mischievous reptile bird made a low burbling sound that alarmed the squire. Nevertheless, the boy squared his shoulders, swallowed hard, and nodded. "I will do my duty for my king and queen, and for Suderra."

By the time full morning arrived in the scarred camp, the Utauks were ready to depart. Seenan and Captain Elcior were mounted and waiting.

Adan kissed his wife, held her for a long moment, and stared with joy into little Oak's perfect face. He was full of wonder and feared for the future. He and all of his people would no longer be pawns. They would fight to control their own fate.

2

༄

THE cold, white expanse was anything but silent. Sunlight from a shatteringly clear sky glinted off silver-crystal armor and long, sharp weapons. The pale-skinned, ivory-haired frostwreths converged on top of the glacier.

Koru, now Queen Koru, stood regal and terrifying beside her battle sleigh. She was a skilled warrior, trained in ruthless combat, but she also held herself with the haughtiness of pure noble blood.

Watching her from where he huddled in the sleigh, Birch found the new frostwreth queen sharp, intimidating, but not so frightening as her mother, Onn. The boy's cheeks were so cold, the skin had gone numb, and curls of frost rose up each time he exhaled. He still had his tattered blanket, but Koru had covered him with heavy white oonuk pelts, as well.

Out in the open, Koru stood by her mages, nobles, and handpicked warriors, watching the thousands of frostwreths file out onto the frozen expanse. Glancing down at the boy, she flashed him a mysterious smile, then turned to her army. She held the spear of Dar, an ancient artifact with bloodstains on its serrated head. Her voice was as penetrating as a winter wind.

"Frostwreths! Celebrate what we have accomplished, but know that it is only the beginning. I am your new queen, and I am your future—not just for the wreths, but for our world." She raised her weapon, impaling the sky.

A howl of enthusiasm rumbled across the snow. In their harnesses, the shaggy wolf-steeds snarled as if they could already smell blood in the air.

"My mother led you astray, but I will lead you forward. You have been restless long enough. Our wreth army is assembled." Koru jabbed the spear upward, provoking another round of cheers and battle cries. She looked sideways at Birch and said in a hard, low voice, "Join me, boy! I want them to see you at my side."

Birch didn't understand her. At first he had thought Koru would kill him as soon as she discovered he had killed Queen Onn with the spear, but instead Koru was pleased. His action had made her the new queen of the frostwreths, and it was their secret.

Pushing the furs aside, but still clutching his woolen blanket, Birch climbed out of the sleigh. He no longer felt the bitter chill as much. He followed the pale queen across the white expanse to a deep blue crevasse that plunged into frozen depths.

A frostwreth mage, Elon, joined them at the edge of the fissure. His pale scalp was patchy and scarred from where he'd been burned in a dragon attack. Elon was a close companion and advisor as the new queen consolidated her rule. Watching the strange, bald man in his blue leather robes, Birch felt the magic resonate through him. Since Koru had accepted the human boy as her companion, her pet, the mage ignored him.

"We will discard your mother's remnants, my queen, so that the frostwreths can focus on their new purpose." He raised his hand in a signal to the crowded ranks behind them. Six small-statured drones scuttled along the trampled path from the ice palace, carrying a pallet with a body wrapped in drab cloth. Queen Onn—the woman who had tormented Birch for so long.

The badly treated drones did as they were instructed and showed an uncharacteristic exuberance as they carried the body to the edge of the crack.

Behind them, the frostwreth ranks stood absolutely still. Koru frowned at her mother's shrouded corpse, as if even this minimal ceremony was a waste of time. She used her sharp nails to tear at the fabric that covered Onn's face, and revealed the slack, sunken features of the dead queen.

Birch peered at the once powerful, bitter woman who had caused so much harm. He remembered the shock on Onn's face when he'd killed her. Now, the dead queen's expression showed nothing, nothing at all, but a shiver raced through him.

Koru smiled at the boy in their shared secret, then she snapped at the drones, "What are you waiting for? Dump her in, or should I make you jump in as well?"

The drones upended the pallet, and the wrapped form tumbled into the cold blue emptiness. Birch felt a fierce satisfaction to see her vanish into the cold depths. The drones chittered among themselves, then tossed the pallet over the edge as well.

The boy kept his expression blank, though he understood what the drones were saying. In their own way, they celebrated the death of the awful queen, who had slaughtered so many of their kind. Birch hoped the new queen would be kinder, and he made up his mind to help the drones if he could.

Koru took his hand as they both looked over the edge of the precipice. Her grip was cold, but held him steady. Seeing the long plunge, Birch felt dizzy.

Straightening, the queen glanced at Mage Elon. "Make sure that she stays down there . . . and that no one can do anything foolish." She glanced back toward the wreth warriors, fixed on the muscular Irri—Onn's lover. He had been a blizzard of anger and undirected vengeance ever since her assassination. Now, he returned her stare coldly.

The mage knelt and pressed his palms against the ice, extending magic into the fissure. A resonant stirring came from deep below as ice calved off, piling countless tons of frozen rubble onto the discarded corpse.

When the ice settled again, Koru spoke in a magic-amplified voice that resounded across the troops. "My mother forgot the words that Kur gave us. She lost sight of our mission, the mission of all wreths. We have been charged with slaying Ossus. The *dragon* is our enemy. Only with our combined strength can wreths hope to achieve our purpose."

Irri crossed his bare arms, and his long hair flowed in the frigid breezes. "Why should we follow you simply because you murdered our queen?"

Koru gave him a withering glare. "That is how wreths have always chosen their leaders. I proved I am stronger than Onn." She glowered at Irri, and the indignant warrior simmered for a long moment before he turned away, his gaze distant, as if snowblind.

Birch felt his heart race, still expecting someone to discover and expose his part in Onn's death. Although Koru had taken the credit and the blame, and the crown, Birch himself had thrust the spear through the queen. Onn had abused him, ignored him, underestimated him. She had commanded the frostwreths when they killed his parents, his little brother, everyone he knew. Birch remembered holding the spear shaft, how it had felt when the deadly point pierced her white skin, plunged into her vital organs. He still couldn't quite believe he had done it, but it made him feel strong. Made him feel *warm*.

And Irri, this arrogant warrior, was the one who had murdered Birch's grandmother Tafira. Irri had gleefully displayed images to Onn, in front of the boy. Birch hated them all. He pulled the blanket tight around his shoulders, more in an attempt to hide than to block out the cold winds.

Koru's voice boomed out so loudly that distant hunks of snow and ice broke loose from slopes and pattered down in avalanches. "In order to defeat Ossus, we will need the strength of *all wreths*—both frostwreths and sandwreths."

A grumble of displeasure rippled through the gathered army.

"Sandwreths?" Irri bellowed. "You expect us to make peace with the children of Raan? You want us to fight beside them? As friends?"

Koru responded with an icy smile. "Sandwreths will never be our friends." She spread her arms. "Therefore, I will march our army south and kill Queen Voo myself. Then I will rule all wreths, for our united purpose."

The idea took the army by surprise. Birch shivered, and the listless drones stood blinking, confused and worried. A great many of them worked inside the ice palace and the glacier warrens, and Birch did not think the small creatures would fare well in a war.

As Koru's words sank in, a rising sound of understanding grew among the cold army. The queen basked in it as she led Birch back to the sleigh, smiling. She said in a low voice to him, "The best way to command loyalty is to give your people what you want and make them think it is their own desire." She nodded to him. Knowing that the new queen was trying to teach him, he nodded back.

Koru climbed into the seat beside him and barked a command. The drones took up the harness ropes, turned the battle sleigh around, and plodded back to the palace.

In her vaulted throne room, Koru led the boy to the small fur-covered block of ice next to her throne and instructed the drones to bring them food. She offered him a thick oonuk fur, but Birch felt warm enough with just his blanket. He sat in silence. Since his capture, Birch had learned to draw no attention to himself. It was the way to survive.

Koru, though, noticed him. He kept his thoughts to himself, not sure that the queen actually wanted conversation. For a time, she paced in front of the throne that her mother had occupied. She carried the ancient spear to the mounting hooks on the wall, but reconsidered. Instead, she took the throne and kept the weapon with her, holding the long shaft across her lap. She seemed distant for a long moment, then turned her quicksilver eyes to Birch. An instinctive chill ran through him.

"You might be very important, boy," she said. "Far more important than I ever imagined."

3

On the frozen shores of Lake Bakal, mourners gathered to say farewell to the slain queen of Norterra.

King Kollanan wore regal furs and leather chest armor covered with a blue doublet that had been Tafira's favorite. He'd left his crown on the bureau back in Fellstaff Castle, and now his gray-streaked hair drifted loose on the chill breezes. In this moment, he was not the king, but a grieving husband.

As people lined up for the remembrance on the forested lakefront, Koll stared across the dark ice surface of the lake to the rubble of the frostwreth fortress, remembering the peaceful village that had once stood there.

His thoughts turned inward to a memory of his beautiful Tafira, unable to shake that last image of her body tied to a tree, her throat cut by a frostwreth blade. Kollanan's heart had shattered like ice in a spring thaw. Now the cracking and settling of enormous fortress blocks seemed to resound with pain.

A Norterran honor guard had marched with him to Lake Bakal bearing the queen's wrapped body on a pallet draped with dried honeysuckle, Tafira's favorite flower. The sweet scent brought a brief smile to his face, followed by a resounding emotional blow. That smell would forever be a reminder, a trigger.

The king's three Bravas stood behind him, all clad in black capes and fine-mail armor, waiting. Elliel, the cinnamon-haired Brava with a rune of forgetting tattooed on her face, stood next to Lasis, a blond-haired man who had served Norterra for decades. The third Brava was the blunt-featured Gant, who had only recently sworn his bond here. Thon, the enigmatic wreth stranger with great powers and greater secrets, remained at the edge of the lake among the silver pines, watching in silence.

Koll heard the people rustle around him, though their voices were no louder than whispers. Their grief was heavy like the overcast sky. He drank in the sight of all of his soldiers, as well as so many mourning villagers, some of whom had traveled for days to pay their respects for their queen.

His vassal lords were shaken, wrapped in a growing dread of what the wreths, or what Konag Mandan, would do to their kingdom. Lord Bahlen looked particularly disturbed. Queen Tafira had been murdered by frostwreths, while many of Bahlen's subjects had been killed by human soldiers, Commonwealth soldiers—supposed allies.

Mandan had done that, Koll's own nephew. Konag Mandan had sent his vengeful army to attack the unsuspecting town of Yanton, out of spite. Many of the refugees were still housed in the nearby wreth ruins, where they had mounted a last defense.

People shifted and began to mutter. Though Koll didn't feel the frigid temperature, others were growing cold and restless. But he would not be hurried, not in this.

Finally, even though he was not ready, would never be ready, he sucked in a long breath, letting the cold sear his throat and lungs, but it could not numb the aching scar on his heart. He raised his war hammer high, and the remembrance party fell into a deeper hush.

He stepped out onto the ice of the lake. "We are here to remember the life and legacy of Tafira, queen of Norterra, and my—" His voice cracked. He stood for a long moment, struggling with the whirling sounds of sadness inside his head, and he breathed again, focused his thoughts. "—my wife, my treasure, my prize from the Isharan war thirty years ago."

He glanced at his vassal lords Ogno, Vitor, Alcock, Iber . . . all of whom had fighting forces ready to defend their counties and their kingdom. Now, however, they faced another enemy, an unnecessary enemy. Their own konag.

Kollanan went to where Tafira lay wrapped in dyed silks with Isharan designs. For all the years she'd been his queen here, he had been convinced the people accepted her, but Koll had been blind to the hatred and prejudice that some of them held in their hearts. Tafira had seen it, yet she ignored it for his sake. Captain Rondo and his brusque escort soldiers from Convera had been filled with spite, though. They had abducted Tafira while Kollanan and his troops fought to save Yanton during Konag Mandan's punitive strike.

Standing at the edge of the ice, he continued, "My wife, my queen was everything to me, and I know she meant much to all of you. In these times, we face the threat of the frostwreths. Their great war may well destroy our world." He lowered his voice, felt infinite disappointment. "I did not think we needed to fear that our own people would become new enemies."

He raised his bearded chin, silently reminding himself that he was their leader, even if he felt broken inside. Yes, it had actually been frostwreths who murdered Tafira, but Rondo and his men had put her into such danger. Kollanan the Hammer had enough reason to hate and blame them both.

"We Norterrans must be on our guard from all sides. I had hoped for unity and trust, that humans could fight together against a common threat. The wreth races are already tearing each other apart, and now it seems that humans are hell-bent on doing the same." His voice became a rasp. "After all, our wreth creators made us to be just like them."

He stroked the fabric that covered Tafira's face. The scattered honeysuckle blossoms were dry and delicate, and a few petals blew away. He remembered exactly how lovely his wife was, as beautiful to him now as when he'd rescued her as a young girl from an Isharan village—her dark hair, full lips, deep brown eyes, the smile she gave him when he deserved it, the furrows on her brow when she worried about him.

He raised his voice so that it echoed around the frozen lake, the lost village, the destroyed fortress. "She loved Lake Bakal! Our daughter lived in this place, our grandsons, so many people . . . so many gone. Tafira will rest here beneath the waters. That is where she would want to be. Whenever we look at this lake, we can remember her, and all those others lost." He felt anger twisting within him. "All those others lost . . ."

Frostwreth warriors had wiped out these people because they were *in the way.*

He heard a clatter and rustle as his soldiers stood at attention, raised their shields, pressed their boots together. He turned to Lasis, Elliel, and Gant. "Bravas!"

The three took the golden cuffs they carried at their waists and secured them around their wrists. The metal prongs bit into their veins, spilling blood down their skin. "The brighter the fire, the longer the memory lasts," Koll said.

Together the Bravas called upon their half-breed magic, summoned fire that engulfed each cuffed hand and extended into a fiery blade. They marched ahead of the king onto the lake ice with their ramers shining like beacons.

Uninvited, Thon hurried after them to remain close to King Kollanan and Elliel, curious about the grieving process, as if he didn't understand exactly what was happening. Four handpicked retainers carried the queen's bier onto the lake ahead of a group of vassal lords.

Reaching a mirror-smooth section of ice, the three Bravas stopped. With the open lake around him, Kollanan absorbed the view, the snowcapped mountains, the silver-pine forests. Yes, this was a good place for her to rest. He knew she always felt at peace here.

The Bravas marked off an invisible rectangle and plunged the three ramer blades down into the ice. The searing fire sizzled through the frozen surface, and steam flashed into the air. The blades cut deeper, down to the water. Once they had carved a large enough hole, the Bravas cut the ice into smaller pieces and hauled them out, creating a blank patch of water like a deep blue grave.

"Tafira will like that," Koll said and turned back to the bier. "She loved this place, so peaceful." His vassal lords stood at his side, reminding him of their loyalty. Thon crouched by the open hole in the ice, touched the cold water, then stood and stepped back. Elliel gestured for him to stand beside her, out of the way.

Kollanan gazed at the wrapped body for a long moment, lost. Tafira had been his dearest treasure for three decades, but Mandan's hatred for Isharans had created this situation. Part of Koll's heart felt the same need for vengeance because Isharans had butchered his brother Conndur even as he sought an alliance with them against the wreths. But Tafira was not responsible for that.

"Farewell, beloved," he said.

The retainers placed the weighted bier in the water, and as soon as they released her, Tafira's body sank into the inky blue depths. Kollanan kept watching, and the colors of her winding fabrics stayed visible for a long time. Dried honeysuckle blossoms floated on the water. In the deep cold, a sheen of ice quickly covered the open water, and the tears froze on Kollanan's face.

Thon went to the edge again. "Let me help." He touched the dark, cold water and summoned his strange magic. In a flash, the lake froze solid in a smooth white patch, sealing over the mark as if it had never been, but the mark would always remain on his heart.

Kollanan let out a shuddering sigh. "Thank you, Thon."

His thoughts continued to spin in circles within circles. Frostwreths had killed her, had destroyed the village at Lake Bakal, and still held his grandson captive. But Mandan was just as responsible for Tafira's death, punishing Kollanan for choosing to defend his own kingdom rather than volunteering his army to fight a reckless war against Ishara.

Koll had many different targets for his anger and vengeance, far too many to choose.

Taking notes in a bound journal she had brought from Fellstaff, Shadri stood at the lakeside and chronicled everything that happened at the remembrance. It was her job as legacier to recount the life of Queen Tafira. The scholar girl felt deeply sad, though she tried to be objective. She lived for knowledge, preserved details so that others could learn, and Queen Tafira had been her mentor, giving Shadri access to everything a curious young woman could want. The queen had been kind and understanding . . . and now she was gone, kidnapped by humans, murdered by wreths.

No matter how much Shadri learned about natural science, or history, or the world itself, she simply didn't understand people.

During the remembrance ceremony, the king's tense body projected a silent shout of sadness. Kollanan the Hammer had been a great ruler, concerned about the dangers his people faced, and he had carried the burden with grace. The uncertain fate of his grandson had left a dark hole in his heart, though, and now she feared the terrible loss of Tafira might break him completely.

Beside her, the awkward mop-headed boy Pokle huddled in a woolen cloak and tattered gloves. He thrust his hands into his pockets and stood close to Shadri as if to share her warmth. Uneasy and shivering as he looked around the dark woods. "I'm not afraid to be here anymore. I can see that the frostwreths are gone now. They'll never come back to Lake Bakal, will they?"

She looked at the fortress rubble not far down the curve of the lake. "That was a resounding defeat. Besides, we still have Thon."

While the vassal lords and King Kollanan returned to their waiting horses, Shadri stayed near Pokle as he wandered along the shore, bending to inspect the pilings of a destroyed dock, the collapsed remnants of an old house. "I remember these places. I grew up here. The frostwreths just . . . erased it all."

"People could return here now, build a new village," Shadri said. "It seems like a very nice place."

He nodded. "Lots of fish in the lake . . . rabbits, squirrels, and deer in the woods. In springtime I know where to find morel mushrooms, and if we look under the fresh snow, we might find winterberries." He blinked. "It would be nice to . . . just to be normal again."

Shadri didn't think "normal" would be so easy to come by, but she didn't dampen the boy's spirit. Despite his lack of learning or imagination, Pokle possessed practical skills. He had survived out in the frozen forest after the wreths obliterated everything else.

The king's remembrance group prepared for the ride back to Fellstaff, and the other vassal lords would return to defend their lands in case the frostwreths attacked or Konag Mandan sent another punitive force.

Shadri and Pokle stayed in the trees, listening to the whisper of evergreens. She heard a rustle of branches and saw small figures flitting in the shadows. Pokle, immediately on his guard, touched the small knife at his waist. Shadri realized that he was ready to protect her, and it made her feel warm inside.

She quickly recognized the diminutive gray-skinned figures. "Just drones, the ones that escaped from the ice fortress. They must have been living in the forest all this time." The creatures scurried closer, peering at them from a safe distance. "King Kollanan says they're friends. They saw so much among the frostwreths and understood wreth daily lives and aspirations. I'd like to talk with them."

Pokle moved branches and pushed forward. "You there! Come closer." The drones bolted off like a flock of startled pigeons. "Maybe next time," he said with a sigh. "We'll be quieter."

Elliel touched the healing ramer marks on her wrist. The sticky blood had hardened into a scab. She put away the metal cuff and donned her gauntlets.

She felt a heavy sadness from the remembrance ceremony, along with a dread of what other dangers might come soon.

Thon walked up, leading both of their horses, and he swung into the saddle. His face had a perplexed expression, deeper than the soft optimism and fascination he often showed. "I am trying to understand the enormity of all I have experienced, Elliel. I feel oddly hollow." He touched his face, unconsciously tracing the tattoo that was almost identical to her own. Though Elliel had her memories and her past back now, Thon still had no inkling of who or what he was. "The emptiness I feel comes from not knowing . . . but the emptiness in King Kollanan comes from knowing too much."

He shook his head, and her heart went out to him. His features were so perfectly formed, the very definition of handsome.

Thon continued, "I am sad for what happened to Queen Tafira, sad for what Konag Mandan and Lord Cade did at Yanton, sad that the frostwreth queen won't let Birch go back to his grandfather. I have great powers in me, I can feel it. You have seen it. Therefore, should I not be able to fix more of these painful problems? When I froze the lake over Tafira's body, it was . . . it was so inadequate." He seemed to be waiting for Elliel to give him answers.

"Many of us, perhaps to a lesser extent, get the same feeling—Bravas, warriors, kings . . ." she said, giving him a sad smile. "You're both powerful and helpless."

"Powerful helplessness," he mused.

She let him work through his turbulent thoughts. Thon had greater powers than anyone she had ever met, yet he was sensitive and innocent. His heart had learned much from her. He was a generous and caring lover, and Elliel cherished him.

"After what happened to Queen Tafira, I feel worried about you." Thon blinked at her. "One unwise decision by a king or warrior could bring harm to you."

Elliel's heart warmed to hear his concern, but she tried to reassure him. "I've been threatened before, and I had to fight. You know I can take care of myself. Why are you worried now?"

"It is not completely rational. I do not understand it."

"Well, I don't understand you either," she said, "but that doesn't stop me from feeling love and respect for you."

He smiled. "Wreths do not teach love and respect. They treat humans as tools to be used and discarded. They care only about waking the dragon and remaking the world, though they do not understand why. As far as I could tell, they do not even read their own histories, so they cannot know what was truly foretold long in the past."

"You and Shadri are working hard to translate and record all of the old documents," Elliel said, hoping to encourage him.

As they rode off following the king's procession, Thon's voice sounded small and troubled. "I am at a loss. I do not know what to do."

Elliel gave him a reassuring touch on the shoulder as their horses plodded onward. "That's what it always feels like to be human."

4

THE nightmares were painful and permanent in Konag Mandan's mind, and he didn't know how to get rid of them. Each time he tried to purge the horrific visions, they returned worse than before.

Still, he painted again. Maybe this time he would burn it out of him.

Vapors of turpentine and thick oil paint mingled as he daubed his brush, swirling scarlet and brown pigments to get the right sickening color of blood. Normally, such odors would have soothed him, but now they only reminded him of the nauseating stench of blood, burned hair, and skin. The smell had struck him full in the face when he'd burst into his father's chamber on Fulcor Island to witness what the Isharan animals had done to him.

Mandan stood in front of his easel, holding the brush with an unsteady grasp. His royal suite in Convera Castle was a spacious room with a large fireplace, a sitting area with a divan, and a balcony that opened to the cool autumn air. His walls were covered with maps of the three kingdoms, but he had plenty of room for his artistic endeavors.

On the canvas he had already sketched out the basics, trying to capture the ghost images in his mind. When his hand shook, the brush produced a skittering lightning bolt of brown and red that strayed outside his guidelines. He stared at the pale canvas, the charcoal lines, a complete mess. All the details were so vivid in his mind, but thus far he had not been able to convey them here. He was a painter! Mandan of the Colors!

He closed his eyes, envisioned his father lying chopped to pieces on the guest bed, blood spattered about as if a child had thrown a tantrum with red paint. Mandan clamped his mouth shut to seal off a scream, damping it to a muffled moan inside. After sucking in deep breaths, he tried to paint again, focusing instead on depicting the bed, the tangled sheets . . . all soaked in blood! He stopped again.

By putting these nightmares down on canvas, he hoped to empty them from his mind, but it wasn't working. Conndur's brutal murder would overwhelm anything else in his father's legacy: his wise leadership, his adventures, his marriage to the lovely red-haired Queen Maire. No, Conndur the Brave's entire legacy would be that his foolish attempt at peace talks with the foreign animals had ended with his assassination.

Mandan daubed the brush again in an attempt to paint his father's face, remembering the man's kind though often disapproving expression. Now, however, the young konag could only remember the eyeless sockets, the dead mouth twisted in agony. He muddled the work and tossed the brush to the floor, where it clattered like a hollow bone. He glared at the ruined canvas. Though the scene was vivid in his mind, the painting was a disaster, as if the artist were a palsied blind man.

He knocked the canvas off the easel, and when it made only a soft thump on the floor, he stomped on it, breaking the pine frame and tearing the canvas. He kicked the mangled remnants aside and stormed out of his suite, making his way to the throne room. Right now, he was too disturbed and too uncontrolled to be a painter, but he was still the konag, the leader of the Commonwealth. No one could take that from him.

He pushed his way into the large chamber, hoping to surprise others who were engaged in questionable business. Indeed, at one of the tables two of his treasury accountants worked at their books, tediously adding sums as a scribe read from a list of accounts. Watery sunlight passed through the tall windows.

Mandan paused as if he expected a sudden fanfare. The treasury accountants looked up and snapped to their feet in a flurry. The throne room was otherwise empty, as was his imposing throne on the dais, although in the smaller throne beside it sat a wisp of a young woman. Her long red hair was clumped and matted now, her gown rumpled. Mandan didn't know how he had ever found Lira beautiful. Now she didn't look like a queen, just a wadded rag of a human being. She clasped a goblet in both hands as if it were a treasure. Mandan knew that it was filled with milk of the blue poppy, the potent drug with which she numbed herself.

Mandan sauntered forward and threw himself into his throne, looking sidelong at Lira. Seeing him, she flinched, then turned her dull gaze away and slurped from her goblet.

He grunted with disgust. "You already act as dead as your father and mother are."

Lira's eyes flew open, and she began weeping. The konag shook his head. "I deserve a better queen than you, a true companion, the love of my life." He slumped against the hard back of the throne, imagining himself as a hero to be written of in the history books, just like Conndur the Brave.

He studied the completed painting he had installed along the wall, a far more successful rendition than the one he had just attempted. The Battle of Yanton. This depiction brought warmth to his heart rather than horror. He had painted the bloody scene as he pictured it, though he himself had not been there. In his imagination, and his painting, the konag's loyal forces stormed an unsuspecting Norterran town to punish King Kollanan for refusing to help against the enemies of the Commonwealth. Mandan had wanted to teach his uncle a lesson, to remind him and his people who their konag was. The painting showed the young konag riding a white horse, raising his sword high so that blood ran down the steel edge. Utho and Lord Cade charged behind him, massacring the traitors. Dead bodies lay all around, while cowering Norterran soldiers begged for mercy that Mandan would not give.

Yes, that was how the Battle of Yanton should have happened, and now anyone who entered his throne room would see history preserved. Soon enough, Konag Mandan planned to send an even greater punitive force to Norterra, before Kollanan could cause any more trouble.

He scowled at Lira. "If your father hadn't failed me, I wouldn't need to raise another army to finish the job."

She startled him with a glare of intense hatred, but the expression quickly fell from her pale face and she slumped again, turning aside.

A tall man dressed in black strode through the open doors that hung on iron hinges. His close-cropped steel-gray hair was neat, his face ruddy. His boots pounded on the flagstone floor.

Mandan began to rise from his throne, as if he were subordinate to his own Brava. "Utho, where have you been? I sent three messages."

"I was busy, my konag." His expression was implacable, and his voice held no regret. "I have been to Rivermouth and back every single day. Many complex preparations for the launch of our fleet." He brushed his black sleeve, pulled off his gauntlet and tucked it into his belt. "I need a change of clothes. Your Brava must cut an impressive figure, and this road dust makes me look like a highwayman."

Mandan ordered the accountants and the squire to leave. They gathered their ledger books and hurried out the door. After they were gone, the young man sulked. "When I summon you, you should come." He meant to sound angry and commanding; instead, it came out as a whine.

"I am sworn to the konag," Utho said, but he sounded annoyed. "My priorities are to do what is best for the Commonwealth." He approached the throne dais and remained respectfully on the bottom step. He cast a disapproving glance in Lira's direction, then looked back at Mandan. "I have a report from the Rivermouth docks. Our navy is nearly ready to launch, forty ships outfitted with armor hull plating. The crews are trained not only in seamanship but in hand-to-hand combat. Our archers practice daily. They know the range of their longbows and they are quite skilled with fire arrows."

"What about our land army? Our cavalry and foot soldiers?" Mandan asked. "I want to send them marching to Norterra before Kollanan moves against us."

Utho's brow furrowed. "Right now I am more concerned with dispatching our sea fleet. We will conquer Ishara, burn their capital to the ground, and sweep across their continent. I have already made up for the ships we lost on our previous assault on Fulcor Island. We'll retake the island garrison before we move on to Serepol Harbor." He hesitated as if embarrassed.

Mandan shuddered to remember that frightening sea battle, where they had lost nearly everything.

Utho continued, "Our invasion force is equal to the one your grandfather Cronin launched three decades ago. Six more Bravas have answered my summons from across the land. We will be invincible."

Restless, Mandan wiped his fingers along his collar, rubbed his neck. "But Kollanan defied my orders! He killed Cade and defeated my army. We can't let that stand! What if he marches on Convera?"

Utho crossed his arms over his chest. "Kollanan the Hammer is preoccupied with his fears about wreths hiding under every bed."

"But he already sent that letter accusing you of terrible crimes, and what you did to Elliel!"

The Brava's voice was flat. "You do not believe it."

Mandan swallowed. "Other people know of the letter, too. Rumors are spreading." He shook his head. "You and I should have read it in private and then burned it."

"That is what we should have done," Utho said. "But people will always entertain themselves with rumors. You are the true konag, son of Conndur the Brave. Remember what the Isharan animals did to your father! You have every right to your revenge against them, and all three kingdoms must fight for that revenge." He stepped up on the dais to stand just in front of the throne. "I set our proper priorities. At the current pace of gathering supplies and arms, our fleet should be able to launch for Ishara soon."

"Am I . . . am I going along?" Mandan could not keep the reluctance out of his voice.

Utho's expression went cold and still. "Of course not, my konag. Better that you remain here to protect the Commonwealth." He gave a quick bow and withdrew from the throne room with a swirl of his black cape.

The young konag saw no point in arguing, because Utho would do as he pleased and then convince Mandan it was for his own sake. He left the dais without bothering to look at his queen again and departed by the side door.

Back in his royal suite, he set a fresh canvas on the easel, picked a new paintbrush, and began to mix colors. He stared at the white field again and called up the dreadful memories so he could try to paint the nightmares out of his head.

5

 ◆

T HE last fires in Serepol had burned out, and anxious people began clearing the wreckage in the streets. The wounded had been tended, and the
broken bodies taken away. Though the godling remained restless, it was contained within the Magnifica temple. For now.

Key Priestlord Klovus could not consider this a victory by any measure,
but he let his followers believe it was, because if their faith faded, the godling
would be weakened, and the entire foundation of the key priestlord's leadership would crumble. All of Serepol had seen Klovus unleash the great godling,
but he had never imagined how much destruction it would cause. He had
meant only to hurt the uncouth barbarians in Ishara's capital, but the collat-
eral damage was gut-wrenching.

While the people were still in shock, the key priestlord retreated to the temple pyramid, taking solace in the nexus of power and faith. The Magnifica
had been his dream for decades, stalled by an empra who had no vision for
the future. In the months since Iluris had fallen into a coma, then vanished,
Klovus had commanded the Magnifica construction to resume at a furious
pace. Now the stepped pyramid towered high, already nearly as tall as the
empra's palace.

The structure thrummed with the power of the godling within. The entity
was weakened now from its exertions, and under his control again. The deity
remained bottled up inside, sealed behind shadowglass in the half world of
its existence.

Klovus stood by altars on the first raised platform above the crowded
square. Throngs came forward, awed by what they had seen the godling do,
the sheer power and the rampant destruction. Both their faith and their fear
had been strengthened. Klovus felt the temple vibrating and raised his hand,
pulling on the strings of power.

Also sensing it, the crowd let out a long moan. "Hear us, save us!"

"I feel your prayers," Klovus shouted, "and the godling feels them as well."

Around the square many building façades had been shattered when the
godling tore open structures to find barbarians hidden inside. Bloodstains
smeared the stucco walls, and Klovus decided to leave them there.

He continued to shout. "The godling keeps us strong and protects us from
our enemies."

The crowd murmured again. "Hear us, save us!"

Despite his bluster, he felt wrung out after what had happened. Everyone had seen the fury of the godling and also noted the key priestlord's inability to control it. They would never forget that, so he chose to distract them by pushing his agenda now. "Yes, our enemies—the godless Commonwealth."

A confused mutter turned into a cheer, growing louder. They had thought the Hethrren were the enemies.

Klovus had dispatched urgent riders across Ishara, summoning the twelve district priestlords to Serepol so they could attend his consecration of the Magnifica, though the construction and adornment would continue for as long as the faith of the people sustained it. The giant pyramid was finished enough.

"We have long waited for this moment. Our warships are ready to deliver the Hethrren to new shores. Rejoice, for Ishara's faith is strong, our people are strong." He drew in a deep breath and bellowed, "And our godling is invincible!"

Arriving at the far end of the square, fur-clad warriors rode forward on sturdy mountain horses, moving people aside so they could approach. Klovus felt a chill, but kept his hands upraised, hoping that Magda would fear the godling enough to listen to him.

As the barbarian leader approached, holding her knotted club like a royal scepter, she grinned to show a file-sharpened front tooth. Her wiry black hair was like greasy smoke around her head. "My Hethrren are ready to conquer." The people backed away, grumbling in fear, but Magda ignored them. She halted her horse at the base of the temple below him.

From the stone platform, Klovus towered over her in his midnight-blue caftan. Why then did he still feel so small? "I will give you a proper enemy so the faithful can use their energies to strengthen our land."

Magda swung down from her horse like a forest panther pouncing on a deer. On thick legs she bounded up the pyramid steps to the stone platform where the key priestlord waited. "Blood is blood, and victory is victory." She leered at him with her hideous teeth and whispered, "I will help you, lover." Magda's face and arms showed bruises turning yellow and purple from where she had been battered in the fray with the godling.

Sweat broke out on the back of his neck. Instead of answering her, he shouted to the people. "Listen! The Hethrren came to Serepol as our mercenaries so they could attack the Commonwealth across the sea. Our godling has helped them remember their bargain."

Magda glared at him, but Klovus dug deep inside himself and found the strength, remembering when the entity had moved through him. He responded to her in a voice as quiet and intimate as she had used. "Let us pray you don't make me remind you again."

He raised his hands higher. "Hear us, save us!" The crowd responded with a roar.

The mounted Hethrren paced around the base of the temple, facing the crowd. Klovus knew the barbarians would never be able to defend their leader if the worshippers turned into a bloodthirsty mob.

"Our warships are nearly ready to launch. We will crew them with our best Isharan sailors and our best fighters, but the Hethrren will be our main fighting force. Hethrren brothers and sisters, when you reach the shores of Osterra, raid the fishing villages, pillage the coast, then sail up the river to conquer Convera. Make the three kingdoms your own."

He saw her hungry look, and he continued, "The godless old world is yours. I give it to you. Squeeze it and beat it into submission, as you wish."

Satisfied now, she smiled. "If your ships take us there, my Hethrren will do the rest."

Klovus happily granted his blessing.

In her hidden chamber beneath the palace, Empra Iluris moaned. She tried to sit up, but her body seemed to be made of dry sticks and paper. Her thoughts were filled with ghosts, whispers, and emptiness. When she blinked, she saw only a darkness that gradually filled with yellow-orange candlelight. Her ears rang, and the voices became real instead of echoes in her head. She felt so weak!

One of the faces in front of her belonged to a young woman with gaunt cheeks and shadows under her eyes. The girl looked so familiar, but Iluris couldn't place her name.

In a flash of memory, she saw this scamp climbing a trellis, trying to break into her royal guest chamber in . . . Prirari District? Yes, in the governor's mansion. This girl had insisted on speaking to the empra.

Cemi! Yes, that was her name.

After that memory came a great hollowness, but she knew that much more had happened. Additional details rolled in, crowding to the front of her mind. Iluris had taken this girl under her wing, talked with her about ruling Ishara.

"Empra, you're awake! Vos, bring her some water!"

A man in tarnished gold armor and a stained red cape bent close to her pallet, extending a cup of tepid water. Iluris remembered her hawk guards, recognized the man's handsome features, a crooked nose that had once been broken—Captani Vos.

She sipped the water, but swallowed only one mouthful before pushing the cup away. Her head resounded with pain, as if cracks still thrummed through her skull.

She recalled striking her head just before everything went black and cold.

She had been fighting somewhere . . . attacked by a man who looked like one of Konag Conndur's Bravas, but wasn't. There had been fire, and his features shifted. . . .

A rush of fear made her gasp as she relived that fight in the locked room on Fulcor Island. A stormy night . . . the man had tried to kill her, and she remembered something else—a surge of power. An invisible force had come out of the air and out of her heart. She had tripped, fallen into a deafening thunderclap of pain and blackness.

"Where?" she asked, breathing the word rather than vocalizing it. She swallowed again and let the moisture ease her throat. "Why?"

Cemi and Vos were at her side, holding her, touching her, as if to make sure Iluris was real. Vos groaned. "We were so worried, Mother. We protected you."

Cemi added in a rush, "You lay near death for many, many weeks. Priest-lord Klovus tried to kill you. Now he's taken over Ishara."

"Or he thinks he has," Vos said. "But now you can return."

Other hawk guards came closer, somehow looking loving and yet filled with murderous anger on her behalf, and ready to move against the traitors who had forced them into this situation. They appeared bedraggled, unshaven, not at all the proud and glorious guards she remembered.

"What . . . happened?" The question was large, seeking many answers.

She could see more now. Turning her head, she realized that she was in a stone-walled chamber, poorly lit. People were crowded here like refugees from a storm.

Cemi explained what had occurred since that night on Fulcor Island, and where Iluris was now. Much of what the young woman said did not make sense to her. The empra tried to make the words fit into patterns within her memory, but she was missing great pieces, like a building with its walls damaged and its windows broken out.

Feeling weak, Iluris wanted to lie back down again, but forced herself to remain upright. From what Vos and Cemi said, she must already have been lying down far too long. She needed to remain awake.

As she struggled to reassemble her existence, Iluris felt a surprising surge of strength, like a fresh cool breeze after a summer rain. She narrowed her eyes, tried to concentrate, to understand where this burst of life had come from. Her vision was flooded with too many images and halos, but she noticed an unfocused ripple in the air that carried warmth and strength and support. It seemed . . . alive and sentient.

She held out her thin hand and curled her fingers in a beckoning gesture. The air rippled around her. "What is this?"

Cemi's face sparkled with wonder. She backed away and spread her own hands, as if to shape the currents of invisible force around her. "We think it's another godling. The people pray for you every day, Excellency. Their sacrifices, their beliefs, their faith in you created something new. This one . . ."

"Your protector, Mother," Captani Vos said. "Just as we hawk guards are your protectors. We have been waiting for you to awaken, but if we wait much longer we will surely lose the city and the entire land. The tipping point is at hand. You must come back to your people. Show them that you still live."

Cemi added, "We've been busy finding allies in the streets, spreading rumors of hope, but we must restore your health and strength." She swallowed hard. "Right now people will see you as just a wisp of a person."

"I will do what I must," Iluris said, still trying to understand the situation. She squeezed Cemi's hand. "And I also have much for you to do, child."

6

೮

I N the Brava training village, Master Onzu guided his wards, half-breed children who would one day grow up to be brave paladins who roamed the land or fighters bonded to powerful men and women. These trainees were his responsibility, and Onzu molded them into *Bravas*.

He gave them combat techniques, tested them with weapons, and most importantly instilled the core of honor fundamental to every Brava. Honor was just as integral to their identity as the wreth blood that flowed through their veins. Every person in the three kingdoms understood a Brava's steadfast loyalty as well as they understood the rise and the set of the sun.

Utho had betrayed everything a Brava stood for, again and again and again.

Onzu stood by his students, preparing them for what he had to do. The oldest one, a wiry twelve-year-old named Rigg, was quick as a cat but had a sensitivity that made him hesitate to inflict pain. As he grew older, Rigg would understand that pain was sometimes necessary.

Just like the pain Master Onzu felt in his heart right now.

As the old warrior regarded them, they waited in wary silence, dreading what their master would say. "My calling should be to stay here and train you. I sacrificed my service to the outside world in order to train more Bravas to protect the Commonwealth. Now even that calling . . ." He shook his shaved head.

The students were well behaved, even the young ones. They stood at attention without flinching, because over the years he had taught them to ignore distractions. When their master spoke, they hung on his every word.

But how could he describe the terrible things he had learned?

Utho had broken his bond, twisted his oath. He had betrayed Elliel, a fellow Brava, making her suffer the consequences of fictional crimes, simply to hide a nobleman's illicit activities. Single-handedly, Utho had imposed the greatest punishment any Brava could face: He had erased her memory, told her that she had committed terrible crimes, and left her broken and guilt-ridden . . . as a cover-up.

But there was more. Hoping to find an explanation, Onzu had invoked rare magic to reveal exactly what Utho did. That was when he discovered his prize student's most world-shaking betrayal: Utho himself had murdered Konag Conndur and planted false evidence, all to provoke a war with Ishara.

That was not the Brava way. His actions demonstrated no honor. His actions eroded the very foundation of their people's values and reputation.

Because Utho had been his student, Onzu was obligated to take care of the matter. That obligation superseded his sworn duty to train his wards. This one corrupt student, a Brava bonded to Konag Mandan himself, could single-handedly cause more damage than any good these students would achieve.

He told his wards what he had to do.

"I'll make arrangements before leaving you," he said. "The nearby village will take you in for as long as need be."

"We will protect the village if it is attacked," said the twelve-year-old, bowing formally.

"Good lad. Saddle my horse. I will ride into town, make inquiries, and pay for your keep. You need not worry while I'm gone."

"We are not worried," Rigg insisted. He was clearly becoming their de facto leader.

"If you have Brava business, shouldn't we all come along?" asked a younger girl.

He smiled at the thought of a leathery old Brava training master accompanied by a batch of children as he confronted Utho, but he was proud of their dedication. "Have I ever given you reason to worry for me? Have I ever lost a battle?" The trainees shook their heads. "Then don't doubt me now."

Though his joints and muscles often ached when he woke in the morning, Onzu remained limber. He trained hard with the children because he would not let himself diminish as a fighter.

When his horse was ready, he sprang into the saddle as if he were no more than a twenty-year-old. He galloped out of the training village, following the forest paths among the beech trees until he came to a stream, beside which a wider path led to the nearby town. Onzu went there every month or two to trade for supplies, though many of the merchants and smiths simply gave him what he needed. They took no money because they were glad to have Bravas close.

As Onzu rode into town, he saw a flurry of activity in the small market square, where people stood around a stranger who looked confused. The young man had drab clothes and raggedly cut blond hair that looked as if he hacked it himself with a dull dagger. The stranger held up his hands, pleading with the villagers for answers.

Onzu was startled to see that the man's eyes had the distinctive almond shape of Brava lineage, though he did not wear traditional black Brava armor. As the training master rode closer, the stranger turned to look at him, revealing the tattoo that marred his face. Onzu knew that complex design all too well.

A rune of forgetting.

The young man's features were similar to his own, though softer. Onzu caught his breath, realizing who he was—his own disgraced son. Onder.

The young man recognized the training master for what he was, but his expression showed no other sign of recognition. "Please!" He pushed past the other villagers. "You're the first Brava I've seen. No one will help me or explain anything. Someone said there's a training village nearby? I came here hoping . . . hoping that—"

"There is nothing for you at the training village," Onzu said in a curt voice. He looked down at the disgraced man from his saddle. "Don't bother to search for Bravas. That part of you is gone. Rebuild your life, make a new legacy."

"That is what they say." Onder touched his face. "But with this mark I don't know what really happened, except for what I was told." He reached inside his tunic and pulled out a stained sheet of paper. "This is a letter signed by a Brava named Utho. He says I was a coward, that I ran from a godling, and that is why I was stripped of my job, my name, my past—everything." The young man's face fell. "I don't remember it." He looked up at the training master. "Could I really have done that?"

"Yes," Onzu said. "Yes, you did. It was in the town of Mirrabay. Isharan raiders attacked, and brought a godling. You and Utho fought against it, but then you turned and ran, leaving Utho to face the monster alone."

"No," the young man moaned. "I wouldn't do that. Why would I do that?"

"Because you were afraid." Onzu spoke without mercy. "The story has been verified by many witnesses."

The villagers stood back listening, muttering.

"What can I do to make up for it?" Onder pleaded. "How can I atone? I'll do anything."

"You already proved that you won't do *anything*," the training master said. "You won't fight a godling. You won't fulfill your duty as a Brava."

"I don't even remember it!"

Onzu rounded on him. "You don't remember what you did? Or you don't remember your duty? Which is it?"

"I will try harder. Can't you help me? Can't you train me?"

The master's words lashed the young man like a whip. "I already trained you once, and you failed me."

The young man looked down at the letter clutched in his hands. "If I don't remember, how can I be the same man?" His voice hitched. "Even if it is true, why would you judge me only by the worst mistake I ever made? A single incident. How does that demonstrate Brava honor?"

Onzu fought back his scorn and controlled his temper. He had come to buy food and supplies, to find homes for his younger trainees, to tell the people that he would be departing on a mission. Now that he saw his disgraced son, however, thoughts spun out in other directions like unraveling threads in an old blanket. He remembered something his own training master had taught him, decades ago. *One moment does not define an entire life.*

"After I finish my errands in town, I have a job for you," Onzu said with a grudging sigh. "You may be exactly the right person to do a Brava duty that no one else can accomplish."

The young man looked at him with an expression of naked hope. "You would do that, even though Utho condemned me as a coward?"

A razor edge of anger sliced through Onzu. "Utho has committed crimes far worse than anything you did."

7

〰

SURROUNDED by heat ripples and mirages, the sandwreth queen gazed across the arid emptiness. Restless and bored, waiting for the end of the world and the reward for her people, Voo brooded about her next move. She was anxious to launch her attack against the enemy frostwreths.

Her warriors and mages were deadly with their weapons and magic, but Voo had a secret advantage—the human army of King Adan, which she was arming with potent shadowglass weaponry. Voo thought she might have enough humans to cause significant harm. Then, once the frostwreths were defeated, Voo and her people could wake the dragon, as Kur had commanded them to do. After millennia of waiting, the end was imminent.

But as she waited in her sandstone palace, she was impatient. Her brother Quo had gone north with a war party to help King Kollanan fight the frostwreths, though Quo's real mission was to find Adan's pregnant wife, who had flouted Voo's summons. While Voo didn't know what she would do with a human infant, perhaps she could use the creature to ensure Adan's cooperation. The handsome young king was often stubborn.

The queen pursed her lips, and the expression turned into a frown. Her brother had been gone a long time, and she'd heard nothing. He was aloof and easily distracted, and she needed him back to help her with the real war.

With a thought, Voo remolded the tower and expanded the balcony with hissing runnels of sand, looping the blocky support columns into more graceful arches. It gave her a broader view toward the bleak volcanic mountains, black peaks like broken teeth. Dust devils and swirls of sand danced across the desert.

Her mages practiced by summoning tatters of magic from the blasted land. They were growing ready to crush the frostwreth armies and rid the world of their stain. Under Voo's banner, the wreths would sweep across the landscape like a blasting sandstorm. Those would be glorious days!

If only her brother would stop dithering and return.

Voo smelled the comforting crackle of dust and heat. Her long golden hair was like threads of intense sunlight. Her coppery eyes blazed as she watched her warriors in formation across the desert. Their augas formed a cavalry with spears and swords, and she would greatly increase her forces with the Suderran army. Surely, even Kur would be impressed.

A gruff voice interrupted her thoughts. "I must speak with you, my queen." She recognized the husky tones of her primary mage, Axus. "I am concerned about the human labor camp, and you must heed me."

She raised her eyebrows. "Oh, I must?" Teasing for now, but she would quickly become incensed.

Axus remained in the tower doorway, neither cowed nor intimidated. He was a tall, thin man with a bald head shaped like a boulder. He wore robes of rust-red leather, dyed with pigments extracted from the blood of those who had died in pain. "I have never been afraid to speak my mind to you. That is what you requested of me."

"At times I find it annoying."

"And yet, you still have to listen," the mage said.

"What is it? You always seem fixated on these humans and their well-being."

"They are a resource, not to be squandered through carelessness." Axus folded his hands into the rune-etched sleeves of his robe. "Humans breed swiftly. That is why they have been so successful rebuilding the world even after our wars. They survived, filled the niches, and built up their numbers while we recovered in spellsleep for thousands of years."

"You are a historian now?" Voo asked mockingly. "A pity we gave all those documents to that strange man Thon. I don't remember you reading them."

"It is common knowledge," Axus said dismissively. "But in the coming war we will surely spend thousands upon thousands of humans. We need them."

"That is what they are for," Voo said.

The mage's shaved head wrinkled as his brows furrowed. "Yes, that is what they are for, but it is foolish to waste them now. Better that we save them for killing frostwreths, not let them die of neglect in poor labor conditions."

With a sniff, Voo stared at the swirling dust devils that rippled across the desert. "I insist on killing some of the frostwreths myself. Their queen is mine."

"I doubt a mere human could kill the frostwreth queen," Axus said.

"What is your point, Mage? I have no time for idle conversation." Actually, she had plenty of time and could accomplish little until Quo returned.

"We sent many shipments of shadowglass to arm the Suderran fighters, but all those human slaves excavating the black glass are dying in unacceptable numbers. The conditions are hard, and we do not get the best productivity from them if we work them to death."

Voo sneered. "Shall we give them perfumes and hot baths?"

"No, but we should manage them better. If you train a crew and let them die of neglect, they will never work again. Then you must acquire and train new humans. But if you keep them healthy by alternating shifts, allowing them to rest and regain their strength, feeding them well enough, then you keep skilled workers who can produce more and more for us." His expression grew harder. "Instruct Mage Ivun to withdraw the current exhausted crew from the excavations, take them back to the canyon camp, and bring in a new crew. You can alternate work crews so that one will always be fresh and productive. You will ultimately produce more shadowglass with fewer workers."

Voo frowned. She didn't like to meddle in however Ivun chose to wring productivity from his miserable captives, although she had to admit that Axus was not wrong. "You make a convincing argument. Very well, I will do so, and Mage Ivun will obey."

"Of course he will."

Voo turned from the desert panorama. The wind picked up around the sandstone tower, whistling through her newly formed arches and pinnacles. "Now I need something from you, Axus. Where is my brother? Use your magic. Find Quo."

His brow furrowed. "I can cast a search, send out strands of magic along the winds, but I will need something of his to forge the link."

Voo reached into her hair, fumbled among the bells and bangles and jewels that she had tied there. She found a small golden disk that her brother had given her many years ago. She yanked hard, snapped her hair, and passed the object over to Axus.

He knelt and placed the disk on the sandstone balcony, then touched his fingertip to the hard stone. As he traced a circle around the bangle, the sandstone dissolved into powdery grains. The mage used the edge of his hand to scrape the loose sand on the bangle and pile it into a cone of grains. The sand sparkled in the bright sunlight.

"This dust compass will point to your brother." He swirled his hand in the air, calling up bright lines of magic. The cone of sand spun, flattened, formed a wormlike cylinder that twitched and extended like a pointing finger. The dust compass quested in one direction, then another. The compass shifted, indicated south, then north, wandering to all four corners of the compass.

"Where is he?" Voo asked.

Axus frowned as he strained harder. The compass wavered, seemingly indecisive, then the needle of sand broke into several small fragments that spun out in different directions. The sand collapsed into loose grains that blew away in the strengthening wind.

"I do not understand," he muttered. "The magic cannot find Quo's location . . . as if he is no longer there."

"If my brother is hiding from me as some sort of childish trick . . ." Voo grumbled. "We will keep waiting until he comes to his senses. In the meantime, I will dispatch a message to Mage Ivun. We can always use humans for one purpose or another. It makes no sense to run these particular wretches into the ground."

8

LOOKING into the sky above the Plain of Black Glass, Glik saw winged creatures that circled far beyond the range of sandwreth arrows. Unlike her beautiful Ari, the wild skas were not connected with a heart link, but still the orphan girl longed for the colorful reptile birds. She had to warn them to stay away from the work camp. Her captors hated mischievous skas, called them spies or little dragons, and tried to kill them on sight.

Glik reached into the pocket of her tattered trousers, found Ari's blue feather that had been knocked loose when the wreths tried to kill her. The frantic ska had barely escaped after delivering a secret message from Queen Penda. Hiding her hand now, she stroked the soft feather. Her heart could still feel Ari. Someday, Glik and all of these bedraggled human captives would find a way to be free.

The slaves, bruised and exhausted, labored under hazy morning sunlight, extracting obsidian from the magic-blasted ground. They were allowed to use chisels, prybars, mallets, and wedges to shatter the puddles of oily midnight, then with cloth-wrapped hands, they carried the fragments up to waiting carts. Glik's hands had been sliced and healed so many times they were a network of scabs and scars. Whenever her blood touched the razor-edged shadowglass, her mind flooded with images, suffocating visions that drove her to the edge of madness.

Wreth warriors mounted on their large reptiles and holding spears guarded the prisoners. Mage Ivun trudged among his humans, barking at them to work harder, while other wreths doled out rations of lukewarm water and occasional morsels of food.

Glik's Brava friend Cheth worked hard, fueled by anger rather than fear. The sandwreths assumed that all humans would happily join their cause, regardless of how the captors treated them. If wreths were supposedly a superior race, the creators of humanity, Glik couldn't understand why they were so stupid.

An auga pulled an empty cart toward the work area, and sullen workers carried fragments of shadowglass, piling them in the wagon bed. Though the crew had worked here for weeks and had already sent many loads of the magic-infused obsidian back to Queen Voo, the blackened plain seemed an infinite source, a giant scar on the landscape.

During the ancient wreth wars, this place had been a vast battlefield, one of the bloodiest clashes of the two races. Here, Glik had seen visions of ancient wreth armies dressed in magnificent armor, opposing ranks of augas and oonuks. A titanic city had stood at the head of this valley where brilliant mages constructed sorcerous machinery to be used against Ossus, exotic weapons and devices. But the wreths had attacked one another instead. The besieged mages in the city had unleashed their arcane weapons, triggering powerful magic designed to kill the great dragon. Instead, that devastation obliterated this whole valley, countless thousands of human soldiers, all the wreth armies and the entire city, leaving only melted blood-drenched glass entangled with magic.

Now, working on her knees in front of an irregular shadowglass pool, Glik held a pick, but she reeled, trying to stave off a vision lurking in her peripheral vision and behind her mind. Inside the circle. Outside the circle.

A wreth warrior nudged his auga closer, and she could hear the reptile's heavy footfalls. "You. Work."

Glik reflexively lifted her tool and pretended to do her duties. Suddenly Cheth was there. "I am helping her." The Brava bent, struck the shadowglass surface with her own pick. Jagged cracks jittered out from the impact point, and the two of them used their tools to pry up black fragments. The orphan girl gave her friend a grateful nod.

Cheth's face was bruised, and scabs ran across her cheek and throat. She glared up at the warrior who loomed over them. "We are all too weary. Haven't you punished us enough?"

"No," said the wreth. "Never enough."

The captives had been treated roughly since their failed escape attempt a few days earlier. Several had been killed as well as a few wreth guards. The prisoners had been rounded up, some beaten, and their rations had been cut, yet they were expected to excavate as much shadowglass as before. Every time she swallowed, Glik tasted dust and chalk. The two carried a load of obsidian and added it to the wagon.

Mage Ivun scrutinized the workers and assessed the growing piles of black glass in the cart, reminding Glik of a beekeeper studying his hive. "Once the load is full, you will receive your ration of food and water."

The laborers looked up suspiciously. Glik's stomach rumbled at the mere mention of food. Cheth glowered back at the wreth mage.

Then Ivun surprised them. "You will need your strength for the journey. We are withdrawing from this site. Queen Voo has commanded me to return to the main labor camp in the canyons, where you will be assigned other tasks. I will pick another group of workers to send back here with Mage Horava." He cradled his withered arm against his chest, but the clawlike limb drooped. The desiccation seemed to be worsening as the mage lost more of his magic.

One worker actually sounded happy, disbelieving. "We're going home?"

Cheth snapped, "It is not home! We're merely going from one prison camp to another."

"You exist to perform whatever the wreths wish," Ivun said. "If not for us, your whole race would never have been created."

"Do not expect me to feel gratitude," Cheth muttered, looking away.

Glik saw more skas wheeling above them, safe and free. She thought about Ari and the message of hope that Penda had sent her via the mothertear diamond in the blue ska's collar. Penda had promised her foster sister that she would try to rescue them. Somehow.

For Glik it was a slender thread of hope, but when a person had nothing else, the impossible seemed more likely. She sketched a circle around her heart. "The beginning is the end is the beginning."

Nothing was impossible, and she would survive another day. They would all find a way out of this.

9

〜

WHEN Adan and his Banner-guard escort reached Fellstaff, he should have been relieved to see the strong outer walls and imposing castle on the highest point of the old city. But as their horses approached the main gates, a pall of grief hung over the capital of Norterra like settling smoke.

Though Seenan carried the Suderran banner high from the lead horse, the people did not flock out to welcome Adan. Farmers worked in the fields harvesting grain or picking late-season fruit from orchards, but they kept a furtive eye toward the walls and the horizon, as if they might need to flee at any moment.

Word passed quickly, and the guards waved them in. His uncle's Brava Lasis cantered up to meet them, granting them a brief nod of respect. "King Adan, you arrive at a difficult time. Come, I will escort you to the keep, but I can't promise Kollanan will see you."

Adan's alarm increased. "Why would he not see me? We have urgent news."

"There is too much urgent news." Lasis glanced away, as if a heavy hand were pressing down on his heart. "Queen Tafira is dead, murdered by wreths, and one of our towns was attacked by Konag Mandan. We are at war on two sides."

Hearing this, Captain Elcior cried out in dismay. Adan urged his horse forward. "Tell us more on the way to the castle."

Adan already knew about the frostwreth threat from the last time he had visited, but the tale Lasis unfolded was appalling. As their horses passed along the cobblestone streets, Adan remained silent and processed the information, knowing that his own news would make the situation even harder.

Around the courtyard, the castle workers turned to their chores with grim focus. On previous visits, he had watched them conversing as they washed clothes in tubs, or peeled vegetables for the kitchens. Now, those not doing castle chores sparred with staffs and wooden swords, trying to prepare for battle. Everyone moved like skittish deer, afraid of predators in every shadow.

At the stables, the young man Pokle—whom Adan and Koll had rescued near Lake Bakal—took their reins. They all dismounted and followed Lasis into the castle.

Adan took a moment to remind himself that he brought joyful news, too—the announcement of his baby daughter. He allowed himself a moment of warmth as he pictured Penda and little Oak. Perhaps his uncle would appreciate the kernel of hope. It was something, at least. . . .

King Kollanan the Hammer sat alone in his throne room to think, but his thoughts just went around in dark circles. The roaring fire in the hearth could not dispel the chill of reality. Beside his blocky wooden seat sat the empty secondary throne, Queen Tafira's throne. His wife had always sat next to him, always counseled him, always loved him. Now, alone with his thoughts and memories, he felt the growing dread of unfolding events.

Alone.

In front of the throne, a heavy table held detailed maps of Norterra, showing the eight counties, numerous towns and villages, known and probable routes east over the Dragonspine Mountains. Other maps displayed roads along the Bluewater River, riverboat landings, and towns along the way. One rough sketch showed the barely charted wasteland regions far north, where the frostwreths lived. On an official map of the three kingdoms, Koll had studied the confluence of the two rivers, the wedge of land that held Convera Castle, where his twisted nephew Mandan ruled. He marked Lord Cade's holding on the rugged northeastern coast, from which the attacking army had originated, the murderers who had preyed upon Yanton. He saw threats on all sides.

A resinous knot of pinewood popped in the fireplace, startling him. Kollanan had been on edge for weeks . . . forever, it seemed.

He heard sounds of people approaching in the corridor, and he closed his eyes for a moment to center his thoughts. Every visitor brought bad news; every report took options away and forced him to react . . . and each such reaction led to more painful choices.

But he could not sit idle. Though he felt hollow after his losses, he was still the king of Norterra and would not forsake his responsibilities. He was the dispenser of justice for his people.

Kollanan drew a deep breath, absently caressed his beard the way Tafira had done, and opened his eyes. For a moment he thought he was hallucinating.

Adan Starfall stood before him, dressed in travel clothes rather than royal garb. He looked dusty, his expression filled with anguish and sympathy. "Uncle, I have heard."

Koll's eyes burned. "Adan . . ."

As he rose from the heavy throne, his stiff joints called attention to his age, slowed down by grief and lack of caring. He was five decades old, but he had never wanted to relax and retire. Now, the very thought reminded him that he had meant to grow old with Tafira in a kingdom at peace, guiding farmers and hunters, miners and craftsmen, villagers whose only worry might be a domestic squabble or an occasional bandit. Memories and regrets boiled around him like deeper shadows in the dark, and he pushed them back. He heaved a breath deep enough to fill the emptiness in his chest. "Oh Adan, I have so much to tell you. I don't know if I can bear it."

Adan bounded up to the throne where Kollanan stood like a tree and threw his arms around his uncle. The two rocked back and forth, shaking with the unexpressed words that clamored to get out. "You don't have to. I know enough for now."

By the time Adan withdrew, Elliel and Thon had also joined them, along with a more reticent Gant. Even the scholar girl Shadri had hurried in with armloads of documents, as if they were a kind of armor.

Kollanan worked through the fog of his grief until his thoughts clarified. He realized there had not been enough time for a messenger to ride to Bannriya with news of Tafira's death or the Yanton attack, so Adan must have come for some other reason.

Kollanan picked up his war hammer, which he now always kept at his side. At one time it had hung on a wall, a relic he thought never to use again. "Adan, why did you come? Tell me what you need to say."

"It's the sandwreths. Queen Voo sent a war party to help you fight at Lake Bakal." He looked away, obviously not finished.

"They did help," Kollanan admitted.

Elliel spoke up. "Thon was the one who actually brought down the ice walls, even if the sandwreths helped."

Koll growled. "And then they would not stay to help us. The sandwreths rode off. If they had stayed, maybe Tafira would not have . . ."

"Quo and his companions had another mission," Adan said, his voice heavy. "Yes, they helped you at Lake Bakal, but their real purpose was to hunt down my Penda. She was hiding among the Utauks so she could give birth in safety."

A flush of heat rose to Koll's cheeks. "They wanted your wife?"

"Voo wanted our *baby*," Adan said. "Quo's party found us at an Utauk camp just as we were attacked by a dragon." He looked away. "In the aftermath, I . . . killed Quo. It needed to be done."

Kollanan breathed harder, absorbing the information. "It needed to be done."

Adan told him more of the story, tempering it with the good news about his baby daughter, and that Penda and her father were riding back to Bannriya. His conversation centered on how the Utauks had obliterated all evidence of the fight with the sandwreths and then headed off. "It'll be some time before Queen Voo knows what happened, if ever, but I needed to warn you. I think we are at war with both the sandwreths and the frostwreths."

"I have been ready for war for a long time." Kollanan walked toward the big map table and sat heavily in a wooden chair. "New enemies keep appearing."

Shadri set down her books and documents beside him, joined by Elliel and Thon. At the throne room door, Lasis, Gant, and the Banner guards remained at uneasy attention.

Koll's heavy heart did not grow any lighter as Adan took a seat next to him, but just having the young man there made the burden easier to bear. "Before it's open warfare with the wreths, though, we have another war to deal with." He rested his elbows on the table and stared at the charts. "I've been doing a lot of thinking—about how dangerous your brother is." As Adan listened in disbelief, he explained how Konag Mandan had dispatched part of the Commonwealth army to Yanton to prey on their own citizens.

He gestured across the maps of the three kingdoms. "Revenge is all that Mandan can see. Yes, the Isharans murdered Conndur, but the wreths pose a far greater threat than the Isharans across the sea." He felt a whirlwind of shadows roaring around him, but he silenced them, opened his eyes again.

"Utho is responsible, not Mandan," Elliel said. "Don't blame the puppet when its master pulls the strings. Utho is the one who dispatched Lord Cade, I am sure of it."

Kollanan looked at Gant, and the Brava's lumpy face twisted into a grimace. "She is correct, Sire. Mandan relished the idea of the punitive attack, but Utho laid the groundwork for it."

Koll growled, speaking what had been on his mind for some time. "Mandan is unfit to rule. Conndur did not provoke the Isharans when he went to Fulcor Island. He wanted to forge an alliance against our common enemy—the enemy we all know." He swept his gaze across the room. "Mandan betrayed the Commonwealth when he demanded that I leave my kingdom defenseless to join his foolhardy misadventure. And it was Mandan who sent soldiers to pillage one of my towns! If we had not been there to defend Yanton, those poor people would all have been slaughtered. And if I had not been out there fighting . . ." His voice broke as a wave of guilt and regret washed over him. He bowed his head.

If he hadn't been forced to ride off on that unnecessary mission, he would have been here at Fellstaff Castle with Tafira. Captain Rondo would never have kidnapped her, and she would not have been out in the forest, vulnerable to frostwreth marauders . . .

If . . .

"You should have been konag, Adan. Everyone knows it."

Uncomfortably, Adan looked at the charts on the table, picked up the map of Suderra. "I . . . I was never meant to be konag. Mandan was the firstborn son. The rules are clear."

"The rules and the people's need are two different things," Kollanan said. "The people of Suderra claimed you as their ruler, and you have been a good king. No one can dispute that you would be a better konag of the Common-wealth."

"And I prefer a sunny day to a rainy one," Adan said, still uneasy, "but one cannot change the weather any more than I can change my brother's blood-line. Mandan may be a bad konag, but he is still the konag."

Kollanan remained silent for a long moment until he said, "Unless we change it."

Silence fell like a headsman's ax throughout the room. Adan paled. "What you're saying . . . we cannot consider it, not at a time such as this."

"Now is exactly the time that demands it!" Kollanan pounded a fist on the tabletop. "And we'd better do it soon. Before long, a third of the Common-wealth army will sail off to Ishara, and we'll need those fighters to defend against the wreths. Mandan must be removed! We need to bring all three kingdoms together before humanity itself is wiped out."

He let out a heavy sigh and sat down again. Everyone looked at him in stunned, uneasy silence. Kollanan rested his hand on the reassuring handle of his war hammer. "And I know exactly how to do it."

10

⊘

THE *Glissand* was barely recognizable, and it made Mak Dur want to cry. After he and his Utauk trading crew escaped Serepol during the godling's rampage, he'd thought they were home free. They raced back to Osterra, but their reception at Rivermouth had been just as bad. The Commonwealth navy commandeered the *Glissand* and turned it into a war vessel. A war vessel!

Mak Dur hung his head and pulled back his dark hair to tie it in a ribbon. Commonwealth sailors crawled all over the deck of his ship, building stockpiles of spears, boat hooks, and pitch-covered fire arrows. They hammered together blinds and shields to protect the vessel from naval combat, once out at sea. The *Glissand*'s mainsail still bore the large circle that marked it as an Utauk ship, a neutral vessel not to be harassed, but now the Commonwealth banner flapped from the mainmast. They had turned his ship into one of their own against her will, forcibly inducted her into their navy, like a young woman being ravished.

Indignant, Mak Dur stood on the dock looking up at the ship, acting as if he was still in charge, but Konag Mandan's soldiers did whatever they wanted.

Beside him, Heith, his navigator, sat sullenly on a crate and picked his teeth with a splinter of wood. He grumbled, "I went to sea to get rich. I left four women who would have married me, but I wanted to sail the seas and see exotic places. I was excited to go to Ishara the first time." He snorted. "*Cra,* the first *five* times! And now we have nothing but the clothes on our backs."

Mak Dur gave him a bitter smile. "The Commonwealth navy offered us their uniforms if we'd like to join."

"*Cra!* I'd rather wear nettles."

Mak Dur watched uniformed fighters drilling aboard the warships being prepared. More than a dozen large Commonwealth warships with copper plating on their hulls and ambush towers on the decks were anchored in the waters of the harbor, and the docks had twice as many private vessels that had been pressed into service, from mere fishing boats to graceful cargo ships like the *Glissand*. At least no other seized Utauk vessels had been brought to Rivermouth. He hoped that his fellow trader captains had made themselves scarce.

Some of the naval ships plied the coastal waters on shakedown runs or engaged in mock battles, while Mak Dur's vessel remained tied up at the docks. The *Glissand* hadn't been out on the open water since she'd been captured, and he knew that she must be as restless as he was.

"I should never have gone on that last run to Serepol. It was too great a risk," he muttered, not for the first time. "The promise of profit made me forget the simple pleasures of freedom."

Sarrum, one of his sailors, came up behind Heith and sat on another crate, gazing at the ship from the dock. He proudly wore orange and gold, the colors of his clan. "It wasn't your fault, Voyagier. The crew voted. We're all to blame."

Heith added, "You didn't force us . . . not like these bastards did. We're back home, but not home."

"The beginning is the end is the beginning," Mak Dur muttered. The other two drew a quick circle around their hearts.

Sarrum said, "Round and round in a circle, going nowhere. That's what we are."

A broad-shouldered Brava with light curly hair boarded the *Glissand* by the gangplank, barely giving the Utauks a glance. Mak Dur had seen him around the ships, a Brava named Arrick. Five other half-breed warriors were at the shipyards as guards or observers. Many Bravas had assembled in the capital to join in the vengewar against Ishara.

Reaching the deck, the Brava man handed a letter to the *Glissand*'s new acting captain, an officious man named Pharion. The captain read the document, then talked excitedly with his Commonwealth crew. Mak Dur noted several other messengers spreading out among the various docked ships.

A soldier in Commonwealth armor ran past where the three Utauks sat, his boots rumbling on the dock boards. Mak Dur stopped him, grabbing his sleeve. "What is it? What's going on?"

"Just got orders to prepare," said the soldier with a grunt, "as if we weren't already doing it." He pulled his arm away, impatient, and nodded toward the *Glissand*. "Is that your ship? We'll need you and your crew ready to depart in a few days' time. Our men will take care of the fighting, and you Utauks can handle the sailing chores."

"We'd be happy to—for a substantial payment," said Heith. "Since the Commonwealth wants to hire our ship."

Startled, the soldier snapped, "It is no longer your ship. We are at war. *You* are at war! Get used to it."

Mak Dur said with a sigh, "I'm the voyagier, and if anyone is going to sail her, it should be me." He hated what he had to do. "And my crew will be aboard." He cast a sharp glance at Heith and Sarrum, lowering his voice. "Would you rather let someone else do it? I wouldn't trust her to anyone else." The two quieted, but did not seem convinced.

"We'll go to Ishara at last, maybe even retake Fulcor Island on the way," the soldier said with a huff, then ran off.

"Mandan's army might be surprised by what they find in Serepol," Mak Dur said, remembering the smoking wreckage the wild godling had left.

"We were held captive there, and got away," Sarrum said, "and now we're prisoners here."

"We're only prisoners because we choose to stay with the ship," Heith pointed out. "They couldn't stop us if we silently disappeared into the night."

Mak Dur reacted with alarm. "Just leave the *Glissand*?" He thought of his crew members, many of whom had been with him for years. Sarrum had signed aboard for the last ten voyages, most of them up and down the Osterran coast. The navigator had been with him longer, but Heith had never been as closely bonded with the ship as Mak Dur was. "The soldiers insist we are part of the Commonwealth navy, whether or not we wear the uniform."

"As Utauks, we're free to make our own choices," Heith said. "Their kings and konags don't command us. It's been that way for a thousand years."

"We make our own choices," the voyagier agreed. He looked at the graceful lines of his ship and felt a warmth in his heart. "Right now, my choice is to stay with my vessel."

11

∾

ATRUE priestlord could feel the land through his senses, as well as through his heart and through the faith of the people. The vibrant soul of Ishara was also manifested in the godlings that took form according to the character of those who made sacrifices and shared themselves.

Priestlord Erical served Prirari District, with its calm landscape of rolling hills, grasslands, cultivated fields and orchards, but he had been summoned to the capital. Key Priestlord Klovus had called all of the district priestlords to Serepol to commemorate the nearly complete Magnifica.

Always content to remain in his own temple with his own godling, Erical nevertheless set off at once. He made the long journey on foot, experiencing Ishara. Although Prirari soldiers would have gladly accompanied him, he traveled without an escort. A priestlord did not need such protection, when his godling accompanied him on his trek. She would keep him safe. Erical was permanently intertwined with the loving force. She gave him strength, and he could walk for mile after mile without needing to rest. Though the other priestlords would likely leave their godlings behind for the commemoration, he did not think he could be separated from her for so long.

The godling from peaceful Prirari manifested herself as colorful swirls of ribbonlike energy, as if distilled from rainbows. Other district godlings, such as the wild deity from Tamburdin, displayed storms and lightning, claws and fangs.

Rutted main roads rolled across the open terrain. He crossed one hill, then another, not sure when he entered Khosun District, but he kept walking. Each footstep gave him the joy of being alive, the fresh air, the smell of grass and flowers, then sparse oak forests that gave way to drier countryside once he reached Mormosa District.

His godling faded and then returned, shimmering brighter. No matter where she wandered, Erical could sense her presence reeling out like a silken thread and then coming back. The road passed through many villages, and the people came out to greet him. They watched the godling with awe, feeling its presence in their town. Some local priestlords brought out their smaller entities to show him.

Whenever Erical slept on a comfortable bed in a proffered inn or dwelling, the godling would retreat to her other realm. On nights when he bedded down by himself in the forest, staring up at the stars, the godling remained beside him, a faithful companion in the darkness like a glowing aurora.

This time communing with the deity allowed Erical to expand his sense of the world. He was disturbed to feel a brooding shadow somewhere far away, like the rumble of distant thunder from dark clouds on the horizon. He'd experienced the ominous sensation several times back in Prirari, a threat that hinted at something looming and dangerous, a vibration thrumming at the heart of the world.

As they traveled, the godling amplified that sensation, and Erical needed to understand what it was. Sometimes at night he peered through the multicolored gauze of the godling's light and tried to focus on that brooding, distant presence, but it always skittered away, like a shadow seen from the corner of his eye. He hoped the key priestlord could provide answers, once he reached Serepol. Maybe together all the priestlords could understand this nascent threat.

Surely they already knew about it?

He was deeply worried about Empra Iluris, the spiritual mother of all Ishara. Grievously injured on Fulcor Island, she had vanished from her palace in Serepol. Rumors suggested she had been murdered and her body hidden, or that she had ascended to the realm of the godlings. Could her disappearance have something to do with that distant evil? Erical had to know.

He slept only a few hours each night, yet the godling let him feel rested and refreshed. He lost count of the days, but he recognized when he neared the capital city. Although his godling became more diffuse to be less obtrusive, the vibrancy in the air drew curious people. Erical waved to them, gave them blessings, saw the wonder on their faces. The capital district had several lesser godlings in addition to the enormously powerful Magnifica godling, but Erical was glad to bring the strength of Prirari as well.

Following the more heavily trafficked road, he arrived at the city and looked up to see the graceful spires of the empra's palace and the Magnifica temple. The large stepped pyramid towered twice as tall as when he'd last seen it, and he couldn't imagine the size of the workforce that had moved so many stone blocks in such a short time.

His godling sparkled brighter, becoming a rainbow force that swept him along and buoyed him up. He rushed ahead without realizing it, practically running as he entered the bustling city.

As he passed the craft districts, warehouses, shops, tanneries, and stockyards, he noticed broken façades on buildings, boarded-up windows, blackened marks of fires that had once raged out of control.

He learned that the Hethrren were still here, unwelcome in the capital city. Priestlord Erical had been unconvinced when Klovus explained his plan to lure the barbarians to Serepol in order to send them off to the old world.

When the Hethrren crossed the landscape from Tamburdin, Erical and his godling had barely deflected the rapacious warriors on their way through Prirari. It stood to reason that the barbarians would not be calm and orderly here either. Erical had hoped the Hethrren would be gone by the time he reached Serepol.

Seeing the damaged buildings, at first he assumed the barbarians were the cause, but the wreckage looked more extensive than mere vandalism and rowdy looting could account for.

Looking down the streets to the graceful harbor, which would normally be filled with trading vessels and fishing boats, he saw a great war fleet with striped sails, ready to launch.

He spoke quietly to his godling. "We have arrived none too soon."

12

〜

AFTER taking over her mother's spacious chambers in the ice palace, Koru set about erasing all vestiges of the previous ruler. She was the new queen of the frostwreths, and her followers needed to recognize it.

Birch followed her into the chill room. Koru had altered the ceiling, which now glittered with sharp icicles in a ferocious display, like countless glass fangs overhead. His hodgepodge clothing kept him warm, and he wrapped the woolen blanket around his shoulders. Mostly, the blanket served to hide his hands so no one would see his carved wooden pig or the makeshift metal knife he had fashioned for himself.

He kept the knife as a precaution, but Queen Koru did not neglect or insult him the way Onn had. He wasn't afraid that she would slit his throat because she grew bored. Still, he didn't know whether to accept her. What did she mean to do with him? Why did she consider him so important? Did he dare trust her?

He took a seat on a block of ice covered with a white pelt, pulled his knees up to his chest, and concentrated on every detail around him. Under the blanket, he held the toy animal, rubbing his thumb along the smooth surface. It was just a trinket made of carved wood, but it reminded him not just of the grunting animals that a pig farmer had kept in a pen in his village, but also of his grandfather, Kollanan the Hammer, a war hero, a brave leader.

When Koru had discovered that the king of Norterra was the boy's grandfather, at first she seemed amused by the fact, and then she dismissed it entirely. "Human kings mean nothing to us," she told him. "Frostwreths have much more important work to do."

Not all wreths ignored humans, though. He remembered his grandmother Tafira used to make yellow candies out of ginger and turmeric and bring a sack of them every time she visited Lake Bakal. But Irri had killed his grandmother and showed off what he had done. Queen Onn, who had ordered the murder, was proud of Irri's success. That was the last incentive Birch had needed to ignite the piled debris of his hatred. So he had taken Dar's spear from the wall by the throne and pushed it right through Onn's ribs. . . .

He squeezed the wooden pig hard in his small hand, still hiding it. Birch made it move across his leg as if it were alive. The pig also reminded him of what his life had been before all the horrors unfolded, before Rokk had seized him as a curiosity while obliterating Birch's family and the entire town. As the memories sharpened, he began breathing harder, faster. . . .

Koru busied herself, reshaping her new royal quarters. She traced her fingers through the air, and lines melted in the frozen floor, sketching out a map that marked the sandwreth territory deep in the desert. She leaned closer to the engraved map, pursing her pale lips. She held Dar's spear loosely in her hand and toyed with the ancient weapon, twirling it as she brooded.

Birch watched her, noting the stains on the spear head. He remembered how the dark red blood had gushed from Onn's side. He remembered the feel of the weapon when he stabbed her. He wished he could have done it a thousand times, but even that wouldn't compensate for the pain the frostwreths had caused him.

Koru turned her icy eyes to him. He hadn't said anything, but she eerily seemed to understand his thoughts. "Boy, what do you think my wreths would do to you if they knew you were the one who killed their queen?"

Birch didn't know if she meant to frighten him or if she was genuinely curious. "You'd be embarrassed if they knew I did it, instead of you."

Koru laughed. "Exactly, boy! You are very clever."

He was aware that she could discard him at any time, or maybe she would set him free. The queen was ready to march all the frostwreths on a long and difficult journey that would end in great battles. Birch couldn't possibly help with that. Maybe Koru would realize he'd just get in the way and would let him go before he became too much of a bother.

If so, the drones would help him survive. The small creatures would bring him food and give him scraps of clothing to keep warm, help him to make his way back to Norterra, back to his grandfather's city of Fellstaff.

On the other hand, if he made up his mind to escape, would Koru bother to chase after him? She had many other concerns. He could slip away without being noticed. The frostwreth armies were busy preparing for the long march. In the manufacturing caves, wreths were building battle sleighs to be pulled by oonuks. Some nobles and warriors would ride in the sleighs, while others would mount the wolf-steeds.

Would they even notice if he escaped?

Yes, Koru would.

The queen paced around the chamber, poking into Onn's possessions with clear disapproval. She melted open frozen curio cabinets and storage cubes. She ransacked her mother's garments, draping some of the webby fabric over her shoulders, ripping many gowns to shreds with her sharp nails. She inspected whatever her mother had considered valuable.

With a tinkle of dissolving ice, Koru broke open one of Queen Onn's transparent cabinets. Inside, she found dozens of cloudy cubes the size of gambling dice. Koru grinned. "Another toy of my mother's." She scattered several of the cubes on the ice floor of the chamber. Like smoke, images wafted up from them, mirages made out of cold mist.

Birch leaned close, intrigued. From one of the cubes, he saw a recording of oonuks tearing one another apart while frostwreth warriors cheered them on. From another cube, brittle and haughty Onn laughed as she caressed the warrior Rokk, who flashed her a lascivious smile. The other cubes projected more images that Queen Onn had wanted to preserve.

Koru picked up the objects, cradling them in her palms. "My mother's stored memories are worthless." She held one of the cloudy cubes between a thumb and forefinger, inspecting one facet, then another. "I should just destroy all of these."

"How do they work?" Birch asked.

The queen turned to him. "Simple enough. Intrinsic magic—here." She extended her palm, and Birch selected two of them. "Touch your thumb to one of the faces. It will store a recording of everything around it, until you tell it to stop."

He pressed his thumb against the smooth face, and turned it around. "It's not doing anything."

"Of course it is, boy. Watch." She took the cube from him and touched the top with her forefinger, and the object projected a misty image of the pale young boy frowning down at it and saying, "It's not doing anything."

Koru laughed at his expression of surprise and tossed the recording cubes back into the broken cabinet. Then, leaning closer, she reached in and withdrew another object, a golden cuff marked with old runes. "Where did she get this?" She bent closer, noting the blood that marked two golden prongs inside the band.

Birch remembered the ramer worn by Lasis, his grandfather's Brava . . . and what Queen Onn had done to the man right in front of him.

Again, Koru seemed to know his thoughts. "You recognize it. I saw the flicker on your face."

Birch had to keep himself useful to her. "It's called a ramer. The Bravas wear them."

"Ah, I have heard of Bravas! Our half-breed descendants. Some wreths took humans as lovers."

"Queen Onn captured a Brava and brought him here into her chambers. His name was Lasis."

Koru held out the golden cuff. "What does this do?'

Birch tried to remember. "Bravas can use the magic because they have wreth blood. They clamp the ramer around their wrist, make themselves bleed, and then call fire around their hand, like a flaming sword."

Koru drew her brows together and looked at the metal band, the sharp prongs. On a whim she slapped it around her wrist and squeezed until the golden teeth cut deep. She raised her bleeding hand, regarded the ramer cuff, and closed her eyes in concentration. "There is magic here. I can feel it. I'm drawing on it. . . ."

Lines etched her face, and her frown deepened. She clenched her fist and pressed it to her forehead. Blood continued to flow, but the ramer did not activate.

"It doesn't work," she said with a huff. "The ramer is flawed."

"Its owner is dead," Birch said. "Queen Onn slashed his throat, but she kept the ramer as a souvenir. I . . . was right there."

The words did not make an impression on Koru. She removed the cuff and held it up. "Apparently, it does not like pure wreth blood. Maybe a mongrel mix is what the magic requires." She tossed the ramer aside, and it landed with a clinking sound against the ice walls.

A flurry of drones entered the chamber with platters of food, and Birch's stomach rumbled. It was long past the time when he should have had a meal, so he rose to his feet and took some of the food without asking. The queen didn't bother to notice.

A moment later, a muscular wreth warrior entered the chamber uninvited, emboldened by anger. Irri wore a blue chest plate and silver scaled leggings. Two ice knives and a wicked-looking hook hung from his belt, as if he had armed himself specifically for this meeting.

Birch felt a surge of both anger and terror. Now his tattered blanket felt too hot.

Indignant, Koru commanded Irri to stop. "These are no longer my mother's chambers, and you are not welcome here. If I choose to take a consort, I prefer one who has not been . . . used."

Irri did not rise to the insult. He planted his feet squarely on the frozen floor and sneered at the map she had etched in the ice. A drop of blood from her wrist had splashed onto the ice near Fellstaff's location.

The sight of blood close to his grandfather's home sent a shiver up Birch's spine. His grandmother was dead. Could there be more bloodshed to come?

Irri said, "The frostwreths go to war soon, Koru. But I warn you—"

She cut him off as if with the slash of a blade. "*Queen* Koru."

He grunted a sound that might have been the word "queen" and continued, "Queen Onn awakened our armies from spellsleep so we could slaughter the sandwreths. Our destiny is to exterminate them, not make peace with them."

Koru said, "I will absorb our wayward cousins into *my* army so that *I* rule them. After I kill their queen, we will see how many others we need to eliminate, but I would prefer to save them for fighting Ossus. Do not forget our true destiny."

"If you refuse to let us kill a substantial number of them, perhaps your own frostwreths will not follow you as queen. Many already question your rule."

"Many? Tell me who they are, and I will kill them myself," Koru said, then added with barbed sarcasm, "You, of course, are not one of them, Irri? You, of course, are my most loyal frostwreth."

He looked away. "I cannot deny the fact that Onn is dead. I know you killed her."

Koru waited for him to explain more, and when he fell silent, she added, "I will take that as your expression of fealty. Now speak no more about wasting great warriors, whether they are frostwreths or sandwreths. I fought a dragon myself, and I know the challenge we will face against Ossus. A warrior must keep his eyes on the true target. In our battle against the great dragon, enough sandwreth blood will be shed to satisfy even you."

Irri grunted, "You have no idea what will satisfy me." He left without being dismissed.

Once he was gone, Birch breathed a sigh of relief. Neither wreth had bothered to notice him or the drones who stood holding their food platters.

Koru returned her attention to the map on the ice floor and continued planning her war. The drones placed food beside her, but she ignored the meal. Birch snatched another plate and withdrew into a corner, where he made himself practically invisible, as he had learned to do beside Queen Onn.

13

ᘒᗺ

FOR the first time in his life, Master Onzu worried that he might not be able to trust other Bravas. His understanding of the universe had shifted when he learned of Utho's corruption, when he observed the actual murder of Konag Conndur through the images projected in the ramer smoke. His mind struggled to grasp the idea of a dishonorable Brava. It was as if the world had suddenly tilted sideways and sent him scrabbling for balance.

Onzu hoped that Utho was the only untrustworthy one, but how could he be sure? Many other Bravas were invested in the vengewar, had answered the summons to Convera. And Utho was the bonded Brava of the konag, whom they were all sworn to protect.

When he guided his horse through the forest back to the training village, Onder followed him, bedraggled but hopeful. The disgraced Brava should have remembered the path, because he had spent years training here under his father. But the young man recalled none of it, thanks to the rune of forgetting. Even these simple memories from his time as a Brava had been stripped from him.

With supplies strung over the training master's saddle and another load shouldered by the young man, they moved at a swift pace. At first Onder pestered him with many questions. "How can I help? What do you want me to do for you?" He was beyond curious, almost desperate. "What is your name? Please tell me."

Finally, the Brava master looked down from his saddle. "I am Onzu. You knew that once." The young man responded with only a blank expression, so the master rode onward. A part of his heart ached to know that his own son could not remember him.

He saw that the young man was repentant and confused. Onder believed that he was a good person and a worthy fighter. He could not accept that he was a coward. But no one could understand their true nature until faced with an actual crisis. In Mirrabay, the young Brava had failed that test when he and Utho faced a godling, and Onder ran. It didn't matter that he could no longer remember.

Even so, seeing the pain, emptiness, and longing that filled his son, Master Onzu felt an unwilling glimmer of pity for him. Perhaps his disgraced son could make up for it in part. The mission he had in mind was well within Onder's capabilities, and no one would interfere with him.

At the isolated village, his wards were always alert. Lookouts in the forest spotted their approach. While the training master was known, the tattooed stranger was not. Onzu heard the appropriate combination of false birdcalls across the trees. His students were perhaps a little too obvious in their birdcalls, but the disgraced Brava didn't notice. Preoccupied with his thoughts, Onder kept his head down as he plodded along.

The hidden path became more apparent among the leaves on the forest floor, and then the beech trees opened up to reveal the cluster of dwellings and the training area. The children were there waiting for their master's return, eager, fascinated, some anxious. A few worked in the garden plot. The oldest boy, Rigg, stood guard, a training staff in one hand and an actual short sword in the other. Onzu noted with approval that he and the other trainees were ready to fight if need be. They regarded the newcomer, who had the half-breed features of a Brava but was not dressed like one.

The oldest girl, Vitora, came forward. "What's that on your face?"

Master Onzu interrupted before his son could answer. "Better hope that you never get one of your own! It is a rune of forgetting, a mark of shame. This man is Onder. As a Brava, he exhibited gross cowardice, so a group of Bravas punished him with that mark, stripping away his legacy and memories."

The trainees looked at Onder as if he were dung they had found on their shoes. The disgraced young man hung his head. "I am sorry. I don't remember. But I . . .." He seemed to come to a decision and raised his head to meet their eyes. "I have a letter written by Utho. I can read you what he says I did."

"What you actually did," Master Onzu corrected in a stern voice. "But I have learned in other ways that Utho's word cannot be trusted."

"If he is not a Brava anymore, why is he here?" asked Rigg. "Are we supposed to punish him? Do we need to guard him?"

"He is going to help us," Onzu said as he dismounted. "I have decided he can be useful."

The young man brightened with hope. "I'll do anything. Just command me. I'll show you."

"I will *tell* you. Things here will change. I'm about to leave, my students will stay in the village, and I'm giving you a separate mission . . . a chance to prove yourself. We'll talk as we eat lunch."

Onder deposited his load of supplies on a wooden bench, the training master untied the bags, and the children helped him unpack. Onzu brought out a fresh loaf of bread and unwrapped a large smoked trout and enough apples to share around. Vitora presented a bowl of red tomatoes picked from their vegetable plot.

Onder tried to help, but the students were like a well-trained army, knowing their tasks as they put together a quick lunch. The disgraced Brava finally sat and just watched, thanking them when they placed food in front of him. They gathered around Master Onzu, who took his seat on the fallen log where he usually lectured.

"First, you need to know that Utho is the konag's bonded Brava. He serves and guards Konag Mandan, and before that he served Conndur the Brave."

The tattooed young man touched the tattoo on his face. "Utho is the man I betrayed."

"Utho has betrayed all of us," Onzu snapped. "Utho lied."

The young man blinked several times. "Then . . . maybe I'm innocent? Maybe this letter—"

"No, the letter is true. When I first heard the news, I couldn't believe it myself, but there were many witnesses in Mirrabay, not just Utho. You did commit the act of cowardice, and you deserved your punishment."

Onder hung his head and nodded.

"Utho's crimes have nothing to do with yours." Crisply and efficiently, the master recounted how Elliel had been falsely accused, her legacy erased to maintain an ugly secret about Isharan captives.

"We hate Isharans," muttered Rigg.

"Yes, we hate Isharans," Master Onzu agreed, "but we hate dishonesty and disloyalty more. Elliel regained her memories and is now sworn to King Kollanan in Norterra. He knows the truth about what happened to her, and he wrote a letter to his brother exposing Utho's crimes against Elliel." Onzu paused and saw that everyone was staring at him. They had all stopped eating. "But Konag Conndur was murdered before the letter arrived. He never learned the truth."

Rigg nodded vigorously. "It was the Isharans."

"It was not the Isharans!" Onzu snarled, surprising himself with his vehemence. "And this is the far greater crime: *Utho* actually murdered the konag, the man he was supposed to protect, in order to trigger our vengewar. I know this for a fact." He paused, waiting for anyone to challenge him. "You saw the other night when I burned the strand of hair and summoned Utho's memories, but you didn't know what you were seeing. That is why everything has changed now. I cannot allow this crime to stand. The three kingdoms cannot allow it."

The disgraced young man stared, wrestling with cavernous unanswered questions. "But . . . why? How?"

Grimacing because the poison was so bitter, Master Onzu described exactly what Utho had done. The trainees looked sickened, and young Onder rocked from side to side, but the training master continued.

Hiding his crime, Utho had summoned all loyal Bravas to Convera, where he would give them their long-awaited war against the Isharan enemies.

"They have been our enemies, yes," Onzu admitted, "but Isharans did not commit this crime." He looked at his young students. "Remember when Utho came here? He dismissed my concerns about the wreths and Ossus, and only focused on the vengewar."

As he thought about Tytan and Jennae, two Bravas who had passed through on their way to Convera, Master Onzu grew even more concerned. Those two had responded to Utho's call by breaking their bonds with sworn lords and riding across the Commonwealth without question. When Onzu had explained how Utho betrayed Elliel, the two had brushed it aside as if it didn't matter. Tytan and Jennae—and how many other Bravas?—were willing to tolerate such dishonor in exchange for the greater goal of vengeance. They chose a situational morality that fit their convenience rather than keeping their vows to act with immutable honor with no gray edges.

Onzu continued his tale. "Although King Kollanan of Norterra knows what Utho and Lord Cade did to Elliel, he does not suspect that Utho is the one who secretly killed Conndur to instigate a war. He must be told."

The training master leaned forward on the fallen log, and turned toward Onder. "Someone has to deliver this news to Norterra. I need a messenger to expose the truth about Utho, to tell Kollanan the Hammer that the Isharans did not butcher his brother . . . that it was Conndur's bonded Brava himself."

He fell silent, and watched Onder.

It took the young man several seconds to realize what the master was asking of him. "Me? You want me to ride with the message?"

"You are a person that no one will try to stop," Master Onzu said. "Other Bravas are so blood-maddened by the idea of vengewar that they won't risk hindering it in any way. They don't question it. I cannot imagine they would prevent a fellow Brava from bringing a message to Norterra, but . . ." He let out a sigh. "But there is much I could not imagine before now. I am almost certain, however, that no Brava would waste a moment on a man with a rune of forgetting on his face."

"You would . . . trust me to do something so important?" Onder didn't seem to believe it, but his eyes held hope.

"The future is always more important than the past. I am willing to believe that *one* scene in the legacy of your life does not tell the whole story," the training master said, hoping he would not regret this decision. "I give you this chance out of mercy and compassion. Please do not make me regret this decision."

Onder straightened, as if he had been given a new life. "I won't let you down. One day maybe I'll earn the right to be a Brava again."

It was unlikely, if not impossible, for a Brava with that rune of shame to come back into the fold, but just as a person needed food and water, he needed hope. Onzu gave that to him.

The training master rose and looked at his students. "I trust all of you. I know that I have trained you properly, even if other Bravas have forgotten their priorities." With a pang, he recalled how diligently he had trained his son years ago, how much pride he had felt when he'd sent the young man off to become a paladin. Now he looked directly at Onder's face and tried to see past the rune. "There may be danger on your path. You must not waver. King Kollanan needs to know what actually happened, so he can make his decision based on the truth."

"Why aren't you going to deliver the message yourself, Master Onzu?" asked Vitora. "Shouldn't King Kollanan hear it from you?"

"I have to ride in the opposite direction."

The young trainees tried to look brave and confident.

Rigg asked, "Where are you going? How long will you be gone?"

"To Convera. I know my duty." He smiled at his trainees. "As for you, I am trusting you to take care of the villagers." He walked toward his dwelling. "I'll once again put on my black Brava armor, my cape, my gauntlets, my boots. I will go to Utho myself and confront him over what he has done. And I will be gone until my obligation is met."

14

IN the throne hall of Convera Castle, the tables and chairs had been pushed aside to clear a large area, and Utho stood on the open floor, wiping perspiration from his brow with the back of his hand. Normally, he and Mandan would have performed their vigorous combat training out in the fresh air of the courtyard, where they could swing swords at each other or at practice dummies dressed in Isharan clothes. But because the day was filled with a cold drizzle, Mandan wanted to train inside his castle.

The throne room was not designed for fighting exercises, but the young konag insisted that he could do whatever he wanted. "Besides, Utho, we never know when or where I might have to fight an opponent. What if an assassin tries to murder me on my throne?"

"Then I would kill him," Utho replied, but nevertheless agreed to spar in the throne room.

Mandan wore a new set of chain mail with fine links polished to a silvery luster. His blue cape had been embroidered with the open hand of the Commonwealth, but his scarlet doublet showed the rising sun of Osterra. Mandan sprang about trying to dodge blows, but the ornate garments made him clumsy and the cape tangled around his elbow. Utho could have killed him ten times over during the fifteen-minute training session, and that made him all the more determined that Mandan never face a duel to the death on his own. Even so, the young man was reasonably skilled as a fighter, though his moves were predictable.

Mandan laughed aloud, pleased with himself. "I am getting better, Utho. You can tell."

"You are getting better, my konag," Utho lied. He would press his ward harder. The young man had to be ready.

Mandan tossed his sword on a table that had been pushed against a side wall, unfastened the heavy cape, and dropped it to the floor. He poured a goblet of cool water from a pitcher on the table and gulped it down.

Without being announced, two dusty Bravas entered the throne room, exuding confidence. Recognizing them as Tytan and Jennae, Utho gestured them forward, and the pair introduced themselves to the konag with a respectful bow. Burly Tytan was not given to deep thought, but he had a strong heart and had created a significant legacy of brave deeds. Jennae was a hardened woman who would have been more attractive if she ever allowed herself to smile. She was a good fighter, though; Utho had seen her in combat. He would not want to be her enemy.

"We broke our bonded service to respond to your calling for the venge-war," Tytan said to Utho.

Jennae frowned, sounding conspiratorial. "We've also heard disturbing stories and gossip about you, Utho." She looked up at him, and he met her gaze. Neither of them flinched. She changed her tone, shrugged, and turned away. "I hear Isharan blood is very good at washing away scandal."

Mandan didn't seem to know what she was talking about, and Utho explained, "Jennae and Tytan are examples of how we need to keep our focus on the real war."

Utho had spent days working carefully to divert Mandan's rage and impatience ever since word had come back about the debacle at Yanton. The young konag still wanted to dispatch armies to the north and quash Kollanan's defiance, but Utho wouldn't allow it. He would soon load the core of the Commonwealth army aboard the naval ships. He wanted the soldiers to save their fighting for the Isharan animals.

Now, sweaty and still breathing hard from the exercise, Mandan stood before Tytan and Jennae. "I am your konag. You are Bravas. Swear your loyalty to me."

The two looked at each other, then glanced at Utho, who nodded without managing to hide his annoyed expression. Both of them bowed.

Tytan said, "A Brava's loyalty is always to his konag."

"It does not usually need to be said," Jennae said with a hint of a scolding tone. "The konag has my loyalty, my ramer, and my blood. Always."

"Good. Many Bravas have answered Utho's call, although many others have been slow to respond. Their ramers should be united against the Isharan animals who murdered my father."

"They should, my konag," Utho agreed, "but sometimes communication is slow and unreliable, and not every Brava has as clear a view of our goal as we do."

"Like Elliel," Mandan said with an underlying sneer.

Utho did not comment, because he didn't want to continue that line of conversation. Instead he briefed the two new Bravas. "Our ships will launch soon and strike the coast of the new world. We will invade Serepol and burn down the empra's palace. We will recapture Fulcor Island on the way. We will pillage their lands and take them for our own."

Tytan muttered, "We'll finally build a new Valaera."

"The war will be glorious," Jennae said.

Mandan climbed the dais and slumped into his throne. He paused to admire the violent painting of the Battle of Yanton. "Utho, you are my Brava, the commander of my troops. You are the best fighter of all of us." He slouched further into his seat. "Even though I am konag, you are best qualified to lead the attack. As we've discussed, I want you to be my general."

The words were exactly what Utho had been planting in his ear for days. Now he kept his voice even so as not to seem too obsequious. "You have faced battle before, my konag, and no one doubts your bravery, but the three kingdoms are facing a great deal of civil unrest. You do not need to command the front lines of our naval strike or ride at the forefront of your troops as we slaughter the Isharan enemy."

Mandan sat up straighter, nodding. "Yes, I am needed here at home."

Utho remembered how terrified the young man had been when fire arrows rained down around the ships from the Fulcor garrison, how he had panicked when the Isharans used a chemical catapult. Mandan had been completely useless in that battle, but Utho could not say so aloud. As a Brava, his charge was to protect the young man at all costs. "Let me manage this vengewar, Sire. I will lead us to victory."

Mandan raised his hand. "You know what is best. You have my permission. Use my Bravas, the Commonwealth navy, and all of our soldiers."

Tytan and Jennae had been watching Mandan, and seemed relieved.

Utho said, "I will issue orders to release the armory stockpiles, distribute the old swords and shields, spears, knives, maces, and war hammers from the catacombs beneath the palace so we can arm every fighter in Osterra."

Mandan smiled. They had both been down in the armory chambers that riddled the bluff above the confluence, inspecting stored weapons from the old war against Ishara. "I'm glad those blades can be of service now. We want everyone ready to fight any Isharan that comes to our shores." The konag paused. "Or they can be used to fight criminals and traitors here in the three kingdoms."

Utho knew what the young konag was considering; he just hoped Mandan wouldn't do anything foolish while the rest of his military force was away conquering Ishara.

15

⚘

INSIDE the walled city of Fellstaff, the silence was suffused with tension rather than peace. Farmers hauling carts to market, merchants, craftsmen, carpenters, and members of the city guard went about their daily activities with a hushed urgency.

After delivering the news to his uncle, Adan wanted to hurry back to Suderra, but he needed to make war preparations with his uncle. War preparations . . . He had come prepared to defend against wreths. He had not imagined there would be a civil war.

Though his guest bed was comfortable and the fire drove away the late-autumn chill, Adan had not slept well. He had thrashed in his blankets, and his thoughts were muddled with nightmares and worry. He grappled with what Mandan had done. Attacking Commonwealth citizens! He and his brother never had a warm or close relationship, but they were both sons of Conndur the Brave, and they served the three kingdoms and ruled their people. As the firstborn, Mandan was always destined to become konag, and Adan had never dreamed of taking his brother's place.

But as a ruler, Mandan was cruel, capricious, and vindictive. Adan had seen those tendencies when they were just boys playing together. Although young Adan had fun enjoying a victory or accepting defeat when Mandan bested him, his brother had not reacted the same say. Mandan experienced no joy in such challenges, only competition, only winners or losers rather than a learning experience that would help both young men grow into better leaders.

As king of Suderra, Adan loved his people and had no wish to become konag of the entire Commonwealth. Kollanan's argument to overthrow Mandan made him uneasy. Adan worried about all the bloodshed that would result. He did not want to send his army against fellow citizens of the Commonwealth, but he understood that Norterra and Suderra had little choice, considering what Mandan had done.

First, however, he had another priority. He had made a promise to Penda.

After he washed himself and put on fresh clothes, he ate part of the breakfast that Pokle had left on a tray outside his door, then went in search of Kollanan.

His uncle was out in the stables. In the crisp morning, Adan could see the breath steam out of his nostrils. Kollanan seemed not to feel the chill. He wore only a sleeveless vest as he brushed his black warhorse. Elliel and Thon kept him company. The other two Bravas, Lasis and Gant, were off on duties of their own.

Adan paused at the doorway, smelling the hay and horses. "I'd think the king of Norterra could hire stable boys."

Kollanan looked up with a small reflexive smile. "Then I wouldn't have the pleasure of tending Storm. I want him to know that I appreciate his years of loyalty." The big black war horse snorted.

Koll's words turned serious. "I sent dispatches across the land. My vassal lords will not be eager to go to battle again so soon, especially if that means a long march over the Dragonspine Mountains, but they all know what needs to be done." He scratched his full beard. "Even the soldiers who were not at Yanton understand what Mandan did. They know it must not stand." He continued to brush the black horse, working out his anger.

Adan thought of Penda and their baby as he wrestled with what he had to say. Koll glanced up, sensing something in the unexpected silence. "I can send escort riders with you back to Suderra. You'll want to begin gathering your army for the march on Convera."

"I need to help some other people first. I've put aside the decision for too long because it was hard, but every day now we have to make hard decisions." Adan paused. "There are many human captives suffering under the wreths in a slave camp in the canyons. I want to free them." He could not drive away the images he'd seen in the mothertear diamond. "We know where they are."

His voice was made quieter by shame because he had done nothing for so long. "I convinced myself we weren't strong enough to fight the sandwreths, and I let all those prisoners suffer. Queen Voo provided my army with shadowglass to make deadly weapons, and I didn't want to provoke her. But we are already at war. I killed Quo. It is about time we make our move before the sandwreths suspect anything."

Kollanan considered in silence for a long moment, but he clearly *wanted* to do something, needing only a target. Frown lines were visible beneath his beard, but he showed his teeth in a hard smile. "My people struck the Lake Bakal fortress, and we showed them we are not to be ignored."

Adan drew a breath. "I could use your help, Uncle. You and your Bravas."

Koll looked at Elliel and Thon. "We could accompany you with a group of fighters, ride quickly south to liberate that camp, while Lasis and my other vassal lords gather the main Norterran army for our long march."

Adan felt the weight of responsibility, and he nodded. "We will ride first to Bannriya and arm ourselves with shadowglass, which is deadly against wreths. We'll need those weapons. Given enough fighters, we can overwhelm the labor camp, kill the guards, free the prisoners." He was sure it would not be that simple, but he had to believe it would succeed.

Thon seemed intrigued. "I helped King Kollanan fight the frostwreths, but that does not mean I side with sandwreths. In fact, until I know who or what I am, I should remain neutral." He gave a solemn nod. "Therefore, I should help attack the sandwreth camp as well. Just to be fair."

Elliel chuckled. Thon did not seem to understand why she was amused.

Kollanan nodded, his decision firm. "We can free those people, and I'll be glad of it." He turned back to his warhorse and began combing the mane. "When we are finished with that task, we can focus on overturning the konag's throne."

16

≈

TRAPPED underground for so long, Cemi felt like a prisoner in a dungeon. She and her companions had hidden for weeks praying for Iluris to recover, watching out for Klovus's murderous schemes. The new godling had helped camouflage their shelter, but Cemi felt that she had been numb and helpless, just like the empra herself. She and Vos had at last begun to make proactive plans.

Now that Iluris was awake, Cemi had to set those plans in motion. The people needed to know the wonderful news.

When the faithful old servant Analera came in with their smuggled food, she nearly bowled the empra over in her joy. "Excellency! Oh, my lady!" She could find no other words, but just repeated herself over and over again. She began bawling, then quickly brought herself under control. "It's time! We must bring our allies together. You have to take back your throne."

"I do not recall surrendering my throne," Iluris mused, though her voice held a faint question, as if she couldn't exactly remember.

Cemi was also enthusiastic. "We must spread the word, tell them all to be ready. Your people are with you, Excellency, but the key priestlord will not relinquish his power quietly. We must be careful."

Analera's eyes sparkled, surrounded by weary wrinkles. "Hear us, save us."

Sitting on her pallet, Iluris seemed weak and wrung out, but the old servant's faith gave her strength. The new godling force rippled along the stone wall, like a fish just beneath the water.

Wearing a drab disguise, old Analera led Cemi out of the winding tunnels beneath the palace. The servant scuttled with surprising speed despite the stoop of her back, the slump of her shoulders. Cemi wore the plain clothes of a washerwoman. Some princess born to nobility might have been indignant to don dirty rags, but Cemi had worn such clothes for much of her life. She blended right in as an unnoticed castle worker.

Analera had allies among the castle staff, but there were also those who could not be trusted, and she helped Cemi avoid them. As she took the young woman through the bustling passageways and workrooms, both of them kept their heads down. Cemi carried a pile of bedsheets on her shoulder, and they moved past the laundry where washerwomen boiled the fabrics in great cauldrons of water and soap.

When they slipped out into the streets of Serepol, Cemi felt liberated by the bright sunlight and fresh air. This was the first she'd set foot outside the palace in a long time, and she felt like a normal person, rather than the empra's ward. Iluris had taken the girl under her wing, tutored her in history, mathematics, government, finances, and made Cemi wear fancy garments, surrounded by a hawk guard escort and smiling sycophants. The young woman never had a moment alone. Now, though, she and Analera were just commoners. They hurried along the wide streets.

"We will meet with some of the empra's strongest supporters," Analera said. Her raspy voice was filled with a new excitement. "I arranged it."

A few blocks beyond the palace, Serepol took on a vibrant character, thriving with everyday business. Cemi looked at candlemakers and coppersmiths, a carpenter assembling a chair seat of woven reeds, a potter pumping his rattling wheel near a kiln that sent up smoke. A wine merchant inventoried his barrels, and a young girl with a basket of eggs went from door to door selling them. A maker of stringed instruments plucked a mournful tune and hummed from the bottom of his throat. Food vendors offered skewers of seasoned lamb, candies made of jellied fruit and honey, blocks of cheese, cinnamon-roasted seeds. One vendor had wire cages filled with songbirds and a long willow switch; any time the birds stopped singing, he would smack the bars and startle them into chirping again.

"Our allies have spread word to their friends and even more friends," Analera said. "This city loves its mother, the empra. Klovus made a grave error when he allowed her to disappear."

"He didn't exactly allow it," Cemi said. "We fought hard, and many of her guards died."

The old woman kept moving and turned a corner. "I remember full well, my lady. Some of my friends had to scrub blood from the walls and the . . . and even the ceiling when the godling smashed some assassins. Once they finished cleaning the room, though, I never saw those workers again." Her voice was heavy, and both of them knew what must have happened to the cleaners. Klovus had eliminated the witnesses. The people of Ishara would turn on him if they believed he had done any harm to their empra.

If Iluris had actually died on Fulcor Island, Ishara could have grieved, but recovered. But she'd come back home in a coma, and then disappeared. No one knew what had happened to her, and when a mystery was too great, people made up their own answers.

The key priestlord's ambitions were too plain. He had brought the rough Hethrren here to the capital city, which they had plundered, before unleashing his godling, which had wrought even more chaos. As Cemi followed Analera on a roundabout path, she noted the damaged structures, broken windows, soot marks. Some of the destruction could be blamed on the rampaging godling, but much was simply callous Hethrren vandalism.

No, the people were not pleased with Key Priestlord Klovus.

Analera led her past a communal well where women filled their water jugs and sullen young sons waited to carry the heavy containers back home. "We are almost to Boorlin's smithy. Follow me."

Ahead, Cemi heard the clang of a hammer on an anvil, saw the smoke of a forge. A grimy, shirtless young journeyman pumped the bellows to stoke the fire.

Analera called, and the blacksmith, a stocky man made muscular from a lifetime of working metal, raised his hammer in a casual wave. His head was shaved except for a tight braid that dangled like a tail from the back of his skull. His eyebrows had long since been singed off. Boorlin sported an iron ring in his left nostril and in his left ear. "You've come about the order from the key priestlord? I am fashioning weapons as fast as I can."

"What order?" Cemi asked in a low voice.

Analera led the girl forward and whispered, "Just a show for eavesdroppers. He knows who I am. Boorlin has long served the empra."

The two women entered the forge yard. Barrels of scum-covered water waited to quench blades after Boorlin shaped them. Two apprentices used tongs to pull red-hot iron from the heat of the forge, while the shirtless journeyman continued pumping the bellows. The clamor drowned out Analera's low conversation with the smith.

She introduced the big man. "Boorlin was commissioned to make the armor for all the hawk guards."

"And a fine job I did! My best work, and I did it for her. I've never forgotten that Iluris placed faith in my skill, and I won't give up my faith in her."

"I promised I would bring more news." The old woman lowered her voice, and Boorlin leaned closer. "This is Cemi, the empra's designated heir."

"She didn't actually designate that," Cemi said. "She was still training me."

"We know who you are, my lady," Boorlin said, then battered the glowing iron on his anvil. For show, he bellowed out to anyone listening, "That is impossible! We are working as fast as we can." Then he bent closer to them, whispering again. "Is it true the empra lives, that she is awake?"

"Yes," Cemi said. "We have to prepare the people for her return, but the key priestlord cannot know. Klovus has his godling, and the other priestlords follow his lead. The city guards are under his control."

"They've come twice to my forge to search for traitors," Boorlin said. "They want to track down those who whisper that our empra will come back."

Cemi's heart felt heavy to learn this.

"They haven't caught anyone yet," Analera said. "Not that we've heard of."

"Oh, you never hear from the ones they catch. Never again," the blacksmith said. "I know of five or six."

Cemi was concerned. "Will they reveal anything? Do we need to move the empra from our hiding place?"

Boorlin pursed his lips. "They have faith, my lady, but they have no knowledge. Nor do I. Not even Analera has revealed all she knows."

The old woman turned to Cemi. "I have said only that Iluris is our true empra, that she lives, and that she will come back to take her place."

"People may be intimidated by the key priestlord, but they do not love him. Their faith in Empra Iluris is far more powerful." Boorlin clanged his iron again, grumbled a loud false complaint for anyone else to hear. His apprentices snickered to one another, then went back to their own labors when the blacksmith glared at them.

His voice was husky but urgent. "The people cannot wait much longer, though. They need to see the empra soon, or they will stop believing. A hot-blooded young man can make promises to his lady for only so long until he needs to add a golden ring." Boorlin made a rude sound. "Though I prefer iron. It's strong, not just pretty."

Cemi looked around the forge district, where a dozen other smithies remained busy, though no one seemed happy to have so much work. Boorlin grumbled as he explained the activity: "Klovus has us making clumsy weapons for his barbarian minions, not much more than cudgels." He picked up a studded iron knob that would be mounted onto a wooden handle. "It's offensive to create such ugly weapons for such ugly people. But once the brutes are armed, perhaps they will simply be gone. Hear us, save us."

Cemi remembered when Magda had stumbled upon their hiding place in the tunnels, but had left them alone, utterly uninterested. From outsiders, Cemi knew that the restless barbarian hordes were just as eager to leave Ishara as the key priestlord was to have them gone.

Cemi smiled with an idea. Though she was anxious to do *something*, she understood the virtue of waiting. "Klovus looks toward the Hethrren to strengthen his position, even though they rarely cooperate. But if they are about to leave, maybe we should wait until they go. Then the key priestlord will have fewer supporters, and we can make our move."

Klovus decided to do more and more of his daily business from the empra's throne chamber rather than the Magnifica temple. He was Ishara's spiritual guide and commanded the godling, yet by performing administrative work in the palace, he also showed that he was the de facto leader of Ishara while the land was without its empra. He was in no hurry to appoint a successor.

He sat at a side table, not quite daring to occupy the throne itself, although Magda had shown no such reluctance. As Klovus stared at reports from the naval captains as well as less optimistic summaries from his spies, he assessed how soon the fleet could depart . . . and how soon Magda and her loathsome Hethrren could be on their way.

While concentrating on the document, he suddenly felt his blood thrum, and gooseflesh prickled down his back. A surge like flames fanned by a gust of wind, the presence of a godling . . . though his Magnifica entity remained quiescent deep within its temple.

He felt a primal force that flowed through the tall doors into the throne chamber. He looked up, ready to call for palace guards if he was threatened. Another priestlord entered, wearing a blue and white caftan. His brown beard had grown long and his hair shaggy, but he seemed clean, energetic. Klovus recognized the priestlord from Prirari District. Behind the man shimmered a colorful energy force that bent and twisted like a multicolored band.

Klovus let out a breath of relief. "Erical! You are the first district priestlord to arrive." The other man walked into the chamber, and his godling flowed after him like a faithful pet. The key priestlord's brow furrowed. "Was it wise to leave your people without their godling back in Prirari?"

Erical gestured behind him. "They are never without their godling, so long as they have faith. I brought this part of her with me, because I'm concerned about . . ." He seemed to have difficulty expressing the words in his head. "I came so quickly because of the dark dreams I have, a dangerous shadow. Don't you feel the evil growing, far away?"

Klovus snorted. "There's always evil. We priestlords must keep it under control. Better that it is distant rather than on our doorstep."

"But this is different, Key Priestlord." Erical strode forward, and the godling became diffuse behind him, spreading out in a fainter mist. "Surely you've sensed it? I see it out of the corner of my mind and in the depths of a restless sleep. Something grows more powerful—across the sea, I think."

"If it is far away, let it stay there. It is difficult enough holding Ishara together." Klovus lowered his voice. "And keeping the Hethrren from destroying our city before I can send them on their way."

Erical bowed but still looked concerned. "I fear this force could become a terrible threat, whatever it is."

Klovus looked back down at his naval reports. "We can discuss it once the navy is launched and our barbarian army is off to fight the Commonwealth." His tone kept Erical from pressing the matter further.

As if his comment had made her appear, Magda pounded on the open wooden door with the head of her club, then strolled into the throne room. Her face was made even uglier by a grimace of displeasure, as if she had eaten a feast of worms and only discovered belatedly that she didn't like them. "My people are impatient, lover—as am I. If you give us nothing else to destroy, we will look closer at hand. Hethrren are not good at waiting."

The key priestlord's heart skipped a beat. He held up the reports and waved them, though he doubted she could read them. "This is a summary from our fleet. Stockpiles of weapons are being loaded aboard as we speak. You will have all of the clubs and spears and swords you need."

Magda raised a fist, looked at it appraisingly. "We have our bare hands if nothing else." She noticed Erical, who met her sneer with a bland expression. "Another pretty man. Shall I have him service me? You yourself aren't much of an enthusiastic lover."

Though Erical did not flinch, the godling brightened and intensified. Magda whirled, noticing the entity. "Ah, another one of those."

"You would be wise not to threaten us," Klovus warned.

The barbarian leader's face twisted. "Among my people, when a woman wants to take a man, it is considered a reward, not a threat. You are very strange cowards."

"We have our own ways," Erical said. "Do you not remember me from Prirari? I fed your armies so you could continue on your way here."

"Ah!" Magda said. "Your supplies lasted us two days, and then we had to raid again."

"Then I kept my district safe for those two days."

Klovus glanced from the priestlord to the pulsing deity to the frustrated barbarian leader. He wanted nothing more than to see the Hethrren depart without causing further damage. He said, "When I raided the coast of the old world, I myself took along the harbor godling. Priestlord Erical, I think you should accompany the warships, bring your godling and make swift work of the enemy."

Magda looked uneasy. "We do not need assistance."

"This is my war." The key priestlord felt emboldened. "I want the godless eliminated. This entity can tear them apart, and there will be enough victims left for you. You will appreciate the added strength, believe me."

Erical looked alarmed. "But Key Priestlord, I came only to Serepol. I must return to my district."

"As you said, a part of their godling will always be with them."

Erical remained uneasy for another reason. "That . . . is the direction from which I sense the evil." Klovus gave him a sinister stare. Resigned, Erical bowed. "Yes, perhaps my godling and I should investigate. Hear us, save us."

Klovus nodded with relief. "The other district priestlords are coming here for the Magnifica ceremony, but you have my permission to depart as soon as the ships are ready."

The barbarian leader grumbled. "I will prepare my people. Give us weapons and ships, and we will make our own victory."

17

∽

THE pens that held the wolf-steeds were hacked out of glacier ice, and the dim light shimmered blue. Despite the frozen walls and scuffed ice floor, the crowded animals made the air thick and fetid. Irri liked the primal smell, which held a promise of violence. It reminded him of the stink of slain enemies.

The snarls were like music and loud enough to drown out the words spoken by his fellow conspirators. His hatred for Koru did not blind him to the fact that she might have allies anywhere.

Irri had easily found six other wreths who despised the insulting end to Queen Onn as much as he did, and he was sure there were hundreds more in the palace and the glacier warrens. "As soon as the bitch is dead, the other wreths will fall in line," he said.

"We all know it," said Mage Qarri. "Wreths quickly forget about a fallen leader. It has always been the way."

"I will not forget about Onn, our real queen," Irri snapped at him. "And she did not forget that we are supposed to kill sandwreths, not write love letters and make friends."

The warriors muttered and nodded, sharing their mutual disdain. Two oonuks bit and wrestled in the pens, attempting to tear each other apart. One of the noble conspirators near the opening lashed out at the animals. "Cease!" Though it was just play, the wolf-steeds were bloody as they reluctantly backed apart. The other beasts looked hungry and angry, as the violence had whetted their appetite.

The mage sniffed. "And who will be our leader once we kill Koru?"

"I will kill her myself," Irri said. "And the more violent and dramatic her death is, the more uncontested my rule will be as I take her place."

Ardo, one of the nobles, snorted. "I want to see the usurper dead, and soon, but why should you be the next frostwreth king? Why not me? My noble blood is more pure."

"Because I could kill you, too," Irri said. "Would you challenge me right now?"

"Not necessary." Ardo turned away with an aloof sniff. He fancied himself a ladies' man, not a ruthless fighter. "But I would like to witness Koru's death, and so would all these others. We are part of your movement. Her defeat should be accomplished in public, not in secret, like when she killed her mother." His companions grumbled in agreement.

Even as Irri and his group spoke in private, drones moved about carrying slop buckets and pulling small carts piled with caribou meat. The small creatures hurried from pen to pen, tossing food to the snarling wolf-steeds. Their chittering language was a low hum, and Irri ignored them.

One of his warrior comrades said, "If you challenge Koru directly and defeat her in combat, why must we plan in secret? Just do it. Enough sneaking around."

Mage Qarri spoke up. "Four centuries ago someone challenged Queen Onn, and he lost. She slashed his throat so deeply that his head nearly fell off." The conspirators chuckled at the image. "And Onn's rule was sound ever since."

One warrior pointed out a different time when a cowardly noble tried to assassinate Onn in her spellsleep chamber. When he was caught, he was flayed alive. Queen Onn did not even know about it until she woke up.

"In recent weeks, more than sixty wreths died in their spellsleep chambers," Qarri mused. "The magic failed, or the mechanisms faltered over the centuries."

"It seems too many to be a coincidence," said one of the nobles.

"Who would assassinate random frostwreths?" Irri snorted. "What would they have to gain?"

The drones chittered and hummed as they moved about. Several of them polished the frozen floor, scrubbing away speckles of blood near the pens. The snarling oonuks tried to attack them, but the bars held.

"When I kill Koru, it will not be a secret thing," Irri vowed. "Everyone will know."

Ardo let out a snorting laugh. "Subtlety and grace are not your strong points, Irri."

The other conspirators muttered as well, but Irri realized he needed to be careful. He had spread cautious whispers, provocative words, and listened carefully to identify those who agreed with him. "I plan to kill her in my own time and place. Her death will be dramatic and clear, but I do not intend to follow the forms. Koru did not challenge her mother, simply ran her through with a spear from behind. That kind of treachery deserves to be repaid in kind." Irri licked his lips.

Four caged oonuks fought over one red leg joint that a drone had tossed in. The small, pale creature stared at the animals in transfixed silence.

"Let us know when you intend to move," Ardo said with a sniff. "I want to be there. I want to watch. And I want to help you plan."

"I do not need your help," Irri said.

The second noble broke in, "If you do not need our help, why did you bring us into this conspiracy?"

Irri's face broke into a smile like cracking ice. "I want you to be there because if I do strike her dead . . ." He pursed his lips. "*When* I strike her dead, it will secure my rule if you all shove your blades into her twitching body before it cools. You can participate in the assassination, as you will all participate in my rule. The frostwreth armies are ready to march, but when I am in command, we will go to war against the wretched descendants of Raan. We will never try to make them our partners."

This made the other conspirators snicker, which in turn provoked the oonuks into a chorus of howls.

One of the clumsy drones dropped his empty meat bucket with a loud clang on the ice floor. Annoyed by the interruption, Irri snatched the drone by its scrawny neck and heaved the pathetic creature over the top of the bars into the nearest oonuk pen. The wolf-steeds roared and fell upon him, but the drone didn't make a sound as the beasts tore him apart. Other drones working among the pens stopped and stared, while some cast glances at Irri and the conspirators. Their expressions were always blank and stupid. Irri shouted for them to leave, and the spooked drones scattered away down the ice halls.

Irri laughed, and the oonuks continued to feed. He turned back to his companions, but they had already finished their planning. They knew what they were going to do.

In the open courtyard before the ice palace gates, Birch listened as the alarmed drones reported what they had seen and heard. The wind had died down, but out of habit he drew his blanket close around his shoulders. The drones' revelations caused a deep chill inside him.

The creatures lived in a cluster of hovels around the towering structure. Sometimes, Birch liked to sit with them. He'd gotten used to the smell, and he liked their company. Koru was so preoccupied with battle preparations that she did not closely watch the boy. But he was watching. The drones were watching.

In their own language, the drones told him about Irri's plans, described how he and his co-conspirators intended to kill the new queen. The drones identified the schemers, and Birch knew who they were. When they told him about their hapless friend being thrown to the oonuks, the boy shrugged off his blanket, feeling a burn of anger. He had always hated Irri.

He had to report the treacherous wreths to Queen Koru and let her take care of them. She would surely execute them all, including Irri. She might even be grateful to Birch.

But then he thought of a better plan, something to make sure she would notice what he—and the drones—did for her. Some drones moved around their stuffy, scrap-filled hovels, while others stared at Birch, waiting for him to decide what to do. He had the drones on his side, and he grew more excited as the details crystallized in his mind.

"We'll do something surprising," he whispered, and the drones understood him. He would take matters into his own hands.

A day later, Birch looked around at the drones, each of them cooperative, willing, dedicated. He knew that not a one of them would question his instructions, since their entire existence was folded around the need to serve and obey. He hoped that they also understood what was at stake.

He held out his hands to reveal a dozen of the translucent recording cubes he had stolen from Koru's chamber, tiny blocks of ice that held wreth magic. "Slip these into the rooms of the ones who are trying to kill Queen Koru. Hide them when you go about your duties." He demonstrated. "Here, just touch the side with your thumb, then walk away. If Irri and the others are talking about their plans, then leave one of these cubes. It's very important."

The drones looked at him, without expression. There was no change in their features. Then after a long, silent moment, they nodded together.

18

ॐ

WHEN the augas wound their way through the canyon maze, Glik shuffled along behind them with all the human workers. Knowing that they were close to the larger slave camp, Mage Ivun did not allow any rest, but pushed on. From their high saddles, sandwreth guards lashed out at the weary men and women.

"I hated the shadowglass camp," Cheth muttered to her, "and I hate this place just as much."

"I hate captivity! *Cra,* if I could just break loose, I'd run and run." Glik looked at the Brava woman's dusty face. "But I want you with me."

Cheth agreed with the idea. "I'd kill as many as necessary to get away."

Glik's feet were sore as she kept moving. The sun pounded down on her reddened skin, but the misery was little different from their days out on the blasted battlefield. "Wouldn't be right to leave these people here, though." She traced a quick circle around her heart. "Fighting all together, maybe we'd be enough. We outnumber the guards."

"I thought about that," Cheth said, "and we would lose. Last time we tried, two Bravas and five human prisoners died."

"Can still plan," Glik said, holding on to the idea, "and dream. A lot more prisoners in the main camp. Besides, maybe we'll have outside help." She didn't know how soon Penda could send the Suderran army.

"I'll be ready," the Brava said. "Either way."

Glik managed a small laugh. Even such a tiny sound seemed a rare thing for her.

A guard brought his auga closer. "Save your energy for walking." He swung his spear, intending to clip Glik on the side of the head, but before the blow could land, Cheth grabbed the shaft. The wreth snarled, trying to yank back his weapon, but the Brava held on. The two glared at each other.

"I can snap your spear," Cheth said in a low voice. "I'll demonstrate if you'd like."

The wreth kept wrestling with the shaft, but Cheth was as immovable as a statue. Finally she released the spear, and the indignant guard yanked it back. Before he could retaliate, Mage Ivun shouted out from the lead auga, "Stop dallying. We are nearly home!"

The prisoners made no response, although the augas snorted. Some wreth guards trotted ahead at a faster pace. Cheth's adversary glared at her, then bounded off.

Ivun called to the bedraggled party, "Tomorrow, we will assign you new work."

Soon, they filed into the crowded camp that was bounded by high rock walls. Hundreds of slaves dressed in rags hunched over tables, sat on the ground, or huddled under awnings. They fashioned shields, spear shafts, arrows, bows; some sewed leather armor, while others made clubs from wood scraps. Forges deep in the canyons produced lumps of iron, which the human slaves used to adorn the shields and clubs. Other metal bits were sharpened into arrowheads.

The returning prisoners brought a wagonload of shadowglass shards, which would be sent to arm the Suderran military. King Adan had supposedly promised that his soldiers would fight for Queen Voo, but Glik knew better.

Before being allowed to rest, she and Cheth were ordered to help unload the creaking old cart. Her hands were cut and blistered, but she carried the black fragments. She kept her face expressionless as she moved with slow, plodding footsteps, as did the other workers. While Cheth delivered a large block of shadowglass, Glik made a show of adding broken shards to the pile, but she covered her movement by hunching a little so she could slip a thin, sharp fragment as long as her hand into the waist of her tattered trousers.

Cheth noticed and gave a quick smile. At the same time, one of the other workers dropped a large shadowglass sheet, which cracked down the middle. The wreths yelled, and the slave cringed. In the distraction, the Brava seized the chance to snatch her own obsidian fragment, which disappeared among her clothes.

"Already got about twenty weapons stashed in crevices around here," Glik whispered. "Been preparing for a long time, but didn't know what to do."

"The more weapons we have, the more fighters we'll have," Cheth said. "Whenever it's time."

Most of the weak prisoners were ill-suited as warriors, although some were forced to participate in basic combat training. They battered one another with sticks and makeshift swords, and if they did not fight with enough fervor, the wreth guards would demonstrate lethal techniques on them.

Cheth glanced toward Mage Ivun's stone dwelling, a smooth-walled structure fashioned from the rock of the canyon. "Better weapons inside there," Cheth said. "The mage still has ramers from any Bravas that were captured."

"*Cra,* we'd have to fight the mage and break down the door." Glik shook her head. "Don't see how that could happen."

"Our lives are built on unlikely possibilities," Cheth said.

Their work crew had been gone for weeks excavating at the Plain of Black

Glass, and no part of this camp felt like home to Glik. Previously, she had made a fabric lean-to that provided some shade in the day's heat and a break from the gusting night winds. Now her old place was occupied by three other prisoners, and she decided it was not worth claiming. "I'm used to sleeping wherever I can find a corner of my own," Glik said. "Home is in my head . . . and it's not here."

Cheth glanced around. "We'll make a new shelter together."

After dark, Glik slipped up to a crack in the canyon wall near another tattered lean-to. In the deep shadows cast by scattered small fires, the girl hid her stolen shard of shadowglass. It would make an excellent knife.

As she turned, she saw a skeletal woman peering at her from under the lean-to. Her mouth was open, her lips cracked. Glik froze, as if she'd been caught murdering someone, but the slave just blinked. Glik gave her a reassuring smile. "Just a weapon. We're preparing. Army's coming to rescue us, but we'll all have to fight."

The woman stared, as if all of her soul and intelligence had been taken away.

Glik continued, "Got other weapons stashed to arm ourselves when it's time!"

The woman slunk back beneath her awning.

Disheartened, Glik returned to Cheth and sat by her. Her friend leaned close to whisper, "I passed word to the other Bravas. They are ready to fight, but the rest of these people . . ." She let out a long sigh. "Weak and broken. They'd just cower if they had a chance to escape."

"Not all of them," Glik said. She felt it in her heart. "When the time comes, we'll do our part. The rest just need a spark."

19

∽

I N the courtyard of Fellstaff Castle, Elliel practiced throwing knives with Shadri, just in case. The scholar girl, though extremely intelligent, was hopeless when it came to physical abilities. She missed the mark at least half the time. Shadri could explain trajectories and rotation and flight curves, but she simply couldn't make the knife point stick into a target.

Thon watched them with interest and did not try his hand. "If I had a knife, why would I throw it at something? More importantly . . . I would not need a knife."

Elliel had to admit he was correct. She stood back and flung her two daggers, one with the left hand, one with the right. Both spun in the air and embedded themselves in the straw-bale target.

Looking at the pair of knives she still held in her own hands, Shadri strode forward and viciously stabbed the bale. "There! I'll be good enough in close quarters."

A runner came into the courtyard, a freckle-faced boy of about twelve. His hair stuck out in all directions, and his eyes shone with the importance of the task he'd been given. "The gate guards sent me running from the wall! There's a man, says he came over the mountains with a desperate message for the king." The runner gawked at Elliel, then at Thon. "He looks like you!"

"Another wreth?" Thon asked.

Elliel pressed closer. "What do you mean? A Brava?"

The boy pointed to his cheek, but couldn't find words.

Realizing that he meant the rune of forgetting that she and Thon both wore, Elliel said, "We'd better go see."

Too exhausted to follow, the runner boy just pointed down the winding streets. "Eastern gate."

With Shadri following at her own, slower pace, Elliel and Thon sprinted down the winding streets to the outer walls and the eastern gate, which was open for daily commerce. The gate sentries had stopped a blond-haired young man who was dusty from many days on the road. The stranger scooped a drink of water from a rain barrel, and someone from the gathering crowd had given him an apple to eat.

The young man looked up at them, and Elliel froze. He did indeed have the distinctive eyes of a half-breed, but he wore a loose brown shirt, trousers held up by a scrap of rope, and mismatched boots instead of formal Brava black. He also had the prominent and damning tattoo on his face.

"Who are you?" she asked.

He looked at her and spread his hands. "My name is Onder. I was a Brava." He pulled out a folded letter as if making a confession. "This tells what happened to me, what I did." He forced himself to continue. "Utho wrote it."

Elliel felt as if someone had stabbed her with an icicle. She remembered the day she had awakened in the back of a cart on a muddy road in the pouring rain, not knowing who she was. Her face felt sore from tattoo needles, and she had found an appalling letter in her pocket that described bloody crimes she had supposedly committed.

She took the letter from his trembling hand. "Let me see it." Elliel knew better than anyone that such letters weren't always the truth.

As she scanned the story, Onder tried to stand straight and firm. "I don't remember it. I can't believe I would do such a thing, but . . . but Master Onzu promises that it is true."

Elliel handed the letter back. The mere fact that Utho had written the words nauseated her.

Onder looked from Thon to Elliel. "You have the same marking as me." He brightened with recognition. "Are you Elliel? Master Onzu told me your story, and everything Utho did to you—everything. Maybe even you don't know it all—which is why he dispatched me here. Utho lies." The young man produced a second letter, folded and sealed. "I brought proof. Master Onzu said this is the most important thing I could possibly do. He gave me another chance. I failed at Mirrabay, and I must not fail again. The future is always more important than the past."

Elliel took the letter. "Then come with us to King Kollanan."

Silence hung like an impending avalanche in the Fellstaff council chamber. After opening the seal and reading Onzu's letter three times without comment, Kollanan could barely keep his turmoil in check as he passed it to Adan. The revered training master's message struck him hard. Koll already felt hollow and hard inside, and this blow reverberated in him like a funeral bell.

Onder fidgeted at the far end of the long table. He had completed his mission and now watched the hurricane of repercussions.

Kollanan distractedly thumped his anger on the table like a pounding drum. If he'd had his war hammer, he would have smashed the table, smashed the wall. "So, it wasn't the Isharans who killed my brother, as we were told. This whole war, the reason why he demanded my Norterran armies, the reason why I defied him, the reason for Yanton . . ." He could not get his mind around it.

Adan said, "My father went to Fulcor Island so he could forge an alliance against the wreths. Utho turned an effort to make peace into a bloody pretext for war."

Elliel and Thon had read the letter, so Adan passed it to the other two Bravas in the room. Lasis and Gant looked offended by the immensity of Utho's betrayal.

"I believe it, every word," Gant said. When the ugly man scowled, his features were even more craggy and unpleasant. "I have seen Utho's decisions and justifications before."

Lasis added, "Utho realized that Konag Conndur would resist him, but his weak son would follow whatever he said."

"And Mandan did exactly that," Kollanan growled. "He wants to send the Commonwealth army across the sea to fight an enemy that we should never have provoked, and then he sent troops to attack Yanton, to slaughter my people." He pounded his fist again on the table, and stood up. "*My people!* Mandan is no true konag at all." Though he lowered his voice, it seemed more threatening. "Now there can be no doubt. Adan, you and I need to bring the three kingdoms together. And Mandan must be removed for the sake of the Commonwealth."

Several advisors sat around the table. Lord Ogno held up his hand, extending the stump of his forefinger. "I lost this finger fighting wreths at Lake Bakal, but I've got nine more of them." He hunched forward. His thick arms were like logs. "Frostwreths couldn't scare us away. I'm ready for this fight."

"How, exactly, do we take the crown away from a konag?" asked Lord Bahlen.

"Do we mean to start a civil war?" Adan asked, his concern apparent in the lines on his face. "Now? We had agreed to free the slaves from the sandwreth labor camp first."

"No, we won't abandon those prisoners," Kollanan reassured him. "We cannot forget the greater threat, however. Uniting the Commonwealth will give us our only chance in a war against the wreths."

Shadri spoke up. "Well, there is a precedent for removing an unfit or unjust ruler. We can quote the Commonwealth charter. Invoke the law. Isn't that better than a civil war?"

Elliel was surprised. "There's a law for overthrowing a konag?"

"Only in extreme circumstances," Shadri explained. "The Commonwealth's three kingdoms, Norterra, Suderra, and Osterra, agreed to unite under the rule of one konag. The Commonwealth itself exists only by mutual agreement. Its primary purpose is to defend its members. Any of those members may call for protection in its time of need. Remember, when King Kollanan dispatched a formal letter requesting assistance against the wreths? Mandan violated his responsibilities as konag when he refused. At the very least, that is grounds for censure, isn't it?"

"You want to scold my brother?" Adan asked.

"Legally, with a decree from two kings." Her words kept coming in a rush. "You see, *we* followed the forms. *We* obeyed the rules, and Mandan refused to do what he was required to do. A konag has legal obligations to his people, and that breach in itself invalidated his legitimacy as a mutually agreed-upon leader. And if that wasn't enough, he attacked Commonwealth citizens! He sent his own army into Yanton, even though any such action requires the agreement of at least two of the three kings. Mandan's scholars and attorneys will point out the clear language to him. He forfeited his mandate. He must resign and surrender the crown to the next legitimate heir." She nodded, proud of her own argument.

Adan frowned, still skeptical. "And how do we manage that?"

"Issue a formal decree signed by two of the three kings. Include a statement of censure. Cite the legal basis for removing Konag Mandan from his reign, and announce that he is no longer konag. It is simple and straightforward."

Kollanan appreciated her analysis, but she seemed incredibly naïve. "Mandan doesn't follow rules very well," he pointed out.

Elliel added, "Don't forget Utho. You will have to remove him before you can remove the konag." Her face flashed with a hard smile. "And I'd be more than happy to do that."

Onder spoke up. "Many Bravas have gone to Convera and enlisted to fight in the vengewar. But they do not know the truth."

Lasis looked at him and nodded. "Utho will continue to deceive them. We may not even be able to trust those wearing Brava black." He showed grudging appreciation for the disgraced young man. "That is why Master Onzu chose his son, a marked man that others would discount. He was right to send you, even knowing your past cowardice."

"But I'm not." Onder paused, thunderstruck, and searched their faces. "His *son*?"

Elliel took the letter back and extended it to Onder, who hadn't read it yet. "That's what his note says."

The former Brava slumped in his chair and scanned the letter. "I wish he had told me. So much I don't know . . ."

Standing beside the table, Kollanan looked around the council room. "This war may determine our survival. We've already started gathering our fighters." He placed a large hand on Adan's shoulder. "But I won't go back on my word to help you liberate the labor camp. I'll put together some of my best Norterran soldiers to ride with us, including Elliel and Thon."

He turned to his other Bravas. "Gant, stay here at Fellstaff Castle to protect and defend my city. Lasis, you and my vassal lords will begin marching the Norterran army toward the Dragonspine Mountains. When we finish our mission in the desert canyons, King Adan and I will bring the Suderran army to join you. Together, we'll cross the mountains, fall upon Convera, and remove Mandan from the throne."

"If he doesn't obey your decree and censure," Shadri said. "Simple and straightforward."

At the end of the table Onder sat in silence, still trying to absorb yet another revelation. Finally, he spoke up, sounding nervous. "I want to go. I want to help. My . . . my father gave me a new chance. One moment does not define an entire life. I might not remember my time as a Brava or the wrongdoing that ended it, but I can still fight, and I . . ." His voice faltered. "I promise I won't run this time."

"Don't make promises you cannot keep," Elliel said, then caught herself. "I apologize. I, too, remember what the emptiness felt like. You may still be a Brava inside."

"He can come with us when the army rides," Lasis said. "He completed his mission for Master Onzu. We will allow him to prove himself."

20

MIDNIGHT at the Rivermouth shipyards was quiet as a strangler. Across the harbor, dull orange lanterns on anchored vessels glowed like fire-flies reflected on the calm water. The *Glissand* remained dark. Waves mur-mured against the dock pilings, and the hulls of naval ships creaked. At any other time, Mak Dur would have found the sounds to be a soothing lullaby, but he could not sleep.

He stretched out on the deck of his ship, saddened that the *Glissand* no longer felt like home. A blanket served as a meager cushion under him, the yarn dyed with the colors of his parents' tribes woven into clever geometric designs that shifted depending on which way the blanket was turned.

Commonwealth soldiers were billeted belowdecks in hammocks and hast-ily constructed additional bunks. Mak Dur couldn't understand why any sol-dier would choose to bed down in those stuffy confines rather than sleeping under the stars. It was one of many things that made no sense to him. The world had turned upside down.

He could no longer take comfort in telling himself that he was still the voyagier and the *Glissand* was still his ship, an Utauk ship. The graceful vessel had been changed—copper plates hammered to the hull, shields and blinds added around the deck to protect archers as they shot fire arrows. Just today, the canvas sail adorned by the Utauk circle—the beginning is the end is the beginning—had been replaced by blue fabric emblazoned with an open hand.

Always before, the Commonwealth symbol had seemed welcoming to him, all encompassing, but now the open hand looked tyrannical, as if to dominate all enemies and all understanding.

Mak Dur refused to abandon the *Glissand* entirely and let Commonwealth sailors take her, for fear they would run the ship up against reefs or crash into fiery battle with the Isharan navy. By order of Konag Mandan, his Utauk crew had been conscripted into the navy. They'd been issued uniforms, but every member of his crew had refused to wear them.

When the newly appointed captain, Pharion, scowled and complained about their appearance, insisting on proper discipline, Mak Dur just laughed. "We Utauks have our own discipline, and this is our ship. I admit we are not strong enough to fight your soldiers and take back the *Glissand,* but my sail-ors are tied to her. They will help you sail only if you treat them with respect."

The tension had risen as his angry crew stood with arms crossed over their chests. Before the disagreement could escalate into violence, Mak Dur had realized that the huffy captain needed to save face, so he offered a concession, telling his men to tie blue kerchiefs around their arms to signify that—on this particular mission—they sailed for the Commonwealth. The crew reacted with grumbling and loud protests in private, but he told them, "Armbands can be removed, and that's less permanent than if the captain decides to chop off a few heads."

Sarrum growled, "So the rape of the *Glissand* continues." He had gone into the cargo hold, supposedly to check for leaks, but he just needed to get away. . . .

Now, lying on the deck, Mak Dur stared at the stars, tracing the familiar patterns there. He heard other soldiers snoring near the bow, a few Commonwealth officers who did sleep on bedrolls on deck. They didn't maintain a watch because the ship was tied up to the dock and no one was going anywhere.

Mak Dur rolled over and was surprised to see two silhouetted figures standing just above him. He started, sat up, but the shadowy men hushed him. The sleeping officers at the bow stirred, then settled down again.

Mak Dur felt no threat from the two, recognizing them immediately. Sarrum hunched, looked around. Heith leaned close enough to speak in the barest whisper. "We've come to a decision, Voyagier. Seawater flows through our veins, and we were born to sail a ship, but we were not born for this."

Sarrum said, "*Cra,* we've had enough. While we were prisoners in Serepol, we had a lot of time to think, and after we escaped from the Isharans, we agreed never to be prisoners again!"

"We won't sail the ship for these people," Heith said. "So we're leaving."

Mak Dur was surprised. "But this is the *Glissand.* You belong here."

"It is no longer the *Glissand,*" Heith replied. "But we are still Utauks. Sarrum and I will slip over the side and make our way overland until we find our tribes, join a caravan. The blue poppies will show us where to go."

Sarrum gestured into the shadows, indicating the archer blinds, the arrow-filled baskets, the stacked boat hooks and cudgels, all ready for war. "These decks will be stained with blood before long. I'd rather be gone from the *Glissand* than see her like that."

"Come with us," Heith urged. "Think of the *Glissand* as lost in a storm. We can do it again. You'll get investors, find other tribe leaders . . . but not now, not like this."

"I can't." Mak Dur's stomach knotted. He had considered the same thing, but he pressed his palm flat against the deck. "I can't just leave her to these brutes."

The two men stood up in the shadows. "*Cra,* we had to ask." Each traced a circle around his heart. Heith pulled out a dagger and cut off the blue arm-band, tossing the fabric over the side. He handed the blade to Sarrum, who did the same.

The voyagier got to his feet and watched his crewmen dart away in a silence deeper than whispers. The gangplank creaked once as they descended to the dock, and then they headed toward the sparse lights of Rivermouth town. Mak Dur could no longer see them, and a large part of his heart wished he had gone along.

After another day of war preparations, the ships were nearly ready to launch. The blue-uniformed crews were at the peak of their enthusiasm, which would soon turn to impatience and restlessness if the fleet didn't sail. More soldiers rode in from the outlying counties, called by Konag Mandan's order.

At midmorning, a loud rumble of kettledrums across the shipyard called the sailors, soldiers, and dockworkers to attention. The naval crews and porters stopped what they were doing and turned to see what was happening. The drums continued, louder and more threatening.

Mak Dur scanned the line of warehouses, taverns, inns, marketplaces, and brothels around the harbor's edge, looking for the source of the sound. Ten Commonwealth soldiers marched in a procession through the streets, led by the officious captain Pharion. Shading his eyes, the voyagier saw that the guards were escorting two prisoners with their arms bound behind them, heads bowed.

The relentless drums continued, and when Captain Pharion and his guard contingent proceeded down the docks toward the *Glissand*, Mak Dur felt a chill. He recognized the Utauk prisoners.

Pharion and his escort marched up to the base of the *Glissand*'s gang-plank. The captain shouted out, his voice loud with self-importance. "In this time of war, all loyal fighters serve to protect the three kingdoms and our konag." He looked at the bound prisoners in disgust. "Ishara is our enemy, and therefore deserters are traitors to the Commonwealth."

"We are Utauks!" Heith shouted. "We are not part of your Commonwealth navy."

One of the guards struck him so hard across the face that blood and saliva flew out. The *Glissand*'s navigator sagged in shock. Beside him, Sarrum yelped as if he, too, had been slapped.

From the deck of his ship above, Mak Dur yelled down in outrage. "Those men are members of my crew. You will release them and return them unharmed."

Pharion looked up at him. "These men are recruits in the Commonwealth military and have deserted their posts. They tried to flee like cowards in the night." His voice grew lower, more threatening. "You, too, will be reprimanded for your insubordination and failure to control your crew." Mak Dur was about to sputter a retort when the captain's words slashed across him. "Choose your words carefully, Voyagier, or you may end up sharing their fate."

He was taken aback. "Their fate? Sarrum and Heith signed no papers with you, swore no oath. They are free to come and go as they please. *Cra,* they're not bound by—"

"They are sailors in the Commonwealth navy," Pharion insisted, "and, as such, are deserters. The punishment for desertion is death."

The rest of the Utauk crew gasped. Mak Dur's face became hot and he could not find words through his rage and fear.

The captain seemed to take pleasure in his duties. "Because they sailed aboard the *Glissand,* that is where they will meet their execution." He ordered the escort guards to push the captives up the gangplank. Heith and Sarrum thrashed, but could not break free.

Mak Dur stalked down the deck to meet them. "I am in charge of this vessel, and my law governs them. Release these two."

Captain Pharion ignored him and ordered his soldiers to throw ropes over the yardarm of the mainmast, one on each side. "We'll need two nooses," he said with a sniff, then turned to Mak Dur. "Or shall I make it three?"

Commonwealth soldiers and sailors came up from belowdecks to watch, and they far outnumbered the Utauks.

"This is not right," Mak Dur said. "The Utauk tribes have always been neutral. If you execute these two, all our people across the land will turn against you."

With a sneer, Pharion shouted to the crowd on the docks, "By order of Konag Mandan, deserters are to be hanged from the yardarm of their own ship, and their bodies shall remain hanging for two full days in the sun so everyone in Rivermouth Harbor can see the penalty for cowardice."

The guards manhandled Sarrum and Heith, slipping a noose over each man's head and cinching it tight.

Mak Dur rested his hand on the knife at his belt, and his Utauk crew was ready to fight, but when he saw all the Commonwealth soldiers with their swords, axes, and spears, he knew it would be a slaughter. The officious captain seemed to be daring them to act. The moment stretched, ready to snap.

As a last insulting gesture, Pharion ordered a blue band to be tied around the arms of the struggling prisoners. Neither Heith nor Sarrum were given a chance to say any final words, to bid farewell to their comrades or loved ones. The Commonwealth guards simply pulled the rope, hoisting the two men up off the deck by their necks. As they rose higher, kicking and squirming, with their hands bound behind their backs, Mak Dur had a sickening vision of an eel caught on a fishhook. The soldiers lifted the victims slowly enough that their necks didn't break, so the noose strangled them slowly. The men turned purple, jerking, shuddering; by the time they reached the top of the yardarm, they had gone still.

Captain Pharion stepped up to Mak Dur, who could not tear his eyes away from his dead crewmates. "You and the rest of your Utauk sailors are confined to this ship until the navy departs. You may not set foot on land."

21

MAKING his way to Convera, Onzu followed the Crickyeth River down out of the wooded hills. He did not look back, keeping his goal in focus like a sharp arrow point in front of him.

For the first two days of traveling, he considered how proud he was of his group of young trainees. He even spared a few moments to consider his son, his disgrace . . . who was now his messenger. Perhaps this was the cornerstone of a new legacy for Onder. They each had a job to do, for the future, for history, and for honor.

Once again wearing his black Brava outfit and finemail cape, like old times, the training master guided his horse into the outskirts of the capital. He saw the city ahead of him and the castle bluff above the confluence of the rivers. Most of the bridges had been damaged or washed away in the floods following the eruption of Mount Vada, so he hired a ferryman to carry him and his mount across the Crickyeth into the lowtown along the wide banks and flatlands. With all the activity of the flatboats and docks, the town was crowded, squalid, and dirty. The area was filled with refugees who had come to Convera in recent months.

Seeing the conditions here saddened Master Onzu. A real konag would have cared for his people. Mandan should never have allowed so many refugees fleeing disaster to face neglect. The konag had recruited many of them into his standing army, but apparently these others were not worth the trouble.

Onzu rode toward the castle like a weapon to a target. He hadn't bothered to eat more than pack food on the way, and his stomach was tight, but he knew his thoughts were sharper when he fasted. He needed his thoughts as sharp as his blade.

As his horse climbed the steepening cobblestone streets, he saw city guards on patrol, but no one would bother a Brava. He did not pause for conversation, was not distracted by merchants, running children, food vendors, or scribes who offered to write down his story, his legacy for the city remembrance shrine. Onzu now questioned the accuracy of all such tales in recorded history. He had discovered that much of what he'd considered the truth was fictional. Throughout history, how many others had there been like Utho?

Though war preparations were fully underway, Onzu assumed that Utho would be near the konag. His hunt was nearing its end.

In his lifetime, he had only been to Convera five times before. As a young Brava paladin, Onzu had spent a decade in the kingdom of Osterra serving justice, doing what was necessary. He had visited the capital when grief-struck Konag Cronin dispatched his enormous fleet to end the Isharan war thirty years ago; back then, Onzu had sailed across the sea, though he hadn't had a chance to fight. That encounter had resulted in peace with young Empra Iluris, when Cronin had been weary of death.

Now, though, Master Onzu knew that Utho would not let this new venge-war end in anything less than slaughter. But the training master could stop his corrupt student and maybe he could stop the war, thereby preventing the massacre of thousands. He would also restore Brava honor for every other half-breed who wore the black and carried a ramer. As he guided his horse up to the gates of the castle above the rivers, he touched the golden cuff at his side.

One of the other times he had come to Convera was to honor his prized trainee, when Konag Conndur had accepted Utho as his bonded Brava. Onzu had attended that celebratory feast, proud of his success.

So many things proved false . . .

As Onzu approached, Konag Mandan's gate sentries snapped to attention, but didn't challenge him or ask his business. Scoffing, the master looked down at them from his saddle. "You won't try to stop me? What if I'm here to kill your konag?"

The guard on the left laughed. "You wouldn't kill the konag. You're a Brava!"

"And Bravas are always trustworthy?" Onzu asked in a barbed voice.

The two guards said "Yes," but eyed him with caution.

The training master sighed, disappointed. "No, I'm not here to kill the konag." He rode past, dismounted in the courtyard, and made his way into the castle.

Many Bravas had come to Convera in response to Utho's summons. He guessed that Tytan and Jennae were already here in the castle, or else down at Rivermouth preparing for war. Onzu himself was prepared for war, though on a smaller, more personal scale.

Inside, he inquired of the castle staff and courtiers where he might find the konag's Brava. He kept pressing until finally someone told him. He felt both relieved and tense. Utho was here.

High above where the Bluewater and Crickyeth Rivers flowed together, the sandstone bluff was honeycombed with passages and storage chambers, including the old armories. The tunnels inside the bluff opened up to barred openings on the cliff face for air circulation and light. In times of great crisis, the cliff windows could serve as ambush points from which archers and siege soldiers could rain down arrows and missiles on invading ships in the river below.

Utho worked alone in the cool tunnels, where he could concentrate and calculate. Many thousands of weapons from old wars had been stockpiled here in armory chambers, and remained until they were needed again. Under Utho's guidance, the young konag had already dispatched bows and arrows, swords, shields, chain mail, throwing knives, maces, and battle hammers to the burgeoning armies. Refugees from the mountains had received ill-fitting armor and heavy shields, many of them still painted with the markings of noble families long forgotten, but the commoners didn't know or care.

Tytan, Jennae, and ten other Bravas were training the ragtag fighters as best they could, including foot soldiers drawn from the surrounding counties. Many were hopeless, but at least they could serve as distractions in a furious fight.

Before the fleet sailed off to Ishara, Utho had come to the armory tunnels for a last inspection of the storage rooms. All the chambers had empty shelves and baskets, except for a few scattered, damaged leftovers. Down here, he felt the weight of the immense castle over his head, but the barred window openings let in fresh air.

Utho went to the nearest window and stood at the bars to look down the sheer cliff to the river below. Distant sounds of barges and small trading ships wafted up from the water, and he saw fishermen in tiny boats working inlets against the bluff. Straight ahead, he followed the Joined River with his eyes and dreaded the idea of enemy ships sailing up to the confluence. But that wouldn't be today . . . or ever. With the Commonwealth fleet, he would wipe out Ishara.

He heard a boot scuffing the stone floor and thought it might be one of Mandan's advisors coming to pester him with some other decision the young konag refused to make. He drew in a breath to speak, turned, and froze.

A ghost stood before him, manifested out of memory, a wiry and muscular old man who looked as if he were made entirely out of coiled springs and drawn bowstrings. Master Onzu stood in his Brava outfit like a midnight shadow with fluid movements and dark secrets.

The older man stepped forward and pulled off his gauntlets, baring his wrists. "I know what you did, Utho, and I have come to serve justice."

Answers came ricocheting at him from different directions. "What do you think you know?" He made no overt denials, because the training master would know he was lying. But what was the accusation? "Ah, you heard about the letter that King Kollanan sent, those claims Elliel made. It is not the full story."

"Oh, I know what you did to Elliel." Onzu took a step forward, his hands still hanging loose at his sides, but he was by no means relaxed. "That is just the beginning. You left a permanent stain on Brava honor. You brought disappointment, and far worse—shame."

"Shame?" Utho said. "Your student is the bonded Brava to the konag himself, to two konags, and I am about to vanquish our enemies after centuries. What greater glory could there be for a training master?"

Onzu unclipped his ramer and squeezed it around his wrist. "You served two konags only because you murdered one of them."

Utho took a step back. By sheer instinct, he reached for his own ramer. "What did you say?"

"You murdered Conndur the Brave on Fulcor Island. You locked yourself in his chamber. You overpowered him. You slaughtered him and made it look like the work of the Isharans." Onzu ignited his inner fire, and the bright torch-blade rippled up from his hand. "I saw every moment of it."

Utho lit his ramer and pushed it into a fiery blade. "How do you know this?" Down in the armory tunnels, the two men were in a confined fighting space, and the curved walls gave them little room to feint and dodge.

"Because the truth cannot be hidden," Onzu said, without explaining further. "I've already sent word to King Kollanan in Norterra. He knows that you're the one who murdered his brother, not the Isharans."

Utho reeled at the revelation. He braced himself. "The king of Norterra has misplaced priorities. He is no longer relevant to what we must do."

"The entire reason for your vengewar is a lie!" Onzu slashed the crackling blade in a provocative gesture through the air. "I cannot let your betrayal go unanswered. As your training master, it is my responsibility, my failure."

"It is not about you, old man. Our need for vengewar has endured for centuries, ever since Valaera. Right now you are splitting hairs."

"No, I am meting out justice. Brava justice." Onzu swung his ramer blade, and he showed his chipped tooth when he smiled. The training master might have looked old, but much of that was a deception to make his opponents underestimate him. Utho knew not to do that.

Onzu threw himself upon his opponent with a savage anger, making it clear that this would be an execution, not a graceful duel. Utho had fought him many times in sparring sessions, and he knew the training master believed that anything less than an all-consuming battle was fair to neither side, nor to the Brava code.

Utho met the ramer blade, slashed with his own, fire sparking against fire. He drove Onzu's weapon to the side, where it scorched a black mark on the sandstone wall. Utho was larger, stronger, and deadlier, but Onzu didn't seem to accept that.

They struck and battled, ramer against ramer. Heat flared, and sparks flew. The air smelled of sweat and lightning.

Grunting with the effort, Utho smashed the training master back against the wooden door of a storeroom, but Onzu dropped down and under the strike. Utho's ramer cleaved the wood instead, burning all the way through and shattering the door into splinters.

"How did you know?" Utho asked again. He knew he had to erase all evidence, remove this man. Master Onzu could cause a great deal of difficulty for him.

"I saw it. I ignited a strand of your hair and extracted the images. I watched you butcher the man you had sworn to serve, Konag Conndur. All Bravas swear to defend the konag."

"And the Commonwealth," Utho said. "Conndur meant to destroy us by suing for peace with the animals."

"You still don't understand the real enemy, Utho." Onzu sounded sad.

"There is more than one enemy, and right now you are my opponent. You would delay me and disrupt the plans for vengewar. You are the one betraying the Bravas."

Taking great insult, Onzu let out a wild cry and pushed forward, hacking with his ramer and singeing Utho's face. Defending himself, he shoved the hot blade back, but Onzu struck and struck, a whirlwind. Utho parried.

The training master pushed him down the corridor toward the barred window opening above the river. He pressed his ramer against Utho's, closer, harder. The incandescent sword came within inches of Utho's face, snarling flames that could sear his flesh. He strained, his lips drawn back with the effort, amazed at the master's vengeful strength. Onzu was relentless.

But while the two fiery blades were locked together, Utho slipped his other hand to the dagger at his side. As the crossed ramers flared, neither blade moving, he drew the knife. Without a second thought, he thrust it under Onzu's breastbone and slammed the blade home into his heart.

The training master gasped and staggered back, the weight of his body pulling the dagger out of Utho's hand. The old man looked astonished. His ramer blade wavered.

Utho used that moment not for gloating or challenge, but just to end the duel. His ramer lopped off Onzu's head, leaving only a smoldering neck stump. The head fell to the tunnel floor, followed by the body, the fiery blade flickering to a few sparks that quickly sputtered out.

Utho stood over his former Brava master, feeling the anger rise. His own ramer continued to shine bright. He wanted to hack this hateful old man to pieces, to destroy him, but Utho had already won. Master Onzu had trained him, made Utho what he was . . . made him strong.

No one else needed to know this.

In three quick strides he reached the window and melted a section of iron bars with a slash of his ramer. He knocked the barrier down with a sharp, hard kick, and the bars clanged and clattered down the rough cliff all the way to the weeds and sluggish water below.

He extinguished his ramer but left the cuff in place. He was breathing hard.

Utho picked up the old man's head in his hands and looked into the eyes. With a grunt, he hurled it like a child's ball out the now-open window. Then he dragged the smoking body, leaving a trail of blood and ashes on the stone floor. Reaching the edge, he looked down at the confluence.

He had never believed that he and Master Onzu would find themselves on different sides. Though he had revered, even loved the man for all he had done, and for the countless other Bravas he had trained, he would not let Onzu become an impediment to the vengewar.

He picked the training master up by the shoulders and lifted him to the opening. With an extra push, he shoved the corpse out into space and watched it flop and tumble through the air. It made a distant splash in the river far below.

22

A T first Adan was glad to be riding, knowing he was on his way home
to Penda and baby Oak. He and Kollanan let their horses gallop for a
while, leading the thirty handpicked Norterran soldiers away from Fellstaff,
along with his two Banner guards and Thon and Elliel. Upon reaching Bannriya, Adan would add many more fighters from the Suderran army, and arm
them all with shadowglass-enhanced weapons. Their strike force would be
deadly against the wreths.

For the first two days of travel, Adan felt eager to complete his promise. It
would be good to free those downtrodden prisoners he had seen in the mothertear images. But as the group passed over the hills into his kingdom, he also
felt anxious about the rest of the Commonwealth, and about his brother.

Master Onzu's shocking letter had revealed just what Mandan and his
bonded Brava were capable of. Utho had murdered their father, intentionally,
and then blamed the Isharans? It was not conceivable, and yet it was true. He
did not doubt the training master.

Thinking of his father brought tears to his eyes, as images flashed through
his mind of the evenings they spent together staring at the stars, mapping
constellations in their books. He and Conndur had discussed history, destiny, the nature of gods and stars.

Now as he lay in their camp under the open night sky, Adan saw a shooting star, a thin slash of light—a reminder of how he had chosen the name
Starfall. What if the wreths actually woke the dragon? What if their god Kur
actually returned to remake the world? What if all the stars fell?

While gathering firewood that night, Adan had spotted a powder-blue
poppy growing alone in tall grasses. He had plucked it, and now held it close
as he tried to sleep, picturing Penda. For a time he stopped thinking of doom
and disaster and settled into a dream about home.

The next day, Kollanan rode close to him, but said little. Occasionally, the
other man brushed his fingers along the shaft of his war hammer, as if he
wanted to hit something. His uncle was wrapped in his own grief, which
was clearly deeper than Adan's. Koll had lost not only a brother, but also his
daughter and at least one grandson. Losing Tafira . . . Adan couldn't imagine
what he'd do if the wreths murdered Penda. Such heartbreak seemed impossible, yet Kollanan the Hammer had to bear it.

The older man seemed hardened and empty. His thirst for vengeance was split in opposite directions—to overthrow Mandan and punish Utho, and to face the evil wreths and help save his kingdom.

"After we free the camp slaves, we shouldn't delay in Bannriya," Kollanan warned. "The Suderran army needs to rendezvous with mine on the western flank of the Dragonspine."

Adan agreed, but he had a reason for his reluctance. "If Queen Voo sees my army ride off, she'll be angry. She believes she owns all my soldiers."

"My heart bleeds for the sandwreth queen," Koll said sarcastically. "She will have to make do."

Adan brightened as an idea occurred to him. "I know she is already upset with Mandan because he spurned her invitation, which gives us a perfect excuse. She feels slighted. If she asks, I'll say that we are going to punish my brother for showing her such disrespect. She is vain enough to believe that is the true reason."

From behind them, Thon called out, "And if I see her, I will thank her for all the historical documents she provided. Some of the tales were most instructive. Shadri promised to translate more while we are gone."

Koll frowned. "Voo didn't exactly give them to you. You coerced her."

Thon shrugged. "She saw the wisdom in providing what I asked. I still hope the documents will yield answers about me and my true purpose."

When they topped a rise and saw the ancient city, Adan felt an indescribable wash of relief to see that the thick walls remained intact. Colorful banners flew from the high points. Seenan and Captain Elcior waved and shouted, even though the horses were too far away for anyone to hear them. Kollanan's lead riders raised their Norterran pennants.

Soon, Suderran scouts raced out to intercept and escort them in through the gates. Xar, Penda's green ska, swooped overhead as if scolding them for taking so long to get home.

Hale Orr welcomed the entire group as their horses entered the castle's main courtyard. Penda's father wore crimson and black silks, his family colors. "*Cra*, Starfall, you brought visitors!" He propped his wrist stump against his hip. "So are we at war then?"

"We've been at war for some time, even though the wreths don't know it yet," Koll responded. "That gives us a little more time to prepare." His voice dropped to deep growl. "And time to take care of other business."

"Unfortunately, we are at war with Konag Mandan as well," Adan said, which astonished his father-in-law. "Suderra must be prepared to defend on several fronts."

Hale laughed out loud. "*Cra*, the vassal lords have already been arming themselves." He raised his eyebrows. "But I thought we were going to fight the sandwreths?"

"We'll do that, too," Adan said.

Kollanan drew his war hammer and rested it casually but ominously on his shoulder. The thirty soldiers from Norterra dismounted, while stable hands took the horses.

When Penda rushed out to greet them in an embroidered Utauk gown, carrying the baby, she took Adan's breath away and he couldn't concentrate on anything else. He swung down from his horse and swept her up in an embrace.

Laughing, she pushed him away. "Let our daughter breathe!"

Abashed, Adan stepped back and brushed off his jerkin, then held out his arms. "Here, let me hold little Oak." When he cradled the infant, she felt tiny and fragile in his arms. She squirmed and looked up at him, and he felt as if clouds had opened up to let sunshine through.

Seenan and Elcior led the Norterran soldier force off to the barracks. Elliel and Thon accompanied the Norterran king, and Hale Orr found them lodgings in the main castle.

Adan, however, wanted to spend time with his wife, his queen. Hom bustled about heating water, scrounging bathing cloths and fresh clothes. Penda tucked the baby under a soft blanket in her cradle, and she fell sound asleep.

Adan kissed Penda and held her for a long time. She smiled at him and said, "We've heard no whispers of sandwreths since I arrived home. Our riders and the Utauk traders have seen no wreth scouts, although we are due for another shipment of shadowglass."

"We will need it," Adan said. "We'll turn the shadowglass against the sandwreths as well." He remembered how it had felt to thrust the obsidian-encrusted sword through Quo's twisted heart. "But we also have to overthrow my brother and hold Utho accountable for his crimes."

"A certain sort of person makes not just one enemy," Penda said, "but many. It becomes a habit."

"Kollanan wanted to march to Convera right away, but I came back here because of my promise. Together, we'll go to the wreth slave camp and free Glik and the others."

Penda brightened. "*Cra,* a good deed can be a more powerful weapon than any sharpened blade."

Three days later, most of his vassal lords came in from the outlying counties, and Adan called a war council. Kollanan was anxious to strike the labor camp and free the prisoners, so they could be on to the next battle. Grief had sharpened his edge of anger and frayed his patience. After seeing his uncle suffer so much loss, Adan treasured what he had all the more.

Xar and Ari joined the meeting, perched on their stand, because the skas would also be an important part of the reconnaissance. The blue ska still had her heart link to Glik and thus could find the orphan girl and the prisoners. The armorers presented a report on how many shadowglass weapons were available, although Kollanan pointed out that any normal blade would suffice against Mandan and his followers.

Adan brought out a small gilded box marked with the colors of the three kingdoms. "This . . . this hits closer to home." He opened the box. "I don't understand what my brother is doing." He revealed the gnarled hand of Conndur the Brave, which riders had brought around Suderra in a grim and bizarre show.

Kollanan turned ruddy with anger. "Mandan sent the other hand to Fell-staff, and many more grisly relics around the three kingdoms to incite our anger. He wanted us to howl for revenge against Ishara. All to start a war . . ." He drew a breath, simmering. "From his first day, Mandan was not a fit konag."

Adan tried to sound more hopeful. "The armies of our two kingdoms will achieve justice and unite the Commonwealth—then we can stand against the true monsters, the wreths."

"Before they manage to wake the dragon," Elliel said.

Penda laid her hand on Adan's. "First, we will free the prisoners. A smaller, but vital victory."

23

⚭

THE new godling thrummed through Iluris and gave her strength. She still felt dizzy and spent the day resting, although she was sick of resting. She drank water and ate a small meal, careful not to strain her shrunken stomach.

Captani Vos doted over her, and she found his voice comforting. She closed her eyes and just listened to him, listened to her heartbeat, and felt thoughts swirling in the empty spaces of her mind. She had trouble connecting them, assessing them. Simple concepts no longer fit together as they should.

As empra, her wit had been quick, and she'd made snap decisions. She could foresee consequences and subtleties, and prided herself on being able to debate any opponent. But ever since she had awakened from the void, thoughts were like loose bits of floss, windblown fluff from wooltrees drifting in the breeze. They touched, dodged, and blew about in random directions. Ideas and realizations came at her intermittently and refused to assemble into one giant mosaic. She saw only little bits of broken time.

Trying to fit his role as best he could, Vos meticulously polished his golden armor and washed the red-dyed fabric of his cape in a basin of water. When he knelt beside her, Iluris placed a hand on his shoulder as she made the effort to sit up. She felt him trembling.

Vos lowered his eyes. "I was so worried for you, Mother. Seeing you lying there, not stirring, it was like . . . like I was sitting vigil at your funeral. But I never gave up hope. We prayed for you." She saw tears in his eyes. "You saved me when I was younger and took me in when my family died of the fever. You gave me a place, and my place will always be with you."

"Your place will always be with *the empra*," Iluris said, "whether or not I'm around." Her voice was still hoarse from disuse. He handed her a cup of lukewarm water.

"We all prayed for you," repeated another guard.

At one time Iluris had known all their names, all their stories. They were her adopted children. But when she looked at this guard, she drew a blank. Instead of names, details, and memories, a hollow ringing filled her head. She looked around. "Where is Cemi? We need Cemi. All of Ishara needs Cemi."

"She is out meeting your supporters," Vos said. His face looked troubled. "We told you that."

"Of course. I only thought . . . she would be back by now. Is she safe?"

Vos looked even more disturbed. "I suggested sending two hawk guards with her, but we could not. No one can be allowed to see us."

Then Iluris did seize upon a memory detail and smiled. "Oh, yes! That girl knows how to hide on the streets and to slip away if she needs to. Don't worry about her."

Vos said, "No one has seen you in a long time, Mother, but your people still believe in you. We have quietly spread the word, finding hundreds upon hundreds who are waiting for you to return. They rejoice to know that you're still alive. Cemi, Analera, and others have encouraged them to increase their quiet sacrifices for . . . for our new godling."

Around them, the faint distortion in the air brightened and thickened like a faint mist as the entity came close. Iluris reached out, spread her fingers, and felt the nebulous force.

Vos's voice shook with emotion again. "It is the honor of my life to serve you. I'm glad I could help you. We will restore you to your throne. Hear us, save us. Ishara needs you—as soon as you are ready."

Iluris sensed the new godling pulsing in time with her heartbeat, and a thrill went down her spine as if its invisible force fired her nerves. The strength buoyed her up, sustained her body, made her blood race. Her breaths came quick and fresh.

She understood that the energy must be different, an outside boost, since she still felt gaps in her mind. Her memory registered a long emptiness after her encounter with the Black Eel assassin on Fulcor Island. Oddly, she could recall with absolute clarity how she'd tripped on a fold of fabric as she tried to escape and struck her skull against a stone bench. After that, darkness reeled out like an unending skein of yarn dyed with lampblack.

Iluris could tell something was not entirely right inside her, but she said nothing to dim the hopeful expressions of the hawk guards. She would let them care for her while she slowly grew stronger and made her plans.

She looked up as a thought occurred to her. "Where is Cemi? Will she be back soon?"

The news of Iluris's reawakening was like a spark set to kindling.

As Cemi slipped through the backstreets of the city, sometimes accompanied by Analera, other times alone, she spoke to dozens of dissatisfied groups. The empra's faithful followers were angry, but needed guidance beyond aimless hope. Having seen the carnage wrought by the Serepol godling, they feared Key Priestlord Klovus. After so much time, though, many had begun to doubt that Iluris still lived, despite Cemi's assurances. Now she gave them bright hope, insisting that the return was imminent.

Intent on keeping their faith and prayers strong, the young woman spoke to a few people at a time, whispering in the corner of a crowded marketplace, meeting in the shadows of a grain warehouse, standing on the pebbled shore of the harbor where old men cast out fishing lines. These were Cemi's emissaries, innocent and innocuous, yet able to spread the word and speak to hundreds of people.

In one of the brothel neighborhoods, Cemi made contact with the most boisterous and faithful of the mistresses, a plump woman named Saruna with painted eyes and enameled nails. She loved Empra Iluris and despised the very idea of Key Priestlord Klovus. "I know what that vile man demands for sacrifices, what he does to those poor girls. Some of my young ladies came here after their parents sent them to him for deflowering!" She snorted in disgust. "That is not how it should be done. I don't believe Iluris would allow it, if she knew!"

Saruna's women felt the same and talked among themselves as well as other pleasure women in adjacent brothels. Because the women were adept at sharing secrets in intimate moments, they also managed to spread the word among their customers that Empra Iluris was indeed still alive and waiting for her moment to return to her throne.

Out in the city, some believers in Iluris were not shy about expressing their skepticism. The rumors had gone on for so long that belief had begun to wane and unravel. A few followers scoffed and walked away from Cemi, resigned to the new situation in Ishara.

The young woman's greater fear, though, came from those who believed that Iluris was awake, but who no longer had faith that the empra would be strong enough to retake Ishara from the key priestlord. Those doubters were most dangerous to the cause of the skinny, teenaged street girl who spoke for the empra.

Cemi knew that if Iluris did not show herself and rally these people soon, she would lose them forever, and Klovus's hold on the city might never be broken.

Fortunately, the Hethrren were about to sail off with the Isharan navy, and it made sense to wait for Klovus's reckless allies to leave. Until then, Cemi hoped she and the people could hold on, keep the faith burning, and maintain the secret prayers that strengthened the new godling.

Walking along the waterfront, Cemi came upon the damaged harbor temple where fishermen and dockworkers made sacrifices to the deity that watched them when they were out on the open waves. The structure had been scorched and splintered during the recent godling rampage, which Priestlord Xion had tried to stop with his own temple's entity. Both had been destroyed.

With their harbor godling defeated and gone, few worshippers came to the temple anymore, yet Cemi saw fresh baskets of flowers, lit candles, gifts of bread and fish, including a strong-smelling mackerel, left on the doorstep.

The door was open and Cemi entered, hearing voices. Inside, she saw a young, calm-looking priestlord addressing a small group of worshippers. She recognized the man's face, but it took her a moment to place him.

Erical gave her an automatic smile of welcome. "Come, this is a place for peace and reflection. We can ponder here, together or alone. Pray to the godlings and take comfort in their company."

Cemi knew he wouldn't recognize her, since she'd just been a street girl when she made a sacrifice several years ago. Even if he did remember her, the priestlord would never guess that she was now heir apparent to Empra Iluris.

Fishermen, shipwrights, and harbor workers welcomed her.

"We were so glad to see someone back in the harbor temple," said a fisherman with thinning hair and a bushy beard.

Cemi stepped forward, keeping her eyes on the priestlord. "You're from Prirari, not here."

"The key priestlord summoned me here." His face looked troubled. "It seems I will be sailing away with the Hethrren in a few days. My godling and I are to help them."

Cemi looked past him to an irregularly shaped sheet of black shadowglass, like an infinite hole falling into the wall. A rainbow swirl of colors appeared from the depths, and she felt a spark inside her heart, an ancient connection. "Your own godling is here." She remembered when she had crept into the Prirari temple and offered it the only thing she could.

"My godling is always with me," Erical said. "And now she is very close."

The spelldoor shimmered, and the shadowglass became more transparent to let the entity flow out, brightening in the air. The worshippers in the harbor temple gasped and smiled.

"I grew up in Prirari," Cemi told him. "I had no parents, and I needed to survive. I sacrificed to the godling once—to this one." As she spoke, the entity brightened, the colors intensified. "It was just a rat, but it was all I had."

Erical smiled. "The godling appreciates every offering, and she remembers you. She is connected to you."

Cemi felt a great warmth, but distinctly different from the deity that protected Iluris beneath the palace.

"All godlings are the same and different, connected by unbreakable strands, yet they roam free, following the needs of their own people." Priestlord Erical sighed. "And my needs are to follow the key priestlord's orders. I don't want to sail to the old world, but Prirari will be safe enough while I'm gone. They have their faith, and the godling will still be in their hearts." He sounded as if he had to convince himself.

Not sure what she was doing, Cemi stepped closer to Erical. Behind him, the godling swirled like an undulating serpentine ribbon. Cemi reached out, and when she touched the colors, the godling brightened as if drawing from her own life force while energizing her in return. She gasped at the sensation.

Seeing what was happening, the others in the temple came forward, expressing their awe.

"This is so different from the harbor godling," said one old woman.

More people entered from the street, sensing something within the newly reopened temple.

Focusing on the godling, Cemi felt her own faith adding power, and she suddenly *knew* that they would find a way to save Ishara, restore the empra to her throne, and bring Klovus to justice.

Deep underground, Iluris blinked awake again, reached out to feel her devoted new godling as it looped around her. The entity suddenly sparkled, as if receiving energy from somewhere else. The hawk guards sighed and chuckled.

Vos said, "Look how strong you can be, Mother! With the faith of the people and the strength of our godling, we will restore our land to the way it should be."

Iluris smiled.

24

BIRCH told his quiet companions what he needed them to do, and they were in a perfect position to glean more details on precisely when and how the conspirators would strike Queen Koru. The creatures scuttled like shadows along the corridors, eavesdropped at doors, and hid like mice. They managed to place image cubes where they would not be noticed, and retrieve them later.

For the most part, Irri and the treacherous wreths paid no attention to the creatures, but three drones inadvertently got in the way and suffered for it. Ardo snapped one drone's neck with his bare hand and tossed the body aside; another drone was boiled from the inside when an annoyed Mage Qarri lashed out with a spell he was practicing; the third victim was caught between two warrior conspirators, who gutted it for mere practice.

Birch felt anguish over the losses, knowing the creatures had been following his instructions, but the drones did what was necessary to help him. He knew they had a silent, secret desire for vengeance against their creators, especially under the rule of Queen Onn. He had watched them sabotage the frozen spellsleep chambers, quietly killing dozens of wreths, and they had never been caught. Now he saw a fierce devotion in their eyes. The drones finally had something they *wanted* to do.

Birch knew he was gambling.

Over the past months, he had shown the drones how to make their own weapons. They had always had deadly materials right at their fingertips— caribou antlers, sharpened bones, scraps of metal—but they had not done much yet. Now, under his encouragement, the drones possessed more than a hundred knives, each one sharpened to a wicked point.

"I promise I'll try to make things better," he said. "But we have to win."

Birch had watched the recorded images from all the frozen cubes, identified each of the conspirators, and learned their plans. He also had proof to show Queen Koru—when it was time. He needed to move first.

In a deepening twilight with the auroras bright in the cold sky, the boy met the drones outside in their dim hovels. Many were naked, while others wore scraps of clothing, pieces of cloth tied over their bodies in a way that seemed more ornamental than practical. But the rags gave them places to hide their knives. The boy hid his carved pig in a safe place and pocketed his own short knife.

Irri and his conspirators had taken time to flesh out their plans to kill the queen, certain that no one suspected their treachery, and Birch was sure that Koru had no inkling of her imminent assassination. He let himself smile for the first time in a long while.

This situation was entirely under his control, and he would make himself valuable to the frostwreth queen. Koru was not malicious like her mother, and if Birch proved himself here, maybe he could convince her to take care of the drones.

Inside one of the stuffy hovels, he outlined the next steps he needed the drones to carry out. "Irri killed my grandmother. He and the others murdered a lot of you. This is our chance, and if we save Queen Koru, I'll ask her to make the wreths not hurt you anymore."

His drone fighters held out their sharpened strips of metal or pointed caribou horns. They had practiced stabbing into the snow or plunging their weapons into the remnants of a tundra ox carcass the hunters had brought in.

"You know how to kill," Birch said. "Tonight, you'll put it into practice. We all have to act at the same time or they might warn each other."

The drones hummed, whispered. They would move like a single organism, all identical; they had been made that way.

"It may take twenty of you to kill each one," he continued.

The drones mumbled, assuring him they had enough numbers.

Birch felt an ache in his heart to know that many of these creatures, his friends, would surely be killed in the sudden battle. The wreths considered them disposable, but he did not. Even with the element of surprise, Irri and his conspirators would fight back and kill innocent drones.

Even so, he did not change his mind, could not. If the conspiracy succeeded and Irri ruled the wreths, he and the drones would suffer far worse. He felt bitter cold again as he imagined what their lives would be like. . . .

As the clear arctic night deepened, the drones filed into the palace and went about their duties, as always. Pale green aurora light penetrated the thick ice walls, adding an eerie glow. When the agreed-upon time came, the drones dispersed like a small army. Instead of their usual frenetic activity and tiny sounds, this time the creatures were silent. This time they were not empty victims. This time they moved like packs of predators.

As the creatures scattered, Birch took the small sack he had fashioned from a scrap of cloth, full of the frozen recording cubes, and made his way to Koru's throne room.

☙❧

In his chamber, Mage Qarri sat motionless, head bowed. He wore blue leather robes adorned with runes, each of which connected to long-unused spells. He rested without sleeping, meditating. He went into a deep trance and pondered the imminent death of the usurper queen. Irri and his companions would slaughter her very soon, and Qarri would have a place at the ruler's right hand.

The mage recalled various spells, feeling the faint threads of magic left in the world. Behind him, he heard a furtive scuffling, sensed movement. He cracked open his eyes, looked through slitted lids, and saw the gray-skinned drones. The creatures were always busy performing incomprehensible tasks that either the queen had given them or they made up themselves. They cleaned and served and generally remained out of the way, though occasionally they were a nuisance.

The mage was annoyed that they had broken his meditations. He had not called for service, had not requested a meal. He closed his eyes and tried to recapture his thoughts, grasping at his center of concentration, and did his best to ignore them.

His eyes flew open again as he realized they were not carrying any food. The drones were acting strangely.

He turned his head, frowning.

They rushed toward him with amazing speed, moving like a blizzard of bodies, nearly twenty of them. It was not conceivable! He saw flashing metal objects in their hands.

The drones didn't make a sound as they swarmed upon him. Qarri raised his hand to ward them off, and a sharp knife slashed his palm open. Before the flare of pain could even register, a flurry of blades stabbed down, a dozen more knives and pointed antlers piercing him in the neck, the chest, the shoulders. A caribou horn slashed across his face. The next one sank deep into his eye.

The drones kept stabbing and stabbing.

Ardo slept with his current noble lover, relaxing before the risky assassination would take place. The supple woman had exhausted him, showing great enthusiasm as she tried to coax out his secret news. Unable to resist, Ardo had bragged that he was about to become vastly more important among the frostwreths. It had been part of the flirtation and seduction, but Ardo refused to tell her any more. He couldn't trust her, at least not this close to when Irri would make his move.

Within a day, Ardo would help slay Koru. After that, he could have any lover he wished. He might even keep this one, since she'd performed with such liveliness. Now, though, he needed to sleep. She curled against him, purring with satisfaction, drawing her long nails across his cheek. "Tell me what you are hiding," she insisted, "or I will consider you no more than a braggart who was trying to bed me."

"I do not care what you think," Ardo said. "I already have what I want."

She playfully slapped him, rolled him over on his back, and climbed on top of him. Her long pale hair flowed down over her shoulders and tickled his face. "Tell me!" she repeated as she straddled him. He surrendered to the sensation, although he just wanted to sleep.

She jerked in surprise. "What are they doing here?" She sounded annoyed.

Ardo opened his eyes and turned toward the door to see a flurry of drones, innocuous creatures that always moved in a skittery manner—but these were running, running toward him. They held knives.

Ardo tried to lurch up out of the bed, but his lover was on top of him, weighing him down. Suddenly, they were both buried under bodies. Crude knives darted and jabbed, and Ardo felt flares of agony, as countless dagger points thrust into all parts of his body.

His lover screamed, and for some ridiculous reason he couldn't remember her name. Then he couldn't remember anything as waves of pain drowned him from innumerable mortal wounds.

Birch had not given the drones specific instructions to kill any witnesses, but the drones decided to stab the frostwreth woman as well.

When he reached the queen's throne room, Birch walked with more pride and confidence than he had felt in a long time.

Koru was on her throne. Bored and impatient, she toyed with the golden ramer on an adjacent frozen table. Scattered across the smooth cold floor were game pieces that she used for plotting her military moves to the south.

As he entered, she glanced up. "There you are, boy. I have not seen you for hours. Where have you been?"

"With the drones." He kept walking at a brisk pace. "My friends."

Koru gave him a curious frown. "You spend too much time with those creatures. It is beneath you. You should be by my side. Have I not done enough to support you?"

Birch kept his expression neutral. "Yes, you supported me."

He reached the front of her throne and opened his makeshift sack to spill the frozen recording cubes on the steps of the dais. "You can watch these later, but each one shows proof of what I am about to tell you—Irri and other wreths want to kill you." He saw her silver-blue eyes go wide with disbelief, but he climbed past her to the wall where Koru had hung the broken spear, reaching for it.

She rose to her feet, suddenly ready to defend herself. "What are you doing, boy?"

"Come with me so you can see for yourself." He pulled the spear off the wall and handed it to her. "You need to hurry. I told them to keep Irri alive. If they could." He knew what the drones were doing at this moment. He was proud of them, and he knew they would succeed. "Then you'll appreciate them more. And me."

The queen took the weapon from him, intrigued. She stepped over the scattered image cubes on the dais and followed Birch as he hurried out of the throne room. "Irri would not dare! I am his queen."

"You can ask him yourself, if he is still alive," Birch said. "The others should be dead by now."

The queen chuckled. "*If* Irri is alive? What are drones going to do?"

He had already gambled everything. From under his shirt, he withdrew the metal knife from his waistband. "I would have helped them with the killing, but I thought it was more important to protect you."

Though the drone attack surprised him, Irri fought back fiercely. Dark blood dripped from half a dozen stab wounds and wide gashes in his body. His right arm hung limp from where the drones had severed his tendons. His abdomen was split open with a long gaping slice.

With a roar, Irri grabbed one drone by the neck, smashed him against the wall, then seized the arm of another drone as its knife plunged into his thigh. Using the creature's flopping arm, he flung the small body like a whip to strike two more, but ten additional drones piled on top of him stabbing, cutting. And even more were coming.

They had made no sound, just rushed into his room. The moment they started attacking, Irri had lunged over the bed and turned to drive them away, but they had tremendous strength in numbers.

A sharpened bone dug into his right breast and stuck there like an embedded thorn. Irri kicked out hard enough to crush the rib cage of one of his attackers, but even as the small body fell, more of them came, and then more.

They cut his legs, slashed his hamstring, stabbed him in the gut again. Now they squeaked and chittered, inane noises that sounded deadly. Like victory.

Irri howled in rage, and a razor-edged strip of metal went into his mouth and slashed through his cheek so that the skin hung in bloody flaps, exposing his teeth.

One jumped on his back and stabbed his spine. Suddenly, his legs went cold, then he felt nothing. His limbs failed him, and he collapsed to the floor, looking up at all the long, decorative icicles on his ceiling.

With his one good hand, he kept trying to fight back, but they stabbed him, disabling him, though somehow careful not to kill him. He lay in a lake of blood and couldn't utter words, only a hoarse gasping. Pain was everywhere.

When he lay completely helpless, the drones stopped attacking, just looked at him with their maddening expressionless faces. The creatures quieted and backed away, leaving him crippled, bleeding on the floor.

When his vision sharpened through the ice haze of pain, he couldn't believe what he was seeing. A boy. Koru's pet human. And he was grinning.

The queen gazed down at Irri, holding her legendary spear like a scepter.

"The others are dead," Birch said, "but he was their leader."

"How can you be sure of this?"

"The drones heard them. I heard them. They pay no attention to us, but we listen. Everything is in the recording cubes. We saved your life."

Koru scoffed. "I could have defeated them myself."

"Without us, how would you have known?"

She scowled down at Irri, who lay like a dying reindeer torn apart by wolf-steeds. He gurgled, opened and closed his bloody mouth. Birch named the other conspirators aloud, the wreth nobles, the warriors, even the mage, all of whom were now dead.

She towered over Irri. He recognized her, and his expression tightened, defiance leaking through all the pain and blood.

"The sandwreths are not our only enemy." She leaned closer. "Now you die knowing that your conspiracy failed. We will feed your body to the oonuks. That way at least you will serve some purpose."

She lifted the spear, stained with the blood of Ossus and then her mother. Looking at the pathetic traitor, she hesitated and frowned. "He doesn't deserve such an honorable weapon." She glanced at Birch with a smile. "Step back, boy."

Birch followed her, and the drones skittered away as well, but remained where they could watch. Irri opened his mouth, but blood came out instead of words.

Koru gestured with her hand, and from the ceiling dozens of long icicles broke off and showered down, impaling Irri countless times.

She put her hand on Birch's shoulder. "I was right to keep you alive and close to me."

Now she was more beholden to him than ever.

25

UTHO felt unbalanced after his clash with his trainer, his mentor . . . a man he had never imagined would become his enemy. How could Onzu, a well-respected training master, have turned against the Bravas' vengewar? Why had he forced Utho to kill him?

With rising frustration, he wanted to slash and destroy anyone else who became an impediment to the Bravas' destiny of a vengewar. Master Onzu was not a true Brava if he could not understand the need to destroy the Isharan animals for what they had done to the colony of Valaera . . . for what they had done to Utho's wife and daughters. He crushed the guilt inside him like a man grinding out the last ember of a campfire. He had no time for guilt, though the repercussions resonated loudly in his mind. He had to launch the Commonwealth navy as soon as possible, before something else delayed them.

The memory of killing Conndur was a twisted secret inside him, walled off and inaccessible, like a castle with its drawbridge raised. He never let his thoughts go there. That bloodshed and violence, the provocative brutality felt as if it had been done by someone else. It incensed him even more to know that Onzu had sent those revelations to King Kollanan in Norterra! Adan in Suderra would surely know, too.

He had already decided to carry out the Isharan invasion without assistance from the two other kingdoms, and he could not let the matter distract Mandan. The young konag's focus already wandered, reacting to petty insults. Utho needed to launch the fleet and be on his way before even more distractions interfered with what he needed to do.

He stalked up from the armory tunnels, sweaty and flushed. No one else knew about the duel. At some point a fisherman or scavenger down at the river might find the headless body, obviously a Brava, but they would not know what had happened. Utho hoped to be long gone before then. The vengewar would be ignited and unstoppable. He would be across the sea.

He emerged from the passages below into the castle proper, making his way through the corridors. He had to push Mandan into action. The time for delay was past, and Utho's determination built like an avalanche sliding down a mountain slope. Nothing would stop him now.

He paused, feeling a droplet on his cheek. He touched it, looked at his fingertip. Blood. Then he touched his black finemail armor and saw more blood.

Onzu's blood. The stains were unmistakable. Once again the training master was stalling him!

He entered a garderobe, found a basin of tepid water, and scrubbed his face. He diluted the bloodstain on his shirt enough that it was not immediately noticeable against the black, then he pushed his way into the throne room like a wolf cornering prey.

Mandan was playing a game with wooden pegs on a board, while Lira sat across the game board from him, with shoulders slumped and a glazed look in her eyes. The young man pestered her to hurry, and she lifted one of her hands over the pieces, let it hover in the air, a wounded bird.

Mandan snatched a game piece and moved it for her, then moved his own. "There, I win. Again." Seeing Utho, Mandan lurched to his feet.

The Brava spoke to him in a tone that invited no argument. "You will ride with me to Rivermouth, my konag. If we saddle up now, we can get to the shipyards before nightfall."

"Rivermouth?" Mandan asked as if Utho had spoken in a new language. "That'll be hours of hard riding. Why not prepare my barge and ride down the river in the morning?"

"That would take too long. I can have horses saddled in minutes. You will address the ship captains, sailors, and soldiers aboard. We must launch our attack on Ishara with the next outgoing tide."

The konag quailed. "But I'm not ready. We have to make sure all the soldiers who remain here are outfitted, our defensive force fully armed. And what if Norterra attacks here while you're gone?" His head snapped up. "Kollanan could be sending a full army to Convera even as we speak! We know he's treacherous."

"We know he is far away," Utho said. "Come with me now." He looked at the young man's rumpled cape tossed on a chair. "I'll send a squire to pack formal clothes and your crown. This is an important announcement. As konag of the three kingdoms, you need to look regal."

Mandan's gaze lit upon Lira. "If it's that important, then my queen should go with me." She did not disagree, showed no reaction whatsoever.

"As long as she doesn't fall off the horse." Utho spun about and went to make preparations for their swift ride to the coast.

The horses raced along the river road, and the party reached the town of Rivermouth without fanfare, on purpose. The escort riders commandeered a shipping clerk's office where the royal couple could change into glorious garments. Meanwhile, runners spread word along the docks, throughout the town, among the ships and crews in the harbor, that Konag Mandan himself would address them before sundown.

It took an hour for the captains to recall their crew members from the town, and servants hurried to dress and prepare the konag and queen. Though Mandan was nervous, Utho coached him repeatedly. Lira was listless from too much milk of the blue poppy, but at least she passively accepted a beautiful gown and let her hair be braided with small white flowers.

When the young konag emerged from the shipping clerk's office, he was resplendent in a blue cape, blue silk jerkin, pantaloons, and polished leather boots. He wore a wide belt and his most elaborate formal crown studded with jewels. Konag Conndur had hated such trappings, but Mandan needed them now.

Utho led the couple down to the main harbor, where crowds had formed on the streets and on the docks, dutifully cheering. The konag looked dazed, as if he, too, had consumed drugs, but he had a nervous energy about him. Sailors lined the decks of their ships. Dockworkers stood at the river's edge and the harbor mouth.

Large armored vessels were anchored nearby in the harbor. It was a far superior force to the one they had recently sent against Fulcor Island. That failure had terrified Mandan and left deep wounds, and now he looked at the large fleet of warships with unabashed astonishment, all of these soldiers sworn to obey his orders. Commonwealth banners flew alongside the flags of Osterra. Utho allowed himself a satisfied smile.

He led the konag and his queen to the main pier, where Mandan turned to face the crowds. Utho stared past him out to the open sea, thinking of Ishara beyond the horizon. Mandan glanced at him as if for permission, and he nodded. The konag took his queen's limp hand. Utho had hoped Lira could manage a smile, but her face remained slack.

Mandan shouted out in a clear voice. "This great fleet reminds me of how my grandfather sent the largest naval force in history to end the last Isharan war. But Konag Cronin did not finish the job."

The young man fed his anger into his words, and Utho felt pleased.

"Today we launch an even greater force to conquer the new world, to punish Ishara for all the crimes they have committed in the past." His voice cracked as he shouted even louder. "To make them pay for the murder of so many innocent citizens over the centuries . . . all the people of Mirrabay. And my father, Conndur the Brave!" He reeled, as if overcome with grief. "The time has come. I command these ships to set sail tonight with the outgoing tide."

Utho glanced up and down the docks and noted at least ten black-clad Bravas on various ships, ready to fight the vengewar. Two marched toward him down the pier—Tytan and Jennae. Utho had other plans for them. They would be displeased when he told them, but he had made his decision.

Mandan waited for the cheers to fade, and his voice faltered. "As your konag, I will be with you in spirit, but my bonded Brava Utho shall command this navy. I must remain in Convera to lead the three kingdoms."

A murmur rippled through the crowd, but Utho could not discern whether the reaction was appreciative or disapproving.

Tytan and Jennae stood beside the konag and his queen. Jennae seemed on the verge of an angry outburst, as she often did, while burly Tytan, practically the size of a warship, was implacable.

Utho turned to them without raising his voice. "I appoint you two to be our konag's new bonded Bravas. While I am gone, stay in Convera and guard him. Protect him from domestic threats and ensure that he makes wise decisions."

Jennae scoffed. "My arm and my ramer are strong enough to fight Isharans. That's why I came."

"Your ramer is also good enough to protect our konag. We have a navy and a trained army. These ships will sail for Ishara, but we cannot leave the Commonwealth undefended."

"There are other Bravas here," Jennae grumbled, gesturing to all the crowded ships. "Pick one of them instead."

Utho's voice snapped at her like the lash of a whip. "All Bravas have sworn their loyalty to the konag. Konag Mandan needs a Brava while I am gone, and I give him two—you two."

Looking at Tytan and Jennae, as if without noticing the tension, Mandan said, "I accept them. Thank you, Utho."

Both Bravas looked unhappy, but Tytan merely grunted. "Our blood and service belong to the konag."

Utho lowered his voice. "Once we crush Ishara, everything will change."

"Stay safe, Utho," Mandan said, his voice sounding young and uncertain. "And come back to me. I need you here."

"Yes, my konag," Utho said. He strode down the docks to the ship he had chosen, leaving the two Bravas with the young konag.

26

ADAN took King Kollanan to visit the weapons shops in the old city, where they watched master swordsmiths and glaziers affix shadowglass, with its deadly obsidian edges, to battle axes and pikes. Larger shards of black glass formed entire spear points; smaller ones were sharpened and used as arrowheads.

"We've made thousands of weapons for our army," Adan said. "Voo thinks we intend to use them only against frostwreths."

Kollanan picked up a shield inlaid with black glass, which could deflect wreth weaponry or magic. "I wish I'd had these at Lake Bakal." He smiled beneath his full beard. "But we did well enough. We know that wreths can die. Shadowglass just makes it easier to kill them."

He set his war hammer on the workshop table, and a leathery old weaponsmith came up to inspect it. Koll said, "Can you add shadowglass to this?"

The armorer picked up the handle, turning the head to inspect it. "I can embed some shards in each end. That might be sufficient." The old man leaned closer. "But it's stained. I can polish and clean your hammer first, Sire."

"Leave it," Kollanan said. "That is wreth blood."

A clang of alarm bells resounded from the western walls, and distant gongs added a higher brassy note.

Koll looked up. "Ancestors' blood, is it a sandwreth attack already?"

"They don't know about Quo's death yet," Adan said. "No wreths escaped, and we erased all evidence. They can't know!"

They hurried to the main gates, where Banner guards stood on the wall, weapons ready. Penda and her father were already there at the lookout point. Xar and Ari circled in the sky, observing. When Adan joined his wife in the shade of the guard tower, she said, "A sandwreth party is approaching."

Hale Orr shaded his eyes, scowling. "*Cra,* at least it's not an army." He touched the black pendant that hung from his ear, as if the small bit of shadowglass might protect him.

Elliel and Thon joined them, taking their places near King Kollanan. She looked toward the Suderran hills and the stark mountains beyond. "The hidden slave camp is out there, isn't it? The wreth party is approaching from that direction."

"Sandwreths always come from the desert," Adan said. "Let's see what this is about."

"They're up to no good," Kollanan said. "Whatever they intend."

Elliel peered intensely into the distance. "There's a mage . . . several warriors and workers. Augas are hauling heavily loaded sledges."

Adan blinked. "Oh, they're delivering another shipment of shadowglass."

"They do not know, beloved," Penda said with a smile. "Queen Voo still believes we are her willing followers. Why should she stop sending us shadowglass for our weapons?"

"How could she be so naïve?" Koll grumbled.

"She's a wreth." Adan remembered how aloof and arrogant Voo had been, how dismissive yet possessive she was. She'd tried to seduce Adan, and when he rebuffed her, she treated him like a pet that had misbehaved. "Human independence doesn't even occur to her."

Penda kept her attention on the approaching party, and her expression showed new concern. "I should stay hidden. They don't know that I've had my baby, or that I've returned to Bannriya."

"I'll let them continue to believe that you're gone," Adan said. "We have to keep up appearances. It will be safest if I ride out and accept the shipment, as I've done before, presenting myself as their happy cooperative ally."

"They may try to deceive you," Koll warned.

"Our deception is greater." He gave his wife a swift kiss. "Go to our daughter and hide yourselves." He looked up. "Kollanan, you too. I do not wish them to know that the king of Norterra is here."

"I don't like this," Koll said.

"Nor I," Adan admitted. "But we can use more shadowglass for our weapons. That's something to be thankful for."

Adan rode out on a chestnut mare accompanied by Captain Elcior and four other Banner guards, as well as a dozen burly porters to take charge of the load of black glass.

Deception did not come naturally to Adan, but in this case it was a matter of survival. Sandwreths had already betrayed the humans. Voo wanted to take Penda and Oak, and they were holding humans in a secret slave camp in the canyons. As for the frostwreths, they had obliterated the village at Lake Bakal, in addition to murdering Queen Tafira.

No, he did not owe their race friendship or honesty.

Outside the city walls, he greeted the wreths and hid his anger behind a convincing smile. On the lead auga, a craggy mage clutched the reptilian mount's saddle horn with a gnarled hand. Haughty sandwreth warriors rode their own augas, spears upraised, as if they feared bandits might attack the caravan. Behind them, more creatures dragged sledges loaded with heavy shadowglass.

Adan pulled his mare to a halt and squared his shoulders, conducting himself like a king as he faced the mage. He recognized the one named Axus.

"The gracious Queen Voo delivers more vital material for her army," the mage announced in a gravelly voice. "Have you made good use of what we already brought? Are your soldiers prepared kill the enemy when Queen Voo calls on them for the final war?"

Adan's expression faltered at the words "Kill the enemy," and his mind flashed to the human slaves, who still needed to be rescued. He would soon face their captors. The sandwreths might seem omnipotent, he reminded himself, but they were also ignorant. He acted with appropriate deference. "Our armorers and weapon makers have been busy. The shadowglass will make us strong for the coming battles."

Strangely, the mage's expression softened. "I have told Voo that humans work better if they are given a hint of freedom. You will be useful when we fight the frostwreths." Axus's rough face showed deep lines, as if someone had chiseled disappointment there. "But I doubt you can aid us when we slay Ossus."

"We humans have enemies of our own," Adan said, thinking of his vindictive brother.

"Human squabbles are not our concern," the mage said.

"And wreth squabbles should not be ours," Adan retorted.

Mage Axus looked disturbed. "Some might hear defiance in your voice, King Adan. Watch yourself." Power seemed to roil around him like faint smoke. "Where are your wife and child? Queen Voo asks. And why has your great Konag Mandan not come to abase himself before her throne, as she commanded?"

Adan chose his words carefully, planning ahead. "My wife is safe, I am sure. She joined her people, the Utauks, in preparation for giving birth. As for my brother . . ." He shrugged. "Mandan sometimes believes he is too important to answer to anyone else."

"Then he does not know the power of Queen Voo. His defiance is unforgivable," Axus said.

Adan replied quickly. "Yes, I will soon dispatch my army to our capital and insist that Konag Mandan respond. We will fight him if necessary." He smiled, emphasizing the solution. "My soldiers will march off to do what we must to punish him for his dishonorable behavior. You can count on us."

"Yes, we can," said Axus, though his expression looked stormy. "Humans were created for a specific purpose. Serve it well."

"All of the pieces are in play, but we have to follow the Commonwealth charter," Kollanan said. "As our armies get ready, we should dispatch a rider with our formal decree removing Mandan from the throne. Then we'll enforce it with our armies."

To Adan, it felt like an irrevocable but necessary step. The kings of Norterra and Suderra, two of the three rulers of the Commonwealth, would write, sign, and seal the document. By Commonwealth law, the decree would serve as formal notice of the konag's heinous crimes and strip him of his crown.

In the council chamber, they took great pains to delineate the charges against Mandan, because they knew the news would be spread widely. The konag's dark rule had shaken the common people, so different from the leadership of Conndur the Brave.

Penda and her father watched the scribes and lawyers write the official document, Kollanan and Adan signed it and affixed their seals. As soon as the decree was finished, Hale Orr ushered in a handsome, lanky man who wore green and tan Utauk colors. "You remember Donnan Rah. He is the best person to deliver the decree." Hale grinned, showing his gold tooth. "An Utauk messenger will get through faster than any military courier."

Donnan Rah made an expansive bow. "At your service again, Sire. And as I ride, I will spread the announcement throughout the Utauk tribes. I hear Shella din Orr's heart camp is moving to Osterra. She will dispatch the word far and wide." After a pause, the messenger said, "The Utauks will stand with you, Adan Starfall and Kollanan the Hammer. Konag Mandan has taken several Utauk caravans, stolen our goods, conscripted our people, and commandeered our neutral trading ships for his navy. This is not tradition."

"*Cra*, it is not!" Hale bellowed. "You can send your documents and quote your Commonwealth charter, for the exact law of it, but all the tribes know what is right and what is true. Inside the circle, and outside the circle."

Penda cradled baby Oak in the curve of her arm, where the tiny girl slept without fussing. "But first . . ." She glanced at the two skas perched on their stand. The reptile birds seemed intent on the discussion. "We have to free Glik and the other captives."

"Mage Axus seems a very interesting man," Thon said. "Will he be at the camp when we liberate the prisoners? I could destroy him, if necessary."

"Who can say?" Adan answered. "We plan for the worst."

"We plan in great detail." Penda reached out her free hand to scratch the green feathers on Xar's head. "Ari can fly out and find Glik, and then map the whole camp with her mothertear. This is a battle we can win."

27

ON the night before the Isharan fleet was to take away the Hethrren at last, the barbarians raided Serepol taverns, brothels, and customhouses in one final reign of terror. That was when Klovus's nightmare began, from which not even the Black Eels could protect him.

While the Hethrren wreaked havoc in the harbor district, Klovus was in the city square, sampling delicacies from a purveyor of spiced honeys. Citizens gave him small offerings to show their appreciation to the great Serepol godling.

Then Magda strode up and grabbed him by the front of his caftan. "Come, lover. You'll miss me while I'm gone, so I will give you a night to remember." He knew everyone had seen him cringe, but Magda didn't care who overheard her. "We should make love once in the empra's bedchamber before I sleep on a wooden deck."

A wave of nausea overcame him, and he felt a flash of anger when he saw uniformed city soldiers just watching him. They actually smiled; one covered his mouth with a hand to hide a snicker. But Klovus had to endure, just to be sure he got rid of the Hethrren. . . .

Somehow, he managed to perform sexually. It took all of his concentration to remember other sweet young women, whose lovely bodies he'd enjoyed in the past. He fought to banish all thoughts of the muscular, smelly, feminine mass in the bed. The act reminded him of rutting with a herd beast. But it had to be done, one last trauma to tolerate in order to ensure Magda's cooperation, so that the Hethrren would leave. He kept thinking of that, over and over. Once he was finished, Magda dismissed him as a tool she had used up.

In the morning, he felt bruised, raw, and disgusted, but he blocked the memories. It was time for the fleet to launch. He gathered his rumpled caftan and hurried to the harbor, while Magda strode off to round up her barbarians.

Arriving early, Priestlord Erical stood on the pier at the flagship's gangplank, still uneasy about the journey. His godling shimmered like a rainbow behind him. The entity looped and drifted, then settled like a faint veil over the deck before she seeped into the hold. Klovus hoped the entity would ensure that the fleet made it across the ocean to their destination.

Shading his eyes in the early-morning sun, Erical looked forlornly at Klovus. "I wish I could stay here, Key Priestlord. I want to join the other priestlords for the consecration of the Magnifica. My place is in Ishara. Our home"—he raised his hand, indicating the godling as well—"is back in Pri-rari District instead of far, far away."

"We all suffer for our duty," Klovus snapped, reminded of Magda's beefy embrace.

Always obedient, Erical bowed, then ascended to the deck.

Klovus knew that the captains and Isharan crews of these warships might also become sacrifices to the greater mission. Once the barbarians ran ram-pant across the old world, would these vessels ever come home? Nevertheless, it was an unqualified victory just to have Serepol, and Ishara, back under his control. With Empra Iluris vanished and surely dead, he could bring the people in line.

He watched the Isharan soldiers standing next to the unkempt barbar-ians, knowing that one of those soldiers was Zaha himself, disguised in unre-markable features. Klovus trusted the Black Eel assassin, had used him as his hatchet man many times. Now, he needed a dependable person to watch over the assault fleet and keep the Hethrren closely controlled. Given Klovus's dis-gust for Magda, especially after the previous miserable night, he gave Zaha permission to kill her, if such an opportunity were to come up. He had other Black Eels to protect him here in Serepol, and they were just as competent.

The harbor crowds were as uneasy as they were animated. Looking out of his depth, Erical stood at the rail of the flagship as the ropes were untied, the gangplanks pulled up. The hundreds of Hethrren had been dispersed across the fleet, and now crowded the decks, shouting. Magda raised her knotted club in a gesture of defiance. She looked directly at Klovus, and he swallowed hard. At least she didn't blow him a kiss.

Out in the harbor, other large warships weighed their anchors, set the sails. Muscular crew members used oars to move the vessels away from the piers. Thanks to Priestlord Erical's godling, a favorable wind nudged the Isharan fleet.

With the ships headed out to sea, the crowd grew oddly louder, resonating with relief. Klovus felt a flush of emotion as he departed from the waterfront, flanked by a pair of his ur-priests. He already felt a heavy shroud of tension lifting from the capital city.

When he reached the Magnifica temple, he climbed tier after tier to the newly finished fourth level. The fifth and last platform was now under con-struction. From this high vantage, Klovus watched the warships sail away.

At last he could consolidate Ishara again. By channeling the Serepol god-ling through the stepped pyramid, he could control everything. He was the key priestlord.

☙

Later that day, in the chambers beneath the Magnifica, Klovus observed the interrogation, wanting to learn if there was any truth to the rumors. His Black Eels had brought in four captives, three men and one woman. He could see by their battered condition that the questioning had already begun.

When he stood before the frightened captives seated on wooden stools, they looked at him with a mixture of hope and fear, exactly as he liked it.

"Key Priestlord!" The woman tried to surge to her feet, but the Black Eels knocked her back down. "I'm just a fishmonger! I sell shells and fresh catch. That's all I do. These men seized me, but I know—"

One of the Black Eels cut her off. "We heard her speaking about how Empra Iluris was coming back to take her crown again."

The woman blinked, not comprehending. "But, of course! Hear us, save us—isn't that what we all wish for? We pray for it every day."

"There are better things to pray for," Klovus said. "The empra is long gone. By spreading such foolishness, you diminish the prayers that feed the true godling." He glanced at the shadowglass panels mounted on the wall, deep black windows that he had seized from the *Glissand*. Behind the obsidian barrier, the godling swirled and simmered, and Klovus could feel its attention on him.

A burly blacksmith named Boorlin grumbled, "We pray for Iluris to return. We pray for her safety. All of Ishara wishes the same thing." The smith's left eye was swollen shut, and his neck showed fresh bruises. The Black Eels would not have used sticks or cudgels, merely their own hands. They could make their skin as hard as stone, if they liked.

Klovus snapped, "Empra Iluris abandoned this city, abandoned her people, and now I am forced to carry that burden. I guide our land and strengthen our people."

"Not in the way Iluris would," muttered one of the captured men, a carpenter. "You brought those barbarians here. They raped my wife."

The key priestlord huffed. "We all make sacrifices. I recruited the Hethrren because of their anger and violence. Would I send a ship full of flower maidens to fight the enemy?"

"Iluris would never have allowed rapists to run free," the carpenter insisted.

One of the Black Eels struck him hard.

"Our empra is still alive," insisted the fishmonger woman. "Everybody knows it. She is among her people. What you're doing—"

A Black Eel punched her so hard he broke several teeth loose. Her head snapped to one side, then lolled, either in unconsciousness or death.

In his heart, Klovus felt an external surge and turned to face the shadowglass, which was a portal to the realm where godlings lived, but he felt sudden darkness twist in his mind. Curious, he realized it did not come from the godling—*his* godling. It was an evil force, a deep stain far away.

Was this what Priestlord Erical had sensed? Klovus shook his head to clear his thoughts and turned back to the captives.

"When can we go?" moaned the third man, looking at his bound hands.

"You are spreading sedition and weakening my authority. You can never go free." Klovus nodded to the Black Eels.

The blacksmith sensed what was coming and pushed himself to his feet. His great muscles snapped the ropes and cracked the wood of the stool, but he didn't have a chance. The Black Eels broke all the captives like kindling, leaving their bodies crumpled and bloody.

The key priestlord's thoughts swirled as he looked at the four dead conspirators. This nonsense had gone on far too long. The citizens of Serepol were left with too many unanswered questions, and unanswered questions gave them unreasonable hope.

"It's time to be done with this," Klovus said. "The whispers and rumors will only gain strength. These four will disappear, but they might become martyrs." He snorted. "Some fools may even say they ascended to the realm of the godlings to join Iluris. It is no longer amusing. I will declare the empra dead, finally, and we will have a funeral." He narrowed his eyes. "Find me an appropriate body."

28

Fellstaff Castle seemed empty, and Shadri was restless. Her friends El-liel and Thon had ridden off with King Kollanan to liberate the sandwreth slave camp. Lasis and several vassal lords had taken most of the Norterran army on a long march toward the mountains so they would be ready to move against Konag Mandan in Convera. Gant remained in the castle, a silent but efficient guardian who sent out scout patrols and drilled the remaining army to protect the city.

Working in the castle library, Shadri jotted page after page of notes in her battered journal. She had spent much of her life wandering the landscape alone, poking under rocks and following her solitary interests. She had wanted to be a legacier, asking questions, keeping records. After Queen Tafira's tragic death, she had written the woman's legacy, recording her life story so it would never be forgotten.

Long life and a great legacy.

Now, though, the scholar girl had other important work. Thon had ac-quired stacks of crystalline sheets engraved with wreth letters, which could only be activated by wreth blood. Before leaving, Thon had illuminated the writing on many sheets, that still needed to be translated. The words and symbols were still there, revealed. Thon was gone, and he could not help Shadri in her studies. Nonetheless, she applied herself to the enormous task.

The enigmatic man still gave her chills after what she had seen in the wreth ruins near Yanton: a huge shadow with great power that had torn apart ma-rauders who broke through the defensive walls. Was he the god Kur himself? A manifestation of Ossus? Or something else entirely? That wasn't a question she could answer by herself.

Keeping busy in the library, she stared at the untranscribed wreth sheets. She could not read much of the language, but did know certain key words and phrases. She wrote notes and identified some of the names she recognized— Kur, Ossus, the two women Raan and Suth. She could identify "dragon" and "evil." Thon had copied the special rune that was his own name, though Shadri didn't expect to find it in these incredibly ancient documents.

She did find one important record, a broken sheet, recording how Kur had issued an anguished pronouncement to the bitterly feuding wreths, just before he vanished from the world: "The only way to destroy the evil is from within."

The rest of the crystal was broken and lost. So far, she had found no further information on the god's final words.

"Not very helpful," she muttered. Searching through the stacks, trying to organize them, she grew frustrated. The wreths had stored the ancient records without protecting or organizing them. She didn't know where to start. Why would they be so careless with their own history?

There was so much about the wreths she didn't understand! She wished she had someone to talk to.

The drones fascinated her as well. They had saved Lasis after Queen Onn slashed his throat and left him for dead. They had helped at Lake Bakal, giving King Kollanan vital information about the wreth fortress. She had seen the creatures hiding in the forests during Queen Tafira's remembrance ceremony. The drones knew countless details about the wreths. If only she could talk to them!

Pokle came into the library with a tray. He stumbled, clattering the dishes, but caught his balance in time. His cheeks burned with embarrassment. "I thought you might be hungry. Here's fresh milk from the dairy, and raisin buns, and . . . and two of my favorite venison sausages, though no one knows how to season them anymore, now that the queen's gone."

When Shadri saw the tray, her stomach growled, and she realized she'd eaten only a small breakfast many hours earlier. "Thank you, Pokle. I was just wishing I had someone to talk to."

Although the young man never had much to say and little knowledge to share, he was a good listener, and he didn't mind her ramblings. "I . . . I brought enough food for two, if we could eat together."

She cleared a spot on the table, and the young man divided up the breads and meats, though they had to share the mug of milk.

"In fact," Shadri said before she could think further, "I want you to come with me on a ride north."

"North? Where the frostwreths are?" He balked. "I . . . I've already been too close to the frostwreths."

"We'll be fine. I want to go back to Lake Bakal to talk to the drones, and you know that place better than anyone." She picked up a new blank journal. "I think they must have a lot of interesting information."

"The drones?" Pokle asked. "But they run and hide. Just like we should."

"This is important. Gant can use the information to protect Fellstaff. Don't you want to be a war hero?" The young man blinked, not sure of the answer, and Shadri pressed. "Have you ever imagined yourself as a hero?"

"Never. When the frostwreths killed everyone at Lake Bakal, I hid in the forest for a long time. I didn't think I was going to survive."

"We'll be better prepared this time, won't we?"

"I don't like this."

She shushed him. "You'll be with me."

The boy bucked up his courage. "Then I'll keep you safe. But we better ride back to Fellstaff as soon as it looks dangerous."

"Of course," she said. "As soon as it looks dangerous to me."

After Shadri explained to Gant what they intended to do, the Brava provided them with two old cart horses to ride. Fellstaff maintained a cavalry for the defense of the city, and the rest of the warhorses had been dispatched east with the Norterran army. Shadri was perfectly happy with the slow mounts. "These will be fine. I wouldn't know what to do with a stallion anyway."

"I cannot spare a scout patrol or a guard escort to accompany you," the Brava said.

She gave a quick shrug. "I camped and traveled by myself for years, and Pokle survived in the wilderness while the frostwreths were hunting him. We have nothing to worry about."

Pokle looked embarrassed. "All I did was hide for a few days before I was rescued."

Shadri frowned at him. "You are a terrible teller of stories."

Gant nodded. "I would be happy for whatever information you discover. You can be my spies."

"Spies," Shadri said, realizing that she liked the sound of the word. "I was just intending to learn, but . . ."

"Spies," Pokle said, as if he couldn't believe it.

They set off from Fellstaff with their plodding horses on the road to Lake Bakal. The mounts were very sedate, and Shadri chattered about whatever struck her fancy as they covered the miles. Beside her, Pokle was pale and tense; she couldn't tell if he was actually listening to her.

"Drones were created by the frostwreths, but that was after so much magic in the world was drained away by the wars. Wreths created humans a long time before that, and so we're better made." She reached over to pinch his freckled cheek, startling him. "The drones are just a pale shadow. But King Kollanan said they were our allies. Oh, they must have stories to tell!"

"I can build campfires," he said, as if it were part of the subject at hand, "but I don't know how to talk to the drones."

"Leave that to me," Shadri said. "First we have to find them."

They camped at night in a small clearing well away from the road. Pokle flinched at every crackle in the fire or rustle in the forest. Shadri told him stories, lectured about human anatomy and the mathematics of music and the history of the kings of Osterra. She talked until he dozed, and made a mental note to continue the story the following night.

On the third day of travel they reached Lake Bakal. The skies were gray and cloudy, and a dampness in the air intensified the cold, but it was not an unnatural freeze. When Thon had brought down the frostwreth fortress, maybe the arctic wave had been broken and the weather would return to normal. Shadri made a note in her journal. "I think the lake might even melt one of these days."

"Winter isn't here yet," Pokle replied. "It'll get much colder before spring." He sniffed, lost in his own memories. "My hunting shack was out here, and my family lived over there." He gestured toward the chaotic rubble where the fortress had overwhelmed what had once been a peaceful town. He shuddered.

"It'll be all right." She reached out to hold his arm reassuringly.

Blushing, he nodded. "I didn't want to come here, but I'm glad to be with you."

Shadri saw flitting shadows among the silver pines, small figures that darted between the trunks. She grinned. "There they are. Drones! Hello, drones. We're friends. We want to talk with you."

Pokle looked where she indicated, but the small figures disappeared, shadows in the forest. Shadri let out a disappointed sigh. "Well, I expected them to be shy. Let's go to the shore and have something to eat. Maybe they'll join us."

"How long do you plan to stay here?" he asked.

"As long as we need to."

They tied the horses to trees, set out blankets on the edge of the lake. Shadri wore a woolen sweater and layers of skirts. Pokle had a warm cloak as well as another blanket; he was always cold since the time he had nearly frozen to death. They sat in companionable silence, pulled food from their packs, and ate. Shadri gazed across the frozen lake and asked Pokle to tell her about the village and the people he had known. He was slow to open up, but soon got lost in reminiscing about fishermen and fur traders, woodcutters and seamstresses. A burden seemed to lift from him as he remembered fond times.

As the young man finished telling her about one of the town's netmakers whose knots could never be untied, Shadri spotted a few drones standing nearby, silent among the trees. Pokle's words stuttered to a halt.

Shadri called out in a quiet, reassuring voice, "Hello there. I want to hear your stories, too. We came here so you could tell us about the wreths."

The drones muttered in a strange language, then they began to form a few words. In a flurry of garbled sounds, she heard them say "wreths," "Kollanan," and "king."

"Come closer." Shadri reached into her pack and pulled out some bread. "I have food."

Though he looked nervous, Pokle remained quiet. Their horses snorted, but did not seem intimidated. The drones approached, wide eyed. Shadri said, "I want to know your stories. I want to understand your language. Tell me about the frostwreths."

The creatures shifted, deeply uneasy. "We're not friends with the frost-wreths," Pokle said, trying to convince the drones. "We hate them."

Understanding him, the drones came even closer.

Shadri began to talk, hoping that the hum of her words was soothing to them, in much the same way as her stories put Pokle to sleep at the campfire. She talked about the ancient ruins she had explored. She talked about Thon and the wreth historical documents she was trying to translate. "I can tell you what I know about the wreths, but there are so many questions. You actually lived among them, so maybe you can help."

She tried to coax out more information, surprised that the creatures knew a fair number of human words, though much of their speech was incomprehensible. Shadri was patient, and they clustered around her. She pulled out her journal. "I need to write all this down."

"We're spies," Pokle said. "This is vital, wartime intelligence."

Shadri kept asking for details. She was persistent and used to people looking at her with blank expressions when she peppered them with questions. She and Pokle sat together listening throughout the afternoon, and in their scattered fashion, the drones told their tales.

29

❦

In the bright heat, Queen Voo pondered her arid domain. The sand and rocks were pure, the sunlight invigorating. Much of the world had been left like this by the ancient wars, with the destructive magic unleashed as armies tore each other apart.

She walked barefoot across the wasteland and saw only raw material. Was this not what the world had been like before Kur made it his flawed paradise? Their god had painted it with the colors and signs of life. She brushed her fingertips along a striated black outcropping. From sand and dust like this, Kur had fashioned the first wreths, had created the beautiful Raan, his true lover, and the treacherous Suth. After he departed, heartbroken by the terrible thing Suth had done to her sister, he had left the wreths to continue his work.

And Voo would do so.

She cupped her hands in the hot sand, letting the grains trickle through her fingers. At some point, her sandwreth ancestors had created the human race, fashioning workers and warriors to serve them. Humans were not as perfect as the god-created wreths, but the land's intrinsic magic had been sufficient to make them acceptable facsimiles. She stared up at the sun, not blinking as the intense light burned into her eyes.

Now, even though the world's magic was weak, her hated rival Onn had made drones as another race of helpers. If the frostwreth queen could do it, then Voo could accomplish the same thing. She wished she had a specimen to study, however. Quo had been instructed to bring one back after his mission to the north . . . if he ever returned.

Pondering her imminent war against the frostwreths, Queen Voo knew King Adan's soldiers were arming themselves to march in front of her army. Mage Ivun's captive workers produced weapons and armor to make the sandwreths even stronger, and they excavated shadowglass for her human allies.

Still, Voo considered the advantage of creating her own drones, countless more expendable fighters for the battlefield. She sniffed the hot air around her. If Onn found enough magic in the ice and snow, then surely the desert could provide as much. Voo and her mages could fashion a swarm of drones to throw against the enemy ahead of the dispensable human fighters with their shadowglass weapons.

Dabbling now, Voo envisioned a proper human form and used her magic to gather pebbles, sand, dirt. She scooped up more material as she sculpted the figure of a muscular fighter. She built the torso out of dust and stone, then fashioned arms, fusing the dry material together. She added muscles, bulking up the figure, although its strength would be intrinsic. She made a head, just a featureless ball, then dabbed her thumbs into it to make eye indentations. Crude, but the basic shape was correct.

Nearby, her auga pawed among the rocks and darted forward to snatch a lizard sunning itself on a rock. The mount gobbled it up, then raised its scaly head, blinking golden eyes at Voo. With a snort, the creature turned, and Voo realized that someone was coming across the desert.

A mounted man came through the heat shimmer, Mage Axus on his own auga. As she waited for him, Voo continued making her drone. The stone-and-dust figure was lumpy but imposing. She imagined a thundering army of such drones following her every instruction. Making such a figure required one type of magic, but bringing it to life required something else entirely. She did not understand how to impart a living spark to the thing.

Voo frowned. The frostwreth queen had discovered how to do it, and the ancient wreths had known how. Unfortunately, the mysterious Thon had taken away all of their crystalline historical records. Though she had not looked at those dusty archives in ages, Voo now regretted surrendering them so easily. Maybe she would go to Bannriya and command Adan to get them back for her. . . .

She made a few adjustments to the sand sculpture so that it was functional if not beautiful. She didn't care about the drone's appearance, so long as it served its purpose. These would be fighters, maybe workers or servants, nothing more—provided Voo could make them live.

The crunching footfalls of the bald mage's auga came closer, and her own mount sniffed the other reptile. They playfully butted heads as Axus dismounted with his report. "I delivered the shadowglass to King Adan, as you requested." He looked at her sand creation, puzzled. "Have you been making large game pieces?"

"For a much larger game," Voo said. "If Onn fashioned her own inferior drones, why can I not make my own here?"

Axus regarded the rough figure. "How will you give it the spark?"

"You will show me how," Voo said. "You are my mage."

He gave her a mild look. "I can tell you that humans already exist, and that humans are far superior to . . . this."

"Then help me make another one. If we perfect this technique, we can expand our army. Let us see the best we can do."

Without arguing, Axus bent down to scoop up more sand and rocks. Voo helped him sculpt a second warrior figure. Voo regarded the motionless figures. Both looked imposing. "And now what do we do?"

"Life does not come from nothingness," Axus explained. "Only Kur can do that. We need blood to animate them, a life force that is tied to the magic in the world." He mage shrugged. "Any life will do." He glanced at the augas.

Voo drew her polished bone knife and slashed the throat of the mage's reptile mount. It grunted and collapsed, dark blood gushing out onto the sand. Voo's own auga took two steps away and looked stupidly at its dying companion.

After dipping her hands into the blood that welled from its scaly throat, Voo went to her sandstone figure. She smeared the red liquid like paint across the statue face, drew another smear down its chest. Axus did the same, marking his figure with bright red.

"And now?" Voo asked.

The mage looked at the two crimson-daubed figures. "Like this." He worked his magic, explaining the technique, and the two rough figures shuddered and began to move. They lurched forward, bent their thick arms, swiveled their crudely formed heads.

Voo grinned. "We can make a huge drone army and turn them loose against the north. We will exterminate the frostwreths one by one until they are all gone!"

The two drone figures staggered a few more steps. They were frightening in a way, but by no means were they nimble fighters. She pursed her lips. "We will have to train them, though."

Then the two figures broke apart. The auga's blood dried in the sun, and sandstone flaked from their molded thighs. One arm shattered and fell off, crumbling into dust. The second drone lurched forward and collapsed into a human-shaped mound of pebbles and crumbs. The drones made no sound as they died, because Voo had not bothered to fashion mouths for them.

Axus watched the disaster with a deep frown, but he didn't look surprised. "You already have your human army. I have told you again and again that they are a worthy resource. You do not need drones, so long as you do not waste the humans."

"We are wreths!" Voo snapped. "I do not *need* the humans either. They are merely a convenience." She scowled at the dead auga and the remnants of her ill-conceived drones. "I do not need to imitate Kur. I have fighters enough." She gazed across the desert, disturbed. "When my brother returns, our army must be ready to march. We can destroy Onn and the frostwreths, and I will have my victory."

Mage Axus nodded. "And then we move on to slay Ossus. Remember our true mission."

Voo seemed distracted. "Of course. We will do that next, and then Kur will return."

She mounted her auga, leaving Axus to stand by his slain reptilian beast. She raised an eyebrow. "If you do not wish to walk, you can try to bring it to life. You might need the practice."

Her auga loped off into the bright sunlight toward her palace.

30

T HE blue ska feather was Glik's prized possession, and she held it like
a talisman. Sitting in the rock shadows at her rickety worktable, she
glanced around to make sure no one was watching. Furtively, she withdrew
the narrow piece of shadowglass she had stolen, a narrow and perfect shard
long enough to plunge through a sandwreth's black heart. But the black glass
was razor sharp, and Glik needed a way to hold it as a knife.

In her camp labors, she used scraps of leather, sewing thick breastplates
to equip an army. Now, she used her sore fingers to cut a length of leather
into a thin strip that she could wrap around the end to cover the sharp edges,
fashioning a crude hilt.

A wreth guard stalked past, but his gaze danced across the camp. The prisoners muttered, bowed their heads, and busied themselves. Before the guard
could see what she was doing, Glik threw a half-finished breastplate on top of
her secret dagger. The guard moved along, aloof in his gleaming body armor,
heading to where a group of other prisoners had been forced to gather.

In the open dirt area at the canyon's wide mouth, a dusty female mage
named Horava climbed into the saddle of an auga. Her rust-red leather robes
wrinkled as she adjusted her position. Three wreth guards mounted up beside her, while a despondent group of twelve ragged humans prepared carts
and harnesses. They carried packs, ready for the long walk to the Plain of
Black Glass. Glick felt sickened, knowing where they were being sent.

Horava was short and thin, apparently a junior mage, and her face held all the
beauty of a broken boulder. Mage Ivun stepped up to her reptile mount, pulling
his withered arm against his chest. "Queen Voo insists that we must not work
the slaves to death." His tone still showed disapproval for the order to withdraw
his workers from the shadowglass fields. "Feed them, do not break them."

"I will find a balance," Horava said. "And I will send back a shipment of
shadowglass in a week or two."

Ivun looked toward his stone-walled dwelling built under a canyon overhang, where he kept the stolen Brava ramers. The dwelling was a luxury he
allowed himself at the camp. "I have my own balance here."

The replacement work crew marched off and disappeared around a curve
in the canyon. Glik knew the difficult conditions the captives would face on
the obsidian plain, but her situation here in the canyon encampment was

no better. "*Cra . . .*" she muttered under her breath, and kept working on her knife.

In an open area nearby, Cheth and the Brava prisoners engaged in combat practice, battling each other with wooden staffs. Ever since some of them had tried to escape out at the shadowglass excavations, Ivun had refused to grant the captive Bravas real weapons, although their weaker human training partners used actual swords. Apparently, the wreths didn't believe they had anything to fear from mere humans.

On the training field, Cheth threw herself against a burly opponent who had no interest in fighting her. Their weapons clattered together, and she drove him back, then eased up and let him press her. Cheth critiqued his defenses. He swung his dulled sword against her, improving with every stroke.

Watching the combat practice, the wreth guard nodded, satisfied, and moved on. Glik felt a measure of satisfaction, knowing that Cheth and the Bravas were showing the humans how to fight against their captors when it was time.

Undisturbed again, Glik slid the leather armor aside so she could finish making her obsidian knife. She laid Ari's blue feather on the blunt end of the shadowglass, then wrapped the long leather thong around and around it, binding it into a serviceable hilt, circle after circle after circle, until the feather was mostly covered. But she knew it was there, like a talisman.

As she worked, Glik hummed her mantra, "The beginning is the end is the beginning." When she was done, she tied off the end, then curled her fingers around her new dagger. The feather and the leather bindings let her grasp it hard in the palm of her hand. She imagined how it would feel to thrust that black point between Ivun's ribs.

Not long ago, the mage had slashed her hand and spilled her blood into a shadowglass bowl so he could share the visions that she'd seen . . . not just the eye of the evil dragon, but that other distant and powerful force. Growing dizzy, the orphan girl began to sink into her memories again. Her vision fuzzed around the edges, and Glik fell wavering into the dream.

Movement nearby startled her out of her reverie, and she saw someone approaching. Instinctively, she hid her secret dagger, but it was only Cheth, sweaty from training and carrying a load of leather scraps for her. Glik couldn't tell how much time had passed.

"Hours of training." Cheth dropped the leather on the girl's table. "Now they want me to work, too."

Glik slid out her dagger to show her friend. Ari's feather poked out from the leather windings, a flash of sapphire blue that seemed to add even more magic to the shadowglass blade.

Cheth approved. "You can kill several of them with that."

"*Cra,* I'll kill as many as I need to."

"They all need killing." The Brava's expression was grim. "I talked with other prisoners, some of the ones I've trained. More of them are ready to fight than we expected. They've been here long enough to know that the sand-wreths will kill them, either by working them to death or tossing them onto a battlefield." Her expression cracked with a hard smile. "I made a convincing argument that it is better to die with the hope of escape."

"Better to *actually* escape," Glik muttered.

"Yes, that would be preferable."

The orphan girl was eager to use her knife, but she was also cautious. "We have to wait for the right opportunity."

Glik felt an unexpected tug in her heart and sensed something nearby, a part of her, yet separate. She sucked in a quick, dry breath, recognizing the heart link! Raising her eyes, she saw a small dark shape wheeling high over-head. She often noticed wild skas, but this one had a close connection. This one was *hers.* "Ari!" she whispered.

The blue ska swirled as if in response to her reaction, but she remained far out of range of wreth arrows.

The ska circled closer and landed in a cleft in the tall cliffs, high above them. Through her heart link, the girl sent out longing emotions, urging her companion to hide before the wreths spotted her. She touched the soft blue tip of Ari's feather on the hilt of the dagger, and their link grew stronger.

Cheth also glanced up, then looked around at other prisoners who were working on their weapons and armor. The guards continued their patrols, and did not bother to look up into the sky.

"Stay there," Glik breathed to Ari. "Wait until dark."

For the rest of the day, she could sense Ari there, waiting. Cheth went about her duties so as not to draw any attention, and Glik worked even harder, even though her thoughts were on her heart link. Her callused fingers were bloody as she sewed more breastplates, but she felt happy to know that her ska was nearby. Those were the longest hours Glik could remember. But at least she had hope.

Finally, after the prisoners had eaten a tasteless evening meal and the camp-fires of scrap twigs and dried auga dung had burned low, Cheth and Glik bed-ded down against the rock wall, extinguished their own fire, and huddled in the shadows. Seeing no guards, hearing only a distant stirring of other prison-ers, Glik opened up her heart link and welcomed Ari, calling the reptile bird down.

With a soft flutter of wings, the ska left her hiding place above and dropped down to land on Glik's shoulder. The reptile bird warbled softly, and the girl stroked her head, preened the sapphire blue scales. "Ari, I missed you so much!" Then she focused on the mothertear diamond on the ska's collar. "Did you fly here by yourself? What happened to my sister Penda?"

Cheth kept watch and nodded when she was sure that they were clear and unobserved. Glik touched the gem, causing a faint shimmering image to spill out: Queen Penda speaking to her.

"We are coming, Glik. We know where you are. Adan Starfall has gathered a fighting force with King Kollanan from Norterra. Your ska will provide the surveillance we need to guide us to your camp. We'll come for you soon, my sister. Be ready for us."

Glik's body filled with a surge of energy, as if lightning crackled through her veins. "It's going to happen! *Cra*, they'll be here to rescue us."

"And we'll help rescue ourselves," Cheth vowed. "We must be prepared. All of us."

Touching the mothertear, Glik played the message again. It was one of the most beautiful things she had ever heard. "I knew Penda wouldn't abandon us." She ran her fingertip along the smooth facets, shifting the magic so that the diamond would record what she said now, telling her sister that she and the prisoners would watch for them and keep their hope alive.

Ari stayed with them for an hour, but Glik feared discovery at any moment. She didn't want to let her companion go, but the wreths would kill any ska on sight. "You have to go. Fly safe and return to Bannriya. Give them what they need."

Ari flashed up into the midnight sky above the canyons. The heart link felt stronger than ever, and a part of Glik went with her—a free part.

Content for the first time in weeks, the orphan girl rested her head against a rock. The sense of joy made her restless at first, but she plunged into a deep sleep . . . a deep dream, a nightmare vision of a battlefield filled with countless screaming warriors, bloodshed and death, bodies hacked unrecognizable. She could not tell if they were humans or wreths. The dream vison became blurry, but she heard myriad voices shouting in triumph.

She woke to the first light of dawn, sweating and disoriented. She traced a circle around her heart, wondering if her vision had been of the past or of the future.

31

⁓

Moving carefully through the near-empty palace in the dead of night, Analera slipped into the empra's quarters and broke open storage wardrobes to gather precious items. Then the old servant hurried down into the dim closeness of the underground, sweaty and frightened, but quite pleased.

She entered the hidden chamber carrying an overstuffed sack. "I brought you something important, Excellency."

Cemi went to see what the servant had brought.

Iluris responded with confusion and uncertainty. "What do I need? Do I not have everything here?" The empra glanced at Captani Vos, who frowned at the distant look on her face.

"See here." Analera opened the sack and pulled out rags and articles of old laundry. She tossed them aside and brought out what was hidden in the sack. With pride, the servant displayed a green ceremonial gown embellished with veils and opalescent cabochon gems bonded to the fabric. "I think this was made for a summer festival. It was locked away, and no one noticed when I took it."

Cemi felt a rush of hope. "Yes, that's perfect!"

Iluris looked at the dress, touched the fabric. "Summer? Of course I remember." Her tone said otherwise, though.

Concerned by the empra's behavior, Cemi stepped forward to take the regal gown and smooth out the wrinkles. "You have to wear it, Iluris. The Hethrren are gone now, and it's time for you to return to the people." She pressed it against the older woman's shoulders.

Iluris reached up to hold the fabric against her. "Yes, summer . . ." she said, her voice distant. "When will it be summer?"

"Not for summer, Mother." Captani Vos came closer, concerned. "You'll wear it when you take back your throne. You have to look like a proper empra. The people are waiting. Are you ready?"

Iluris released her shaking hands, and Cemi caught the gown as it dropped. The empra touched her temples and squeezed her eyes shut. "I . . . can't. My head . . ." Her skin turned pale and gray, and her expression fell slack.

The empra collapsed, crumpling like a discarded garment.

In an eyeblink, Vos got his arms around the empra before she could hit her head again. As if she weighed nothing, he lifted her and gingerly carried her to her old pallet and covered her with a blanket. "You need to rest, Mother. Rest and recover."

He stood, and his face was haunted. Sweat burst out on his forehead. His eyes met Cemi's, and she knew they shared the same thought. Iluris could not battle Key Priestlord Klovus like this.

With the Hethrren gone, the entire city was safer, and the empra's palace was certainly quieter. Klovus was glad for that.

His skin still crawled from the memory of sharing the empra's spacious bed with Magda. He never wanted to enter that room again or glance at the rumpled sheets. He ordered the soiled, contaminated bedding removed and burned. The pillaged throne room bore signs of rough use where the barbarians had pried away gems and gold, favoring the gaudiest ornamentation rather than the most valuable.

But at last he was rid of the Hethrren, and Iluris could be written off. He felt as if he had come out of a wilderness. After he made his forthcoming announcement and dispensed with any lingering expectation of the empra's return, Ishara would embark on a new future.

He had waited too long to offer answers about Iluris, which had only let rumors and false hopes fester. Gossip and unrealistic belief took the place of truth, and now Klovus needed to establish his own truth. He would show them a corpse, hold a respectful funeral, and that would be the end of all the nonsense whispers.

Today, he would shift the people's praise and faith toward himself and away from the rosy memory of Iluris. Today, he would show the doubters what they needed to see.

He stood inside the empty and echoing entryway of the palace, marveling at the silence, the grandeur. From here, emprirs and empras had guided the land for centuries. The key priestlord had always been a separate role, but Klovus was strong enough to bear that double burden.

It was not his actual goal, however. If he could find a cooperative candidate, he might crown another ruler to serve in his stead. Cemi could have been an appropriate puppet, but she had disappeared along with Iluris. The girl was too unruly and ill-educated anyway, and he did not trust her to be submissive enough. . . .

Ready for the day's grand ceremony, he brushed his soft hands down his blue caftan. After Priestlord Erical's departure with the fleet, two more priestlords had arrived from their districts, joining the three already in Serepol for the consecration. He cast a glance at the newcomers, Neré from Tamburdin District and Dovic from Sistralta.

Dovic was quiet and respectful. "I'm here to serve, Key Priestlord. The journey was hard, and the roads were bad, but I am grateful to be in Serepol for the empra's funeral ceremony in addition to celebrating the Magnifica."

Klovus let out a petulant sigh. "Empra Iluris seized so much construction material and so many workers from the Magnifica temple, she could have fixed some of those roads."

Neré was a thin, hard woman who served in the wildest and most remote district of Ishara. Her long brown hair was bound in a pair of tight braids, like halter ropes on each side of her head. When her lands were harassed by the Hethrren, Neré had disappointed him, incapable of using her own godling to stop the threat. She was weak, fearing that the entity might rampage out of control. Of course, Klovus himself had unleashed the Serepol godling, which had led to disastrous results. . . .

Klovus was not willing to admit his own failings, though. "Both of you, come with me. The people have already gathered to bid farewell to their dear, lost Iluris. The other priestlords are at the Magnifica steps."

He stepped out from under the arched entrance, letting the sunlight bathe him like applause. Ten uniformed city guards fell into place while Priestlords Neré and Dovic remained a step behind him. He set off at a brisk pace down the wide boulevard toward the nearly finished Magnifica pyramid. He felt strengthened to see the huge, somber crowd, to hear their loud voices as he marched past.

"Hear us, save us," the people chanted.

"Hear us, save us," he responded, his words echoed by the priestlords behind him. There would be no more prayers to Iluris, not after today.

The enthusiasm sounded weaker than he hoped, though. Despite his best efforts, the key priestlord knew the people did not love him as they had loved Iluris, but that would change. After the godling debacle, at least they feared him. He strutted along, taking note of the flowers growing on street corners, the ornamental trees, the swept flagstones of the wide promenade. He rarely bothered to notice details of the city. Serepol was quite beautiful.

Reaching the temple square, he approached the huge stair-stepped ziggurat. The three other district priestlords stood together on the first platform above the crowd. Numerous ur-priests had taken strategic positions around the square. City guards made a pathway for Klovus at the main steps. He looked up at the imposing stone blocks, and the Magnifica seemed to throb with the power of Serepol's godling—*Ishara's* godling.

Construction scaffolding remained on the upper levels, and Empra Iluris's funeral pyre had been laid out on the uncompleted top platform. Even from here, he could see the body draped in colorful silks, familiar outfits taken from her palace quarters. He climbed the steps and found himself out of breath by the third level.

All five of the district priestlords followed him up the steep stairs, and he worried for a moment that the crowds would flow up as well, eager to weep around the body of their beloved empra. If they came too close, they would see a dead old woman and know it wasn't Iluris. Although the worshippers milled about near the base of the pyramid, they remained cowed, muttering instead of applauding, watching him.

Klovus stopped one level below where the corpse was arranged on the pile of wood. He had to catch his breath, and disguised it as a moment of silent contemplation, then turned to look out at the sea of people. So many subjects . . . so much faith, so much potential. He raised his arms, and the dark caftan made him look like some kind of great bird.

"People of Serepol, people of Ishara!" He touched the presence of the godling that thrummed through the massive temple, and his words were amplified, becoming loud waves that rumbled through the air. "You knew this sad day would come. You have waited and worried and believed, but it was not enough."

"Hear us, save us!" the people moaned in eerie, spontaneous unison.

"On Fulcor Island Empra Iluris was tricked by the godless Konag Conndur, who sent an assassin to kill her!"

The people grumbled, and he twisted their grief, fed their emotions. The godling within the temple also grew stronger. He stifled his smile to put a grave expression on his face. "But our dear empra clung to life as we rushed her home. Our best doctors tended her. We isolated her, hoping that your prayers and her heart would be strong enough." He drew a deep breath and made his somber announcement. "But Iluris finally succumbed to her injuries. Our empra is dead. She is gone."

Moans of dismay rippled through the crowd, even though they all knew why they were here. His voice boomed out, hammering home the point. "Today, we bid farewell to our empra, but we do not forget what the Commonwealth did to her. Even now, our Isharan navy and our Hethrren allies are sailing to wreak our revenge upon the godless old world. Enemy blood will flow, and Iluris will at last receive justice."

The crowd grew more vociferous, and their cheers became a war chant rather than showing awe for the key priestlord's authority. The waves of anguish and despair increased, but the sound buoyed up Klovus.

Leaving the other priestlords on the level below, he climbed the final set of steps to the partially completed apex platform that held the old woman's bier. Klovus stood before the corpse and bowed his head, as if in reverence. The replacement corpse was a suitable match, about the same height and age as Iluris. Her hair had been cut in the style the empra had worn.

He probably did not need to worry. How many of her subjects had actually seen Iluris up close? How many of them remembered precise details? This body would do. The Black Eels had found someone to serve the purpose.

After a suitable time for a silent, sincere prayer, he turned from the pile of dry wood and raised his hands again. "Farewell to our empra."

With his fingers he summoned a little bit of magic to ignite the dry kindling. Flames began to lick the wood in the pile, eating the twigs, building into a respectable blaze. Gray-white smoke curled up. In the plaza below, the people muttered and mourned as if they were a single mind. The fire consumed her colorful garments, blackened and peeled the corpse's flesh.

When he decided he had stayed long enough, and the stench was growing stronger, he descended to the fourth level to join his other priestlords. There, they all looked up to watch the rising blaze.

Klovus called upon the godling to make the event more spectacular. The entity emerged from the core of the temple and swelled up through the heart of the pyramid, manifesting as bright fire. The pyre on the apex platform roared into an inferno, curtains of orange and white so hot that Klovus flinched. The waves of heat rolled out, intense enough for the whole crowd to feel.

Within seconds, the funeral pyre consumed the false Iluris, turning her and all the wood to white ash. Just as quickly, the godling withdrew and pulled the fire back with it, leaving only a steaming mound of powder.

The crowd was swept into silence by their astonishment. Klovus seized the moment, and his voice boomed out again. "I am your key priestlord. I lead your thoughts and prayers, and I will guide Ishara until such time as we find a new emprir or empra for our land. The godling holds you in its protective embrace. Continue to feed it with your prayers and sacrifices, and I will lead you to victory. The old world will fall, and Ishara will be stronger than ever."

His priestlords cheered. Around the plaza, his city guards cheered. And the people also began to cheer.

Klovus felt magnanimous and satisfied. They were in his hands now.

32

❧

BIRCH and his quiet drones had ended the frostwreth conspiracy, but Queen Koru rooted out several more traitors who muttered defiance of her plans to unite the wreths. She executed the others herself, freezing their bodies into blocks of ice while using spellsleep magic to maintain their heartbeats. Thus, she kept them alive to endure a slow suffocation, adding to her satisfaction.

The boy stood silent beside her, watching the last few victims die slowly inside their ice. He had thrown in his lot with her. He gathered his courage, knowing this was the right time. "I want something from you, Queen Koru."

Her head snapped back in surprise. "You think you can command me, boy?"

Birch did not let his gaze waver. "I stuck the spear into your mother and put you on the throne. I saved you from Irri and the others who wanted to kill you. I should be able to ask a favor."

Her expression pinched, and her eyebrows drew together. "Continue. What do you want?"

"Queen Onn killed many of the drones just because she was angry. I watched her do it." He shuddered at the memory of Onn's rampage, slashing with her ice blades, hacking apart dozens of drones, leaving the small bodies strewn in blood on the throne room floor. "Please don't kill them anymore, like your mother did."

Koru considered. "The drones were created to serve."

"But they didn't do anything wrong," Birch said. "And she killed so many of them." He swallowed hard. He felt strangely light-headed with the boldness of his request. "I just don't want them hurt like that."

Koru looked at the motionless drones standing behind the boy at the edge of her frozen throne room, their expressions empty. "They work for me," she said. "But, yes, it is foolish to slaughter them on a whim. It is wasteful." She lifted her chin and sniffed. "Very well, I see no reason to harm them, so long as they do not get in the way."

"They won't." Birch looked at all the drones, his friends. They fidgeted, made low sounds of agreement.

"All right, that is enough for now," said the queen. "Go!" The drones scattered, but Koru kept Birch with her. "Not you, boy—join me as I review our troops."

She extended her hand to take Birch's small one. Heading out of the throne room, they strolled past the last few traitors inside their ice blocks. Behind the rippling surface, Birch saw one set of eyes still flickering, still dying. Koru left them all behind.

She explained as they walked along and emerged into the breathtaking cold on the open balcony. "My wreths were led down a road of mindless vengeance for too long. Queen Voo has done the same thing to her sandwreths." She shook her head. "But I recently fought a dragon, and I know how hard our final battle against Ossus will be. I will not fail the destiny of my race because the descendants of Raan and Suth have too much hate to work together. If I can unite our race, we will destroy Ossus." She showed her teeth in the flash of a smile. "First, though, I must cut out the rot in both frostwreths and sandwreths."

From the open speaking balcony, they watched milling warriors across the frozen wasteland. Hundreds of wolf-steeds wore collars and saddles augmented with spikes. The bright reflections on polished crystal and metal armor made Birch dizzy. The din of the army was thunderous as the wreths prepared for the expedition south.

He pulled his blanket around his shoulders, imagining it as a cape, and he stood at the queen's side, so everyone could see that this was where he belonged. The wreths knew that if anyone harmed Birch, they would face Koru's wrath.

The queen drew in a deep breath, and her voice rippled out like a cold wind from the speaking balcony. "We waited thousands of years for this. Now it is time."

The frostwreths pounded weapons against shields and let out bellowing war cries. The ice trembled as if about to crack.

"We will conquer the sandwreths and make them a part of our army." The roars and excitement diminished with this pronouncement, but Koru shouted even louder. "All wreths were created by Kur! *All* wreths were given the same mission. My mother deluded some of our own people and they forgot themselves. Now those traitors have been dealt with. The sandwreth queen has also deluded her people—and I intend to kill her as well." She raised the spear of Dar. "Today we march. We will retake this world that was made for us."

The army rumbled out a roar of approval, but Birch made no sound. He wrapped his hand around the wooden pig in his pocket, his hand hidden by the blanket. He wanted to ask Koru what would happen to all the human settlements that the army would encounter. Queen Koru did not seem to have considered that.

❧

As the army rumbled across the north, Queen Koru rode in a sturdy, imposing sleigh adorned with hooks and spikes. Birch sat in the front seat, swathed in oonuk furs as well as his own blanket. As the sleigh swept onward, she didn't seem to notice him next to her, but he noticed everything around him.

Elon, a hard mage wrapped in blue leather robes, sat on the other side of him. The man's skin was pale, and his bald head sported the prominent burn scar. Now he spoke in a gruff voice. "In the time that our journey takes, my queen, will the sandwreths be able to build defenses against us?"

"I cannot guess what Queen Voo will do. She has been a fool in many ways. Maybe we will take her by surprise."

The oonuks strained against their harnesses, pulling the queen's sleigh along with a whisper and scrape. Twenty armored sleighs glided over the frozen ground, while warriors rode wolf-steeds in the second wave behind them. Sleek foot soldiers sprinted along, covering miles without resting.

Pack sleds carried the supplies, and several hundred drones also scurried along for support to perform menial labor when setting up camp. Birch had convinced Koru to leave most of the drones behind, pointing out that they would just get in the way on a battlefield, and that she would need to feed them on the journey.

She had looked at him curiously. "I had not considered that. Very well, we will take only the ones we need for basic work. I promised not to harm them." Birch knew the drones could keep up and would forage along the way.

He watched the landscape rush by and knew they were riding down toward Norterra. He might even see Lake Bakal again, and the prospect dredged up uncomfortable thoughts. He finally asked, "What will you do with me? Will you ever let me go?"

Koru looked at him with pearlescent frozen eyes. "You are full of surprises, boy. Maybe you can surprise me some more."

Since she hadn't answered his question, he persisted. "Will I . . . will I ever go home? Back to my own people?"

She frowned. "Why would you want that?"

"Because . . . my friends, my family."

Koru laughed. "I know altogether too much about family. Be thankful your mother was not like mine!"

"My mother is dead," Birch said in a sharper tone than he had ever used with her. "Just like yours is."

Pretending not to hear, or just ignoring the comment, Koru turned away from him and looked at the landscape.

Before long, the ice and snow gave way to tundra dotted with stunted trees, which eventually became thicker and darker stands of silver pines.

Seeing the forest made Birch long for his family's home in Lake Bakal, a large house with a steeply sloped roof so that snow would slide off. A fireplace in every room and a warm oven where his mother would bake bread and tarts.

He thought of Tomko and his friends, his grandmother Tafira ... and King Kollanan. Of all those people, only he and Kollanan were still alive.

The frostwreths had let him be among them, but they paid little attention to him, preoccupied with their own concerns. Even Koru. With the group of drones accompanying the wreth army, Birch thought he might have a chance to steal away. What if he just ran into the forest when they stopped to camp one night? Should he try to escape? The queen had not said she would ever let him go.

Or would he do better staying with Koru? He was safe enough with her, now, and she even listened to him sometimes. As the great army marched through Norterra, he thought that maybe he could keep her from hurting other people, just as she had grudgingly agreed to leave the drones alone.

Wouldn't that be the better decision, for him to stay here?

Or should he just run?

Riding in the sleigh, he felt cold like the patches of snow around him.

33

⁐

"I AM already sick of war." Lord Ogno let out a snort as he looked at the Brava riding beside him. "But, I'm good at it, and if Kollanan the Hammer needs me, then I know what I have to do."

"We all know what we have to do," Lasis said in a solemn voice. He raised his head, listening to the large Norterran army behind them as they traversed the long road heading toward the mountains.

Ogno swatted at a fly buzzing around his head. "Each time I come home from a battle, my wife is enthusiastic to see me, and that makes up for all the inconvenience."

Once dispatched from Fellstaff Castle, the main army traveled eastward at a steady march. The numbers in their ranks grew as they passed through the adjacent counties, like a snowball growing larger as it rolled down a winter hill. After they passed the town of Yanton and its adjacent wreth ruins, Lord Bahlen joined them with fifty handpicked soldiers. Though he was uneasy to leave his bruised people, vengeful anger forced them to ride with the Norterran army.

When Bahlen joined Ogno and the king's Brava, he said, "Any of our towns could have been the target. This time it was Yanton, next time it could be somewhere in Lord Teo's holdings or Vitor's, or any other. But if we win this fight now, then we will never have to fear another bloody betrayal like Konag Mandan's." He sounded resigned, but resolute. "And once the bad konag is replaced, all three kingdoms will stand against the true enemy."

Lasis was quiet as they traveled through the burned-out remains of Yanton. He saw the smashed windows, the blackened roofs. Some buildings were nothing more than stone chimneys and charred beams. Lasis worried about the security of Fellstaff, and not just from a frostwreth attack. What if Mandan sent some other rogue force to burn the outlying farmlands or lay siege to the capital city? He told himself that Gant would keep the people safe.

Although Lord Cade had led the marauding army into Yanton, Lasis laid the blame squarely on Utho. Elliel had the most personal reason to hate Utho and would join the Norterran army as soon as she finished her mission with Adan and Kollanan. But any truth-loving Brava would make every effort to destroy the man who had so violated their principles. Including Lasis, if the opportunity presented itself.

He nudged his horse to pick up the pace, and the army traveled onward. He wanted to waste no time, even though it would be weeks before Kollanan and Adan could join them with the additional armies.

During the day's travel, a contrite-looking Onder worked his way through the ranks and guided his horse next to Lasis. The former Brava wore a sword at his side, a leather breastplate, and a leather-and-steel helmet, traditional armor and equipment issued by the Fellstaff quartermaster. Though his eyes and features marked him as a half-breed, the young man dressed like a cavalry soldier of modest means.

Lasis acknowledged him, but remained preoccupied with opponents and threats.

Onder's pale expression accentuated the stark tattoo. "I wish I could have fought for Yanton. I would have driven the enemy back, maybe saved a lot of townspeople." He looked down, frowning. "I saw all the new graves when we rode through."

"There will be many more graves before this is all done," Lasis answered. His hand unconsciously went to the new ramer at his side. Onder did not have one and could not use the Brava weapon, despite his bloodline.

"I . . . I wouldn't run," Onder said. "You know that."

"I don't know, but I can hope. Determination isn't proof."

Onder said in a small voice, "Let me earn the right to be a Brava again. Elliel broke her rune of forgetting, and you respect her." He lifted his chin. "I want to earn your respect, too."

When Lasis responded, his voice carried a tone of rebuke. "Elliel was betrayed, and the rune of forgetting she suffered was unjust. She never actually shirked her honor, despite the false accusations made against her. When her memories returned, she was vindicated. For you, it is different. Without doubt, you did commit an act of cowardice, whether or not you remember doing so."

Onder bowed his head. "I cannot deny it, though it breaks my heart. Wiping my memories does not change my nature. I asked Master Onzu, my . . ." He paused, as if still processing the information. ". . . my father not to judge me by the single worst moment of my life. I want to show that I am better than that. If Elliel received justice, what I seek is redemption. Isn't that a worthy goal?"

Lasis faced forward and rode on. "We shall see."

On a weed-overgrown spur of the road, the army came upon a cluster of ancient wreth ruins, where local farmers and villagers had scavenged the perfectly cut stone blocks from the walls to use for their fencelines and dwellings. Lasis directed the troops to spread out and make camp among the abandoned buildings.

The place seemed haunted with history and dark memories, but the broken structures provided adequate shelter. Lasis was content to spread his blanket in the grass of an overgrown courtyard with buckled flagstones and collapsed pillars.

Outriding hunters had brought in two stags and four wild turkeys, which roasted over fires to supplement the rations in the supply wagons. Lasis let other soldiers eat the fresh meat, since he didn't mind chewing on pack bread and nuts. Water from the nearby creek was cold and refreshing.

The Brava sat alone surrounded by hundreds of Norterran warriors and their mounts. Their voices filled the air with boisterous games of chance; some sang bawdy folk songs while others joined in on the refrain.

Lasis drew into himself, as a Brava could. He recalled the days when he had been a paladin in Norterra, riding from village to village, helping whoever needed his assistance. He represented the justice of King Kollanan, tracking down bandits, rescuing lost children. Once, he caught a young arsonist who liked to start forest fires in the dry season, one of which had burned a mother and three small children in a forest hut. Lasis identified the man by the fascination in his eyes as he stared at dancing flames and flaunted the scalded red marks on his cheeks and hands; Lasis had not been at all reticent to strike the killer down with the purifying flame of his ramer.

His heart ached at the loss of Queen Tafira, and Lasis considered it a failing on his own part, even though at the time he had been protecting Yanton against Lord Cade's marauders. It was not a mistake he had made, nothing he could have predicted, yet still Tafira was dead. This army would soon be joined by Suderran soldiers, and they would face even more harm and bloodshed in Convera. It all weighed heavily on him.

Carrying a bowl of beans topped with a lump of camp bread, Onder sat next to him. Lasis did not express any welcome for the disgraced Brava, nor did he chase him away. Onder seemed contrite and persistent. "I could go sit with the others, but you're the only Brava here. Can you tell me some stories? Were you a brave paladin?"

"I am a Brava, not a storyteller."

Seeing the young man's obvious disappointment, Lasis sighed. "Yes, I was a paladin for years before I made a formal bond with King Kollanan."

"You must have won many victories in the king's name." Onder chewed a mouthful of beans, then dabbed at his mouth with the hard bread. "How did you get that scar on your throat?"

Lasis lifted his chin and rubbed his fingers on the long lumpy line. "I don't think about it much." He closed his eyes. "The frostwreth queen did this to me. When I scouted Lake Bakal, wreth warriors and mages overwhelmed me, took me to their frozen palace where Queen Onn tortured me. When she grew bored, she slashed my throat and left me to bleed on her bed. She dumped my body outside in the snow and cold."

His breathing accelerated as the memories grew more vivid. "But Bravas are not weak. The shock sent me into a sort of spellsleep, kept me just barely alive. Drones found me, helped me, healed me, and I made my way to Fellstaff."

Onder's eyes were wide and bright. "You were brave."

"I had to be. I'd learned that the king's grandson was still alive and held among the frostwreths, so I had to make it home to tell him." The young man was enthralled, but Lasis looked aside. He spoke to Onder in a grave tone. "Understand what we are up against. The godling you faced in Mirrabay was there because of the old enmity with Ishara. Now, I'm leading our army over the mountains because Konag Mandan has a grudge against us. Those wars are unwise at the moment, but we must win them. But the only way to ensure that humanity truly survives is to defeat the wreths."

Onder gave a quick nod. "I'll do that, too. I'll fight whatever I have to."

With an explosive laugh, Ogno strode through the wreth ruins, drawing attention. He had found a garden with weathered statues of wreths rendered mostly featureless by time. "If these are the only wreths we can find," he bellowed, "then damn it all, I will defeat the wreths!"

He shoved one of the statues, toppling it into a fallen stone pillar. The figure's head shattered off, leaving a broken neck stump. He roared out with laughter and heaved another statue. "We will crush all of you and grind you into stone dust."

Another toppled statue cracked in several places. Jumping onto the stone body, he stomped on a carved arm and broke it off. "And I'll keep doing it until I find one of you that bleeds."

By the time he turned to the next statue, other soldiers had gotten into the spirit. They all joined in, finding more wreth relics they could smash. Before long, the ancient city was nothing more than wreckage.

The following dawn the Norterran army moved out again.

34

〜

As the world teetered on the edge of disaster, King Adan wondered how long this quiet moment with his wife and baby daughter would last . . . but no one knew how long anything would last. He cherished each second he spent with his family.

He and Penda had retired to their quarters, where she nestled Oak in the crib. On his crossbar near the open window, Xar hissed at the squire Hom, taunting the boy as he brought the king and queen their dinner. The green ska flapped his wings and nearly made Hom spill the plates.

Penda scolded her pet. "Leave him alone, Xar. We know you are fierce and intimidating, but you'll wake the baby." She stroked wisps of hair from Oak's smooth forehead. The infant scrunched her face, but remained asleep.

"S-sorry for the disturbance, my queen," Hom stuttered. "H-he doesn't scare me."

Xar hissed again, and the squire flinched.

Adan sat back in his chair. "I am surrounded by battles, large and small."

The ska grew even more agitated, ruffling his feathers. On his perch, Xar craned his neck toward the open window and turned his faceted eyes to stare deep into the cool, dry night.

Penda suddenly touched her chest. "Oh . . . I can feel—"

A flutter of blue wings appeared outside the window. Hom set down the tray of food and scuttled off.

Penda hurried to the window just as another ska landed on the stone sill. "Ari's back!" She leaned close to the blue reptile bird. She whispered, "Did you find Glik? Did you scout the camp?"

The ska made a warbling sound, partly a purr and partly distress. Penda scratched the soft sapphire scales on Ari's throat, touched the mothertear collar to activate the diamond. The first set of images spilled out, showing Glik's gaunt face and hollow cheeks, though her dark eyes were suddenly bright. The orphan girl's words were hushed, yet excited after hearing Penda's message. She promised she and the other prisoners would be ready, whenever rescue came.

Penda let out a long breath. "*Cra,* we are really doing this, my Starfall. We can save them."

Adan smiled at the blue ska. "You are a very brave spy, Ari." Xar gave an indignant trill because he hadn't received a separate compliment. "If her sur-veillance shows the camp layout and the number of wreth guards, we'll know exactly what to expect. Our strike force has everything we need."

Penda felt hard determination. "What *I* needed was to know that Glik is still alive."

∾

In Adan's council room the ominous tooth and dark triangular scale were on display as grim reminders of Queen Voo's capricious dragon hunt in the desert. King Kollanan and several vassal lords joined the meeting to discuss final plans for the assault. Excitement was palpable in the air.

The handpicked fighters, both Norterran and Suderran, had armed them-selves with shadowglass-enhanced weapons, checked their armor, and now waited for the time to move out.

On their stand, the blue ska preened her blue feathers, while Xar perched next to her. Adan picked up the dragon scale and rested it on its hard edge. It was the size of a dinner plate, a mere token from the dissolving reptilian corpse slain by the sandwreths.

Sitting beside Adan, Penda projected Ari's misty images, which Koll and the battle commanders scrutinized. The route for the army's approach was plain as the ska flew over the tangled canyons, arrowing toward the hidden slave camp. Sunshine lit the red rocks and cast shadows in the deep clefts. Adan felt as if he were flying, swooping down for a closer view, rising up on unexpected thermals.

"It is a maze," grumbled Fen Halc, a vassal lord who had served in the Commonwealth army before retiring to lands in Suderra.

"That means they won't necessarily see us coming," added Glenaro, a pale-skinned lord who flushed readily, showing his emotions.

Kollanan turned to Adan, his expression hard. "Mark down every detail and have your scribes make copies so that our strike force can distribute maps."

Bright-eyed, Thon stared at the terrain flowing in front of them. "I under-stand the cracks and canyons, the secret pathways." He gave Elliel a knowing smile. "I will not let us get lost."

Now, the ska's fresh views showed hundreds of human prisoners, exhausted, dirty. They clustered in squalid hovels, hunched under tattered awnings. They performed tasks for their aloof captors, creating weapons and armor that would likely be given to Adan's own fighters. It seemed that Queen Voo thought noth-ing of it, thought nothing of him or the rest of the human race, except for how she could use them.

It was a blind arrogance he hoped to use to his advantage.

Kollanan leaned into the shimmering view as if he were like Kur looking down on his world. Ari's images centered on a cliff wall as the ska found a hiding place in a rock cleft from which she could watch the groups of laborers.

Cradling baby Oak against her shoulder, Penda sighed at the sight of Glik crouched in her own dirty shelter. "We will come for you soon," the queen whispered.

Elliel stood next to the Norterran king, also assessing. "It's helpful to see the sandwreth guards and defenses, as well as the prisoners—potential fighters—in this labor camp."

"They don't look much like fighters," Glenaro muttered.

"The wreths expect humans to be weak and subservient," Kollanan said.

"But they aren't beaten," Penda said. "Glik isn't beaten, and the Utauks will feel the same way, even though times look dark." She traced a circle around her heart.

Kollanan jabbed his finger into the shifting images. "I see only about fifty wreths to maybe three hundred prisoners. Most wreths are warriors, but there is a mage or two. Those will be harder."

"But not impossible," Thon said. "We fought five mages at Lake Bakal. I know what to do."

"And this time we have shadowglass weapons," Adan pointed out. "They don't know about that advantage."

Elliel flashed a thin grin. "I see Brava captives there. We can count on them."

Koll picked up his war hammer from the table. "This is good news, Adan. That camp is not a fortress, but a sad and dirty prison settlement. Fifty wreth warriors and a mage or two against hundreds of us armed with shadowglass, and all the prisoners fighting for their freedom? Ancestors' blood, we can win this!" His hand rippled through the shimmering images. "We'll ride in, bottle them up, free the prisoners—and kill the wreths. They will never know what happened."

Elliel warned, "We can't let any wreths escape—not a single one—or they will bring word to Queen Voo that humans attacked them."

"We'll have to hide them, too. Just like I hid her brother's body." Adan gave a grim nod. "She can't know that I turned against her. If we eliminate all the witnesses, Voo will surely blame the frostwreths. That would be her automatic assumption."

"*Cra,* she'd never imagine humans could fight back!" Hale Orr leaned back in his chair. At the sound of his loud voice, both skas fluttered their wings.

"We can't let any of them get away," Elliel repeated. "Everyone needs to know this before we ride out. Some wreths did escape when the Lake Bakal fortress fell. Queen Onn learned what had happened, and she . . ."

Kollanan's face turned dark. "And she murdered my Tafira. We won't let that happen again." His face sagged with grief and his eyes welled with tears.

Hale grumbled, "*Cra,* you're damn right it won't happen again."

"The wreths will know sooner or later," Adan said, resigned, "but the longer we keep the secret, the better for all our people."

He knew how important it was to free the human slaves in the images. At the same time, the Utauk messenger was on his way to deliver the decree to dethrone Konag Mandan, which would surely start a civil war. As soon as they freed the slaves, he and part of the Suderran army—which Queen Voo considered *her* army—would ride east toward the mountains to join with the Norterran army to face Mandan.

He felt as if he were playing a complex strategy game while blindfolded. Penda placed her hand on his. The monstrous dragon tooth was sharp and ominous on the table in front of them, reminding him of yet another set of enemies and threats to the world.

"You'll do this thing, my Starfall," Penda said. "It is what must be."

"It is what must be," Adan responded.

Kollanan and everyone around the council table echoed the words with a thunderous shout.

The horses were saddled at sunset and the strike force gathered to head out. They would ride fast and hard toward the desert, crossing the easy terrain by moonlight. Adan expected they could reach the edge of the rugged canyons by dawn, hole up under the light of day, and ride out again in darkness.

As the soldiers prepared to move, Kollanan mounted his warhorse and rested the hammer on his shoulder, as if he might need it at any moment. His face had a forlorn expression. "I'll lead them out, Adan, so you can have a few moments to say goodbye."

His hollow voice reminded them all that he hadn't had a chance to say goodbye to Tafira.

Penda looked regal and beautiful, holding the baby just outside the stable. Adan swallowed a lump in his throat and stepped forward to embrace his wife. She wrapped her arm around his neck and pulled him close for a kiss.

Adan needed no stronger reminder of what he was fighting for, why he was doing this. "Even though you ride at night, Starfall, do not expect to stay hidden. With more than two hundred riders, your group will not be invisible. The sandwreths might see you coming."

He kissed her again, then leaned down and kissed Oak on the forehead. He didn't want to leave them, but he had to. "But we know the sandwreths—will they even bother to be watching?"

35

O N the open sea the Isharan flagship led the fleet toward the old world. The battering-ram fist at the prow thrust forward, ready to fight.

Priestlord Erical inhaled the salty spray that sparkled up from the wake, making brief rainbows in the sun. In Prirari he'd been to lakes and rivers, but this wide, empty ocean was new to him, both frightening and exhilarating.

His godling shimmered around the mainmast, rippled the red-and-white sails, and permeated the hold as her temporary lair. Erical could sense that the entity was uneasy as they sailed farther from the land that was bonded to her by threads of faith.

The old world had no godlings because the land was weak and drained from the ancient wreth wars. How could his godling survive so far away, and how could he survive without the godling? His heart was uncertain.

But as Erical faced the wind, hearing the snap of canvas sails, he also sensed the entity's joy of discovery, the strength and wonder of the ocean that she had never before experienced.

The ship's captain stepped up to him, a humorless man named Gaus with a square-cut beard. "Your godling gives us smooth sailing, Priestlord. We should reach Fulcor Island by this afternoon."

"It will be good to be on land again," Erical said with a sigh.

The captain chuckled. "It has only been two days! And Fulcor is just a stopover."

"Hear us, save us," the priestlord muttered.

Though the sky was clear, the breezes were strong enough to stir the waves. The deck rose over a wave and gently rode it down. The Isharan sailors were unaffected by the swells. They climbed the rigging, strolled barefoot across narrow yardarms, fearless. Erical, though, felt dizzy, as if he'd had too much hard cider after the orchard harvest.

The Hethrren were far worse off. The barbarians were scattered among the ships in the fleet, a few dozen on each. Back in Serepol, they had raced aboard the vessels as if already conquering territory, but now many of them clung to the deck rail or huddled in misery by the supply crates. Magda bent over the side of the ship and retched out a great stream of vomit, as if to prove that she could be more seasick than any of her companions.

Captain Gaus shook his head. "I hope the Hethrren aren't as worthless when we reach the old world. If we were attacked now, the enemy would conquer every Isharan ship."

Magda groaned like a wounded cow and spewed more puke overboard.

A few hours later, a lookout shouted, "Land ahead! Fulcor Island!" The Isharan sailors moved about, preparing for arrival, while the barbarians struggled to recover themselves.

Magda braced herself enough to clap a meaty hand on the priestlord's shoulder. She squinted into the distance. "I am eager to get off this ship and start claiming territory."

"This is only Fulcor Island," Erical said. "Just a rock."

When the island outcropping came into view, he was not impressed with the jagged gray edifice protruding above the waves. He saw no hint of green, only the pale walls of the watch outpost that had stood for centuries, conquered and reconquered many times.

Magda grimaced at what she saw. "Klovus deceived us. I brought my people across this terrible ocean to claim that stump of rock? Who would want it?"

Erical wished he could explain why this island had been fought over so many times, one bloody overthrow after another. It did not seem worth a ship's time even to pause there.

Captain Gaus stepped up. "Fulcor is strategically important, the midway point between the old world and the new, a foothold for our soldiers to stave off an invasion whenever the godless come."

Magda grunted, clearly not convinced. "As long as it feels solid beneath my feet."

Seeing the striped Isharan sails, the soldiers in the Fulcor garrison raised celebratory banners from the watchtowers. Gaus said, "Most of our ships will anchor out beyond the reefs, but we'll take this vessel and two others into the harbor cove and meet with the garrison commander to tell him our plans."

Magda looked impatient. "Does this island have enough fighters to make a difference? Not that we need their assistance. No matter. We will take them."

Captain Gaus stood ramrod straight. "These soldiers were assigned to defend and hold Fulcor. It would not be within my authority to take them away and diminish the strength of our hard-won garrison."

Magda swiped her forearm across her mouth, removing a fleck of vomit. "We are about to invade the old world. Why would you be afraid of them coming to take this rock?" She flashed a smug grin with her sharp teeth. "They will be too busy."

Gaus did not flinch. "You have not yet proved you can conquer an entire continent."

With a guffaw, the Hethrren leader rapped her twisted club on the deck, leaving a divot. "Maybe we should leave your Isharans here on Fulcor Island and do all the conquering by ourselves, just to show you."

Now it was the captain's turn to sneer. "Good luck sailing these ships when you're all puking over the deck rails."

Erical stepped between them. "No need to create another war. I have heard so much about the Fulcor garrison, I'd like to see it with my own eyes." He glanced at the barbarian leader. "And we want to stretch our legs."

Even though the flagship was one of the largest naval vessels in the Isharan fleet, the captain and the navigator expertly guided it through the reef channel and into the narrow harbor cove. Erical used just a wisp of the godling's magic to push with breezes and currents so the ship smoothly arrived at the main dock. He gazed anxiously up at the high stone walls that protected the outpost. Steep metal-and-wood stairs led up to a cleft above, the only entrance beneath the towering fortress walls. Burn marks stained the rough stone, and the steps themselves had been repaired recently.

Magda walked down the gangplank and stood on the dock boards, unsteady. Her face still looked a little green from seasickness. She craned her neck, assessing the steep climb.

The gruff captain noticed and snorted. "Don't make me carry you up there. If you can't climb a set of stairs, how can you conquer a continent?" He began bounding up the rickety cliffside steps.

On the walls above, Isharan soldiers crowded the lookout points. Some waved at the visitors, while others remained on guard, wary of the shaggy barbarians with the Isharan sailors. Magda stomped up the stairs as if trying to break them with her anger and determination.

Erical held the railing, ascending one step at a time. He glanced down to see that they had climbed well above the top of the flagship's mast. The other two vessels were still tying up to the docks and lashing sails to the yardarms. The presence of the godling refreshed him like a breeze, and he did not feel weary at all by the time they reached the crack in the rock beneath the fortress. They slipped through the gated opening and walked under the walls until they emerged into the open courtyard of the garrison.

The Isharan soldiers had donned fresh garments and stood in ranks as the garrison commander, a thin veteran named Wota, bullied the soldiers into formation and brought them to attention. With Erical and Magda beside him, Captain Gaus presented himself. "Garrison commander, the Isharan navy has launched to conquer the old world."

"So many ships," said Wota.

"Thirty-six," Gaus said proudly. "Some are ranging widely on patrol."

Magda squared her shoulders. "And they have my Hethrren aboard."

Wota frowned, clearly considering the brutish woman to be unappetizing.

The flagship captain explained in a clipped, disapproving voice. "Key Priestlord Klovus saw fit to make an alliance with the Hethrren tribes to help conquer the godless lands."

Magda's lips parted to show her filed front tooth. "We are conquering it for ourselves, but we may leave some pieces for you to pick up."

Uninterested in the Hethrren leader, Wota concentrated on the rainbow haze of the godling that flowed behind Erical. The garrison commander's voice sounded wistful. "I am glad to see a godling here again. We recaptured Fulcor Island with the help of Priestlord Xion and his godling." He gave a formal, appreciative bow to Erical, and the entity brightened with pride. "How is he? Did he return safely to Serepol?"

Erical felt an ache in his chest. "There was an incident in Serepol. The main godling went out of control, and Priestlord Xion and his godling were both killed."

Magda sneered. "Klovus wanted to intimidate my people, but his godling damaged his own city at the same time. I think he learned his lesson." She laughed.

Wota groaned, crestfallen. "I am sad to hear that. Xion was a good man. My garrison welcomes you regardless." He indicated his ranks of soldiers. "These fighters will pray and worship to make your godling powerful. Hear us, save us."

His soldiers repeated the chant, and the godling thrummed, reinforced by the faith that had been waning as they journeyed farther from Prirari. Erical let out a contented sigh. "Thank you. We have a difficult battle ahead of us as our ships sail to the Commonwealth, and my godling needs to be strong."

The garrison commander announced, "My soldiers will also make blood sacrifices so that victory is assured."

"Victory is already assured," Magda said with a huff. "My people are ready to conquer the land, and we are eager to get off the sea."

The garrison soldiers bared their arms and took out fighting daggers, while others gathered pots and urns to collect the blood sacrifices. Erical flushed at the show of support. In Prirari District, most of the sacrifices to his godling consisted of barrels of cider, portions of the harvest, even crafts and artwork. A blood sacrifice was not the usual offering, but here it was made with the earnest will and devotion of the soldiers, and its potency was unquestioned.

Wota barked orders and segregated ranks, assigning volunteers to step up in an orderly fashion. They slashed their palms or arms, splattering red liquid into the basins. "Hear us, save us!" they chanted. "Hear us, save us!"

Magda watched the spectacle with wry amusement. "I would rather shed the blood of an enemy than weaken my own army."

"They are not weakened," Captain Gaus said, as if insulted.

Erical sensed the tingle grow inside him. "My godling is grateful for the renewing strength they impart."

Then one of the watchmen bellowed from an observation tower on the garrison wall and waved a yellow banner urgently back and forth. Lookouts ran to their posts at corners of the wall, scanned the watery horizon to the west. They also began waving yellow flags.

"What is that about?" Magda said.

Garrison commander Wota was already moving. "They have spotted non-Isharan ships." Ignoring his visitors, he sprinted up the stone stairs, followed by Erical, Magda, and Captain Gaus. Once they reached the top of the thick wall, Erical stared out to sea. The godling sharpened his focus, and he could see tiny dots of ships approaching—a great many of them.

"It's the Commonwealth navy," he said. "Sailing toward us."

36

〰

IN their camp by the frozen lakeside, Shadri woke up, stretched, and was startled to see many small figures in the silver pines just watching her, holding cherished objects. When she sat up, they approached her with odds and ends, many of them incomprehensible. Fascinated by the unusual creatures, Shadri returned their curiosity with curiosity of her own.

Pokle, though, was unsettled, suspicious of the drones. Each night he laid his blanket near Shadri's and sat up late, keeping watch until he dozed off, which left him red eyed, weary, and cranky in the morning. It took Shadri a while to realize that he was jealous of the attention that she gave the drones.

On this morning, the young man snapped awake, saw them in the dawn light, pawed his ragamuffin hair to brush off leaves and dry grasses, then stalked off muttering, "I'll find us some breakfast." He didn't even glance at what the drones had brought her.

Shadri sat on her blanket and adjusted her skirts, welcoming the eager feral creatures. "What have you bought me today?"

She had spoken at length with the drones over the past two days. They understood human speech, and she had learned some of their words. The creatures communicated in an odd dance of sounds, words, gestures, and puzzled looks.

The first one came forward and offered her an empty bird's nest. She looked at it, puzzled. "I don't understand. Is this a special nest?" The drone left without attempting any explanation.

One brought a small, still-wriggling trout scooped up from a creek, and she smiled. "This will make a fine morning meal over the campfire coals. Thank you." She looked around to call out to Pokle, but he was gone.

The next drone brought her a mottled yellow aspen leaf; others brought tangled yarn, a broken bit of pottery. One carried a button carved from an antler, and all the drones seemed to revere it. The next had two rib bones from an elk. One gave her a mud-covered rock that had no special significance she could see. Shadri thanked them all.

The previous day, the drones had presented to her a wooden cooking spoon, some jewelry, and a child's embroidered dress. When Pokle saw the objects, he turned pale, as if he might be sick. "They took those things from the houses in Lake Bakal! From the people who died here. They were friends of mine. They . . ." His shoulders had bobbed up and down, as if wrestling with an invisible snake.

"It wasn't the drones who hurt them," Shadri said. "They're trying to survive here in the forest, just like you did. They probably scoured the rubble for anything they could use." She softened her voice, understanding how much Pokle was hurting. "They don't know the significance of anything they found, do they? Just like magpies collecting any intriguing object." Afterward, though, Pokle had avoided the drones even more than usual.

Still blinking the sleep from her eyes, Shadri looked at the drones who were brave enough to come close, while others crouched among the trees. She set the twitching trout near the coals of the campfire, waiting for Pokle to come back.

"I wish you could explain what you're thinking." She picked up the mud-covered rock. "There must be a story here." She smiled encouragement. "Let's try to tell some more today." She pulled her journal out of her pack.

She had furiously been writing down notes. Back in Fellstaff, she would assemble them into some meaningful history, though she had to guess at many things, either because she couldn't understand the words they said, or because the little creatures failed to provide enough details. Shadri would create the legacy of the drones and their time with the frostwreths, and she couldn't wait to share it with King Kollanan and his advisors . . . whenever they returned from their war.

She hummed to herself, rereading her words. "Yesterday, you told me about Queen Onn and her warrior Rokk." The drones stirred, muttered at the mention of the name. She knew they didn't like Rokk. Onn's warrior lover had massacred many of them, as had the queen. The drones talked about how Onn would swallow them up in the ice floor of her palace or create frozen monsters to devour them, as if it were a game. They seemed more ashamed than horrified.

In halting phrases, they described how they had helped build the giant ice fortress, constructing their own hovels out of scrap material, deadfall wood, and skins from animal carcasses they found in the forest. They talked about the ferocious wolf-steeds they were forced to tend, though many lost their lives doing so.

She also learned that the drones had been created by magic somehow, and they could not reproduce. Strange. Shadri remembered working with a doctor named Severn in the town of Thule's Orchard, and together they had dissected human bodies to understand the workings and purpose of the internal organs. Because Shadri was a young woman of seventeen years and her monthly courses had started when she was thirteen, she knew about her own biology. Though in theory wreths had created humans, Shadri knew how babies were made and how they were born.

But what the drones described was not at all how human children came about. Through twisted magic, the creatures emerged fully formed out of membranes in the glacier walls, like unnatural wombs. It was both amazing and distressing.

She used her stylus to add more notes. "You've told me so many extraordinary stories." She looked at the dirt-crusted trout, which had by now stopped flopping about. "I'll listen to more tales today, but then Pokle and I have to go home."

She knew the young man wanted to get back to Fellstaff Castle, nervous to be far from the defensive walls. He saw threats everywhere, unable to forget the sweeping destruction the frostwreths had caused here. Shadri thought Pokle a bit too skittish, but maybe he was the one exhibiting common sense. She knew she wasn't wary enough, since her interest in everything blinded her to obvious dangers. After all, the world might be in its final days, if the wreths managed to wake the dragon. Maybe she should be more worried. . . .

She could not tell if the drones were disappointed that she would be leaving. "I'll share your stories back in Fellstaff, though." She pursed her lips. "I wonder if drone legacies have ever been written down before?"

Suddenly, the creatures around her glanced at one another like spooked deer. Shadri looked up from her writing, realizing that something had changed. The drones communicated in low murmurs with palpable anxiety. They twitched and fidgeted, shifting positions, while some of them disappeared into the trees.

"What's the matter?" The ones that had brought her offerings spoke urgently, but in their panic they forgot all their human words. Unable to understand what they were saying, Shadri held up her hands. "Slower. Try to tell me what you mean."

Like frightened quail, the drones bolted, leaving her behind at the lakeshore. She picked up the mud-covered rock, as if it could summon them back. "You haven't finished yet." But the drones were gone.

Moments later she heard a crashing sound, like a bull moose rampaging through the underbrush. Pokle came running, knocking branches out of the way, tripping through shrubbery. He was wheezing and breathless when he got to the camp. "We have to get out of here. They're coming!"

Even now, her curiosity won out over caution. "Who's coming? Tell me."

"I watched from an overlook, but none of them saw me." Pokle grabbed her arm, tugged it. "We need to hurry. I'll get the horses."

She stuffed the journal inside her pack and grabbed her blanket. "Tell me what's going on."

"The frostwreths are marching—a whole army!"

"Another war party?" Shadri said. "You think they're coming to make a camp at Lake Bakal?"

"Not just a war party!" Pokle's face was white as the snow. "I think it's *all* of them."

"Take me to the overlook. I want to see for myself."

"It's too far away, and too dangerous! We need to get out of here."

"If it's a whole army, they won't be here that quickly," Shadri said, trying to be calm. "And you said they didn't spot you. Gant will need as much information as we can bring him. We're spies, remember?"

The boy looked around, studying the thick silver pines, and hurried over to one with low-hanging branches. "Can you climb a tree?"

Shadri scoffed. "Of course!"

He put his foot on the low branch and scrambled up, stepping on the boughs, hauling himself higher. As Shadri followed, she remembered all the times she had climbed the pear trees near her father's shop in their village. Looking around from the top of the tree had sparked her interest in exploring the land. Now she climbed and climbed, scratching her hands. A lump of pitch made her palms sticky, and she wiped it on her skirts.

Pokle climbed so high that the pine began to sway, but Shadri pulled herself after him until both of them had a good view from the high boughs.

"There. See?"

Shadri looked to the north beyond the high mountain lake and saw the figures moving forward, rank upon rank. Front lines of bounding white oonuks, a vanguard of armored sleighs, flashing blue and silver armor, weapons, flowing ivory hair. "There must be thousands," she said. "Who knew there were so many frostwreths in the entire world?"

"I told you it was all of them," Pokle said.

The enemy army moved at a determined pace, bending around the mountains. As Shadri studied them, she realized where they were going. "They're not headed here to rebuild their fortress. No . . ." Clinging to the top of the tree, she finally felt true alarm. "They're marching south. Toward Fellstaff!"

37

❧

THE horses wound their way through the desert canyons after dark. The moon had not yet risen high enough to illuminate the rocky floors, but the soldiers' eyes adjusted to the gloom and shadows. Overhead, the starry sky was a slash caught between high rock walls.

Many side routes led to dead ends, but they had Ari's surveillance maps, and Thon led the way without the slightest hesitation.

Such confidence let Adan focus on the imminent battle. He patted the mane of his chestnut mare, more to reassure himself than the horse. The hundreds of fighters in the strike force were tense and silent, keeping their weapons muffled and their words to themselves. The only sounds were the jingle of tack and the click of hooves on the rocky ground.

In their two days of travel, Adan believed they had not been seen, and he felt a cautious confidence. The wreths had no inkling that their slave camp was about to be attacked. This would be their only chance.

Above them, the blue ska flitted ahead and circled back, clearly anxious. Normally Ari would have given a piercing cry, but she knew to be silent.

The first riders reached a bend in the canyon, and Thon reined in his horse with Elliel beside him. The rest of the raiding party stuttered to a halt, restless in their saddles. Thon turned back as Kollanan and Adan approached, and he spoke in a loud whisper. "We are almost there." His face lit with a grin. "Just beyond this curve the wash widens out and is joined by a tributary canyon. That is the main entrance to the high galleries where the human prisoners are kept."

Adan peered into the canyon shadows, trying to discern details. One sharp protrusion looked like a man with an overlarge nose, and he recognized it from Ari's original images.

Kollanan removed his war hammer from its sling and rested it on his shoulder. He looked at Adan with an expression as hard as the rock outcropping. "We brought down the fortress at Lake Bakal. Let's liberate this pitiful camp."

Elliel spoke calmly and tactically. "Once we begin the fight, our army has to spread out, make sure none of the wreths escape down side canyons. We have to cut them off and exterminate them."

"Wreths would not think to run from humans," Thon said. "They will fight without imagining that they will lose."

Adan nodded. "Penda promises me that Glik and the other prisoners will also defend themselves, but let us not be overconfident. These are wreth warriors and mages." His throat was dry. "Our army won't get out of this unscathed."

"I'm not overconfident," Koll said. "Just confident enough."

Adan looked back at all the mounted soldiers that filled the canyon behind them, Kollanan's fighters from Norterra as well as his own Suderran warriors. He slid his shadowglass-inlaid sword out of the scabbard and held it up. Faint starlight caught on the obsidian.

He spoke so that the first ranks could hear him, but he didn't dare shout the battle cry he felt within his heart. "This is the sword that killed Queen Voo's brother, who wanted to take my wife and child. Tonight, it will kill many more wreths." He thought of freeing Glik and all the prisoners. "Tonight we will do a good thing."

Kollanan turned his hammer in front of him, admiring the shadowglass inlays. "We cannot let a single wreth escape. Not one." The reminder was passed along to all of the human fighters.

Ari swooped overhead, urgent, impatient. All the soldiers drew their swords, set their shields on their forearms. The sound that came out was not a war cry, but a determined murmur that Adan found heartening.

"It will be a surprise as it needs to be." Elliel removed her gauntlet and clamped the golden cuff around her wrist. The ramer ignited in a flare of fire. It served not just as a blazing sword, but a beacon for the attacking army.

She urged her horse forward, with Thon right beside her. The two kings followed, spurring their mounts into a charge. With a building clamor, the strike force surged toward the slave camp.

The moon had just risen over the top of the canyon walls when Glik awoke to augas snorting in their paddocks. She had been lost in a dream in which she attacked her enemies, slashing with her shadowglass dagger. The dream was so vivid she could feel Ari's feather against her palm. She had laughed with her victory.

She heard the increasing sound of rumbling in the canyons.

A few wreth guards prowled among the human prisoners who slept on patches of ground or huddled under meager overhangs. The warm breeze picked up, and Glik sensed the change in the air. Something was coming.

She drew a quick circle around her heart.

The augas grunted again. A wreth called out a question instead of an alarm.

Glik could hear galloping hooves coming closer. Horses sounded so different from the reptilian mounts. And a rising chorus of shouts—human voices!

Cheth was instantly awake and sat up, flashing her eyes toward the orphan girl. "It's time. They're coming at last."

Glik sprang to her feet, threw her dusty blanket aside, and darted to the rock cleft to retrieve her hidden knife. The shadowglass nicked her fingertip, reminding her how sharp it was, but she grasped the leather-wrapped hilt, felt the gentle kiss of the ska feather. This was exactly the weapon she needed.

Now the shouts grew louder, a storm of riders rushing through the canyon toward the camp. The wreths scrambled about, confused. Glik yelled loud enough to waken the sleeping captives. "Get ready to fight!"

The prisoners roused themselves, some questioning, some eager, some terrified. Sandwreth warriors snatched spears and swords and bounded toward the mouth of the canyon, as if they were joining in a game.

Human soldiers galloped into the camp, a stream of hundreds. The orphan girl saw no banners or colors, just raised swords that had an oily black cast. And in front, like a torchbearer, rode a Brava woman, her hand engulfed in fire.

Cheth laughed with anticipation. "Bravas! Time to fight."

The wreth warriors were not at all regimented, but accustomed to one-on-one fighting. Facing the unexpected human charge, they struggled to form a defensive line across the mouth of the canyon, but the human rescuers crashed through. In the lead, the Brava's fiery ramer caught a wreth full in the face, cleaving his head in two.

The camp augas were riled, charging back and forth. Several broke loose and blundered into the wreth warriors; one stomped on a wreth and broke his leg. The warrior lifted himself halfway to his feet, but one of the riders—Adan Starfall, Glik recognized—killed him with his black-inlaid sword.

Cheth grabbed the iron-hard wooden pole that propped up their lean-to awning. Planning ahead, she had already notched the end of the staff, and now she fitted it with the obsidian point she had hidden, making her own shadowglass spear before dashing out to join the fight.

Without thinking, Glik followed her friend into the fray, while the guards faced the hundreds of human soldiers. Behind her, she was pleased to see other slaves rising up, many of them with weapons they had stashed, while others simply picked up rocks to throw.

The wreth guards did not give a thought to the prisoners in the camp behind them.

In the starlit sky Glik saw a blue ska sweep in with a loud cry, and she felt a surge through her heart link, which gave her all the energy she needed. Glik sprang forward and plunged her shadowglass dagger into the back of a wreth.

The shadowglass bit deep, and the warrior fell as if it were a poison blade. The girl snatched her weapon free and rushed to find her next victim.

The human strike force slammed into the prison camp, and the battle was engaged.

38

Even though the *Glissand* no longer belonged to him in any meaningful way, Mak Dur refused to give up. He and his ship were inseparable, and he was still the voyagier, even if the Commonwealth had taken over.

As the fleet sailed from Rivermouth, each day held a taste of dread. For so many years, Mak Dur had been proud of every scrap of wood, every strand of rigging, every stretched sail. The *Glissand* was beautiful and perfect, and his crew worked hard to keep her immaculate, scrubbing the deck boards, painting and varnishing the ornamental wood. But now the deck boards seemed to be stained with invisible blood, and whenever he looked at the rigging ropes, he could only think of nooses and his two friends dangling from the yardarms. His ship would never be the same; her soul had been bruised.

He knew, though, that news of the gruesome, unjust punishment would have spread far and wide among the Utauk tribes, along with reports that Utauk trading ships had been seized and inducted into the Commonwealth navy. Shella din Orr would know what had happened before long. Things would change. If Heith and Sarrum had simply been allowed to vanish among the tribes, nothing more would have come of it, but now the widespread Utauks would be forced out of their generations-old neutrality. Their way of life was at stake.

The *Glissand* sailed along with the Commonwealth warships for the terrible vengewar against Ishara. According to Utho, first the fleet would hit Fulcor Island and then move on to Ishara itself. But Mak Dur knew that a similar number of Isharan war vessels were ready in Serepol Harbor. A great deal of destruction, mayhem, and bloodshed was still to come.

He stood at the bow and stared at the scattered ships, with their bright sails, an enormous fighting force cutting across the blue waves. He had grown up among the thick forests and rugged hills of Norterra, but he had made his way to Convera, seen the ocean, and felt the call of the sea. He had become a sailor and finally a voyagier with his own beautiful ship. He wondered what would have happened if he'd chosen differently, decided to wander the hills and forest trails as a caravan leader rather than a ship captain. Settling down, he might have taken a wife, had children. But the sea was Mak Dur's calling, his true mistress.

Clad in black, the konag's bonded Brava came to stand next to him. The voyagier did not acknowledge him, and they both kept quiet, each for his own reasons. Utho was always grim and reticent, and Mak Dur was angry at his situation.

Finally, the Brava asked, "How close are we to Fulcor Island?"

"I don't know," Mak Dur retorted. "You murdered my navigator."

"But if he had been allowed to desert your ship, he would not be here either." Utho's expression was not angry, but implacable. "You are the voyagier, and you are not incompetent. How close are we to Fulcor Island?"

Mak Dur's shoulders sagged. "*Cra,* it should be very soon. Within hours."

As if on cue, his lookout shouted from high on the mainmast, "Ships! Ships ahead."

Other voices resounded from the first vessels. Mak Dur shaded his eyes and peered toward the horizon. The lookout's voice rang out, "Fulcor Island just off to starboard!"

Mak Dur removed the viewing tube from his belt and peered through the lens.

"What ships?" Utho demanded. "What do you see?"

Mak Dur twisted the barrel and aligned the lenses. A group of sailing ships sprang into view. "Lots of ships. Red stripes on their sails." He lowered the tube. "I warned you that the Isharan navy was preparing to set off."

Utho seized the viewing tube. "We have forty armored war vessels, which should be more than enough to strike whatever they send after us." He peered at the oncoming vessels and his expression darkened. "I count maybe twenty enemy vessels, but they are widely separated, sailing our way." He swept the viewing tube in an arc. "Ah, and more of them at Fulcor Island." He handed the tube back. "When I tried to recapture our garrison the first time, I did not bring enough ships. I intend to make up for that lack of foresight."

The rocky bastion of Fulcor Island came into view as the Isharan navy sailed to intercept them. Distant shouts rang out across the water, attenuated by the spaces between the Commonwealth ships, and bright blue flags flew from the masts, followed by red battle pennants.

Mak Dur scanned the ocean again, noting more enemy vessels approaching. "Our forces are about evenly matched."

"Not evenly matched," Utho scowled. "They are Isharan animals and we serve the konag. Our ships have several Brava fighters. This time I will recapture Fulcor Island." His lips twisted as if he didn't remember how to smile. "It will be our most important battle."

Mak Dur shaded his eyes and peered across the water. "Why? It is just an ugly rock that happens to be in a convenient place."

The Brava looked at him as if he'd been insulted.

The voyagier pressed. "I thought our objective was to strike Serepol and conquer Ishara. Why even engage in a battle here? On the vast sea, we could space out our ships and simply slip between the enemy vessels like water through a sieve. Then we'd reach Ishara unscathed."

"And we would leave the shores of Osterra vulnerable. We engage the enemy here." Utho's pale lips hardened into a firm line. "By the time we reach Serepol, they will have nothing left!"

He took the viewing tube again, pointed the lens toward the island. He ignored the activity as soldiers prepared for a battle that was still hours away in the slow dance of a naval engagement.

"Our fleet will fight the enemy on the open water, and we will sink them," Utho said. "But I'll take your ship and several others and head directly to Fulcor. We will capture the garrison by ourselves."

High on the walls of the stronghold, Priestlord Erical tried to catch his breath. He felt alarm as he watched so many Commonwealth ships closing in on the island. An entire war fleet heading for Ishara!

His godling enhanced his senses, made the priestlord feel stronger and larger, as if he had a view from the clouds down upon the enemy navy. "They have dozens of ships." The garrison commander and Captain Gaus both shaded their eyes, trying to see. Erical took a moment for a methodical count. "At least forty."

"We can defeat forty ships," Magda said. "My Hethrren are aboard." She stomped an impatient foot on the stones of the wide wall. "But we need to be out on the water!" She growled at Gaus. "Take us back to the ships. I want to be in the thick of battle, not hiding here like a rabbit in the underbrush."

Gaus glanced at Magda. "Surprisingly, I agree with the Hethrren leader. My warships are ready to fight, and I need to be at the bow shouting orders and guiding maneuvers. I do not intend to watch from a lookout post."

Garrison commander Wota swept his gaze across the fortified garrison. Lookouts continued to bang their gongs and alarm bells, and the soldiers ran to take up their positions, gathering bows and arrows, loading catapults, stacking baskets of missiles to hurl down on any invaders who tried to climb up from the harbor cove. "We will defend Fulcor. We won't let the enemy overrun us."

Magda strode toward the cliff stairs, swinging her club as if to strike any garrison soldiers who got in her way. She grabbed Erical's arm. "Come, little priestlord. Bring your godling, and we'll make short work of those other boats."

Erical could feel his unsettled godling through the air, and her uneasiness made his insides twist. Some godlings were fierce and destructive, but Priestlord Erical had never been in a battle before, and neither had the entity. He wasn't sure how it would affect either of them, but his deity had just received many fresh blood sacrifices. She felt energy and a rising battle enthusiasm, and those emotions set her on edge. Erical braced himself.

Gaus shouted back to the garrison commander, "If we sink all those ships before they reach Fulcor, your soldiers can make themselves useful by throwing a celebration feast for us."

Magda bellowed to a few Hethrren who milled around the courtyard, having followed her up to the garrison. They were not pleased when she commanded them to rush back aboard their ships. "This ugly rock is better than a wobbly boat," one of her men grunted in a clear challenge. He had thick braided hair and a missing front tooth. "I am staying here."

Magda punched him in the face so hard she knocked his head back. "We came to fight, and the enemy is out there! Or would you rather plant a garden in the dirt?"

The warrior pressed a palm against his already-swelling eye. "Now you made it harder for me to see! How am I supposed to chop off heads?"

"Just swing your blade when you get close enough. You'll hit something."

Captain Gaus ignored the barbarians as he rushed down the cliff stairs to the docks below. He shouted toward the flagship, "Enemy warships approaching. Prepare to set sail!" The crew had already heard the alarms above, and were setting the sails, tightening the rigging, preparing the oars to push off. The barbarians thundered up the gangplanks, waving their weapons.

Gaus put the burly Hethrren to work at the oars, and they rowed the flagship out of the narrow cove and into open water. Erical could feel the angry, churning godling inside him and inside the ship. She helped move them forward and added breezes to the stretched sails, while the navigator called out directions to thread their way around the dangerous reefs.

The flagship raced out to the main fleet, while three warships remained at the mouth of the cove to guard the garrison. Gaus flew signal pennants to communicate with his dispersed warships, setting up for battle.

Erical gazed ahead at the Commonwealth fleet. The enemy ships spread out in discrete battle groups aiming for specific targets, with several of them arrowing toward Fulcor. He drew a deep breath, sharing thoughts and feelings with his godling. The entity also drew energy from the rising battle fever across the Isharan fleet.

For the first time in his life, Priestlord Erical felt hungry for violence.

39

✺

WHEN Cemi and Analera rushed back into the hidden chamber, their dismay was palpable. Iluris instantly knew that something terrible had happened. She lifted her shaky body from the pallet to stand, though her body felt hollow. "What is it, child? Have the Hethrren departed yet, as you promised?" Iluris drew upon all her strength, supported by the ethereal godling that swirled around her like a safety blanket.

Cemi paused, confused by the comment. "Yes, Excellency. The Hethrren sailed away days ago. The key priestlord sent them to attack the Commonwealth. Don't you remember?"

"I don't think that is a good idea," Iluris said in a faint voice.

Suddenly, she wavered as if her life force had stumbled into an unexpected pothole in the street, and the new godling also reeled. Yes, she could sense it herself now. There had been a significant change in the core of the city, in the hearts of the people. She whispered again, dreading the answer, "What's happened?"

"Klovus just held your funeral and burned a great pyre with a body that he claimed was you!" Cemi blurted out, breathless. "From the Magnifica, he told all of Serepol that their empra is dead."

Iluris formed a bitter smile. "It is not the first untrue thing that man has said. He will find me to be less dead than he would like."

Analera groaned. "Excellency, it is terrible! The people were already distraught, and now they've lost hope. Hear us, save us!"

"It changes everything," Cemi said.

Captani Vos flushed with anger. "I will have that man's head."

Analera and Cemi described the giant crowds in the temple square and the funeral pyre. "All the people believed."

"Of course they believed." Iluris sighed. "It has been so long since they've seen my real face, how many even remember what I look like?" She touched her sunken cheeks. She was just a whisper of the glorious leader she had once been. Yes, she had finally awakened and her external wounds had healed, but she was not herself. Iluris could tell something wasn't right inside.

The new godling helped her, energized her, and she felt the entity permeating the underground chamber. The godling stretched out its tendrils to all the places where dedicated followers believed, and Iluris felt the truth: The funeral spectacle had turned their beliefs to ashes.

Even so, Iluris continued to think like an empra—she was glad that she could still do that, at least. Thoughts and consequences, connections leading to important decisions, rolled out inside her mind. "The people have held out hope for so long, and you all have encouraged them. My true followers prayed for me and believed in me, and through their faith created a new godling."

She extended her hands in front of her, and the strange misty presence sparkled brighter.

"Your godling," Cemi said.

"Ishara's godling," Iluris corrected. "A reflection of the people's true spirit, but because of this false funeral pyre, they have doubts." She clicked her tongue against the back of her teeth, breathed in the thick air of their chamber, where too many people had been confined for too long. "And as they experience doubts, so the godling will weaken."

"We have to move soon, Mother," said Vos. "Come back to your people."

"We will help you to be strong enough," Cemi said.

Iluris drew her brows together, trying to find the words. "I am the empra, and I will be as strong as I have to be." She spoke in a forceful voice, but then her vision faded alarmingly around her. She felt she might faint, but she couldn't allow that!

Vos said, "Some of your greatest supporters have been arrested by priest guards and never seen again. Still, many maintain their belief in you."

"I would challenge Key Priestlord Klovus myself," Cemi said, "but now we have you back! The godling will help. The faith of the people will help." She paused. "But you have to give them something."

Iluris knew, though, that if Serepol saw her as she was now, barely able to walk or even stand, their dismay would destroy her chances. Klovus would seize the weakness, and she doubted her rule would ever recover. She swayed on her feet, and Vos rushed to take her arm, propping her up.

"For now, this is the best I can do." Though it took all her energy to maintain her composure, Iluris unbound her rumpled hair, which had been covered by bandages for far too long. Shaking her head, she let the strands fall long and loose. "Captani Vos, your dagger please."

The hawk guard didn't hesitate, simply handed over his gilded knife. Iluris tugged on a clump of hair and slashed it off, then cut another thick lock, and another until she had four. She extended her palm, and Analera took one of the locks, holding it like a religious object.

Iluris said, "Give strands of my hair to my strongest followers. Show it as a sign that I am still truly here and promise they will see me soon."

Cemi took another lock of hair, skeptical. "But how is this proof? Such strands of hair could belong to anyone. What standing do I have when I say that the pyre was just a trick, that the body in the pyre wasn't really you?"

"Because that hair does come from me," Iluris said. "My followers will sense the truth, if they have faith. Remember, the godling draws its strength from the deep moral character of the Isharan people, from their warm hearts, their compassion, their respect. They will know."

Cemi accepted the locks of hair, wrapped her fingers around them, and nodded. Analera pressed one lock against her chest.

"I will go with them," Vos said in a voice that allowed no argument. "The people can look in my eyes, and they will know what I say is true." He averted his gaze out of respect. "If that is acceptable to you, Mother?"

"These other hawk guards can keep me safe here," Iluris said. "Reassure my people, Vos. They feel despair because of what they think they saw."

Cemi also showed renewed resolve. "We will make them see. Many still believe in you, and their faith is strong. They've held on for this long, and they won't be shaken so easily." She lowered her voice, leaning closer to Iluris with concern. "But we have to prove what we say, and it truly must be soon. Each day your promised return becomes more of a memory and less of a threat."

Iluris concentrated, forcing clear focus through her fuzzy mind. When she called upon the new godling, it brightened, became more sharply defined. The others in the chamber sensed the sudden strengthening of the deity, and they were impressed.

Iluris said, "It will be soon, I promise. I already have a plan, and it will certainly rattle our dear Klovus."

40

❧

THOUGH Kollanan had seen images of the slave camp, he was still appalled to see the conditions with his own eyes. It only intensified his rage to destroy this place, and to destroy the wreths. He swung his war hammer, comforted by the weight of its deadly end and the newly inlaid black shadowglass. His warhorse snorted, familiar with riding into battle.

The raiders charged forward, guided by the flare of Elliel's ramer. She and Thon moved like a plow through the disorganized ranks of sandwreth guards. Behind them, gaunt prisoners stirred awake, uncertain, but then Kollanan watched a transformation pass through them. The cloud of despair that hung like smoke from a greenwood fire now lifted, changing to a wave of hope. The prisoners sprang to their feet, found anything that would serve as a weapon.

The wreths tried to stand against the surprise attack, but not quickly enough. The thunder of horse hooves resounded from the canyon walls. Adan galloped beside Koll, raised his obsidian-inlaid sword as they surged into battle.

A line of warriors pulled their augas into place, raising spears, bone swords, golden axes. The lumbering reptile mounts looked up with dull eyes as the humans charged toward them.

A sneering wreth pushed his auga toward Kollanan and raised a curved sword for a vicious blow. But Storm collided with the reptile, making it rear up. The sandwreth slashed and missed. Koll felt the whistle of the ivory blade in front of his face, and he put all his strength into the swing of his war hammer. The heavy weapon slammed into the enemy's chest, caving in his breastbone like a rotten squash. The wreth gaped as the shadowglass collapsed his heart. He fell off the auga, and the freed mount careened off, trampling a second sandwreth.

Koll continued his charge and swung his hammer right and left, cracking an enemy skull, crushing a spine.

Deeper in the camp, some of the prisoners retreated to shelter, while others snatched up fallen weapons or rocks. Seeing them fight sent a pang through Kollanan's heart, reminding him of everyone the wreths had swept away at Lake Bakal.

Finally taking the attack seriously, the sandwreths called in reinforcements. From the ska's surveillance images, Koll knew that no more than fifty wreths were here in the camp. By his count, the rescuers had already killed six—and they were just getting started.

Adan took off to the right, finding his own enemies to engage. He shouted out to encourage the captives as they rose up, "We are here to free you. You all come home tonight!"

A wreth warrior sprinted toward him on foot, then faltered as he recognized Adan. "It is King Adan of Suderra!" His voice was filled with confusion. "But you fight for Queen Voo."

"Humans fight for themselves," Adan said. "We fight to survive. We fight to be free." His shadowglass sword cut through the wreth's neck, cleaving all the way down to his heart.

"We also fight for revenge," Kollanan added, but the words were for himself.

As a Brava, Elliel did not need shadowglass weapons. She had her ramer. Her hand tingled with the energy summoned from her half-breed blood, and the fire brightened. When she swept her flaming sword to decapitate a wreth warrior, his long hair caught fire as the head fell to the dusty ground.

Thon bounded into the attack without restraint, and his abilities surpassed any that the other wreths could bring to bear. Smiling, he spread his fingers and whisked his palm sideways. The invisible force snatched a sandwreth out of his auga saddle, spun him in the air, and slammed him against the canyon wall, leaving a stain redder than the rock.

Desperate prisoners threw fist-sized stones at the wreth warriors. The blows caused few serious injuries, but the distraction helped. One enraged wreth woman turned on a pair of prisoners harassing her, lifted an ivory-tipped spear to slay them, but Elliel rode her down and killed her with the ramer.

The rescuers yelled for the prisoners to get to safety, while they continued to fight the wreth captors. Elliel lost count of the wreths she had slain. Her personal numbers did not matter, only completing the task.

Mounted human soldiers rushed ahead to cut off side canyons and block any escape routes. The wreths were astounded rather than panicked, crippled by disbelief that mere humans would have the audacity to attack this encampment.

Thon seemed to be enjoying himself as he struck out at the sandwreths, testing his own capability. He knocked them down in front of the galloping warhorses, where they were trampled. As the wreths lay broken and groaning, emboldened slaves rushed forward and stabbed or pummeled them to death.

Four more wreth warriors bounded in from a tributary canyon, as if thinking they alone could overwhelm the entire human strike force. Thon sprang down from his saddle, and let the horse keep running on its own. He turned to the mouth of the side canyon as the defiant wreths raced toward him. Thon touched the ruddy rock walls, closed his eyes, and pulled the cliffs together like curtains of stone, sealing shut the side canyon and trapping the four warriors.

Thon flashed a smile at Elliel, but she said, "Need to stop them from retreating through the back of the canyon. Don't let them get away."

Thon's expression darkened, and he touched the newly sealed walls. His long dark hair crackled with static electricity, a rumbling noise began, and a deep vibration spread through the sealed canyon. The upper cliffs folded over from above, collapsed inward, and buried the trapped wreths. Thon crossed his arms over his scaled silver breastplate and gave Elliel a satisfied nod. "Done."

Ahead of Elliel, a tall, muscular prisoner—a woman with close-cropped hair—fought with great vigor. She wielded a spear fashioned from a hard tent pole with a shard of shadowglass at the point. The woman slashed a guard with the obsidian edge, leaving a deep wound, and turned to look around her. Seeing the prisoner's eyes, Elliel realized that she was a Brava!

The woman saw Elliel, too, and her eyes locked on the blazing ramer. She offhandedly dispatched her wreth opponent with the shadowglass spear, then bounded closer. "I am Cheth, one of five Bravas here." She showed no reaction to the rune of forgetting on Elliel's face. With her spear she indicated a rock structure tucked into a nearby alcove. "Mage Ivun keeps our ramers in there. Help me get them back."

Elliel responded with a hard smile. "Thon, help us!"

Two wreth warriors tried to block them from the mage's dwelling, but both Brava women engaged them. Between the ramer and the shadowglass-tipped spear, they dispatched the guards and cleared the way.

Thon joined them at the sealed structure, and Elliel gestured with her chin. "Open that. Split the wall."

He touched the flat stone wall, pressed his fingers and palms hard against the surface. "It is protected, sealed with magic. . . ."

"Can you break it?"

Thon looked at her and sniffed. "Of course. I was just making a point."

He slammed the side of his hand against the rock, and the wall popped like a soap bubble. The stone fell away to reveal a chamber much larger than the building itself, extending deep into the alcove. Ivun's vault was filled with arcane objects, exotic furniture, stacks of crystal sheets, chemical vials.

Several other prisoners joined them—all half-breeds. Elliel spotted the golden cuffs on a shelf and passed them around to the eager Brava captives. Cheth clamped one band around her wrist and summoned the fiery blade. She admired the flickering glow coming from her hand, and her green eyes shone. "Now we can finish this!" With a laugh, she bounded back out into the chaos of the slave camp.

Four more Bravas followed her, armed with ramers.

Leaving the mage's dwelling, Elliel and Thon suddenly found themselves facing a bald man in the leather robes of a mage. He raised one withered, clawlike hand and sketched invisible lines in the air. "Half-breed fools cannot stand against a mage. How do you think you were captured in the first place?"

"You did not capture me." Elliel lurched toward him, swinging her ramer, but Ivun thrust out his hand. A hard shock wave hit her and pushed the ramer back. She stumbled, lost her balance, and fell to her knees.

As the mage pressed his attack, Thon intervened. "You will not harm her." He called up his own magic, blocking the way, but Ivun pushed back with unexpected strength. Thon seemed surprised by the sheer vehemence of the counterattack.

The mage pressed, and Thon concentrated to raise a stronger shield against his opponent. Ivun pulled back his lips to show clenched teeth as he strained harder. His withered arm drew closer to his chest, as if he were draining himself with the effort.

The mage's eyes suddenly bulged, and he stumbled forward. Ivun opened his mouth, and blood blossomed up to spill down his chin. He gasped, tried to walk.

Behind him, Glik raised her shadowglass dagger and plunged it down again, stabbing deep into the base of Ivun's neck. The black knife sank into his spine, and the mage sprawled forward, dead on the ground.

Thon stepped back, relieved, but clearly shaken.

Cheth bounded over the mage's body and swept up the orphan girl in a hug. "He deserved it."

But Ivun did more than just die. His corpse folded in upon itself, his skin wrinkling, his entire body withering like his clawed arm until he was only a shriveled husk.

Cheth turned from the young girl and nodded. "Now, let's finish the rest of them."

41

〰

When the sea battle was engaged, Utho felt great fulfillment. He paced the deck wishing the *Glissand* could race across the waves like a galloping horse, but a naval battle was nothing at all like a cavalry charge. Rather, it was a slow choreographed dance as ships used the currents and breezes, shifting sails and tilting rudders to bring their vessels within longbow range, hoping their own archers could shoot farther and more accurately than the enemy could.

The Utauk voyagier was a reluctant captain, but he did know his ship. The Commonwealth officer formally in charge, Captain Pharion, was so arrogant and useless that Utho had quietly commanded him to stay out of the way once actual battle was joined, preferring to leave operational decisions to Mak Dur.

Hours passed, and the *Glissand* and three designated vessels closed in on Fulcor, while the Isharan fleet moved their dozens of warships up against the Commonwealth navy. Utho concentrated only on the key island—*his* target. Across the Commonwealth fleet, the other Bravas as well as highly trained Commonwealth soldiers would engage the enemy and set Isharan ships on fire. Utho had his own needs.

He could see the high stone walls of the garrison adorned with Isharan banners, which sickened him. Several Isharan warships had already escaped from the harbor cove, sailing away and aiming for the heart of the Commonwealth fleet, but a few remained to guard the narrow harbor opening.

Utho knew every inch of the place. Fulcor Island was a part of him, and his time serving there had made him who he was—Utho of the Reef. During the Isharan blockade decades ago, Utho had slipped down to the reefs at low tide, made his way across the treacherous water to the enemy ships, and set them on fire. He had saved the garrison and freed the besieged soldiers.

And while he'd been defending the island, another Isharan force had struck Mirrabay and murdered Utho's wife and two daughters.

He needed to return to Fulcor Island and leave his permanent mark in blood. He had to be the one to tear Fulcor from the clutches of the enemy. For Konag Mandan, for the Commonwealth, but most of all for himself.

As the *Glissand* drove with deceptive grace toward the bleak island, passing markers and following the safe channel through the reefs, Utho watched the greater naval battle engaged out in the open water. As Mandan's fleet closed in, volleys of fire arrows streaked like shooting stars, rising up in a perfect curve to ignite the striped sails. Commonwealth longbows had a greater range, which gave them a momentary advantage, but soon enough, when the ships drove together, the Isharans would be able to shoot their own fire arrows.

As the *Glissand* sailed relentlessly toward the Fulcor harbor cove, Utho silently counted the wisps of smoke rising from the fleet on the open sea. Mak Dur stood next to him, troubled. He said, "At least fifteen ships are on fire."

"This engagement will continue long after nightfall," Utho said with a hint of wistfulness, but he turned nonetheless toward Fulcor Island. "By then the garrison will be ours. That is our battle for now."

Of his four ships that sailed to take the island, three held Bravas—Wendir, Arrick, and himself—and he considered one ramer to be worth at least fifty swords. He rubbed the scars and scabs on his right wrist. He knew his fellow Bravas were just as eager as he to eradicate the Isharan animals from the garrison.

Out in the open water behind the Utauk ship, thick smoke rose from damaged vessels as more of the Isharan fleet joined the fray. Several enemy ships were entirely on fire, but so were some of the Commonwealth vessels. The Isharans had begun to fight back with devastating effectiveness.

He tried to will the *Glissand* to greater speed. Foamy lines of water marked the dangerous reefs, but his four ships kept well clear. His focus became sharper, narrower, and he thought only of the battle to come. He breathed harder, felt his pulse quicken. When it was time, he clamped the golden cuff in place and ignited his ramer. Two flaming swords were raised by the other Bravas on the companion ships.

His ships closed in on the Isharan ships that guarded the mouth of the cove. Abruptly, the tedious approach became a blur of speed and confusion as well as a slow-motion strategy game. One of Utho's four ships collided with an Isharan defender and tossed grappling hooks over so that Commonwealth soldiers could swarm onto the enemy deck.

Unrelenting, the *Glissand* and its companion ships broke the Isharan blockade, leaving the enemy vessels in flames, but in doing so one of Utho's vessels crashed aground on a reef. The Brava Arrick and many fighters left the stranded ship and transferred aboard the two remaining ships.

Utho commanded Mak Dur to keep sailing into the cove, followed by the last vessel. He knew that he had enough fighters to capture Fulcor Island, and the other two Bravas were still with him. The fight was just beginning.

Finally entering the narrow harbor, the *Glissand* and the last Commonwealth ship sailed beneath the high cliffs. The Utauk ship ground against the rocks, suffering serious damage by the time it reached the docks, and then the defenders on the walls above began raining down fragments of stone, burning oil, and a hail of fire arrows. The voyagier shouted for his crew to put out small fires in the sails and on smoldering patches the deck. The stern mast was engulfed in flames.

Utho let Mak Dur and his Utauk crew handle that problem. He was interested only in the garrison.

Before any ropes could be thrown across to tie up the ships, Utho leaped onto the planks. He led the soldiers toward the steep metal stairs that ascended the cliff. The next step was clear. His fighters would crash through and into the garrison.

Emerging from the cleft in the thick wall above, Isharan defenders swarmed down the cliff stairs to stop the advance, but Utho charged headlong to the base of the steps. Hundreds of soldiers disembarked from the two ships in the harbor cove, joined by the bright orange swords of two more ramers.

Three Bravas . . . they could do it.

Starting to climb the steep and narrow stairs, Utho left a swath of bodies behind him. His vision became a red haze. As he climbed higher, still battling Isharans perched on the steps, he looked down at the docks and saw that the *Glissand* was on fire. They had destroyed the Isharan guardian vessels at the mouth of the cove, but at a cost. At the damaged Commonwealth vessel that had run aground on the outer reef, he saw more fighters disembark in landing boats, rowing furiously to join the fight at Fulcor. Others simply jumped into the water and swam toward the docks.

As he reveled in the glorious fight all around him, Utho allowed himself a cold grin and climbed toward the cleft in the rock that led to the barred stronghold gates. Out at sea, the rest of the Commonwealth fleet was engaged in a great and complex battle against the Isharans.

A chill swept over Utho as he spotted a storm, not in the sky but upon the waves. Ships—Mandan's ships—were tossed about and wrecked by a tremendous force. He uttered a curse of disbelief. The Isharans had unleashed a godling against his fleet! A godling!

Utho screamed in frustration, but he could not fight that battle so far away. No, he would take the Fulcor garrison and make the Isharans pay with a great deal of blood.

With her inherent energy from the recent blood sacrifices, the godling stoked the breezes and made the flagship surge through the waves. Priestlord Erical felt the same energy inside him, as if he were part of the Isharan warship. The Hethrren could sense it as well. Spoiling for a fight, the barbarians stomped back and forth, flexing their muscles, leering at the Commonwealth fleet.

Captain Gaus was amazed by the speed at which his ship streaked away from Fulcor Island, pushed by the godling's energy. It entered the fray like a wolf charging in among sheep. The Isharan soldiers raised their swords and shouted against the godless Commonwealth. Their bloodlust was contagious, and Erical felt his entity swelling, growing more and more eager.

The navies had collided in the vast open-water battlefield, ship after ship altering course, picking a target. Fire arrows sang through the air like sparks from a grinding wheel. They ignited rigging, sailcloth, deck boards.

One Isharan ship rammed into an opposing Commonwealth vessel with its clenched-fist prow, and both sets of fighters swarmed the decks in a flurry of swords and blood, screams and death.

Each slain Isharan sailor was like a sacrifice, and Erical's godling accepted the blood and strength. She swelled larger, angrier, lashing out in a storm of rainbows and primal lightning linked to the worshippers that fed her . . . and to the priestlord himself. His godling lashed about like an eager dog straining to be free, wanting to lunge—and so Erical released her.

He closed his eyes and breathed a sigh as the deity exploded outward like a white squall. A shimmering whirlwind surged onto the nearest Commonwealth ship, racing up the masts, snapping the yardarms like twigs, smashing the deck hatches. The godling plunged down into the hold and burst out through the hull boards in a multicolored eruption, rocking the ship, tipping it sideways. In a froth of foam and spraying water, she bounded to the next enemy vessel, diving under the water and cracking its keel from below.

Erical could no longer control her, but he laughed with the joy of destruction, of victory.

Building up a great curling whitecap, the godling rolled toward the next ship and slammed into the side, capsizing it. Bodies flew into the air like dust motes, many of them broken and torn apart. Other victims tried to swim to safety, but the godling swept over them and pulled them under and deep.

She was a boiling cauldron of sparks, steam, and aquatic fire. Erical watched her, clenching his fists. His heart twisted in knots of exhilaration and nausea, but he did not try to stop the destructive deity. She roiled forward, finding more targets.

Magda cheered beside the priestlord, pounding her club on the deck. All the Hethrren hooted in a wordless resonant chant, and even that adoration gave the godling more strength and obsession. She continued to expend her energy, her corporeal presence—Erical could feel that—but she was not inclined to stop. The rainbow entity tore through more masts, rigging, sails . . . splintering, shattering, sinking.

In the extensive battle, though, more than half of the Isharan navy was also damaged or sunk. Some ships had already been rammed or on fire before the godling came among them, but other Isharan ships were unintentionally damaged by the fury of their own entity. Though he tried to communicate with her, to rein her in, Erical could not reach the godling through her red haze of energy. She destroyed the enemy, caused absolute chaos among the ships. No one could stand against her.

And Erical loved her.

As the warships reeled and sank, the priestlord wiped away the tears that streamed down his face. Shaking, he held on to the rail and turned to look back at Fulcor Island.

The garrison there was also burning.

42

Maps of Norterra covered the throne room wall, and Mandan studied them for vulnerabilities. He had ordered his cartographers and librarians to bring the overall chart of the kingdom showing the mountains, rivers, lakes, and forests, as well as detailed segments of trade routes over the Dragonspine Mountains, a street-by-street layout of Fellstaff, and a plan of King Kollanan's castle.

With Utho gone off to destroy Ishara, the young konag wanted to do something he could show his mentor when the victorious navy returned home. Determined to bring another punitive force against his intractable uncle, he ordered his Osterran vassal lords to send additional troops to expand his marching army.

Not all of his lords were pleased with the order, reluctant to give up their own security. Mandan paid little heed to their whining.

Two of the fussy lords stood behind him now, Judson and Drune. They waited, fidgeting, while Mandan continued to scrutinize the maps, imagining villages in flames. He finally turned from the charts and fixed his smoldering glare on them. "The reason I requested your soldiers, gentlemen, is so that I can prosecute an attack against Kollanan the Hammer, who defied his true konag's order and thus put the entire Commonwealth at risk."

Judson and Drune each skittered a step back, but Mandan stepped even closer. "Do you intend to defy me as well? That would not be wise."

Only Lord Judson stood his ground, while Drune took shelter behind the larger man's broad shoulders. The konag sharpened his voice. "I've had quite enough of any vassal lord who questions my authority as konag, the ruler of all three kingdoms."

Judson was a round-faced man with a square body. His brown hair was cropped so short that it was barely more than fur against his skull, but an extravagant walrus mustache drooped below his chin. A bright copper bauble was twisted and braided in each tip of the whiskers. Judson thrust out his lower lip. "Why no, my konag! But these are dangerous times, and your order would gut the defenses in our own counties. We can barely protect our holdings as it is."

"Is it not more important to protect Convera?" Mandan demanded. "To stamp out rebellion in the Commonwealth?"

Lord Drune, a frail-looking man with overlarge eyes, seemed old enough to be Judson's father. "But our Bravas have left us for the vengewar, Sire. My holding has only a skeleton force of guards, a small cavalry, a few hundred armed soldiers, and that is not enough to march against Norterra—"

"If we all join together, it will be enough." Mandan's anxiety increased. Why did everyone defy him? Did they dare push him around because Utho was gone? He was still the konag!

The thought of Utho made him glance toward the throne room doors, where his two new Bravas stood at attention, as always. Tytan and Jennae had accepted their role as bodyguards, though the woman's morose demeanor made it clear that she would rather have been slaughtering Isharan animals.

Following Mandan's gaze, the two vassal lords glanced at the black-garbed warriors.

"My own Bravas will lead our punitive strike once all the armies are gathered, but first I need your troops!" Mandan tried to make himself intimidating, the powerful leader of the Commonwealth. "Tell me that your forces are on the way, as ordered . . . or shall I have you escorted back home to lead the soldiers yourselves?"

"Our, uh, soldiers have . . . been informed of the summons, my konag," said Judson. "But Lord Drune and I were hoping we could make you see reason."

It was exactly the wrong thing to say. Mandan's nostrils flared. Tytan and Jennae approached the visiting vassal lords, simmering with the potential for violence.

Mandan's automatic response was to lash out and emphasize his authority, but uncertainty made his voice grow shrill. "As konag, I alone establish priorities for the Commonwealth. It is not my purpose to explain every decision to underlings. It is your *duty* to follow my commands!"

Mandan's father would have scolded him for such an overbearing attitude, but Conndur the Brave had never been as much a mentor as Utho had been. While his father always seemed disappointed in him, the Brava was more patient, showing his loyalty toward the konag and to the crown prince. For the hundredth time, Mandan wished Utho were here, but he needed to prove himself.

His expression tightened as he thought of his fragile queen, with whom he'd been so suddenly smitten, only to realize he'd just been fooling himself. Lira was not the woman he had imagined her to be, not warmhearted like his mother. The girl might have been similar to Maire in appearance, but their hearts were so different.

Right now, Queen Lira was probably huddled in their royal suite, in a stupor from drinking milk of the blue poppy. Someday, she would take too much and succumb to a "sleeping sickness," the way Maire had done. He gritted his teeth. That day couldn't come soon enough.

He spoke gruffly to the recalcitrant vassal lords. "While Utho and my great invasion fleet conquer Ishara, the rest of my army must gather here in Convera. I will command them myself." He gestured toward the bloody painting on the wall that depicted the Battle of Yanton. He needed to build his own legacy, make his own decisions, not simply hide in the shadow of his bonded Brava.

Lord Drune fidgeted. "Back home, Sire, my army is positioned to defend against outside threats. Both King Adan and King Kollanan warned about the returning wreths. What if wreth armies come marching—"

Mandan rounded on him. "What if I have a headsman lop off your head so I can give your county to a more amenable lord?"

The skittish man paled, and Mandan was pleased to see the reaction. The two Bravas regarded him with approval. The young konag smiled, prepared to continue his lecture, when noises in the corridor interrupted him, hard boot-steps coming at a brisk and confident pace. Tytan and Jennae turned toward the open doors, as if expecting an attack.

A visitor strode in unannounced, flaunting distinctive Utauk garments in green and white. His long brown hair had been tied back in a ponytail, and he held a wide-brimmed leather hat in one hand. He was a handsome, thin-faced man with a cleft in his chin, perhaps ten years older than Mandan, and he seemed aloof, even rakish.

Mandan suddenly recognized him. "I know you. You came bearing an ulti-matum from the sandwreth queen." He felt sick as he remembered Queen Voo's demand that he rush to the southern deserts so he could bow and scrape be-fore her. Mandan had dispatched one of his vassal lords instead, and the angry queen had returned the man melted and crammed into a box, but still alive. Mandan's skin crawled as he thought of the horror. "What does Voo want now?"

"I am Donnan Rah," the man said with a flourish of his hat. "Yes, I de-livered Queen Voo's message at the request of your brother, King Adan of Suderra. The Utauks, however, have no allegiance to the sandwreths, and my message is not from Queen Voo, sir."

Mandan realized that this man had not bowed or even formally acknowl-edged his rank. "Sir"? Not "Sire"? Not "my konag"? He was immediately on edge.

The messenger continued, "I bear a decree for all to hear." He reached into his travel-dusted jerkin and pulled out a folded document. With a snap of his wrist he opened the letter and held it out so he could read aloud. He seemed overbearing as he spoke, pitching his voice with heavy import. The words rolled out as if he didn't even need to read them.

"By decree of the rightful kings of Suderra and Norterra, and by the laws laid out in the Commonwealth charter, Mandan, who sits on the throne in Convera Castle, is no longer deemed worthy to wear the crown of konag."

Lords Judson and Drune audibly gasped and stepped away from Mandan, as if he had just shown symptoms of a terrible plague. Tytan and Jennae bristled, and their expressions darkened.

The Utauk messenger kept speaking in a firm voice. "For his failure to provide requested aid to the kingdom of Norterra against the frostwreth threat, Mandan is delinquent in his duties as ruler of the three kingdoms. By dispatching an unprovoked force of murderous marauders to attack an innocent town in Norterra, Mandan has demonstrated that he lacks the humanity necessary to be a good ruler, and is therefore unworthy of the crown."

Donnan Rah cleared his throat, pausing to let the words sink into the ominous silence in the throne room. "For these and other crimes, Mandan is hereby removed from his position and will be sent into exile, unless additional punitive measures are required. King Adan Starfall and King Kollanan the Hammer will march their armies to Convera in order to secure the new rule and ensure a peaceful transition of power."

Mandan felt as if he would explode. The pair of vassal lords looked at him in horror and confusion, and he was suddenly outraged that they had witnessed the reading of this humiliating message. "This is . . . treason!"

Lord Judson muttered, "It is not treason if you're no longer the true konag."

Mandan spun in desperation, searching for Utho, and his gaze fell upon the two other Bravas. They would have to do.

Donnan Rah held up the letter again and spoke in a rush as if he knew his time was short. "Furthermore, the Brava Utho has been found to be responsible for far more heinous crimes. Not only did he betray and disgrace his fellow Brava Elliel, an innocent woman, Utho stands accused of murdering Konag Conndur the Brave with his own hands."

The last words struck like a boulder hurled from a catapult. Reeling, Mandan shouted, "Isharans butchered my father on Fulcor Island! I was there." The thunderclap of horrific memories roared up, nearly blinding and deafening him. He could never forget that night.

"No, that is not true. Utho is the one who killed him, although he made it look like the Isharans were to blame. The Brava training master Onzu discovered the truth and sent the information to King Kollanan."

Tytan and Jennae glowered, both of them deeply alarmed. They placed hands on their sword hilts, but didn't seem to know which enemy to face.

"No, the Isharans killed him," Mandan insisted. "Not Utho."

Donnan Rah repeated what he'd been told. "You were deceived as well. Utho sealed himself in the konag's bedchamber on Fulcor Island and hacked

him to pieces so that it would look like the work of Isharans. He wanted provoke a vengewar . . . exactly the vengewar that he now fights."

"Seize him," Mandan cried. "Take that messenger and silence him!"

Jennae ripped the decree from Donnan Rah's hands, and the young
konag continued to roar until his throat was raw. "Lock him up! Stop him
from spreading these vile lies any further." Mandan's head pounded, and
he couldn't see, even though he blinked and blinked. "No one else can be
allowed to hear that message."

"But it has already been widely—" the Utauk began in a haughty voice,
and Tytan struck him across the face, a blow hard enough to split his lip and
knock out one of his teeth to clatter like an ivory bauble on the floor of the
throne room.

The Brava woman snatched Donnan Rah's arms and pulled his elbows
behind him. He wriggled in a futile attempt to break free. "That is a legal
decree, drawn from the Commonwealth charter. *Cra*, I'm an Utauk. We are
neutral—"

"One cannot be neutral in accusing the konag," Mandan said. He couldn't
think of what to do. How could anyone even consider that Utho had murdered Conndur the Brave? The two were friends, bound companions! Mandan recalled the blood, the scattered body parts, the look on his father's dead
face, the stench of death. Utho could never have done that! Only Isharans
were capable of such cruelty.

He barked orders to the Bravas. "Make sure that no word of this gets out."

He swung his gaze to the vassal lords, both of whom had turned pale,
staring in disbelief and uncertainty. Panic rolled off them, but he also saw
a flicker in their expressions. They actually thought such nonsense might
be true! Not only did they think Utho capable of such crimes, but they had
heard the decree stripping Mandan of his crown.

In his own studies, he had of course read the charter, and he compre-
hended the basics enough to realize that this political maneuver could rip the
Commonwealth apart. Mandan would have to stand up against these traitors
and prepare for the rebel army that would be on the way.

He growled at Tytan. "Place the Utauk in a prison cell beneath the castle
and secure these two vassal lords."

"Sire, we've done nothing!" squealed Lord Drune.

"We are your loyal subjects," Judson said, puffing his lips and jiggling the
ornamental baubles at the tips his mustache.

Mandan could never let them go now that they had heard the decree. Either man could let the news slip, spread dangerous rumors. What if they
decided to throw in their lot with Adan and Kollanan?

"Place them in separate rooms where they can contemplate."

Tytan and Jennae drew their long swords and loomed over the intimidated lords.

Mandan continued, "The first thing I want these two 'loyal' men to do is write a letter to be dispatched to their holdings. They will order their armies—all of their armies—to march to Convera right away. We must prepare before those invaders come over the mountains."

43

As Utho continued up the cliffside to smash his way into the garrison, followed by the two other Bravas and hundreds of Commonwealth soldiers, he heard the cold breeze whistle around the cliffs like distant screams. Maybe it was indeed distant screams. . . .

From his high, precarious position on the cliff, he glanced out to sea and felt a sickening anger as the monstrous godling rampaged across the water like a wild bull made out of storms. The unnatural entity snapped the masts of Commonwealth ships, shredded the blue sails, capsized the armored vessels. The wreckage of the fleet looked like a stand of deadwood flattened by a tornado.

Because he was too far away to fight the thing, Utho let loose a howl of frustration. No matter how well armed the ships were, they did not stand a chance. And he could not help!

But he could take Fulcor.

He glanced down and saw the two blazing ramers of Wendir and Arrick, heard the clamor of hundreds of vengeful fighters working their way up the cliff stairs. Utho reminded himself that his battle was here. The garrison gates were his foe. He shouted to the Bravas on the landing just below. "We take the fortress. Throw out these vermin."

Wendir looked battered from fighting even before they reached the harbor cove. Her face was red with effort and with anger. "Once we have the garrison, we can defeat the rest of them. Fulcor!"

Utho bounded up the last stairs to the sheltered cleft and the secure gates inside. He did not know how the Isharans had captured the garrison in the first place. He had left a skilled Brava here as watchman—Klea—but she had failed. This time, he and his fighters would take over the fortress. He was Utho of the Reef, and today he would be Utho the Conqueror.

From above, the Isharan defenders continued hurling rocks and shooting arrows. A barrel of oil tumbled over the verge and fell spinning end over end as it caught fire from a rag wick. The barrel crashed down on the dock far below and shattered in a spray of oil and splinters. The fire caught on the second docked Commonwealth ship. On the adjacent pier, the *Glissand* was still burning, its sails smoldering, although Mak Dur's crew scrambled to save their vessel.

An arrow whizzed past Utho's face as he clung to the metal stairs, and he lashed with his ramer, burning the arrow. A storm of projectiles buzzed around them like angry hornets, and the fiery blade struck several more away. Behind him, his soldiers raised their shields, but not before at least three were caught by the barbed shafts and toppled over the edge, dropping to their deaths.

Ignoring the screams as his fighters fell, he charged faster, plunging into the rock cleft, just as five Isharans emerged from the shadows. The fools thought they could command the bottleneck here, that they could stop the onrushing Commonwealth army. Only five of them? Against *him*?

He threw himself into the cluster of defenders, striking them with his incandescent blade, shattering their shields, melting their swords. He killed them all, one after another, and kicked their smoldering bodies aside so that he faced the thick gate that blocked the passage into the fortress.

Wendir and Arrick arrived behind him, and their ramers illuminated the shadowed cleft. A swarm of Isharan soldiers on the other side of the iron-reinforced barricade hurled insults as they swung shut the heavy gate. Utho noticed the repaired hinges, the charred wood of the door . . . and realized that the barrier had been severely damaged when these Isharans wrested the garrison from Klea.

The defenses had not yet been restored to their previous state.

Utho used his ramer like a battle ax and smashed at the blackened wood. Beside him, with her fiery blade, Wendir melted the iron hinges. Cherry-red rivets popped out of the scorched wood. Working together, the three Bravas pummeled, burned, and chopped, until the gate shuddered and cracked. The last iron hinge groaned, unable to hold the weight, and the heated metal twisted and broke. Utho kicked hard with his boot, and the other two Bravas slammed against the barrier, which finally toppled inward.

Utho was the first, followed by a wave of soldiers like enraged hornets. They charged through the passageway and up into the garrison in a sudden swirl of bodies and weapons.

The foreign defenders faced them, wearing red capes and scaled armor, wielding curved Isharan swords.

The sharp tips of so many blades pointed toward him looked like a forest of spines, but Utho flung himself into the mob without hesitation. "I am Utho of the Reef—and Fulcor is mine!"

He, Wendir, and Arrick drove back the first lines of defenders, killing many and scattering more. Behind them, Commonwealth soldiers flooded inside, ready for battle. They filled the enclosed parade ground in front of the keep, and within moments any coordinated military plans fell into chaos.

Some of these fighters had been with Utho during the previous attempt to recapture Fulcor. Back then, they had tasted shame and defeat, watched many comrades killed and ships sunk. Today was their own private vengewar.

The garrison became a bloody free-for-all. The Bravas mowed down their opponents two and three at a time with their ramers. The air roared with screams and the clash of metal against metal, and the sounds echoed within the stone walls.

Isharan archers from lookout posts fired arrows down into the invaders, but Isharan and Commonwealth forces swiftly mingled so that arrows could no longer be used.

The garrison commander, a man distinguishable by his golden breastplate and distinctive insignia, stood on the stone steps in front of the keep. He bellowed orders, trying to direct his forces into a defensive phalanx, but his words were cut off in a gurgle as a thrown dagger blossomed in his throat. Arrick, who had hurled the knife with his free hand, turned to Utho with a satisfied nod.

The Isharan garrison commander collapsed into the arms of his horrified troops. They roared in outrage and dove into the fight, and Utho and his companions were glad to oblige.

As Commonwealth soldiers swarmed in, bodies fell everywhere. Though Utho was swept up in a blood haze, he realized that their casualties were horrific, but he did not count the cost. The only thing that mattered was retaking this garrison. If he was the only one left standing at the end of the day, then so be it.

In the melee, Utho spotted a bland-faced Isharan foot soldier who fought like a madman, slaying Commonwealth attackers right and left. Holding a sword in each hand, he fought with equal dexterity. Corpses began to pile up around him like a fortress wall of flesh, but even as the dark-haired man fought and killed, his expression remained empty. He showed no fear, no anger. His moves were swift and liquid.

Utho decided to kill him.

A Commonwealth soldier threw himself against the exceptional fighter, somehow slipped through the man's defenses, and landed a solid sword strike. The edge of the blade hacked into the Isharan's arm, and should have sheared through the skin and bone—but the steel merely clanged off the bared biceps as if it had struck stone! The sword skittered harmlessly off the enemy's skin, and the expressionless Isharan used that moment of surprise to skewer him through the heart.

Grinning, Utho pushed his way through the battle, one hand hacking with the ramer, the other swinging a sword, clearing a path to his target.

The other two Bravas spread out in the courtyard, wreaking more carnage. Wendir shouted, rallying soldiers behind her and gesturing with her ramer to charge the doors of the keep. Suddenly, an arrow buried itself deep in her shoulder, despite her finemail armor. She staggered and stumbled, looked at the shaft in amazement. Her ramer sputtered as her concentration flickered.

At that moment an Isharan warrior thrust a spear into her side. The Brava gasped, her knees sagged, but she had enough strength to bring her sword around to decapitate the man who had killed her. Then she collapsed to the ground. Her comrades howled and surged forward. Arrick ran after them, ramer blazing.

Utho pursued the dark-haired foot soldier. The man offhandedly killed two more Commonwealth fighters, and then the Brava was upon him, driving him back to the steps that led up the defensive wall.

"It is necessary to kill you." Utho smashed down with his ramer, but the Isharan fighter blocked the blazing weapon with his sword. He danced sideways and backward, then sprang onto the stone steps, gaining height over his opponent.

Utho lurched after the man, undaunted. The steel of the Isharan's sword glowed orange from the ramer's fire, and the heat transmitted through the hilt, surely burning his hand, but the man didn't flinch. The Isharan struck at Utho with his other blade, and Utho parried with his own sword. Pressing forward, the Brava drove his opponent higher up the steps toward the top of the wall.

The battle raged in the parade ground below, but Utho's concentration was focused on his mysterious opponent. The two dueled with a weapon in each hand; steel clashed and skittered, driving one blade back, then parrying.

Utho was amazed at the power of this bland-faced fighter. His ramer heated the other sword, now yellow-hot, and still the opponent gripped the hilt. Utho slipped the flaming blade down and struck quickly, burning the man's exposed arm. But instead of cutting into soft flesh, the ramer fire merely left a scorch mark, as if the skin were polished marble.

The Isharan fighter grunted, and Utho hammered him again, amazed. "Who are you? What are you?"

The enemy parried each blow. "Few know my name." He wasn't even sweating with the effort. "And you could not comprehend what I am. But I know you, Utho of the Reef—Brava from Konag Conndur's retinue. Conndur was found dead in his guest quarters here. Did you fail to protect your konag?" The man gave a thin smile. "I was there."

The words made Utho flinch, hesitate. The enemy slashed the red-hot steel past the Brava's face. Utho ducked back just in time, the heat stinging his eyes. As he stumbled, the other man retreated up three more steps, reaching the open expanse of the wall. Utho bounded after him.

"Others say that it was Utho who tried to kill Empra Iluris," the man taunted. "But you are not good enough for that." He lashed out, as if his words were a barbed whip. "Only a Black Eel assassin could meet such a challenge."

"Black Eels are only rumors." Utho struck with the ramer, missed as the assassin slipped away. "What is your name?"

On top of the wall they continued their reckless, furious battle high above the waves that crashed against the reefs. Utho had spent countless hours on guard watch here, staring at those reefs, always alert for enemy Isharan warships. His ramer slashed across the Isharan's chest plate and ripped a smoking line through the leather.

The man's skin was not harmed, and he said, "Our names do not matter, but if you must take it to your grave, let your legacy say that it was Zaha who killed you."

The name meant nothing to Utho, merely foreign sounds. "Your name will be forgotten."

The Black Eel said in a cool, emotionless voice that was somehow more unnerving than a scream, "I am the one who wore your appearance when I attacked Empra Iluris. She fell thinking it was *you* who had killed her."

Utho swiped a gloved hand across his brow. "You did my work for me. I would have been happy to kill her, along with all the Isharan animals."

Zaha stood at the lip of the wall, fighting with both swords, and Utho countered with his own blade and his ramer. Unexpectedly, Zaha flung one of the swords directly at him. The hilt flew toward Utho's face, and he instinctively brought up his sword to defend himself.

In that moment, Zaha tackled the Brava, using all his strength, weight, and momentum in the collision. Somehow, his skin had turned to stone.

Both men toppled backward off the wall, plunging into open air. In the instant of freedom as they fell, disoriented and floating, Utho focused his attention. He drove the flame of his ramer into the center of Zaha's chest, a molten impalement that pierced even the hardened flesh. The weapon burned through the Black Eel's heart and sprouted out the other side.

Falling to the open water and the reefs, Utho held on to the dead man, using his hardened body as a shield as they crashed into the foaming water.

44

A COLD wind accompanied Queen Koru's army, adding a dustfall of snow that created a pristine white path for them as they headed south. The frostwreths marched day after day. The oonuks dragged the battle sleighs or carried armed riders, never seeming to tire.

After the first several days, the accompanying drones spread out from the main army. They had learned to dance out of the way and remain unobtrusive, to avoid becoming food for the wolf-steeds. Koru had issued instructions to her wreths that they were not to harass the drones. Birch knew that all the drones could have fled, vanishing into the wilderness, but instead they chose to race along with the frostwreth army. They stayed for him.

As the pale army covered mile after mile, Birch no longer felt the cold under his thick furs. He would take out the carved pig and rub his thumb over its smooth wood, and he also had his small, sharp knife. Koru had let him keep it.

The army came upon Lake Bakal, and his heart leapt as he looked around the familiar scenery of the area around the village and the lake, where he had grown up . . . the place where the frostwreths had unleashed their winter magic like a frozen wildfire to destroy everything he had known.

Beside him in the sleigh, Mage Elon frowned at the remnants of the collapsed ice fortress. He extended his hand and spread his fingers to pull on small threads of magic that remained in the air, then shook his head in disappointment.

The army didn't pause there, however, but skirted the frozen lake and moved on. Koru's concentration was wholly dedicated to reaching the desert lands as swiftly as possible. When she saw Birch staring at the remnants of his home village, though, she reached out and touched his cheek, puzzled. Only then did Birch realize that tears were rolling down his face.

The queen sounded almost sympathetic. "Why this reaction, boy? It makes no sense. Are you not impressed with our glorious army?"

Birch wiped away his tears, reminding himself that the frostwreth queen wasn't cruel. She just didn't understand. "This was my home. My parents lived here, and so did Tomko and my friends. My schoolteacher was here, and the nice old fisherman who let me ride in his boat. And the trappers who came in with their pelts. There was a man who gave me apples, and . . ." His voice cracked as the memories grew more vivid. Around him he saw things as he remembered them, not as they were right now. "And we had a cat who liked to lie in the sun. But it's all . . . it's all . . ."

Koru looked around, frowning. "Yes, I can see there was a human settlement here, but it's gone now."

"Because frostwreths killed them all!" Birch said. "The town isn't here anymore!"

"Rokk was the one who did that," said Koru. "My mother ordered it, because she wanted to build her fortress here. And she failed in that as well."

"They're still dead," Birch muttered.

"I did not give that order," Koru repeated. She nudged Elon, who pushed the sleigh to greater speed so they could leave Lake Bakal behind. "Now you are with me, and you have opportunities greater than any human could conceive. Think of what we are about to accomplish. Are your circumstances not better than you ever imagined?"

Birch withdrew into himself, surrounded with silence for a long moment. But Koru waited, and he knew she expected an answer. Finally, he found the courage to shake his head. "No."

"Foolish boy." She seemed irritated as the army continued its march.

As they went south, they passed empty villages, where the people had packed up and fled. The frostwreth queen didn't notice anything amiss, but she mused about her expedition to Mount Vada, where she had seen rivers of lava as the world gave birth to hideous dragons, fragments of Ossus himself.

Birch thought of when he had traveled with his mother, father, and Tomko to visit Fellstaff Castle. He remembered the Norterran towns they passed through, especially one old woman who made cherry preserves from her orchard, a goat herder who let the boys play with his animals, a surly innkeeper who disliked children. On one trip to see his grandparents, Birch and Tomko had sat on a log, dangling fish lines into a creek in a contest to see who could catch the biggest trout.

Now he stared at empty barns, fallen paddocks, dry brown cornfields, and vegetable gardens that should have been harvested by now. A dairy cow lowed as if relieved to see people approaching, and several sheep wandered loose. Oonuks fell upon the animals and devoured them.

The queen's sleigh glided along, lifted by a mist of frozen air. The next villages grew closer together and more populated. Some terrified people hid in the forests or fled across the fields, while a few brave but foolhardy men stood ready to defend their homes.

Koru glanced at the defenders, looked down at the boy, and then back at her army. She issued instructions for them not to attack or provoke the humans, as if they were beneath the notice of the frostwreths, and for that Birch was glad.

Soon, the enormous army approached a large city surrounded by high walls. The outlying lands were covered with harvested fields, open pasture-lands, and orchards. Birch could see many people rushing to the protection of the walls. From guard towers and sentry points he spotted flashes of sun-light on armor, human soldiers standing ready.

"Quite a large cluster of human hovels." Koru sounded almost impressed. "I find it remarkable that your people could accomplish such a thing."

Birch was proud to share what he knew, remembering what his mother had taught him. "It is called Fellstaff, the capital of Norterra." This was where his grandfather sat on the throne. Birch wondered if King Kollanan could save him.

From the high wall, Shadri stared out at the frostwreth army that rolled for-ward in a haze of white frost. A glimmer of snow covered the fields, and some of the orchard trees died as the army passed.

Beside her, Pokle's hair stuck out in all directions, even though he had tried to paw it into place with his fingers. The young man glanced at Gant's grim and ugly face as they stood watching. "See, we told you it was a huge army! Hundreds of them."

Shadri knew that Pokle simply did not understand his numbers. "I mark it as several thousand, don't you?"

The Brava stared at the ominous force. "Many thousands."

"That's a lot," Pokle insisted.

They watched and waited, looking at the obdurate wall of enemy fighters coming toward the city. Gant said, "My mission is to protect the people of Fellstaff, but I expected to have more time."

The city's remaining soldiers had been stationed on the perimeter, swords drawn to guard the barricaded gates. Archers lined the high walls.

"We're doomed," Pokle said. "We'll all be wiped out."

Shadri's annoyed glance cowed him more than the frostwreths did, but his conclusions were not wrong. She just absorbed the number of wreth war-riors, mages, wolf-steeds, battle sleighs. She jotted down the details in her journal, but wondered who would ever read the notes she left.

As the huge force approached Fellstaff's northern wall, though, something astonishing happened. The frostwreth army divided in two and continued marching, spreading to skirt the great city. Rather than laying siege to the capi-tal, the frostwreths simply rolled onward, passing on either side of the city, like a river current splitting around a rock.

Even Gant's mouth dropped open. His hand rested against his ramer cuff, ready to ignite the fiery sword and fight as many as he could—but he did not even draw the weapon.

"They're just . . . ignoring us!" Shadri said.

"It's a miracle," Pokle cried.

The frostwreth army did not even slow down as they diverted around the city.

45

AFTER the *Glissand* had crashed against the dock in Fulcor's harbor cove, Utho and the Commonwealth soldiers abandoned the damaged ship and raced to what would surely be their deaths.

While they charged off to their own battles, Mak Dur had no interest in the garrison or the bleak island. His vessel was burning! He had to save his ship. He rallied his crew, and every one of them got to work, though some of them found a moment to tear off their blue armbands.

Running from the bow, the voyagier looked up at the flames that danced along the rigging. The lower corner of the mainsail had caught fire. "Cut the ropes! We have to get the sail off."

One Utauk scrambled up the ratlines with a dagger in his teeth. He scampered across the yardarm and hacked at the ropes until the burning sail dropped free. Mak Dur and two other sailors caught the end of the fabric, but the flames kept licking upward. Two troublesome ropes still held the sail to the mast. "Cut it free!"

Still balanced on the yardarm, the Utauk slashed one more rope, grabbed a corner of the sailcloth, and jumped. He swung down, dangling, and then cut the last rope. He let go at the last moment before crashing into the mast, and dropped to the deck. Mak Dur and his companions dragged the burning canvas over the side, tossing it into the water.

Arrows rained down on them from above, some covered in burning pitch. When the projectiles thunked into the deck boards, Mak Dur was reminded of a violent hailstorm at sea. One sailor yelped when an arrow struck his shoulder, but he yanked it free.

On the adjacent dock, nearer the cliff stairs, the second Commonwealth ship was fully engulfed in flame. It had been severely damaged when it limped into the harbor, and a burning barrel from above had sealed its fate. Flaming oil exploded across the decks, and many Commonwealth sailors dove overboard screaming; others were killed by a barrage of arrows.

Next, the Isharans concentrated their attack on the *Glissand*, even as Utho and the attackers stormed the fortress above. More missiles pelted down, and a large rock shattered one of the ship's yardarms and punched a hole through the deck. Mak Dur cursed up at the garrison wall, and then cursed Utho and Konag Mandan for trapping his beautiful ship in this impossible situation. Now it looked as if they would all perish in this foolish conflict.

His crew had retrieved every bucket they could find, tied ropes to them, dropped them down to the water, and hauled up load after load to douse the flames. More rigging rope had to be cut free. The crew moved swiftly in their loose Utauk garments, but at the moment Mak Dur wished they had heavy armor to protect them. An arrow zipped over his back, barely missing his neck, and clattered on the deck in front of him. He kicked it aside as if it were a viper that had landed at his feet.

A veteran crewman fell when an arrow struck him in the breast, and he spilled his water bucket. With projectiles raining all around him, Mak Dur raced to the man and dragged him to the meager shelter of stacked crates.

Stones and shards continued pelting down. One sharp rock clipped the voyagier on the side of his head, stunning him. He fell to his knees and touched a shallow gash that bled profusely. He cursed again, and focused on the arrow in his companion's chest, glad to see that the barbs hadn't penetrated far into the skin. "It's not deep."

"*Cra*, hurts like a demon turd," the sailor hissed.

Without warning Mak Dur yanked it free. The other man cried out and blood began to flow, but the voyagier pressed the sailor's shirt against the wound. "Hold that. Take shelter." More arrows pattered on the deck, and he howled up at the sky. "Damn you!"

The bombardment tapered off when the Commonwealth soldiers managed to break into the garrison and engaged in fierce combat up there. Black smoke roiled up from burning structures inside the fortress. Several dead soldiers—from both sides—crashed down the cliffs, from the walls above.

The Utauks fought their own battle at the docks. Flames began climbing the *Glissand*'s foremast, like a tall tree in a forest fire. If his crew didn't work together to extinguish those flames, arrows or no arrows, his beloved ship would sink right here in this bleak foreign harbor.

Out on the open sea beyond the reefs, he could see that most of the Commonwealth navy had already been wrecked, so many ships smashed and sunk. He'd been busy trying to rescue his ship, but he now watched with horror as the godling wrought havoc throughout the fleet. But many Isharan ships had been destroyed as well, some burning, some smashed. Mak Dur felt a chill, remembering the carnage that the Serepol godling had caused in the Isharan harbor, not long ago.

He drew a circle around his heart. "The beginning is the end is the beginning." Groaning below him, the injured sailor repeated the phrase.

❦

Out on the water Priestlord Erical felt wrung out, frayed, and euphoric. He couldn't believe what he and his beloved godling had done. Around him, ringing in his ears, the howls and mayhem continued. The fighting was not over yet, but Erical didn't think he or the godling could do any more. They were both spent.

Now it was up to Magda and her Hethrren.

The godling had rampaged across the enemy navy, flinging ships about, shattering hulls, splintering masts like a child having a tantrum with his toys. Captain Gaus had barked orders for his crew to shift the sails, align the ropes, pull the rudder. With a push of godling magic, the flagship drove toward the nearest Commonwealth vessel, even as the weary deity ranged wider over the waves, showering up waterspouts and drawing down lightning. Connected with the godling, Erical could feel her expending the prayers, faith, and anger of the Isharans, the blood sacrifices she had been fed.

The flagship careened toward its target, and the barbarians lined up at the rail, bellowing challenges, waving clubs, spears, and swords. The godless sailors waited for them, already terrified. Captain Gaus intended to ram them with his prow's iron fist, but the Commonwealth captain tacked to the side, turning so that the Isharan ship merely caromed off the hull.

But the vessels were close enough, and Magda took four running steps across the deck, leaped up on the rail board, and bounded across to the other deck. She landed on her thick legs and then became a fury, swinging her club, cracking skulls, smashing faces. More Hethrren swarmed over with blades, broadaxes, spiked clubs.

The godless soldiers fought back, killing several barbarians, and enraging the Hethrren. Magda slaughtered twice as many after seeing some of her companions fall.

Left behind on the flagship, Erical slumped in an exhausted daze. His godling had gone mad, doing things she had never done before, burning bright with the fuel of Isharan anger. She overextended herself, but did not retreat.

Finally when the priestlord sensed that the entity's presence was wispy and ethereal, he grew fearful. They were far from the sanctuary of Prirari, and she could not hide behind the shadowglass window and recover in her own realm. "Return to me," he whispered. Nearby, the clamor of battle on the Commonwealth ship was deafening, but he knew she would hear him through their bond.

Magda and her Hethrren killed every enemy sailor and threw the bodies into the sea. After they dispatched the last fighters, they took glee in spilling oil across the blood-soaked deck and setting the ship on fire. Magda was laughing as she bounded back aboard the Isharan flagship, ignoring the flames that rose behind her.

Captain Gaus scowled at her. "That was a perfectly good warship. We could have commandeered it for the Isharan navy."

"We have our own ship," Magda said.

Gaus growled. "And we lost dozens here in the battle."

She just huffed, not caring.

Erical crouched against the side wall and concentrated on the gossamer threads that connected him to the godling. "Return to me before it's too late."

The entity was little more than misty fragments when she coalesced near him on the deck, just a spark compared to the rainbow bonfire she had been during her rampage. His godling would need to recover. Right now as the deity swirled around him, Erical gave her whatever strength he could, but the Isharan survivors would have to sacrifice to her.

Joined with him, she brightened and shimmered in the air above the deck.

When Erical rose to his feet on shaking legs, he turned in a slow circle to survey the damage to the Commonwealth fleet. Some vessels were burning, some shattered, some listing sideways and sinking. Farther away on Fulcor Island, he saw, the garrison buildings were also on fire. "Such destruction," he said.

Standing nearby, Captain Gaus scratched his thick square-cut beard and wiped blood from his forehead. "Far worse than I imagined. I will never underestimate your godling, Priestlord."

"I'm not sure she could do it again," Erical said. "We should sail home. She needs her own land, her temple, her worshippers. Otherwise, she will fade away."

"Sail back home?" Magda bellowed. "After this victory?" She raised her bloodied club. "You are a ridiculous little man."

Erical shook his head. "It is not possible for us to continue now. We can't go to the old world."

"We have to conquer our new lands!" Hearing their leader, other Hethrren stomped on the deck.

Gaus shaded his eyes and looked around the carnage in the water. "I count ten Isharan vessels still intact. It is not enough of an invasion force."

"Ten ships, but the enemy has none!" Magda said. "We smashed them all. If we go to the old world now, they'll have no one to defend them."

Erical pointed to the burning Fulcor garrison. "Shouldn't we go there? Help those people?"

"They're on their own." Magda drew herself up, menacing the captain. "The rest of your ships have many Hethrren aboard, and that's a fighting force better than anything in your history. The battle here is finished, and victory is ours. We won't stay to pick up the pieces or help the weak and dying." She glanced across the water, saw the red-striped sails of the few intact

Isharan warships. "Send your signals, Captain. We take these ten ships and sail onward."

Gaus remained silent for a long moment, considering. Erical wasn't sure whether the captain was intimidated by Magda or whether he agreed with her. In the end, he ordered the signal flags raised, calling the remnants of his navy.

The ten ships set their sails and headed west toward new lands to conquer.

46

After he seized the treasonous decree and imprisoned the Utauk messenger, Konag Mandan retreated to his quarters to sulk. Utho had instructed him never to let others see his weakness or his immature moods. Only his bonded Brava could talk to him like that, and despite his annoyance at the comment, he realized that it was the right advice.

He missed his mentor's counsel, but knew that a konag had to make his own decisions, even difficult ones. He tried to imagine what Utho would say about the open rebellion from Norterra and Suderra.

Sitting in his royal suite, he hunched in the chair before the roaring fire. The chill in his bones went deeper than the cool autumn air. The fire in the hearth seemed hungry, and he was eager to feed it. He read the insulting decree over and over again, rankling at the unfair accusations Kollanan and Adan made against him and Utho. They twisted what had really happened and shifted all blame from themselves! His uncle and brother were the ones who had broken the Commonwealth charter, because neither of those kingdoms had responded to *his* call for assistance in the war against Ishara. As kings, they were responsible for protecting the entire Commonwealth, but instead they wallowed in petty local problems and tavern stories about ancient races and dragons.

He glowered at the letter. His eyes couldn't seem to focus on the terrible things they accused Utho of doing. Why would a bonded Brava kill his konag? It was simply impossible, absurd.

His thoughts returned to that horrible night again and again. No Brava—no *human!*—could possibly have done that to a good man like Conndur the Brave. Only Isharan animals could be so ghastly. The fact that Adan and Kollanan would blame *Utho* for such heinous violence only proved how corrupt they were. They could not be allowed to destroy the three kingdoms like this. Mandan wouldn't let them.

Utho would never do such a thing.

Would he?

He crumpled the decree and threw it into the fire, watching as the paper browned and blackened. Even the fire seemed reluctant to destroy the message, and it took a long time to burn. Mandan gritted his teeth. Why did everything resist him?

Lords Judson and Drune had been locked in guarded guest quarters. His initial instinct had been to toss them into the dungeons along with Donnan Rah, but even his new Bravas advised against the impetuous action. "Your vassal lords are not traitors like those other kings, Sire—not yet," said Tytan in his deep voice. "They merely overheard a false accusation, through no fault of their own."

Jennae had scowled, as she always did. "Next time we will make sure no one enters your presence with such nonsense." Her face looked pinched. "Even so, the two lords cannot unhear the words spoken in front of them. They must be detained."

"But a dank cell may not be necessary," Tytan interjected. "Let them demonstrate their loyalty."

Mandan had conceded. "Yes, I will view it as a test. If they write letters and summon fighters for my army, they may remain in guest quarters, under guard." His face had darkened. "If they refuse, they belong in the dark dungeons with the other rats."

Judson and Drune had obediently dispatched their letters calling their standing armies to Convera, and Mandan was sure their soldiers would arrive forthwith. It gave him enough time to plan how to put down this rebellion, which would likely involve marching his military force over the mountains. He had to move before his enemies did.

The ashes of the decree flaked down into the coals, but its dark stain did not go away. Civil unrest remained in the Commonwealth. Even now, Kollanan and Adan were gathering their armies to oust him from the throne.

And Utho was far away across the sea!

He was startled to hear a low chuckle behind him. He lurched out of his chair and spun to see Lira sprawled on a divan, as if she had collapsed and lain there in a silent stupor. Now she propped herself on one elbow and looked at him with acid in her red-rimmed eyes.

"It's all falling apart for you," she said. "Like a collapsing house. Your first bad decision knocked away a support beam, and then others fell, and the Commonwealth keeps crashing down." She laughed louder. "It keeps crashing down—because of you!"

Mandan snapped, "You don't know what you're saying."

"You sent my father to attack Norterra. Now he's dead and the whole Commonwealth is turning against you. You shouldn't have done that."

He spun toward her, expecting her to flinch and cower as she often did, but this time her expression was defiant. Had she stopped drinking so much poppy milk? He preferred her in a useless dreamlike state.

"That Utauk messenger brought the terrible news." She levered herself into a sitting position. "Don't you think he spoke to other Utauks along the way?

Of course he did! Don't you think the castle servants are whispering about what happened? Everyone knows, Mandan." She snickered. "They know the world is falling out from under you, and it is all your fault."

Lira laughed again, and he struck her hard across the face, knocking her back into the cushions. A red splotch appeared on her pale cheek from the blow.

She sniffled, then forced herself to sit up again. "I'm your queen, and I will fall with you. Because of you!"

He felt cold and horrified as he realized what she had said. Had the rumors actually spread out of his control already? He had seized the Utauk messenger, locked him away so he could not reveal the damning message to anyone else . . . but what if Donnan Rah had already spoken to his Utauk friends? What if they distributed the rumor like a pestilence?

He thought of the countless Utauk trading caravans, merchants, and travelers that wound their way across all three kingdoms. What about all the vendors in the public markets who bought Utauk goods, the innkeepers who lodged riders, Utauk processions that did business in the capital city and then camped along the river roads?

And what about the barge captains, the workers plying their trades up and down the Bluewater and Crickyeth Rivers, and the cargo ships that sailed down the coast? They would all be talking.

Mandan felt his skin crawl. How could he stop it?

He turned away from Lira, who huddled back on the sofa, nursing her fresh bruise but satisfied with the harm she had inflicted on him.

He had few enough soldiers left in Convera after the great navy sailed off to Ishara. How would his smaller standing army react if they heard the lies about Utho murdering Konag Conndur? Mandan knew his mentor better than anyone, better even than his father had. Utho was loyal, dedicated, and had saved Mandan's life several times already.

Tytan and Jennae, his new protectors, did not believe Utho could have committed such crimes—but others would, and he could never stop the whispers. Maybe some of his soldiers would desert in the night, forsaking their duty to defend the Commonwealth and simply riding away.

Mandan needed to take action before the rumors could undermine him further. He strode to the entrance of his chamber and flung open the heavy door. As the iron hinges creaked, he felt a chill. The sound reminded him of the door to his guest quarters on Fulcor Island, when he had crept out to discover his butchered father. . . .

Utho would never have done that.

Mandan called out for the two Bravas, and they rushed in to see if he was in danger. He announced, "I trust no one else. My own soldiers may be weakening, and I need to do something about it. That Utauk messenger spread the word among his own people before he delivered the decree to us. I'm sure of it." He growled deep in his throat. "For that reason alone I should chop off his head."

"Shall I?" Jennae sounded eager.

"Later. First I want you to dispatch teams into the city. If the Utauks are spreading sedition, we have to snuff it out. Go to the markets, ride along the river road, round up all of the Utauks, detain any caravans."

Tytan looked troubled. "Are you certain, my konag? The Utauk tribes have always clung to neutrality, and they have served—"

"They've been spies for generations, I am convinced of it! Their trading ships traveled to Ishara even during the war. What were they telling the foreign empra about us?" He shook his head as he stood at the door. "I want them where I can control them. Silence any further rumors."

The two Bravas set off, shouting for captains of the city guard and preparing to enforce the konag's orders.

Several hours later, though, they returned to Mandan, disturbed and defeated with their report. All of the Utauk tribes had packed up and vanished. They had disappeared from Convera like a puff of smoke.

Shifting on his throne beside the red-themed painting on the stone wall, Mandan felt queasy with anger and uncertainty. He understood just how much he had depended on Utho's wise counsel, but now he feared that Utho himself was the problem.

It couldn't be true.

The decree sickened him, as did the thought that the vanished Utauks were even now spreading foul lies throughout Convera, maybe across the entire Commonwealth. Not only did Adan and Kollanan want to remove Mandan from the konag's throne, but also they accused Utho of murdering Conndur and declaring war on Ishara.

He wanted answers, wanted to make firm decisions and have every person in the three kingdoms obey him. Instead, he felt as if he had been propped up in a blocky ornate chair. Tytan and Jennae remained in the throne room, ready to guard him against attack—the very idea of which would have seemed ridiculous, but for the accusations and unrest already spreading in the streets.

"I don't believe it," Mandan said.

"You should not," Jennae replied.

Two burly dockworkers appeared at the throne room accompanied by a bearded fisherman. All three seemed distraught. The dockworkers carried a long and heavy object wrapped in canvas.

Mandan rose from his throne. "What is this?"

The thing inside the long burden oozed liquid that seeped through and stained the fabric. The smell arrived faster than the men did. Tytan and Jennae stepped in front of Mandan, ready to drive off any unwanted visitor.

The bearded fisherman carried a basket, which also stank of fish slime and rot. "It is something you must see, my konag."

"He found this caught in the weeds just beneath the bluff," said one of the dockworkers, nodding toward the man in the front. "Called us to help him bring it in."

The fisherman said, "I take my boat up against the sandstone because I like to catch fish in the weeds there. A lot of flotsam washes up right above the confluence."

Uninvited, the dockworkers trudged forward with their heavy package, which was as large as a rolled rug. Or a body.

"Take that away. It stinks," Mandan said.

Openly defying him, they dropped their load on the floor. It made a soft but ominous thud. Mandan stepped down from the dais, glaring at his two Brava guards. "Take them away. I don't want to see it!"

The dockworkers pulled the stained canvas aside to reveal a bloated, headless body that had been in the water for some time. It was dressed in Brava black, clearly identifiable.

"Don't know where it came from, Sire," said the second dockworker, "but it was in the weeds right below the window openings in the bluff above." He paused as if his meaning weren't clear. "The passages right underneath your castle."

The fisherman opened his basket and stepped forward. "And this head washed up in the eddies around there. See, the neck stump is cauterized—cut through with a hot blade." He lifted the swollen, fish-pecked head of a dead man, bald and unrecognizable. The stump had clearly been seared by ramer fire. "Don't know who it is, but it seems to me like one Brava killed another."

The first dockworker said, "Cut off his head and dumped the body from above."

"Another Brava . . ." Mandan muttered, then sucked in a quick gasp. "Utho killed him!"

The three men backed away. "Utho," the fisherman said.

One dockworker said in a harsh whisper, "The konag's bonded Brava!"

"Get them out of here," Mandan yelled.

The three men fled, and Mandan realized too late that they were leaving the decapitated corpse behind.

Utho . . . Mandan couldn't believe it, even if the answer seemed obvious.

He knew that the dockworkers and fisherman rushing away would believe it. Before long, the rumors would spread throughout Convera.

The stench of the dead Brava nauseated him. His eyes stung, and he couldn't see. The young konag stumbled away from the dais. Tytan and Jennae called after him, but he couldn't hear, couldn't concentrate. He rushed away to find a place where he could lock the door.

47

❧

CEMI believed in Empra Iluris. To her, that made the locks of her ash-blond hair feel magical. She had faith that her mentor would return to power, and the people needed that encouragement as soon as possible . . . but Iluris still seemed strangely weak and disoriented. She wasn't ready to overthrow Key Priestlord Klovus—physically or mentally—but she needed to be. Meanwhile, Cemi had to keep faith burning among the loyal citizens.

Strands of the empra's hair seemed to tingle in her hand as Cemi and Analera moved through the streets, meeting their contacts, spreading the word with more urgency than ever. But in the days since Klovus had lit the false funeral pyre, the faith of the people had been shaken. Cemi resolved to change that.

Captani Vos accompanied them, wearing a plain brown jerkin that left his muscular arms bare. He hid a knife in his jerkin, but left the long sword behind, and he seemed to feel naked without his armor. As a hawk guard, he normally kept his dark hair neatly trimmed and his face shaved and oiled, but after he had hidden for so long underground, his hair was shaggy, and a beard covered his cheeks. He looked rough and haggard, and could easily be mistaken for a common tradesman.

Analera clung to her lock of Iluris's hair. "This should convince them, shouldn't it? I can feel the magic of the empra's presence."

"It may convince some of them," Cemi said quietly, "but we've made promises for too long. After that funeral pyre, the people are discouraged and have no reason to believe us anymore." She shook her head. "They need to see Iluris herself, but if they see her as she is now, they may still give up. You and I support her." She swallowed hard. "But how can she fight? She can barely stand for a few minutes."

Vos glanced around the streets with hunted eyes. Temple guards went about the key priestlord's business, and priestlords were accompanied by an entourage of ur-priests and acolytes. Vos placed a firm hand on Cemi's shoulder, and she absorbed the warmth of his touch. He looked at her with great concern. "I will protect you both—for as long as it takes." He lowered his eyes and sighed. "But how can we make Mother Iluris strong enough?"

"The new godling will help her." Analera pointed to a small gathering square in front of them. "We expect many of the empra's strongest followers up ahead, because we sent out the word. Their faith hasn't faltered yet." She clutched the lock of hair in her hand. "We just need to give them hope again."

They entered the square through a warren of Serepol's back alleys that had not been touched by the godling's rampage or the Hethrren ransacking.

A crowd had gathered, drawn by a common cause. Men, women, and children dressed in varying garments, from all professions, all strata of society. Cemi was glad to observe how many had responded to the message they had sent. These people were still faithful to Empra Iluris, still clung to a spark of unrealistic hope. They chanted in hypnotic unison, "Hear us, save us! Empra Iluris, hear us, save us!" They waved banners from the palace. Someone had even constructed an effigy of a regal-looking woman dressed in the bright imperial clothes Iluris had often worn in public.

"She is not dead," shouted someone. "Our empra will return."

"Hear us, save us. Hear us, save us!"

Analera held up the lock of hair. "Iluris lives! She sent you a part of her as promise that she will come back. You will see soon." The crowd stirred, responding to strangers on the perimeter. The old servant handed a few hairs to a wine seller she recognized.

Moving quickly through the crowd, Cemi and Vos passed out a couple of hairs to one supporter after another.

Vos leaned close to Cemi, concerned. "We must remain alert. We may need to leave quickly."

Analera pushed forward, waving the lock of hair like a talisman. "This belongs to Iluris. The key priestlord lied to you all! Her body did not burn. Her hair did not burn. Your empra is alive."

Some people shouted out, ecstatic with the news. "She did not burn! Empra Iluris is alive. Hear us, save us!" Even though Cemi knew the words to be true, she could see that the people's belief was desperate.

"Then why won't she show herself? Where is she?"

Cemi looked around the square, troubled. The empra's supporters had never been so open before. Cemi, Analera, and Vos had wanted to encourage them, but so loud a response could not be wise. The people's faith swelled so that it fairly sparkled in the air. The cheering became boisterous.

Cemi heard horses, the jingle of armor, city guards approaching. The crowd stirred. Vos grabbed Analera's arm. "Come, we must drop back into the alleys where we can hide."

"No, we have to pray for the empra," the old servant said, yanking her arm free. "To strengthen the godling. And to make her stronger."

The crowd continued its chant.

Cemi felt a great urgency at the sound of the armed city guard approaching, closing off exits from the trading square. "He's right. We don't dare let ourselves be captured and interrogated."

The wine merchant waved his strands of Iluris's hair, shouting with an undertone of awe. "This belongs to the empra. I can sense her!" He ran into the crowd just as several ur-priests and armed temple guards closed in.

"Disperse!" a gruff squad leader bellowed. "Or Key Priestlord Klovus will bring his godling to clear you out."

"So he can destroy the rest of the city?" another man yelled. "We already learned our lesson!"

"This gathering is out of hand," Vos warned in a quiet voice, urging Cemi to the alley. "Was it too soon? She will be strong enough any day, I am certain."

Cemi shook her head. "We've been telling them that for too long."

As ur-priests and soldiers rode into the square, confusion swirled through the crowd. Many dispersed, running away, but a few stood defiant, and the ur-priests directed the guards to arrest them.

Dismayed, old Analera called, "But it is time! The empra promised she would act soon." She turned to Cemi as Vos tried to whisk her away. "We need to prepare the way."

For weeks, Cemi had inspired supportive groups around Serepol, but they needed something concrete to cling to. When Iluris awakened, Cemi had naïvely expected an instant solution to the crisis. But the empra had been sleeping for so long, and remained so weak and frail, that not even the strange new godling could magically restore the crown.

Chamberlain Nerev had tried to put Cemi forward as the new empra, and Klovus had murdered him. Too late, Cemi realized that she should have stepped forward then and made her claim before the key priestlord secured more power. But she had clung to hope for Iluris—not a false hope, but a misplaced one—and Klovus took advantage of the power vacuum.

Analera scuttled beside them as they discreetly escaped the square. "Come, we have to go to Boorlin's forge. He was one of the empra's staunch advocates before he disappeared. Our supporters still gather there to gain information so they can go out and spread the word."

Vos muttered with displeasure as they moved through winding backstreets toward the blacksmiths' district. "Boorlin and the others have surely been killed."

"No one has seen his body," Analera insisted. "Our people have faith that he will come back, just as the empra will."

Inside the split-rail fence that bounded the smithy, apprentices still worked the bellows and pulled hot steel from the furnace. Many unlikely people had already gathered around the forge, and few of them looked as if they were in the market for a fine new blade. Several members of the crowd recognized Cemi and Analera.

"We thought the empra would be with you," said one bald man with a sunburned pate. He sounded deeply disappointed. "You said she was coming."

Cemi said, "Soon the empra will reveal herself to Serepol, and she will prove the key priestlord to be a liar and a conspirator. Our rightful ruler will be restored to her throne, and we will be Ishara again." As she spoke, Cemi felt a stirring inside her . . . the new godling. Strength grew in her words, and she raised her voice, building the inspiration. This was how a real empra spoke to her people. Iluris had often coached her, but this was the first time Cemi really felt it in her heart. Her words resounded across the crowd. "I have seen Iluris myself! I've spoken to her. She has recovered from her terrible injury, and every day we work together, discussing how to make Ishara stronger."

"Then why does she hide?" asked a man with a thin voice. "Why is she not here with us?"

"We need her!" someone else wailed.

"Hear us, save us!"

"She's not hiding," Vos said in a loud, clear voice. "She is preparing."

Cemi felt larger than life. She maintained her confidence in front of the supporters, but she could not forget how Iluris sometimes sat staring blankly at the stone wall, how she would touch her face as if she didn't believe she was really there. Once, Cemi had watched the empra extend her hand and stare at the unmistakable tremor, concentrating until she quelled the shakes.

"Soon," Cemi insisted. "It will be soon. You'll see." She took the lock of hair and handed it to the person next to her. "Iluris gave this to me just today. She wanted you to feel it, to know she is with you."

In wonder, the man passed the talisman to the next person and the next, and they muttered and they believed. The apprentices at the forge stared, and their faces were lit with amazement, though covered with grime and soot.

"Spread the word. I know we've made these promises again and again, but now Iluris is awake. She has returned—and you will all see tomorrow." She swallowed. There, she had committed to a time. Vos looked at her in quick surprise, then gave her a confident nod.

The people sighed with relief, some cheering, others laughing and embracing.

Then city guards rode in. Someone had revealed their quiet plotting, and armed soldiers carrying the key priestlord's banner surrounded the district. The alarm went up among the conspirators, and the people scattered.

Vos grabbed Cemi's arm, pulling her with him. Analera pushed Cemi away so hard she stumbled. "Go! Get yourself out of here. I'll find my own way."

The guards galloped in, waving clubs and striking down unarmed citizens. Some soldiers used swords to hack at those who resisted. Screams rose up. The apprentices fled the forge, dropping tongs and hot iron as they bolted out into the streets. Fire caught on the structure of Boorlin's smithy, and flames rolled up, accompanied by black smoke.

"We need to separate." Vos rushed Cemi away. "You are the empra's heir. You must stay safe!"

"Analera!" She was dismayed to see the guards seize the old servant along with a dozen other captives, but there was nothing she could do.

Vos's face darkened as he rushed the young woman through the streets. "We are in great danger. Analera knows where the empra is hiding, and they will torture the information out of her!"

Cemi felt her resolve harden, though. "Now there's no question about it. Iluris has to return to save us all."

48

Blood flew through the air, mixed with shadows and violence. Glik fought by instinct, slashing with the shadowglass dagger and killing wreths. The bright Brava ramers became a focal point for the most intense battles.

Then, as so many sandwreths died around her, one by one, Glik's eyesight turned fuzzy. Feeling detached, she saw echoes, memories, and visions. Grand battles and epic struggles from the past now resonated through magical fault lines in the land.

Barely aware of what she was doing, the girl thrust her obsidian knife forward, felt it cut through flesh—wreth flesh. She had hurt another one.

She blinked, and everything became clear: blood spurting, a golden-skinned warrior looking at her in astonishment. Injured but not killed, he lurched toward her with murder in his eyes, but before he could reach her, he stopped short as a flaming blade sprouted from his chest and sliced downward through his body. The warrior died with a grunt, and smoke boiled out of his mouth.

Cheth stood back, satisfied. "I know you could have killed him yourself, girl, but why waste time?"

Barely holding on to reality, Glik gasped. Her friend rushed to her and clasped her shoulder. "Have you been hurt? Are you all right?"

Glik smeared spatters of red from her cheek, felt the warm liquid as it dried. "Is anything all right?"

Cheth laughed. "Of course! There aren't many wreths left alive. We will kill the last of them soon."

Around her, the girl heard the battle din fading. Her fellow captives fought using whatever weapons they had, many of them snatched from the dead hands of fallen sandwreths. Hundreds of armed human riders swept through the narrow canyons to hunt down any enemy stragglers.

The wreths remained incredulous not only that humans were winning, but that they would fight back at all.

Angry and confident, two sandwreth nobles walked in among the human fighters, as if they could single-handedly punish these upstarts. In seconds, both wreths were cut down and killed. Butchered slave masters lay sprawled in dark pools of blood on the canyon floor.

King Kollanan stalked along, patient and deadly. He swung his war hammer into the shoulder of an approaching enemy who was more methodical than nimble. The warrior looked in shock at his shattered bones as Kollanan swung again and crushed his head. The king continued walking, impervious to the sounds of battle, and delivered a final blow to any wounded wreth who could still fight.

"Three more down that side canyon," Adan shouted to anyone who could hear him. "Cut them off! We outnumber them."

"None will escape," Kollanan growled. His eyes faded from a flare of bloodlust to a dull resignation.

The human fighters tracked down and slew the last of the sandwreths. Glik watched the bodies fall, recognizing most of the guards who had abused the slaves. She felt no sympathy for them. She hated them all.

The battle was over more quickly than Glik expected. She was shaking with exhaustion, a wash of terror, and the exhilaration of survival.

Ari fluttered down to land on her shoulder, and she felt a joyous surge in her heart link. She stroked the sapphire scales, scratched under the reptile bird's chin, and ran her fingers under the mothertear collar. "*Cra*, I'm so glad to have you back! We're together again, inside the circle." She finally allowed herself to believe, and she looked from the ska to Cheth. "Is it over? Are we free? Are all of these prisoners free now?"

The Brava remained ready to strike with her fiery ramer, but she found no more targets. All the sandwreths were dead.

King Adan rode up to them, covered with blood and sweat. "You're Glik. I remember you." He smiled down at her. His long sword, inlaid with shadowglass, was streaked with runnels of red.

"My sister promised that you would rescue us," Glik replied.

"Sorry it took so long." His expression darkened. "So many innocent humans subjugated by the wreths. Queen Penda will be very happy to see you . . . and it'll be your first chance to see our little daughter Oak."

Glik brightened. "Penda had her baby!"

"Even in the world's most terrible times, nature takes its course."

Cheth used her free hand to brush sweaty brown hair from her face. "We'll be glad to ride away with you, Sire."

"We may be exhausted and ill fed, but we're tough." Glik drew a circle around her heart. "And we are ready to be free."

The other Brava woman, Elliel, joined Cheth, and the two surveyed the carnage in the aftermath of the battle. "We'll take all of the prisoners to Suderra," Elliel said. "But we have to move soon. We can't stay here."

Thon was beside her, his dark hair flying loose, his fierce smile full of satisfaction.

On Glik's shoulder, the ska flapped her wings and burbled to Thon in recognition, though the reptile bird also seemed disturbed. When Glik looked at the mysterious wreth man, she felt energy simmer inside her, as if an earthquake were happening in her mind. Reality split into cracks, breaking into fragments and visions.

With a puzzled look, Thon stepped toward Glik, curious about her as well. The girl tried to say something, but then like black water flooding over her consciousness, evil welled up and engulfed her. Suddenly, she could see nothing but an avatar of anger and death, rippling black scales on a reptilian body as large as the world itself. She saw flashing fangs the size of sharpened trees . . . a dragon, but more than that—it was all dragons? No, more than that. Great wings like thunderheads pounded down, and Glik could not escape.

The slitted eye of the dragon, as big as a lake, roiled with impossibility. Ossus! Out on the Plain of Black Glass, she had seen part of the world dragon, the blight torn from the soul of a god. Ossus had stared up at her from the obsidian pools, and now some poisonous essence of the dragon exuded from Thon himself.

With a shriek, Ari flew up into the air in front of her, but Glik could barely see through the sheen of shadows. Groaning in pain, Thon staggered backward, pressing a palm to his brow.

Cheth shook Glik's narrow shoulders, breaking the contact between them. "Don't go drowning in visions now, girl! We have to get away from this place."

Glik gaped at Thon in horror and astonishment, and he stared back at her with equal confusion.

"What are you?" she whispered.

"I do not know. Please—did you see any clues in your vision?"

The orphan girl turned away, with a shudder. "Not sure you want to know." She circled her heart again and again, muttering, "The beginning is the end is the beginning."

Kollanan rode up to them on his black warhorse, resting the war hammer on his shoulder. "They're all dead, Adan." He scratched his beard, which was encrusted with blood. "Now we have to pick up every one of our weapons, take away our dead, even rake the ground—leave no evidence of who defeated the wreths."

Adan moved among his soldiers, calling for teams to count the rescued prisoners, triage the wounded, tend the injuries. "Identify those who can ride themselves and separate the others who have to be carried back." His expression flickered with sadness, then hardened again. He glanced up at the starry sky, knowing dawn would arrive before long. "Recover all our dead, and do it quickly. They must all be brought back with us."

Kollanan stayed beside him. "We have to collect all the tack, any scrap of broken armor, leave nothing that the wreths can trace back to us. How many horses did we lose?" His voice became deepened with sorrow at what they would have to do. "We need a pyre to burn the dead animals, or Queen Voo will know."

Adan shouted to the soldiers. "Take the wounded and the freed captives and ride, get a head start while others take care of what must be done here. Burn the slave hovels and anything else that'll catch fire. Every scrap!"

Kollanan rode among the fighters, supervising as they set fires, leaving the wreth corpses where they lay. The raiders combed the ground, picking up any shard of a broken human weapon while Elliel and Thon helped load the injured fighters on horses to be rushed away to medical attention. Dead human soldiers and slaves were reverently wrapped and also prepared for the journey back to Bannriya.

Dawn cast faint yellow light through the canyon shadows as smoky fires spread through the wreckage. Staying far away from Thon, Glik found a soldier who let her ride in front of him. Cheth chose a horse that had belonged to a fallen Norterran soldier.

King Adan rallied everyone who had stayed to erase all signs of battle. "We freed these people, but it is just the beginning. We have to free the rest of the human race and save the world."

Kollanan grunted and wheeled his black warhorse about. "We'll do what we need to do."

49

Lasis led the Norterran army along the trade roads, through autumn-bare forests and dry grassy hills, on their way to establish a base camp in the foothills and wait for the Suderran army to join them. Then, led by Kings Kollanan and Adan, the combined military force would cross the mountains and overthrow Mandan.

Lasis felt torn in many directions. For Kollanan the Hammer, his sworn duty was to dethrone the twisted konag. For himself, he wanted vengeance on Queen Onn for what she and the frostwreths had done to him. And for all Bravas, the long-standing blood feud remained against the Isharans, who had massacred their colony so long ago.

He longed for the simpler days of riding as a paladin to protect Norterra against local troubles, rather than facing grand-scale threats on which the fate of kingdoms rested.

Lord Ogno rode up beside him, and his brow so furrowed that it made his bald pate wrinkle. "Once we set up camp below the mountain pass, we could be waiting a long time. I want to wring Mandan's neck! Right now!" Suddenly the big vassal lord paled. "Ancestors' blood, did I just speak treason? He's still the konag until we've overthrown him." He looked from Lasis to Lord Bahlen, who had joined them.

"The decree has surely arrived in Convera by now," Lasis said. "Legally, he has already been stripped of his crown."

"He is not my konag." Bahlen shook his head, scowled. "Mandan of the Colors surrendered his right to rule on the day he sent soldiers to burn my town." He looked weary and defeated. "I did not intend to abandon my people. If the frostwreths come against us now . . ."

Lasis looked far ahead as they rode along. "That is always a risk. In order to strike one deadly enemy, we may leave ourselves vulnerable to another."

Ogno held up his hand, looked at the stump of his finger he had recently lost in battle. "When Kollanan came to Norterra, he just wanted a quiet rule. Many settlers in my county were veterans from the last Isharan war. Aye, I enjoy a good bloody battle as much as the next man, but I had hoped to tend my pigs and my cherry orchard for the rest of my days."

Bahlen glanced at him. "I enjoy the cherries from your county."

Ogno chuffed. "And your people make the best crock pickles." The big lord looked immensely sad. "Such small pleasures. Will our lives ever be normal again?"

"Not any time soon," Lasis said and nudged his horse to a faster pace.

By midafternoon the army came upon a large Utauk camp, with a dozen wagons, numerous spacious tents, fire circles, and communal areas. From the distinctive colors, he recognized that there were several tribes together in this traveling group. During his days as a paladin, Lasis had often bedded down with traveling caravans.

As the army approached, Onder trotted up to him with a report. Eager to show his worth, the disgraced Brava often rode ahead of the main army as a scout. "This is their heart camp. Shella din Orr is with them, the matriarch of the Utauk clans."

Lasis was pleased to hear this. "I know Shella. She is a wise woman." Considering, he turned to Onder. "Go, ride to the heart camp and tell her that I would enjoy having dinner with her to exchange information."

The eager Brava galloped off toward the camp. Lord Bahlen frowned. "Should we tarry here, Lasis? If we continue to march, we could make several more miles today."

"The Utauks hold more knowledge than any remembrance shrine I've ever encountered," Lasis said. "It will be well worth our while to hear their news."

Ogno said, "The heart camp passed through my county six months ago, and I learned more in those two days than in a dozen council meetings."

As the Norterran soldiers set up their own camp and riders ranged out to hunt for supplies, Lasis, Bahlen, and Ogno joined the Utauk matriarch in front of her large tent. The ancient woman sat cross-legged on a multicolored rug, apparently more limber than she appeared.

Lasis brought her some candies made from honey and beet sugar mixed with fruit preserves. "To share and be shared."

The old woman smacked her lips. "*Cra,* you remembered these are my favorite! The best thing I can eat with so few teeth." She popped one of the sweets into her mouth.

Lasis noted a burned patch on her large tent. "Did a fire sweep through your camp?"

"Worse than a fire," she cackled. "We had a dragon."

Ogno let out a burst of laughter. "A dragon!"

Lasis remembered. "Yes, King Adan told us about the dragon on the night Penda gave birth. We did not expect the heart camp to be heading this direction, though."

"We intend to cross over the mountains and head into Osterra," Shella said. "Many Utauks trade in the capital city, and I want to see the ocean again while I still have days in my life."

They all exchanged stories as they ate their meal in front of her tent, and the matriarch shared reports she had received from reconnoitering skas. "Convera is in great turmoil since an Utauk messenger delivered a decree from King Adan and King Kollanan, stripping Mandan of his crown."

Ogno grumbled, "So, we will not be a surprise then."

"An army this size was never going to be a surprise," Bahlen pointed out.

"The forms were required by the Commonwealth charter," Lasis said.

Old Shella seemed deeply troubled as she slurped her bean-and-grain mash. "The konag thinks he can silence the decree. We've received word that he imprisoned Donnan Rah."

"That sounds like Utho's doing," Lasis growled. "He is a disgrace to Brava honor."

The old woman shared a toothless grin. "Utho sailed away with the Commonwealth navy to fight Ishara. He left Mandan alone, and the konag is not prone to making good decisions." She clucked her tongue against her gums. "Donnan Rah announced the decree on his way to Convera, just in case the konag tried to stop him. Word spread quickly. We Utauks rerouted our caravans and withdrew our commerce from Convera. The effects will not be noticeable right away, but people will feel the pinch soon enough."

"Do you think it'll be enough?" Bahlen asked. "Mandan attacked my town, murdered my people. We cannot let him get away with it."

Lasis ate a few bites of savory stew. "That sort of message will inflame the people in the market district, on the lowtown docks along the rivers, merchants and travelers throughout Osterra. By the time our joint armies arrive, Konag Mandan may be weakened enough to crumble."

Shella din Orr hummed to herself. "*Cra,* that would be the simplest solution."

After the meal, she asked her nephews to bring out the maps her people had compiled. The matriarch took great pains to show them the best routes over the mountains, indicating which roads had been blocked by the eruption of Mount Vada. Lasis consulted with the lords, and together they chose a large open park at the base of the mountains where the army would wait for the allied kings before the final push over the passes.

The army roused at dawn, packed their things, and moved out. Lasis kept them marching two more days at a distance-eating pace, and on the morning of the third day the Brava saw a jagged line on the horizon—the Dragonspine Mountains and the smoking mass of Mount Vada.

50

WAVES boomed against the reefs like battle drums. The sharp rocks, like teeth in massive jaws, ground up the bodies in the water.

Utho clung to the broken corpse of the Black Eel assassin. His ramer was extinguished, and blood still oozed around the cuff. Though Zaha had somehow hardened his skin to stone, he was dead by the time they struck the water, a hole burned through his heart.

Plunging from the high wall of the stronghold, Utho had grappled with him as they fell, wondering if it would be his final battle, but the Black Eel's strange body had cushioned the impact. The currents flung them into the jagged reefs.

Coughing and choking, Utho released the dead assassin, then tore off his black finemail cape, which was an anchor dragging him down. Whitecaps rushed against the reefs and cliffs, and Utho was helpless flotsam. He struggled to swim, and his body scraped against the rough rocks. The body of Zaha, no longer hardened by magic, was torn to ribbons, and Utho was not sorry to see the corpse sink.

Fighting still raged up in the garrison, but his battle here was a private one, just trying not to drown. He fought and flailed until he made his way to upthrust rocks on the edge of the island. Breakers still foamed against the rugged shore, and seaweed and anemones poked through the cracks, but he found a sheltered niche and clung to it. Another wave sloshed over him, and he coughed, spitting out water, flinging wet hair from his eyes.

Overhead, he saw curls of smoke, heard the clang of metal, the clash of swords. The garrison was on fire and probably the keep and the barracks. There would be nothing but ashes and fallen timbers if he ever made it back up there . . . if anyone else survived.

He peered up the bare cliff, wondering if he had the strength to climb. But he realized it was impossible. The rocks were sheer and the garrison wall much too high. Fulcor was impregnable, which made it even more desirable as a strategic fortress. His anger and frustration became intense enough that the ramer cuff sputtered around his wrist and then flickered out again. He was stranded here like waterlogged driftwood.

He looked out to sea, where the wreckage of hulls and masts, rigging and deck boards was strewn across the water in the aftermath of the naval battle.

Many Isharan warships had been sunk as well, but he saw the striped sails of a small armada drifting away, ten ships or so. Though their fleet had been decimated, the Isharans had a godling.

They had a godling!

And they were sailing toward the Commonwealth.

Utho was trapped here at the waterline, unable to fight any enemy but the ocean. The waves continued to swirl around him, making it impossible to move. He railed against the universe and cursed this pathetic end to his legacy. Better if he had just died a hero, falling from the wall.

Leaving his sheltered niche, he tried to swim, hoping to work his way around the island to the harbor cove, but the furious undertow caught him and smashed him into the reefs again, slicing a deep gash in his arm. Because he was a Brava with enhanced healing abilities, the blood flow soon stopped, though it weakened him. Some of his ribs were cracked from the fall, and he felt pain like jagged glass in his sides as he tried to swim. He retreated to the sheltered cranny again.

In the citadel high above, the sounds of fighting had diminished, though the smoke was thicker. The entire complex must be ablaze. Out in the water, the surviving Isharan warships sailed out of sight, and Utho waited miserably to die. . . .

Two hours later, the tide went out, and he did find a way to move. The low tide exposed slimy, moss-covered rocks around the edge of the island, revealing a route to the reefs, and he felt unexpected hope. Yes, he was Utho of the Reef. He would do it again. He worked his way along the stark shore, painstakingly heading toward the harbor cove, a few feet at a time. If he could inch around the perimeter and get to the cove, he could find whatever ships remained, maybe even climb the cliff stairs to the garrison.

A Brava should not dream of failure, but he had tasted too many setbacks. If the Isharans somehow won because of their dark magic, because of their vile godling, Utho would make them pay, even if he was the only one left alive.

Whitecaps curled in, smashed the rocks, and then retreated, exposing a few more inches of the sea-swept rocks. Taking advantage of the lull, Utho flung himself across the gap. He grabbed the next boulder, seized a hunk of seaweed, and struggled around to the next outcropping. He pressed himself against the cliff, holding on as waves came in again. They were weaker now with the low tide, but the obstacles remained slippery. A sneaker wave slipped in and slammed him against the cliff, stunning him, threatening to wash him out to sea, but he managed to keep his grip on a handhold. He ignored the pain, the bruises, the gashes.

He waited, timed his next move, and then struck out for an upraised finger of reef. The rocks were high enough that Utho could sit for a couple of minutes trembling as he rested. He caught his breath and wasted no more time. He did not want to be stranded when the high tide came.

After hours of tedious, painful struggle, he clambered around a rock corner and saw a slash in the high cliffs—the sheltered harbor cove! Here, wreckage clogged the water: splintered boards, dead bodies, broken hulls. Greasy smoke wafted up from the docks as well, and he saw both Commonwealth and Isharan vessels smashed or burned.

Eventually reaching calmer waters, he was able to swim, though as he struck out he felt the depth of his weakness. Utho had never been so exhausted, and this time he didn't even have the energy of victory to buoy him up. He found a scrap of hull planking as long as his arm, and clung to it, glad for the buoyancy.

One vessel, the *Glissand*, was tied up to the nearer dock. It was damaged, its sails tattered and hull scorched. He felt a strange relief to see people moving on the deck, climbing the masts. He tried to wave and yell, but the background noise of workers shouting and making repairs was too loud.

Utho swam on, nudging a bobbing Isharan body aside. A Commonwealth vessel tied up to the adjacent dock had burned, its hull gutted, the sails gone, the masts like blackened skeletons.

The *Glissand* was the only ship that appeared even partially intact. He struck out toward it, ignoring the pain in his ribs, finding strength somewhere inside him. Some sailors spotted him, pointed down at the water. An Utauk man, Mak Dur, came to the deck rail, stared at Utho, giving no sign of welcome. Finally, he shouted down, "I thought it might be a shark coming to feed on the bodies, but instead I find a Brava."

"Throw down a line and help me up," Utho called. "Why are you not helping to fight in the garrison?"

"*Cra*, everyone's dead up there! The buildings are burning. It was my duty to save the ship—*my ship*." Mak Dur directed some of his sailors to lower a rope ladder down the hull.

When Utho was hauled aboard, dripping, he saw fifteen bedraggled Commonwealth soldiers, many of them injured, working with the Utauks, cutting away charred ropes, sawing out damaged deck boards. Two sailors returned in a small rowboat loaded with planks salvaged from the other wrecked ship, and the lumber was raised up to the *Glissand* for repairs.

Utho was barely able to stay on his feet, looking up to the fortress walls above. "All dead?"

"We climbed up there to have a brief look, but came back here, where our real work is," the voyagier said. "It is not my problem. They slaughtered each other."

"At least their godling didn't come here," said another Utauk sailor.

A Commonwealth soldier groaned, which broke the scab on a large cut across his cheek.

Utho felt his anger swell to hear the report, but he had enough room inside for more anger. "I saw some Isharan ships sailing toward Osterra." He looked around, and the urgency rose in his voice. "Repair the *Glissand* as soon as possible. We must set sail!" He looked desperately at the Utauk crew, the wounded soldiers. "We have to get to Osterra. The invaders are on their way!"

Mak Dur shot him a glare filled with withering insult. "Repair? *Cra,* what do you think we've been doing?" He gestured up at the mainmast. "Are you blind as well as injured? We'll set sail as soon as I'm sure the *Glissand* can stay afloat."

"Then I will help," Utho said, "and the repairs will go faster."

51

HOLDING on to the thick rigging rope as she stood on the prow, Magda leaned out over the water and looked down at the split waves where the white foam flowed. She turned her face to the wind and saw only open water ahead. She paid no attention to the smoke rising from the ever-dwindling dot of Fulcor Island.

"How long will it take to get to the enemy shore?" Magda asked.

Harried and upset, Captain Gaus gazed at the ruined and sinking ships they were leaving behind. He worked his jaw. "You are abandoning a large part of our Isharan navy. Countless sailors are still alive in the wreckage. We must rescue them."

Magda spat over the rail. "They're weak and defeated, as broken as their boats are." She turned to the striped sails of the ships following them, counting quickly. "Ten ships and many Hethrren fighters left. It's enough to conquer the Commonwealth."

Gaus stood firm. "We'd have a stronger force if we rescued the other fighters. Let's take a day, circle back."

"No," Magda growled. "If you take a day, that wastes a day."

"What does it matter?" he demanded. "The old world will be there tomorrow, and the day after. My crew—"

"By the day after tomorrow, that land will be ours," Magda said. "Can't we make these boats go faster?"

Red-faced, Gaus snapped, "Our sails are damaged. Some of the ships have splintered masts or snapped yardarms. My navigator is dead! My first officer is dead. Many of our best sailors were lost in the battle." His voice carried a tone of insult. "A ship doesn't sail itself, and your Hethrren know nothing about seamanship." He let out a rude snort. "Nor about disciplined fighting. Your warriors are not a real army. I am the captain of—"

She seized the front of his jerkin and tossed him over the side, like so much garbage. Gaus barely had time to squawk as he plunged into the water. The flagship rushed swiftly across the waves, leaving him behind.

Other Hethrren guffawed, while the remaining Isharan crew let out a roar of dismay. Some rushed to the starboard side; others ran to the stern, calling the captain's name. One sailor with officer's insignia shouted, "Take down the sails! Turn about. Drop the landing boat to retrieve the captain."

Sailors rushed to the rowboat that was tied up to the deck, but Magda snorted like an angry bull. "Stop! We sail on."

"But, the captain!" the officer shouted. "He'll drown."

"Or maybe sharks will eat him," Magda said. "I am captain now."

Angered, the sailors drew together, but the Hethrren also gathered, flexing their muscles, showing their sharpened teeth. Though they did not outnumber the Isharans, the barbarians' violence and self-confidence outweighed the resolve of the crew.

"Anyone who argues is useless to me," Magda said. "Toss them overboard if they make trouble."

The tense Isharan crew shifted into an uncertain stance, and their resistance crested and faded. The distraught officer said, "But you don't even know how to sail! You can't navigate."

Some Isharans stood at the stern, shading their eyes and trying to find the struggling captain in the foaming wake as the ships sailed onward.

Assessing the remaining ships, Magda was sure her people on the other vessels would grow impatient with the Isharan captains and get rid of them as well. "I don't need to know how to sail as long as one of you remains alive." She raked her glare across them all. "Besides, I have my priestlord and my godling. What more would I need?"

She saw Erical hunched on the deck as if in a daze. Magda had seen what the unrestrained deity could do to enemy ships. Why would she need any weakling Isharan fighters when she had that?

His beautiful godling had triumphed in every way, had defeated the godless fleet and cleared the sea around Fulcor Island. Now the Isharans and the Hethrren could do exactly as Key Priestlord Klovus had commanded.

Yet Erical felt deeply wounded by the experience. He sat on the deck, feeling a stiffness in his joints, a shaking exhaustion in his mind and heart. The godling simmered in the hold below, greatly weakened after such an expenditure of energy.

Though surrounded by sunshine and open air, Erical felt a darkness inside. The deity brooded about what she had done. She was linked to her priestlord, and to Prirari District, far, far away. With all of the bloodshed and devastation she had caused, she now questioned if this was what her people, her worshippers, and Erical wanted.

But he himself had driven the godling to do it. He had communicated with the deity, made sure she understood what he wanted . . . even though he hadn't really wanted it. He had been caught up in the moment, in the heat of battle. He had felt enraged, liberated, and the godling took her cues from him. Wanting to please her priestlord, she had smashed the enemy ships, torn

Commonwealth sailors to pieces. Erical had felt so exuberant at the time, and now it sickened him.

As a priestlord, he had stained himself forever. He closed his eyes and hung his head, wishing he could just sink into the deck boards.

As the ten ships sailed away from Fulcor Island, he paid little attention to the drama occurring between the barbarian leader and Captain Gaus. The Hethrren had never obeyed orders or respected ranks, they did not understand military ranks or the authority of a captain, and they did not understand nautical duties or the nuances of a sailing ship.

Erical knew only that they were sailing away from his godling's carnage, and the entity belowdecks amplified his guilt—a fundamental shift in what the godling was, and what the priestlord was. Even if she rested and regained her strength, would she ever be the same again? The deity twisted and glimmered in his mind, but her rainbow colors seemed muddier. With each moment, they grew farther from Prirari, the lifeline that bound the godling to the world.

When Magda threw the captain overboard, Erical was startled out of his reverie. He watched the panic among the crew, but Gaus was gone. The priestlord realized that the barbarians had just taken control.

Erical groaned and sent his thoughts down to the godling. Oh, he could surge her power, make her come blasting up through the deck to exterminate Magda and the ruthless Hethrren in moments. But did he dare unleash the entity again?

He heard the thud of heavy footsteps and focused his thoughts again. The ugly barbarian woman loomed over him. "Priestlord, use your godling to make us sail faster. Call upon her powers."

"No." Seeing Magda stiffen, he feared she would tear him limb from limb, or maybe just toss him into the waves like the captain.

"If you defy me, I will break you," she said.

"My godling is too weak and needs to rest. Aren't you satisfied with what she accomplished back there?"

"Not satisfied enough. Your godling feeds on sacrifices?"

Erical gave a weak nod, and the Hethrren leader bellowed to her followers. "Take knives, bring buckets, shed blood."

"No . . ." Erical said, but his voice was small. "She doesn't want that."

"We need your godling, so we'll give her blood—our blood." She snorted. "And the blood of these Isharans, if she prefers that taste."

Considering the request trivial, the barbarians slashed their forearms and spilled blood into basins, which they passed around until the containers brimmed with red liquid.

Though the Isharans were accustomed to making sacrifices for a godling, they resisted the orders because Magda had killed Gaus. But they could not resist all of the Hethrren. Blood flowed freely, spilling into buckets and bowls, and the offering was poured down into the cargo hold. Despite his unease, Priestlord Erical could feel the entity regaining strength, absorbing the offered life essence, whether or not she wanted to. Erical found that he felt more vibrant as well.

When enough blood had been shed to satisfy Magda, she stood before the priestlord, planting fists on her hips. "That should be plenty. We need winds. Have your godling make a strong breeze to push us faster. I want to conquer those new lands."

Erical swallowed. "You . . . want my godling to summon a storm? To call great winds?"

"I want your godling to push these ten ships all the way to the shores of the Commonwealth. Am I not clear enough?"

"I haven't called a storm before," the priestlord said. "I can't be sure what will happen."

Magda scowled. "You know what will happen if you refuse me, little priest-lord. So what is your choice?"

Erical looked at the blood spattered on the deck from careless sacrifices and sent his thoughts out to the godling. "I don't know what she can do." By now he could no longer even see the smoke from the island garrison or the wreckage of sinking ships. "But I will do as you command."

52

MASSACRED, my queen," said the sandwreth warrior. Appearing on the smooth sand before Voo's desert throne, he hung his head as if his confidence had withered away. "They are all dead, the entire work camp in the canyons." He was accompanied by a female warrior even taller than he. She remained silent, struck dumb by astonishment.

Voo leaned forward like a viper about to strike, her topaz eyes wide as she waited for the rest of the report. "This is a poor joke. Are you attempting to amuse me?"

The female warrior burst out, "It is true, my queen. We arrived yesterday to deliver supplies and found the canyons silent and empty. Wreth corpses everywhere, the human slaves gone—presumably stolen."

Her companion added, "Some of the sheer walls were melted by powerful magic. All the hovels were burned to the ground. Mage Ivun's dwelling had been shattered. A complete massacre, no survivors."

Voo came to her feet. "Why did the mage not save my camp?"

"Ivun was dead. We found his withered husk. The other mage, Horava, was not there."

Acid roiled in Voo's stomach. She knew that Mage Horava had taken another group of workers up to the shadowglass plain, but whoever attacked the canyon camp had been more powerful than Ivun. She squeezed her fingers tight like the legs of a dying desert tarantula. She struggled to find words, and she knew who had caused such a disaster. "The frostwreth queen struck us before we could attack her. What about the weapons my slaves were making? Can they be salvaged?"

The male warrior bowed in shame. "All gone."

Voo lashed out, releasing a magic of rage that pulled a scouring cyclone of sand from the floor, whipped around the boundaries of the throne room, and tore at these two bearers of terrible news. The queen felt stunned and confused, helpless. No, not helpless. Never helpless. But shaken to her core, nevertheless.

Voo let the sandstorm die down and said, "Send twenty wreths—nobles, warriors, and a mage. Investigate!" Her lips twisted in a snarl. "Learn what you can about the attack . . . and how we can strike back at the frostwreths."

The two warriors departed with their orders from the queen, and then, as if summoned, Axus strode into the throne chamber with a swirl of rust-red robes. Hot winds surrounded him like a nimbus of stray magic. His feet left wide divots in the newly smoothed sand, but he made the marks erase themselves, covering his path.

"The frostwreths attacked us!" Voo said, then her lips quirked in a thin smile. "Perhaps it is in retaliation for how my brother attacked their ice fortress." She shook her head, distracted again. "Quo is taking much too long to return, and I grow annoyed with him."

Axus bowed, delivering news of his own. "A riderless auga was just found in the desert, my queen. It may reveal some information."

"What does an auga have to do with any of this?"

"The beast's saddle bears the markings of Quo's party."

Now Voo was interested. "It was just wandering in the wasteland? How did it get loose?"

"I believe it was coming home by instinct, my queen. Whatever happened, it lost its rider. But there are . . ." Axus looped his fingers in the air as if tracing unseen designs. "There are ways to determine what this auga has seen, where it has been."

"Then bring the creature here. I will have answers." Voo stalked back and forth in front of her throne. "Our labor camp was attacked, and our war with the frostwreths has finally flared into a blaze. At last!"

Before long, Axus returned leading a gaunt reptile mount. The dusty auga stumbled on its three-toed feet, exhausted. It flicked out its black tongue as if tasting danger in Voo's presence. The creature looked stupidly around on the clean sand of the floor.

Voo scoffed. "How can this beast tell us anything? It has the brain of an insect."

"It has eyes, my queen. It does not have to understand what it sees. It will show us."

He stepped up to where the auga stood at the foot of Voo's throne, as if waiting to be fed. Standing just behind its wide head, Axus raised his empty hand, with fingers outstretched. He chopped down in a hard blow, using his hand like an ax, and the crack of the creature's splitting skull was a sharp report in the chamber. With a final grunt, the auga collapsed dead onto the sand. Its muscular legs folded up, and its jaw plowed a furrow in the floor.

Axus knelt beside the dead reptile, placed both hands on the cracked head, and pried open the scales and bone to expose the creature's brain. The grayish-pink tissue was folded like a crushed desert flower. The mage bent closer and sniffed, while Voo watched.

"Where has it been?" she asked. "And where's my brother? If this auga was with their party, tell me what happened."

"One moment, my queen. I can draw forth the memories and learn." He dipped his fingers into the soft brain matter, then pushed them in up to the last knuckle. He twitched his hands, closed his eyes, and hummed.

Voo watched, her entire face a frown. Axus looked first intrigued, then concerned, then appalled.

Queen Voo lurched down from her sandstone dais and joined the mage on the other side of the slain auga. "Tell me!"

"See for yourself. I brought the appropriate memories to the surface."

While he kept his fingers immersed in the gelatinous tissue, Voo dropped to her knees and shoved her fingers into the auga's brain beside him. "Show me."

She began to feel the images, sights, and memories wafting up. Like noxious fumes, they stung her eyes, but then she saw the visions herself, seeing what the auga had seen. Voo watched her brother and his sandwreth companions join the weakling humans in Norterra, riding to the frostwreth fortress on the shores of a frozen lake. Through the uncritical eyes of the auga, she watched haughty Quo slaying frostwreths, spilling their blood. She saw the ice fortress crumble and collapse—and after that victory her brother and his party rode away on their real quest, to find Penda and take her baby.

That was when Voo's true horror began. Quo did indeed find the young woman, in an Utauk camp that was under attack by a dragon. The monster killed many humans along with some sandwreths. It was a reminder that their ultimate enemy was Ossus, but Voo would deal with that after all the frostwreths were killed. . . .

Then the auga's memory images showed *King Adan* standing above her wounded brother. But instead of helping Quo, as he was required to do, Adan was defiant. "You will not have Penda or my baby. I *can* stop you." His voice held an undertone of strength that Voo had never heard.

Adan's sword was inlaid with black glass—exactly the kind of weapon she had instructed him to make, so that he could kill frostwreths.

The auga, *this* auga, had been injured during the dragon attack and wandered around the Utauk camp, understanding nothing but still seeing, still remembering. And all of those memories were still inside its brain.

Adan leaned closer to where Quo lay wounded. "I know about the labor camps you hide in the desert. The human prisoners you have taken."

Voo was so shocked to hear this that she almost yanked her hands out of the auga's brain. Instead, she thrust them deeper, insisted on seeing more, seeing all.

Adan held his sword in a threatening manner. "Someday, legends might say that you died fighting a dragon . . . or maybe no one will remember you at all."

Voo gasped as her human servant, her supposed ally, thrust his enhanced sword through her brother's heart. The auga wandered away, not understanding what it had just seen.

The queen screamed in her throne room. She lunged to her feet, held out hands dripping with gore, but in her mind the blood was Quo's blood. "King Adan murdered my brother!"

The mage remained kneeling, his hands still embedded in the reptile's open skull. "Adan and his humans knew about our labor camp. You heard the tone in his voice."

Voo gasped as the realization struck her. She hadn't even considered the possibility. "This cannot be true! No human would be powerful enough to massacre . . ."

"They have shadowglass, my queen. And I did warn you about abusing the prisoners, making them hate us when a true alliance would have been much more effective."

Voo took Mage Axus by surprise. With a burst of magic she flung him against the far wall of the throne room. "Humans killed my brother! Humans slew the wreth warriors in our labor camp and stole our slaves." She let out a wordless ululating cry.

Axus gradually picked himself up and looked at the queen, careful not to anger her further.

"We must get revenge—and now."

53

∽

IN the hour before midnight, Convera Castle was dark, but Mandan's thoughts were darker. He had waited impatiently for a flood of armed forces to arrive from the surrounding counties, but the response was abysmal.

That afternoon a ragtag group of fifty fighters rode in from Judson's holding, responding to the captive lord's written demand. The soldiers were a motley crew, carrying only dull weapons and wearing patchwork armor. They clearly resented being pulled from protecting their homes and families, even to serve their konag. Annoyed, Mandan had ordered new Commonwealth colors made for them so they would fit in with his larger army.

No troops had yet arrived from Lord Drune, despite his letter. Drune made the excuse that the distance was greater and the roads were often muddy. Mandan kept the vassal lord locked in his "guest quarters."

If Conndur the Brave had sent out a call for military support, every able-bodied fighter would have rushed across the three kingdoms to pledge their lives and swords. Mandan was infuriated that he did not command the same respect, but no matter how many times he reminded the people that he was konag, no matter how often he railed against the passive insubordination, he could not change how they responded.

Throughout the day he had received reports from patrols in the market squares, the docks, and the lowtown warehouse districts. The Utauk traders had scattered like roaches under a bright light, but even with them gone, the people had spread the news about his crown being stripped from him. Now, everyone in Convera knew about the two rebel kings and their ridiculous decree, as well as the malicious accusations about Utho. The headless Brava body found in the river had also been blamed on Utho. Some audacious citizens had even appeared outside of the castle demanding to know who had truly murdered their beloved Conndur the Brave. They seemed ready to tie a noose for Utho, who wasn't even here to defend himself.

In response, Mandan sent criers up and down the streets to shout denials. Bills posted around the city declared the accusations false and treasonous, threatening arrest for anyone who supported the rebellion.

Jennae disagreed with his tactics and was not afraid to say so. "With your criers and leaflets, you only give fuel to the rumors." Tytan did not comment, though he clearly felt the same way.

"I am putting an end to the sedition!" Mandan snapped.

Jennae turned away. "And yet you have not silenced any rumors, only raised more questions."

Another group of agitators crowded on the remembrance shrine steps, flanked by the stone lion statues, also demanding answers. Chief Legacier Vicolia had been given a proper response to deliver, but instead of issuing the approved statement, she closed and barred the doors of the shrine and refused to face the crowds.

Mandan's father had been a hard teacher, though he tried to be a loving mentor. Even so, Conndur's interactions with his son had been laced with disappointment. Whenever crashing thunder and lightning drove the young man into instinctive terror, the konag had dismissed his trauma. Only Utho had understood and tried to comfort him. Utho . . .

He refused to believe that the loyal Brava had killed Conndur the Brave. Now, late at night in his royal suite, his heart beat faster, and he took another gulp from his second goblet of mulled wine, sloshing the heavily spiced liquid in his mouth before swallowing it.

When his goblet was almost empty, his thoughts turned warm and fuzzy. Mandan walled off his doubts, but a nagging part of his brain wondered what sacrifices Utho would have made to spark his long-awaited vengewar. Just how far would he have gone?

Mandan shuddered, blocked those thoughts, and finished his wine.

Lira crept up beside him in a wispy blue gown. Her red hair was disheveled, but he could tell she had made a small attempt to improve her appearance. She had washed her pale face, though her eyes remained puffy and dulled by the poppy milk. At least the drug kept her quiet, not weeping and complaining all the time.

"The city is unsettled." Lira seemed edgy, as if made of broken glass. She surprised him by taking his empty wine goblet, almost solicitous. "The people don't know what to believe. The Utauks spread the news about the decree, and now everyone knows you've been stripped of your crown."

"That is not true!" He lashed out at her, but she skittered away, taking the wine goblet with her. "My people should know what to believe. I am their konag. They watched the chief legacier crown me, and my name is inscribed at the remembrance shrine."

She shuffled off to pour him more mulled wine and answered in a low voice. "My name was chiseled beside yours on the day we were married."

He slumped in his chair and closed his eyes, as she picked up the wine jug. The fire crackled in the hearth, shedding waves of heat. Mandan couldn't remember what time it was, or if he'd been served dinner. He knew that some of the serving staff had vanished, running away in the night. He groaned with frustration.

Lira returned with the wine, and he was pleasantly surprised that she had served him. A konag should be able to count on his queen. He took the goblet, smelling the cloves and dried orange peel, a delicious scent with just a hint of bite.

She gave him a thin smile. "When you lead your army up the river road and see the rebel forces moving against Convera, all the soldiers will believe you. They will be loyal. You'll see."

He swirled the mulled wine and gulped it. "I know."

Lira watched him, and his wine-fogged mind took a moment to realize that was unusual. He rolled his tongue around in his mouth, frowning, and took another swallow of the wine. The spices seemed stronger at the bottom of the jug, and he detected a strange taste. Leaning forward in his chair, he peered down at the dregs in the goblet, saw that the red wine looked murky.

Lira chuckled. She seemed frenetic, more awake and alive than she had been in a long while. "Now you will sleep, Mandan. Sleep forever!"

He tried to lurch to his feet, scowling at the goblet. "What did you do?" He tossed the cup aside, and it clanged on the floor.

"It's warm and gentle," she said. "You'll just drift off and float like a river barge on the current." She grinned and leaned closer.

He tried to reach out and grab her, but his arms felt numb. His lip was swollen, slurring his words. His tongue didn't want to move. "What did you . . ."

But he already knew. She'd given him milk of the blue poppy, a strong dose of it.

Lira said, "That's more than even I have ever taken!" She leaned close and then danced away. He wanted to strangle her, but the wispy young woman wasn't afraid of him, did not feel threatened. Something was terribly wrong. This was the same drug that had killed his mother. Lady Maire had consumed far too much poppy milk and drifted off into eternal sleep.

"You'll find it pleasant," Lira taunted, coming close again. "And that's more than you deserve."

He could feel her warm breath close to his face, then he couldn't feel his cheeks at all. Everything was so numb! His thoughts were thick with fog. His vision closed in like a thunderstorm, then narrowed to a pinpoint. He lurched forward, but his body betrayed him.

Laughing, Lira had a spring in her step as she hurried toward the door, abandoning him.

Mandan slumped out of his chair and sprawled on the floor near the discarded goblet. Then the blackness of unwilling sleep strangled him.

Lira hadn't felt such a lightness in her heart since her wedding day. She darted along the castle corridors as if she had nothing to hide. Mandan had swallowed so much of the drug—and he wasn't accustomed to it. He would die just like his mother.

Over the past couple of days, Lira had weaned herself off the poppy milk as her plan became clearer. She would huddle in her chambers or creep to the throne room when Mandan insisted, pretending to do whatever he commanded.

But not now. That nightmare was over. She was the queen, and the castle staff treated her with respect. This late at night, the halls were mostly empty. Many times, she was too dim and drug-fogged to notice when servants, retainers, and courtiers made way for her. But now Lira didn't want to be seen. She slipped along back passages, took a hidden servants' staircase, and worked her way down to the castle's lower levels.

She had considered freeing Lords Judson and Drune, throwing herself upon their mercy and begging them to take her away . . . but if Mandan did indeed die from the poppy poison, those vassal lords would not save her. No, Lira needed to extricate herself from the court intrigues and the power plays and run far away. They would know she had done it. Even if Kings Kollanan and Adan marched into Convera and took the throne, would they forgive her for killing a konag? Lira would not take the chance.

She still couldn't believe that she had poisoned him. Lira had once thought she loved the shining young man, but it was merely a glare of foolishness, like sunshine reflecting off polished metal. He had shown her his true character very soon after they were wed.

Now he was dead, and she had to get away.

She could think of only one man in the castle who spoke truth without fear of the consequences. Donnan Rah could rescue her, take her away to someplace she might find sanctuary.

Lira slipped into the tunnels beneath the castle. For a long time these stone-walled chambers had been used to store old weapons, but now they were a dungeon. In his years of peaceful rule, Konag Conndur the Brave had little use for political dungeons, but Mandan and Utho had repurposed some of those cells. Now the Utauk courier was locked inside, and Lira knew where to find him.

She took her own torch because the tunnels were dark. The Utauk courier had been left in blackness. She hung the torch in the sconce outside the barred doorway of his cell and whispered his name. She slid back the bolt and tugged with both hands, swinging the heavy door open.

Donnan Rah blinked at her, confused and wary. "Who . . . ah, Queen Lira."

Even though they were alone, she spoke in a hushed voice. "Come! I'll save you." She realized there should have been guards here, but many people had abandoned their posts. Mandan had called all competent fighters to join his army, and perhaps he had called away the guards. Or maybe they just stopped following a konag who had been stripped of his crown. "I'll help you escape, but only if you take me away. We have to go far from the castle."

The Utauk man raked his fingers through greasy hair, trying to regain his dignity. He brushed off his stained tunic and stepped out of the cell, blinking in the glare of the torchlight. "That doesn't explain why you are you freeing me."

"Because I have to get away. I need to leave Mandan."

The courier looked troubled. "Has he beaten you?"

"He's done many things to me and left both obvious and invisible injuries. But I . . . I tricked him into drinking milk of the blue poppy. I think I killed him."

Donnan Rah was instantly wary. "Then you're right—we have to get out of here. How soon do you think they'll find him?"

She grabbed the torch and led the way back up the passages. "We'd retired for the evening, but he . . . he is the konag. Someone is always troubling him for something, so we have to go." She tossed her lank hair and realized that her blue gown was not at all adequate for hard traveling. She had not packed any supplies. "I am poorly prepared for this."

The messenger squared his jaw. "We will make do. We'll need to find the Utauks. Most of them left the city, but at least we can ride out of Convera."

Lira tried to sound strong. "Please take me away and hide me among your people."

Donnan Rah gave her a gallant bow as he walked down the passage after her. "It would be my pleasure to do so. Our people will be glad to have the queen of the Commonwealth as their guest. Inside the circle."

Mandan's guts twisted, and he retched again, coughing, choking, and spewing out more vomit. Nausea tore at his stomach, turned him inside out. The poppy milk leached into his mind, froze his thoughts, numbed his muscles.

He tried to crawl forward and collapsed into the sour-smelling pool. He tried to scream, but managed only a faint sound like a mewling shoat. His throat felt as if it had been torn wide open. His vision blurred and crossed, then went black again, but he awakened a few minutes later, twitching and thrashing.

Eventually, he felt his hands tingle. His spasming legs jittered on the floor, tapping his fine royal slippers on one of the woven rugs. He made a strangled gasp again, still without words. His thoughts had spiraled upward in a whirl-wind of euphoria, but now his head pounded as if Kollanan were trying to pound his way out of his skull with the famous war hammer.

Mandan let out a croak again and attempted to crawl. He heard a thumping at his door and did not at first realize that it sounded different from the pound-ing in his head. He tried to respond, but no sound came out. The knocking continued, then eventually went away.

Mandan began sobbing, trying to regain his strength. Instead, he drifted into unconsciousness again . . .

Only to be awakened by repeated hammering on his door. He managed a hollow hoarse sound when he tried to give a wild shout. Finally the door was flung open, and Tytan stood there dressed in black. The Brava bounded forward to kneel over Mandan. "My konag! What happened?"

"My wife . . ." he managed to say. "Queen Lira . . . Find her."

54

THE rescue party came over the Suderran hills from the deep desert, racing back toward Bannriya. They rested for only an hour at a time as they headed to safety behind the city walls.

Safety . . . Kollanan thought he might never feel safe again, never calm, never at peace. He felt as if he'd been dropped into a dogfighting pit.

He did not feel overjoyed by their victory, nor had he kept count of the wreths he'd killed, though he did derive a sense of satisfaction from rescuing the human prisoners. His arm ached from swinging his hammer. "We will never again be *in the way*," he muttered bitterly to himself, remembering what the frostwreth queen had said, dismissing the entire town of Lake Bakal.

In front of him on the saddle was a scrawny, hollow-eyed woman from the slave camp. She said her name was Irundel, and she was an Utauk by the look of her. For no reason whatsoever she reminded him of his daughter Jhaqi. Blood had dried on her ragged clothes, and she sat mostly in silence during the long ride home. Koll was glad for that, not interested in cheerful chatter. Around them, other rescued captives talked incessantly, delirious with relief, but Kollanan had never been good with conversation even during happier times, normal times. Oh, he had been able to talk with Tafira for hours, but now who could he talk to?

Hearing him mutter, Irundel turned back to him. "What did you say?"

"Nothing. I was talking to my own ghosts and memories."

"We all have them." Beyond that, she remained quiet and stared ahead as they covered the miles. At least she had survived.

After the battle at the canyon camp, the rescue party had counted the dead and loaded the bodies of their fallen comrades onto horses for the journey back. Although only fifteen humans had fallen, compared to more than fifty wreths, it was a large number to any king's heart, and the losses felt like a personal failure. Eleven of the casualties were from Suderra, and the other four had followed Kollanan down from Fellstaff, trusting his leadership. Now they wouldn't be going home.

In war, all victories were tempered with sadness, and he reminded himself that those fifteen casualties had been the price for all these captives. The math was clear, as was their absolute victory, but human lives weren't counted like a merchant's commodities.

Kollanan hardened his heart and made up his mind that he would always be at war now, until the end of the world . . . or until they managed to save it.

He and Adan had succeeded in rescuing the slaves, but as soon as they returned to Bannriya, the soldiers would be off again, marching to intercept the Norterran army and join in the war against Konag Mandan.

And then, even after they succeeded, even after Koll put Adan on the Convera throne, uniting the three kingdoms again, all the armies would have to stand against the wreths. It felt as if it would never end.

This was what he had to live for now.

On a bright sunny morning hours before noon, the outriders gave a shout to signal that they had seen Bannriya. Adan rode up beside him, showing clear relief. "We made it home, Uncle. We did what we needed to do. Thank you."

Koll gestured with his chin. "Go, gallop ahead. You should be the first. Let them celebrate our return." Grinning, Adan urged his horse forward, and as he galloped off, Kollanan whispered after him, "Your wife and daughter are waiting for you."

Irundel glanced back at him, saying nothing, but he could tell she understood his comment.

When Storm crested the last hill, the refugee woman straightened in the saddle, craning her neck. "As an Utauk, I have slept under the sky most of my life, but I'll be glad to have a soft bed, a warm fire, and food prepared in a kitchen. Inside the circle again."

"That much we can promise you," Koll said.

The soldiers let out a cheer and increased their pace. Kollanan saw flags on the watchtowers and heard a brassy fanfare of celebration from the gates.

The triumphant party returned, and the city responded with a happy uproar. The wall sentries could see how many riders approached and they would know that the mission had been a success. As Kollanan guided Storm toward the gates, people rushed out of the city, calling out for loved ones. Soldiers and refugees dismounted and threw themselves into the arms of welcoming citizens. Hale Orr and Queen Penda rushed out to greet Adan at the gates. Colorful skas circled overhead.

Watching the reunions, Koll could only think of his family—his grandson Birch still held prisoner among the frostwreths. He thought of Jhaqi and her husband, of Tomko, of Tafira . . . He wanted to share in the joy of these people finding their loved ones after such an ordeal. He stared at them, longing to feel the same thing. He saw one young soldier find his sweetheart, wrap his hands around her waist, and swing her in the air as he recounted his stories about the battle. The laughter rang in Koll's ears, and he remembered Tomko's childish giggling when he played with the carved wooden animals his grandfather had made for him and his brother. That boy's laughter was forever silenced.

Kollanan's sadness was always with him. Although he did not join in the celebrations, he could see the elation around him. Despite himself, he experienced a hint of happiness from the prevalent mood.

Adan swung Penda around as if she were no more than a little girl, and delight lit both of their faces. Her green ska circled overhead, whistling and chirping. Hale Orr cradled a baby girl in one arm, and pounded his son-in-law on the back.

Kollanan could only watch, could only remember. Irundel waved at the crowd from the saddle, though she knew no one here in Bannriya. He swung her off the saddle and helped her to the ground. "They will be happy to welcome you. Tell your story."

She thanked him, then disappeared into the swirl of the crowd. As he sat in the saddle, Kollanan the Hammer fought another battle within himself, a struggle just to keep the tears from flowing.

During the raid on the wreth camp, Queen Penda and her father had prepared the Suderran military for the long march eastward, loading supply wagons, preparing camp tents, issuing weapons and armor, seeing that the cavalry horses were tended. Adan's army was ready to march for their rendezvous with King Kollanan's army, and the battle to unite the Commonwealth.

Adan was proud of the extensive preparations she had completed, but he teased, "I thought you'd ask me to stay with you a few days and rest."

She let out a sigh. "We cannot rest. Even here at home, no one has rested." She placed the baby in his arms as they walked together into the council chamber. Kollanan, Elliel, Thon, Hale Orr, and many others already waited for them.

Adan took a moment to marvel at his daughter, feeling such an unexpected sense of amazement at her delicate strength yet vulnerability. His daughter. His child. The future. The baby stirred but remained asleep. He said, "We can't ever give up. My army will ride out to the Norterran forces and gamble everything on our next victory. I know there are many struggles to come. That's as far ahead as I can think now."

She stroked his cheek, brushed his reddish-brown hair back behind his ear.

Hale greeted them, his loud voice drowning out the others. He held up a piece of paper. "I counted the days since we dispatched Donnan Rah, and I know the route. I know how fast he can ride." He looked at the stony-faced King Kollanan, who sat in one of the large chairs at the long table. "He should have reached Convera at least four days ago. Mandan has received the decree by now."

"Then we have followed the forms in the charter, and war is on," Koll said. His war hammer rested on the table in front of him, still stained with wreth blood.

"Then Utho knows what we're trying to do," Elliel said in a low growl.

"Unless he already launched his vengewar," Adan said. "That's what started this, and why Mandan demanded that we all send our armies to help him fight. Because . . ." His voice caught in his throat. "Because he thought the Isharans killed our father."

Adan took a seat beside Penda, still cradling the baby. "Our army should make good time as we ride up to join the Norterran forces at the base of the mountains. Our kingdoms will enforce true justice in the name of the Commonwealth."

"Mandan will not surrender easily," Koll said, but it was not a warning. "I look forward to convincing him."

"And Utho must face justice," Elliel said.

"I can't leave Bannriya entirely vulnerable." Adan said. "We just attacked the sandwreth prison camp. Even if Queen Voo doesn't suspect our involvement, she'll be upset if I take 'her' army far away."

Penda snorted, "*Cra*, you know I'll tell her you've gone to punish Konag Mandan on her behalf. That will mollify her."

Adan looked at Elliel and Thon. "With your powers, I'd like you two to stay here in Bannriya to protect my city and my kingdom. And my family. Our armies should be more than sufficient to face Mandan."

Elliel shifted uncomfortably. "I am the bonded Brava to King Kollanan, and I must accompany him." She paused, flicked a glance at Thon. "And . . . personally, I won't give up a chance to fight Utho. My own vengewar is against him."

Thon took her hand and met Adan's eyes. "If Elliel goes, then I go with her."

"Five other Bravas were rescued from the camp," Hale Orr pointed out. "One of them is close friends with the girl Glik. And we have the Banner guards. We'll have enough protection." He touched the shadowglass pendant in his ear. "But it will not be an easy thing to stay here and hold these walls if the wreths come."

"Do what you must, Starfall," Penda said, "and come back to me and your daughter."

"As I always have." He leaned over to kiss her. "As I always have."

The army rode out the next morning.

55

THE key priestlord's guards and ur-priests had forcefully dispersed six more public gatherings of people chanting the empra's name. The funeral pyre should have put an end to such nonsense, but crowds still prayed to her and called for her return. Klovus's guards had raided a blacksmith's forge, where much of the sedition was being planned. The smith had already been interrogated and disposed of, but the rebels were such fools that they returned to the same place. He hoped he had at last rooted them out.

His Black Eels interrogated the new group of prisoners seized at the forge, but learned little. Klovus could not understand why they still clung to their fantasies about Iluris, despite all obvious facts to the contrary. Why didn't they offer faith and prayers to him instead? Had he not shown them how powerful his godling was?

Klovus found them ridiculous, ignorant complainers duped by a silly story. Even so, he needed to understand why they believed such nonsense, because if he could understand their gullibility, perhaps he could convince people to believe *in him* the same way.

Even now, chanting crowds were gathered outside the Magnifica, but here in the chambers beneath the temple, Klovus wanted a last word with the prisoners before he publicly put an end to this nonsense. He had to stop people like that from undermining his guidance.

One old woman was bound and beaten, her face bruised, her lip split. Blood trickled down her chin. Her name was Analera, and she had apparently been a palace servant for most of the empra's life. Klovus paced in front of her, trying to remember if he had seen this old crone in the palace before. "So you served Iluris when she was still alive."

"Iluris is still alive," Analera said. "And she will return to defeat you."

Klovus tried to sound reasonable. "I am not the enemy."

Analera worked her lips as if to spit, but she had no moisture in her mouth. "You and I define enemies differently."

"Ishara's enemy is the Commonwealth. If you question that, then you have no faith in our land or in our godlings."

The servant's shoulders slumped. "Maybe there is more than one enemy."

"Maybe you and your followers are trying to make Ishara fail. We've already dispatched the Isharan navy, and the Hethrren warriors will conquer the old world."

"I will rejoice when the empra sits on her throne again."

The Black Eels stood motionless, observing but saying nothing.

Klovus roiled with frustration. "Why do you insist she is still alive? What evidence do you have?"

"I have a lock of her hair," Analera said. "Your man took it from me because he knows what it is. He is afraid."

Klovus sniffed, looked at the Black Eels. One of them reached into a pocket and withdrew a clump of ash-blond strands. "She carried this with her, Key Priestlord."

Klovus rubbed the hair between his fingertips. "You say this belongs to Iluris?"

"It comes from the empra of Ishara," Analera said. "It has magic."

"It comes from *a woman*," Klovus said. "It could be anyone. How can you be so gullible?"

"Because I know."

"All of Serepol saw her funeral!" he roared. "A blazing pyre on top of the Magnifica. We all watched the empra's body burn."

Analera scoffed. "We saw *a woman's* body burn, but we are not so gullible."

Klovus could see by the hardness in her eyes that nothing would shake her recalcitrance. He felt weary and disappointed, rather than infuriated. "I will not let myself be troubled by the delusions of a fool such as yourself."

He called out to the Black Eels. "Snuff out this continued delusion that weakens us. They have committed crimes against Ishara, trying to undermine our government in a critical time, misleading the people into offering false prayers to a dead woman. They steal energy from Serepol's true godling, the soul of all Ishara."

Klovus liked the sound of the words as they rolled out of his mouth. Yes, he would use them in a short while. "Call the people to the palace, and bring all of the new prisoners there. They weaken us by raising doubts. We will hold a public execution in the main courtyard and get rid of these last distractions."

By now, the priestlords from most of the Isharan districts had arrived in the capital, and this was the perfect opportunity to bring them all together. The palace courtyard was wide open beneath the graceful soaring towers. In the past, Empra Iluris had stood on the high balcony above to be seen by her subjects.

Klovus wore a fresh blue caftan adorned with a golden amulet that denoted his position. The other priestlords surrounded him, wearing the colors of their districts, flanked by rows of his ur-priests. City guards lined the perimeter of the courtyard, garbed in the colors of Ishara with an added blue sash that showed their loyalty to the key priestlord. This was a perfect way to end the unrest.

Not long ago Klovus had stood on this very platform to announce how the empra was attacked on Fulcor Island. Horrified, they had listened to him as the comatose woman was whisked into the palace to be held under guard and out of sight. He had reassured the populace with his commands, his grief, and his inspiration. At the time, young Cemi could have claimed to be the empra's chosen successor, but she had not seized the chance.

The rebellious prisoners were marched into the courtyard, hands bound behind their backs, faces bruised, hair disheveled. Ten in all, a good round number to make his point, including old Analera.

Klovus stepped up, pausing to acknowledge his district priestlords, knowing each one. As the crowd noise rose to a loud thrum, the key priestlord could feel his godling growing stronger, extending tendrils of energy from the Magnifica temple.

Aided by the deity, his voice boomed out. "These prisoners tried to weaken Ishara!" The crowd's murmur swelled, but they seemed uncertain instead of furious. "They damage the land by confusing our beliefs and diminishing our godling. They want you to waste your prayers and energy, diffuse our strength, distract you from our true enemy."

He paused, feeding on the ripple of emotions in the crowd. The prisoners stood with hands bound. Analera glared at him through a puffy eye.

"But there is a way they can strengthen us all. We will feed their blood to the godling, and thereby have them repay their crimes." He raised his hands and felt the entity surging through his veins. It made him powerful, invincible. . . . Even so, he felt unsettled, as if the godling's thoughts did not align with his. The mood of the crowd was not as triumphant as he wished it would be. He knew he had to guide them, shape their prayers. "These prisoners refuse to let our people move on. They weaken Ishara. This is not what our beloved empra would have wanted."

Suddenly, another voice boomed out from high above. "Do not speak of what I would want, Klovus!" The words came out with a resounding crack.

The key priestlord looked around in surprise. The crowd gasped, and he heard a whooshing sound like a simultaneous indrawn breath from a thousand throats. People pointed upward, staring at the palace towers.

"You do not rule Ishara," the voice continued from overhead. "There is only one empra."

Klovus craned his neck and saw an amazing shining figure, a beautiful woman standing tall on the speaking balcony high above—Iluris herself! Everyone recognized her in her familiar gown, a fabulous dress she had worn during the summer festivals. Her jeweled crown caught the sunlight.

Klovus reeled, at a loss for words. He felt a swirl of power inside him, a twisting retreat accompanied by a surge of unrestrained joy—emotions that came from the entity. The Magnifica godling also recognized Iluris. She was really there!

The woman continued to speak, her voice clear and distinct. "Why did you take my loyal subjects prisoner, Klovus? They have done nothing except continue their faith in me." Her voice was amplified as if a godling energized her words—another godling? An aura of power swirled around her as she extended her hands from high above.

Klovus squinted to see if this was some kind of trick. He could see Iluris, *knew* it was her. Somehow she must have been hiding in the palace, waiting to humiliate him. Her very presence made the people question him. Once they saw the empra and knew she was alive, his declarations would be proved false—his funeral pyre, his consolidation of power. He had just cemented it all, tightened his hold, strengthened Ishara.

The crowd began chanting at once, "Hear us, save us! Hear us, save us!"

Analera cried out. The prisoners on the execution dais struggled to raise their bound hands.

"Free those prisoners!" Iluris ordered. "Guards, hear my command!"

Before the key priestlord could say anything, the Serepol soldiers pulled out their daggers and rushed forward to slash the bonds, responding like puppets to the empra's whim. Analera shook her wrists to restore circulation. Two of the prisoners bolted into the crowd.

"Stop them!" Klovus shouted, but the guards took no action. Empra Iluris stood over them on the balcony—no one could deny that she had truly returned. "Find her!" he hissed to his ur-priests, and at least they responded to his orders. "Into the palace. Go find her."

Reeling, afraid the crowd might become a mob, might turn against him, Klovus shouted to the gathered people. "Iluris has spoken to us—but is it really the empra, or is this some trick? We must not be fooled."

The shouts drowned him out, though. He didn't dare defy her more openly, not now. In dismay, he watched the rest of the prisoners scatter, and people folded around them, hiding them.

Sickened and angry, finding it hard to breathe, Klovus stared up at the high balcony. He wanted to scream at Iluris.

She smiled down at him and beamed out at the crowd.

Then she vanished in another flash of light.

56

HISTORY was buried deep in the desert outside Queen Voo's palace. Sandwreth warriors marched out in scaled armor with crystallized-bone spears. The saddles and headgear of their augas were adorned with long spikes. Voo had girded herself for war, wearing high boots, a shining chest plate, spined shoulder guards. She was armed with her sword and two smaller knives.

Surveying her army, though, Voo felt a pang. Her brother should have been there among them. Quo, his mages, and his warriors should have returned after crushing the frostwreth fortress. Her military force should also have included the Suderran army, with shadowglass-inlaid weapons for killing frostwreths. Yet the humans had betrayed them, raided the slave camp. And they killed Quo! Adan the traitor!

She stood in the bleak wasteland, staring at the undulating dunes like an arid ocean. The angular shadow of her palace towers fell across the desert, pointing to where the artifact was buried. She needed it now.

Pulling on her magic, the queen scooped the glittering grains away. Powder shot upward in a curling plume. She dug deep, excavating the legendary shield. Deeper . . .

"Help me, Axus."

Her mage added his magic to hers. With the army watching, the two of them dug through centuries of piled sand. Sandwreths did not care much for history or legends, did not revere curios and relics, but this shield once belonged to the ancient warrior Rao, a wreth hero who had injured Ossus and driven him deep beneath the mountains.

Voo and Axus curled their arms and with a mighty heave ripped the triangular shield from under the mounded dunes—a single scale from the dragon at the heart of the world, copper with black stains.

Voo held the relic by its edges and felt an unfamiliar reverence. The artifact was cool from being buried so deep, but it warmed quickly under the pounding sun. She turned the rippled surface and stared at it, but it drank her reflection.

The queen did not need to see herself. She understood how beautiful she was to others—wreth men, even humans. Anger rose again as she remembered how Adan had rebuffed her advances on his last visit. She should have taken him by force and killed him afterward.

Yes, it would have been far better if she had killed him.

She held up Rao's shield and showed it to the large sandwreth army. They raised their spears or swords. The augas shifted and snorted. With the loss of her human army, she now wished she had been able to manufacture thousands of drone fighters, but that effort had failed. She lifted her chin and decided that her sandwreths would be enough to exterminate the humans who had betrayed her and killed Quo.

She slipped her arm through the band on the back of the shield and drew the artifact close against her chest. If Rao had wounded Ossus so long ago, then he was a fighter Voo should emulate. She was the queen of the sandwreths. No enemy could stand against her—particularly not King Adan. She would fillet him slowly into a thousand tiny strips of meat, keeping him alive for as long as possible.

That was something Quo would have enjoyed. . . .

Leaving the crater they had excavated in the sand, Voo swung up into the saddle of her auga. The reptile mount rocked from side to side as it plodded forward.

She shouted to her troops. "We have long been preparing you for war. We even engaged in a dragon hunt. Now, we destroy the human infestation in Suderra—for practice." She grinned. "And after we obliterate Bannriya, our forces will march north to destroy the frostwreths."

This elicited a great cheer from her warriors, nobles, and mages. The front line of reptile mounts picked up their pace, trotting across the open desert. Behind them came countless lines of warriors, some mounted, some jogging across the blasted terrain. They kicked up a wall of dust and sand, which the doomed humans in Suderra would see coming. Voo wanted them to know the sandwreths were riding toward them. She wanted them to dread their fates.

Silent on his own mount, Axus paced her. Voo glanced at him, then looked ahead at the rugged mountains. "I intend to level their city, leave it smoking rubble. We should have done it before." Her brow furrowed as memories came, Quo accompanying her during that first visit to the human city. "When we emerged from the desert, I was surprised that humans could have scraped out an existence like that. We should have conquered them then."

"That would have been a waste of workers and resources," Axus cautioned. "As would massacring all the inhabitants now. Why not simply kill Adan as punishment, and then use the people as our laborers, our foot soldiers?"

"How could I trust them?" Voo asked. "How can I let that defiance stand?"

"Yes, they should die, but why not let them serve a purpose? Let them die fighting frostwreths—for us. Our relationship with humans could have been more effectively managed. If you had kept them happy, we would not be wasting time now. We could be heading due north to our real enemy."

Voo slapped her palm against the triangular shield, making only a hollow sound as if the scale drank sound as well as light. "I thought you insisted that our real enemy is Ossus."

The mage made a dismissive gesture. "We have enough enemies. But if you had not antagonized Adan, he would never have dared to kill your brother. He would never have been driven to attack our labor camp."

Voo dismissed his accusation and lashed out. "They will all die, and then the frostwreths will die!" She sniffed. "Afterward, we can finally wake the dragon."

She recalled how she and Quo, Axus, and those other mages had pushed their magic deep into the southern mountains, causing Ossus to stir. She inhaled the searing air, letting it burn her nostrils, throat, and lungs. Yes, she was eager to destroy Ossus, too. So much to do, she thought. So many to kill.

"Why are you fond of these humans, Axus? You keep trying to save them."

"It is simple enough to understand. I would rather *spend* them than waste them."

She remembered the vision she had pulled from the brain of the slain auga, especially Adan's expression as he thrust the shadowglass sword into her brother's heart. Her black fury dispelled any sense of logic.

"I might have listened to you in the past, Mage, but now there is no other answer. King Adan and his subjects must suffer the penalty for defying me."

She kicked her auga, and it lurched forward. Behind her the sandwreths rushed across the desert toward the walled city.

57

∽

GATHERING courage from the waves and air around him, Priestlord Erical stood at the bow and closed his eyes. He lifted his face to the clear sky and spread his arms wide, inhaled a deep breath of the sea breeze, let the sunlight warm him. He opened his eyes and saw no clouds at all.

Erical had never been so far from land in his life, and he felt the glory of the ocean, the majesty of the waves. The open expanse of blue-green water reminded him of the prairies back home, the fields of grain waiting to be harvested. He thought of patches of sweet lavender outside of villages, bees humming around orchard blossoms in the spring. He and his godling had made Prirari District a perfect place of abundant game, fertile farmlands, free-flowing streams. His people were at peace, happy and satisfied, and they revered their godling. Drawing from their prayers, the rainbow entity had quelled severe storms, diverted tornadoes, controlled heavy floods. Once during a bad drought, Erical had prevailed on the entity to bring enough rain to irrigate crops.

This was different, summoning strong winds out on the sea, but he thought he knew how to do it, and his beloved godling was willing to try.

As he imagined Prirari and longed for home, he thought of his faithful worshippers, could envision them chanting as they gathered in the temple. "Hear us, save us!"

Now standing on the deck, he could feel the deity waking, rising down in the hold. She drew comfort from him, and he gave strength back to her. His memories of home calmed her, encouraged her. Although he had left a small part of her behind for the worshippers, the entity was with him here. When he opened his eyes, multicolored light was glowing from beneath the deck boards.

The breeze curled back into Erical's face, and he grimaced at a sudden foul smell as Magda stepped close, thumping her club on the deck. Even after days out on the ocean, her furs still smelled as if they came from a rotting animal. "Call the winds, Priestlord. Bring us a windstorm to carry my ships to the shores of the Commonwealth."

The striped sails had already caught the godling's breeze. Uneasy Isharan sailors clustered together, but only one officer found the courage to confront the barbarian leader. "This is not necessary. We are already traveling at a good pace, and it takes skill to work the rigging, to shift the sails and rudder so we reach our destination. And you killed our captain."

"I am your captain," Magda said. "You don't have enough skill to find an *entire continent*? I saw your maps. If we sail west, we will find our destination."

"But summoning a storm is dangerous. What if—"

She struck the officer full in the face, knocking him backward. "Maybe I *want* a storm to ravage the enemy shores! It will drive our ships all the way to the old world, and my Hethrren will emerge as furious as any whirlwind. Won't we, little priestlord?" She glowered at him.

But Erical was focused on the godling, knew the entity was strong again, eager. He had consoled her, and she wanted to please him now. "We already have a satisfactory breeze. Can you not be satisfied? I am not practiced in this form of magic. Always before, I wanted to calm the weather, not stir up a wind."

"Then learn a new skill, or you are of no use to me." She scrutinized her club. He didn't think she would be so brazen as to threaten him. If the Hethrren harmed him, the godling would go wild and probably slaughter everyone aboard the ship. But Magda was not in the habit of thinking through the consequences of her actions.

On other ships in the ragtag Isharan fleet, the barbarians had already killed haughty or reluctant Isharan crews. The Hethrren were ready to raid the three kingdoms, but Erical was not convinced this invasion would even survive to reach the far shore.

"Are you afraid?" Magda sneered at him.

In fact he was. Erical looked her directly in the eye. "You should be."

He closed his eyes and connected with the godling, summoning her so that more rainbow light leaked from the hold below. The central hatch burst open, and the deity rose up like a sparkling morning mist.

"Use what you can," Erical whispered under his breath.

The godling understood grasslands, orchards, and farm fields, but here in the vast ocean there was so much power in the waves and currents, the churning engine of the tides and the wind.

Magda looked around and grimaced. "Do you need more blood?"

The priestlord tasted bile in the back of his throat just thinking of the recent sacrifices, the bloodlust and violence that had fed his godling. "No, I have enough."

Together, he and the entity reached out into the open air, drawing on the sea. They summoned a storm.

The skies darkened as the godling's force materialized clouds from the water and mist out of the air. She stirred and strengthened the winds, added to the waves and built the ripples into whitecaps. Flickers of blue static arced through the godling's core, reflected by great bolts of lightning that raced from thundercloud to thundercloud. The storm descended upon the ten ships, and the winds produced a raging current.

Magda gripped the bow rail, looking for the unseen coastline of the old world. She howled with glee, and the other barbarians joined their shouts with hers. For a moment, the war cries from two nearby ships were even louder than the gale, until a boom of thunder drowned them out.

Aboard the flagship, Isharan sailors clung to the ropes or huddled beside crates as icy rain pelted down. The godling continued to unleash energy that enhanced the storm, built it up.

The wind whipped Erical's hair, tugged at his shirt. The entity, which had so relished destroying Commonwealth ships and killing all those people, now called upon a similar wanton energy. Her recklessness brought about a rising storm that Erical felt slipping out of control.

Lightning lashed down, and a jagged bolt blasted a nearby Isharan ship, exploding the foremast into a shower of splinters. Even in the downpour, the ship caught fire.

The waves bucked and heaved. Erical slipped to the deck and cast about for anything to keep him stable. He reached for a crate, but it slid on the wet boards. The rain continued to pound and spray.

He begged the godling to calm the storm, but she could not do it. The raging weather was out of her control. The sky became so black, the rain so thick, that the priestlord could see none of the nearby ships. Blinding electrical bolts struck down like spears hurled from above. A detonation of thunder roared around them.

Magda seized the priestlord's shoulders and yanked him to his feet. She screamed in his face, "Make it stop."

Erical's teeth chattered as the rain became freezing cold. "I can't! The godling can't."

The wind moaned around them, shredding the sails and snapping the rigging. The storm skirled even higher, and the Hethrren leader snarled in frustration. She shook him violently. "Then you are useless."

Erical tried to grab for a handhold, a moment too late. Magda flung him over the side of the ship. He yelled, but all sound was snatched away in the hurricane. The wild presence of the godling, a shimmering and incomprehensible force in the storm, swooped away from the ship and down as Erical plunged into the waves that drove the battered ships far from him.

58

On a horse stolen from the castle stables, Donnan Rah rode with Lira away from Convera. She hunched forward, pressing her cheek against the thick mane. The gelding's rich scent reminded her of grain dust, of straw in a barn . . . of times she had gone riding with her father into the headlands. She held on, squeezing her eyes shut.

In the saddle behind her, Donnan held the reins of the well-trained horse, which surely would have been used in the coming war. He guided the horse through the night streets, working their way out of the city. By now the castle was far behind them. "For rescuing me from that dismal dungeon, my lady, it is my honor to rescue you in return." The man leaned close, keeping his voice low as he whispered in her ear. "I'll take you to safety among my people. The Utauks will repay your kindness and make you welcome. Inside the circle."

Lira shuddered, knowing that Mandan would be angry with her, and then she remembered that he was almost certainly dead. She had killed him.

As they rode away, she felt her terror and helplessness drain away, along with her strength. She was awed to consider what she had done. Her husband was dead! She had seen him collapse. Mandan . . . her handsome Mandan, *Konag* Mandan of the Colors—who had charmed her, swept her away from her home, from her parents. Oh, the glorious wedding, the gowns, the flowers, the delicious pastries! She'd been convinced that he loved her.

But their wedding had been held without her mother or father. Lira had been all alone, grieving yet clinging to her future as queen of the Commonwealth. It should have been a beautiful, magical tale better than any of her legacy books, but the glamour faded quickly. Mandan's charm had twisted into harsh treatment. Endearments turned to insults, which swiftly became beatings.

And Lira had murdered the man she thought she loved . . . the konag of the three kingdoms. She closed her eyes, clung to the gelding's neck, and she wanted to disappear.

Donnan Rah wound the horse through the outer districts of Convera, reaching the Crickyeth River and all the docks and pilings where flatboats could tie up. Only a few lights shone from the dwellings and shop yards, a lonely lantern burning over the door of an inn. The Utauk messenger wisely kept them away from the main streets, choosing darker thoroughfares. Lira jumped at every sharp noise, expecting alarms to ring out at any moment.

"We need to take the river road west and north up into the foothills," he said. "We'll follow the Crickyeth, which is more rugged, but it'll take us to the Dragonspine Mountains, where we should find some Utauk caravans."

She nodded, absorbing his words in silence. The man helped her to keep her balance. She was glad to feel him in the saddle behind her, steadying her.

She glanced back at the looming shape of Convera Castle on the bluff above the rivers. Lights blazed from the windows, more torches and lanterns shining than she had seen only a few minutes earlier. At this time of night, the castle should have been mostly dark.

"I think they know," she said.

Donnan Rah clucked his tongue against his teeth, encouraging the horse to greater speed. "I don't dare risk finding a ferryman. He'll remember taking us, and the city guards are bound to ask. But I've heard that one of the bridges across the Crickyeth is repaired."

He rode along the docks and up the riverbank, scanning ahead until he saw the span of a new bridge. In the moonlight, Lira thought it looked rickety, with rough boards filling in spaces where the finished bricks and wood would be placed, but Donnan Rah was sure it would be passable, at least for one horse. The gelding's hooves clattered across the planks, which wobbled alarmingly.

Below, a few night fishermen had tied boats to the bridge pilings, and they called up, hearing hoofbeats on the wood. Neither rider answered. When they had crossed to the other side, Donnan Rah urged the mount to a full gallop along the main road.

"We'll run for a few miles, then settle into a steady pace." His voice was rich and reassuring. "We're safe now, my lady. At dawn we can hide in the forest."

"My husband will send soldiers after us," she said, then again realized that Mandan would not be issuing any further orders. "Or someone will."

"We'll cover our tracks." Holding the reins in one hand, he traced a circle around his heart. "The beginning is the end is the beginning."

In a quiet voice, she said, "Maybe they won't realize what happened. Maybe they won't come searching for us at all."

"No matter what, the queen is missing. Sooner or later they'll find I'm not in my dungeon cell, and someone will guess at least part of the story. Until we come upon an Utauk caravan or at least a few traders, we'll be on our own."

They galloped on in silence, and Lira just clung to the horse, desperate to get far away. Before dawn, they retreated into the forest sheltered from the road and did not risk a campfire. Once during the day they heard a soldier galloping furiously along the road, but he did not see them hidden in the trees. He didn't pause, simply raced away, leaving a trail of dust to mark his passage.

They had brought no food, clothing, or supplies with them, because there hadn't been time, but Donnan Rah foraged for berries, found a few small apples, even a patch of wild onions. They drank water from a creek. Lira was miserable, but she had been miserable for quite some time.

As the following dusk settled in, they set off again, but around midnight, after they had covered many miles, the queen felt ill. Until now, she had been distracted by grief and terror, but something was definitely wrong. Her stomach twisted, and she had to dismount three times to vomit. A clammy sweat broke out on her forehead, and she trembled with fever. "Am I dying?"

He felt her forehead and frowned. "Not dying, but you may feel like it. I understand that for a very long time you consumed milk of the blue poppy. We Utauks are quite familiar with it. In fact, we plant poppies to mark our hidden trails." He became more serious. "Your body craves it. You feel ill without the drug."

"But I don't have any. I didn't bring my bottles."

"And you shouldn't have any. You must ride through the sickness, just as we ride along the road. You will need to be very strong."

She groaned and shuddered. Once again, she wanted to die.

She lived in misery for the next two days. They rested and hid at a campsite on the edge of a forest meadow, where Donnan Rah cared for her. She could keep none of the meager food down, but he brought her water.

Eventually her fever broke and her nausea dwindled, although she felt wrung out like a washerwoman's rag. Donnan Rah found some yellow blossoms and willow bark, which he boiled into a tea and made her drink. The taste was awful, but it made her pounding head feel better and soothed her upset stomach. She thought longingly of the poppy euphoria, the sense of being lost and not caring, but as she considered drinking the stuff again, her stomach knotted, and she just groaned.

Finally, Lira felt well enough to eat, and could walk without swaying or stumbling. That night, they rode off again, aided by moonlight, and after traveling for hours in the darkness, they saw fires ahead. Donnan Rah pulled the horse off the road and told Lira to stay there as he crept forward to investigate.

He returned a short while later grinning. They mounted the horse and he guided it toward a large encampment. Wagons and tents surrounded a bonfire and many smaller cookfires. Lira saw colorful banners, a flag with a single circle emblazoned in the middle. She heard singing. She asked him, "Are we safe?"

He laughed. "Those are Utauks—we can travel with them. Ah, this is what I've been waiting for!"

As he guided the gelding into the firelight, the Utauks spotted him. They stopped singing and rose from their cookfires. Lira looked around, intimidated. So many Utauks with different tribal colorings!

Though Donnan Rah's garments were tattered and stained from his time in the dungeons, the people recognized his tribe markings, and he recognized the camp.

"This is better than I thought!" He wrapped his arms around Lira's waist, holding her up as he rode toward the main bonfire. "We've happened upon Shella din Orr's heart camp. We'll be more welcome than you've ever felt anywhere." He gave a loud laugh. "This is your new home!"

The smiling Utauks enfolded themselves around the new arrivals.

59

EVEN after Adan and the Suderran army departed, Penda did not feel alone in the city. Glik remained close to her, telling stories and seeking comfort. The girl curled up in the great royal bed, remarking that she had never experienced such a ridiculously soft mattress or such extravagant blankets.

"I hope it doesn't make it too difficult for you to sleep," Penda said in a teasing tone. "You can always choose the floor if you prefer."

Glik tugged the comforter close. "I'll manage." Both skas were perched on their stand, watching over the baby in her cradle. Penda blew out the candles, and Glik curled up in the queen's bed. Before long, she was dozing, consumed by dreams and visions, but Penda remained awake. It was so quiet, so warm, that for a moment she was reminded of what peace and security felt like. But Adan was gone.

The orphan girl wrestled with the blanket in the middle of an intense nightmare, and Ari flapped her wings, letting out a shrill sound. Glik jerked awake, and Penda was pained to see the shadows around the girl's eyes in the glow of the hearth. Her gaunt face had not yet recovered from malnourishment and constant fear. Penda tried to soothe the girl by stroking her ragged-cut hair. "You're safe. It was just a nightmare."

Oak began to cry, and Penda got up to rock the baby in her arms.

Glik tried to process what she had dreamed, what she had seen. "Oh, much more than a nightmare. So many visions!" She rubbed her eyes. "Even worse out at the Plain of Black Glass because of all the poison magic that seeped into the ground! So much blood, so much history." She circled her heart again and again, an exercise in exerting calmness. "Heard the echoes of screams from thousands of years ago. All the wreths and human slaves slaughtered there." She sniffled, wiped the back of her hand across her nose.

"Saw the dragon too, hiding underneath the shadowglass. Black pools were like windows . . . into evil. Deep in the world and leaking out, more than just a dragon." Alarm filled her small face. "Little bit of it lives in everyone."

Penda pulled the scrawny girl into an embrace, holding Oak in one arm and wrapping the other around her adopted sister. She could serve a purpose like the high, sturdy walls of Bannriya around her. "We can find a way to fight it, both inside and outside." She sighed. "I wish my Starfall were here. The city walls are strong, but his heart is stronger still."

Still troubled, Glik shifted on the rumpled sheets. The hearth light was just enough for Penda to see her distress. "Saw another presence in the shadow-glass, too, something just as powerful. Opposite of the dragon. Couldn't tell if it's better, or just different. Something terrible."

"Too many terrible things in the world," Penda said. "I'm glad we have each other."

Surprised and concerned, Glik looked up. "*Cra*, I forgot! All the prisoners were freed in the main canyons, but another group went to work at the Plain of Black Glass! A dozen or so slaves, three wreth guards, and a mage."

Penda was alarmed to hear this. "And they're still there? Harvesting shad-owglass?"

The girl nodded. "I think so. We have to save them!"

Penda pressed her lips together. "We can't just ride up there and free them. Queen Voo might figure out who liberated all the captives from the canyons."

"We have to!"

Penda felt deep concern in her own heart. "We will call a council tomor-row and see what we can do. You say it's only one mage and three guards?"

Glik drew a circle around her heart. "Yes. And twelve captives. We can break them free. Queen Voo ordered the guards to keep them alive."

Since neither of them could sleep, Glik told stories about the work camp, the things she had been forced to do as a wreth slave, conversations she'd had with Cheth, how she treasured the blue feather that had fallen from Ari. The girl finally drifted off again, snuggled against the queen.

Penda tried to sleep as well, thinking about Adan out there with the army, heading toward a confrontation with his brother. Tonight, far away, he'd be sleeping on the hard ground. She missed Adan, but she had her responsibili-ties, and this city was in her charge now. She, the Banner guards, Cheth, the other freed Bravas—they would keep the city safe. They had to.

The next morning after she had nursed her baby and joined a breakfast with a few advisors and vassal lords who had stayed in the castle, she began to discuss the remaining prisoners up at the shadowglass camp. Then Hale Orr stormed in, his face an odd mixture of anger and panic. He lifted the stump of his left hand as if it were a club. "They are coming, dear heart! Scouts galloped in from the western hills—it's a sandwreth army. Thousands of them, on their way here! You can see the harbinger dust roiling up from their march. *Cra*, Queen Voo must have discovered what happened."

Penda left the alarmed advisors and lords at the dining table and bolted for the staircase that led up to the castle's observation tower. From there, the highest point in Bannriya, she could see the enemy coming. She remembered the terror of that first unexpected dust storm, the horrific winds that had swept in from the deserts, bringing the sandwreths back for the first time in thousands of years.

This would be worse.

Glik raced after her, taking the stone stairs two at a time, while Hale huffed behind them. Out in the open air of the platform where Adan liked to look at the stars, Penda shaded her eyes. She felt her skin crawling even before she saw the dust raised from hundreds and hundreds of sandwreths rolling over the line of golden hills and heading directly toward Bannriya.

Glik drew a circle around her heart as she swayed backward in a trance, and Hale caught the girl as she fell against him. Glik mumbled, "This is what we feared."

Penda drew a cold, dry breath. "It is what we expected."

The orphan girl stared off into an unimagined distance. "I saw this. A huge army, great walls. Terrible battles."

Alarms resounded from the watchtowers as word spread throughout the city. Penda and her companions observed from the high platform. She raised her voice. "We are ready. We are not helpless. Call the Banner guards, arm our defenders with shadowglass weapons. We'll show the sandwreths that we are not weak and vulnerable."

Soldiers galloped through the streets, rushing to the gates and walls. Queen Penda, who had been among the Utauks out in the hills, was back in her place in Bannriya. Now she braced herself beside her father and concentrated on her Utauk luck, any hint of magic she could use. "Bannriya has stood for two thousand years, and it will stand for a thousand more."

"I'll be more confident if it stands through tomorrow, dear heart," Hale said.

They made their way to the wall above the western gate, where the largest group of defenders had gathered. Penda walked among them, trying to display a confidence she didn't feel inside. Her throat was dry, and her eyes ached from what she saw out there.

Glik ran forward when she saw Cheth among the waiting defenders in position at one of the watchtowers. The Brava woman marched toward the queen dressed in full black cape and finemail. Cheth's entire presence was intimidating, but the oncoming sandwreth army was far worse.

The armored augas rumbled forward, with Voo in the vanguard. The sandwreth queen, beautiful and haughty, led a full-fledged army far larger than Suderra had ever seen. Obviously, this was no mere visit like the previous times. And the queen's aloof brother was no longer with her—because Adan had killed him.

The army crushed the landscape as they approached, and Queen Voo guided her auga directly up to the barred gate. She waited below the city walls, craning her head back so that her coppery hair streamed behind her like a brushfire.

Summoning her courage, knowing the entire city—in fact all of Suderra— was counting on her, Penda stepped into view, looking down at the desert army.

The sandwreth queen reacted with surprise. "Penda Orr, the woman who calls herself queen! You have come out of hiding."

Penda decided to be cool, as if this were a mere conversation over pastries. "I am home among my people after my long journey." She had left the baby under the care of nursemaids back at the castle, but Voo could easily see that Penda was no longer pregnant.

"By now, you have delivered your baby. Bring it to me!" Voo demanded.

Cheth's face grew stormy with anger, and Glik hissed, but Penda forced herself not to budge. Now she sharpened her words. "Bear your own child if you want one so badly, but my daughter belongs to me. Leave us alone."

"You *all* belong to me!" Voo shouted.

Though she let none of it show, Penda felt sick with dread. Why did Voo want her baby so much? Was it only because the sandwreth queen did not like to be denied anything? Or did Voo want a hostage to help her control Adan?

Rising anger made the wreth queen's voice shrill. "And where is my army, my human army that King Adan promised?" She raised a stark black shield on her left arm. "I know he killed my brother. I know that you attacked our camp in the canyons!" Her words echoed out like the roar of a storm. "For that, your lives are forfeit. Bannriya will be razed to the ground."

"And you enslaved and abused hundreds of humans," Penda said.

"*My* humans!"

Hale Orr turned pale next to her. Sweat blossomed on his forehead. "*Cra . . .*"

Penda quirked her lips in a cold smile and called down from the high wall. "This world no longer belongs to the wreths. Your race nearly destroyed it, then you ran away into hiding. This world belongs to humans now. Go back to your desert wasteland."

Voo was apoplectic with rage. Behind her, hundreds of augas pawed at the ground with clawed feet. The sandwreth warriors raised their weapons and demanded vengeance, as if their rage alone could flatten the walls of Bannriya.

"Where is my army?" Voo shrieked.

"*Your* army is behind you," Penda responded, "and I know where mine is."

At her signal, hundreds of archers rose up from behind the walls, flashing thousands of shadowglass-tipped arrows.

"It should be enough."

60

THE frostwreth army had split apart and marched around Fellstaff as if the city didn't exist, didn't matter. Shadri knew the wreths could easily tear down the walls and buildings if they decided to attack. But they had just gone on their way.

The people of Fellstaff had escaped the jaws of death and didn't understand how. Those thousands of warriors with all their armor and weapons, battle sleighs and ferocious oonuks, had traveled down from the northern wastelands, then simply ignored them. Humans were not their target.

"We scared them off," Pokle said. "They saw our walls and knew they couldn't get to us!"

"I don't think it was our walls," Shadri said.

Wreths were famously capricious. Shadri had spent time in their ruined cities and pored over Thon's documents, but she still could not comprehend the mindset of the ancient race.

Other people in Fellstaff cheered Gant, as if the Brava deserved credit for saving the city, but he was as perplexed as anyone. He came to speak with Shadri in the castle library, crossing his arms over his chest. "Fellstaff is a rich city. They could have taken everything from us. Oh, we would have fought back, but against that force we would have lost." He lowered his voice. "How do you explain this, scholar girl? You've done more research than anyone."

Shadri shook her head. "Maybe they weren't interested in anything we had to offer."

Gant admitted with an exasperated sigh, "I can only conclude that, for the time being at least, Norterra is safe from that particular threat." His lumpy expression became ruddy with deep-seated anger. "Now we just have to worry about whatever Konag Mandan might do to us." With a swirl of his black cape, he left the library.

As Shadri and Pokle looked after him, the scholar girl became even more determined to make sense of it all. Thon was gone with King Kollanan, but he had left many crystal sheets, half-translated documents from the archives of both sandwreths and frostwreths. She knew enough of the language and writing to continue her work. She would figure out something.

"It's lunchtime," Pokle said. "Aren't you hungry?"

"I'm hungry for knowledge," she said, but saw that he didn't understand what she meant. "I need to keep studying these records. I have a lot of work to do."

Pokle gave her a solemn nod. "I know you do. I'll see what the kitchens are making. It'll be special—just you wait and see."

Shadri was glad to have peace and quiet after the young man bolted off, although she also liked his company. She settled in with sunlight streaming into the reading room. She arranged her paper, her ink, and her notes.

With Thon's help, she had compiled a guide to translating wreth runes, and she knew which particular symbols to look for. She wished Thon could be here to help, then a shudder went down her spine as she recalled the great shadowy form that was somehow connected to him, the nightmarish presence in the ruined wreth city that had slaughtered the marauders. Despite his curiosity and seeming innocence, Thon had a dangerous facet to his being. Either he didn't know about it, or he truly didn't understand.

Shadri took it as her mission to unlock that riddle, understand the wreths.

She dug into her studies, picking up the broken sheet and rereading what she had transcribed. According to this, Kur had said, "The only way to destroy the evil is from within." Had he gone away, isolating himself so he could confront his own evil, away from his creations? But if he had purged all evil from himself, then what evil remained "within" him?

Maybe there was little point in studying vague, ancient legends too closely.

Thon had sorted the crystal sheets and used his blood to activate many lines of prose, but much remained untranslated, and many more sheets were entirely unilluminated.

She copied the symbols she recognized and painstakingly transcribed the ones she didn't, gradually piecing together the threads of a narrative. She mulled over the legend of Kur, who had created the wreths, and then the wreths had created humans, as well as the poor drones she had met at Lake Bakal.

Humans were different from the drones—not so passive, not so helpless. In the thousands of years since the wreth wars, humans had built their own civilization. They were not as violent as the wreths and not as meek and passive as drones. Humans were predators and gatherers, hunters and farmers, warriors and builders.

One of the new half-translated documents retold the story of how Kur had extracted his innate evil to create Ossus, and then simply left the dragon to be defeated by someone else. Was it meant as a test of his creations? Or just an abdication of responsibility? Had he created an enemy that he knew he could never defeat?

The only way to destroy the evil is from within.

She had her own questions, too. If the dragon had been separated into a tangible form, and if the wreths were supposed to destroy it, then why were the wreths themselves so full of evil? She tapped fingers on one of the blood-stained crystal sheets. "And it's not just wreths," she muttered, remembering what Lord Cade had done to Elliel, remembering Utho's betrayal. Those actions were surely evil, but they had nothing to do with the dragon or the wreths.

She sat back and wondered. Was evil inherent in every creation, or was it created by their personalities? Humans were neither exclusively passive nor violent, not just harvesters or killers. Did they have to be one or the other?

After Kur extracted the dragon from himself, a supposed triumph, he had seemed weak and unable to face his own flaws. He no longer had the strength, or the *desire,* to be a god anymore. He had left the wreths to confront the problem, to win or lose and create their own destiny. He had simply gone away, tasking others to fight his great battle.

What if even a god needed both aspects, a soft compassion and a hard edge? What if Kur had irreparably weakened himself by erasing his dark side, which left him fragile and indecisive?

How she longed to have a legacier here, or dear Queen Tafira, so she could debate these possibilities. Right now, Shadri was extrapolating a great deal from only the handful of words she could translate.

And dragons had been seen—more than one. With so much evil growing, splitting, and cracking open, what if Ossus had fragmented, so that pieces of him were emerging? Because the great dragon had no balance to hold himself together?

Her head throbbed from the work of reading the strange symbols, filling in the blanks. She found a detailed description of the ancient command Kur had given the wreths. There were many different versions, but this one was clear, stating that once Ossus was destroyed (and she noted the passive, not that once the "wreths" destroyed the dragon, but only once it "was destroyed," attributing no specific agent to do the deed), then "a better world" would come. Intrigued, she checked her work, verified the words. It didn't say specifically that the god would return, annihilate the existing world, and create a new one . . . only that there would be "a better world."

"Well, that makes a lot of difference," she said, exasperated. She picked up other disorganized sheets, trying to arrange the same sources together, but it seemed a hopeless job. One answer was clear, though, and she shook her head. "The wreths haven't even read these in ages. They don't care about their own history."

When Pokle came in bearing a tray with soup and some boiled eggs, Shadri couldn't contain her ideas, needing to tell *someone.* Even though the young man could provide little scholarly input, she rattled off her thoughts, growing more and more excited as she talked.

Pokle listened, drinking in the words, or maybe just letting them run off him. After Shadri finally ran out of steam, she looked at him, hoping for his opinion or advice.

The young man grinned and said, "I like stories about dragons."

61

W ITH the empra's dramatic reappearance, Serepol was in an uproar, and
Key Priestlord Klovus had to respond. Before long, the unrest would
explode.

Klovus was appalled to see the vision of Iluris on the high balcony above
the execution platform. He had always had a nagging sense that she might
still be alive. Zaha had been given orders to kill her on Fulcor Island, but he
had failed. Even so, Klovus had seen blood leaking out of her cracked skull,
and she had been comatose on the voyage home and for long afterward. She
couldn't possibly have recovered from that injury.

But from what he had just seen, Empra Iluris was more than just recovered. The tremendous power she had exuded from the speaking balcony, the
shimmer around her, the roar of energy! It was as if she had joined with a
godling's force—but Klovus controlled the Serepol godling. He would have
known! It made no sense.

Now, as he hurried toward the Magnifica, he could feel the powerful entity
moving through him. Oddly, though, the Serepol godling felt an unfortunate
empathy for Iluris, sensitive to the prayers and faith of the people. If Iluris
returned now, she would ruin the future of Ishara.

Klovus had been concerned that Cemi might gather enough followers to
pose a threat as the empra's heir apparent. But he had never expected to see
Iluris herself. . . . The crowd's delight, excitement, and adoration offended
him. "Hear us, save us. Hear us, save us!"

Having actually seen her on the palace balcony, many people quickly con-
cluded the funeral pyre had been a sham. By reappearing in front of everyone, she had made Klovus a fool—or they thought he was actively involved
in her disappearance.

As the execution ceremony descended into chaos, he acted quickly, needing to get the crowds away from the palace before they turned into a mob
against him. He called a grand and loud procession to move toward the great
temple, where they could supposedly pray for Empra Iluris.

As he moved off, though, he whispered harshly to his temple guards, who
included at least two nondescript Black Eels. "While I distract the crowds at
the temple square, ransack the palace. Find her! We need to stop anyone from
seeing or hearing her again. Capture her."

One guard asked, "Capture, Key Priestlord?"

He hissed his answer. "Soon enough she will go back to being dead, but I want to interrogate her first. We must understand what she is up to." He made sure only the temple guards and ur-priests could hear him. "Go over every inch of the palace. You know she's in there. Turn over every wardrobe, break into every cupboard, every locked chamber, every storage room until you find her."

Leaving them to follow his orders, Klovus strode into the crowd, raised his hands, and added his voice to the exuberant chants. "Hear us, save us!" The crowd rejoiced in the affirmation that their beliefs had not been in vain. But angry doubts would set in very soon. Klovus's thoughts raced as he tried to imagine how to deal with this disaster.

Worshippers flocked in from the side streets, filling the temple square. Klovus went straight for the Magnifica steps, showing false excitement while his heart raced and he tried to hide his panic. The district priestlords were pleased to have seen Empra Iluris, unaware of how the underpinnings of power had changed in Serepol.

He ascended the stone stairs, and the murmur of excited chatter made his stomach churn with disgust. The crowd noise sounded so different from the somber responses whenever he spoke to them. From the second platform above the square, he turned and regarded them all. Beaming for the crowd, he raised his arms in celebration, still indignant that the conspirators had escaped execution. Certainly, they would cause more trouble.

As the crowd fell into a simmering silence, he drew in a deep breath and knew exactly what to say.

Meanwhile, a determined invasion occurred in the empra's palace. Bland-featured Black Eels led search parties through the arched entrance into the reception hall. Ranks of temple guards pushed into the main throne chamber, the anterooms, the banquet halls. Silently, the Black Eels spread apart, rushing into the guest quarters, the now-empty offices of Chamberlain Nerev.

Some of the guards were uncertain why the key priestlord was not rejoicing in the empra's return. Others, who had rounded up and interrogated outspoken rebels in the streets, understood the complications posed by her unexpected return. Some searchers simply let their penchant for vandalism run free.

Some palace servants tried to stop the indignity as guards searched the kitchens and larders, finding ample opportunity to seize food and bottles of wine or fermented cider. Others broke windows, kicked in cupboards, smashed open wardrobes, and walked away with silver and gold curios.

Yet they found no sign of Empra Iluris.

As the key priestlord's lackeys flooded through the palace, ransacking rooms, overturning beds in search of the empra or her co-conspirators, smashing furniture, at some point a candle was knocked over onto a pile of parchment, or a smashed lantern spilled burning oil, or a torch caught on a hanging tapestry. In almost no time, flames rushed along wall hangings, caught on bed coverings, ignited furniture.

The Black Eels continued their search even as the fire raged, but they found the empra's suite empty, the speaking balcony clear, her bedchambers vacant. The smoke thickened.

The palace had stood for centuries, home to a succession of emprirs and empras, but the fire knew nothing of history or reverence, and it kept burning.

High above the temple square, Klovus used the godling to amplify his voice to a thunderous boom. "Your faith has kept Ishara strong, and I have led you through these turbulent times."

The crowd responded, "Hear us, save us."

"And now the spirit of Empra Iluris has given us a sign. Even after you all witnessed her funeral pyre, she appeared to us in a vision so that you could see how important it is to follow my commands."

The apparition had said no such thing at all, but Klovus spoke with such great confidence that many would soon doubt their own memories.

"The spirit of our beloved empra is always with us, and she is restless because we have not yet destroyed the Commonwealth murderers who struck her down. She demands revenge."

The crowd responded with automatic anger, but not as loud as he had heard before. They were still too awed by what they had seen.

"Iluris speaks to me," he proclaimed, a comment so audacious that no one would challenge him.

"Hear us, save us!"

The key priestlord's own representatives were mixed in among the crowd now, and they picked up the shout. "Hear us, save us! We have faith in you, Key Priestlord Klovus." The chanting roared louder. He raised his hands again, lifting his gaze toward the palace—

Where he saw curls of smoke spilling out of shattered windows, a blaze that was growing stronger. The palace was burning!

People in the crowd turned, shouted the alarm. Many began to rush back through the streets, hoping to help fight the blaze. The crowd that had been in the palm of his hand only moments earlier now watched in dismay as the fire engulfed the towering structure.

Hidden again deep beneath the palace, Cemi was overjoyed. "Iluris, that was perfect! The people desperately needed to see you, at last. You saved Analera and the others from execution!"

"I saved them for now, but I need to save the rest of my people." Iluris sounded both vigorous and exhausted. "Ishara needs a new empra, a strong empra, but I am almost used up." She touched the girl's shoulder. "You have to be ready, Cemi."

"But you're back now! You revealed yourself," Cemi said. "Everything will change! No one can deny that you're still alive. You'll expose Klovus, overthrow him."

The older woman shook her head. "I offered them a glimpse, but now I must give them a government."

Above, searchers were rushing through the palace, smashing doors and breaking into rooms to find the hidden empra, but her bolt-hole had been safe for many weeks, and the new godling maintained their protective illusion.

Before long, though, Iluris felt her head pulse and throb, and the godling around them stirred in alarm. She sensed smoke, though she could not actually smell it. "My palace is burning!"

Captani Vos reddened with anger. "Is the key priestlord trying to smoke us out? I can't believe even Klovus would dare such a thing."

"The violence was clumsy, not intentional," Iluris said. The godling communicated with her, showing what was happening above.

"The blaze will not reach down here," Cemi said with forced confidence. She was also connected with the new entity, and her eyes were glazed. "It's all burning. The flames are growing."

Behind her eyes, Iluris saw visions of the fire scorching rare paintings, burning beautiful curtains and woven artwork, destroying ancient furniture. "Klovus would not do this on purpose. This will harm him as well."

She felt dizzy and faint. Standing on the balcony and speaking in her giant voice had drained her. It was necessary, Iluris knew, but she had very little energy left inside her. "Cemi, you have to do this. Save what you can . . . but I will pave the way. We can stop the blaze. The godling can do it . . ."

Iluris closed her eyes and fell backward into the entity's unseen embrace. She called upon the faith and energy with which all of the worshippers had imbued it, and Cemi helped to guide the act.

With a whipping whistling force, the new godling swirled up from the underground levels and raced like a whirlwind through the palace. As a smothering breeze, it rushed through rooms and passageways, snuffing out fire, engulfing smoke. It enclosed the blazes, suffocated them, and moved on to other burning rooms, chasing the fire. The flames flickered out as the godling expended its magic.

Afterward, the godling showed Iluris from its point of view what had become of her home. The palace was charred, stained, and broken. She could see what the godling saw. The damage left a great wound in her heart.

But it also gave her anger and determination.

"Now we must plan the next step and move quickly. It is time to emerge from hiding and go among the people," Iluris said. "Our land will have an empra again."

62

❧

KING Adan's army crossed the land at a swift pace, heading toward the Norterran troops on the western slope of the Dragonspine Mountains. The cavalry led the way, while scouts raced ahead to spread the word and commandeer necessary supplies. The soldiers covered many miles, and each of them knew it would be a tiring journey with the prospect of a hard battle ahead.

As he rode along, Kollanan kept his focus as sharp as an arrow point. Long ago, he had made grand, hopeful plans for his kingdom of Norterra. He had worked with his brother Conndur, and the Commonwealth had prospered for decades, troubled by nothing more than a few local disputes. Citizens traveled and traded as they wished, and paladin Bravas like Lasis administered justice or resolved squabbles when necessary.

After the Isharan war in his youth, Koll was content with his legacy and wanted to be remembered as a good king with a devoted wife and a loving family. That dream had been shattered, as if a rock had been thrown onto the thin ice of a frozen pond. All shattered . . . the united Commonwealth, the long-forgotten wreths, his dear brother murdered by his own bonded Brava. And now the land was facing a civil war.

Closer to his heart, closer to his home, so many were dead, although Kollanan kept the faintest glimmer of hope that Birch might still be alive. As he rode along under a clear sky, he didn't notice the bright sunshine all around him. . . .

Elliel and Thon rode at King Kollanan's side like bodyguards, engaged in their own conversation. Kollanan admired how they always found something to talk about, but their clear love also served as a raw reminder of his own losses.

That afternoon, the army camped at the fringes of the western foothills. Large command tents were erected for both kings. Across the camp, other soldiers laughed and sang, played gambling games, and boasted about their abilities. They chattered about wives and sweethearts, and their descriptions grew more beautiful with each day they traveled farther from home.

Kollanan surveyed the numerous fire rings, the gathered soldiers, their stacked shields, their swords, many of them inlaid with the shadowglass provided by Queen Voo. The obsidian rippled in the gathering darkness, but did not reflect the orange light from the campfires.

He kept to himself, but Adan came to sit with him, sharing a meal of Utauk camp food that made even the bean and sausage soup into a feast. Kollanan acknowledged his nephew's company, though he wasn't sure he had the energy to act sociable.

Adan made some suggestions about strategy, but they had made a plan, and there was little else to say until the joined armies moved over the mountains. "By now, everyone knows what Utho did, what Mandan did." Adan frowned down at his bowl. "Do you think the people of Convera will overthrow him before we even get there?"

Kollanan finished his meal and set the bowl aside near the campfire. "I trust that the Utauk messenger got through, but beyond that I cannot say. Ancestors' blood, there's little chance that this will be a simple thing . . ."

He picked up a twisted dry branch from the pile and cut off a hunk of the wood with his dagger. He turned it this way and that, imagining what animal figure might lie inside. He began to whittle away flakes of pale wood, flicking them with enough vigor that they fell into the flames and burned in quick bright sparks.

"I wish Mandan wouldn't make this into a war." Adan shook his head. "Somehow I can't accept that he knew Utho was the one who killed our father."

Koll dug deeper with the sharp edge of his knife, cutting out a lump of wood. He began to see the shape now, knew it would be another pig, like the ones he had carved for Tomko and Birch. "Maybe your brother just wanted to be konag."

Adan savored a spoonful of his meal. "Do you think he was that ambitious? Mandan always resented his schooling, complained about meetings with vassal lords and counselors. He was pampered, not power hungry."

"He was a spoiled, weak brat." Koll let the anger bubble up from his chest. "He was older than you, but he had the emotional maturity of a child." He stopped carving for a moment to look intently at the king of Suderra. "Conndur wanted you to succeed him, Adan."

"We already talked about this. I rule my own kingdom." He looked away. "I never wanted more than that."

"You rule Suderra well, and you can do the same for the Commonwealth." With the point of his knife he fashioned a snout and formed lumps of ears. "You grew up with him in Convera. You both had the same tutors. Was there ever a time you truly felt that Mandan was more worthy of the throne than you?"

"All he wanted was to paint," Adan admitted. "He valued his comforts and wealth, but I didn't see him as greedy for more. Now he sends for people to fight and die for him because of perceived insults. He lets others do his thinking and planning for him without considering the consequences of his decisions Why? I . . . don't know what he wants."

"Your brother is a man of few aspirations and little courage," Koll said. "And those are not qualities that make a good king."

"It's a cruel joke that he has such a talent as a painter, yet is forced to wear the konag's crown."

"Not for long. He'll have plenty of time to paint in exile, where he can cause no more damage."

Kollanan continued carving, adding more anger with each stroke. Flecks of wood spun off, and the animal took shape—a boar.

"I almost sympathize with Mandan," Adan mused. "I never wanted to be a king either. I could have spent my life observing the night sky, plotting the patterns of the moon and charting the stars in the heavens. . . ."

"We don't always get what we want," Koll said. "Gazing at the stars might seem important, but leading all of humanity takes priority."

Adan frowned. "Mandan never liked to join me and my father on the observation deck. He said he was bored, said he was cold. He didn't have the patience to make precise measurements." He ground his teeth together. "Once, after we'd argued, he found my journal filled with detailed maps of the sky, drawn with the most meticulous care. I had spent years creating it, compiling every star-mark with the greatest precision." Adan flushed. "And he . . . with a fine brush and black paint, he added dots to the pages, random stars wherever he wanted. It took me weeks to discover what he had done. My maps were ruined because I couldn't tell which were the real stars and which were his angry markings. Years of detailed observations, ruined."

Kollanan scoffed. "Such a cruel and petulant man to lead the three kingdoms? I think not." He continued carving. This conversation reminded him of evenings spent with Tafira, talking about mundane matters or sweeping consequences. How he missed her! Though he felt broken and cold inside, he would fight his battles and achieve his victories, but after all he had lost, Koll wondered if he could be salvaged, if he could be entirely human again . . . or even if he wanted to be.

He looked down at the animal he had carved, hoping someday he would give it to Birch.

Koll said, "Mandan is corrupt and dangerous, and he must be removed from power. I will do everything I can to make that happen."

He looked down at the new wooden animal. It was good work, but he could always carve another one, if he ever saw his grandson again. He tossed the figure into the campfire and watched it burn as he thought of the war—the many wars—to come.

63

Dark clouds gathered over Bannriya, a swirling storm and an ominous hush. But it was more than thunderheads, more than dust clouds—the darkness accompanied the sandwreth army as they laid siege to the city.

From the high wall, Penda stared across the terrifying force of augas and wreth warriors, the forest of spears and swords. Cold rushed through her veins like a sudden ice storm, and she traced a finger around her heart, but could not complete the circle. A supernatural fear worked its way through her that might signify the end of this ancient city and the collapse of Suderra.

Arrogant and impatient, Queen Voo looked up at the humans on the parapet high above her. "Open your gates. Surrender your city, or we will knock down these walls."

Penda thought about her baby back in the castle, the future she should have. If the sandwreths battered through the walls and ransacked Bannriya, little Oak would be only one of countless victims. Penda had to stop that from happening. She steeled herself. She was the queen of Suderra, and she would lead them.

"Our walls have stood a long time," Penda shouted back. "They can withstand you. Our shadowglass weapons will kill you."

Captain Elcior shouted for his Banner guards to raise their shadowglass-tipped spears, ready if the wreths came at the walls. Archers held their arrows steady.

Penda said in a lower voice, "We have no wish to fight. Do not force us."

"Oh, we will not fight you," Voo mocked. "We will simply kill you all for what King Adan did."

Xar swooped overhead, whistling and clicking, soon joined by Ari. The orphan girl hurried up beside Penda, just as agitated as the reptile birds. Glik pointed up in the sky where dozens of wild skas had appeared, flying together beneath the thick clouds that congealed like greasy smoke. "Look!"

Hale Orr gazed at the enemy army. He was dressed in crimson and black, looking like a military commander in uniform. "*Cra*, there must be a way to make her see reason." The small shadowglass pendant in his ear dangled like a teardrop of midnight. He turned to his daughter. "Let me go out and parley with her, dear heart. She knows damned well how much shadowglass she sent us. I can negotiate something." He grinned, showing his gold tooth. "I am an Utauk after all."

"Look at that army, Father! What could you possibly have to bargain with?"

"Common sense." He shrugged. "What good does it do for us to point arrows at them, while they shout at us from outside the walls?"

Though her father was filled with confidence and bravado, Penda remained troubled. "I would not count on common sense to outweigh vengeance for the sandwreth queen. Adan killed her brother, and we overran their slave camp."

"Then I'll have to count on my Utauk luck." He propped the stump of his hand on his hip and she was reminded of how he had lost the hand in a knife fight.

"Utauk luck has failed you before."

"Utauk luck failed me once, long ago. It can't happen again."

Cheth looked at Hale Orr. "I will accompany your father as a Brava escort." She patted her side. "Now that I have my ramer again."

Glik said, "There are other Bravas here on the wall, too."

Cheth responded with a stony expression. "Hale Orr, you will have an impressive escort."

Tears stung Penda's eyes as she looked at the vast enemy army, and she knew something had to be done. With their magic, the sandwreths could indeed crush Bannriya and kill everyone. Including her sweet baby. "Do what you can, Father."

She embraced him, felt the strength in his hard barrel chest, and remembered when he had held her as a child, rocked her and told stories about her mother, who had died years earlier.

Cheth and the other two Bravas rushed from the wall to prepare.

"We will resolve this," Hale called back to her. He always believed he could talk people into anything, but wreths were not humans. "I love you," he said, then hurried after the Bravas.

Penda brooded, then finally spoke to Glik. "Run to my quarters in the castle and tell the nursemaid to bring Oak. Whatever happens, I want my daughter here with me."

Glik flinched, and the skas overhead swirled in the sky as if in reaction. "Is that wise? You know Queen Voo wants the baby."

"She can't have my daughter, but there's no hiding her." Penda did not want to admit that if everything fell apart, if the sandwreth army did crash through the ancient stone walls, she wanted to hold her baby.

Overhead, the black clouds seemed darker than ever.

☙❧

As the gates swung open Hale Orr rode out on a well-mannered gray horse, with two Banner guards leading the way carrying Suderra's yellow flag. Dressed in black, Cheth and her fellow Bravas sat tall in their saddles, while the flamboyant Utauk man smiled and reminded himself to be prepared for anything. Hale began to sing an Utauk song of luck and love and the choices between them. He doubted the wreths would understand such things, but the singing put him in a good mood, and it was better than howling out a primal war cry.

The wreth army was vast, their armor dazzling despite the clouds overhead. Queen Voo sat on her auga, her spear held like a signal, her dragon-scale shield across her chest. She grimaced at Hale Orr and his small negotiating party, which was clearly not what she had expected.

Warriors glowered at him as he came forward with a welcoming grin. Axus shifted on another auga beside the queen, but she ignored her resolute mage, her warriors, and everything else except for Hale Orr. She frowned as the gates swung closed behind the party. The two Banner guards glanced nervously over their shoulders, as if trapped.

Showing deference, Hale dismounted and set the reins on the saddle. He used his good hand to sweep aside his black and crimson cape to reveal that he carried no weapons. Behind him, the Bravas did not ignite their ramers, nor did they dismount. The Banner guards held up the flags, waiting.

Hale made an expansive gesture. "Queen Voo, I am here to have a discussion. You remember me, the father of Queen Penda Orr? We dined together when you were our guests in Bannriya Castle."

"I vaguely remember you," Voo said. "Humans are so often indistinguishable." In a smooth movement, she slid down from her auga and stepped forward to face him. "You have come to surrender to me."

"I've come to negotiate." He glanced up at the sky. The wreths glowered at the circling skas, twenty of them now. "I would like to reach a resolution. We do not want to use our shadowglass weapons to kill your army."

"And you want to save your puny city," Voo said.

Hale shrugged. "In any good negotiation, both sides benefit."

The queen seemed to crackle with heat. "Then we can resolve this quickly. Have Penda Orr bring me her baby. I asked for it before. I demand it now."

Hale tried not to show his dismay. "That will not be possible, Queen Voo. Why would you want an innocent baby?"

"My brother came to take Penda and the baby, and Adan killed him. Therefore, the lives of Penda and Adan are also forfeit."

Hale huffed. "You cannot have my daughter or her husband. Or the child."

"You took my slaves!" Voo roared. "Killed my camp guards."

Hale tried to remain calm, smiling. "But you enslaved the human captives in the first place. How will you atone for that? If you hadn't taken them from their homes, none of this would have happened. We were already arming ourselves to serve as part of your army. What more did you want?"

Axus muttered, "As I told you, my queen."

Hale was surprised by the mage's reaction.

Voo flashed an angry glare at Axus, then turned back to Hale. She said, "All humans are mine from the moment of their birth and from the moment of their parents' birth. As a subservient race, you are meant to follow whatever commands I deem appropriate. And you—" She sniffed at Hale Orr. "You flaunt these colors. You grin at me. You strut forward to 'negotiate,' when you should be groveling." She raised her dragon-scale shield. "I command you to kneel before me."

Hale swallowed. The three Bravas shifted on their horses. "*Cra*," he muttered under his breath. "And if I kneel, will that end this dispute? Will you withdraw your army without further threat to Bannriya? If so, I would happily pay that price."

"It is not a price. It is an obligation," she snapped. "You will kneel before me, because I command it."

His famously disarming smile faltered. "Queen Voo, I remind you of the thousands of shadowglass arrows pointed toward you at this very moment." He glanced back at the city, where he could see the figures lined on top of the walls.

Cheth spoke a low command from her saddle, calling to her comrades. "Bravas!" She clamped the ramer around her wrist as did the others, igniting their blazing swords.

The skas let out piercing cries, and increasing numbers of them joined the group overhead.

Curious, Voo looked at them. "Half-breeds with fiery blades? Is that intended to intimidate me?" She turned back to him. "I told you to kneel."

"We can negotiate this, discuss what each side really wants," Hale said. "Let us be reasonable."

"Reasonable!" Voo waved her hand sideways as if it were an ax blade. Hale heard a loud wooden snap before he felt the pain. His leg bones shattered. His legs folded as if he had far too many joints, and he collapsed in a tumble. He sprawled face-first down on the ground—and then the roar of agony exploded inside.

Grinning, Voo lifted her hand again, twisting her fingers and curling them like the legs of a dead spider.

With a wild cry, Cheth galloped forward, slashing with her ramer, and the other Bravas were right behind her.

Mage Axus threw an invisible wash of air, knocking the Bravas aside just before their ramers could cut down Queen Voo.

Hale howled in pain. He rolled, tried to get up, but his legs were useless.

Ignoring everything else, Voo strode toward the man, intent on making an example of her victim. She sneered at him while the Bravas battled a surge of sandwreth warriors. Somehow, Hale had the presence of mind to reach behind him with his good hand. He pulled out the shadowglass dagger he had hidden there, because for all his bluster and confidence he did not trust sandwreths.

Voo wore high boots, but her thighs were bare. Hale slashed upward, cutting a red gash across her upper leg. The queen recoiled, her mouth open in an O of surprise at what the shadowglass had done. Blood spurted from the cut.

It was enough to make Hale forget about the pain for just a moment.

Voo twirled her bone-tipped spear, and as he struggled to get up, she plunged her weapon through his chest. "There, just the way my brother died," she said.

"No!" Penda screamed from the wall as she watched her father fall.

The Bravas attacked in a raging fury. Their ramers flashed like a lightning storm as Cheth and the others drove back the wreth mage and numerous warriors. The Banner guards tossed aside their yellow flags and drew shadowglass swords to defend themselves.

The Brava attack was vehement enough to drive back the wreths for just a few seconds. "Take him!" Cheth shouted.

Penda could hear the words, despite the distance. The Banner guards killed two warriors who were unprepared for the shadowglass. One Brava leaped down from his horse, yanked Queen Voo's spear from Hale's chest, and snatched the body from the ground.

Penda screamed from the high wall. "Father!" The baby in her arms was crying, and Penda also wept, her body shaking with grief. "No!"

Glik hugged her.

Below, the Bravas used their blazing ramers to battle the wreths. The Banner guards took Hale's body and galloped back toward the city, while the Bravas covered their retreat. Cheth and her companions fought hard, against an overwhelming tide of wreths.

High above, Ari and Xar circled squawking and whistling, and then flashed down toward the sandwreth army.

Penda felt her heart link fraying, tearing.

Glik moaned and staggered, gasping for breath and lost in a sudden trance. "It's too many . . . all of them!"

The black clouds darkened and countless small shapes burst out of them like a swarm of locusts. Xar and Ari plunged toward the battlefield below, followed by thousands upon thousands of wild skas. The reptile birds attacked the wreths by the hundreds, harrying them, pecking, clawing.

The wreth army churned in disarray, their augas charging off in panic. The skas formed a blanketing defensive wall so that Cheth and the other Bravas could break free and retreat.

Soldiers on the wall called for the gates to be opened. The skas continued to harry the wreth army until all of the riders were safely behind Bannriya's walls with their grim burden.

64

～⌾～

MANDAN slept off the effects of the poppy milk, and awoke feeling sick and shaky. His mind was clearer, though, and his outrage was strong enough to force him into motion.

When the castle searchers reported that the Utauk messenger had also escaped, the konag knew that Lira must have fled with him, plotted with him. The rebellious decree from Kollanan and Adan, the obvious collusion of the Utauks, and the assassination attempt against him—all part of a widespread conspiracy. His own queen was working with them, as well as his brother and uncle. While he'd been consumed with trying to build defenses and gather his army, the venomous snake Lira was right next to him, plotting his downfall.

Hunched on his throne, Mandan dry-heaved and his head pounded. Recovering himself, he looked up as the two Bravas marched in with their report. He felt a rush of excitement. "Did you find Lira? I want you to bring her back alive, though she will not stay that way."

"We have much to report, my konag," Tytan said, sounding evasive. "Our scouts are trying to track the Utauk rider. We suspect the queen is with him."

"Of course she is with him!" Mandan snapped. "She betrayed me. She's probably even his lover."

The big Brava grumbled. "We are searching for Utauk caravans or camps. They all communicate with one another. Someone will know what happened."

Jennae's voice was a low hiss. "The Utauks disappeared, left the city all at once. It is obviously coordinated."

"You should have stopped this," Mandan said. "You should have known ahead of time."

Jennae's eyes flared with indignation, but Tytan spoke first. "We were dealing with larger problems in Convera."

"You had an entire army for that," Mandan said.

"Not an entire army," Tytan replied. "So far, your vassal lords provided only about a third of what we expected. In addition, the number of desertions has increased, including among the castle staff."

"Deserters! Find them. Punish them."

"Word has spread about the decree from Suderra and Norterra. Some of them believe the charges, and no one wants to be in a civil war."

"Lies," Mandan said. "I'm the konag. They must believe me over anyone else."

Although Jennae became stony and unreadable, Tytan seemed uneasy. "They are beginning to lose confidence in you, Sire. And if Utho was truly the one who killed Konag Conndur..."

"Oh, of course Utho didn't do that!" Mandan had told himself the same thing repeatedly, and each time he believed it a little more. "Isharan animals killed my father. Everyone knows that! And now Queen Lira tried to poison me. She's in league with the rebels Adan and Kollanan. We must find them and defeat them."

Jennae spoke up. "We have an idea, Sire. A scout just reported a large Utauk camp on this side of the mountains, heading down the river road."

"A large camp?" Mandan chewed on the words. "That must be where Lira and that messenger were heading. Those tribes all stick together. Gather two hundred soldiers right away. We have to ride before they disperse."

Tytan was surprised. "Two hundred soldiers, Sire? For what?"

"To overrun the rebel camp, of course," Mandan said. "And to capture my wife, if she is there."

"I'll go," Jennae said. "I'll ride fast and bring back Queen Lira if she is there."

"No, I'm going myself, and I will take my army." He glanced at both of his black-clad guardians. "Two hundred Commonwealth soldiers and two Bravas will be more than enough."

The mounted force rode out that afternoon. Mandan wore full armor and a fine cape in Commonwealth blue embroidered with the rising sun of Osterra. Whenever he saw the open-hand symbol on his shield, he thought of his own hand prepared for a brutal slap across Lira's face.

"We move fast and hard up along the river! As long as it takes!" he shouted. With a jingle of tack and a rumble of shod hooves, the soldiers rolled out of Convera Castle, making an impressive charge through the city streets. They rode single file across the repaired bridge, and then galloped hard along the wide road.

Though he cut an imposing regal figure, Mandan felt ill experiencing more than the aftereffects of the poison and several times broke out in a cold sweat. The hard riding made him feel like vomiting again. His skull pounded, but he forced himself to think about the victory ahead.

As he rode with the war party now, he knew it was about time he participated in a real battle. He had only been at Yanton in his imagination, but he was with the Commonwealth navy at its shameful defeat at Fulcor Island and it had made him reel with terror, had given him nightmares. This time it would be different. These were mere Utauk spies, motley traders, traveling family groups. They would be like sheep, and his army were hungry wolves.

On the second day of hard riding, scouts reported they had seen the Utauk camp ahead—cookfires and bonfires, numerous tents and carts, horses tied to trees. "At least a hundred Utauks, Sire," said the rider, whose sweaty face was crusted with road dust.

"And we are two hundred," Mandan said. "Utauks should give us no trouble." He kicked his heels into his horse's side, and the soldiers raced ahead, swords drawn. When they reached the open meadow filled with tents and wagons in the deepening twilight, heard the singing and camp chatter, Mandan yelled, "Attack. Attack the enemy!"

The war party swung into the camp like a giant hammer. The outriders hacked with their swords, cast torches into the tents. Startled family members ran screaming.

Mandan yelled in his loudest voice. "We declare the Utauk tribes to be traitors and subject to the konag's justice." His horse snorted, skittish from the clamor. He struck its flank with the flat of his sword, making it rear up and strike down with its hooves.

The Utauks scrambled about like a stirred-up anthill, grabbing tent poles, old swords, brands from their bonfires. They stood back-to-back to defend themselves. Mandan could have had archers kill them all, but he preferred to see his swordsmen hack them down.

In front of the main tent, an ancient woman sat cross-legged on a rug, raising sticklike arms. "I am Shella din Orr and these are my people. What have we done?"

Mandan galloped toward her, recognizing the leader's name. She looked pathetically weak, confused. "You kidnapped my wife! Where is Lira?"

"We kidnapped no one," said Shella din Orr. "Utauks are neutral. You must stop this now."

Two children let out shrill screams as riders chased them into the trees. Tytan and Jennae ignited their ramers and struck down tents, killing men and women who tried to defend themselves.

Two bearded Utauk men stepped up on either side of the crone. "We will defend our mother."

Mandan laughed. "You can try. Where is Lira?"

"Our tribes are peaceful traders, as it has always been," Shella said.

"Your tribes participated in a conspiracy. Your messenger is in league with two rebel kings."

"This is beyond your authority," said the old woman. "You do not rule us!"

So Mandan raised his sword and struck her down. He blinked, startled by what he had done. Though he had trained with Utho many times, she was the first person he had actually killed by himself. Yes, he had hacked away at straw-filled dummies dressed in Isharan clothes. Despite her political clout, this old Utauk woman was not a powerful opponent.

Mandan chopped again, and the blade bit through her leathery skin and cut off her head.

The two bearded men threw themselves on Mandan, and he slashed back and forth with the sword, cutting only one of the men, missing the other.

In an instant, Tytan was there. The Brava man struck down one of the men with his ramer, while the other staggered away, wounded.

Throughout the burning camp, Utauks were screaming, moaning. Seeing their leader killed seemed to drain the strength from them. "Shella din Orr! Oh, Mother."

Mandan was pleased to see the many bodies sprawled on the ground, their tents blazing, their wagons smashed and overturned, their horses butchered. The Utauks were in shock.

He heard a scream and a struggle. Jennae came forward holding her ramer high and dragging a thin woman in a fine blue gown.

Mandan was startled to see her rich red hair, her pale skin. For just a moment he saw a flash of his own dear mother, but then anger reddened his vision. Lira was a betrayer, not a loving woman like Lady Maire.

"I found her, Sire. We can take the queen back with us after we've finished punishing the Utauks."

Lira's face was blotchy and red. Tears poured down her cheeks. He found her weak and pathetic.

All of Mandan's plans evaporated when he saw her, and a new idea emerged. He felt nothing for Lira. She wasn't even worth tormenting. He didn't need revenge, because she didn't deserve the effort.

Considering the number of Utauks in the camp, he began to realize the extent of the plans against him, how the wandering tribes must have spread sedition, turned villages against him, even his own vassal lords. Donnan Rah had spread lies that weakened his rule. It was too much shame to think that Lira herself had participated. Had her love for him been an act all along?

Mandan scowled at her, then looked at Jennae. "I do not see my queen. She is less than nothing to me. All I see is a field full of treacherous Utauk snakes." Another thought crossed his mind. "Utauks . . . like the woman who seduced my brother Adan. She probably turned him against me, too, and all of Suderra." He sucked in a deep breath, not doubting his decision. "For their betrayal, they should all die."

With a loud cry, a man rushed out from between the trees. Donnan Rah! The messenger sprinted forward as if to rescue Lira, but a Commonwealth soldier intercepted him and thrust a sword between his ribs. The Utauk man gasped, staggered, and pitched forward onto the ground. His hand reached out, still clutching for something he would never reach.

Lira wailed to see Donnan Rah fall, and Mandan heard immeasurable treachery in that noise. "She chose to come here. Therefore, she is not my queen. She's an Utauk. Kill her."

Without the briefest hesitation, Jennae swept her ramer through Lira in a smooth arc just below her ribs, cutting the young woman in two.

Mandan felt nothing but smug satisfaction. Now he had no queen. . . . He was the konag, and he was alone.

65

⁓

WAVES boomed against rocks nearby, but Priestlord Erical could not open his eyes. He choked and coughed, spitting out salty water. He felt himself lifted by the water, washed higher up onto the rocky beach.

The storm had passed, breaking open the clouds and leaving clear blue. Bright sunshine penetrated his eyelids, magnified by the water that nudged him up onto the beach and then pulled him back, taunting. Erical blinked and tried to see, but another foamy wave sluiced over him. The force rolled him over, dragging him across the rough pebbles. He choked again, tasted blood, then more salt.

He had struggled for so long engulfed in the ocean, swept away by the storm that lashed the Isharan vessels, capsizing some, driving one hull against another in a splintering crash drowned out by the rolling drumbeat of thunder. He remembered hearing Magda's roar as the battered ships were hurled onward, leaving him behind, flailing, splashing.

The godling had embraced him like a shimmering blanket and buoyed him up against the malicious whitecaps. She was strong enough to save him, though weakened from the magic she expended to create the hurricane. Erical had been pulled so far under that even the entity could barely reach him, but her energy surrounded him in a bubble. Dizzy, uncaring, unconscious, he had let himself vanish into the water, the storm, and the darkness. He felt no fear, only a warm, tingling comfort to know that the godling would save him—if it was in her power.

Now, awakening alone on an unknown shore, Erical had no idea how much time had passed. He lay in the amniotic afterwash of sun-warmed shallows that eased him up on the beach until he could get to his hands and knees.

As he crawled, he tried to see, but the sunlight was too bright, the pounding in his head too violent. He coughed, spewing out more of the seawater he had swallowed. He worked his way higher onto the shore, finding clumps of seaweed and dried grasses. A twisted driftwood trunk served as an anchor, and he slung his arm around a broken branch. He was crusted with salt, aching in more parts of his body than he could count, and alone.

He plucked at his sodden clothes and let out a harsh chuckle, finding irony in the situation. He was the priestlord of Prirari District, where by custom the people did not believe in immersion. Now he had been immersed beyond imagining in a vast ocean and hurled onto a foreign coastline.

With an effort, he looked beyond the driftwood log and the ocean emptiness behind him. He felt sad and distraught—and then he recognized a different sort of emptiness. His godling's comforting presence was missing.

Erical pulled himself up in alarm, looking desperately around. He felt empty, even more lost. Finally, he felt the gentle tendrils of the entity rediscovering him. She was weak and diffuse, and he knew that she must have expended most of her life energy to carry him through the water to safety.

Now that he was conscious and thinking of her, the godling seeped back into the wakening world. He helped her, letting her pull joy and power from him as well. Erical drew in another deep calming breath, and the godling swirled inside him. As he exhaled, the deity strengthened, brightened. Although he still shuddered with weakness, just knowing she was still with him gave him resolve and stamina.

Erical braced himself against the driftwood and pushed himself to his feet. Around him, clumps of green, rubbery kelp shriveled in the sunlight, like the matted hair of an undersea maiden. Rushing waves provided a constant white noise.

The rocky beach extended far in both directions, though the shoreline curved toward a high sharp point, where stronger waves beat themselves into white foam. He saw none of the other Isharan vessels, though he knew that several of them had been wrecked in the storm. Erical had not wanted to come on this voyage in the first place. The godling belonged back in Prirari. *He* belonged back in Prirari. Was this really what Key Priestlord Klovus wanted? It seemed a fool's errand to him.

Erical's lips were cracked, his throat parched, and his stomach was empty and knotted with hunger. He shouted, "Hello!"

Booming waves answered him. Gulls circled overhead, sounding an alarm that only other birds could hear. Erical closed his eyes, felt the faint godling, and found the strength to shout out again, even louder. "Hello!" He slumped back down onto the driftwood log, muttering, "Hear us, save us."

Then the godling sent a thrill of surprised energy through him. He blinked and looked up, able to sense something through the deity.

A figure came around a nearby corner of rocks, a young girl of no more than ten years, with a basket slung over her shoulder. The girl hiked up her skirts as she picked her way among the tidepools, gathering shells. She moved with nimble fingers to seize a scuttling crab, which she thrust into her basket. Intent on the crannies, she knelt on the weedy rocks and plucked mussels from the pool. She worked her way closer as Erical stared from a distance. The noise of the surf was too loud for her to have heard him.

But when he raised himself to his feet, the motion caught her eye. She looked up swiftly, astonished. He took a step closer. "I won't hurt you."

The girl backed away, clutching her basket. Then she turned and ran.

I won't hurt you?

Erical did not recognize this place, but it was surely the Commonwealth coastline. He had brought a godling along with a war fleet and bloodthirsty barbarians who intended to conquer the three kingdoms. *I won't hurt you?*

He didn't even know if the girl could understand his language. Within him, the godling seemed diffuse again. Driven by hunger and thirst, he worked his way around more driftwood, seaweed, and piles of kelp, heading in the direction the girl had fled. Surely she had come from some fisherman's hut, maybe even a village.

Waves lapped against the rocks, and he realized the tide must be coming in again. He should find a way to climb high enough that he could rest without fear of drowning. He stumbled around the rock promontory and saw the unfolding line of the shore extending into the distance. *North,* he thought.

People were coming toward him, six or seven men following the young girl, who led them back. Erical stopped and stared, hoping they hadn't come to kill him. He had no strength to fight. As the figures approached, he raised his hand in greeting.

66

With the strength of numbers, skas harassed the sandwreths, lashing out at them with talons and snapping with needle fangs. The wreths, driven into a frenzy, fought with ineffective jabs of their spears and slashing swords.

Mage Axus retaliated with turbulence, throwing winds to scatter the skas in the air. Other wreth mages erected invisible protective walls to deflect the wild, unexpected attack. Queen Voo's archers killed many of the skas, but the colorful creatures kept attacking the wreth army until the Bravas and Banner guards had returned Hale Orr's body behind Bannriya's walls. Then, as if released from their mission, the reptile birds dispersed up into the clouds.

The city gates ground shut, leaving the wreths stunned for a long moment before they responded with a resounding surge. Not bothering to form ranks, warriors and nobles charged the city without an obvious strategic plan. Nursing the deep wound in her leg, Queen Voo anticipated the mayhem and destruction about to unfold.

As the sandwreths came closer, Penda clutched her baby and shouted out, "Archers, lancers—ready!" She heard a clatter as a thousand soldiers took positions on the wall. Full baskets of shadowglass arrows stood at every firing station. Over the last month Adan had made sure his army possessed tens of thousands of weapons ready for battle—but it was not the battle that Queen Voo expected.

Beside Penda, Glik leaned over the wall, staring down. "*Cra,* they still believe we are defenseless!" She raised her shadowglass knife, which had already killed wreths. "If they come up here, sister, I will die before I let them get to you and Oak."

Penda felt a warmth that washed away some of her shock and grief at her father's death. "None of us will go quietly. A great many wreths will die before they breach these walls."

As the wild army howled closer, she scanned the countless obsidian sparks that tipped the arrows nocked on drawn bows. For such a ruthless and powerful person, the sandwreth queen seemed incredibly naïve. Not even a drunken Utauk trader would be so gullible as to arm an enemy.

Penda brought her hand down. "Loose!" A black blizzard of arrows showered out. Projectiles peppered the arrogant warriors, and the wreths recoiled as if they had been stabbed with acid. Warriors spilled from their augas and sprawled onto the ground, and their reptile mounts died as well. Countless wreth foot soldiers rushed the gates with extended spears, and another rain of arrows mowed them down. Sandwreths fell by the dozens, then the hundreds.

Voo shrieked in disbelieving fury, and Penda responded with her own battle cry, a loud long sound that expressed anguish at her father's death and a vow of protection for her people. The air was filled with the thrum of bowstrings, the whisper of countless arrows, and the screams of dying wreths.

The initial assault lasted half an hour before the reckless fury of the wreths spent itself. Penda could not tear herself from the walls, though she longed to go where her father's body had been laid out just inside the gate. She wanted to touch his hand, caress his face. Because she could not go down yet, she did the next best thing, stroking the cheek of his baby granddaughter, touching her tiny fingers and tracing a small circle around Oak's heart. "I'll miss you, Father. The beginning is the end is the beginning."

Finally, the momentum of the attack was broken. Wreths tripped over the bodies of their fallen comrades, and their augas stumbled as they retreated. Mage Axus sent a moaning whirlwind that curled back like a signal, and Voo's army withdrew out of arrow range, leaving a grisly new barricade of bodies piled along the wall and in front of the thick gate.

Penda's face felt hot, and tears evaporated on her cheek as if she could will away the sadness. Even seeing the sandwreths draw back gave her no sense of victory, no trickle of happiness. She clutched Oak against her breast and rocked back and forth, just as her father had long ago rocked her.

With a flutter of colorful wings, Ari and Xar returned to wall parapet and preened, as if proud of their work. Glik praised them both and traced a circle around her heart.

Bloody and bedraggled, Cheth returned to the observation post on the wall. She trudged as if carrying a heavy burden on her shoulders and stood before Penda, silent for a long moment. She had removed her ramer, and blood was drying on her wrist. She lowered her eyes. "We could not save him, my queen. We should have interceded and killed that bitch before your father spoke a single word to her." The Brava ground her teeth together. "We need to kill them all."

"Voo won't stop," Penda agreed. "She has been hurt and humiliated, and she will not rest until this city is ground to dust."

"Hale Orr tried to negotiate, but her mind was already made up. She came to destroy Bannriya, and now she knows that it will cost her dearly."

"It can't cost enough to pay for what she did." Glik sniffled. "Father Orr was always good to me."

Before long, Voo and Axus rode back to the wall, picking their way through the mounds of corpses around the gate. The queen shouted up to them, "You have made your certain defeat more painful! I will take pleasure in ripping down these walls stone by stone, killing your people one at a time, splitting their heads open, crushing their chests, chopping off their limbs, or slicing their bellies open, while I make you watch. And then I will still take your baby."

Realizing that Voo could now see Oak in her arms, Penda could not control herself. "I can't count how many times you've threatened to knock down Bannriya's walls. It will never happen. We will slaughter you." Common sense fought with her need to inflict more harm on this woman. "Just as Adan executed your brother—by thrusting a sword right through his chest. Quo only whimpered."

Queen Voo writhed like a rattlesnake thrown onto a hot rock. She roared at the mage beside her, and Axus raised his hands to summon immense power that welled up from the ground beneath Suderra. The city walls trembled.

Cheth said in a low voice, "That was not a wise thing to say, my queen."

But as Axus worked his magic, he faltered in surprise. Bannriya's walls shook, and then the vibrations subsided into silence. The sandwreth army stirred, as if the soldiers sensed some outside danger. Queen Voo stared off toward the northern hills beyond Bannriya. "Come with me," she told Axus, then whirled her auga about and rode back to the heart of her army.

At the same time, Bannriya's northern lookouts raised signal flags, relaying messages, and shouts rang out. Penda looked around, and Cheth stared into the distance, trying to see.

Glik was baffled. "*Cra,* what is it? What made them stop?"

"What *could* make them stop?" Penda asked.

Below, the mage also withdrew from the gate, leaving his attack unfinished. Queen Voo summoned her wreth warriors to form them into ranks. The huge army began to draw away from the city, leaving their dead behind.

It took many scattered messages and confusing reports before Penda learned what was happening. Taking the baby, she ran with Glik and Cheth toward the far end of the city, with Ari and Xar circling over their heads, to where she could look toward the hills. Amazed, she shaded her eyes, squinting toward a vast military force, an army at least as great as the sandwreths— marching south.

Glik couldn't understand. "Is that King Adan returning? Did he bring Kollanan's army with him too?"

Penda knew this was not her husband's force. The colors were wrong, the ranks looked different. When she discerned the front lines of furry white mounts and pale warriors in blue and silver armor, she swallowed hard.

"*Cra*," Penda whispered, drawing a circle around her heart. "Those are frost-wreths."

Wave after wave of pale wreth soldiers marched over the hills from the north, heading straight for Bannriya.

67

⤸

THE ruins of the Fulcor garrison were as burned and scarred as Utho's heart. Standing inside the compound again, he took in the damage on the walls, the collapsed observation towers, the charred timbers of the keep.

He considered how much time he had spent defending this fortress against Isharan animals. Now gulls circled, screaming and fighting over scraps of flesh, even though the birds were already engorged with the unexpected feast. Corpses were strewn everywhere, many in Commonwealth blue, even more of them in Isharan uniforms.

A soldier with cuts on his face and a bandaged hand stepped up in front of Utho, looking shocked and hollow eyed. "What do we do with all the bodies?"

"Leave them for the birds. They'll all be picked clean soon enough."

The man was at a loss for words, and he looked down at the blood-soaked bandage around his hand. He had lost two fingers in the fight. "Even our comrades? Should we not give them a burial at sea? Write down their legacies—"

"They're dead, and we have no time. Salvage whatever weapons you can. Make sure our surviving soldiers are well armed, because we still have more fighting to do."

The injured officer was again confused. "Fighting? But we've killed all the Isharan prisoners. There are no enemy survivors." He forced a victorious smile. "Fulcor Island is ours again."

"Fulcor is as dead as these soldiers." Utho felt cold and hollow just to admit that, but it was true. This garrison, which had changed hands numerous times over the centuries, was just an empty shell. He could stay here and lay claim to an empty rock—but not when his homeland was under attack.

The Isharans—and their godling—were sailing toward Osterra!

Ignoring the injured soldier, he climbed to the top of the wall, taking the steps two at a time. He gazed out to sea, where wreckage still drifted about after the naval battle.

The other two Bravas, Arrick and Wendir, had died in the battle here. He found their bodies, viewing them with disappointment rather than grief, and he was able to use Arrick's cape and gauntlets to replace the parts of his Brava uniform that he himself had lost in the battle and the fall down to the water.

Down in the harbor he could see the activity as Mak Dur's work teams furiously made repairs to the *Glissand*. Three damaged ships had been brought

closer to the island, barely seaworthy. With massive effort, time, and resources, they might be salvaged, but right now the Utauk trading vessel was
the only one close to sailing, and he could not wait any longer. He had to get
back to Rivermouth, to Convera . . . to Mandan. He stared at the horizon,
saw dark storm clouds rolling over the sea.

The sight of ten Isharan warships sailing away still haunted him. He imagined those inhuman warriors crashing their ships up against the shore, invading innocent coastal towns . . . like Mirrabay.

He had left the young konag with only two Brava guards, thinking the
land safe while he conquered Ishara. But Mandan was impetuous and often
made capricious decisions based on emotion rather than careful planning,
and he would be woefully unprepared to face an Isharan invasion. Utho
needed to be there, to lead.

Though he had long dreamed of his vengewar, that idea had shriveled like
a bright flower under the baking sun. Utho had to put aside his obsession for
now and rush home with whatever ships and fighters he could find.

Knotted with impatience, he descended the cliff stairs to the docks, as if
his very presence could hurry along the repairs. Workers from the garrison
above used ropes to lower crates of salvaged supplies: strange-tasting Isharan
food, coils of rope, baskets of swords and arrows.

Cool breezes whistled through the cove. Shouting voices, the rasp of saws,
and the pounding of hammers all made the construction sound urgent.
Other wrecks were stripped of usable materials, picked clean like the bodies
of dead soldiers. Sailcloth was spread out on the *Glissand*'s deck while Utauks
and Commonwealth soldiers sewed up the rips, cut out burned sections, and
patched them with fresh canvas taken from other ships.

Utho was their true leader, but he was not a sailor or a shipwright, and
Mak Dur was in charge of the repair plans. Even though the voyagier and his
crew resented being pressed into Commonwealth service, their goals aligned
with Utho's.

He climbed onto the deck as another rowboat pulled up with a load of
extracted hull boards. Paying no attention to the Brava, Mak Dur shouted,
"We'll use that wood to shore up any weakness inside the hull, but what I
need most is rigging rope. We are ready to hang our sails!"

"How soon can we depart?" Utho demanded as he strode across the
deck.

The voyagier flashed a glance at him and spoke with undisguised disrespect. "As soon as humanly possible—and not a moment sooner, or we'll sink
out in the open water. You'll take a lot longer to swim back to Osterra."

Utho could feel violence brewing within him, but it would not serve his
purpose to lash out. "Then give me a realistic answer." He looked at the re-

stored masts, the yardarms mounted in place, the ropes being strung through pulleys to lift heavy sailcloth. "Ten Isharan vessels sailed west. If we do not get to Osterra soon, it will be too late."

Mak Dur looked at the nearby vessels, assessing the damage. He drew a quick circle around his heart. "Tomorrow." He had obviously been thinking about it a great deal. "She'll be seaworthy enough tomorrow. My crew is willing to chance it."

"Good. Then I'll crowd as many fighters aboard as I can." Utho frowned. "We don't have enough surviving soldiers to fill more than one ship anyway."

The Utauks worked by lantern light all through the night, while soldiers filled and carried water barrels from an intact cistern near the Fulcor barracks. More wood, rope, and nails were carried aboard and stacked on the deck so Mak Dur's crew could continue less vital repairs during the voyage.

At dawn, with the outgoing tide, the *Glissand* moved out of the harbor cove with Utauks and soldiers working the oars. On the open water, they stretched the patchwork sails and caught favorable winds. In yet another measure of defiance, the crew had painted a circle on the new mainsail, marking it as an Utauk vessel again. Utho didn't care about petty insubordination. Once the ship reached Rivermouth Harbor, he and his soldiers would have their own battle, and the voyagier and his recalcitrant crew be damned. He had to get back to Mandan.

The crew threaded a delicate path among the guardian reefs and the broken hulls of sunken ships. Mak Dur said bitterly, "We would have had an easier time if my navigator hadn't been hanged."

"Yes, it would have been better if he'd not tried to desert," Utho replied. "If you must, take consolation in knowing Captain Pharion was also killed in the fighting. I won't whimper about what might have been."

The *Glissand* headed west, catching a swift current and a brisk breeze. The thick seams on the repaired sailcloth looked like scars left by a battle-field surgeon. By late afternoon, a rainstorm and choppy waters tossed the ship about. Some of the repairs cracked, and the hull sprang a leak, but the Utauks were able to repair it enough. Commonwealth soldiers formed a bucket-brigade line from the hold, bailing out water that seeped through split hull boards.

The vessel sailed on.

Utho remained at the bow throughout much of the next day, staring ahead as if his force of will could draw the coastline closer.

Finally, on the third day from Fulcor Island, his heart filled with dread to see rolling black smoke on the horizon. Mak Dur joined him, raising his viewing glass, which he handed to Utho. The Brava pressed the cylinder to his eye, adjusted the focus, and looked toward Rivermouth.

He spotted several Isharan ships. The harbor and the shipyards were in flames.

68

"Hear us, save us," Iluris said.

The empra seemed to be muttering to herself, calling for strength, but Cemi chose to take the phrase as reassurance. She responded bravely, clearly. "Hear us, save us."

Captani Vos added his voice. "Hear us, save us. Your people are ready, Mother."

"And they are angry," Cemi said.

Although the new godling had extinguished the raging blaze, the palace was still gutted and damaged. Everyone knew that Klovus's reckless ransackers had caused the blaze, just as the key priestlord had unleashed the Magnifica godling, which had also damaged the city.

Seeing the smoke coming from the palace, the crowds had rushed from the temple square, scrambling to fight the fire with a line of water buckets from the fountains and animal troughs. It had been a hopeless fight, until the new godling miraculously snuffed out the fire, and even Klovus could not explain it or take credit.

During the turmoil after the fire, Vos and his hawk guards used the opportunity to slip Iluris out of the catacombs and into the city, *her* city. After spending so much time rallying the faith of the people and spreading the word, Cemi knew of safehouses where they could hide the empra. It was happening at last!

She and the hawk guards donned normal working clothes and set up residence for themselves and Iluris in the back rooms of Saruna's brothel—a place no one would look, run by one of the empra's staunchest supporters.

Mistress Saruna was a plump woman with painted eyes and enameled nails. She expressed her deep honor to help save her beloved land. She and her working ladies took care of their special guests, and not a hint leaked out into the streets. Though they were away from the palace, Cemi felt more comfortable now than in all the time they had hidden underground.

Vos grumbled that the quarters were inelegant and unseemly, not fitting for an empra, but Iluris dismissed his concerns. "Anyplace in Serepol, anyplace in *Ishara,* is part of my domain." She also reminded him that whores were particularly good at keeping secrets.

Saruna was as protective as a lioness with cubs. From the back rooms of the brothel, Iluris wrote messages, each one sealed with a blob of candle wax to which she affixed a lock of her hair. "They will know it's me," she said.

The empra touched the center of her chest, and Cemi could feel a thrill of energy surge inside her. She saw the candlelit air in the back chamber shimmer and ripple as if through flawed glass. The new godling was with them, subtle and hidden.

After expending so much energy to extinguish the palace fire, though, the presence had been faint, like cobwebs of faith. With the renewed attention of the people, the entity grew stronger again. Mistress Saruna and her brothel women sensed a joy and happiness, and they even made small blood sacrifices. Public excitement about Iluris fed strength to the godling, and Cemi knew it would accompany the empra in her restoration.

The citizens were abuzz since Iluris's appearance on the speaking balcony. So many of them had seen her, and they remembered the scolding she had delivered to Klovus. The whispered movement supporting Iluris had gained strength. Runners even raced to adjacent districts, telling the story.

Loyal merchants and couriers carried hidden letters, spreading the word far and wide, accusing the key priestlord of deceiving the people, igniting a false funeral pyre and lying to them that the empra was dead. Vos was convinced that many members of the city guard would shift their allegiance once they saw Iluris in the flesh. The weight of Ishara's history and traditions would drive them.

Cemi, Vos, and Iluris sat in the back room of the brothel, finalizing their plans. Ever since her grand appearance, the empra had looked washed out. She would occasionally stare off into the distance, then shake her head and come back to the matters at hand. Cemi touched her hand, reassuring her. "You will be back, and you will lead them."

"Ishara does need an empra, Cemi. I have taught you enough, and you will learn the rest—just as I did. Once we put the key priestlord in his place, leadership will fall to you."

Cemi balked again. "Even if I am to be your successor, you will still rule as empra for a long time. You will keep training me."

"You are already more prepared than I was. Accept what must be," Iluris said. "We both know what Ishara needs."

In an effort to recapture the attention of the people, Klovus called a gathering around the Magnifica temple to demand sacrifices and prayers. He had ordered expanded construction crews to complete the gigantic pyramid. He was joined by many district priestlords, all of them eager to see the Magnifica consecrated.

Cemi attended, keeping her eyes and ears open. In the temple square, she slipped in among the milling people, curious to hear what the key priestlord would say. She smelled stone dust along with pungent sweat and body oils mixed with perfume. Thousands had gathered, per Klovus's request, but the citizens were angry, not joyous. They wanted Empra Iluris, and Cemi smiled.

After climbing the stone steps above the crowd, Klovus bellowed out his speech. "Our Serepol godling will shelter you, comfort you, and protect you. You saw a vision of our beloved empra, so you know that Ishara is still strong. I will guide you all. Hear us, save us!" he shouted, and a halfhearted response came from the restless crowd. "Hear us, save us."

Near Cemi, a man with a thick mustache shouted out, "Empra Iluris is alive. She will come back." Others muttered and made similar comments.

Cemi worked her way among them, invisible and nimble just as she had been as a street girl. "Iluris is alive," she said to two women, clearly sisters, as she moved past them. "I've seen her." She hurried along, repeating her words and knowing others would say the same thing.

Klovus agitated the crowd by sending his ur-priests among them to collect sacrifices. They carried curved knives and urns to capture the blood, calling for volunteers. When only a few complied, the ur-priests became more insistent. Temple guards grasped men and women and slashed their forearms to collect blood. "Everyone must give their due for Ishara!"

Cemi managed to duck and evade them, feeling the secret protection of the new godling flow around her, just as she could also sense the throbbing Serepol deity that inhabited the Magnifica temple.

While blood sacrifices spilled out, the people dutifully chanted and prayed, responding to the key priestlord, though many of them whispered Iluris's name. Feeling the sacrifices strengthen the empra's new godling. Cemi smiled. This was not what Klovus intended.

As the key priestlord struggled to rally the worshippers, Cemi sensed the great Serepol godling growing restless. The temple entity was a terrifying enemy, while the new godling, Iluris's guardian, exuded bright optimism.

The key priestlord's voice strained and became hoarse, commanding greater sacrifices, greater prayers. Cemi felt her young deity flow through the crowd, touching them, even interacting with the Serepol godling. The two powerful entities twisted, flowed, and sparkled, measuring each other. Briefly, Cemi worried that they might battle each other right here, just as the Serepol godling had defeated and incorporated the harbor godling. Instead, Cemi felt something stranger—a layered harmony between the two forces.

Klovus didn't realize what was happening as he called upon the people, but the crowds in the temple square sensed both godlings . . . and the two entities responded to the surge of attention. The Magnifica vibrated, its foundation stones, large as houses, shuddering and trembling.

On the pyramid platform, Klovus struggled to keep his balance. The temple square quaked. The district priestlords and local ur-priests scurried about, raising their hands, afraid the godling might break loose and wreak havoc again.

Cracks split the flagstones, and people yelled as they fled to the connecting streets. As the Magnifica square emptied of worshippers, the tremors quieted again.

Cemi ran panting back to Saruna's brothel with her news. Her face was flushed and her thoughts scrambled, yet now she felt a strange confidence. She didn't know what had just happened, but she had felt the mood of the people, heard their prayers, and sensed the reactions of both godlings.

Ishara was ready for Empra Iluris to return.

69

THE frostwreth army crossed the dry Suderran hills, riding on a wave of frost that curled the brown grasses and cracked trees. Riding in the lead sleigh drawn by wolf-steeds, Queen Koru stared ahead, her pale gaze piercing the distance like a dagger.

Under the clear skies Birch stood in the front of the moving sleigh, balanced so he could see the hills, roads, and empty villages. He had never been this far south. Now that the air was warm, he had thrown off the oonuk pelts days ago, and his blanket lay crumpled beside him, no longer needed.

Mage Elon scratched his burned face. "Our first destination is up ahead, my queen."

Koru exhaled tendrils of steam, cold vapor from cold lungs. "We have not reached the desert yet."

"No, but our enemy has come to meet us here. I can sense them. The sandwreths are close . . . many of them."

Koru sneered. "How would Voo even know we are coming for her?"

A mounted frostwreth scout bounded toward the lead sleigh. He tossed his long, pale hair and gestured toward the blur ahead. "It is a human city, large and impressive."

"Like the one they called Fellstaff," Koru said.

"I think it's Bannriya," Birch said, feeling a glimmer of eagerness. "My grandfather showed us maps, told me and my brother all about it."

"Why is that place important?" the queen asked.

Before the boy could answer, Elon said, "Because the sandwreths are there."

Koru's expression darkened. "Faster! Move like an arctic wind."

As the cold frostwreth army approached the ancient city, Birch spotted another enormous force camped outside the western wall. He could discern lines of reptilian mounts, the gold and copper of sandwreth armor.

Koru was delighted to see the opposing force. "This will save us the time and annoyance of traveling through the desert. I hope Queen Voo is with them, so I can chop off her head." She grinned down at the boy.

Previously, she had seemed uninterested in Bannriya, but now she wanted Birch to tell her what he knew. He said, "Adan is the king there, just as my grandfather is the king of Norterra."

She still didn't seem to see any significance to what he was saying, but as her battle sleigh raced onward, Koru frowned. "If the sandwreth army is here, does that mean King Adan allied himself with our enemies? Do I have to destroy their city as well?"

Birch didn't know the answer, but he didn't want to see Bannriya harmed, or any of the people inside. Before he could make a plea, though, the scarred mage beside him spoke up. "Doubtful, my queen. It appears the sandwreths are attacking the city."

"Then we will give Voo a proper enemy to fight," Koru said.

The frostwreth army closed in like an avalanche rolling down a mountainside.

The spear of Dar lay on the seat beside her, much more than a ceremonial artifact. Considering how often the queen caressed it, Birch knew she was anxious to wield the legendary weapon. It reminded him of how he would reach into his pocket and stroke the carved pig.

Koru mused, "Today will be a battle like the one when the sandwreth queen dueled with my mother, long ago." She showed her perfect white teeth and traced a fingertip along the wide spear point. "Voo slashed her cheek and left a permanent scar."

The enemy army outside the walls swirled like a dust storm as the frostwreths came over the hills. Voo's forces were suddenly in turmoil, unable to form ranks. They were obviously agitated, as if recovering from an unexpected blow. Birch hoped that the humans from Bannriya had hurt them badly somehow.

Queen Koru gave an impatient shout, and the slavering oonuks bounded ahead. The sleigh's runners scoured across the ice-lubricated ground. Birch stared at the city's high walls, seeing clustered people watching in fascination and terror. Yellow banners flew high, as if in defiance.

Koru paid little attention to the capital city, though. "There she is!"

At the vanguard of the sandwreth army rode a regal-looking woman on an auga. She wore copper and gold armor with swatches of dark leather. A dark triangular shield rested on her left arm and she carried a spear in her other hand.

"Queen Voo." Koru pulled on the reins of the wolf-steeds and ground her battle sleigh to a halt. She stood up and shouted, "Voo! I come to challenge your leadership."

The other queen pulled her auga to a halt and regarded the opposing force. Her gaze skated over the countless cold warriors, then fixed on Koru. "Who are you? You are not Onn—I remember cutting a gash in her face."

Koru took the spear of Dar and stepped out of her sleigh. Mage Elon joined her, while Birch remained in his seat, trying to be invisible but watching every moment.

"Onn was my mother," Koru said. "I killed her, and now I rule the frost-wreths." She paused a beat, then her voice boomed across the gathered armies. "And after I kill you, I will rule the sandwreths as well. They will follow me, or my army will destroy you all."

A sandwreth mage in red leather robes joined Queen Voo, remaining astride his reptile mount as Voo mockingly dismounted. She held her dragon shield casually and swung her spear like a swagger stick as she approached the battle sleigh. Birch noticed that she walked with a limp from a deep wound in one of her legs, crusted over with a fresh scab.

The harnessed oonuks growled and slavered, but Voo did not appear intimidated. Elon stood next to the bristling white beasts and shouted, "Queen Koru has issued a challenge! She will fight and kill the sandwreth queen."

"Then she will die," Voo said. Laughing, she sprang forward like a panther, sweeping her spear sideways in a surprise attack.

Koru spun out of the way like a curl of wind and eluded the downward slash of Voo's weapon.

The oonuks pulled at their traces. Koru caught her balance and bounded forward again, graceful. Her metal and crystal armor shone like quicksilver, and she clearly relished the challenge. Though she had no shield of her own, she tossed the legendary spear of Dar from hand to hand. Taunting, she twirled it, then jabbed at the air.

Voo danced out of the way, limping despite her cockiness. She caught her foot on a rock, and lurched to the side just as Koru viciously thrust the spear point, barely missing Voo's ribs. The serrated edge skimmed past and just nicked the copper and leather armor.

The sandwreth warriors hissed like desert vipers. The frostwreths cheered with lively energy.

Koru pressed her advantage, swinging her spear and thrusting again. Voo brought up the dragon shield just in time. The ancient spear point and the dark reptile scale clashed, and blue-black sparks spat off. The two weapons clanged again. The frostwreth queen drew back her lips with intense concentration and effort. Voo flung her long hair out of the way, the metal bangles and rings jingling with a musical tone.

Grim-faced, Elon stepped forward, ignoring the wolf-steeds that strained at their harnesses. He raised his hands to summon swirls of sparkling magic, while his counterpart Axus prepared his own. The two mages merely built up defenses for the two queens, however, and did nothing to interfere in the crucial duel.

Birch did not trust the sandwreth queen. This was the first time he'd ever seen sandwreths up close, but he could sense that Voo was evil . . . just as Onn had been. Although he could not cheer for the cruel frostwreths, he felt that if Koru was victorious here, he had a better chance of staying alive. As would the humans, and the drones that followed the pale army.

The frostwreth forces prepared for battle, bellowing resonant war chants, raising their weapons. The sandwreths hammered their weapons, bone and metal against wood, to make an eerie hollow sound. The oonuks howled, and the augas grunted, flicking out their black tongues.

But the main event was the vicious duel between the two queens.

Voo hammered her spear at Koru's face, and the frostwreth queen bent backward with impossible flexibility. The razor edge whistled past her face. "You won't mark me as you did my mother." Koru slammed her spear point against Voo's shield with such power that it drove the other queen back.

Voo staggered, then winced as the deep wound in her leg broke open, spilling blood. She responded with fury, a sandstorm of energy. Raising her shield, she smashed forward like a battering ram, then swiped her spear sideways. Koru blocked every single blow.

Birch glanced up at Bannriya's walls, saw all the figures watching. He longed to take refuge with them, to be among humans again. He had wanted to escape up north when the frostwreth army marched past Fellstaff, but he had decided to stay. Now, these were King Adan's people inside that ancient city. Again, he could try to run away, but he doubted he would remain unseen, even with both wreth armies so preoccupied.

Voo laughed as a particularly close blow struck Koru's armor and left a dent, but even as Voo chuckled, Koru slashed her spear upward with all her might, tracing a red furrow across the other queen's cheek.

The sandwreth reeled backward and touched the blood on her face. "It does not mar my beauty!"

Fifty sandwreth warriors kicked their augas and surged closer. They charged toward the dueling queens, intending to overwhelm Koru, but a wave of air knocked them back. Mage Axus—their own mage—lifted his hand and raised magical barriers to keep Voo's warriors away from the duel. Elon regarded him in surprise, but gave a satisfied nod. The frostwreths howled for blood, pushing forward as well, but Elon restrained them.

This was between the two queens.

After being wounded, Voo became a whirlwind of fury, flinging blood from the cut on her face. She swung her spear, thrust her shield, and smashed the side of Koru's head. The frostwreth queen staggered away to shake the ringing pain from her ears. Voo spun and raised her spear and shield to deal a death blow.

But in the instant her back was turned as she twirled, Koru struck with the spear of Dar. The spear point, stained with the blood of Ossus and the blood of Queen Onn, pierced Voo's spine just below her neck. The sharp point cut through leather armor, sliced skin, and embedded itself between two vertebrae.

The sandwreth queen sprawled forward, her face filled with astonishment even before the pain could strike.

Koru leaped in as her rival fell face-first on the trampled ground. Voo twitched, tried to make her arms work. She crawled forward on her elbows, using the edge of her shield dug into the dirt, but her legs were useless. Her arms barely functioned.

Koru wrenched the legendary spear free, twisting it to do more damage, then stood over the fallen queen. She relished the moment and stomped her armored bootheel as hard as she could on the bleeding wound high on Voo's back. A loud crack of bone rang out into the sudden gasp of silence.

Voo lay twitching and gurgling, trying to move her arms or legs. Koru looked toward the ancient human city, then turned to her frostwreth army. She raised the spear of Dar in victory.

70

FROM her vantage on the walls, Penda watched the two armies. Frostwreths and sandwreths faced off as the rival queens began their deadly duel. Bannriya's yellow-and-red flags snapped on high poles from the watchtowers, but an odd hush settled over the open battlefield.

Glik shaded her eyes, then pointed urgently. "Penda, look down there! See the frostwreth sleigh? A boy in front—a human boy."

Penda had been watching Koru and Voo try to kill each other, but now she looked where the orphan girl pointed. "Why would she have a human boy?" She suddenly remembered what King Kollanan had told them about his grandson. "Wait, could that be Birch?"

Cheth and two of her Brava companions came up, still encrusted with dust, sweat, and blood spatters. "We are ready to ride out again, Queen Penda. If need be, we will ignite our ramers and fight."

"Fight on which side?" Penda asked. "Neither race of wreths cares about humans."

"I'd prefer to kill more sandwreths, if it's all the same to you," Cheth said. "After what they did to me—to all of us." She looked at Glik.

Below, the two queens dueled, smashing with spears, shouting. Both wreth armies were restless, but waited as Koru and Voo vied for control.

"No." Penda drew a circle around her heart. "Let them do all of the killing."

Then the frostwreth queen struck her rival in the spine, and Voo sprawled on the ground, twitching and helpless.

Penda drew a long breath. "Now we will see what happens."

Paralyzed, barely squirming, Voo looked pathetic.

Standing over her, Koru relished her victory for a brief held-breath before howls and roars erupted from both armies. She raised the spear of Dar, which had once again tasted the defeat of an enemy. The two armies were poised on the verge of a final battle.

Voo clung to life with thick blood flowing from the grievous, paralyzing wound. Dust caked the blood from the lesser slash on her cheek. Her eyes swirled with hatred, and she grimaced with fury, but her arms and legs were useless meat attached to her body. "I will kill you," she gurgled.

"Empty words." Koru snatched the dragon-scale shield from Voo's limp arm. She recognized the artifact, and even the rising threat of the two armies did not dampen the power that tingled through her hands. She reached a decision. "I despise you, Voo, but I will not kill you. Rather, I will keep you with me, impotent and helpless—as a reminder to the sandwreths." She smiled. "To *my* sandwreths."

Ignoring Voo's useless struggles, she raised both ancient weapons, letting blood run down from the spear point. "I bear the shield of Rao. I hold the spear of Dar. I am the queen of all wreths." Her words echoed across the battlefield, and the simmering warriors, nobles, and mages listened. "I defeated your weakling queen and now I take her crown . . . just as I also wear the frostwreth crown. For the first time in thousands of years, our race has one leader, one queen . . . and one mission."

She stared across the infuriated sandwreth army, which looked ready to charge forward. She had already convinced her frostwreth army of what she intended to do, and now she had to control the other race.

Oonuks continued to howl at the sky. The frostwreths grumbled challenges, shifted their weapons, and the sandwreths hissed and snarled back at them. Mage Axus swelled up, and his ominous magic flickered. Lightning created rings of storm energy around him, while Elon and ten other frostwreth mages constructed a wall of power to flatten their enemies.

But as Mage Axus looked down at his writhing queen, his coppery eyes swirled with calculation. He spoke to Koru, though his words were a loud announcement to the desert army behind him. He pointedly gave a bow of respect to the pale queen. "You issued a challenge and defeated our queen in combat. Therefore, what was hers is rightfully yours." He raised his hands, letting his wall of magic fade. "That means the sandwreths are yours to command."

Behind him the desert army uttered their displeasure at the mage's declaration, but Axus whirled toward them and roared out, "Queen Voo was weak. Look at her now!" An amplified, hot wind carried his words. "She wasted too much effort trying to fight other wreths . . . our own people. Voo's bad decisions brought pain and death to her own sandwreths because she scorned the humans, who should have been our allies." He gestured toward the clustered figures on the high walls of Bannriya.

Unexpectedly, Mage Elon added his voice. He stepped away from the wolf-steeds and the battle sleigh. "Every wreth knows that our destiny is to slay Ossus, so that Kur will return to make a new world. We would be fools to weaken our forces before we engage in our most important battle."

Koru stood silent with her shield and spear, watching, listening. She glanced back at the sleigh to make sure the boy was safe. She smiled at Birch, aglow with victory.

Mage Elon continued his pronouncement. "I have seen dragons emerge from the mountains." He touched the burn scar on his face. "They were mere fragments of Ossus, and still they were terrible and mighty. It will take all wreth forces together if we are to achieve our sacred goal!"

Koru turned from the sandwreths and faced down her own army, feeling their volatile moods shift like a weather pattern. She remembered the poison that had turned Irri and his conspirators against her. She willed them to recognize her leadership, her air of command that seemed to rise up from the land itself.

"We fight together—all wreths." She glanced over her shoulder at the human city of Bannriya. "All fight together." She felt giddy at the prospect of the long-foretold confrontation. "And slay the dragon at the heart of the world."

From above the sealed western gate, Penda could hear the wreth armies. The two great forces had not thrown themselves into a final massacre, as expected. Instead, they were like two fighting dogs at bay, snarling yet held apart by unseen leashes.

Cheth stood coiled with energy, her hand resting on the ramer at her side. Waiting.

"*Cra*, what are they doing?" Glik asked. "Did the frostwreth queen unify the races?" Xar and Ari flew overhead, as if to protect their humans.

Captain Elcior had sent his Banner guards to form a large force just inside the gate as a last line of defense. Now the guard captain spoke to Penda in a husky voice. "We feared the sandwreth army before, but if those forces are now united, they can grind Bannriya to rubble."

Penda whispered, "Let's wait. I prefer to think there are other possible outcomes."

The victorious pale queen rode one of the shaggy wolf-steeds toward the gate, with Mage Axus on her right and Elon on her left. As they approached Bannriya, the defenders on the walls gripped their shadowglass weapons, ready to rain death down on any attackers. Then Penda saw that the young human boy sat in the saddle in front of Koru. Unharmed. A hostage? A threat?

The party stopped before the high gate, and Penda looked down from the parapet, holding little Oak in defiance. Would the frostwreth queen also demand her baby?

Koru called in a loud, intense voice. "I am queen of the frostwreths . . . of all wreths. I wish to speak to my fellow ruler, Queen Penda of Suderra."

Whispers of surprise traveled down the lines of observers on the walls.

"What does she want with us?" Cheth asked.

Glik muttered, "Careful, sister. It's a trick. These are *wreths*."

"I know they are wreths." Penda came forward in full view, cradling the baby against her side. "I am Penda Orr, wife to King Adan Starfall. Your armies have invaded our kingdom. What are your intentions?"

"My armies have no interest in you," Koru replied. "Now that we are joined, we will ride to the Dragonspine Mountains to wake the dragon. Ossus is the only enemy that matters."

Penda considered, turned to look at the Brava woman, at Glik, at the Banner guard captain, all of whom looked as perplexed and confused as she felt. After a moment, she called down, "Who is that boy with you? Is he your prisoner?"

Distracted, Koru glanced down at the child, stroked his hair. "This boy? Just a human child taken from a frozen village in the north."

The boy looked up to meet Penda's eyes, and a ripple of emotions washed over his face. He did not look harmed or abused, though he seemed apprehensive.

"What is his name?"

The boy answered for himself. "Birch!"

Penda steadied herself. "Free him and give him to us."

"He belongs with me," the queen said in an offhand voice, then changed the subject. "I hear that Voo armed the Suderran army with shadowglass weapons. She was always foolish, but your soldiers could be useful to us. Give me those fighters and we will all ride together."

Penda said, "Adan Starfall has already led our army to the mountains, where he will join a force from King Kollanan of Norterra." She said the name intentionally so the captive boy would hear it. "We have wars of our own."

The frostwreth queen seemed surprised, but satisfied. "If they have already marched toward the mountains, we shall intercept them on the way. Then all of us can wake the dragon together."

Queen Koru wheeled her oonuk about, taking the boy with her. The shaggy animal bounded back toward the core of the two gigantic armies, followed by the pair of mages. Before long, the combined wreth army shifted, preparing to move out.

Penda lifted her hand to the sky and reached out with her heart link. Within moments her green ska fluttered down. She called for a strip of paper so she could write an urgent message to be tied around the reptile bird's leg; Adan could not activate the mothertear, but he could read her note. He had to know.

"You must fly, Xar," she said. "Bear this message to warn Adan Starfall. And tell King Kollanan that his grandson still lives and is with the wreths."

71

As the Utauk camp burned, Konag Mandan's soldiers finished rounding up the few scattered animal tenders, caravan merchants, hunters, mothers, and children. Tents went up in blazes brighter than the scattered bonfires, and the sounds of screams, neighing horses, jingling armor, and clashing swords began to diminish.

Mandan was delighted to discover that one of the wagons carried books, ledgers, and maps. By the light of a hanging lantern, he sorted through the volumes and pored over descriptions of roads and trails. A treasure trove!

He thought of how easily he had killed Shella din Orr, supposedly the leader of all the Utauk tribes. Mandan had shown them the consequences of defying the konag's command, of kidnapping and corrupting his queen. By spreading insidious rumors, the Utauks were responsible for much of the unrest in the three kingdoms.

Ignoring the sounds outside the wagon, he paged through charts, traced the rivers and streams, compared written accounts to corresponding maps, and studied the main passable road over the mountains. He leaned closer, fascinated by the great detail. This was vital information.

Jennae strode up to the wagon's open door, and orange light spilled from her ramer. "The threat has been eradicated, my konag. Several riders managed to escape and many children ran into the forest. Would you like us to hunt them down?"

Mandan was sure they would spread more wild stories that made him out to be a monster, but when he thought of all those children lost in the trees with no adults, no supplies . . .

"Let them starve." He looked down at the logbooks, charts, and maps. "Send all of this back to Convera Castle. The Utauks have withheld important intelligence from our armies." He shook his head.

Jennae glanced at the carnage in the camp, her face lit by crackling ramer fire. "One of the men . . . a nephew of the old tribe leader has been wounded, but you should hear him before he dies."

Mandan scoffed. "You want me to take down his legacy? Write it so he's remembered for all time?"

Her expression became pinched. "You'll want to hear his information,

Sire, I promise you." She stepped away, then spoke in a sharper voice. "Hurry, he doesn't have long to live, although I'm not sure he realizes that."

Mandan glanced at all of the books and scrolls, wishing he could just stay here and study them. Once back home, he planned to spend many evenings absorbing these volumes. It would be easier to concentrate without the whimpering Lira bothering him all the time. She had adored him until the Utauks poisoned her thoughts, turned her against him. Justice had been served. . . .

He followed Jennae to the remnants of a large fire in the middle of camp. Heavy iron cauldrons were overturned, soup spilled into the ashes and across the ground. Unappetizing puddles lay near dead Shella din Orr and the body of one bearded man. A second man lay propped up in a half-sitting position, a sword wound deep in his guts. Blood trickled out of his mouth.

The man's agony made Mandan queasy, but he was just an Utauk. As he sat on the ground, squirming, he looked at the young konag with glassy eyes. Recognition and anger crossed the bearded man's face. "I am Burdon," he said, as if Mandan would care about his name. "You killed our grandmother. You killed all of us."

Mandan frowned. "You deserved it for what you did. Utauks will no longer spy freely across the Commonwealth."

Jennae stood with her ramer upraised, listening, and Mandan flashed her an impatient glance. "What was so important here? He's dying, isn't he?"

"We're all dying," Burdon rasped. "Even you."

Jennae kicked the man in the shoulder, and he groaned, coughing more blood. "Tell him what you said to me!"

"Large army . . . gathering on . . . other side of . . . mountains," Burdon said. "A double army. King Adan's forces will join King Kollanan's." He tried to smile, but the expression turned into a grimace of pain. "You are not konag!" The Utauk man turned his head away as if he could not abide to look at Mandan's face. "You cannot survive."

Mandan's anger flared. The insolent decree was one thing, but his brother and uncle had actually sent a full invasion force, as he feared! "I will stop them." He shouted to the Commonwealth soldiers and any surviving Utauks. "I am the rightful konag. I, Mandan of the Colors, rule the three kingdoms."

With a jerky movement, Burdon lifted a shaky, blood-streaked hand to touch his chest and tried to draw a circle. "The beginning . . . is the end . . ."

Jennae struck with her blazing sword, and the sizzling heat of the ramer and the stench of burning meat wafted into Mandan's face. "Why did you do that? He would have died soon enough."

"I wanted to kill him. We have other things to do," she said. "A rebel military force is heading to Convera. We will need a larger army than this to stand against them." She gestured to the Commonwealth cavalry soldiers that had formed the strike force.

Tytan approached, his hair tangled, his black finemail cape askew. He lowered his burning hand and extinguished the ramer. "We're done here, Sire, except for a little mopping up. We should put out these fires and salvage any camp supplies. Our soldiers will need the provisions."

Mandan remembered what Jennae had said, and made a swift decision. "Tytan, I want you as my messenger. I trust you."

The big Brava blinked in surprise. "Of course you trust me, Sire. I am a Brava, and you are the konag."

The words warmed Mandan's heart. Yes, he was the konag. "Take a fresh horse and ride back to Convera. In my name, gather all the military forces in the capital, all the soldiers from the surrounding counties, then march them here so we cross the Dragonspine together. We must root out the rebel army like an infestation of rats."

Tytan seemed troubled by the slaughter this night, but his loyalty to Mandan was without question. He gave a brusque nod. "As you command, my konag. I will set off at first light."

"We cannot waste any hours! The enemy army might be marching even now."

The Brava bowed, acknowledging the order. "At once, then." He grabbed a horse and rode off.

Mandan scowled at the dead Utauk man as well as Shella din Orr, then scanned the wrecked heart camp, letting his eyes linger with satisfaction on smashed wagons, burned tents, slaughtered horses and people. He looked up at Jennae. "Handle the rest of this," he said and returned to the large wagon with all its books and maps.

Leaving the smoldering camp the next morning, Konag Mandan and his soldiers rode along the river road. A few narrow flatboats passed by, their captains waving at the large military force. Mandan didn't think the rivermen were Utauks, but he couldn't tell. He wondered what sort of stories they would spread once their boats reached Convera.

Jennae traveled beside him. "Tytan will rally the rest of your army. They will come."

"Of course," Mandan said.

Jennae continued in a sour voice, "But your action leaves Convera vulnerable. The navy went to Ishara, and you will take your army over the mountains."

"I would rather go to the enemy than wait to be attacked at home," Mandan said. "Utho will crush the threat in Ishara, but right now I have to put down this uprising! Why would I leave soldiers to lounge about the barracks at home? I may need all the fighting forces I can muster."

"Indeed you might, Sire." Jennae stared at the road ahead.

His frontline force moved into the foothills on the east side of the Dragon-spine range. Jennae passed the order to the advance scout riders.

Mandan said, "Find a good place for a long-term camp. We'll wait for Tytan to bring the rest of my army. Then we will cross the pass and sweep down on Adan and Kollanan like a pack of wolves."

Ahead, Mandan saw the dramatic broken cone of Mount Vada, the impressive peak that had exploded with fire and lava. The ground still trembled with angry energy, but the vibrations did not make him consider turning back. His anger toward his uncle and brother was greater than his fear of any dragon beneath the mountains.

72

With his tattered clothes and bedraggled hair, Erical posed no threat to the fishermen. They did not look at him as a dangerous Isharan invader—in fact he doubted they even recognized the style of his clothes. Why would they know what an Isharan looked like? As residents of the seashore, they were duty-bound to help castaways or shipwreck victims.

As soon as the rescue party found him, Erical realized anew how hungry and weak he was. The godling gave him a flicker of strength, though she herself was as wispy as a mist in late morning . . . drained and so far away from her beloved worshippers.

His voice was barely a croak as he spoke. He tried to take a step toward the people, but his knees gave out and he dropped to the rough beach. The pain seized his attention and he couldn't remember what he was about to say.

"He's dazed," said one of the rescuers. "Get him back to the village."

Another man said, "He needs something other than salt water in his stomach."

Two men draped his arms over their shoulders and carried him along. Erical could barely move his feet.

The little girl who had found him spoke to a bearded man, who seemed to be in charge. "I have to go, Cetor. Tide's coming in, and I don't want to miss all those green mussels." She darted off.

They supported Erical along the beach and up a steep dirt path to the headlands. He saw scattered homes, and in the distance a village with a small harbor. He was asleep before they got there.

When he awoke, disoriented, he felt sore and battered, his body covered with bruises and scabbed-over cuts. Lying on the strange cot, he closed his eyes and let out a sigh. "Hear us, save us." He could sense the godling's presence, but she seemed far away.

"What's that you said?" An old woman bent over him with a crooked-toothed smile. Her face was wrinkled and weathered and her gray hair hung in twisted lumps that reminded him of the kelp strands on the beach.

Erical shook his head and said the first thing that came to mind. "I can't remember."

"I cleaned a nasty cut on the back of your head, and it's no surprise you've lost your memories. Storm hit the coastline a few days ago. Must have thrown you overboard. I can't believe you're still alive."

Erical lifted a hand, saw his fingers shaking. "Barely."

"Many people lose their memories after an ordeal like that. No shame in it. Sometimes your past comes back, and sometimes you just have to make a new legacy."

He searched for words. If he continued to claim a loss of memory, then that would take away the need for other uncomfortable answers.

"What is your name?" she asked. "Do you remember that at least?"

He didn't want to live without a name, no matter what. "Erical."

She pursed her lips. "An odd name, but at least you remember it. Were you on a ship by yourself, a fishing boat? Were there other crew? Family members?"

"I don't know," he said again, realizing the power of the answer.

The old woman frowned. "I ask because we need to know how wide we should search. There may be other castaways, other bodies washed up on the beach. You'd want to know, wouldn't you?"

"I want to know . . . a lot of things." Erical tried to sit up. She had tucked blankets and rag-stuffed pillows beneath him. His body ached in dozens of different places. "What is your name? Where am I?"

She smiled. "I'm Mystia, the windcaster. If you had any memories, you've probably heard of me. This drafty shack is a good place for my work." The woman continued before he could even ask her what a windcaster was. "The village is Windy Head, the southernmost port town in Osterra, though it's been quite a while since any Utauk trading ship docked here. I've heard the konag took all the ships for his navy." She made a scoffing sound. "Good thing our fishing boats are too small, so they're still here to do their work."

She went to the hearth, where a small pot hung over low coals. "Fish-head broth with some wild garlic." She brought the pot closer and dipped a wooden spoon into the liquid.

"I don't think I've ever had fish-head broth," Erical said. Fish was a very small part of the Prirari diet.

"Oh, you remember that detail, do you? Well, if you had tasted my fish-head broth, you'd remember it."

He slurped from the spoon, and the broth was indeed delicious, and not just because he was so hungry. His stomach wanted more, but Mystia wagged a big-knuckled finger at him. "Not too much, now. And we won't have fresh fish for a while, since that storm damaged many of our boats." She clucked a tongue against her crooked front teeth. "I did a windcasting, and I can usually gauge the weather without mistakes, but that storm did not show. Town leader Cetor is upset with me because I've never missed such a heavy storm before." She clucked her tongue again. "I don't think it was a natural storm."

Erical felt a chill. "Maybe not."

The windcaster seemed to enjoy talking with him, glad for the unexpected company, and she also enjoyed the sound of her own voice. He gathered that Windy Head was far south of Rivermouth and Convera Castle, and also far from any rumors of war. She mentioned no Isharan raids, not even in years past. Erical was glad for that. Considering the fury of the godling's storm, he couldn't imagine that any of the Isharan warships had survived, especially if the Hethrren brutes had killed all the competent captains. Erical felt no sadness in his heart over the lost vessels, which had been intent on laying waste to the coast.

After Mystia fed him again and he rested, he felt his strength returning. He sat up on the cot and thanked her. "Please give the people of this village my thanks as well."

The windcaster gave a dismissive snort and offered him strong-smelling cheese and pickled seaweed. She sat next to him and they both ate. "It is a human duty to save whoever the sea casts upon our shores. Someday, sure enough, our fishermen may be shipwrecked and need the help of others."

Once again, Erical thought of how the Hethrren would have smashed any fishing villages and set them on fire. Key Priestlord Klovus had often bragged about his raid on a town called Mirrabay, where he'd used the harbor godling to devastate the docks, boats, and homes.

He was glad that had not happened here at this village. Was he the only survivor of the entire war fleet? His godling had saved him. Was that the only reason he still lived?

Erical walked around the shack and decided he felt strong enough to go outside and breathe the sea breezes. He felt isolated here and strangely at peace.

Later, Mystia sat outside in a rickety chair, facing the fresh winds that blew in from the sea and were concentrated on the point of the headlands. She had built a fire of dried seaweed, which released thick, rank-smelling smoke. Resting in the chair, she held a flat wooden lap board, on which she had tacked a clean piece of paper. She held a blackened lump of charcoal between two soot-covered fingers and leaned closer to stare into the smoke that blew into her face and stung her eyes. She used the charcoal to sketch across the paper, drawing curves, circles, twisted loops of whatever the wind and smoke showed her.

Stretching his legs, Erical stepped up to her. "What are you doing?"

She sniffed. "You don't remember anything, do you? I told you I'm a windcaster." Mystia frowned at her jumbled attempt at artwork, peered back into the smoke, and added another set of lines. "The seaweed in the fire comes from the ocean, the winds come from the air, and together they form the weather. The smoke combines both, and it has magic."

She sketched furiously, adding large black areas and then light wispy lines. "These are all the patterns I see in the wind and smoke, and it helps me determine what is in store for us. That way I can warn the people in Windy Head if something terrible is coming." She shook her head. "Except I failed to see that recent storm."

When she was finished, the windcaster studied her incomprehensible sketch, then handed the wooden board to Erical. He attempted to interpret what he saw, but failed. "What does it mean? I am not a windcaster."

"That is for certain." Mystia reached over and tapped the charcoal scribbles with a big-knuckled finger. She spoke in a solemn voice. "I see an ill wind coming."

73

As the *Glissand* sailed toward the embattled Rivermouth harbor, still taking on water, Utho clutched the rigging ropes. His face felt hot, and he wished his anger could drive the ship faster.

The patchwork sail belled outward, stretching the canvas and making the Utauk circle look like a target. He no longer needed the viewing tube to see the disaster unfolding ahead of them. Parts of the Rivermouth docks and shipyards were on fire!

"Arm yourselves!" he shouted down the deck, and his surviving Commonwealth soldiers grabbed their swords, shields, bows. They donned leather armor and helmets, adjusted their chest plates. After scavenging what they needed from the Fulcor garrison, Utho had pulled together a hundred soldiers with only minor injuries, who were ready to throw themselves into battle again. Only a hundred fighters . . . he would make sure that was enough. They had to defend the three kingdoms, save Convera, save Konag Mandan.

Several burning warehouses sent raven feathers of smoke into the sky, where the breezes twisted and dispersed the sooty haze. Two Isharan ships had run up against the empty piers, and he could see that the enemy vessels were also on fire. They looked as if they had been battered and pummeled even before reaching Rivermouth. Two Isharan warships . . . but Utho had seen ten of them sailing away from Fulcor Island, and he felt a hollow dread in his chest. Did that mean the other eight ships had already sailed up the Joined River to Convera?

Utho squeezed the hilt of his sword. He would ignite his ramer once he jumped onto the docks. As the *Glissand* sailed closer, he spotted a few skirmishes taking place along the waterfront, but the fighting seemed dispersed, as if the brunt was already over.

"Faster!"

Mak Dur scowled at him. "How? We're already pushing my ship as fast as she can go, and she's falling apart. *Cra,* unless you can summon some kind of Isharan magic, we have to depend on Utauk luck—and my skills as voyagier."

Mak Dur and his crew showed their expertise as the ship skirted a sunken Isharan wreck at the mouth of the harbor where the river spilled into the sea. That accounted for three ships, but he didn't know what had happened to the other seven.

He remembered how the Isharan animals had razed Mirrabay, twice. . . . He swallowed back his primal rage, remembered the godling they had used there. He had seen another one of the horrific entities smashing their fleet at Fulcor. "Faster," he muttered, but it was more a personal prayer than an angry shout.

Mak Dur yelled to his crew. "Bring us close enough to throw down ropes. Pick any empty dock."

Utho pointed to a pier opposite the two damaged Isharan ships. "That one's open. Just get me ashore!" He glanced toward the anxious fighters milling about with their weapons.

The Utauks manipulated their once-graceful vessel, using oars to guide the ship in. From the hold, crew members were hauling up buckets of murky water, yelling that more repairs had broken loose. The damaged ship was taking on a great deal of water, but Utho needed the vessel to hold itself together just a little longer.

Several of their oars were cracked, and one snapped in half as they drove the ship toward the dock. Barely under control, the trading vessel ground up against the pilings, cracking hull boards. The dented copper hull plates scraped along with a hideous sound.

Utho drew his sword and leaped to the side. "Close enough!" Without looking at the fighters on the deck, he swung himself over the side while the ship was still slowly coming to rest. As soon as he landed on the pier, he was running, his finemail cape flying out behind him as he went to defend Rivermouth.

On the adjacent dock, he saw that the half-sunken Isharan ship was empty, all the enemy fighters having abandoned it to pillage the harbor. Utho spotted the nearest knot of fighting, port workers and town guards brawling with Isharan soldiers outside a smoldering warehouse. In addition to uniformed Isharans, he spotted muscular creatures that looked as if the enemy had used magic to fashion barbarian warriors out of mad bulls or shaggy bears.

Shouting their own battle cries, the Commonwealth soldiers disembarked behind him to run pell-mell down the pier to defend the town.

Utho reached the end of the dock, seeing twenty or thirty foreign fighters locked in combat with Rivermouth defenders. Bloody corpses lay sprawled along the waterfront. He paused to clamp the ramer around his wrist and ignite the flaming sword. He raised his traditional sword in the other hand, ready to hack down the invaders. He bounded toward the skirmishes, and the defenders let out a cry of surprise and relief to see the Brava ramer.

The barbarians turned as Utho came at them. They had clubs, cudgels, and heavy axes, not a single delicate weapon among them. Two of them turned to face him, drawing back their lips to show filed teeth. They grunted in voices that were more animal than human.

Utho's first slash severed one of the clubs in half, and in the follow-through he cut off the other barbarian's battle ax along with the hand of its wielder. Four more barbarians charged at him as if they thought they could defeat a Brava and his ramer. They snapped at him with sharp teeth, trying to rend his flesh like wolves. Before the rest of his soldiers could join the fight, Utho had killed most of the uncouth enemy.

The local defenders were weary and bloody, and while Utho dispatched the brutish fighters, they turned their attention to the uniformed Isharan soldiers. The Isharans did manage to kill a dockworker who used a boat hook to defend his city, but the other townspeople killed the rest of the raiders. With Utho and his reinforcements from the *Glissand,* the tides of battle swiftly turned.

The last burly barbarian careened toward him with a thick club. He seemed to think he was invincible, but Utho's ramer proved that he was not. The dead brute crashed to the ground like a felled ox. His sharpened teeth bit the ground.

The town defenders stood panting, bleeding, and exhausted. Their eyes were glazed, their faces drawn.

Feeling pain and desperation, Utho looked inland up the river, sure that more Isharan ships had already sailed up the waterway toward the confluence. He had to get to Convera before it was too late!

Utho strode up to a man who looked more like a fisherman than a soldier. "How long ago did they arrive? How many ships?"

The man blinked as if Utho spoke a different language.

"When? And how many of the enemy?"

"This morning at dawn," the man said.

A woman streaked with blood added, "Six ships . . . no, seven I think. One was sunk just outside the harbor, but the fighters swam to shore. We managed to wreck and burn two more at the docks."

"We fought them as best we could," said the fisherman, "but our harbor was almost empty with the whole Commonwealth navy gone. We had nothing left here."

"What happened to the other ships?" Utho demanded. "Did they get away?"

The woman gestured up the river. "They sailed toward Convera. Four of them."

Exactly what he had feared most. Four ships left . . . out of ten. What about the others? He wondered if they were attacking elsewhere along the Osterran coast. He thought of Mandan at the castle, unskilled as a military leader, though a decent swordfighter. Tytan and Jennae would advise him, help him, but surely there wasn't enough of an army left to stop a full Isharan invasion. Four warships sailing up the Joined River!

He shook his head, running calculations. It would still take them time to sail against the current to Convera. "I need a horse, a fast horse! I'll ride there myself."

The Rivermouth survivors seemed too disoriented to offer him the help he needed. When he raised his fiery ramer to emphasize his demand, someone finally got him a fresh horse, and he mounted. Without a second thought, Utho left the other Commonwealth soldiers to put out the fires in the harbor town. Kicking his mount into a gallop, he hunched forward in the saddle. He raced up the river toward Convera, afraid he would find the konag's castle in flames.

From the tilted deck of the *Glissand,* Mak Dur watched the waterfront fighting continue. He saw the warehouses burn and the last of the invaders fall, many of them to Utho's blazing ramer. He and his crew, though, were just happy that the unwanted soldiers were gone from his ship.

His beloved trading vessel felt quiet and calm, but she wasn't the same. Too much damage had been done, not just from the fighting at Fulcor Island, but also from the modifications that had turned the *Glissand* into a warship. Down in the hold, his crew worked frantically to repair the new breach in the hull, where makeshift patches had split open, and water was pouring in. Ramming against the Rivermouth dock had caused even more damage.

While Utho ran off to fight in the harbor town, Mak Dur dropped down into the hold with a lantern, where he watched the frantic efforts, but his sailors were up to their knees already. Unstoppable sprays of water jetted between breached hull boards. Two more boards cracked, and the whole ship let out a creaking groan, as if his poor *Glissand* were sighing in pain. He felt heartsick. She was like a mortally wounded animal.

Utauks had very little magic beyond the bit of good fortune or coincidence where luck ran in their favor, but Mak Dur had spent enough time aboard his vessel that he could sense a connection. After so much damage and abuse, the *Glissand* was giving up. The ship's spirit had already been broken after being seized in Serepol Harbor and forced into the Commonwealth navy, then two of her own crewmen hanged from the yardarms.

Tied up to the Rivermouth dock, the *Glissand* continued to take on water, already swamped. She was in need of great repairs—repairs that Mak Dur could neither complete nor afford.

He felt the sad anger. This was not why he had become a trading-ship captain, not why he reveled in the joy of bringing goods to port, seeing the delight on customers' faces as they pawed through coveted items and haggled for the best prices. He had not become a voyagier to go to war, not for either side. He drew a circle around his heart.

"I am going ashore, and all of you can do the same." He looked at his poor vessel. "I do not know if she'll ever sail again . . . or if I'll be back."

In the dim hold, his crew stood in the water, looking hopelessly at the damage. "*Cra,* Voyagier, are you abandoning your ship?"

"As I've been told so many times, she is no longer my ship. You should all get to safety ashore." He leaned down and kissed the smooth wood of the hull, then climbed the steps to the open hatch. Tears welled in his eyes as he walked along the deck, saying goodbye—for now—to his precious *Glissand.*

He disembarked and walked down the damaged dock into the harbor town, where citizens ran about putting out flames, gathering fallen bodies.

No one paid attention to him. Rivermouth seemed deserted, wounded. As he walked along the harbor front, he turned back to look at his listing ship, saw how tilted her deck looked as more water flowed into her cracked hull.

So much damage . . . so much hurt.

Mak Dur's heart and his determination had also been broken. He looked inland and walked away from the waterfront.

He was an Utauk, born to travel, explore, and trade. Both Ishara and the Commonwealth had betrayed him, and now so had the sea. He had grown up in Norterra. Maybe he would spend more time there.

He made up his mind to head into the hills, where he would find other Utauks. He would live with them and perhaps become a caravan leader somewhere. For a time.

But he knew he would return to his ship. When he was able.

74

✑

As key priestlord, his greatest weapon was the Magnifica godling, power-ful and ever present, which could slip throughout the city like the wind. Klovus needed to use that weapon now to hold the gullible people together, to channel their thoughts and faith away from their foolish belief that Empra Iluris would return as their savior. He would cement his power and end this distraction.

He had sensed something very disturbing that day in the temple square, his own godling rising up, but encountering resistance. The faith and energy of all the Serepol believers channeled . . . elsewhere. It had to stop.

His Black Eels had done everything they could, listening, spying, quietly questioning potential witnesses in back alleys. Although his special assassins were the best possible killers and protectors, they did not have the right kind of powers. He finally needed to use the great godling, his godling—and he had to hope that this time he could control it.

After the last time, he knew what a tremendous risk he was taking.

He called his visiting district priestlords, eight of whom had arrived in the capital by now. Two of them, Adas from Ishiki District and Romuro from Janhari, had brought along fragments of their godlings, faint manifestations that shivered behind them, though not the core of the entity, as Priestlord Erical had done.

He and the eight district priestlords met in the chamber beneath the Magnifica. On the thick stone walls, sheets of shadowglass were mounted like windows into a dark eternity, and through the black glass, Klovus could connect with the great godling.

The priestlords obeyed Klovus, but seemed uneasy to be in such a deep chamber, rather than out in the open temple square. The wall blocks contained old stains of long-dried blood, which made them uneasy. Down here, Klovus had watched his Black Eels train, had seen them battle against a part of the godling—to demonstrate their powers and to test fighting techniques.

The key priestlord paced in the confined chamber. "I brought you here to the very heart of the Magnifica temple because I may need your strength. You will serve as a buffer to help me control what I'm about to do. Just in case."

"Hear us, save us," muttered Priestlord Neré from Tamburdin.

Priestlord Dovic from Sistralta seemed out of sorts. "And what do you intend to do that is so dangerous?"

"Release the Magnifica godling again," Klovus said. As he spoke the words, tangled sparkles of light appeared within the shadowglass panes, and he knew the godling was watching him. "There is an imposter in the city who claims to be Iluris. She is disrupting Serepol and all of Ishara."

"An imposter?" asked Adas, as if the idea had never occurred to him.

"How do you know it's an imposter?" Dovic added. "Many people saw her."

Klovus felt a flush of anger. "I know because Iluris is dead! Therefore, the woman who appeared must be false. Anyone spreading this sedition is causing great harm to Ishara. We must find this imposter and her conspirators, expose them and bring our people back onto the straight path."

As they continued to comment under their breath, the key priestlord focused on the deity inside of him. Just by looking at the shadowglass panes he could feel the godling awakening, ready to spread out. The priestlords would do as they were told, as would the godling.

It was long past midnight, and the city would be quiet. The godling would sweep out into the night like black smoke, hunt down the lair of Iluris, then extract her.

He closed his eyes and made the godling surge within him . . . much as when he had dispatched the deity to hunt down the Hethrren, but with more control. He had learned an important lesson. Tonight, Klovus needed to keep the godling reined in, rather than turning it loose to tear apart the streets and buildings like a hunting dog ripping open a badger hole.

The priestlords fell silent, realizing what he was doing. Klovus's mind was already journeying like a passenger along with the huge roiling force that swirled out of the Magnifica. The godling emerged and raced above the rooftops of Serepol, and the key priestlord felt liberated, powerful, swift. Distantly, he knew the other priestlords were there, but they had no connection with the godling, as he did.

Find where the empra is hiding, he communicated directly with the pulsing force. He felt his thunderstorm limbs, the lightning that flowed like blood through his body. The godling lunged and twirled like a rising tornado, spreading out over the city. *Find Empra Iluris and destroy her.*

But as the godling diffused over the craftsmen's district and the market squares, racing above subsidiary temples where lesser godlings simmered, Klovus felt resistance. The entity hesitated.

The key priestlord pushed with his mind again. Inside the stone-walled chamber, his physical body clenched his fists, gritted his teeth. The godling spread wider, probing, looking for Iluris, sensing its own connection with the empra of Ishara.

Where is she? Klovus could sense Iluris. He knew the old woman was hiding, and the godling knew it, too. *Find her!*

The godling was everywhere, a part of Serepol connected to the faith of the people. To Klovus's relief, the deity did locate Iluris, but that relief evaporated when the key priestlord could not learn where she was. His frustration built, but his increasing anger only seemed to generate more resistance from the godling.

The entity spread out like an angry turbulent storm, but it was brought up short by an invisible force—not just a leash, but a barrier, like a wall of glass that kept it from moving against Empra Iluris.

Klovus strained. He couldn't understand this. *I control you. Find her!*

But his tenuous grip on the godling began to slip, and he found himself losing control again. Losing control! He experienced a flash of terror. If the godling broke free and went on a rampage in the middle of the night, tore up and flattened entire sections of the city, the people of Serepol would blame *him* again.

But to his surprise the godling did not attempt to rampage. Instead, it resisted the key priestlord's command. The entity pushed back against his commands to expose Iluris, refusing to damage the city. The deity had been perfectly willing to go berserk and slaughter as many Hethrren as it could find, but this one woman—a frail, old, and injured woman—seemed strong enough to defy the Magnifica entity.

With a hollow realization, Klovus knew it wasn't Iluris's strength pressing back—it was the godling's own reluctance. Previously, he had loosed the deity against barbarians, against enemies of Serepol.

The Magnifica godling did not consider Empra Iluris to be an enemy.

Klovus wrestled for control, but the godling turned around and roared back into the pyramid, coalescing and funneling itself into the temple like water pouring down a drainpipe. In a rush, it plunged back behind its spelldoors and shadowglass barriers.

As he came back to himself in the deep chamber again, Klovus found himself weak, shaking, and gasping for air. When he saw all the priestlords looking at him, he recognized confusion, fear, even disrespect in their expressions.

"We tried to help you control it, Key Priestlord," said Dovic. He shrugged. "But the godling didn't want to cooperate."

Klovus felt great humiliation, knowing that every priestlord here had seen him fail.

75

⮵

B ECAUSE it was her skill and her duty, Shadri continued searching for answers in the old wreth documents. She was a scholar, a legacier ... maybe the only one who could understand vital information about the ancient race—or about Thon. To her, that was the most important part.

Elliel was deeply in love with the enigmatic man. Shadri was a little jealous of the bond they shared, but Thon was not a normal person, not human, not even a wreth, not exactly. Maybe he was himself a god.

Shadri had considered the possibility before, only to discard it. But should she? Elliel had found him inside Mount Vada, sealed for millennia inside a crystal-lined chamber. Could Kur have erased his own memory in despair and buried himself, as one story suggested? But Thon did not act like a god.

In the wreth ruins near Yanton, Shadri thought she had seen him *change,* thought she had seen a glimpse of an enormous reptilian monster, but could she be sure what had happened and what it meant? Thon seemed genuinely unaware of his origin or purpose, but he did not seem evil.

Here in Fellstaff Castle, Shadri spent her days in the library, and Pokle brought in cushions where she could nap if she needed to work late. When the skies grew cloudy and dark, she would light candles by the reading table. She left the library only occasionally to go to the privy when she realized her bladder was about to burst.

Now, she studied the documents Thon had left, rereading her translations, trying to decipher unfamiliar words and runes. It would take weeks if not years to sift through so much disorganized historical material. The wreths had not bothered to refer to their own source documents, ignoring their real history. They simply passed along spoken legends and perceived destiny for centuries. Wreths were created by their god and carried a great purpose, while humans were just a *made* species, beings created to serve them.

Shadri wondered if humans had the potential to accomplish far more. If the Isharans could create their own godlings out of the magic inherent in the new world, couldn't humans somehow spark their own souls? Make their own destiny?

Maybe *humans* were the ones meant to destroy Ossus.

Supposedly, Kur had said, "The only way to destroy the evil is from within."

What did that mean, specifically? From *within* what? Mental? Physical? Spiritual? The Utauks had some phrase about being "inside the circle."

Maybe Shadri was overthinking this.

She scratched her cheek and picked up a cup of fresh milk, drinking it down. She didn't even remember when Pokle had brought it for her. She looked up now and saw the eager-eyed young man just standing at the door, watching her. She smiled at him, and he nearly fell over.

Pokle flinched when Gant strode to the library door, standing twice the size of Pokle. "I came to see what you've learned, scholar girl. I read your notes about the drones. It makes me understand the cruelty of the frostwreths a little more." He glanced at the crystal sheets on the table in front of her. "Do those hold more answers? What do you need from me?"

"Oh, I have paper, and I have time." She picked up some of the original pristine sheets, which Thon had not yet activated. "These could be helpful, too, but they're still bound by wreth magic. I can't read them, unless Thon activates the letters with his blood. The writing is locked inside the sheets." She sighed, imagining all the answers that might be hidden in the ancient documents. "So, I just keep busy reviewing the work I've already done."

"The wreth records require Thon's blood?" Gant asked. "Thon's alone? I find that difficult to believe, since the wreths didn't know he existed underneath Mount Vada."

She flushed. "Oh, sorry, I meant wreth blood."

Gant considered. "I'm a Brava, a half-breed. My wreth blood may be diluted, but it still flows through my veins. Might it be sufficient?"

Shadri pursed her lips. "Well, these are simple documents, aren't they? Not sealed by powerful magic. We can try—"

Before she finished her sentence, the Brava startled Shadri by slipping the dagger from his belt and slashing across his thumb. As red liquid bubbled up, Shadri snatched the top crystal sheet and held it under his hand just in time for the first drops to splash onto the surface. The glassy sheet grew warm, and the runes began to shimmer and come alive, activating in layers. Glowing letters rose into the air.

"It worked! Now I can read them."

Gant held up his bleeding finger. "Bring another sheet."

She fumbled through the delicate records and realized she had forgotten to note which ones came from the frostwreth archives and which from the sandwreths. She decided it didn't matter now. She gave him sheet after sheet, more text than she could translate in days.

As she flipped through the stack, one discolored crystal caught her eye, sandwiched between two thicker documents. She slid out a thin rectangle of dark glassy material, not quite black but murky, as if its information were somehow shadowed. Candlelight did not shine through it.

"That one looks important," Gant said, milking the ball of his thumb to squeeze more blood out. His frown of concentration made his lumpy face look like a wadded-up ball of human features.

"Let's see, shall we?" Shadri brought it under the Brava's bleeding hand. A thick red drop splashed onto the murky crystal and spread out like thin oil to cover the entire surface. The sheet became warm, then so hot that Shadri nearly dropped it. Hissing in surprise as much as pain, she turned to the reading table and set it down, then stepped back to watch.

Scarlet wreth runes blossomed in the air, growing brighter. Shadri picked up her ledger and lead stylus, scribbling the letters as fast as she could. The markings changed before her eyes, flashing past too quickly. The thin coating of Gant's blood darkened and bubbled.

With a startling *crack,* the crystal sheet broke, then split again, crumbling into sharp-edged shards. The projected runes flickered like angry fireflies, losing their shape and coalescing into different lines that joined and flowed and formed something new. The lines and designs created not words, but a figure . . . a face. A wreth face.

As it twisted and clarified in the air, Shadri recognized the features and gasped. The image was Thon, locked inside an incredibly ancient document!

His projected head rotated, an expressionless face, but Shadri could not mistake his face. The shifting lines brightened before suddenly turning dark, the opposite of the first image—positive light, then negative light. Thon became something more than a wreth, more than a monstrous and inhuman creature, but the images alternated so fast they became a blur, and she couldn't understand what she was seeing. Wreth-dragon-blank-Thon-dark reptilian form . . .

With a squeak, Pokle darted out of the room, but Gant continued to watch.

Shadri spoke aloud, thinking through her ideas. "I think . . . I think this means Thon is neither Kur nor the dragon. He's something else, something more."

Glowing runes appeared, forming a message that she struggled to read. The letters throbbed and blurred, as if they couldn't contain their own meaning. With her stylus, she scribbled down what she could glean as quickly as possible. "It says he was hidden away as . . . hope. A catalyst? A counterweight? I don't know what these words mean!"

Desperate, seeing the glowing runes in the air begin to fade, she tried to read faster. Gant dripped more blood onto the broken shards on the table, but it didn't help.

Shadri squinted, breathing hard. "It says that the instructions were sealed away in the crystal chamber with Thon, in case anyone should find him. Otherwise, unless the mark is erased from his face, he will not know." Her brow furrowed, and she looked at Gant. "What does that mean? This is a terrible plan, if you ask me. Why would Kur do that? Elliel didn't find any instructions!"

Gant frowned, as if she were demanding actual answers from him. An elaborate answer.

"There's more, but I don't know what it says!" She huffed, felt the pressure of the Brava staring at her.

Thon's image curled and then dissipated like smoke on a breeze, and the crystal sheet dulled, became unreadable again. Gone. The scholar girl looked at the runes she had managed to copy, which had yielded a handful of answers and hundreds more questions.

"This is significant." She looked up at Gant. "In fact, it's real progress." Shadri quickly made up her mind. "I need to get this information to Thon. He's been trying to find out who he is, where he came from, and whether he has a purpose. This is at least part of an answer. Maybe it'll help him make a breakthrough. It might make all the difference! Can you ride with me? Take me to the Norterran army, wherever it's camped?"

"When you need more blood, I'll be happy to give it." The Brava licked the wound on his thumb. "We leave in the morning."

76

⧛

MOVING swiftly along the foothills, King Adan's army soon reached the large Norterran encampment near Mount Vada's western slope.

"One more step in the journey," Adan muttered, knowing it was something Penda would have said. He missed her, missed his baby daughter, missed a normal life in peaceful times. He leaned forward, tightened his grip on the reins. He couldn't have those things again until he and Kollanan overthrew his brother and brought together all three kingdoms against one enemy . . . a great enemy.

Seeing their long-awaited reinforcements approach, the Norterran army rose up and cheered, waving banners with the mountain symbol of the kingdom. Adan was surprised and pleased to see others waving the open-hand flag of the Commonwealth, and he nodded to himself. Yes, even though the combined armies intended to move against Convera, these forces represented the true ideal of the three kingdoms bound by a common cause.

As the weary Suderran troops arrived with their packs, tents, and supply wagons, the base camp doubled in size. The well-entrenched Norterran soldiers helped prepare for the additional people by digging latrines, gathering wood for campfires, sending out hunting parties to bring in more wild game. There were thousands of troops, but they would eat well enough, and they would not wait here long.

Kollanan guided his black horse, accompanied by Elliel and Thon. The raid on the canyon slave camp and the long ride overland had left Koll with grim determination and little desire for conversation. Now, in the combined camp, his expression seemed clearer, as if merely seeing his loyal subjects again eased some of his inner pain.

Staring ahead, he said, "I remember a large battle camp like this, after our first landing in Ishara so many years ago. Conndur and I had a sense of justice in our hearts. We thought we knew the rightness of our battle." He scratched his beard. "Now I don't even remember what the squabble was about, some disagreement or insult between our father and Emprir Daka."

"This time it's different," Adan said. "We know what Mandan and Utho did, and we know we have to protect the Commonwealth."

"And then we stop the wreths." Thon hunched down, looking serious. "I will help however I can. Elliel and I make a good team. We will figure it out."

"We don't have to kill all of the wreths, like at the slave camp," Elliel said. "We just need to prevent them from murdering more humans."

"And stop them from waking the dragon and destroying the world," Adan added. "Don't forget that part."

"We'll kill plenty of them, if they *get in the way*," Kollanan said, his eyes smoldering. "A thousand wreths need to die for my Tafira, and a thousand more for Jhaqi and her husband. And more for Tomko. And for whatever has happened to Birch. . . ." His voice caught. "That will just be the beginning."

A Brava rider approached from the fringes of the Norterran camp, the pale-haired Lasis, who had established the base camp. "Sire, your army is rested and ready. We are glad for our Suderran allies and ready for you to lead us over the mountains."

Kollanan surveyed the countless tents, the smoking fires. "You've done well, Lasis, but there are many battles to come. Ancestors' blood . . ." He seated his hammer against his saddle.

They all rode into the bustle of camp preparations, where the activity reminded Adan of carpenter ants in a log. They ate dinner beside a cookfire, and Lasis summarized their preparations. The stories that the Suderran subcommanders told about their victory at the wreth slave camp reawakened worries in Adan's heart. What if Queen Voo had not been fooled?

He went to his command tent early, not because he was sleepy, but because he wanted to avoid further conversation. He sat outside and read a book of legacies by lantern light for a while, but could not concentrate on the stories of old human heroes. His thoughts wandered.

Circumstances were rushing around him, and he wondered if this combined army could reach Convera swiftly enough to stop Mandan from starting yet another bloody war that would result in the deaths of many thousands. He shuddered. Provoking a war with Ishara was unwise at any time, even to avenge the murder of his father, but it was unavoidable now. Adan knew the provocation had been fabricated by Utho himself. Utho needed to be stopped and punished for a thousand crimes.

Humanity's real war needed to be against the wreths—and instead he had to waste time and blood to stop his own brother!

Before he bedded down, Adan heard a flutter of wings and looked up to see a ska circling over his tent. With a hooting cry, Xar landed on a nearby bush and cocked his head to look at him with faceted eyes. The reptile bird dropped to the ground and strutted in front of Adan.

"Did Penda send you?" He saw the collar around the green ska's neck and knew the mothertear would contain preserved images, possibly a message from his wife. But since Adan was not an Utauk, he could not activate it.

Penda had found another way, however, as she'd done before. Xar paced back and forth, as if flaunting the strip of paper tied to his left leg. Adan reached out to take it, but the ska scuttled away, taunting him. "Yes you're very clever, Xar. You're a good ska. I need to read the message. That's why Penda sent you."

The reptile bird dodged him twice more before Adan managed to grab him. He tugged at the threads binding the curl of paper. Xar let him keep fumbling, but once the message was free, the indignant ska hopped away and groomed his ruffled emerald feathers.

Adan leaned close to the lantern light and read Penda's tiny writing, describing how the sandwreth army laid siege to Bannriya, how Queen Voo killed Penda's father, and how the frostwreths came to stand against them. Every sentence conveyed staggering news, and he had to read the last line twice before rising to his feet.

The boy Birch was with the frostwreths, held by the queen.

He ran to find Kollanan.

Koll searched for something to brace himself as his entire world went unbalanced. He grasped the fabric of his tent, and still almost stumbled. He regained his footing and read Penda's note again, while Elliel and Thon pressed closer. Lasis faced outward, as if to defend his king.

"My grandson is still with the frostwreth queen," Kollanan said. "And she brought him with her on the army's march."

Adan said, "There may be reason to hope. The frostwreths did not destroy Bannriya. And Penda says your grandson seems healthy."

"They are headed toward us," Lasis said.

"Birch is alive." Koll felt as if he needed to say the words several times before he could believe them. "The queen holds the boy hostage."

"But she kept him alive," Elliel pointed out. "That is something, Sire."

Lasis shook his head and said with a bitter undertone, "It doesn't sound like Queen Onn."

"Birch is *alive,*" Koll said a third time. He looked around as his heart raced. He had not felt so excited, so determined . . . so *whole* since his life had shattered. He seized the war hammer that rested near his tent. "Saddle up Storm. I will ride! I mean to intercept the wreth army and challenge this queen."

Adan gasped. "They'll tear you apart!"

"That is my grandson, and he is the only descendant I have left. I am going to save Birch."

Lasis stepped forward. "I ride with you, my king, as your bonded Brava. I . . . I have faced the frostwreth queen alone before. We have a debt to settle."

"I'm also your bonded Brava," Elliel said. "We'll all ride together."

Koll looked around the camp, then at Adan, and shook his head. "We can't lose all the Bravas. Elliel, stay here with Thon to protect the army." He snorted. "Thon probably has enough power to defeat an entire army himself, if he can figure out what to do. Lasis and I will go together. This is not a problem to be solved through force of numbers."

Disturbed, Adan frowned. "You're being unreasonable, Uncle. The wreths are already coming here. We can face them with our combined forces."

Kollanan would not be swayed, though. His vision had funneled down to a single focus, one clear mission. "Sometimes one must be unreasonable." He glanced up at the sky, judged that the moonlight was sufficient. "I don't want to wait until dawn."

The disgraced Brava Onder hurried up, leading Kollanan's saddled warhorse. The young man looked nervous, but earnest. "I . . . I could be of use—"

"Lasis and I ride together," Koll said, "and that is all." Impatient to be off, he swung into the saddle, as another horse was brought for his Brava.

The two riders trotted through the sprawling camp, weaving their way around campfires and tents, and picked up speed once they got to open terrain. Koll was not about to consider coming to his senses.

77

👁

As the wreth army swarmed across the landscape, Voo was dragged along with them, bouncing on a flat pallet. The terrible spinal injury had left her legs and arms useless, and she was little more than hauled garbage. She felt as if she had been buried up to her neck in sand, leaving only her head exposed and aware. She could grimace and snarl and curse, which only reminded her how helpless and weak she was.

She wished Koru had just killed her with the spear of Dar. Her deadweight body experienced no pain. She felt nothing . . . except for the vengeful hatred that boiled inside her brain, and the painful awareness of how her own wreths had abandoned her.

The haughty frostwreth queen rode ahead in her armored sleigh flanked by frostwreth warriors on white wolf-steeds, while augas carried sandwreth warriors who had betrayed their own queen. Although the two races remained separate divisions of a vast army, they all pressed toward the Dragonspine Mountains.

As her sledge jounced along, Voo spat out venomous, ultimately pointless words, and her impotent fury made her feel ridiculous. The sledge, which was better suited for hauling a load of shadowglass, jostled across the rough terrain, drawn by an oonuk that would happily devour Voo if given the chance.

Unable to contain herself, she let out a wordless scream at the sky.

A frostwreth warrior bounded past her on another oonuk, looked down at the fallen queen, and let out a mocking laugh before racing ahead to catch up with his companions. Voo rolled her head from side to side and gnashed her teeth. Her sledge hit a rock and jolted hard.

Leading the united wreths, Koru raised her spear and set up a cheer that was echoed by frostwreths and sandwreths alike. As Voo twisted her head, she could just see the usurper queen in her obnoxious triumph. The other wreths began a resounding chant. "Ossus! Ossus!"

Voo was horrified to hear her own sandwreths join in. "Ossus! Ossus!"

One of the augas plodded up next to her, and she tried to roll over and look, but her body wouldn't respond. Her shoulders twitched, but that was all. At last she could see Mage Axus riding high, frowning at her with disappointment and pity.

"You betrayed me!" she screamed at him, but he didn't flinch.

His mount kept pace with the oonuk hauling her sledge. "You were defeated," he said. "Wreths are led by the victor, as it has always been."

"I was tricked and betrayed, first by the human Adan, then by you and my own sandwreths."

"It is not betrayal to follow wreth traditions." Her mage sounded flippant. "Koru vanquished you. That is how we always choose a new leader."

"She's a frostwreth!"

Axus gave a maddening shrug. "She proved stronger than you."

"I ruled for thousands of years. Even when I descended into spellsleep, no one challenged my rule. No one dared."

"And now someone has," the mage said.

"No daughter from the line of Suth has ever led our people," Voo roared. "Their betrayal goes back to the very dawn of history."

"When have you ever heeded history?" The mage let out a disbelieving chuckle. "Do you even know how Dar and Rao fought Ossus together?" The grim mage scowled at her as if offended to see her wretched state. "Do you even remember our reason for existence?" He let out a heavy sigh. "I warned you, my queen. You wasted far too much time obsessed with the frostwreths, and ignored our true mission. But some of us remember what Kur told us to do."

Voo wasn't hearing him. She spoke in an urgent, conspiratorial whisper. "Koru lets you get close to her. You have an opportunity! Use your magic, make her heart burst into flame! Turn her mind to dust." Voo snickered, wrapped in her own thoughts. For just a moment, she forgot about her paralyzed body. "Make this right, Axus."

"And what if it is right?" the mage asked. "The wreths have come together in the greatest army the world has ever seen. Even the humans are gathered at the base of the mountains. We are about to challenge Ossus. That is what wreths were meant to do."

"Then kill me! Be done with it. I should have died when Koru defeated me." Her eyes shimmered. "Kill me . . . please."

Axus frowned. "Koru left you alive for a reason. I would not challenge my new queen." He added the last words with a bitter viciousness, then spurred his auga out of her view.

Voo screamed again.

At sunset, the wreth army ground to a halt. The wolf-steed that had hauled her sledge was disengaged from its traces and left to roam among the other oonuks that hunted in the foothills. Queen Voo was simply abandoned where she was; no one paid attention to her as the wreths set up their fires and boasted of how they meant to single-handedly slay Ossus.

One of the drones, the inferior beings created by the frostwreths, approached her with a bowl of gruel. It squatted next to her in silence, and Voo turned her head away, but she couldn't evade the creature's ministrations.

Clearly following orders, the persistent drone jammed a spoonful into her mouth. She spat out the gruel, which only smeared the mess across her chin. The drone scraped it up with the side of the spoon and fed her again.

Throughout the feeding, she willed herself to sit up, to move her arms, to raise herself off the ground, to slap the insolent drone, but nothing happened. She might have felt a twitch, or maybe she just imagined it. Finished, the drone left without a word or sound.

After the creature departed, another figure crept forward, the small human boy that Koru kept as her plaything. He was pale and quiet, but seemed to be fascinated by her. He hunched next to her pallet. "You are a sandwreth queen?" His brow furrowed. "I thought you'd be more impressive."

"The lowliest sandwreth is more powerful than any human!" Voo snapped.

"I am the grandson of the king of Norterra," the boy said. "And you don't look very powerful to me. Queen Koru says that when we awaken Ossus, maybe she can feed you to him, and then your poison will kill him."

Voo was disgusted with the child, a feeling that reflected her disgust with herself. She tried to squirm, but could not evade the boy's probing gaze. He spoke in a low, sharp voice. "I know the wreths did terrible things." He leaned even closer.

In her mind she reached out with one hand, curled her fingers into a claw, and grasped the boy by the throat to throttle him. But her arm didn't twitch. She couldn't even see her hands. Her magic was a weak glimmer, and she could summon none of it.

The boy taunted her with a powerful secret. "I could kill you if I wanted to. Right here." He leaned even closer. "I am the one who killed Queen Onn."

"You are too weak to do that," Voo sneered.

"Oh?" Tilting his head to one side, he gave her a mocking smile. "In that case you should feel completely safe." With a low chuckle, he sauntered away.

Voo raged inside, commanding her injuries to heal, willing her body to lurch up so she could attack. No one in the wreth camp paid attention to her shout, or the boy who had provoked her.

But Voo was certain—completely certain—that this time she felt her hands twitch.

78

∽

AFTER the wreth army moved onward, Bannriya held a subdued celebration of survival and relief. Queen Penda ordered the city stores opened. Wine merchants distributed barrels of their finest vintages, and bakers made a special knotted honeybread normally reserved for holidays.

Finally feeling safe, Utauk caravans arrived from the outer counties, and the marketplaces were filled with haggling and rejoicing. Penda knew the leaders had been hiding in the hills, watching the walled city to see what would happen with the wreths. Now, they rushed in to restore trade and help with repairs.

More importantly, the Utauks came for the funeral of Hale Orr.

Penda acknowledged the exhausted relief felt by all of Suderra, mourned the loss of her father, and was sad that Adan couldn't stand beside her during the lighting of the funeral pyre. Even Xar was gone, having flown off to deliver his message to the army.

Penda had her daughter, though, as well as her friends, subjects, and extended family among the Utauk tribes. All their hearts were as one.

She traced a circle over the center of her chest as she left the castle for her father's remembrance. "The beginning is the end is the beginning," she whispered. Penda wore a crimson and black gown and her delicate crown as the queen of Suderra. Today, she was benevolent ruler and grieving daughter.

With Ari perched on her shoulder, Glik fell in beside her foster sister. "Inside the circle and outside the circle."

Penda smiled at the girl and felt a little less alone. Yes, she also had Glik. It would be enough until her Starfall came home.

All around the square, the Utauks had erected tents, but for right now all commerce had stopped. Every Utauk came to pay their last respects to Hale Orr, as did several Suderran vassal lords. In many council meetings, her father had made his opinion known, and Penda was pleased to see the respect he had earned from the other lords.

She had considered leaving Oak back at the castle, but she wanted her daughter to witness this, whether or not she could remember her grandfather. The thought reminded Penda with a pang that the baby's other grandfather, Konag Conndur, was dead as well.

As she approached the main market square and saw the dried wood neatly stacked for the pyre, her heart seemed to stop beating. The visiting Utauks had made bundles of kindling sticks, each family tying the bundles with their own family colors, which made the pyre look like a rainbow. Her father's body was laid out on top of the wood, draped in the black and crimson of his tribe. A thin rectangle of silk covered his face, but she could still see his ear and the tiny shadowglass pendant that he wore, supposedly for luck.

Penda wanted to offer a moving eulogy in loving detail, recounting his legacy, but when she saw the shrouded body, her words evaporated. "He was my father," she said. "I loved him. I will miss him." Her throat closed on a sob, and she couldn't get out another word. Glik moved closer and put an arm around her, and Penda hugged Oak tight.

She hung her head, then nodded. With a burning brand, one of the men lit the kindling at the base of the mound.

As the fire rose up from the base of the pyre, an Utauk man came forward. He wore gold and brown colors, the Tomah clan. "Hale Orr was my friend. We rode horses together when we were young. We captured wild ones and brought them to market." The older man grinned. "One of the horses bit him on the shoulder."

Another man stepped up. "Hale and I went camping when we were just learning to fend for ourselves. I made stew over the cookfire and was adding fire peppers when he made a joke. I laughed so hard that I accidentally dumped far too many in his bowl. I didn't tell him, and he . . ." His voice hitched. "He insisted on eating the entire serving, peppers and all, just to be polite. His face turned red, and sweat dripped into the bowl, but he never criticized me. He did not let me cook again for the rest of our trip." The man looked down. "I haven't eaten fire peppers since."

A third man braced himself and came forward. "I knew Hale Orr. I . . . I was the one who challenged him to a knife fight. I won." He looked away, ashamed. "That is how he lost his hand."

"It was Utauk luck," Penda said. "Bad luck for him."

Balanced on Glik's shoulder, Ari flapped her sapphire wings. As the fire grew larger, the orphan girl spoke up. "I have no father, but Hale Orr was like a father to me. He even scolded me once." She smiled. "What more could a daughter want?"

Penda responded with a faint smile of her own. "What more could a daughter want?"

In all, nineteen Utauks gave brief remembrances, telling parts of Hale Orr's legacy as the funeral pyre swelled and consumed the body. Eventually the fire died down to coals, leaving a mound of ashes. It seemed to take a very long time, but as the Utauks continued to share story after story, Penda didn't want it to be over.

At last, many hours later when the sun dropped behind the hills, she ordered a group of Utauks to gather the ashes and put them in a special leather sack. "The beginning is the end is the beginning," she said. Holding her baby, she walked with Glik back to the castle.

Glik awoke sweating in her bedchamber. Her ska shrieked and trilled, flying around the confined room in an attempt to escape. The girl sat up blinking, but she didn't see the room. Instead, she saw a nightmare vision. Something was happening—or would happen—out on the Plain of Black Glass. That place was a center of power, a calling, a warning.

Cheth, who was in the adjacent room, pounded on Glick's door, then kicked it open and bounded in. She found her shaking. "You're safe. It was just a dream."

"Not just a dream! I never awake to anything that is just a dream."

Ari battered her wings against the stone walls, as agitated and restless as her bonded human. Glik called her close, trying to soothe the ska.

"I was out on the shadowglass plain again." She blinked up at her Brava friend and reached to the small table at her bedside, where she kept the obsidian knife, its hilt wrapped in leather around the blue ska feather. "Remember, the last group of workers are still there, still slaves."

Cheth's expression darkened. "I remember when they left. It is only one remaining camp. Do you think Mage Horava is still there? Is that what you sense, some unleashing of magic?"

"If the prisoners are still there, we have to free them. We can do it now! But . . . but, that isn't what I felt." Glik traced her finger around the center of her chest. "Inside the circle, outside the circle. I sensed something so far outside the circle, something I don't understand."

Glik felt the looming reptilian eye spying on the world, but also that other brooding presence. "There was such power—enough power to break the world."

"You're safe here in Bannriya. I promise I'll protect you. No need to worry."

"Not just to protect me! There's so much more darkness and anger. Have to get those people away from there. And . . ." Her teeth were chattering, and she took measured breaths to force a quietness upon herself. "And that place is calling me. I have to go back."

"Sounds like I should keep you as far away as possible," Cheth said.

"I know what I know," the girl insisted, climbing out of her bed. "Freeing the other slaves is reason enough, isn't it? The ones like us?"

"We can take a troop of Banner guards and ride together," Penda said from the doorway, where she had been listening. "We talked about it before, and it's my obligation as the queen of Suderra. We should have gone days ago, but the wreths . . . and my father."

Glik put her head in her hands. "*Cra*, I don't understand why I have to go there, but I know. I just know! I saw giant monsters and dragon eyes."

"Then we will go. A troop of Banner guards and a Brava should be enough against a small camp like that," Cheth said. "But I don't know what to do about giant monsters and dragon eyes."

"I'll be with you," Penda said, and her expression fell. "I have my father's ashes. I'll scatter them on the way. He'd want to be in the open land where all the tribes roam."

Ari finally calmed enough to settle back on Glik's shoulder. The ska nudged her dark hair, and the girl stroked the blue feathers.

Cheth lowered her voice. "I never wanted to go there again, ever."

"This time it'll be different," Glik said, not really meaning that things would be better. She felt a powerful tug-of-war in her mind, and she squeezed her eyes shut, lost in the trembling visions.

79

⟁

AFTER days of resting in the windcaster's shack, Priestlord Erical felt strong enough to accompany the old woman into Windy Head. The town folk were quite curious about him. Erical knew that his coloring was different from theirs, his features plainly Isharan, although the villagers didn't seem to know what an Isharan looked like. Erical did not point out the differences. The fishermen, tavern owners, and craftsmen just assumed he came from far away.

Cetor, the town's leader, hung tangled nets on racks near the water, where he painstakingly sorted and repaired the strands. Erical remembered him as the head of the rescue party that had found him. Cetor spent most days out on his fishing boat, but once each week he spent a few hours tending, untangling, and mending his nets.

Erical and Mystia paused to see the town leader before they went back to her shack on the headlands. Cetor raised his eyebrows, regarding the stranger. "You still can't remember anything, eh?"

Erical looked away. "Just a few images, no details. I'm sure my old life wasn't all that interesting."

The town leader tugged on a rough tangle and finally got the net unraveled. In a good-natured voice, he said, "We will make up our own answers, then, so it won't be a mystery anymore."

The priestlord felt the wispy godling in the air, touching him from the inside and sparking the energy of her affection. He knew that none of these other people could sense it. "I can't wait to hear what you come up with," he said with a smile.

The old windcaster made him carry the provisions she picked up in town, a package of flour, two onions, and a pair of knives she had sharpened at the grinding wheel. She carried a mesh sack of fresh green mussels, which she would wrap in seaweed and steam over coals.

Beyond the town's small harbor, Erical saw fishing boats out where they could catch schools of silverfish. Boisterous singing came from an inn on the waterfront, though it was only midday.

He marveled at what he saw. This land was so different from Ishara! Key Priestlord Klovus had led people to believe that the old world was a devastated place drained of magic, where the godless lived a bleak existence. To his surprise, Erical liked these people.

He realized the rescue party had been under no obligation to save him. Mystia was not required to give him food and shelter, or tend his injuries. The people of Windy Head did not show an automatic hatred toward Isharans, as he had expected. Instead, they lived their days and worried about parochial concerns.

His godling was far from her worshippers and the strength their gentle sacrifices gave her, but he sensed that the entity appreciated this place as well. And with Erical's contentment, he could feel the faint godling presence grow a little stronger, too.

He and the windcaster bade the town leader farewell, letting him go back to knotting and unknotting his nets. Before they could set off, though, the town's bell sounded an alarm. Cetor looked up from his nets and out to sea with deep concern. "Is it a storm? The skies are clear."

Erical's gaze ran along the coastline, then inland and to the north, where he saw curls of smoke rising. "There, something's burning!"

"Maybe a grass fire in the hills." Cetor hurried back to the wooden town hall, which was no larger than a house.

Erical and the old woman followed him. Mystia said, "My latest windcasting showed something dangerous, but I couldn't tell what it was."

A windblown farmer rode into town on an old plow horse and shouted, "Raiders coming down the coast. We're being attacked!" The old nag wheezed, having never been pushed to such desperate service, and the farmer seemed just as out of breath. "I was delivering my melons when I saw the smoke. Raiders are hitting the farm holdings!"

Cetor pressed him for further information, and the farmer sputtered, "They're on foot, and shaggy like animals. Attacking everything! They killed Chilson and his wife, slaughtered their flock, set the cottage on fire. I saw it from the outer stone fence, and I think the raiders saw me. So I cut the traces, left my wagon and my melons behind, and rode my horse here to sound the alarm!" His voice cracked.

Erical felt a chill, knowing exactly who the farmer was talking about. "They must have survived. The storm drove the ships apart, but some could have crashed on the shore." Reaching a decision, he raised his voice. "They'll burn and pillage every village up and down the coast."

Cetor gave him a curious look. "*Now* you remember?"

"Some . . . enough," Erical admitted. "They will be ruthless. They grant no mercy. They are called Hethrren." He swallowed. "From Ishara."

The old windcaster turned to him in surprise. "I think you have a much longer story to tell us."

"I do, but the important part is that we have to prepare. I don't know if we can stand against them. I have seen the Hethrren fight." He gestured around him. "Windy Head is not an armed camp. Do you have weapons, soldiers, guards? How can you defend yourselves?"

Cetor let out a bitter laugh. "We have fishing nets and oars." He paused, frowned. "Even better, we have many boats! We should evacuate our people out to sea where these raiders won't reach them."

"If the town is empty, they'll burn and destroy everything," Mystia said.

"But the people will live, and that's better than letting them all die in the streets." Cetor strode into the town, shouting to rally the people. Signal flags waved in from poles on the docks, and the nearby fishing boats headed back toward the Windy Head harbor.

Over the next few hours, more panicked refugees rushed in to town, yelling about the advancing force of barbarians. One old woman even rode a goat, swatting its flank to urge it to a faster pace.

As Erical listened to story after story, he guessed that fifty or so Hethrren were storming down the coastal road, ransacking whatever houses they found, setting fields on fire, killing livestock—conquering their new land.

The town leader rounded up townspeople to evacuate them. One surly old fisherman hobbled about with a makeshift crutch, which he waved in the air. "This thing is sharp enough. I can stand here and jab at the raiders."

"They will kill you," Erical said.

"They just might," the limping man replied and poked at the air again. "But maybe I'll get a few of them first."

The town leader urged the injured man to the waiting boats. "I would rather have you alive to rebuild. Go to safety."

One man herded three children in front of him to the evacuation boats. Some people escaped into the hills to hide from the marching Hethrren, while others rushed to form a clumsy, makeshift defense of Windy Head. "They'll be here in an hour!"

Mystia stood looking out at the water. "I'm not sailing out there. I have my shack on the headlands, and I'll make my stand there. Maybe you should come and defend me." She held up her woven sack. "Somebody has to help me eat these mussels."

The air to the north was thick with smoke like black stains. Erical felt dismayed rather than frightened, and as those emotions twisted, he felt the godling surge within him, a rush of power that he could tap into, even here.

"I may be able to help defend you after all," he said, turning to the town leader. "I have a secret that even the raiders will fear. Get everyone else away, and I will go face them."

"Not alone, you won't," Cetor said. He glanced out at the water where two more fishing boats rowed off, then set their sails. "As long as the innocent are well away, I can stay. I want to see who dares to attack my town."

Erical breathed harder, faster, felt the burn of the godling in his lungs like a crisp wind. He strode along the streets toward the edge of town with Cetor and Mystia following. Ten other fishermen joined them with splintered oars and sharp boat hooks. One clean-shaven man with weathered cheeks said, "I use this to club marlin. It'll crack barbarian skulls just as well."

Erical thought of Magda and her twisted club. "I'd be happy to see that."

As they awaited the oncoming raiders, Windy Head was mostly empty of people. Twenty or so determined villagers had armed themselves to defend their homes, and they gathered in the road that led into town. Standing together, they watched the enemy come toward them.

Erical's vision suddenly became sharper, magnified—and he realized the godling was enhancing his abilities.

The barbarians strode along, fifty warriors who had survived the godling's storm that had flung them to the coast. The Hethrren, fierce but bedraggled, stretched their lips to show sharpened teeth. They wore salt-caked furs and brandished spears and cudgels, even broken tree branches; some just carried rocks. Many held smoldering torches they had used to ignite the farmsteads and fields along the way.

In the lead, Magda lurched along on her thick legs, casually swinging her club. She seemed to think that just because she had burned a few farmhouses and grain fields she had conquered an entire continent. When her barbarians spotted the town and its defenders, they let out a grunting howl and jogged forward for battle.

Several fishermen groaned, but stood their ground. Erical could hear town leader Cetor breathing hard beside him, but he held his boat hook without flinching.

When Magda noticed the priestlord, she hesitated in her strutting charge. Erical inhaled and felt the godling feeding on his faith. He and his beautiful deity could do this together. He sensed her waning, but he held on to her, connected with his heart, his mind, and his sheer devotion. Even though the entity sensed great danger, she stayed to protect him, shimmering with rainbows that grew sharper, more visible.

Magda marched within shouting distance, leering at him. "It is the little priestlord! Did you swim all this way?" When Erical didn't answer, her face clenched. "Your godling's storm nearly destroyed us, scattered our fleet, wrecked some of my ships on the shore."

"You forced me to do it," Erical said.

"You should have controlled the thing. I warned you." She looked at the town's makeshift defenders while scattered fires continued to burn behind her. "I think you betrayed us, Priestlord. You abandoned Ishara, and now you stand with these weaklings."

"Betrayed you?" Erical scoffed. "I never wanted to be part of your invasion in the first place. Key Priestlord Klovus was just trying to get you out of the way, and apparently my godling and I were an acceptable sacrifice." When he spoke, a rainbow shimmer folded out of the air, as if the breezes themselves had turned into prisms.

The old windcaster cried out in surprise, and Cetor looked at him, astonished. "You are from Ishara?"

Before Erical could make excuses or explanations, Magda roared out to her followers, "Kill the people! Burn the town—then we move on to the next one. But the priestlord is mine." Waving her club, she strode toward the defenders, snarling at Erical. The fishermen and the town leader held their crude weapons in a solid line, trying to remain steady.

Erical stood empty-handed in front of them. He had no weapon but his godling.

As Magda lunged toward him, the godling drew on the remnants of her power, swelled, and retaliated. With an invisible storm of howling wind and shattered-rainbow glass, the intangible deity transformed into the violence she had previously used against the Commonwealth navy—violence that Magda herself had initiated.

The Prirari godling had learned how to kill and how to destroy, and she used those skills to rip into the oncoming Hethrren. The rampaging entity expressed all the rage and destruction they had placed into her with their own sacrificed blood.

Erical couldn't guide the godling, couldn't control her, but his own thoughts and emotions rushed out into the air. The deity surged into the raiders, picked them up, broke their limbs, pummeled them into the ground. An invisible, implacable wind split Hethrren skulls like rotten fruit. She tossed barbarian bodies in all directions like tattered dolls.

Magda herself yelled and swung her club into the air. Howling, gnashing her sharpened tooth, she flung herself at the entity in defiance. She charged in, as if she could destroy the shimmering deity by sheer force of will. She smashed with the club, poked into the whirlwind.

But the godling snapped her weapon in half, ripped the lower end out of her hands. The barbarian leader still roared, flailing with her fists, and the godling slammed the pointed end of the club like a stake through her thick chest.

Magda spouted blood through her teeth, and she clawed at the stake. The godling lifted her into the air, where she floated, her arms and legs dangling and twitching. She still tried to claw at her enemy.

With a sharp wind, the entity snapped the barbarian leader's neck and twisted her head all the way around until it was backward. Magda crashed to the ground in a broken, bloodied heap.

The few remaining Hethrren were aghast. Some scattered toward the hills, while others ran forward in one more attempt to kill Erical, but the godling used up her final shreds of energy to pulverize each one of the enemy attackers, as if they were no more than insects.

When they were all dead, Erical stood panting, sobbing, without a scratch on him. None of the other Windy Head defenders had been harmed either.

To his deep dismay, the priestlord saw that the sparkle in the air was very faint now. His precious godling, so far from home, so far from her followers, had expended every last bit of energy to save him and to protect the town he had come to care for.

Erical felt drained, weaker and shakier than when he'd first awakened on the rocky beach. His beloved entity was no more than a feathery presence, a thin, ruffling breeze through his hair.

The godling came to him, a last breath of rainbows, and swirled around him in a loving embrace, a final embrace. He frantically looked around, tried to find a knife to shed a little blood, to give her a sacrifice and keep her alive. The other defenders were standing too far away, so he scratched at his arm, clawing with his fingernails, but he couldn't draw blood before she faded.

Her entire presence expanded like an evaporating mist and dispersed into the air and land.

Perhaps, he thought, she would add a little more magic to the tired old world as she went.

80

Following narrow roads or faint trade pathways, crossing open terrain where necessary, Kollanan and Lasis raced to intercept the oncoming wreth army. Koll had never pushed Storm so hard, not even when he raced home after finding the frostwreths at Lake Bakal, everyone frozen to death. He would never forget seeing the little boy's body covered with ice and snow, his small hand clutched around a carved wooden pig. . . .

It wasn't Birch, though, but rather one of his friends, frozen in an instant by the evil wreths. . . .

Now Koll had fresh confirmation that Birch was alive! He had tried to rescue the boy twice and failed both times, which only incurred the frostwreth rage. He could not drive away the image of Tafira tied to the tree, her throat cut by vengeful wreth warriors.

What chance did Birch have among them?

Though disheartened, Kollanan had never entirely given up, but he could see no chance to liberate his grandson. Now, though, he had a spark of renewed hope. If he barged into the wreth camp, at least he might see Birch one last time.

Lasis galloped beside him. They paused to water the horses at streams, ate pack food in the saddle, and rested no more than an hour each night. Koll would have kept going until he collapsed, and a Brava could go on forever, but they were careful not to ruin the horses. They still had a long journey ahead—and then they had to face the wreths.

Lasis said, "I will fight at your side, my king, and defend you to the death. My greatest duty is to rescue Birch alive." He rubbed his fingers along the thin white scar at his throat. "But if there's any possibility, I intend to kill Queen Onn for what she did to me."

"A shame she can only be killed once," Kollanan said, knowing the cold-hearted queen was as responsible for Tafira's murder as Mandan and his brutal escort guards were. So much had died inside him and around him.

They came upon the huge army sooner than expected. Frostwreths and sandwreths moved like a flood across the land, heading toward the Dragonspine Mountains. The two men topped a rise at sunset and looked out at the sprawling military camp as the wreths stopped for the night.

Shading his eyes, Koll scanned the ranks, thousands and thousands of the ancient race. He spotted an impressive tent structure that stood out from the other tents and lodges, and he knew instinctively that it was the headquarters of their queen.

Koll mused aloud as he stared ahead, "At another time, I might be convinced to listen to the voice of reason." He unslung his war hammer and held it in front of him, inspecting the embedded shadowglass. He rested it on his shoulder, ready to go. "But not now."

Lasis clamped his ramer around his wrist and ignited the torchlike blade. With a nod to each other, the men urged their horses into a gallop and charged toward the enormous wreth army.

Outside Koru's tent, Birch quietly listened to the queen discuss war plans with her mages and warriors. One of the drones delivered a meal to him, and the boy nodded his silent gratitude. Many of the small creatures still moved throughout the camp or foraged widely in the hills. True to her promise, Koru had left them alone, and the drones still followed the army.

The wreth force had traveled south from the frozen wasteland through Norterra down to Bannriya, and now back east, where the rugged mountain range lay ahead. Riding in the battle sleigh, Birch did not find the rigors particularly horrible. He was fed and reasonably warm, and he was more confident of his survival now than when Queen Onn had abused and ignored him. Koru sometimes even talked with him about what she planned to do, how they would wake the dragon within the mountains. Birch didn't know what his fate would be if that happened.

Day after day, he rode silently in the front of the sleigh, looking at the unfamiliar landscape and wondering where he was. Birch had a lot of time to think and remember, but at least he was not afraid anymore. Koru seemed to consider him some kind of a talisman, a good-luck charm.

After a long discussion inside the queen's pavilion, Mages Axus and Elon rose to their feet, while Koru lounged on furred cushions. She watched Birch as he wolfed down his meal, and as soon as he finished the last spoonful, the drone took the bowl away and vanished.

Then shouts rippled through the camp, and the boy looked toward the lines of wreth tents, the separate makeshift corrals for augas and oonuks, and saw a bright light in the gathering gloom at the edge of the large camp, a distinctive fiery sword—a Brava's ramer! He jumped to his feet, excited.

"What is this?" Koru sounded curious.

A scout raced to the queen's tent, gave a perfunctory bow, and presented a gruff report. "Strangers, my queen—a human and a half-breed. They rode right into camp, and they seem unafraid."

"Unafraid? What do they want?" Koru asked.

The two mages stood next to her in their dyed leather robes, watching and pondering. The warrior scout seemed amused. "They demand to see you, Queen Koru."

Koru chuckled. "Demand?"

"One of them says he is the king of Norterra."

Birch's heart raced. His grandfather! "I knew he would come."

Koru glanced at the boy, then shrugged. "Bring them here."

Consumed with vengeance and anger, Kollanan sat tall in Storm's saddle. He carried his war hammer while Lasis kept his crackling ramer poised and ready. The wreths thought so little of humans that they didn't even disarm the two men as they passed through the swarming camp. Koll felt the weight of his shadowglass-enhanced weapon and knew how deadly it would be. He hoped he got a chance at the queen, and he hoped he could at least glimpse Birch.

Lasis held the ramer like a torch, leading the procession. As they neared the large pavilion, the Brava shouted out, "The king of Norterra!" Rather than showing any sign of respect, the frostwreths and sandwreths simply watched the riders pass, feigning disinterest.

Numb and focused, Kollanan breathed hard, saw a tinge of red around his vision, but he rode forward.

Ahead, the frostwreth queen emerged and stood tall and cold to face him, emanating as much power as beauty. Two mages flanked her, one in rust red, the other in blue. Wreth warriors stood armed and protective, though the queen looked as if she needed no guards.

Kollanan paid little attention to any of them as soon as he saw Birch step up behind her. The boy looked toughened and scrawny, but alive. Not injured, not abused. Joy filled him. "Birch!" He tried to make it a shout, but only a whisper whistled out of his mouth. His heart nearly broke.

The boy grinned. "That's my grandfather!" He looked pleadingly at the frostwreth queen, and she drew herself up. Pale hair flowed around her head in a crackle of magic.

Kollanan had already unconsciously made up his mind, but now the determination was clear. He would do what he needed to do to free this boy, make any sacrifice necessary. It did not matter what happened to him—did not matter at all.

He leaped to the ground and strode forward, holding his heavy weapon ready. "I am King Kollanan the Hammer. You took that boy hostage. Free him, or you will all die."

His demand was so preposterous that the wreths were taken aback. The dour mages looked at him as if dissecting some unknown creature.

Lasis joined his king, holding up the ramer and ready to die with him. But he leaned closer, and his words astonished Koll. "Sire . . . that is not Queen Onn."

Kollanan flashed him a glance. "What do you mean?"

"That is not Queen Onn. I do not know her."

Birch could barely restrain himself, but one of the frostwreth warriors held him back. Kollanan stood before them glowering, threatening.

The frostwreth queen stepped closer. "I cared for this child, but I did not kidnap him. He served me in . . . interesting ways."

Kollanan could not stop the words from pouring out. "The frostwreths destroyed Lake Bakal, killed my daughter and her family. They took Birch with them. Frostwreths murdered my queen, my beloved . . ." His voice cracked. "My Tafira."

Oddly, the pale queen simply regarded him, unruffled. "I did none of that. You are thinking of my mother, Queen Onn—but she is dead now. I am Koru, and I rule the frostwreths. I rule *all* the wreths."

Kollanan shouted, "The wreths took everything from me!" He was unable to control his anger, needed to vent the rage that had swirled inside him for so long. "Have you not taken enough?"

The queen—Koru—stepped up to stand face-to-face with him. Her frame was slighter than his, but she had the coiled energy of a whip. "As I said, I did none of those things. The wreths who led that attack on your town by the lake are also dead. Irri, the warrior who slew your wife, has been executed. I—" She looked down and actually touched Birch's shoulder. "*We* killed Irri when he betrayed me. My mother kept this child as a pet, and she treated him badly. But he survived, and I have even grown somewhat fond of him."

"She's telling the truth, Grandfather," Birch admitted, then he turned a meaningful glance at Koru. "But you don't need to hold me anymore. I want to go home . . . or at least I want to be with my grandfather. The king of Norterra."

Koru looked perplexed. "The boy has earned my respect. He served me well." To his surprise, Kollanan found her strangely unthreatening.

Birch looked at her. "He is the only family I have left. Please?"

Queen Koru looked at the boy with a softening expression. "You did say something about that." Then she turned back to Kollanan. "I have no hatred for you, king of Norterra, nor any humans. My mother is dead, and the despised Queen Voo of the sandwreths is also defeated. I have my own mission."

Koll could barely find his voice. "What are you saying?"

The frostwreth queen spread her hands while her two mages continued to stare. "When we marched past Fellstaff, we left your city alone. We just came from Suderra, but I caused no harm to Bannriya. I simply united our two wreth armies, and now I lead them on our true cause." She sounded almost sad. "I do not need the boy anymore . . . if he would like to be with you."

With a wistful smile, she released Birch, giving him a gentle nudge. He bounded toward the astonished Kollanan and threw himself into his grandfather's arms.

Unable to hold on to his war hammer, he loosened his grip and let the heavy weapon slip to the ground. He didn't care. His heart felt as if it were melting. He began to sob as he wrapped Birch into a big bearlike embrace.

81

Utho's nightmare was that someday Isharan ships would reach the Osterran shore and sail up the Joined River to Convera. If that ever happened, he would know that he had failed, that all Bravas had failed in their sworn duty to protect the Commonwealth and the konag.

He pushed his horse hard along the river road, leaving the *Glissand* and his remaining soldiers behind in Rivermouth. He had to get to Convera Castle, to reach Mandan . . . but he feared he was too late, in so many ways.

Even though they had overwhelmed the Fulcor garrison, the Commonwealth navy had been resoundingly defeated. His vengewar against Ishara had crumbled without even reaching the foreign shores, and now he was back in Osterra, desperately trying to salvage what he could.

He lashed the horse, venting his anger. Hooves pounded along the road for hours, and at last, looking up the wide river, he saw the bluff rising above where the Bluewater and the Crickyeth Rivers came together.

And he saw that the enemy attack had already arrived. He howled aloud and kicked the horse hard. The city was burning in places along the riverside. Bulwark defenses directly below the castle remained intact, but four Isharan ships had plowed into the lowtown docks, where ships came up from the coast and barges and flatboats sailed down the rivers with loads of produce, livestock, grain, lumber, or quarried stone. The lowtown area was made for easy docking and unloading of commercial boats; wide areas formed livestock pens, and tall warehouses were open for storing goods. By its very nature, the lowtown was vulnerable to attack, and the Isharan monsters had taken advantage.

One of the new bridges over the Bluewater River had already been smashed, part of its span in flames, but Utho had to get across the water to Convera and the castle. From the opposite shore, he was angry and dismayed to see frantic fighting in the marketplace near the river. On the invader ships, the striped sails were tattered and the hulls looked battered, but the vessels had crashed to shore and disgorged their deadly crew. Utho grasped his ramer cuff but did not ignite it yet—not until he came close enough to kill.

Though the bridge was burning, he spotted a ferryman on the riverbank, gazing at the fighting across the water from a safe distance. Utho dismounted from his exhausted horse and bounded up to the ferryman. "Take me across! I need to defend Convera."

The man quailed at the imposing Brava. "I can't go there! Those barbarians are slaughtering everyone!"

"That's why we need to fight back."

"I-I can't. They'll seize my boat."

Utho drew his sword. "Then *I* will seize your boat."

The ferryman leaped out of his small craft and scuttled away down the riverbank. Utho ground his teeth in disgust and climbed aboard, steadying himself. His foam-flecked horse just stood on the bank trembling.

Utho turned his back, settled onto the wooden seat, and took the oars. He pulled himself across the slow river current, aiming for the main fighting and the burning lowtown docks. Several Isharan soldiers were hacking at tradesmen, fishermen, porters, but Utho was glad to see the townspeople fighting back with whatever weapons they could find. The muscular barbarians lumbered among the defenders like maddened bulls, smashing pottery, cargo crates, and windows, wrecking market stalls, overturning food carts.

Utho rowed harder, breathing hard, and no one even saw him coming, a lone man dressed in black. When the ferryboat careened into one of the piers, he sprang out, climbed onto the wooden slats, and finally ignited his ramer. Holding his sword in the other hand and roaring a challenge, he ran toward the Isharan animals he wanted to kill. As he saw the mayhem, the burning buildings, the butchered townspeople, he could not help but think of his own family slain in Mirrabay decades ago.

As soon as he entered the fray, he hacked down barbarians one by one. No enemy could stand against his ramer flame or his sword. The Isharan soldiers—battered remnants of what must have been an army—looked disheartened as they made their last stand at the riverfront. His fiery blade beheaded one of the Isharans, who seemed to accept his death, then Utho used his sword to stab through a barbarian's thick pelt and between the ribs.

Seeing the Brava's charge, the townspeople fought back even harder. Their numbers doubled as people rushed from shuttered homes and barricaded doors, wielding sticks, pitchforks, cattle prods. The tide of battle swiftly turned.

Although citizens of Convera stood up to fight, he was disheartened to see no Commonwealth soldiers among them, no uniformed fighters from the konag's army. Why wasn't Mandan there, rallying his troops against the enemy? The young man should have been wearing his best armor, his Osterran colors, waving his blue Commonwealth flag.

With a growing anger, he glanced around the last skirmishes, searching for other bright ramers. He had left the two Bravas here to defend Convera! Where were Tytan and Jennae?

He shifted his fury to another barbarian, as ugly a woman as he'd ever imagined. She came at him with a stone-tipped mace, and he struck so hard that his ramer cut off her arm and burned through her chest in the same arc. After her body fell, he kicked it for good measure. He turned, listening to the crackle of his ramer and holding up his bloodied sword in his other hand in search of another target. He saw only exhausted and red-faced defenders. Some of them cheered. Others looked stunned.

Smoldering warehouses filled with bolts of cloth and hay bales produced a lot of smoke, but the capital city was not the inferno he had feared. Convera had not, in fact, fallen to the Isharan attack.

But Utho still didn't understand. He demanded of the people staring at him, "Is the konag safe? Where is the Convera army?" Now that most of the fighting was over, the patchwork defenders regarded him differently. When no one answered him, he lashed out, "Do you hear me? I am Utho, the konag's bonded Brava. How could our army allow such an attack here, without mounting any defense?"

"We know who you are," one fisherman said, his voice full of acid. He held a long-handled hatchet designed to split kindling rather than enemy skulls. "Utho!" Surprisingly, his face twisted into hatred, and he spat at the Brava before he dropped his hatchet on the ground with a clatter and stormed away.

Utho was stunned. He'd never been treated in such a way before. This was bizarre and unbelievable. "Why are there no defenders to this city? Where is Konag Mandan?" He guessed that the young man had barricaded himself in the castle and ordered the two Bravas to remain at his side. Utho couldn't believe Tytan and Jennae would have let Mandan look so cowardly.

"The konag rode off with his Bravas," said a prune-faced old fishwoman. She had blood on her rags of a dress, and she held a knife in her hand. "They led a raiding party to go slaughter an innocent Utauk camp."

Yet another incomprehensible thing. "Why would Mandan attack Utauks?"

The fishwoman continued, as if she relished delivering bad news. "Then he took the rest of his army into the mountains, leaving Convera defenseless."

A grizzled man said, "He declared a civil war against King Adan and King Kollanan."

Utho felt deep dread. "Why? Why would he not wait?"

The fishwoman sneered. "Because they sent an official decree that revealed the crimes Mandan committed. They stripped him of his crown." She stepped closer to him, looking like a viper. "The whole kingdom also knows what you did, Utho! Murderer!"

He stepped back blinking. The ramer was still hot, blazing from his hand. "What do you mean?"

"We know you killed Conndur the Brave," she screamed at him. "Butchered him on Fulcor Island. Murderer!"

The other people growled and grumbled, forming a wide circle around him but fearing to come closer. "Murderer . . ." someone else said. "We even found the headless body of another Brava—one that you killed."

Utho took a moment to recover from his shock. They had found Master Onzu? And was he the one who had revealed the truth about Conndur's death? It must have been the old Brava trainer! Even in death, Onzu still caused problems. Utho felt a flash of humiliation, but he crushed it. These people didn't understand anything about what Utho had sacrificed, what he had accomplished.

Other townspeople were glaring at him, and he could tell they all knew. Meanwhile, Mandan was gone, Tytan and Jennae were gone, and the whole army was gone, leaving the city vulnerable. He had to rectify this!

"Murderer!" the fishwoman screamed at him again, waving her bloody dagger as if she meant to kill him herself.

He turned and cut her down with the ramer. The other townspeople, still hot and bloody from fighting Isharans, gathered against him, angry and threatening. As he raised the flaming sword, they scattered and left the woman's smoking body on the ground. He looked down, surprised at himself, then disappointed. He'd killed an old woman!

No one dared follow him as he left. He stalked through the merchant district, stole a strong horse, and mounted up. He needed to reach Konag Mandan and his army. He had to stop the young man.

And he had to explain.

82

QUEEN Penda and forty soldiers left Bannriya and set out for the Plain of Black Glass, while Captain Elcior remained behind to watch over the city. The heavily armed Banner guard, along with Cheth, should be a strong enough force against three wreth warriors and a mage, but they knew better than to underestimate the strength of the enemy.

If they were even enemies anymore . . .

The sandwreth captors could not yet know that their Queen Voo had been defeated, or that the combined wreth armies had moved on and were no longer in conflict with humans.

Though this group was making the journey at her insistence, Glik felt uneasy. Her stomach roiled, as if she'd eaten too many fire peppers. Picking up on Glik's apprehension, Ari frequently left her shoulder and circled above the group, scouting for hazards. From her exotic and incomprehensible visions, Glik knew that the greatest danger lay in the dark magic that seeped through the shadowglass pools.

Seeing her troubled expression, Penda said, "We will do this without bloodshed if we can. I'll tell the wreths what's happened and hope that they release their captives."

Glik heaved a sigh. "What if they don't believe you?"

"Maybe they will."

Cheth pulled her horse up alongside them. "They will." The Brava rode ahead, a powerful figure who looked so different from the dusty captive at the wreth labor camp.

Since it was the way of her people, Penda brought the baby along on the journey. With a fabric sling, she lashed the infant against her as they rode, and Oak traveled well. Glik wasn't surprised, since the little girl was still an Utauk child. In addition to the protection of the Banner guard, Penda had brought the young squire Hom to help tend the baby. His brother Seenan was among the uniformed soldiers.

The Plain of Black Glass called out to Glik, and she could not turn away. This was something she had to learn, had to face. She dreamed at night as they slept under the open sky with her ska perched on a branch overhead, and she nearly drowned in confusing, overwhelming visions of looming shadows, slitted eyes, dark and ominous scales, a monstrous presence rising out of the ground.

The orphan girl did not fear for herself, but for the future, for the Utauks, for the whole world . . . and for little Oak, whom she already considered another sister.

As her party rode onward, Penda listened to the whisper of dry grasses, the wind in her ears and stirring her hair, and she thought of her father.

Even though Bannriya's walls had protected humanity for thousands of years, she felt liberated to be under the open sky again, riding her chestnut mare. She straightened her back, tilted her face up to the fluffy clouds, and stretched out her hands. With her eyes closed, she seemed to feel her father's presence there, and everywhere.

When she spotted a flower-spangled meadow with a creek running through it, she knew her father would have liked it here. She glanced at Glik, and her adopted sister seemed to know what she was thinking. They both traced a circle around their hearts. Penda called a halt. Cheth and the Banner guards asked no questions, just pulled up their horses.

Penda dismounted and opened her saddlebag to remove a large leather sack. When she touched it, her fingers tingled. Her father's ashes, powdered and packed after the pyre in Bannriya square. "This is where he will rejoin the land."

Cheth gave a solemn nod.

Penda walked with the sack, holding its loose sides and loosening the drawstring to open the mouth. Ari circled overhead like a herald for the remembrance.

Standing by the creek side and listening to the murmur of the water, Penda reached into the sack and flung a handful up into the air. "Return to the sky you always loved, Father. Share and be shared."

As the fine ashes glittered and dispersed in the breezes, Penda took a second handful and tossed it into the creek, where the grains danced on the surface of the water and rushed along into the burbling current. "Return to the water, cool and refreshing. Share and be shared."

Glik also took a small handful and sifted the ashes into the creek.

Penda held the sides of the half-empty sack and shook it, scattering the pale ashes onto the flowers, wild herbs, and grasses in the meadow. "Return to the earth, to the growing and living things that refreshed you so much. Share and be shared."

She closed her eyes and lowered her head. Tears streaked Glik's face. "I'll miss you, Father Orr," the girl said.

Penda drew a circle around her heart and folded up the empty leather sack.

Two days later, Glik recognized the terrain, and her heart felt heavy. With Ari perched on her shoulder, Glik rode close beside Cheth, seeking the Brava's company.

Cheth stared ahead, her expression drawn tight. "I never wanted to come back here, but at least this time it is my choice."

"And mine," Glik said. "Though in a way, this time there is more to fear."

"We'll free those prisoners, do not worry," the Brava said, but the prisoners weren't the source of Glik's anxiety.

The first scout galloped back to the troops, causing a flurry of uneasiness in the line of riders. "And the work camp?" Penda asked. "The prisoners? Did you see the wreth guards and human captives?"

The scout said, "I made sure I wasn't seen, but I can say there's no encampment, just ruins. The place looks abandoned."

"We'll see for ourselves," Cheth said, urging her horse into a trot.

When they crossed the rise and came upon the glossy black devastation, Glik shivered. She closed her eyes. "*Cra,* so much magic was released here it boiled the dirt and bones into obsidian."

Queen Penda gave an audible gasp as she stared at the terrible vista. She had never been to the place before. "I can sense the power, too. You both lived here for weeks?"

"You could barely call it living," Cheth grumbled. "We worked." She indicated where parts of the blasted plain had been excavated. Old fire circles and a few wooden posts of auga corrals marked where the prisoners had been kept.

In the hollow resounding emptiness, Glik spotted three figures far out among the black rocks—wreths, with their augas nearby. She identified a mage and two sandwreth warriors. "Where are all the others?" She feared the worst.

"Our force should be more than sufficient," Cheth said, looking back at the line of Banner guards. She and the queen rode forward to face the few wreths, with Glik beside them. Ari took flight with an indignant series of clicks and chittering. The soldiers remained in ranks, a show of strength, and baby Oak stayed behind with Hom.

Glik identified Mage Horava, who had led the dozen prisoners from the canyon work camp not long before the rescuers arrived. The bald lump of a woman sat in the ruins of what had been a campsite. She hunched in her rust-red leather robes, which were covered with runes that now looked entirely impotent. Horava stared out at puddles of hardened obsidian, glossy smears of black glass among the rubble. Two wreth guards stood nearby, looking defeated and uneasy as Queen Penda and her companions rode forward.

Glik peered across the expanse of broken obsidian, remembering that there had been one more wreth guard and twelve hapless humans sent to work here excavating the shadowglass.

As Penda approached, one sandwreth warrior braced himself, holding a jagged bone-tipped spear, as if he refused to be intimidated by the human fighters. The other wreth guard already looked lost.

The queen sat high in her saddle as she looked down at Horava. "I am Penda, queen of Suderra. I came with these troops to free your human captives." Her brow furrowed. "Where are they?"

"Gone." The ugly wreth mage looked helplessly at her hands. Her skin, normally a coppery brown, was now the color of washed-out dust.

"Gone where?" Cheth glowered at the mage, then at the two warriors. It was clear Horava didn't remember either the Brava or Glik as former prisoners.

"Gone," the mage said, with an indecisive gesture toward the hills.

Penda held up her hand. "Queen Voo is defeated. The frostwreth queen struck her down in a duel outside Bannriya. The wreth armies are joined, and they rode off to the Dragonspine Mountains."

Mage Horava looked up. "I know . . . at least most of it. I saw it within the shadowglass. When we heard nothing for so long, I sent one of the guards to get information. He hasn't returned. But one of the human captives . . ." The mage leaned forward and peered into a dirty, stained swatch of obsidian. She used the sleeve of her rusty robe to polish the gritty surface, revealing a clean, deep black.

Glik felt dizzy, but she saw no visions in the revealed shadowglass. Not yet.

Horava said, as if she were talking about a change in the weather, "I shed the blood of one of the humans, spilled it here, and saw what I needed to see." Her shoulders slumped, and her expression made her face look even more unpleasant. "After that, there was no reason to keep the captives anymore."

"You killed them?" Cheth asked, anger building in her voice.

Horava seemed confused. "No. There would be no purpose to that."

"Then where are they?" Penda looked around the empty Plain of Black Glass.

"Gone," the mage said, as if she didn't care about further details. "Some ran away. Then a caravan of humans . . . they called themselves Utauks . . . skirted the hills, and we let the remaining prisoners join them. It does not matter."

In a gray daze, Glik walked forward alone as her ska circled above. The girl focused her attention on thermal ripples in the air. She sensed the magic—a power—that tugged on her like a rope, but also repelled her.

Inside the circle. Outside the circle.

Glik turned and asked the mage, "Why are you still here?"

The two wreth guards looked away. Mage Horava glanced up, as if noticing the girl for the first time. "Because we are bound here. I have to stay. I see . . ." A sudden light snapped on in Horava's eyes. "You! You are the girl with visions. Mage Ivun made you show him."

Glik touched the wrapped hilt of the shadowglass dagger at her side. "Mage Ivun is dead. I killed him."

The news caused no visible shock or dismay. Horava merely looked down at the cleared shadowglass in front of her. "The visions are still here. We are waiting."

"Waiting," said one of the guards. He sounded dubious.

Glik felt the pull inside her, the anticipation and dread . . . the power that oozed up from the ground. She looked over at Penda. "The mage is right. This is the real reason we were drawn to come here." Her visions swirled around her, and she needed to have the answers. "Something is about to happen . . . but it has nothing to do with these wreths."

"Leave us alone," said Mage Horava, and she and her two wreth guards wandered deeper into the obsidian wasteland.

Penda considered for a moment, then signaled to Cheth and Glik. "Come, we have our own business here."

The queen and her Brava went back to the troops, directing them to set up their own camp, far from the forlorn wreths.

Glik walked away by herself, tugged by the power all around her. Relieved, at least, that the other group of prisoners seemed to be safe, she still needed to be alone. She approached the shore, where broken black mirrors shimmered but did not reflect the sunlight. Magic bubbled like a cauldron coming to a boil, and it seemed stronger than before.

Over many centuries, the flat expanse of obsidian had broken and weathered. Rocks uplifted through the shiny crust created countless separate pools . . . empty vitrified voids. She heard a hollow whispering in her ears, an eerie call. Penda and Cheth called after her, while Seenan and Hom just stared, awed by the stark landscape.

Glik picked her way among the boulders, careful not to cut herself on broken slabs of shadowglass. She climbed an outcropping that rose above the ancient battlefield, and she knelt precariously where she could watch the black wasteland. This place of ancient battle had become a reservoir of pain and death, a gateway to some incomprehensible place.

As the girl peered down—and *down*—all the black pools, like scattered oil slicks, shifted, flowed together, changed . . . and suddenly opened. They were filled with eyes. Countless eyes. Huge and sinister eyes. Slitted, flaming, reptile eyes, all of them staring at her, blazing at her.

Glik squeezed her own eyes shut and reeled backward, stumbling on the uneven surface. She slipped, began to slide off the outcropping, and barely caught her balance. In the dim distance, she heard Penda shouting, saw Cheth running toward her.

Glik grasped the outcropping, afraid she would slash herself on the broken shadowglass, but even her body seemed far away as she was consumed by the vision. The eyes were inside her looking out at her, looking deep into her heart, and then staring through Glik's own eyes and thoughts.

She knew this was what had called her here.

She felt hands grasping her, voices shouting—Penda and Cheth calling out her name. "Come back, little sister!"

Glik kept blinking, but saw only darkness and myriad stars. They were strange stars . . . like an entirely different creation, a different universe.

She fought her way back to herself, following the friendly voices that shouted for her to return. Cheth helped her down from the jagged outcropping. Glik blinked, and when she spoke, her words came out in a hoarse rasp. "Our journey here was not wasted. We needed to come here. I needed to see for myself."

Ari swooped above her, clearly agitated. Penda's dark eyes were wide and alarmed, and baby Oak was crying.

"The coming battle is fraught with more danger than any war the Commonwealth has fought," Glik said. "And it is imminent."

83

⌘

THE change began slowly, subtly, as excited whispers rushed through the streets of Serepol. The empra's believers had heard promises many times, but now it was real. Iluris was returning!

After being saved by the empra's miraculous appearance on the palace balcony, old Analera found her way back to one of the rebel cells. The people hid her, helped her recover. Each day the loyal servant became more angry and determined. When she finally reunited with her group at Saruna's brothel, she hugged Cemi and Iluris. Analera wanted to run shouting through the streets—and so they turned her loose. It was time.

Iluris was stronger than any time since awakening. She inspected Cemi, her heir apparent, touched her cheek. Satisfied with what she saw, the empra nodded. "Yes, we are all ready. Shall we go?"

The brothel mistress looked regal in her gaudiest clothing for her new role. She had donned brilliant purples and reds, and draped herself with gold chains and gems given to her by lovestruck customers. She dressed her hair in lacy scarves, and directed all of her women to do the same, painting and perfuming themselves, carrying veils and ribbons.

Saruna dispatched her ladies through the city with a specific mission. The women were used to gathering attention, drawing the lusty gazes of men and women. Everyone noticed them. Everyone listened. And they spread the word. Iluris was coming!

Saruna's women called out to every citizen of Serepol, telling them to come to the main plaza in front of the burned-out palace. They darted along, flirting, tantalizing with few details. Because the rebels had already been primed, large groups of people began to move, gathering to express their hope.

Saruna was used to controlling rowdy men and drunken women, and now she acted with the grace and poise of Ishara's most skillful ambassador. When the brothel mistress flung open her doors, Captani Vos and his restored hawk guards emerged, resplendent in their gold and scarlet uniforms as they marched in front of and behind their beloved empra in a grand, unexpected procession.

"To the palace!" Captani Vos shouted out. His fellow hawk guards raised their defiant voices, "To the palace—to the empra's palace."

The brothel mistress had rummaged through her chests and wardrobes, selecting garments that were worthy of an empra. Now Iluris walked with grace, head high, a vision of authority and beauty, the absolute depiction of what the land of Ishara believed in. She exuded a staunch energy. Her head was wrapped in dyed scarves studded with enough jewels and bangles to serve as a makeshift crown.

Analera and Saruna walked in positions of honor just behind the hawk guard escort, as Empra Iluris and Cemi moved into the widening streets, finally revealing themselves.

Cemi was starry-eyed, unable to believe the beautiful, colorful gown and veils she wore. Previously, she had been uncomfortable in the formal garments Iluris made her wear in the palace court, but now the young woman knew it was necessary. She felt beautiful. She felt proud.

For some time, she had been worried about how frail the empra was, showing little of her previous vigor, but now Iluris was alive and strong. Cemi was convinced that the land would be restored, that Ishara would return to peace and prosperity.

They marched with a bold confidence, but the rumors traveled ahead of them. City guards scrambled to intercept them—no doubt following the key priestlord's orders—yet as soon as they saw the shining empra, many remembered that she was also *their* empra, and they backed off. The hawk guards drew their weapons, ready to strike down anyone who attempted to stop their march.

Walking beside Iluris, Cemi felt even more elated as she sensed the new godling's invisible force of faith rolling down the streets ahead of them. The vibrant entity gently nudged the excited crowds aside so that Empra Iluris encountered no resistance.

The older woman stared straight ahead, surrounded by her own thoughts, and seemed a bit stiff and brittle to Cemi, who longed to talk with her. But Iluris was too focused for conversation, as if she needed all of her energy to maintain this illusion of health and strength. Iluris looked utterly regal.

Cemi felt a huge swell of love for this woman who had done so much for her. Her own beliefs fed the godling ahead of them, as did the joy of the crowd. From the sidelines, the people chanted, "Hear us, save us. Hear us, save us."

Old Analera whispered to Cemi, "They've all given sacrifices. See how many wear bandages on their hands and wrists? They prayed to the empra and to our godling." She gestured, and the shimmering presence ahead of them seemed to grow stronger as the celebrating voices boomed out and the populace could sense it.

Delighted with the attention and adoration, Saruna waved to the smiling crowds, showing off her rings and lacquered nails. More city guards followed them and some ran ahead, folding themselves in as part of the empra's escort, while others rushed off to report to Key Priestlord Klovus. Nothing stopped Iluris from reaching the fountain plaza in front of the palace, *her* palace.

Cemi marveled at the difference since the last time she was here. It had not been so long ago that Analera and other outspoken rebels had been brought here to be executed.

Saruna and her colorful women dispersed among the crowd, spreading their happy news, making people smile and laugh. Vos and his hawk guards fanned out, a plainly visible line of protection.

Iluris ascended the speaking platform with careful footsteps. At the third step, she turned and extended her hand. "Come, Cemi. I want you at my side. Our people need you." The young woman felt intimidated, but she climbed up next to Iluris.

When the crowd fell into a hush, Iluris spoke in her kind but firm voice. The barely tangible godling circled them like an invisible guard dog, and refreshed them like a soft rain in spring. The entity amplified Iluris's words.

"I am alive, and I have returned," she said. "I'm sorry it has been so long. I was attacked and badly injured on Fulcor Island."

"Treachery!" someone shouted from the crowd.

"We hate the godless!"

"It was treachery . . . but treachery from Key Priestlord Klovus," Iluris said. A ripple of disbelief coursed through the crowd, then the murmurs changed to angry growls. She continued, "He wanted to remove me as empra and turn your anger to a war against the old world."

She smiled gently. "But I am not so easily killed." Everyone in the plaza fell silent, completely attentive. "I now do what I should have done long ago. I should have made it clear to all of Ishara." She placed her arm around Cemi's shoulders, squeezing in a surprisingly maternal gesture. The young woman remained silent, not sure what her mentor was doing.

"For months I searched all thirteen districts of Ishara to find my successor—and I found her." She looked down with a warm smile. "Cemi." She took the girl's hand, raising it up, joined with hers. "This is your next empra. I have decreed it."

"Hear us, save us!" the people chanted.

The new godling wafted above them on the sound, as if celebrating the announcement. Cemi felt dazed, but she had to be ready. Empra Iluris sounded strong, but she clung to her last vestiges of energy, only with the help of her godling.

The people roared and cheered, "Empra Cemi! Empra Cemi!"

Iluris raised her voice again. "We have more work to do—for Ishara! Follow me now to the Magnifica." Her words caused another swell of uncertainty and confusion, and the empra's voice filled with iron anger. "Klovus has corrupted the godlings and he deceived many of my loyal priestlords. He used the power of *your* beliefs and *your* faith for his own ends. The godling in the Magnifica belongs to Serepol, belongs to *us,* not to him! Follow me now."

She descended the dais, and Cemi hurried after her. The hawk guards folded like a shield around their empra and her heir. Captani Vos led the way as the crowd surged away from the burn-scarred palace, traveling the main boulevards, some of which still showed damage from the Serepol godling's recent rampage.

Iluris walked with brisk footsteps, the picture of restored strength. The people's beliefs also magnified the new entity. Cemi felt as if she were walking in a silent vacuum beside the empra, while cheers and chants cascaded around her.

The new godling danced and swirled ahead, parting the crowd and sweeping them along in its undertow after the empra's procession passed. The excited crowd reached the temple square, where the imposing pyramid was nearly complete.

The empra strode forward in front of her guards now.

Klovus's temple guards stood around the perimeter, uncertain and uneasy. Ur-priests crowded the main steps with other district priestlords on higher levels, looking down at the approaching crowd and the regal woman in the lead.

With a swirl of her vibrant garments, the empra advanced with Cemi just behind her.

Klovus waited for them on the stone platform, looking down with defiance and disdain as the dedicated believers flowed toward him, along with a group of his own followers whom he had summoned. He raised his hands and shouted, "Imposter! Do not be fooled. That is not your empra!"

The people muttered and shifted, taken aback, but no one truly doubted that the real Iluris had returned. They sensed the new godling around them, even if they didn't understand exactly what it was.

When the key priestlord raised his voice, though, Cemi felt the roaring strength of another force: the Serepol godling that shored him up, augmenting his words and his charisma. The rippling deity rose out of the huge temple, a powerful entity that had fed on the prayers and beliefs of an entire continent, amplified by the Magnifica.

As the people gasped in confusion, Cemi sensed the new godling, Iluris's godling . . . *her* godling growing stronger as well.

Klovus shouted to the people, "I have led you through this time of turmoil. Ishara needs a strong leader in our great and final war—and I am stronger!"

Iluris paused at the base of the temple, giving him a chance to speak, before she flowed forward with graceful steps, borne along by an invisible current. The new godling and the beliefs of the people rushed along with her, lifting Iluris up the Magnifica steps.

She spoke in a quiet voice that circulated around the square like a roar. "You may be strong, Klovus, but *I am Ishara*."

84

AFTER four days of hard riding from Fellstaff, Gant, Shadri, and Pokle finally arrived at the army camp. Despite her aches and exhaustion, not to mention the grit on her face and in her teeth, Shadri could hardly wait to share her news.

She wanted to reveal the mysterious knowledge she had gleaned from the crystal records, hoping that the insights would spark a reaction or memory in Thon. Even just knowing some of the answers warmed her heart. Her purpose in life had always been to dig into questions, gather data, and record what she learned. Knowledge was its own reward, but this knowledge might also save lives.

Shadri had told Pokle the story several times during their days of riding. He always listened, nodding. She was pretty sure that what she was saying wasn't overly important to him, that he was happy just to hear her voice. He didn't grasp the nuances of her explanations. When she suggested that Thon was a fulcrum, a catalyst, a counterweight, Pokle didn't know any of those words. Still, he was attentive, so she used the conversation as practice for when she finally presented her discovery. She knew she tended to dither and wander off on tangents, and she didn't want to make that mistake with this vital news.

Once Thon knew, he could act on whatever it meant—and so could Elliel and King Kollanan. "The only way to destroy the evil is from within." Whatever that meant. Maybe once Thon understood more about himself, he'd be able to direct his powers.

The mountains loomed just beyond the gathered camp. Mount Vada smoked and simmered. Thon had been found inside it, preserved for thousands of years, marked with the rune of forgetting.

As they reached the camp, Gant's distinctive black garb was enough to draw attention. He led Shadri and Pokle around the small fires and tents, past soldiers who were bored, uneasy, or impatient. Elliel emerged from one of the tents, and Shadri waved with excitement.

The Brava woman showed sudden concern. "What could be so important as to drive you here?" She looked up at Gant, her brow furrowed. "You've ridden hard."

Thon stepped out of the tent to join Elliel, looking at them curiously.

Shadri slid down from her horse, intending to bound toward her friends, but her legs cramped, and she winced as she rubbed her thighs after the long ride. "We learned something in those crystal sheets—something about Thon. Is King Kollanan here?"

King Adan emerged from one of the command tents, hearing what Shadri had said. "He's not here, but you can tell us what you've learned."

Another half-breed man came to the edge of the group, and Shadri remembered Onder, the tattooed Brava who had brought Master Onzu's dangerous message. He quickly said, "King Kollanan received word that his grandson is still alive and with the wreths. He and Lasis rode off to find them."

Gant looked astonished. "The king rode off to the frostwreths?" He touched his ramer. "I should have been there."

Still trying to work out the cramps in her legs, Shadri hobbled forward. "I learned about something that Kur left behind, a gift or a weapon. I couldn't understand a lot of the runes, but I translated some. And, Thon—your face was locked inside one of the sheets. It projected among the runes."

"A wreth face?" Elliel asked.

"No, Thon's face!" Shadri tried to contain her excitement. "The record was degraded and confusing, but I think . . . I think I know more about what he is."

Thon's face did not look hopeful. He frowned in concern. "It may simply be more confusion. First we thought I might be Kur himself, and then maybe I was a manifestation of the dragon."

Shadri said, "When I was hiding in the tunnels beneath the sinkhole, remember I found an ancient carving—a twisted shape of a dragon and a man combined. I think the answer is both and neither." She waited, but her tale did not make the answer any clearer for them. "I don't think you're Kur—sorry—but you're not Ossus either. You're something . . . entirely different. You have dual aspects—hard and soft, creation and destruction. A balance, a focal point. Good and evil. Predator and harvester . . . just like humans are."

Thon tossed his long dark hair. "You will fill me with self-importance, scholar girl, if you tell me that I am everything to all people."

"Not that," Shadri said, impatient. "I think maybe Kur made a mistake when he purged all evil from himself, every dark emotion. He thought it would purify him, but the purity actually weakened him. He needed to be tempered, not purged. Steel is harder than pure iron." She glanced up again, seeing more people crowded around. "What if he needed both aspects to truly guide the world? The hard and firm decisiveness as well as the kinder part? A person cannot stand on one leg for long."

Thon frowned, deep in thought. He clearly still did not understand.

Shadri continued. "One of the records said that the *hope* was sealed inside the crystal vault—I think that means Thon, whatever he is. There were supposed to be instructions, some other kind of record or an engraved sheet, in case somebody found him."

Elliel swallowed, and she looked stricken. "The walls were crumbling, the mountain shaking. I barely got Thon out. If . . . if there was a book of instructions, it is permanently buried in Mount Vada, and likely destroyed in the eruption."

Thon's shoulders slumped. He reached up to press a palm against the rune of forgetting, as if he could hide it. "I will never remember by myself."

Shadri said, "The record said that if you could erase the rune, you would know everything."

"How do we do that?" Elliel said, raising her voice with frustration. "Cover it up? Use . . . lye or acid?"

King Adan stepped forward. "This whole army is about to cross over the mountains to challenge my brother for the konag's throne. How does this information help us? What should we do with it?"

Elliel said, "What should Thon do with it?"

Taken aback, Shadri looked at the king of Suderra, at her friends, and saw the questions on their faces. "I don't know what you should do. I was just bringing new information, so you could learn. It was a very good story."

Shadri and Pokle were taken to a troop campfire where they could lay down their bedrolls, and the scholar girl would keep telling her story to anyone who would listen.

Gant felt a great concern. As night set in, he surveyed the line of dark mountains. Scout riders had returned with reports that Konag Mandan had an army of his own just on the other side of the pass. And if Mandan was there, Gant knew that *Utho* would likely be there as well—Utho, who had brought dishonor to all Bravas, who had ignited this civil war, whose obsessive hatred of Isharans had brought them to this impasse.

Utho . . . one man, one *Brava* had caused so much pain and suffering.

Gant had done his best to serve Lord Cade honorably. But the man was dishonorable and twisted, yet Utho was a far more significant menace than Cade. Gant realized that if one man could bring an entire continent—two continents!—to war, then perhaps one man could stop it.

One Brava. Himself.

As full night settled in and the camp quieted, Gant saddled up his horse, determined to ride off into the darkness. He did not intend to tell anyone his quest, but Onder intercepted him before he could leave. The earnest young half-breed faced him. "Where are you going?"

"I have a mission to accomplish," Gant said.

"A Brava mission! Let me join you."

"You are not a Brava."

"I was," Onder insisted. "And I can still fight. Please, let me assist you."

"I am riding right now. I cannot delay."

"Then I'll ride now, too."

Gant frowned at him, not sure what to think. "I cannot stop you."

"I'll do whatever you need me to."

Gant paused, assessing him. "What can you do?"

The question took the disgraced young man off-guard. "A wise man once said, 'The future is always more important than the past.' I understand that you doubt me. I was a coward in my past. I cannot change that. But I will do everything in my power to be a good man—and a brave man—in the future. I may never regain my status as a Brava, but you *are* a Brava. I place myself at your service. I will do whatever you require of me. I swear on the honor of the Brava I wish to be."

With a dismissive snort, Gant turned his horse and trotted out of the camp. Moments later, Onder, having saddled his own mount, raced after him.

Gant looked straight ahead and kept riding. "Don't get in my way."

"If that's what you require, that is what I will do." Onder let his horse drop behind by a few paces, and they headed quietly into the mountains.

85

Riding without pause—not to rest or eat or drink—Utho was forced to abandon his near-dead horse at a tiny village. He stopped outside a small stable, lurched inside without a word. In full view of the angry stable manager, he swapped the saddle to a new horse, cinched the belt tight, swung himself up, and rode away on the stolen steed. The entire village could not have stopped him, if they'd tried.

On the fresh, skittish mare, Utho rode even faster up into the foothills where he would find Mandan and his army.

The people in Convera had heard the rumors, and they knew his secret. Onzu's body had been found. There was no way Utho could quash it now. Therefore, *Mandan* likely knew the truth, too. The young konag had stubbornly refused to believe his uncle's first letter, which exposed what Utho and Cade had done to Elliel. But this was different. So much different.

Inside his head, he practiced his explanation, or more likely the argument, he would have with Mandan, and he could imagine many ways this would not turn out well. He had not found an acceptable resolution by the time he reached the Commonwealth encampment at the base of the mountain pass.

He saw a thousand or so fighters total, though the konag's main army should have been much larger. These soldiers still remained loyal to Mandan, or at least followed orders without thinking overmuch.

Seeing them camped out in the foothills, and knowing that Isharan animals had rampaged through Rivermouth and struck the unprotected capital city, Utho felt his anger flare. Because of this foolish misadventure, Convera had been left vulnerable, undefended, and Isharan ships had raged up to the confluence. He was annoyed at the young man's lack of forethought, at his outright stupidity.

Mandan was petulant, easily insulted, provoked into unwise actions. He had commanded this fighting force to follow him here, but he didn't know how to lead them, was inexperienced in planning the tactics of a large battle. What did Mandan plan to do after he crossed the mountains? How would he fight the united armies of two kingdoms? He would be marching to his own destruction.

Utho wanted to shake the young man by the collar, and scream at him for such a reckless decision. Isharans in Convera! Rising bile drove away his horror of knowing that Mandan now knew who had really murdered his father. . . .

As he spurred his horse into the camp, Commonwealth soldiers rose up, staring at the windblown, black-garbed visitor. Many recognized him with surprise and then open contempt; some backed away, while others wore a look of disgust or hatred. That told him the rumors had spread throughout the konag's army as well.

He clenched his expression tight and guided his horse toward the konag's command pavilion, speaking to no one. He owed no explanations to these underlings.

Tytan and Jennae emerged from the tent. Both Bravas looked morose but intimidating. When they saw him, their faces filled with questions. Tytan demanded, "Why are you alone? Has the war with Ishara been won so fast?"

Jennae's lips quirked in a smile. "Did you crush them?"

"Our vengewar was . . . inconclusive." Utho approached the tent. "I must see the konag, now."

The two Bravas stepped aside with clear reluctance. As he passed, Tytan said in a low voice, "Mandan knows. An Utauk courier brought a decree from King Adan and King Kollanan, stripping him of his crown." His expression hardened. "And accusing you of killing Conndur the Brave."

Jennae's voice hissed and spat like a kettle boiling over. "It was the Isharans! You won't convince me otherwise."

"Mandan is my concern." Utho could deal with rumors later, reshape the story, create a different legacy. Though he had slain Onzu, the training master's poison had spread like gangrene throughout the Commonwealth, but Utho could not let it rot within the konag himself.

He yanked aside the hanging flap without announcing himself. "My konag, I have returned—and much has changed."

The command tent was spacious and comfortable, not like the rough traveling camp endured by Commonwealth soldiers. The dim enclosure was filled with hangings, cushions, blankets, furniture, a long table lit by three lanterns.

Mandan looked up at him from his chair by the table. He appeared very young and terrified. He opened his mouth in surprise, but couldn't speak.

Utho kept his voice firm. "You need me now, Mandan. More than ever."

The young konag's expression went through a whirlwind of changes—first delight to see his Brava, then confusion, a wave of relief, then terror, followed by a rise of anger. "I received a message. They told me terrible things!"

"The world is filled with terrible things, and sometimes a man's duty is terrible." He let the flap fall behind him. "These are terrible times, my konag—times when great legacies will be written, if you make the right decisions."

"They said you murdered my father," he blurted out. "But I saw his body!

All the blood. He was chopped to pieces . . . and his face! His face!" Mandan screamed.

Utho loomed there, thinking of all the times he had imagined this confrontation, all the different ways he had played it out. A coward would have simply lied. A coward would have denied the story with such force that a weak person like Mandan might have believed him. Utho had such dominance over the young konag that he could have pummeled him into submission, no matter what the evidence was, no matter how convincing the tale might sound. He could have done that.

But Utho of the Reef was not a coward. "I am your bonded Brava, Sire. I have always been there for you more than for anyone else. I'm sworn to defend the konag with my life, and to do what is best for the Commonwealth."

"The Commonwealth? How can you defend the Commonwealth if you murdered my father? I know what you did! You swore to defend my father with your life!" Mandan wailed, racked with grief and doubt. "Is it true? You killed him! Why would you do that?"

Utho took a moment to compose himself, to calm his voice. "Because what Conndur was doing would have destroyed the three kingdoms. Your father meant to betray our entire land to our worst enemies. I had to choose between protecting a deluded, mistaken man . . . or supporting his successor, my protégé, a new konag who would serve the Commonwealth and save us from the Isharans."

Mandan looked pale and confused. "But all the blood! How could you do that?"

"Remember the Isharan animals! You know what they do!" Utho roared. "Even now, while you've been off here with your camp, Isharan ships reached the shores of Osterra. They set Rivermouth on fire, then sailed up to the confluence to ransack Convera." He strode closer, a crucible of fury. Mandan flinched, then cowered backward.

Utho continued to shout. "And *you* allowed it! You left your city defenseless! You withdrew the soldiers, took the army away on this folly. If I hadn't arrived in time to save our capital, the animals would now be in your own castle."

Mandan began sobbing. "But why? What was I supposed to do? You weren't here!"

Utho lowered his voice, shifting tactics. He knew what Mandan needed now. His voice was more paternal. "I wasn't here, but I came back. I fought and defeated the raiders in Convera, and I saved the land. I did what needed to be done, just as the death of your father was necessary to trigger the vengewar. He was one sacrifice—yes, a terrible sacrifice—for our very future."

Mandan was gibbering and confused. "But what am I supposed to do?

There's a civil war here. I had to stop Adan and Kollanan, or they would have torn the Commonwealth apart." He blinked his puffy red eyes, and tears streamed down his flushed cheeks. "You weren't here! And I didn't know what to do. My uncle and brother turned against me, tried to take away my crown. My own queen betrayed me. The Utauks have all disappeared." He pushed himself out of his chair, shouting helplessly at the Brava. *"And you weren't here!"*

Utho felt a small measure of pity for the young man, who was being driven mad by conflicting emotions and difficult decisions. Mandan had always been weak and malleable. Utho had shown great patience with the boy's irrational fears of thunder and lightning, with his whimpering inability to make firm decisions.

Mandan of the Colors was a weak konag, and the only thing that would save the Commonwealth was an implacable advisor to make the necessary decisions.

"I am here now, my konag," Utho said in a much gentler voice, "and I will tell you what to do."

Mandan blinked at him, but he still looked frightened. "How can I trust you? You murdered my father!"

It was time to be harsher. "If I leave you, then you'll have no one. No one! You must listen to me because you know I will tell you the right thing to do."

"What . . . what happened to the war with Ishara? What about our navy?"

Utho would not lie to him now. "Our navy is destroyed. The animals unleashed a godling at Fulcor Island and sank most of our ships. I came back with a few survivors and saved Convera. Now I will save you."

Mandan was horrified by the news. "My navy is sunk? All my soldiers dead?"

"*A godling*," Utho repeated, "but we stopped them at our shores."

Mandan began to laugh, a frayed and edgy sound. "Then your vengewar failed. It is finished."

"*I* define the vengewar!" Utho roared, and the young konag collapsed, missing his chair and falling to the floor of his tent, terrified, nearly unresponsive.

The Brava stood over him, waiting. "Good. Now you will listen to me as I issue more orders. I will take command of the Commonwealth army." He lowered his voice. nodding to himself. He desperately needed a victory, and so did Mandan. The obvious battle was right before them.

"I will order our fighters to push forward into the mountains. We will descend like a hunting hawk on the traitors there. I mean to end this civil war even if I have to kill both kings myself."

86

A T dawn on the Plain of Black Glass, Glik jerked awake as Ari took flight from a nearby boulder. Her first reaction was alarm, but then she felt a wash of surprise funneled through her heart link.

Rubbing her eyes, she climbed to her feet and stretched, feeling refreshed as she looked into the empty sky, even though her night had been filled with incomprehensible dreams. The brooding threat of this scarred place indicated impending changes to the whole world.

The wreth mage and the two remaining warriors ignored the human troops, taking their augas to another part of the obsidian wasteland. Horava and her companions posed no open threat, showed no interest at all. The rough-featured mage wandered among the shadowglass reservoirs, peering into the black emptiness as if searching for answers. The wreth warriors struck their spears against the obsidian with a hollow clacking sound, and that was what had awakened Glik.

She let her gaze travel past Ari's beautiful feathers and scales, to the skas higher overhead riding the thermals. They had flown in from their eyries in the distant crags. Glik remembered climbing up to those high wild peaks, bloodying her hands and knees, scrambling up cliffs until she wormed her way into the reptile birds' nests to find Ari's precious egg. That had made all the effort worthwhile.

Penda joined her as she also gazed up into the sky, and they watched the wheeling skas for a moment. She obviously missed Xar, who had not yet returned after delivering the urgent message to Adan Starfall about Birch. "Skas harried the wreths at Bannriya after my father . . ." She took a breath. "Do you think these are the same ones? What is their connection?"

"No one knows how many skas there are." Glik looked across the rubble at Mage Horava, where she was hunched over a shadowglass pool, then glanced up at the tiny figures high above. "They seem to be ignoring the wreths now. The sandwreths called them little dragons, saw them as spies, as vermin." Her voice turned bitter. "They killed skas whenever they could, but Ari got away."

The girl closed her eyes, feeling her strong heart link with her pet, but these wild birds had their own sharp, primitive energy and recklessness—innate mischief, like little knots of chaos.

Suddenly, Mage Horava looked up at the wheeling reptile birds, and one of the warriors shook a spear, but it was an empty, halfhearted threat.

Many of Glik's visions prominently featured skas, but the reptile birds remained an enigma. Why did the wreths hate them? Suddenly, she felt something shift in her mind and in her heart. The bright morning around the blasted site became darker, as if the light were bending into the future and the past.

"Oh!" Penda swayed beside her. "Do you feel it?"

Before Glik could reply, sounds and visions began to roar around her. She drew a circle around and around her heart, muttering the words to her chant, but she felt lost, adrift . . . reeling up in the open sky like one of the reptile birds, but flying without anchor or stability.

Penda reached out to clasp Glik's hand. "*Cra,* what am I seeing?"

Glik laced her fingers around her foster sister's. The two of them were together, sharing the hallucination . . . or was it a revelation? Something changed at the heart of the world. Reality was cracking like the shell of a ska egg. As she gasped, a flood of visions became more than just images. They were also information, history—direct knowledge.

She saw the Plain of Black Glass as a blood-drenched battlefield stained with harsh magic. She was looking far back in time to the early history of this place, when the landscape had been wounded by the countless centuries of wreth battles. They had driven Ossus deep underground, but the evil was not destroyed, and then the wreths devoted their energies to a long war of extermination against one another.

But in Glik's vision now, the wreths were gone. She saw human settlements below as she flew on the winds of time. At first they were no more than squalid encampments, as the war survivors picked up the pieces and eked out a living, but as the visions rushed forward, year after year, decade after decade, the blistered land grew softer, tinged with green. It became more fertile, recovering. The human settlements grew larger, more prominent, more populated. Water flowed in streams; forests flourished until they covered the hills.

Overhead and all around, Glik sensed the deep, slumbering presence of evil—Ossus—but it wasn't the only dragon. Lesser dragons were abroad, still fearsome, but as the humans formed a community, their own government, a prosperous life, and a thriving race—entirely without wreths—the dragons faltered, faded. They crumbled into a thousand small pieces that were intrinsically different, changed forever.

Now, surrounded by a storm of history, Glik swirled around in her premonitions, trying to understand the knowledge pouring into her. As humans healed the world, the fragmented dragons broke apart, and broke apart, and the only remnants that survived became skas. The reptile birds were the tiniest parts of the gigantic dragon at the heart of the world, flickers of what had once comprised all the evil and violence inside Kur. The core of Ossus might remain under the mountains, but over many centuries it had diffused, seeped into the hearts of those left behind, the surviving wreths and even some humans.

But the skas themselves were different.

In her vision, Glik saw countless flocks of reptile birds cruising across the open sky, clustering together into a remembered shape, then drifting apart. Ari was among them now, darting up and down. Her heart link with Glik was warm and strong.

The visions snapped like a stretched rope, and the girl collapsed, cutting her knees on the shadowglass that covered the ground. Penda swayed beside her, holding on to her shoulders. "Did you see?" she asked.

Glik bit her lip and nodded. Her throat was dry, her eyes burned.

"Did you understand?" Penda pressed.

Glik was trembling. "*Cra,* I know some things, but maybe . . . maybe it just can't be understood. Skas? Little dragon fragments that were changed?"

Cheth bounded up to them, very worried. Apparently, the Brava had been shouting herself hoarse, but neither Penda nor Glik had heard her. Hom also hurried over to them, alarmed to see so many skas circling overhead. "I don't like them," the young squire said. "They always pick on me."

"Skas might be mischievous, but they're harmless," Cheth said.

"Not when there are thousands of them," Hom said. "Remember what they did to the sandwreths at Bannriya!"

Glik got to her feet and wiped blood from her knees. Her blue ska landed on her shoulder, and she folded Ari into an embrace. "I was so worried . . . I'm still worried. What's going to happen here?" The reptile bird burbled as Glik stroked her head, looked at the faceted eyes. "Why were we called to this place?"

Penda let out a happy laugh and stretched out her arms. Another ska flew toward her, beating emerald wings to land on the queen's extended forearm. "Xar, you came back! You delivered my message to Adan Starfall?"

The green ska chittered and whistled, pleased with himself. Penda leaned closer, looked at Xar's faceted eyes. "Is Adan all right?"

"Are any of us all right?" Glik asked.

Overhead, dozens of skas circled above the Plain of Black Glass, waiting for something to happen.

87

IN the army camp, Elliel was the first to notice that Gant was gone. Though she did not particularly like the other Brava, they had a common bond, a shared shadow cast by Lord Cade. The painful memories still stung inside her mind. Gant had replaced her in Cade's service, and he had eventually seen the dark core of his bonded lord. He also knew the dishonorable, dreadful things that Utho had done. . . .

But Gant had departed, telling no one where he intended to go. Elliel continued searching the camp. Growing more concerned, she asked the other line commanders, and one thought he remembered seeing the Brava ride off the previous night, accompanied by Onder.

Why would those two have gone anywhere together? Did Gant think he had some mission to complete alone? Arrogant confidence?

"Soon, there will be fighting enough for everyone," Thon said. "I can feel it emanating from the earth itself." He was quieter and more introspective than usual after what Shadri had told him, trying to understand what it meant for him. He spread out his fingers as if to sense the land, then suddenly grinned. "Ah, they are coming, all of them! They may arrive sooner than I expected."

Rushing in, scouts reported the approach of an enormous wreth army. King Adan quickly called a council of his war commanders and all the vassal lords. "Queen Penda sent a message telling us what to expect," he said. "It's possible they do not intend to destroy us. But it's time to prepare."

Lords Ogno, Teo, and Bahlen rallied their troops, forming ranks to stand against the enemy force, though Xar's message had said the wreth armies, united under one queen, were not intent on punishing humans. They were coming to the Dragonspine Mountains with a different goal entirely.

And that might be even worse.

Getting ready for an important parley with the new wreth queen, Adan donned his finest cape and his crown. Elliel glanced at Thon. "We should ride with the king, just in case."

"There is no telling how I might be needed." Thon's brow furrowed. "Even after what Shadri told me, I still do not understand my place. The wreth records are so scattered and contradictory, I do not know if I can believe any of them."

She reached out to touch his tattoo. "You will know what to do."

Mounting up, she and Thon rode with King Adan to meet the oncoming wreth army. Elliel was astonished to see the size of the marching forces, bronze sandwreths and pale frostwreths, warriors, nobles, and mages.

Ogno also joined them, squinting ahead. "I want to know what they've done to Kollanan the Hammer."

Lord Bahlen and Urok, his bonded Brava, also rode with King Adan. "Kollanan's anger was fierce, and his hope was small. He might have provoked a war after all."

"We'll hope otherwise," Adan said, spurring his horse forward. "And we hope that he still lives."

As they trotted toward the front ranks of the wreths, Thon stared ahead, intent. He showed a genuine smile again. "We do not need to worry! All is well."

Elliel rested her right hand on her ramer cuff, then was astonished to see the bright line of another ramer igniting near the front of the enormous army, the black-garbed figure of a Brava, Lasis riding in the vanguard of the wreth forces.

King Kollanan accompanied his Brava, looking proud and confident, rather than defeated—an expression Elliel had not seen on his face for some time. On the saddle in front of him sat a young boy—surely his grandson—safe and happy. Koll raised his war hammer high in greeting.

Adan laughed out loud. "Not what I expected! Not what I expected at all."

Elliel bedded down with Thon, as she did every night. In other times, she was happy to lie under the stars with her lover next to her, considering all the bright lights. Here in the army camp, though, they accepted the privacy of a canvas tent, just like so many other soldiers.

The mystery of the universe did not concern her as much as the mystery of Thon. She pressed herself closer against him, and they made love slowly and quietly, so as not to disturb anyone else. Outside, she could still hear soldiers singing campfire songs about lost sweethearts.

Afterward, with so many wreths spread out against the mountains and knowing Konag Mandan's army was on the other side of the range, she just looked into Thon's eyes, drinking in the beauty of his face, the perfection of his form.

Though the night was chill, they were both naked with only a thin blanket, sharing body warmth. She marveled that he was with her, that he had saved her by restoring her memories. Because of him, she knew she was not a criminal, not a murderer.

But Thon's memories, Thon's *reality* and his past, were still locked inside his head. Without words, she traced a fingernail along the patterns on his face. "I could change your tattoo, too . . . connect the lines, complete the unlocking design if you tell me how."

"My rune is not exactly the same as yours, and I cannot remove it," Thon said. "I think my past and my purpose are still here." He touched his forehead, then slid his hand down to press a palm against his smooth chest. "And here. But the rune blocks them, and there must be a reason. Shadri gave us part of the answer, so we know—or at least suspect—that Kur must have made me for some purpose. Should we trust him?"

With a sigh, Elliel leaned her head against him. For everyone else, she could be strong, invincible, but here with Thon she allowed herself to be soft. "Why wouldn't we trust him? Kur created the race of wreths and created the whole world."

"Does that mean he's infallible?"

She shook her head. "It sounds like Kur made plenty of errors. Shadri thinks it was a mistake for him to purge all his darkness and evil, because that weakened him, and then it was loose in the world."

Thon kept wondering, "But if I was Kur, maybe I would have been ashamed enough to lock myself inside a mountain after that. 'The only way to destroy the evil is from within.' Does that not make sense?"

"Or if you are the dragon, the sum of all evil, then we should never have let you loose." She forced a nervous laugh. "I can't believe it, though. You're too loving, too beautiful."

"But if I am something else . . ." His face looked young and innocent, and Elliel's heart went out to him. "Then my purpose is nigh. Surely these must be the times for which I was created? A balance? A fulcrum?"

"Let's not rush it." Elliel held him, not wanting anything to change. This moment was so perfect right now. Shadri had given them such confusing information.

Thon said, "I am ready, for whatever may happen."

Elliel felt desperate as she kissed him, stroked his hair, and pulled him close. She kissed him harder, touched his skin. "Make love to me again. Now."

Thon chuckled. "You think you can command a god or a dragon?"

"I know how to make my lover pay attention to me."

"Then I will obey your command."

They held each other and lit their inner fires, but even though Elliel pushed her thoughts away and tried to distract herself, she felt that something was changing. Events were reaching some kind of conclusion, all the questions adding together into some strange decision. They each had a rune of forgetting, a bond unlike any other, but Elliel and Thon were very different, no matter how much they had shared.

As she drifted off with his arms around her, she closed her eyes and just concentrated on the moment. But she could feel the ground rumbling beneath them.

88

WHEN she inhaled deeply, the empra felt strength swell within her, the energy of the godling as well as the faith of the people, *her* people. She was swept along, borne on her destiny. When she shouted to Klovus, her voice was stronger than it had ever been. *"I am Ishara!"*

In the temple square, the new godling shimmered next to her. It had been manifested and strengthened by the shock, grief, faith, and hope of all those who refused to accept that their empra had really left them.

Iluris moved toward the Magnifica. Previous key priestlords had wanted to build such an enormous temple, but Iluris had stopped the construction because she would not risk concentrating too much power in a single place, in a single godling. Now Klovus demonstrated precisely what she had feared. He was a fool, and he was out of control.

Her new gowns, the fine and colorful silks, scarves, and glittering bangles, tingled and crackled around her. The empra's very presence was filled with static electricity, sparks ready to snap out and shock anyone who came close. Temple guards took up their positions, including archers who stood ready with bows, sharp arrows nocked. But they all hesitated, just watching as Iluris approached.

Through a strange haze, she realized that Cemi accompanied her, right at her side, and Captani Vos marched ahead of them, defiant and protective as if he considered himself an entire army embodied in one man.

At the base of the Magnifica, she spread her hands to let the force of the deity flow through her. Iluris knew she held the real power to defeat the key priestlord, even if he was connected to his enormous godling.

Klovus stood on the stone platform above. "I lead the people," his voice boomed out. His midnight-blue caftan billowed around him as if in a wind storm. "I guide their prayers. I made the godling strong—Serepol's godling, which will defend us against our enemies."

Iluris answered in a normal voice, yet the words were amplified so that everyone in the temple square could hear her. "But what if *you* are Ishara's enemy, Klovus?"

The other district priestlords had gathered around the pyramid to support the key priestlord, but some of them now looked uncertain.

"Hear us, save us," the people chanted. More and more crowded into the square, pressing shoulder-to-shoulder as they joined their voices in the familiar chant. "Hear us, save us." Some prayed to the key priestlord, to the obviously powerful Serepol godling, but others shifted their faith to make Iluris strong. Her new godling expanded, ready to face its rival, its counterpart.

When Klovus shouted, thunder cracked in the sky, and the huge temple trembled. The scaffolding and piles of construction stone on the uppermost platform fell apart. Stones blasted up in the air and whirled around like dry leaves, and large bricks pattered down the steps.

A cyclone of wind and dust swirled from the heart of the Magnifica with a roaring sound, accompanied by black smoke and cracking lightning. A column of countless eyes, predator eyes, insect eyes, and bright human eyes, roiled aloft. The Serepol godling was an outburst of uncounted sacrifices and prayers, anger and bloodlust channeled against the enemies of Ishara—enemies as defined by Key Priestlord Klovus.

The Serepol entity turned itself inside out, fashioning innumerable screaming faces, unrecognizable visages of those the godling had killed in its last rampage. The snarling mouths were full of fangs, and the myriad eyes flashed with angry fire. The godling rose like a titanic shadow behind the key priestlord as he descended the steps toward Iluris, inflamed with confidence.

The empra felt her own strength, her own godling, and she did not doubt that she could be just as strong. "Hear us, save us," she whispered under her breath and stepped forward. Something did not feel quite right inside of her. Even so, it was time to act.

Disorientation and blurriness thrummed through her mind—not pain exactly, like when her skull had cracked and blood saturated her brain. She had drifted for so long in limbo without thought or awareness, and now she had to find the strength to win this last battle. She had expended so much just to get here, just to *begin* this confrontation. She would have enough.

Her new godling gathered energy from the prayers of the crowd. The people might have been awed by the Magnifica godling, but they also remembered how the thing had wrecked their city, destroyed so many buildings, taken so many innocent lives. Seeing Iluris restored, seeing the shimmer and halo around the empra as she faced Klovus, their beliefs surged to make her new godling equally inspired.

Iluris climbed the stone steps to meet the key priestlord halfway, and Cemi and Vos flanked her. She turned her attention to the young woman, her chosen successor. Since the first few days of talking to the street girl from Prirari District, Iluris had been convinced that Cemi had the wisdom, the imagination, and the balance to be a good ruler.

Even as the battle loomed in the Magnifica square, Iluris turned to Cemi with great maternal warmth. "Our land is in good hands with you," she said.

"You will know what to do. Do not doubt yourself. I am touching one candle flame to another wick."

"What do you mean?" Cemi said, alarmed.

Already the new godling was taking form, building into a swirling cyclone. Iluris could sense the presence all around her—not just as a protector, but a part of her, a stronger part . . . and Iluris could hold on no longer. A red splash of pain filled the void behind her eyes. Her thoughts recoiled as something burst inside her head.

"I am Ishara!" she said with her last breath as she fell into the godling's whirlwind.

Iluris didn't feel that she was giving up. There was no surrender involved in what she did now. Simply by letting go, she was becoming stronger, becoming something more.

The new godling took her into itself, absorbed her, and grew even more powerful. Her dwindling consciousness flowed into the rising entity, fed it, guided it—and Iluris met her purpose.

She was Ishara. And Ishara was strong.

Cemi's heart and thoughts didn't seem to be her own as she was swept along in events that would change the whole world.

The new godling, the protector, the presence that had saved them from the key priestlord's treachery, now grew stronger as Iluris faced her nemesis. The fledgling deity blossomed, became more distinct and terrifying, as if it had undergone some kind of metamorphosis. The old empra drifted along with it, confident but somehow ethereal, fading. Iluris had been pale and wispy, as if partially made out of mist, but Cemi had watched her mentor grow strong enough to wrest power from the priestlords.

Cemi had prayed for that day, because she wanted to save Ishara. Now, though, concern flared within her as Iluris was swept into the burgeoning entity and became lost. "No, not yet! You have to stay strong."

She watched in dismay as the godling encompassed Iluris, enfolded her. The old woman held out her hands and closed her eyes, and just let herself be carried away. Iluris *dissolved* in the godling's embrace, and her form became a shadow within the pulsating unstoppable force.

Cemi felt it in her heart. The connection was still strong—no, even stronger. Iluris was still there, and the godling was there. Cemi could feel them both inside her, connected to her . . . the power of Ishara, the destiny of the empra, the beliefs of all the people.

Around her, she heard a deafening roar of shouts, screams, cheers. Not just the crowd in the Magnifica square, but all the thoughts and emotions bottled up in the godlings themselves.

Rather than cheering with triumph, though, the young woman felt sad. All she could think of was that Iluris was gone—not dead, but changed, now a part of the deity. The godling rose, rippled back, and Cemi felt a warmth, a comforting scent, Iluris's presence making the deity stronger in a way that the wounded empra could not have done in her old body.

Cemi understood that although Iluris had awakened from her coma, she was not completely healed. She clung to life only out of her sense of duty. Now as a final sacrifice, she had surrendered herself in order to enhance the new godling, to give it a better chance against the enormous Serepol entity that had been corrupted by Klovus.

"No," Cemi moaned and drew a heavy breath. "No!"

The key priestlord charged down the Magnifica steps with the Serepol godling behind him. He was suddenly in front of Cemi and Vos, a looming presence strengthened by the roaring impossible force.

Cemi shouted her defiance at him. "I am the empra! I am Ishara, and we will take back this land."

With his scarlet cape whipping behind him, Vos drew his sword and stood beside Cemi as her loyal defender.

The other priestlords around the temple cried out, but Cemi couldn't hear what they were saying. City guards shouted, some of them still choosing to side with Key Priestlord Klovus.

A sudden rain of arrows clattered around Cemi and Vos. Archers were firing at them! The godling's wind sent most of the projectiles spinning harmlessly into the air like bits of straw. But one of the arrows struck Vos in the chest, sinking deep. He let out a cry of pain and stumbled, and blood blossomed from the wound.

Cemi whirled, distracted from her singular focus. "Vos!"

As the captani fell, clutching at the arrow, Klovus lunged forward and grabbed the young woman. Cemi squirmed and fought, as she had learned to do in the dangerous streets of Prirari, but the key priestlord was surprisingly strong. In his hand he held a razor-sharp dagger used for spilling sacrificial blood. He pressed it against her throat until the cold edge bit into her skin. One quick slash and he could kill her, spilling her blood over the flagstones in front of the temple. His own godling would feed, and hers would diminish.

"Now this is ended!" His voice was a snake's hiss. "If you control that godling, then tell it to surrender, make it fade away. The Magnifica godling will keep Ishara strong." He pressed the knife harder. She squirmed, but could not break free of his grip. "Or I'll just kill you now and end it that way."

The storm of battle rose across the temple square as the two godlings fed on the violence around them.

89

⮑

TRAVELING over the mountains through the night, Gant and Onder followed the trade road, which had been partially cleared after the eruption of Mount Vada, at least enough for two riders to get through. In the moonlight, the horses picked their way past fallen trees, took roundabout paths to avoid rockslides, always climbing higher toward the pass.

Onder cast frequent glances at Gant's craggy face, but both of them kept quiet. The Brava did not scorn him because of his rune of forgetting or his past cowardice; Gant didn't seem to care much about Onder at all, barely even acknowledged the young man's presence.

As they pressed on, Onder quietly promised himself that he would make a difference, that he would change. Was a person's entire destiny defined by a single mistake? He refused to accept that.

Finally just before dawn, in darkness so thick they could barely see the way ahead of them, Gant surprised him by saying, "I was there in Convera on the night you received your tattoo. We met in the remembrance shrine after dark. You were brought before the other Bravas, and we heard the story of your cowardice at Mirrabay. You admitted it yourself."

Onder felt as if rats had suddenly made a nest inside him. "You were there? I don't remember you."

"Of course not. That is what the rune of forgetting does."

The young man remained silent, riding along and just listening to the horses on the rocky road. A pine bough brushed against his shoulder, startling him. He asked, "Do you . . . do you want me to leave you now?"

"I didn't want you to accompany me in the first place." After a moment, Gant's tone changed, not hurtful, not bitter, merely matter-of-fact. "I've fought many times, faced many dangers . . . and made many mistakes, too. I had the poor judgment to bond myself to a vile man like Lord Cade. Should I be defined forever because of that poor choice?"

Onder mouthed the word "No," but in the darkness the other Brava couldn't see him. "No," he said louder.

"Then who am I to accuse you, now?"

They crested the pass just at sunrise, and looked out across the land of Osterra. Dawn's glow broke over Mandan's large army camped several miles

ahead down the slope. Tents and tall poles flew banners of the Commonwealth and Osterra.

Gant led his horse to a line of windblown pines where they could stay out
of sight. He nodded to Onder. "We will rest here and prepare. When I face
Utho, I intend to be at my best."

While Gant rested in the trees, the young man brought water from a nearby
snowmelt stream and killed a brindle whistlepig that sat too curiously among
the rocks. He skinned the furry rodent and prepared a meal, but Gant would
not let him build a fire, sure that someone in the konag's camp would see the
smoke. So the two men ate the flesh raw, washed down by the cool water and
some tundra berries that Gant had discovered nearby.

Onder reminded himself that they were Bravas. They could survive.

Gant used a dish of water and his sharp dagger to scrape stubble from his
rough face, then he scrubbed dust and stains from his black armor and cape.
Onder also shaved while looking at his reflection in the water, seeing the tattoo. For the first time, he simply accepted the markings, which told everyone
he met that he had committed an act of dishonor, and rightfully so. If anything the mark should serve as a reminder to him to be humble. A reminder
to act with honor. It was no longer imperative for him to remember everything he had done. Rather, he needed to make a new legacy—forward, not
backward.

By afternoon, Gant drew himself up, brushed off pine needles, and stood
tall, ready. "We'll be there at twilight. That's the time I have chosen."

The two men mounted up again and headed down the mountain path toward the army camp. As the sun cast long shadows behind them, the two did
not try to hide. Onder still considered himself to be a Brava inside, and this
was what Bravas did.

At the edge of the konag's camp, Gant glowered at the blue banners flying
with the open-hand symbol, as if insulted that Mandan continued to carry
the mantle. He turned to Onder. "Whatever occurs here, you are the witness.
You are the one to remember what happens." He nodded to the army, noting
that they seemed ready to move out the next day. "I am counting on you to
ride back and report to Kings Kollanan and Adan."

The young man inhaled deeply, preparing his mind and body as he looked
at the opposing military force. He wanted badly to prove that he was a man
of honor. He would serve with integrity, even if it cost him his life. "I'll fight
at your side. You can't defeat them all yourself."

"I'm not going to defeat them all. I intend only to defeat Utho." Gant narrowed his eyes. "Onder, I command you not to be a fool. This mission is more
important than either of us. You swore to do whatever I required of you."

Gant waited for a long, tense moment.

Finally, Onder said, "If that is what you require, that is what I will do. I gave you my oath."

Gant nudged his horse, and the two rode in among the troops, who huddled around campfires or squatted in front of low tents, sharpening swords or tinkering with armor, bored and unhappy. The soldiers looked up as the pair arrived, but no one dared to challenge a Brava and his companion. Onder wondered if they had stopped questioning whatever the konag did.

Gant headed to the heart of the camp and the command tent. He shouted out a challenge as he came closer. "Where is Konag Mandan—and Utho?" He dismounted and glowered at the tent, which was closed up even though the sun had barely set. Any other leader should have been out among his troops. Onder dismounted as well.

The tent flap parted, and Utho emerged like a bear coming out of a cave. He wore his black garments and carried his sword unsheathed. Looking at him, Onder felt his heart skip a beat. He half expected a wave of recognition and memories to flood back into his mind, as had happened to Elliel. He'd fought alongside Utho at Mirrabay, and he had fled in panic from a horrific godling. But his past remained just a blank void inside him.

Behind Utho stood a young man with a gaunt face and bloodshot eyes. Though he was the supposed ruler of the three kingdoms, Mandan crouched behind his Brava as if to take shelter.

Utho fixed his gaze on Gant, ignoring Onder, as if he were invisible.

"What do they want?" Mandan asked.

Utho turned, lashed out at the young man. "I warned you not to speak. This is too important—I make the decisions." The konag crumpled.

Onder was astonished, and his hand strayed to the hilt of his sword, but it was a far cry from a ramer. Gant responded in a gruff voice, "If you are a Brava, your absolute loyalty must be to your konag. And this is how you treat him?"

"I treat him as he needs to be treated," Utho said. "I am his mentor, and the Commonwealth is in my hands."

"That's not the way it's supposed to be," Onder objected, though he couldn't decide which one disappointed him more, Mandan or Utho.

When Utho glanced at Onder, it seared him as if the Brava had shoved a torch into his face. "I'd recognize you even without the tattoo on your face, coward. You left me when we needed you most. You were afraid." He spat out the last word as if it were a ball of poison.

"I know," Onder said. "I accept who I was and what I did. Now I am what I aspire to be."

With a quick laugh, Utho turned back to Gant and jerked his chin. "You remember him as well. You were there when we gave him the rune of forgetting."

"I heard you relate the story," Gant said, then lowered his voice. "And I have heard far worse stories about you, Utho."

Two new Bravas approached from the far side of the camp, Tytan and Jennae. As the female Brava stalked forward, she glowered at Onder, and the young man felt a deep chill. Had she been there for the tattooing as well?

"What is he doing in this camp?"

Onder turned toward her, trying to remember. "I came with Gant."

Though Utho did not take his gaze from Gant, he spoke to Jennae. "That man is not a Brava. He is a coward and a disgrace. Remove him from my sight."

Onder prepared to resist, but Jennae cuffed him on the side of his head, making his ears ring. She seized him by the back of the neck and dragged him away, past other campfires.

Gant still focused on Utho. Gant said, "He is free to do as he wishes. I did not ask him to come."

"Then why are you here, Gant? I hear you are a traitor to the Commonwealth as well. You were with the konag's forces at Yanton. Why didn't you defend Lord Cade?"

The ugly Brava drew himself up. "Because he didn't deserve it. When I learned what he had done to Elliel, my honor could not abide it." He strode forward, building himself up. "And that was before I learned the truth about you, Utho." Without breaking his gaze, he clamped the ramer around his wrist and ignited the fiery blade.

Tytan stepped forward, on the defensive, but Utho remained in front of the konag's tent, implacable.

Mandan cringed by the upraised flap, wide eyed. "Kill him, Utho!"

"I intend to." He readied his ramer.

Jennae dragged Onder far enough from the konag's tent and pushed him with a mighty heave. He couldn't get his feet under him and sprawled across the dirt. The Brava woman flashed a glare at him. "Leave now of your own free will, coward, or I'll cut off your legs and make you crawl back over the mountains."

Onder picked himself up and retreated a few paces. His horse was still at the konag's tent. Aloof, Jennae turned to watch Gant face off against Utho, as if Onder demanded no more of her attention.

Outside the main tent, both opponents had their ramers ignited, fiery swords summoned from the magic of their half-breed blood. Utho held his steel sword in the other hand.

Onder didn't have a ramer, but he did have the same blood inside him. He had the same magic, whether or not it was locked away. He touched his sword, considering whether he should attack Jennae, challenge the Brava woman. No, he decided. She would kill him like a bug.

He had promised Gant not to do anything foolish. He had a mission to watch what happened and deliver his report to the kings, no matter how much he wanted to join this combat.

"I fight for Brava honor," Gant declared as the crackling weapons clashed. "Cade is dead, but his memory remains. Your legacy will mark you for what you are."

Utho did not laugh, did not boast, but kept battling, striking hard with the flaming blade. "Those who write the legacies are the ones who preserve history. And I will decide what's to be written."

"No," Onder whispered as he watched. "I will tell everyone what happens here."

Jennae turned and glowered at him.

Gant hammered with his ramer, catching Utho's weapon, pressing one against the other. Sparks flew, and the flames curled up. Gant grimaced with the effort and kept pressing. Utho slashed with the long sword in his other hand, but the craggy Brava caught the steel edge on his burnished belt, and the sharp edge glanced off the hilt of the dagger on his hip.

Metal clanged, and Gant broke away, drawing his knife and hurling it. Utho swirled, flaring his cape as a shield, and the point of the knife plunged through the finemail. Utho ran forward, sword in one hand, ramer in the other.

Gant braced himself and held up his fiery blade. Utho struck at him like a carpenter swinging a mallet. He slashed with his ramer, then swept back with the steel sword, then with the ramer again. Gant blocked every blow.

Onder watched, his heart breaking, wishing he could help. He had promised. *I command you not to be a fool.*

Gant struck back with his ramer, driving Utho aside. His fiery sword heated Utho's steel blade, making it glow.

Tytan stood watching, not moving, not speaking, while Jennae stalked back toward the tent as if she might strike Gant down from behind.

"Kill him, Utho! Kill him!" Mandan chanted. The konag's whining seemed to strengthen Gant, who struck even harder, fighting so brazenly that Utho staggered back two steps.

Onder held his breath, felt a thrill rise in his heart, but soon questions whispered in his mind. If Gant defeated Utho, wouldn't Jennae and Tytan just rush in and strike him down anyway? Master Onzu—his father—had warned him that some Bravas could no longer be trusted. Wouldn't Konag Mandan call his loyal forces to surround and kill the outsider Brava who had challenged him? If that happened, should Onder try to defend him?

I command you not to be a fool.

Utho faltered under Gant's onslaught, staggered back on his heel. His knee began to buckle under the relentless pummeling. Gant took advantage of the falter, raised his ramer for the death blow.

But it was just a feint. In the flicker when Gant thought he had won, when his confidence left a small opening, Utho thrust his ramer into the other Brava's chest, burning through his heart. The smoldering blade protruded from Gant's back in a flaming spike.

Utho ripped his ramer sideways and cut Gant's body core in half. The other Brava was dead before he struck the ground.

Gasping, Onder stumbled backward as a scattering of cheers passed through the camp.

Utho stood over his victim and held his ramer high. Jennae and Tytan came forward. Mandan ran to him from the tent, laughing. He raised both hands in the air. "We are victorious!"

The rest of the konag's army muttered and stood watching, as if they weren't sure what to think.

Onder gripped the hilt of his sword, breathing fast and hard. There was no time to stay and mourn Gant.

King Kollanan and Adan needed to know. He had promised. He wasn't a coward. Utho had ordered him to go, and Jennae had thrown him out.

Before they could think about him again, Onder slipped away from the camp, hoping no one would notice him. He needed to flee—but not as a coward. He had a mission to complete.

He had to make his way back over the mountains, rush to the combined camp with his terrible news, and warn them that Mandan's army was ready to march.

This was what Gant required of him.

90

〰

"This will not turn out well," King Adan said as he watched the wreth army spread along the base of the mountains, covering the foothills.

Kollanan glanced at his nephew's concerned expression, then he turned back to watch the endless ranks of wreths with their wolf-steeds and augas. Their mages had spread out along the uplift, as if looking for weak points in the world. He stroked his beard. "No, it will not turn out well at all, Adan."

He did not consider Queen Koru a friend or an ally, but she had given him back his grandson, and that changed everything. After releasing Birch, the queen no longer seemed interested in Kollanan, though. She had no further business with humans, now that her huge force had arrived at their own destination. She kept looking hungrily at the Dragonspine Mountains.

The Norterran and Suderran army sprawled along the foothills, but the wreths concentrated on the slopes of Mount Vada. The hollow shape of the blasted peak was imposing, with several prominent fissures running down its flanks. The mages seemed to revel in the anger that simmered beneath the range.

Kollanan watched as the wreths crawled over the rocks, placing their hands flat against the surface of the world, probing and prodding. They used their magic to stir up turmoil, like a fool poking a sleeping guard dog.

Birch stood at his side, then wrapped his arms around his grandfather's waist in a big hug. "What will happen to us if Kur remakes the world?"

Kollanan tousled his hair, still unable to believe the boy was here with him after so much time. "I wish they had all just gone back to killing each other, like the two queens did."

"Queen Voo isn't dead. She can still move her head and twitch a little," Birch said. "She's very angry at how helpless she is."

Koll gave him a fierce hug back. The boy was like a single bright star on a dark night. Birch had told him about his time in captivity, how Queen Onn had tormented him, but he insisted that Koru was not as evil as the other wreths. When he told his grandfather how Irri had killed Queen Tafira, both of them wept together. But then the boy's face had taken on a hard and surprisingly predatory look when he explained how he and the drones had killed Irri and his fellow conspirators. Birch had looked around them into the forested hills.

"The drones followed us all the way. They are around here, watching. They can help, too."

"They already helped me when we attacked the ice fortress," Koll said.

He felt so proud of the boy, yet angry and empty, thinking of what Birch had been through, what he'd survived. He gripped his war hammer with such strength he thought he might splinter the handle, then he felt love and relief instead. He looked down at his grandson, and his vision blurred with tears. "You're here now, boy. You are safe. You are with me."

He wanted to forget about the grandiose plans for war, the politics of the three kingdoms. For a while, just a while, he wanted to be with this boy, to enjoy life and appreciate things again, but he doubted he would have that chance. Not for a long time at least.

Though Birch was young, the ordeal had hardened him, made him more mature than any little boy had a right to be. His childhood had been another victim of the frostwreths.

Even if Queen Koru was different, she was still a wreth, and wreths did not act in humanity's best interests. . . .

The mountains were jagged and dangerous, but Koru knew that the greatest danger lay beneath them. Now that her grand army had arrived, she could feel the darkness in the air, a smell of smoke and sulfur lingering across the landscape. Her two primary mages stood beside her, Axus and Elon. Together, they represented the combined magic of the frostwreths and sandwreths.

The queen turned to them. "Now that we have finally arrived, we must face our destiny." She paused, then raised her voice. "But we must not be fools! We cannot summon Ossus and just wave weapons and shout at it. We need the means to destroy the dragon. Is our army enough?"

Axus bowed. "My queen, in ancient times when our people prepared for the great fight against Ossus, the early mages developed profound and impressive weapons. These magical devices could concentrate and wield incredible power, enough force to crack open the world and shatter a dragon."

Elon's pale brow furrowed. "I read of such things in the ancient crystal records. I viewed the designs." He turned to look at Axus, as if consulting the other mage. "I believe I know how to construct them."

The sandwreth mage looked troubled. "Those weapons were unleashed many ages past—only once. The children of Suth built those weapons and turned them against the armies of my ancestors. . . ." He paused to push back the anger in his voice, his instinctive disdain for the progenitors of the frostwreths. "They unleashed that terrible power on other wreths instead of against the dragon." He looked away. "All that remains there now is a great plain, melted and sullied by the blood of countless victims—from both sides. That is where our laborers now harvest shadowglass."

Koru only heard the part that was important to her. "The power of these weapons is evident, so we must create them here." She lashed out at the two mages. "But instead of turning them against our own people, they must be used to kill Ossus!"

Axus and Elon looked at each other in a long tense moment, then they nodded. "Yes, we will work together."

"We can build these weapons."

All together, seventy of the most powerful mages, frostwreths and sand-wreths, worked side by side in a line that extended along the foothills at the base of simmering Mount Vada. Axus called upon his magic. He shouted, and his voice boomed through the air. "Make the machinery!"

As she watched the preparations, Queen Koru took pleasure in standing beside the wretched, paralyzed Voo, who lay on the rough ground. Koru smiled to herself and pointedly ignored her former rival.

The sandwreth mages pulled forth soil, rocks, and sand to build up and fashion solid curved arcs, sturdy yet graceful frameworks. Beside them, the frostwreth mages drew moisture from the air and the ground to create large disks of ice, which they polished and curved into enormous interlocked lenses, which they mounted in the sand-rock frameworks, completing the devices.

Along the most vulnerable cliffs and peaks around smoking Mount Vada, the mages erected pylons and armatures, called forth ice lenses, and assembled intricate magical machinery that even Koru did not understand.

These weapons had been designed in the most ancient of days, yet never used for their true purpose. Working together, the mages finished their work in a short time. In addition to their own magic, they had a greater power to shake the world and wake the dragon. And destroy it.

Camped around the mountains, the human armies observed them, while they rallied to face their own enemy, an insignificant enemy. Queen Koru was not worried about them or their trivial squabbles, but as she regarded the lines of soldiers, with their tents and campfires, she thought of the human boy and wished he were here to watch this great victory.

The queen felt strangely unanchored without Birch. She hadn't realized how much she welcomed the boy's presence. But why? He was small and weak, ineffective, yet if not for Birch, she would not be queen of all the wreths. No other person had dared to challenge, and kill, Onn, but the boy—a little human boy!—had slain Queen Onn with the spear of Dar. Who would have expected that? By being quiet and unobtrusive, yet observant, Birch had exposed the plot to assassinate her. He had saved Koru's life.

He had slain her mother, stopped a conspiracy to kill her, and commanded the drones—drones!—to eliminate some of the most powerful and treacherous frostwreths.

And because she owed him a great deal, she had allowed him to rejoin his grandfather. She was perplexed at herself for surrendering him so easily, but she had paid her debt . . . not that a wreth should feel obligated to honor debts to a mere human.

Birch had surprised her, helped her, even amused her. Why had he wanted to be back with his grandfather, with his own people? There was no understanding it, but once Ossus was destroyed and Kur remade the world, all the humans would be gone anyway. A distant smile crossed her expression, and she was glad she had let the boy go where he wanted, at least for the time being. . . .

She turned away, ignoring the human soldiers and their camp, not worried about what they were doing. Koru sneered down at Voo, who lay so pathetic and helpless, thrashing her head from side to side, either because she was trying to see or denying what was happening.

Koru said, "I will keep you alive to watch, Voo. And only when you know that we have succeeded, then I will kill you." She turned away with a sniff and shouted to her mages. "Summon your magic and activate the machines. We must shake the world." She drew in a deep breath. "And rouse the dragon."

Watching the frostwreth queen's preparations with keen interest, Adan asked, "Do you think they mean us harm?"

"Not at the moment," Koll said, "but they may harm us even so."

Elliel and Thon stood side by side close to the kings, ready to fight, if need be, but the wreth warriors made no move toward the human army.

The preoccupied mages had erected large devices made of sandstone and ice at strategic locations against the mountains. Now, they began sending sharp magical jabs deep into the ground. Even from this far away, Adan could feel the ground trembling beneath his feet.

A lone rider galloped out of the mountains from the pass, frantically waving. His shouts were dampened by distance, but the army folded open to make a path for him. The rider saw the two kings and headed directly for the vantage point from which they were observing the wreth movements.

Koll recognized the prominent mark on the young man's face.

Flushed, panting, and drenched with sweat, Onder pulled his horse to a halt and gasped, "Gant is dead!" His shoulders heaved as if he had run as hard as his horse. "Utho killed him. The two dueled and . . . and Gant lost. I had to steal a horse to get here. I had to tell you! Gant made me promise to tell his legacy, and to warn you."

Elliel snatched the horse's bridle. "Utho killed him? Why would Gant go by himself? What did he mean to achieve?"

"He wanted to bring justice—to end the war and save lives. Utho is the cause of this rift in the Commonwealth."

Elliel's face darkened. "We know that! All Bravas should have gone together to confront Utho." She seemed incensed. "I should have been there, after what he's done!"

Onder gave a solemn nod. Gant felt a measure of responsibility for enabling some of Utho's misdeeds when Gant worked for Lord Cade. "I would have fought at Gant's side, too, but he commanded me not to be a fool." He hung his head. "I didn't want to run, but I swore an oath. I had to bring you this information." He snapped to attention, drew a breath. "The army is ready to march. After Gant was killed, Mandan's forces started to move, and they are not far behind me. They'll be coming over the pass. You must prepare!"

Kollanan felt a chill in his heart again, but his blood burned hot. "We have been waiting for this. Let him come to us, and we'll strip him of his crown. Our army will defeat theirs."

Adan looked uneasy. "I'm reluctant to kill Commonwealth citizens in cold blood. They are still loyal to the three kingdoms, as they understand it. If I am going to be konag after all this is over, then they'll have to follow my rule."

"You have to establish your rule first," Koll said. "Word has spread, and everyone knows of our decree. They all know what Mandan did and what Utho did! Any soldiers who still stand with Mandan now have made their choice."

Elliel hung her head. "Gant should have waited. We could have gone together." Her voice hardened. "I'll be very disappointed if I don't get my chance at Utho."

"We all want our chance," Kollanan said. "He killed my brother."

"And my father," Adan said.

"It is amazing that one man committed so many crimes and created so many enemies," Thon mused before turning his attention back to the wreth mages and their enigmatic labors. "However, what those mages are doing is of far greater concern. Perhaps it is best for us to stop the destruction of the world first? And worry about punishing Utho and Mandan afterward?"

He suddenly grimaced and shuddered, as if something had seized his heart and started shaking it. He gripped the sides of his skull, gasping.

Elliel flung her arms around him, as if her own physical presence could give him strength. "What is it? Do you feel the dragon stirring?"

Out on the open hills, the mages scrambled about, like a disturbed anthill.

Birch pointed to the sky. A swirling mass approached from the west like a huge swarm of locusts—flickers of many different colors. Koll's brow furrowed.

"Skas," Adan said. He had sent Xar back to Penda several days ago. Now hundreds of the reptile birds rolled in like a storm front.

Soon the air was filled with clicking and humming, a cloudburst of skas that broke, and then the flying creatures poured down like a heavy rain. They flew in and around, startling the horses and human soldiers, but the bulk of the flock swarmed over the wreth encampment.

Kollanan could hear the roars of restless oonuks, the grunts of augas. The mages were disrupted in their preparations at their strange devices. Wreth warriors swung their weapons, trying to batter away the swarm, and they fired countless arrows, killing many skas, but the flying creatures kept rushing in.

Adan was amazed, but not afraid. "The skas are no threat—not to us."

"Maybe they'll help," Birch said.

Thon kept clutching at his chest, gasping for breath. Elliel held him up, trying to assist him, and he finally grew steady again as the spasm of pain and confusion passed. "Something is calling me." He looked at Elliel and blinked in amazement. He tried to explain. "There is a great force inside the mountain, sparked by the magic. Those mages are trying to unleash it."

"Are the wreths attacking *you*?" Elliel asked.

"I do not believe so." Thon had regained his balance, though he still breathed heavily. "Perhaps they are awakening something in me. I am trying to understand it." His strange eyes sparkled with dismay. "If another human army is coming, should we not all join forces to stop the wreths? Maybe together we can prevent the mages from waking the dragon. The consequences would be so terrible, and . . ." He pressed a palm to his chest again. "Am I the key to stopping them? Or am I a key to fighting Ossus? How will I know before it is too late?"

Elliel held his gaze. "I know *you*. You will do the right thing when you need to."

Adan spoke up. "Meanwhile, we all do whatever we can to keep the world safe."

Kollanan felt a weight in his heart. "Neither Utho nor Mandan will listen to reason. They're blinded by their own vengewar." He lowered his voice. "Just as I was nearly blinded by mine. Here is what I can do. There's a better chance the wreth queen will listen to a warning if it comes from me. *From us.*" He placed an arm around Birch's shoulders. "My grandson and I will go and speak with Koru. It's worth a try."

91

THE mountains trembled with the power of possibilities. The elaborate magical weapons had been fashioned using the elements at hand, and the structures were ready. They began to creak and move.

Queen Koru joined her two lead mages, those who could draw on both sandwreth and frostwreth magic, using the last shreds of power that survived inside the land.

Rather than feeling victorious, though, she experienced bittersweet regret. The old wars had destroyed so much of the world's potential, when all wreths could have been unified from the start. If her ancestors had simply combined forces to do Kur's bidding, thousands and thousands of years ago, the world could have been perfect all along. The wreths had squandered so much.

It angered Koru to think of the lost opportunities, the long-faltered destiny of her race, and as her fury rose, the burgeoning magic in the air seized upon her anger and strengthened it. The sensation was an odd ricochet inside her mind. She clenched her pale hand until the sharp nails bit into her palm.

Axus and Elon called upon their fellow mages to use the weapons. The large machinery began to glow, and the wreths had their own powers as well. The mages lined up, raised their fists, and after a united pause, pummeled the ground with balled fists. The blow sent shock waves deep into the mountains, a shuddering spasm that plunged to the roots of Mount Vada.

Smoke and lava simmered, then spurted like blood from an open wound.

Elon said, "We can feel the darkness and the evil, my queen." Though he bore burn scars from his previous dragon encounter, he was energized with anticipation. "We are bringing it to the surface. Our own powers and the new machinery will shake the mountains, and then we turn the weapons against Ossus."

Koru gestured toward her vast army, and let her gaze drift over the sprawling human encampment. "We will disturb the dragon's slumbers and make him face us." She twisted her lips. "And he will die."

Just then, to her disgust, clouds of wild skas swirled in, hissing, clicking, taunting. The creatures were annoying, tiny fragments of the great dragon, bits of debris like the cast-off scales of a snake . . . little dragons and spies, merely mischievous rather than evil. The humans seemed to have reached an accord with them, an incomprehensible symbiotic relationship.

As if attracted to this final battle, knowing Ossus was about to emerge, the skas were suddenly everywhere. The wreths' powerful work continued, and the angry warriors killed many of the reptile birds, but it was like smashing ice moths in the night. Instead, Queen Koru shouted for her mages, nobles, and warriors to prepare for the important conflict.

"Wake, Ossus!" Her words resonated around the peaks, and thunder boomed in the sky in response to her cry. "Wake!"

Crippled Voo was still impotent and helpless, lying paralyzed on her pallet. As an added torment, a pair of warriors had propped her up to watch the culmination of the work here. Koru no longer enjoyed seeing the miserable ruins of a once-great queen. Voo was as irrelevant as a drone.

Axus and Elon held up their fists and brought them down again. The line of mages did the same. Huge ice lenses, mounted in curved sandstone armatures, began to turn and hum.

The air rippled around them, the light in the sky changed and bent. The magic waves shuddered deep into the mountains until the ground rumbled, and the huge brooding evil stirred. Disturbed by the wave of magic, thousands of skas scattered into the air with a flurry of colorful wings.

"Again!" Koru said, and the mages hammered into the mountains.

As Kollanan and his grandson rode in among the wreths, he did not feel as lost as he had been the first time with Lasis. "We've got to make Koru heed our warning," he said to Birch. "You know her."

"She listens to me. Sometimes," the boy said. "When she wants to."

Storm did not shy from the wolf-steeds or augas, and Birch looked around the large army camp without fear. Koll wore his fur-lined Norterran cape over his shoulders, and his war hammer was lashed beside him where he could easily draw it, but he made no threatening gesture. He cut an imposing figure as king, although wreths were not easily impressed.

He raised his voice to the warriors around him. "Where is Koru? I must speak with your queen. It is an urgent matter."

The nearest sandwreth warrior regarded the king of Norterra with little interest. "She has many urgent matters." Nevertheless, after a pause, he nodded toward the line of mages and their strange machinery.

Near the cluster of robed figures, Kollanan saw other wreths and the tall pale figure of the queen. He nudged Storm forward, and skas swirled around the king and his grandson.

The mages made the ground thrum. Smoke poured into the sky from Mount Vada, thickening the air with the smell of burning and ashes. The Dragonspine range shifted in a long series of convulsions.

The mages did not even look up when Koll approached and sprang down from his warhorse, and the boy jumped down beside him. The king removed his war hammer and carried it like a scepter of office, not as a threat.

Queen Koru turned to acknowledge him and brightened to see Birch. "You have come to observe our triumph."

"I've come to beg you to reconsider," Koll said. "Let the dragon lie sleeping. Isn't there already enough evil awake in the world?"

A cackle came from nearby. "Even the human shows no respect for you, Koru!"

Kollanan looked down to see a sandwreth woman propped up on a pallet like a sack of grain. Her head rolled from side to side and her face grimaced, but the rest of her body didn't move. Koll did not hide his scorn. "Queen Voo. You look much . . . *less* than when I saw you in your desert palace."

She snarled at him, unable to move.

Queen Koru laughed, then dismissed her helpless rival and turned back to the king. "What should I reconsider? Our race has been distracted for thousands of years, and now we are finally going to achieve the purpose ordained for us."

"To what end?" Koll asked. "You've already fought dragons, and they caused you great harm. Why would you bring more of them?"

The frostwreth queen blinked as if she couldn't understand him. "Because this is what Kur tasked us to do."

On the ground Voo laughed again, and Kollanan stepped past her pallet, intent on the frostwreth queen.

"Even if you do wake the dragon, and even if you do succeed in killing it, then the world would be destroyed. And my entire race would be gone."

"The new world will be better." Koru tossed back her long ivory hair. "It will be perfect, the way Kur wanted it."

"Isn't it better if we all do our best to fix the world ourselves?" Koll asked.

Now Birch came forward, pleading. "Please don't wake the dragon. There's enough pain in the world. Give everybody a time of peace. Wouldn't that be better?" The boy was drawing on his connection to Koru, to foster her affection for him. "That way I could still visit you."

The cold queen raised one hand toward Birch, then paused and let it drop. She raised her chin and squared her shoulders. Behind her hard expression, Koru looked somewhat haggard, and she did not want her decisions questioned. Her tone sharpened. "This is our race's reason for existence. This is the command that our god gave us. We created humans a long time ago to help us with this specific task, and I cannot worry about your race. If we don't destroy Ossus, then Kur will never return! We have to bring him back."

"Why should my people care about Kur?" Kollanan demanded, feeling the frustration and anger. "He didn't create us. He didn't save us. The human race had to survive on its own after the wreths ruined the world. We did just fine."

She turned away from him, as if she no longer saw him or Birch. She spoke over her shoulder. "Are you staying? You are welcome to watch. The boy may want to see."

Queen Koru gave her signal, and the mages swung their immense machinery, pouring energy into the ice lenses. The destructive weapons pounded more magic into the mountains.

As his full army moved out, Mandan knew what he was expected to do, his *obligations* as konag. Riding along in his fur-lined cape and regalia, holding his sword at his side to lead the true army of the Commonwealth, he knew he wasn't ready for any of this.

In his heart, he did not rely on Utho, treacherous Utho, murderous Utho . . . but Utho was all he had. Mandan felt pulled in many directions, torn apart, but he forcefully reminded himself that he was the *konag.* He whispered it to himself again and again, and he clung to it.

The grim Brava rode beside him, reaffirming his faithful support, even if Mandan could no longer believe in him. He could no longer believe in anything.

Except that he knew that Adan and Kollanan had turned against him. They were the enemy, and they had gathered an army to march on Convera. Even if he didn't have faith that Utho truly served him as a loyal bonded Brava, he was certain that Suderra and Norterra had turned against him. His brother and uncle had sent their despicable decree, and now he, Konag Mandan of the Colors, would lead his army to victory and crush the rebels.

It was his duty as konag.

After serving so many years as his mentor, Utho understood him like no one else. . . . Next to him now, the Brava seemed to read Mandan's thoughts.

"Our army will overwhelm the enemy forces. We will destroy the treasonous kings, and all their subjects will once again show fealty to you, my konag." He paused, then added, "As do I."

Mandan thought of his painting of the Battle of Yanton, with the dead bodies of defeated rebels strewn around . . . how he had imagined himself high on a horse and waving his sword, killing all those who defied him.

"Will there be much fighting before they surrender?" Mandan asked.

"Not if they are wise, my konag," Utho said. "But I trained you in vigorous sword fighting, and you are highly skilled with a blade. You are more than a match for any enemy you might face." After a hesitation, he added, "But I will protect you."

Mandan touched the hilt of his sword and felt suddenly dizzy. Utho had made the same promise to Conndur the Brave, and yet he had killed him.

Mandan kicked his horse sharply, urging it to greater speed, as if that could help him outrun the sudden images of his slaughtered father.

Behind him, his hundreds of troops pressed inexorably forward, picking their way over the pass. The army wound along the rough road, taking sharp switchbacks until they reached the great vista down the western slope of the Dragonspine Mountains.

He expected to see two small armies camped there, a motley group of rebels that needed to be defeated. Instead, he saw a huge fighting force, vastly larger than he anticipated. Thousands of foot soldiers and cavalry, supply wagons, and lines of tents that flew the banners of Suderra and Norterra.

He also saw another incredible force, something not human. They were exotic creatures in metallic armor, cold whites and blues and glinting coppers and golds. They rode on monstrous beasts and constructed exotic machinery. They hurled magic into the mountains and made the ground shake.

Mandan gasped. "Those are . . . those are wreths!" His skin crawled as he stared at the enormity of the opposing army born out of legend. "Those are wreths," he said again, and his voice trailed off into a whisper as his army thundered behind him over the pass.

Utho glanced at him, then glared ahead, as if he didn't see. "We know our enemy," he said. "Ride."

92

ⴲ

IGNORED on the ground, Queen Voo felt helpless, furious. The anger in the world pulsed beneath her, a dark energy that was at once destructive and rejuvenating.

She felt her arms twitch again, and that made her smile in surprise. This was a long, agonizing time coming. Voo had been defeated, shamed, and humiliated in front of her people. Koru dragged her along with the army for no purpose other than to continue tormenting her, to remind the sandwreths that their once glorious queen had fallen.

But the usurper queen was also a fool for not killing her outright. That hint of compassion or need for sustained vengeance would be her downfall.

Now, with Koru and all her wreths distracted, Voo clenched her teeth and *willed* her legs to move. They bent at the knees, shifted. Her arms stirred.

Nearby, the Norterran king argued with Koru, as if he could simply convince her to turn her back on the wreths' destiny. Voo remembered when the bearded man had come to her desert palace along with Adan. Kollanan had requested her help against the frostwreths, which was why she had sent Quo off to join them . . . and her brother had died. Adan had killed him.

And that weakling human child Birch had dared to claim that he had murdered a wreth queen, so Voo should fear him. Her lips drew back, and her spine arched. Her muscles were coiled, full of energy, ready to kill.

It had been long enough.

Voo had suffered a grievous wound to the back of her neck, and her spine had been severed by the legendary spear of Dar—surely a mortal blow for any human, and a crippling wound for any half-breed. But she was a sandwreth, and a *queen,* and Voo possessed incredible wreth healing powers, deep magic that permeated her blood, her skin, her bone.

During all the time she had been dragged along, ignored, considered weak and helpless, irrelevant, Voo had gradually—oh, so gradually—regained her strength and movement. At night when the fires died down, she would twitch her fingers, curl her hands, flex her toes.

Horns and war cries sounded out. Wreths and humans shifted, preparing for a great clash if the dragon did emerge.

And now while Koru commanded the mages and enforced her will, while the bitch had her back turned, Voo lunged up from her pallet, using all the energy and strength she had regained. They didn't expect her. . . .

Kollanan remained consumed with his need to convince Koru. It was their last chance before open, world-shattering war.

As he considered a new tactic for convincing the wreth queen, out of the corner of his eye he saw Voo move on the ground. Her legs swung to the side. She used an arm to lever herself up as she sprang to her feet. Somehow she had a long knife held in her talonlike hands. Queen Koru's back was turned.

Birch spun, also saw her. His eyes went wide as Voo raised the blade. He lunged toward Koru as if he could knock her out of the way. "No!"

Kollanan was already moving.

Voo's mouth opened in a silent scream. She darted forward like a snake.

Queen Koru turned, startled as Kollanan leaped between the two queens and swung his war hammer. The shadowglass tip whistled through the air and smashed the side of Voo's head in a tremendous blow. The shadowglass caved in her skull. Her neck snapped to one side, and Voo collapsed even before Koru could drop into a defensive position.

Kollanan stood with his bloodied weapon. It felt heavy in his hand. Birch ran to his side, safe, staring at the dead sandwreth queen.

Astonished, Queen Koru laughed. "You saved me. You killed the queen of the sandwreths, King Kollanan!" A thought crossed her mind, and she smiled down at the boy. "Just as your grandson killed the queen of the frost-wreths. My mother." She chuckled, but it was a disoriented sound, as if she couldn't quite believe what had happened. "Once again, I learn that humans are not to be underestimated."

Kollanan heaved deep breaths as other wreths came running to stare in amazement at the dead Voo. Looking down at her bloody head and bent neck gave him a strange sense of justice done.

He reached out to enfold his grandson in a great hug, sure that he had done a good thing . . . even though it might still be the end of the world.

Struggling with feelings of helpless desperation, Adan watched the wreth mages work their giant exotic machinery, building up ripples of magic that made the air shimmer and twist with invisible cyclones of embedded power. Other mages simply bunched their fists and hammered down into the ground, sending shock waves that shuddered and surged. The mountains themselves stirred, convulsed.

Kollanan had been gone a long time, and the wreths continued without pause. Adan didn't know how much longer he could wait—especially since Mandan's army was on the way.

He rode up and down the lines of his restless cavalry troops. His army was ready, their weapons, shields, and armor prepared. The horses snorted, feeling the tension in the air. The fighters spoke nervously, and some pounded on their shields to make loud sounds of defiance, though not sure where to direct them.

Elliel rode up to him, resplendent in her black finemail armor. She held a sword in one hand and had the ramer cuff ready for whenever she needed it. Her face had gone pale, which made her stark tattoo seem more fierce. She gestured toward the mages and the wreth warriors as the ground shook again, and heavy smoke belched out of Mount Vada. "They are trying to bring about the end of the world—how long should we give them?"

Adan stared at the frostwreths and sandwreths, the sprawling encampment and the large pavilion where he knew Queen Koru directed her troops. "We have to give Kollanan a chance."

Thon was also there, his deep sapphire eyes intense. "Do not wait too long. Once they wake the dragon, it will be too late, and I cannot promise to save you all." He touched the mark on his face. "I have great potential, but it is all locked inside."

Lasis galloped up, joining them. With Kollanan gone, he reported to Adan. "I have word from our scouts, Sire. Mandan's army is marching over the pass at a swift pace." He frowned. "A foolishly swift pace, if you ask me. They will be exhausted by the time they reach us."

"My brother will find the strength for battle when he gets here," Adan said.

"As will Utho," Elliel said.

Lasis continued, "We cut down trees to block the road, which will stall their horses and wagons, but they have enough soldiers to clear the blockade. It won't be long."

Adan looked toward the wreth machinery, the line of mages. The ground trembled again with a sharper shock. "This is a problem we need to deal with first."

He shaded his eyes. His uncle had been gone a very long time. The wreths could have killed him already—how would Adan know? Queen Koru had done them one favor by releasing the boy, but she was by no means sympathetic to saving the human race.

At the nearest grand device, the huge sand-and-stone framework shuddered and thrummed as magic built up in the ice lenses. The mages tending the structure raised their arms and shouted, calling out indecipherable spells.

The lens spun and then released a huge thunderclap of force the color of lightning. The blast erupted into the ground and diffused, spraying in all directions like a flash flood striking a boulder. The ground shook as if someone had struck a giant iron bell.

A distance away, another of the strange wreth devices also thrummed and blasted its roar of power, as if trying to rip the mountains apart.

Onder rode up on his nervous horse. The young man's lips were pressed together in determination. "King Adan, we have to fight!" He looked to Lasis, drawing strength. "We must stop this from happening."

The ground rumbled and rocked, and the horses snorted, pawing at the dirt. The human soldiers let out a roar of impatience and dismay.

Reaching a decision, Adan raised his sword. "We will not sit by and let the wreths bring about the end of the world. Go! We must destroy those devices. That should buy us some time."

Elliel and Lasis ignited their ramers as Adan led his armies forward, surging into the preoccupied wreth forces. The soldiers from Suderra and Norterra raised their swords, and mounted archers nocked arrows to their bowstrings. The vanguard flooded into the opposing camp.

The wreth warriors were dispersed, not in ranks at all, and focused on the work of the mages, anticipating what might emerge from the mountains. The human army charged through the camp without pausing to engage the wreth warriors. Adan led them straight to their target—the line of magical apparatus that vibrated and glowed as they emitted magical power.

The wreths were slow to respond to the unexpected advance, but when they did raise their weapons, they were deadly and powerful. Reflexively, they hurled spears and lunged in with long curved blades, cutting down horses and soldiers alike. Adan leaned over the saddle and charged forward.

Beyond the camp, dazzling intangible force exploded from additional magical machinery. The rippling blasts pounded into the mountains and cracked open cliffs.

With Elliel riding close alongside him, he raced toward the nearest machine. It had paused, its power fading as if the device needed to rest and restore its power, while individual mages hammered the ground with their fists and sent vibrations deep underground. Lasis led another group of riders with his blazing ramer.

As he plunged into the thick of the fighting, Adan had a brief image of his sweet daughter Oak, of Penda, of his entire kingdom, but then he locked his heart upon this giant, powerful construction. He knew that if they didn't stop this outpouring, then he would have no home, no family, no world to go back to.

With a loud shout, he raised his sword. Elliel lifted her crackling ramer blade. Concentrating on their work, the mages ignored the human strike force. As he galloped past, Adan struck with his sword, hitting a blue-robed mage in the back and cutting deep. The wounded mage collapsed and lost control of his own magic. He jittered and flailed, bleeding on the ground.

Human archers loosed volley after volley of arrows into the wide smooth surface of the ice lens, chipping divots into the perfect curvature, which sent sparks and cracks throughout. Some fired projectiles at the mages, who easily deflected them.

Adan raced up as the sandstone framework seemed to shudder with uncontrollable power. He hacked down with his sword blade, chopping a large chink in one of the structural arcs. Arrows again peppered the surface of the lens as it rotated, building up power.

The mages screamed in surprise and dismay as the lens crazed and cracked. Instead of flowing outward, the magic crackled within the ice itself, setting off a firestorm of static.

Elliel came in beside Adan, and after he had chipped into the sandstone support, her fiery sword burned directly through the armature. The frame broke, and the device began to collapse. The lens tilted as it whirled wildly and crashed down on two mages.

Lasis and a dozen riders attacked another one of the strange, pulsing machines.

Now the wreth warriors rallied, turning to defend the line of mages. Too long restrained, they howled their bloodlust as they were finally released to fight. The human soldiers spun about and defended themselves as the giant magical construction collapsed and flared behind Adan.

Elliel turned about with her ramer and faced the howling wreths. "Go, Sire! Get to safety."

"I'll fight alongside my army!"

The Brava hurled herself at two sandwreth warriors who came at them on charging augas. Her ramer drove them back, knocking one off of his reptilian mount and killing the other. An angry roar raced through the wreth troops, and their indignation turned to boiling fury.

Adan heard their shouts as the word went up. "Queen Voo is dead! The human king killed her!"

This news sparked even greater fury, and Adan couldn't understand what he was hearing. The wreth armies had already been engulfed in a black poison of revenge just waiting for release, and now their attack became even more furious.

Incomprehensibly, though, as the enemy forces roiled with violence against the human army, Adan watched a pale frostwreth warrior plunge his ice-tipped spear into the back of a sandwreth riding beside him.

"Queen Voo is dead!" he yelled. "Kill the sandwreths!"

Even as the wreth armies fought against the forces of Suderra and Norterra, they also turned on each other, igniting their ancient rivalries.

Onder rode in on his horse and struck down a frostwreth warrior who lunged at King Adan. "We'll defend you, Sire!" Moments later, a sharp sandwreth pike hurtled toward the disgraced Brava, but the weapon struck and killed his horse instead. The animal collapsed and threw Onder, who bounded to his feet, slashing with his sword among the wreths.

Adan, Elliel, and Thon charged away as the fighting roiled around them. Enemies closed in. Elliel's ramer took down two more wreths, and she tried to move Adan from the thick of the battlefield. Lasis fought not far away.

Adan heard loud cries coming from the mountains, a new wave of shouts. An icy chill ran down his back as he saw the line of mounted soldiers riding down out of the foothills from the pass. The soldiers made a loud clamor by pounding sword hilts against the metal bosses on their shields. They flew the banners of Osterra and the Commonwealth. At the front of the new army, Adan saw three bright ramers, a trio of Bravas leading the charge.

Konag Mandan's forces had arrived.

93

◈

THE new godling rose up in an ethereal, omnipotent force, and the crowd around the Magnifica roared in both excitement and dismay. The spirit of Empra Iluris and the faith and hopes of so many people transformed the godling, made it blossom.

Held hostage on the temple steps, Cemi thrashed like an angry wildcat, but the key priestlord had an arm around her torso, crushing her close. She tried to pull her throat away from the dagger's edge, but Klovus drove his knee into her back, forcing her down. "Your blood will gush out and feed my godling."

The huge temple rumbled as the Serepol deity rolled out, unfolding itself in thunderstorm waves. It was powered by the atavistic energies from countless sacrifices, innumerable chants and prayers, so much magic and anger coalesced together.

Both opposing deities were fueled by the outpouring of faith, conflicting beliefs, and a confused purpose. Together, they became clashing whirlpools of violence and fear.

Cemi's fear was mitigated by her anger and certitude, which gave her strength. Nearby, Captani Vos had collapsed with bubbles of blood forming on his mouth, the arrow shaft protruding from his chest and making a sucking sound with each breath he gasped. Despite his grievous wound, he struggled toward her, but Cemi could not break free of Klovus's grip.

She knew what the empra would have done. She hissed, "Iluris chose me as her successor, and today she named me in front of the people in Serepol." Cemi gritted her teeth, squirmed against the razor edge at her throat, then shouted louder, "They know that I am the rightful leader of Ishara!"

"You were never more than a placeholder," Klovus scoffed, and his hold remained firm. "No matter what that old woman said, they can see my godling—the godling they created!" His grip was iron hard, as if he drew strength from the Magnifica entity. "Sacrificing you will make my godling even stronger."

"The empra chose *me*!" she said. "And we have the strength of a godling as well."

The new godling brightened until it seemed as powerful as the Serepol godling. Cemi had watched Iluris sacrifice herself, letting the swirling force of Isharan magic absorb her. The godling drew from Cemi and gave to Cemi, and both of them grew more powerful.

Captani Vos crawled forward, leaving a wide trail of blood. He coughed red splashes on the flagstones. Klovus ignored the hawk guard, pressed the knife so hard against her throat that Cemi felt a rivulet of blood trickle down the front of her neck. The two godlings faced off, opposing black clouds that exploded with lightning and anger. Storm winds whistled around the square. Electrical energy crackled everywhere, and Cemi's hair extended in every direction and whipped around her face. Her skin sizzled.

The deities circled like hounds in a dogfighting pit. Cemi remembered how the Magnifica godling had fought, defeated, and consumed the harbor godling, which had stood up to defend Serepol.

Needing to give her defender strength, she called out through her heart. Even without closing her eyes, Cemi let her vision flow outward and upward, combining with the new godling. Ishara itself was inside that presence, as was the remnant of the beloved empra, and Iluris wanted to help fight.

In this battle, Klovus was no longer significant to her.

Feeling the change in his captive, the key priestlord gave a victorious laugh, and Cemi felt him tense for the death blow. She held her breath, expecting to feel the hot sting of the knife across her throat, but suddenly he shrieked in pain. He staggered back, howling, waving the dagger.

Vos had ripped the arrow from his chest, then lunged upward with the last of his strength to ram the sharp point through the caftan and into the soft center of the key priestlord's groin. Klovus wailed, holding his crotch and trying to stanch the flow of blood.

The second she broke free, Cemi jabbed him in the stomach with her elbow, and he collapsed into a mass of bleeding misery.

The two circling godlings swelled, as if fresh fuel had been tossed into a blazing fire. The smoke and lightning, the winds and snarls grew more intense. The shapeless mass of the entities filled with faces of all manner of dead people: defiant and peaceful, men and women, rich and poor, young and old.

Cemi heard a voice ring out inside her head, the familiar voice of Iluris—no longer weak, dry, and raspy as it had been since she awakened in the tunnels beneath the palace. *I am Ishara!*

Cemi echoed, "I am Ishara!"

The two godlings both drew strength from hearing the voice, and Cemi felt a change around her, as if the weather had turned. Her ears popped. A crackle of static electricity rippled through the air, but to her it smelled like fresh rain, bringing excitement, confidence, victory.

She realized with surprise and wonder that the two godlings were not intent on destroying each other. They were separate aspects of Ishara, both drawing from the magic that was the soul of the land. The Magnifica godling and the empra's new godling threw themselves at each other, though not in battle.

They combined and fused.

Together, they were more powerful than the strongest godling that had ever existed, dual manifestations of Ishara, created by worshippers who prayed to the great temple of their faith, as well as those who prayed for their leader Empra Iluris. The unified entity was driven by the absorbed empra, energized by the entire land of Ishara, and strengthened by the countless faithful in Serepol.

Cemi understood that Ishara needed both—faith and leadership.

Vos had collapsed, bleeding heavily from the deep wound in his chest. Key Priestlord Klovus hunched and wailed, clutching at his groin. He ripped out the arrow and raised one bloody hand in an attempt to impose his power and discipline on the godling.

Ignoring him, though, Cemi dropped to her knees beside the hawk guard and grasped his hand. "Vos!" He squeezed her fingers back. She pressed down on the chest wound, trying to stop the bleeding. "Vos . . ."

As empra chosen by Iluris, though, she also had to save the land. Cemi drew herself up and prepared to counter what Klovus was doing. Just being near Vos made her feel stronger and more confident.

She extended her mind to the combined godling and whatever remained of Iluris inside. She drew upon the faith and the chants of the gathered people, and she fought back against Klovus.

The Magnifica temple shuddered and trembled. Cracks appeared in its enormous stone blocks, and its foundation shifted.

The combined godling snatched up the key priestlord and lifted him from the temple steps into the invisible whirling embrace of a hurricane. The force also lifted Cemi, yanked her away from Vos, and she found herself swirling in midair.

Gasping in shock, Cemi felt all of her muscles tense. At any moment she could be dashed to the ground or smashed against the temple wall. The godling could do whatever it wanted with her. She wished for Iluris's strength, and suddenly she felt her mentor's presence, letting her know that she was safe. Relief flooded through Cemi as she realized the godling would not harm her. She was chosen and had an incredible future ahead. Forcing herself to relax her muscles, Cemi let go and abandoned herself to the experience.

Klovus twisted and screamed, his face drawn back in a grimace as he struggled. He used everything he had to impose his will. The godling whipped the two of them around, faster and faster, and although Cemi was buoyed up like a feather in the wind, Klovus thrashed and screamed.

The more he struggled, the more life began to drain from him; the more he tried to control, the less control he had. As Cemi watched, the life was drained out of him, the very essence of his existence, by both godlings, acting in unison. The key priestlord shriveled into a mummified husk, spinning in place, little more than the gray rags of a man that broke apart into fragments that were lost in the wind.

Cemi flew along for what seemed like an hour, feeling energized, optimistic. Then with a slow and gentle touch the godling deposited her onto the ground next to Vos.

Her people cheered with a roar even louder than the storm of the godlings.

94

୭

WHILE fighting the wreths and watching his brother's army come over the mountains, Adan thought of all the strategy sessions and war council meetings in which they had discussed confronting the konag.

Now it had come to this.

"Armies to me!" he shouted. His Banner guards raised the flag of Suderra side by side with the flag of the Commonwealth—the real Commonwealth. He kicked his horse into motion, riding farther from the frenzied wreths. Elliel and Thon charged beside him, keeping the king safe. They watched the seemingly endless stream of mounted soldiers, led by three Bravas.

Elliel said in a cold voice, "Utho is there. He has to be."

Adan knew she was right. "Mandan will be with him."

Farther down the foothills, another of the strange machines throbbed a rippling blast of magic into the crags, and the mountains rumbled. Adan knew their main target should be those incomprehensible devices, but Konag Mandan's army was hurtling toward them. He wished he knew what had happened to Kollanan.

He tossed his cape over his shoulder, knowing that the whole army would be looking toward him, even as they fought the wreths . . . who were, in turn, fighting one another after the death of Voo. But why? What had Kollanan done? Frustrated sandwreth and frostwreth warriors turned to attack the humans. Augas and oonuks charged in, bearing armored fighters.

Seeing the wreth forces spread out along the mountains, maybe Mandan would realize the true danger at last, after denying it for so long. It seemed like a lifetime ago when he and his uncle had traveled to Convera to warn about the wreths, begging Konag Conndur for assistance. But Utho had made sure their concerns were dismissed, so as not to interfere with his vengewar.

As he led his front ranks on the charge forward, Adan fixed his eyes on the dishonorable Brava who rode in the lead with his ramer raised high.

The Norterran and Suderran armies shifted to defend themselves from the flank as the Commonwealth forces rode toward them. Wreth warriors charged in to break the human ranks, seeing no difference between one human force or another.

Utho galloped closer, shouting to the ranks behind him, "Strike down the rebel kings! This army belongs to the rightful konag!"

Mandan looked angry, as if he had been whipped into a frenzy and bullied into action. Dressed in his spotted cape and heavy crown, he mechanically lifted his sword as if he were in a play.

When Utho noticed Adan leading the charge to intercept him, a dark smile filled his face. He spurred his horse forward, slashing his ramer in the air.

Seeing Utho, Elliel could not tear her gaze from the dishonorable man who had ruined her life, disgraced her, and made her believe an awful lie for so long. The ramer cuff bit into her wrist and fire pushed out around her hand into a white-hot blade that drew upon her blood and anger.

As the wreth mages continued to work their magic, she could feel dark rumblings underground—which fed the blaze within her. One of the remaining machines turned its ice lens and sent a throbbing blow into the world, and beside it, several mages used their fists to hammer the ground, setting up resounding shock waves.

King Adan had already begun his charge, so she urged her horse forward. Her ramer shone brighter. As a sworn Brava, her responsibility was to protect the king, and she had additional goals.

Utho stormed toward Adan, who raised his sword, ready for the clash, but even a king's blade could not stand against a ramer. Elliel pushed her horse harder, closing the distance.

Mandan galloped behind the treacherous Brava as if he wanted to be close at hand when Utho killed his brother, but Elliel shouted a challenge and cut in front of Adan. "Utho! I declare my vengewar on you." Her horse reared, and she struck sideways at him with her ramer.

Surprised, Utho met her blow, fire rippling against fire. When he recognized her, his face twisted into a look of disgust. "You should have stayed forgotten."

"My duty was stronger!" Elliel slashed with the hot blade again, a flaming extension of her arm. Sparks flared into Utho's face, and he flinched. His skittish horse lunged aside and tried to throw him. Utho clawed at the saddle with his black gauntlet, but he was flung from the horse. Somehow, he managed to land on his feet, planting his boots apart.

Without hesitation, Elliel sprang from her own mount and stood to face him.

Utho yelled over his shoulder, "Mandan—Adan is yours! It's your duty as konag to execute him for his treason."

Flustered, the young man swirled his cape and leaned forward in the saddle. He swung his sword without conviction, screaming in a thin voice, "Adan!"

Elliel saw King Adan ride forward to duel his brother. She had intended to protect him, but Adan's swordsmanship was stronger than Mandan's, and Utho was the greater danger, the strongest poison. By eliminating the dishonorable Brava, she would not only save Adan, but the three kingdoms. It was what she needed to do.

Mandan's other Bravas thundered past, only two—a burly man and a sour-faced woman. Of all the Bravas in the three kingdoms, she wondered what had happened to the rest. Utho had called all the half-breed warriors to join the war against Ishara. Had no one else stayed to fight for their konag?

The human armies clashed around her, mingled with the turmoil of attacking wreths, and it felt as if the whole world was exploding. But Elliel had only one goal now, one opponent, one mortal enemy.

She struck at Utho, pushing back the other ramer with such outrage that he staggered, but he dug his heels into the grass and fought back with equal fury, his face twisted.

The ground shook, but it might have only been her pounding heart. Her focus narrowed to Utho alone. Her hatred for this evil man flared brighter. Her need for justice strengthened her ramer, and she struck again and again.

When Mandan came at him with his sword slashing and eyes blazing with irrational fury, Adan saw only a stranger.

He and his brother had often scuffled in childish brawls, responding to some insult or other. Utho had provoked the two sons of Konag Conndur, trying to toughen them. Even then, Adan had felt an unfairness in the way Mandan handled his disputes, how he would wail for help the moment the odds turned against him, when a braver person would have fought his own battles.

As the older son, Mandan was always destined to become the next konag, but he had shown little interest in statecraft, economics, agriculture, commerce, or military tactics. Unlike his brother, Adan had listened attentively to Conndur's discussions about leadership, and he had taught himself to be better. That was how he became a good king to the people of Suderra. He did not have other ambitions until his brother failed so profoundly as a leader.

Until Mandan's Brava mentor had killed their father to trigger a war.

Now as the horses came close enough together, the two men raised their swords and fought. The fighting was not elegant. They hacked and hammered at each other. The steel blades clanged, and Mandan winced, cringing away.

Adan struck again, and the force of the slash would have cut off his brother's head, but Adan hesitated, pulled his blow at the last moment. Something stopped him.

Mandan wheeled his horse around and came charging back. "I am the konag! Not you!"

"You sacrificed your right to be konag. You do not *deserve* it," Adan shouted back. He brought his horse close enough for their saddles to crash together. With the flat of his sword, he deflected a blow.

Now Mandan fought him with greater strength and skill, but he was like an abusive man pummeling his wife. Adan parried blow after blow with far more finesse. Sparks flew from the edges of their swords.

"I trained to kill Isharans!" Mandan said, his voice shrill. "You should have fought them with me! You should have brought your army so we could sail across the ocean and defeat them."

"You should have defended the Commonwealth," Adan said in a quiet, hard voice. "Instead of attacking your own people."

Nearby, Elliel and Utho dueled with their ramers, flashes of fire like a relentless lightning storm.

With all the force he could manage, Adan shouted, "Utho murdered our father—you know that! You were there, you found his body. You saw what Utho did, and yet you fight beside him!"

"I don't believe it. I refuse!"

Adan saw his brother's expression flicker. "You read the decree. You know Utho did it to push us into a bloody war with Ishara!"

"Utho is loyal to the Commonwealth," Mandan cried. "He would never do that. Or if he did . . . he had to! He's loyal to the konag. He's my Brava."

Their horses circled while the two young men battled, their swords slashing, parrying, beating each other down. Adan knew he was the better swordsman, but his brother was furious and desperate.

With an unexpected sweep of his sword, Mandan slashed Adan's arm, drawing first blood.

Adan realized he had a weakness that his brother didn't have. He had compassion.

95

THE wreths retaliated against the human army to protect their mages, even though several of the strange ice-and-sand machines were already ruined, toppled over. Onder was glad he had helped, and if he'd had his own ramer, he could have single-handedly destroyed more of the devices.

Now, though, in early afternoon the battle turned into a hurricane of confusion, with wreths and humans battling, as well as frostwreths against sandwreths, and humans against humans. Seeing his chance, Onder rushed in to defend his comrades, to battle for the three kingdoms, and push back the wreths. Though he wore traditional Commonwealth armor and colors and wielded a normal sword, he could still act as a true Brava would. In his heart, he was a Brava and would fight like one.

An auga thundered toward him, carrying a sandwreth rider with a bone-tipped spear. Onder braced himself for the clash. The cold steel of his sword gleamed in the sunlight.

The oncoming warrior thrust with his spear, but Onder countered with his sword, deflected the tip, and hacked a notch into the shaft. Annoyed, the wreth twirled the spear, raised it to dispatch his enemy, but Onder darted in to fight close up, where the long weapon would be useless.

While the wreth snatched for a crystal dagger at his side, Onder stabbed him through the ribs, shoving the sword's steel point deep. The wreth coughed a gout of blood, and his face suddenly sagged with astonishment.

Onder wrenched his sword free as the wreth slid off to crash to the ground. Hoping to save some comrades, the young man ran among the wreths, fighting them, holding his own.

The konag's military was in disarray as they encountered two separate enemies with no clear-cut battle plan. Onder spotted bright ramers among the human soldiers, fiery shafts wielded by true Bravas.

The closest one, a big male Brava, was Tytan, whom Onder had seen outside Mandan's tent just before Gant lost his life. Now Tytan moved on his own, as if independent from the konag's main army. He charged in to fight the wreths. Although there were Norterran and Suderran soldiers nearby, the Brava man concentrated on the other enemies, as if he couldn't stomach murdering members of the Commonwealth. Brash and powerful, he swung his ramer like a cudgel, waded in among frostwreths and sandwreths—and found himself vastly outnumbered.

Seeing him, Onder knew he had to help a fellow Brava, had to stop the wreths from waking the dragon, had to protect his comrades. He had to *be a Brava*! Angry, arrogant warriors turned to stand against Tytan as he fought like a fury, striking down five opponents. But there were more than even his ramer could defeat.

Knowing this was his last chance, Onder yelled, "I'm coming!" He had no ramer, but he had his sword. He fought his way closer, striking right and left, pushing forward, but Tytan was overwhelmed by wreths. Three warriors surrounded him—frostwreths attacking with crystal blades, sandwreths with bone-tipped spears.

An icy sword pierced the Brava's side, and as he buckled, a sandwreth spear punched through his chest armor. A third wreth followed through and struck Tytan down with a clean blow before Onder could get there. The big Brava collapsed, still trying to raise his ramer, but the flame flickered and sputtered out. He sprawled dead on the battleground. The wreths moved onward, ignoring the corpse.

Weeping at his inadequacy, Onder ran to where Tytan had fallen. "I couldn't come faster! I tried to help you. I . . . I failed again." He reached the dead man, hoping for some final word or phrase to add to Tytan's legacy. But the Brava was dead, his arm extended in front of him on the bloody ground. His ramer was extinguished.

Onder stared at the bloodstained cuff, glanced at his own sword, and drew a quick breath as an idea flashed through his mind. He reached for Tytan's wrist, worked the catch, and released the ramer. Heart racing, he held the metal band, looking at the golden fangs.

Half-breed blood activated the magic . . . a Brava's blood. And Onder was a Brava, at least by blood.

Onder got to his feet again, steel sword in one hand, ramer cuff in the other. More wreth warriors raced toward him, a lone and vulnerable soldier wearing Norterran colors. The clash of armies created a deafening din, and there were so many shouts of pain and roars of challenge that he couldn't think straight.

He might never earn the right to be called a Brava again. But was it enough to be a Brava in his heart? Or was his Brava magic lost to him forever?

There was only one way to know, and he could make a difference. There was little chance he would survive, but he would fight the wreths. He had to stop them! It was the honorable choice.

Two pale warriors stormed toward him on snarling oonuks. Onder faced them, shouted a challenge. He clamped Tytan's ramer around his wrist, pressed until the prongs cut into his veins, spilled blood. As hot red liquid ran down his arm, Onder dug deep within himself, searching for the Brava magic he needed to summon ramer fire.

The wreths closed in, raising their weapons. Three sandwreths joined them, mocking him.

Onder lifted his hand, clenched his fist, focused on the blood flow, and *pushed.* Sparks and tiny flickers appeared around the rim of the band, little more than candle flames. They sputtered, brightened a little, and then went out.

He stared at his hand in dismay. Blood seeped from under the beautiful gold cuff and trickled down his arm.

The wreths arrived, bloodlust on their faces, weapons raised. The oonuks snarled, and the augas grunted.

"No!" he screamed. "I am a Brava."

He still held his sword in his other hand, knowing it would never be sufficient against five opponents.

"I am a Brava," he said again, defying the universe. He might not be accepted among them, but being a Brava was in his core, beneath his skin. His identity was in his blood, not in the tattoo on his face. He'd been born a Brava, the son of Master Onzu, whom he had disappointed. He'd been trained in the best fighting skills with sword, knife, bow, spear—and ramer! Whatever skills were left to him, he would use.

He focused his entire being on the golden band around his wrist, Tytan's ramer cuff. He pictured Tytan in his mind. *I'm sorry I couldn't save you. I want to save anyone I can.*

Yes, he had shown cowardice—once. He had fled the godling in Mirrabay. *One moment does not define an entire life,* Onzu had said. *The future is more important than the past, and the now is most important of all.*

"I am a Brava!" Onder whispered one more time, raising his hand. A flicker of fire appeared around the golden edge. Tears fell unheeded from his eyes. His heart swelled, his blood burned—and at last the ramer ignited.

Flames spilled out to engulf his hand and extended into an incandescent sword. *Thank you.* He felt light on his feet again as he sprang forward into combat. He felt stronger, and he felt *alive* as the five wreths surrounded him.

Onder saw nothing but the bright ramer and his targets. He threw himself forward, slashing with the hot blade while parrying and thrusting in the other direction with his sword. He struck down one of the wolf-steeds, caught a sandwreth full in the face with the steel, then pierced another's chest with the ramer. He ripped both blades free and struck again and again. He heard himself howling like a wild animal.

But more wreths joined the fight, using their crystal spears and curved swords. He saw their twisted faces. Ten against him . . . twenty, and still Onder fought. His ramer incinerated a spear thrust at him, and he battered back a long blade of fossilized bone.

The sharp edge of a serrated spear slashed his upper arm, and another blade grazed his side as he twisted out of the way at the last instant. He felt the acid pain, the burn of spilling blood. He slashed with the ramer, breathing hard, suffocating as they pressed in.

"I am a Brava," he said under his breath, and he concentrated on the fire sprouting from his hand, kept it burning bright and deadly. He would fight to his last breath, as the wreths engulfed him, clamoring for his life.

There were too many. He felt himself falter.

Then a slash of blinding fire caught the nearest wreth warrior from behind, cutting him down. A frostwreth fighter turned and snarled, and his head flew off, leaving only a smoking stump. The flare of a second ramer slaughtered three more wreths as they reacted in astonishment to this unexpected attack.

Onder didn't understand, but he had no opportunity to think. He took a deep breath and simply fought.

Then he saw Lasis. King Kollanan's Brava cut his way in through the enemies, fighting like a controlled storm. As the wreths reacted to this new threat, Onder felt a burst of energy. He sucked in a lungful of hot air filled with blood smoke, and killed another one.

Lasis met his eyes, and Onder saw a glow of pride in the other Brava's gaze. Within moments, the two of them dispatched most of the wreth attackers and drove the others off.

Onder panted. "I thought I was dead."

"You may still be," Lasis replied. "But at least you showed who you are. You are a Brava again."

"Yes," Onder said. "Thank you."

96

⚮

THE battlefield surged with gusts and eddies of combat. Skas swirled overhead. The armies of Suderra and Norterra braced against the oncoming flood of Mandan's soldiers, both sides waving the open-hand banner, claiming to represent the Commonwealth.

All the while, wreth forces attacked the humans and defended the mages and their remaining great machines that hurled wave after wave into Mount Vada. Their furious output shook the sky, knotted the air, and pulled in thick clouds of smoke and thunder. The mages raised their voices, shouted louder, and the air picked up the roar, transmitting it into the mountains for an even more tremendous rumble.

To Thon, the battle was deafening, confusing, and fascinating. The violence and bloodshed unleashed in every direction seemed to be strengthening Ossus, awakening him. He could sense it—the evil once contained in a monstrous reptilian form began to spill out like a flash flood into the hearts of these fighters, both wreths and humans.

Revelations awakened in Thon. He finally felt the depth of power and potential he contained. His destiny, however, was still uncertain. He still didn't know his purpose or abilities. What was he *supposed to* do? He could feel events building to a crescendo, and the answer was ready to explode into his mind. *The only way to destroy the evil is from within.*

Within what?

Behind him, Mount Vada was a behemoth of stone, a cone whose top had blasted away to spill the hot blood of the earth. He had been sealed inside that mountain, part of the Dragonspine range, part of the world. He had been within, and now the volcano seemed to be destroying itself. But that was the result of wreth magic. If he were a god, why would he bury himself with his memories gone, waiting for uncounted centuries with no answers? Or if he was a manifestation of the dragon itself, then what remained inside the mountains? Were the wreth mages trying to awaken something in *him*? No, he was sure now that neither answer made sense. As Shadri's studies suggested, maybe he was something else entirely, a catalyst or a balancing point, entombed next to the ancient dragon.

He didn't know, and he was desperate to reach his destiny, to stop the disaster—if that was his purpose. He wanted to scream. "What am I sup-posed to do?"

The shaking ground and roaring air, the clamor of the battlefield did not give him answers.

What he did see, though, was a personal crisis. Wild-eyed, Elliel threw her-self against the despicable Utho, the man who had betrayed her . . . who had *hurt* her. Thon realized he had to defend her, his closest friend, the woman with whom he shared a rune of forgetting, the woman who had taught him how to love.

Elliel's ramer flashed as she used all of her strength to drive the dishon-orable Brava back. He retaliated with ramer and sword. Though Utho didn't possess the vengeful, abused anger that Elliel did, he demonstrated an un-canny rage. He swung his ramer, then the sword in a deadly rhythm, pound-ing Elliel blow after blow after blow.

When she screamed in frustration, her tattoo stretched against her cheekbones. She staggered backward a step, faltering. Thon ran to help her, knowing that Elliel would resent him if he deprived her of her re-venge, but he would not let her fall. She was weakening under Utho's fierce attack, though he wasn't sure she realized it. He knew he had to save her. "Elliel!"

Another Brava galloped in front of him, a muscular, sour-faced woman who looked hardened by battles and by life itself. She wielded her own bright ramer to intercept Thon and faced him with a haughty snarl. "I've heard of you, wreth man. You serve Kollanan the traitor."

Thon recognized her as the one named Jennae, ally of Utho, loyal to Konag Mandan.

Behind her, he saw Utho strike at Elliel with his ramer, followed by the sharp steel of his sword. She barely defended herself in time. One foot slipped on the bloodied grass.

Thon felt an urgent need to get to her.

Seeing Jennae as no more than a minor obstacle, he tried to pass her, but the Brava slashed at his face with her ramer, intending to slice off his head. He recoiled, snapping his head back, but not quite in time. The white-hot fire of Jennae's blade scorched the side of his face, burned off the skin, blinded him in one eye.

And seared off the tattoo.

Agony exploded through him unlike any pain he had experienced before. Thon staggered back, trying to blink away the red flash. He lashed out with his hand, felt magic rise inside him like a steam explosion. His anger, his knowledge, his revelations, exploded out of him in a cyclone of magic. *His magic.*

He struck Jennae with a blinding black wall of force.

Behind his eyes, he could see and sense only a coiled mass of black scales and long fangs. He heard a reptilian roar of resounding fury. Primal rage seemed to erupt out of him.

The impossible destructive force pulverized every bone in Jennae's body, twisted and crumpled her until she was no more than a soup of meat, blood, and bone fragments.

Thon hurled her out of his way and staggered off, collapsing to his knees as he clutched his burned face.

Elliel's ramer pressed against her enemy's, but her leg buckled. Even though she fought with all her might, Utho was stronger. He wore an expression of absolute focus, as if he had walled off the weakness of uncontrolled anger. He saw Elliel as an obstruction to be removed, a stain to be erased.

She remembered what this man and Cade had done to her. There could be no understanding, no forgiveness. Utho had to be defeated. But even as she pressed back against his ramer, he hacked at her with his sword. Elliel dodged, barely avoiding the blow. She could not let him win!

Behind her, she heard Thon's howling voice and whirled in time to see him running toward her—and Jennae striking his face with her fiery blade. Elliel screamed.

Utho lurched in front of her, grinning. He had seen Thon fall, and he raised his ramer for a death blow, but Elliel summoned all her half-breed strength, all her restored memories, all the painful wrongs that Utho had inflicted on her. More than anything else, she needed to get to Thon, and she screamed as she struck back against the Brava man. She crashed her ramer against his steel blade, and pushed, heating the metal to an orange glow. Utho parried with his own ramer, trying to cut her in half.

Out of the corner of her eye, Elliel saw Thon stagger away and collapse. She had to get to him! Her incandescent blade brightened with a flash of intensity, and she caught Utho's ramer arm just below the elbow, burning through skin, muscle, and bone. His forearm dropped to the ground with the blazing cuff attached. The ramer sputtered and went out.

Utho let out a deep-throated scream, and reeled backward. Blind with pain, he flailed with his heated steel sword, trying to drive Elliel away and save himself.

She could have killed him then, but Thon had collapsed nearby, clutching his burned face. She screamed Thon's name, desperate to get to him, and Utho bounded back into the swirl of human fighters, clutching the smoking stump of his arm.

Elliel needed to hunt him down and kill him for all he had done—but she knew what was more important. She ran to Thon.

More of the konag's military charged in, struggling to maintain ranks while raising their banners and swords. Yelling, they crashed against their rivals like an ocean wave breaking against shore rocks.

Adan needed all of his training and physical strength as he fought his brother. He had never expected to see such venomous hatred on Mandan's face. He fought like a man possessed, his eyes glazed and no longer recognizable, as if sheer violence could somehow eclipse the dread knowledge that his own mentor, his own bonded Brava, had butchered their father.

While the din of battle roared around her like a tornado, he and Mandan stood as if in the eye of the storm, their muscles aching, their arms and joints vibrating from each sword blow. The air smelled of blood, churned dirt, sweat, and fear.

Sparks flew as their blades clanged together. "Why do you hurt your own people?" Adan shouted at him. "The konag is supposed to rule justly, not destroy!"

"You're trying to break apart the three kingdoms and ruin me." Mandan swept his sword sideways with inartful vigor, and Adan danced out of the way. He slapped the point of the konag's weapon away. Mandan stumbled, lost his balance, and then spun.

Again, in that moment Adan could have killed him, but he hesitated. "You don't need to do this, Mandan. Let's all work together to stop the wreths. Can't you see what's going on around us? Call off your army."

"My army!" Mandan shouted. "*My* army."

"*The konag's* army," Adan retorted, blocking his brother's wild blow. "Our father would never have done this! You know that Utho killed him."

Mandan's face twisted as if a raging fire burned inside his head. "He had to die." His voice was strangled, cracking. "Utho said so."

Adan braced himself, deflecting each blow his brother struck. "Utho corrupted you. Utho betrayed the three kingdoms. Utho serves only himself." Steel rang again. "You are just a tool to him."

Mandan flung himself like a wild animal toward Adan, as if he knew the words were true but he had to defy them somehow. He lunged.

And Adan ran him through.

Thrusting the pointed steel under the king's chest armor, he drove his sword into his brother's heart.

As Mandan fell, his heavy weight dragged Adan's sword down. Astonishment at what he'd done made Adan's fingers go limp, and he dropped his own sword. The dying konag collapsed to the ground, the blade still protruding from his chest.

Everything froze in a prismatic moment, a shard of time. Around them, the deafening battle continued. No one understood yet what had happened. No one realized the konag was dead. He dropped to one knee. "Mandan . . ."

An echoing bellow repeated the name. "Mandan!"

Utho charged forward like an enraged bull, knocking fighting soldiers away, and struck with his sword—a real sword. His ramer was gone, and Adan suddenly saw that the Brava's right arm had been cut off, leaving only a smoking stump below the elbow. He was still an incredibly formidable opponent.

Utho covered the last distance in an instant, his face full of rage and despair. He tore his gaze away from the konag's body and swung toward Adan. In a smooth movement, he swept back his sword for the killing blow.

Adan was unarmed, his blade still in his brother's body. He could not defend himself, but he refused to accept death. He dredged strength from within himself and imagined that he heard the voices of his beloved Penda, the sounds of his baby daughter.

"Stop!" he shouted in a commanding voice that struck Utho as hard as King Kollanan's hammer.

The Brava glared at him, lifted his blade. "I will kill you and be done with this!"

"No you won't." Adan felt a new strength inside, a new realization. "Remember who you are. You are a Brava—you serve the *konag*."

Utho froze, as the realization struck him like a bolt of lightning.

"And I am the konag now." Adan squared his shoulders, felt his blood burning with strength. "You must be loyal to me."

97

OLDING the bloodstained spear of Dar and the dragon-scale shield, Queen Koru appeared energized. Her blue diamond eyes sparkled and her lips spread in a laugh as she looked at Kollanan. "Exhilarating, isn't it?"

With Voo dead at their feet, Koll could not comprehend what she was doing. Why would she allow a civil war to surge among her own troops? Around him, he heard the wreths shouting. "Voo is dead! The sandwreth queen is dead."

Koru seemed to revel in it.

His pleading with her to stop her efforts to wreck the world had failed, and he had seen Adan lead the charge to destroy the monstrous magical devices. And, with the arrival of Mandan's forces, the entire battlefield had become a free-for-all.

"Your army is going to break apart. Look at them!"

The wreth queen raised her hands and drew a deep breath, as if inhaling a fresh spring breeze. "Do you not understand? It is Ossus," she said with awe and delight. She seemed to thrive on it.

The rage and recklessness of the combatants was fed by an external force—a poison that they didn't even realize was affecting them. Koll could sense dark and rippling emotions that oozed up from the ground like swamp water, affecting everyone around him—humans and wreths. His head pounded, and waves of nausea churned inside him.

Birch retched in the dirt beside his grandfather. He shivered and his teeth chattered.

Koru gave him a brief, sympathetic glance. "We are waking the dragon! Evil is rippling out, and we have to withstand it, smother it—in order to accomplish what we must." She jabbed her ancient spear at an imaginary enemy. "Now we destroy the dragon and remake the world."

The air filled with the sounds of clashing weapons, shouts of rage, rumbling voices, cries of pain, and the clamor of countless skas. Shadows and anger became tangible, congealing into an oncoming storm.

Birch looked pleadingly at Koru. "You don't need to destroy this world. You're making things worse!"

"Yes . . . it is happening."

Struggling to control the external revulsion that invaded him, the bloodlust rippling like a heat storm through the air, Kollanan looked at Voo's dead body. He felt no remorse or shame for killing her, but he worried that it had triggered a reaction in the Dragonspine Mountains.

The news of Voo's death swept like a stampede through the combined army. Oonuks howled. Frostwreths celebrated and shouted, mocking their desert cousins, who were infuriated. The anger of the sandwreths transformed their enthusiasm for battle into a frenzy of revenge. They turned on the frostwreths, even as various parts of the human army battled among them.

Several of their exotic machines had been disabled by Adan's efforts, but the wreth mages stood united as they probed the unstable mountain, making seismic jabs with spears of dark magic. Another rotating ice lens shimmered and crackled, blasting away.

Undisturbed by the death of his former queen, Mage Axus shouted to his comrades, "The calling builds in strength! As the dragon rises, our magic likewise grows stronger."

Mage Elon lifted his hands from the shaking mountain rock. "Conditions are perfect. Even our fighting wakens Ossus!"

In the face of absolute chaos, Kollanan's heart flooded with dread. Mandan's army had crashed into the Suderran and Norterran forces. The wreths were killing one another and indiscriminately attacking humans, no matter what banners they flew. Fighting flared everywhere, and he could do nothing to stop it, could see no path to victory, however defined.

All the animosity fed upon itself, manifesting as a physical force of unstoppable turmoil. The poisonous hatred of wreth versus wreth, brother versus brother, human army against human army, resonated in the world. An intense storm of evil swirled and expanded, drenching Kollanan with rage and despair. Deep inbred hatreds refused to dissipate, and most fighters did not want them to.

But Koll was not helpless. He could do one thing, achieve one little victory—a victory that mattered so much. In addition to being king of Norterra, he was also grandfather to Birch. His main goal was to keep the boy safe.

"Birch, come with me—we have to go."

A sandwreth warrior bounded toward him, raising a curved bone sword, his face curled in vehement hatred. "You murdered our queen!"

Storm reared up in front of them, whinnying a loud warning. Koll pushed Birch behind him and swung his war hammer at the reckless sandwreth. The shadowglass weapon sank into the enemy's chest, leaving a bloody crater.

Queen Koru seemed oblivious to the attack. Grasping her spear and shield, she screamed to her mages. "Use the anger! Harness the power, draw upon it all." She laughed at the cracking, shaking Mount Vada. "Wake! Wake the dragon!"

Storm rolled his eyes in panic. Kollanan grabbed the saddle horn with one hand and snagged his grandson with the other. "Let's go! We have to ride!"

The boy did exactly as Koll told him. The king leaped into the saddle behind him and shouted back to Koru, "You will die if you stay here."

She glared at him as he wheeled the horse about. "This is where we must fight Ossus. Hatred and evil are the catalyst." Her shout was clear even over the rumble of cracking mountains. "This is what Kur asked of us!"

Birch said, "But you are already strong. This is a good world. You don't need Kur to destroy it."

All of the mages acted together, throwing one sustained cycle of hammering shock waves deep into the mountain range. Their remaining magical devices blasted again.

And at last Mount Vada broke.

Axus and Elon howled in triumph, a sound echoed by the other mages. They lurched to their feet, raised their hands to the sky. They could all feel it.

The black warhorse reared. As he tried to calm him, Kollanan felt a blow to his stomach, a searing pain in his heart. The ground rocked. Huge boulders tumbled down the mountainside. The slopes of the mountain cracked and burst. Gouts of scarlet lava sprayed upward, and angry billows of black smoke belched out.

As the quake strengthened, fissures split the battlefield. The feuding wreths turned toward Queen Koru, their weapons faltering, while the mages continued to celebrate. What they had triggered could not be stopped.

Koll was sure the mountain would explode again. He remembered how the fire and ash during the first eruption had wiped out mountain villages and mining towns, destroyed roads, killed countless people. He ducked, shielding his grandson with his body.

"Hold on!" he shouted. Birch wove his fingers through the horse's black mane, and they galloped away from the shuddering landscape.

The ground rocked and lurched, and Koll could imagine dragons pushing their way out from beneath the surface. Cliffs began to fall, and the jagged line of mountains slipped apart as the upheaval grew and grew.

Although their powers had started the upheaval, the mages were helpless against it. Several nearby mountain peaks exploded like pots boiling over, ejecting house-sized boulders into the sky, and projectiles rained down onto the combined armies. Struck by falling rock, two more of the giant magical machines collapsed. A river of lava gushed out of a widening fissure at the base of Mount Vada, and a jet of steam spurted into the air.

Hunched over, fearing they would be crushed by a boulder plummeting from the sky, Kollanan urged Storm to greater speed. The black horse galloped, bounding over widening cracks in the earth. Birch held on for dear life.

Behind them, where they had triggered the breach in the mountain range, the wreth mages crumpled, unable to protect themselves. A wave of incandescent lava swept over them and the ground swallowed them up.

Queen Koru seized one of the wolf-steeds and threw herself onto its back. She kicked it in the sides and bounded away, both of them howling. She held the dragon-scale shield above her head and brandished Dar's spear, calling her wreths together for the final battle.

As the mountain split open and Kollanan raced away, he cast a glance over his shoulder. Something dark and scaly with sharp wings began to emerge from the gaping wound in the mountain.

98

~

AFTER the two rival godlings had coalesced above the Magnifica, the anvil-shaped storm of prayers and rage, hopes and fears, was deafening, suffocating, and incomprehensible to any human mind.

But the storm of hands was a powerfully gentle grasp that had carried Cemi aloft and now deposited her safely at the front of the temple. After the intangible force withdrew, her skin and hair crackled, and her mind filled with wondrous thoughts. The world was spinning, throbbing, and she felt too giddy to think. Though unharmed, she swayed, took two steps forward, and collapsed next to Captani Vos.

He lay bleeding on the ground. Blood bubbled from his mouth, and a wheezing sound came from his chest each time he tried to breathe. Vos had saved her, but the arrow to his chest had made blood gush out of him, and into him. Despite the hawk guards' best efforts to tend him, he was dying.

The large crowd in the temple square had fallen into a stunned hush. Many had fled, hiding within the city, knowing full well that the gigantic deity could smash every building in Serepol to splinters and rubble. Instead, the godling just roiled and waited.

For decades, Empra Iluris had refused to let the ambitious priestlords build the Magnifica because she feared adding so much power and faith to a single godling. After thwarting her wishes, even Klovus had been unable to control the gigantic deity that he had fostered, and his unleashed godling had laid waste to portions of the city.

This dual manifestation was far stronger.

Cemi couldn't imagine how anyone might exert authority over a titanic godling twice as strong. But she had felt both godlings. She knew what they *were* at their core. And she, Cemi, was the empra, clearly designated by Iluris. The double-godling reflected the beliefs of the populace, the faith of all Ishara.

Now, *Cemi* was Ishara, and she knew deep in her heart that the people were good, brave, loyal, and honorable. Some people, of course, were twisted, uncaring, and corrupt, but that wasn't the real raw material that made them what they were.

"I am Ishara," she whispered, thinking of Iluris, thinking of all of them. Her skin tingled, her hair crackled and drifted around her head as if from a small lightning storm.

Cemi clutched Vos's hand, felt it move. His grip was weak, his skin gray and cold from blood loss. She had to save him. Even with the roaring hurricane that towered above Serepol, her focus, her crisis was here.

Vos blinked up at her, and she could see he was fading. She extended her hand, letting it hover above him. Energy continued to crackle and bubble through her veins—the godlings' energy. Her love for the leader of the loyal hawk guards reflected back into the vast entity, strengthened and reinforced what it already had as part of its existence.

When she lowered her hand and touched the deep wound in Vos's chest, the godlings' strength flowed into Cemi, and Cemi's strength flowed into Vos.

The deities could shape and create, manipulate the magic in the land and the people, and now she realized that it was a simple thing to stop the flow of blood, to seal the wound. The thick red liquid that Vos had spilled was itself a sacrifice, giving strength to the godling, and the godling now reciprocated. Cemi healed Vos.

He blinked at her in wonder, and she stared down at her red-stained hand. She took his hands and helped him to his feet, and he was more than healed. She felt a new bond with him now, heart and mind, a connection fashioned by the crucible they had both passed through.

Even though she had used some of the energy in the air and within the deity, the very fact that she had done it to save someone else seemed to strengthen the godling even further. She was no longer afraid of it. It, too, was Ishara.

Vos stood beside her, strong and energized. Together, they beheld the breathtaking immensity of the united being. Around the temple square, she heard the crowd's droning chant. "Hear us, save us. Hear us, save us."

The district priestlords had gathered around the temple's foundation, but they backed away, intimidated. They had witnessed the return of Empra Iluris, even if it was just long enough to transfer her powers and beliefs into her chosen successor. Seeing Cemi, they sensed what she was and added their voices to the chant, solidifying her hold on the throne, while also making the unified godling even more terrifying to them.

Cemi realized that it was her godling—*Ishara's godling.*

She did not know how long the tense moment lasted, whether it was hours or barely a second. The godling loomed over her, waited for her.

"Now we are strong," Cemi whispered to Vos beside her, but her voice boomed out like a thunderclap, and everyone heard. She suspected that the words resonated across the entire land.

Someone from the crowd shouted, "Now we can face the Commonwealth! Now we can defeat them, no matter what they bring against us. We can save Ishara."

Similar words were picked up and shouted. Several district priestlords squared their shoulders and looked ready for battle. "We can bring our god-lings as well!"

At this talk of war, Cemi felt exhausted and disappointed. "There is indeed great evil in the world. Yes, I know it." With her heightened senses, she could feel the darkness brooding, growing—far away, yet still a tremendous threat. "But the true danger we face is not the people of the Commonwealth, but something else. Something terrifying."

She saw it in her mind now, like a black fire burning across grasslands, drinking up the light, spreading poison. That true nexus of evil and danger threatened the existence not just of Ishara but of the world itself. Her heart wrenched with alarm.

The combined godling was not a horrific monster that could reel out of control and harm her people. It was her greatest weapon, her greatest de-fense . . . perhaps even a force strong enough to save them all.

When she raised her hands, she watched the godling grow even larger, even stronger, though it was already beyond her comprehension. It towered over the giant Magnifica pyramid, which the people had built with their sweat and blood, which they had empowered with their sacrifices. Deep inside the temple were the spelldoor portal and all of the shadowglass panes through which the godling could emerge from its strange realm inside the universe.

The combined deity twisted and swirled, stretched to the top of the sky in a thunderstorm spiral, then it retreated—looped around and dove through the top of the Magnifica, crashing down into the huge temple, with all its spelldoors and shadowglass.

The stones around the temple shook beneath their feet. Vos grabbed Cemi and rushed her across the temple square to safety. All the district priestlords ran as far from the temple square as they could.

With a collapsing explosion, the godling plunged deep, vanished through the center of the world . . . and pulled the entire pyramid down with it. Stone blocks, bricks, and dust spun in nightmare whorls of debris, before being sucked down into the collapsing crater.

Vos and Cemi fell together against the wall of a perimeter building and stared as the Magnifica vanished. The air reverberated with the ripples of residual power from the united godling. It was gone, far away.

99

⤨

THE ground wrenched and convulsed beneath Elliel's feet as she staggered toward Thon. Though she reached him quickly, it seemed to take far too long.

Dazed and reeling, Thon had collapsed to his knees, the skin of his face horribly burned and sloughing off.

Elliel extinguished her ramer flame and dropped beside him. Wrapping her arms around his shoulders, she pulled him close and rocked him, and he let out a croak of agony. The eye on the burned side of his face looked like a badly cooked egg, but his other eye flared deep blue.

"Elliel . . ."

"I'm here. I'll keep you alive. We'll find a way to heal you."

As if he didn't hear her, he touched the crackled skin, through which moist red meat showed. Sickeningly, Elliel was reminded of a venison haunch roasted over an open campfire.

Then she realized the wound had destroyed the complex tattoo that blocked his memory.

When Thon spoke, his voice held as much wonder as pain. "But now I see. . . . It begins to make sense." He breathed faster. "All my knowledge, all my past sealed away. That barrier is now cracked." When he smiled, the burned skin split open, which worsened the bleeding. "I need to know it all. Now or never. This is why I'm here. I must . . ."

"Hush," Elliel said, leaning close. Tears flowed down her cheeks. "I'll keep you safe. I can make a bandage, a poultice, but first I have to take you away from the fighting."

Thon struggled against her, pulling back. "No, not away from the fighting—I need to go to the heart of it. The . . . the only way to destroy the evil is from within." He turned so he could look at her with his good eye. His expression was still determined, but it softened a little. "I am glad you are here, Elliel, but I have a mission, a purpose. I have to understand or . . . or I will fail. And Kur wouldn't want that."

Even with the battle around them, she continued to hold him, giving Thon her strength. "I love you. You opened the world to me."

"You did the same for me," he said. "You opened my eyes to priorities and emotions. You offered me unconditional love. You showed me how to value life and people in ways that no wreth even considered before. Maybe even Kur himself did not know how to value them."

Thon pawed at his belt and slid a knife from its sheath, and she was surprised to see it was a shadowglass blade. "This is what I need, because I need to know."

"Shadowglass is dangerous to you! Where did you get that?"

"From King Adan's armory in Suderra. I thought it might be useful. Right now—" He struggled with the pain and seemed to be working himself into a trance. He climbed to his feet, and she helped him.

"Give me the knife," Elliel said, reaching out. "You shouldn't—"

But Thon released some of his magic to nudge Elliel away from him. Though he was as gentle as possible, the force was irresistible, and she staggered back. Thon lifted the shadowglass dagger to his face. "The old records said the rune has to be removed."

"No!" Elliel cried, but not in time to stop him.

With the obsidian's razor edge, Thon began to cut away the burned skin on the left side of his face. "I need to know, and I will pay the price no matter what it costs."

He sliced off the crisped skin, the charred tattoo, leaving half of his face a red and glistening wound. Holding the scrap of skin in his fingers, he frowned at it as if trying to read a page from a damaged book. "Shadri said that I was likely neither god nor dragon, but a catalyst or counterweight, or both or something between. . . ." His blind eye stared; even the lid had been burned off. He blinked his other eye and gasped as memories came flooding back.

Around them, the opposing human armies clashed, and the entire world shook and cracked, but Elliel only paid attention to the man she loved. She longed to know what he was and how she could save him, how she could bring him back to her.

One side of his face was still as handsome and perfectly formed as the features of a god who had created the wreths. Even with the hideous wound on the other side, she could not see any ugliness within him.

But Thon *changed* as she stared at him. His mind seemed to unfold with revelations, knowledge that had been locked away, but always there. Elliel remembered the same experience after her own tattoo had been neutralized. She'd been lost for so long, had forgotten who she was, but she always felt the weight of those sealed memories.

Now Thon exploded with understanding. At last he had the answers to the questions he had carried for so long.

"After creating the dragon, Kur understood what he had done, but too late," Thon said, a whisper of wonder as he collected his new thoughts. "By extracting his dark thoughts, his anger, his jealousy, he meant to perfect himself, but in the process he reduced himself to so much less than he had been." When

Thon looked at Elliel now, his single gaze pierced her heart. "It was as if he had filed down a perfectly honed blade, blunting the edge. It was less dangerous, yes, but much less of a knife." He shook his head. "But the wreths, Kur's own creations, forced him to do it."

As Elliel listened, fascinated and horrified, the words rolled out of him. Thon told the stories he now remembered, assembling information only hinted at in Shadri's fragments, research, and scattered legends. "Kur loved his wreths, but they broke him with their selfishness, their jealousy, their hatred . . . Raan and Suth, the poisoning of Kur's own daughter. Their failings made him despair. After removing every bit of darkness from himself, he no longer had the heart to be a god. He wanted to erase his entire creation, but he had made himself too weak to fix the problem.

"The evil and darkness was not gone, was not safe. The poison of Ossus was no longer contained within a single god, but flowed out everywhere, creating more dragons, corrupting wreths, harming all of us. And Kur could not defeat it."

"Then what are you, Thon?" Elliel demanded. "What are you supposed to do that a god can't do?"

"Kur could never repair the damage he had caused, and so in desperation he gave that task to his wreths, hoping that someday they would accomplish what he could not. But he was, however, strong enough to create something else before he left, a last chance. He created . . . me." Thon touched the red wetness on the side of his face as if he still expected to find the tattoo there. "Before abandoning us all, Kur left something that could help in the final hour."

Elliel looked up, saw the tremendous battle all around them, countless fighters killing one another, allies turned into enemies, and the wreths trying to summon the most monstrous dragon the world had ever seen.

"He left me behind so I would be here when the world needed me most." Thon looked at the shadowglass knife that still dripped with his blood. "In a sense I am an unexpected weapon." His smile only enhanced the horror on the other side of his face. "A last binding thread to keep the world from tearing itself apart, a weapon annealed against uncontrollable evil." He wiped the dagger on his chest. "Kur was not enough. The wreths will not be enough. I am the last necessary element."

He stood straighter, and Elliel saw that he was gaining strength, drawing it from somewhere. She wondered if the violence in the earth, the shaking ground and exploding mountains, was feeding him, bringing him to life.

"I can stop the world from ending," he said.

A deafening blast split the air, and they looked up to see what was emerging from Mount Vada.

❧

Koru slid off her oonuk and planted her booted feet far apart, taking a stance that would keep her stable even as the mountains cracked open. She held the legendary spear, much the way her ancestor Dar must have used it to wound Ossus long ago. She seated the shield on her arm. "Frostwreths, sandwreths—this is our destiny. This is how we satisfy Kur!"

The wolf-steed bounded off, whining in terror. Most of her mages were already lost, and all but one of the ice-and-sand machines destroyed. Her warriors faltered in their fight as they stared in awe toward Mount Vada.

Energy roiled up from the ground. Part of Vada's western slope collapsed to gush out more lava, which ran down the rocks, steaming and hissing. But Koru's gaze was fixed on the huge shape that clawed its way out and unfolded angular wings, a jagged triangular head, and a powerful black body larger than a sailing ship. It snapped open its jaws, displaying rows of curved teeth. Spines extended like barbed spears from its head and saw blades ran down its back.

With flickers of fire running along its scales, the dragon flapped its wings and heaved itself out of the lava. It steamed and smoked as it took wing from the erupting mountainside.

"Prepare to fight!" the queen shouted. "All weapons. Wreths must stand together against the dragon." The wreths forgot their hatred for one another and raised their weapons to face the real enemy.

As her words rang out across the din, though, something else moved within the split mountainside: the reptilian form of a second dragon as large as the first.

Then, a peak adjacent to Vada also cracked open to expose gaping caverns, widening fissures, and more orange lava. A third dragon burst free, steaming and smoking as it lunged into the air, ready to destroy.

Above the vast battlefield, countless skas swirled around, buzzing and shrieking, thousands of fragments of dragons.

More and more of the mountain range cracked open, as if the peaks themselves were enormous eggs. In all, nine great beasts emerged and took to the skies, as the world unleashed a terrifying harvest of dragons.

Even Koru experienced fear now. If killing all of these beasts was truly the wreth destiny, it seemed impossible for them to achieve victory. Against this? In all her years of planning for this final confrontation, even she had never imagined that so much pure evil could possibly exist in the world.

But she kindled a fire in her heart, resolved to do what their god had commanded.

The storm of dragons directed their anger and hatred at the gathered armies spread out below them.

100

~∞~

As the mountains rumbled and split open, and dragon after dragon burst into the air, King Adan faced a threat far different from clashing armies or monsters from the heart of the world.

Looking at Utho, he put all his force of will into the words. "I am your konag!"

The Brava stood before him holding the smoking stump of his arm as if he didn't know what to do with it. In the other gauntleted hand, he gripped his long sword, which dripped with blood. His face was ashen and twisted like a nightmare drawing.

Mandan lay dead at their feet, his blood soaking into the ground. For a frozen instant Adan was trapped in a microcosm of tragedy, a pivotal moment. The bonded Brava had broken his honor to follow an obsession. Where was his core?

Utho raised his sword.

Adan repeated, as if it were the coup de grace, "You are a Brava, and I am your konag!"

The battlefield was trampled and churned as the Osterran forces crashed against other citizens of the Commonwealth. Sandwreths and frostwreths tore each other apart. Dragons emerged from the mountains and took to the skies.

But Adan stood balanced on the sharp point of decision, afraid to move lest he fall away. Utho seethed at him, then glared at Mandan on the ground.

Adan felt hollow and shattered, but he had done what was necessary. As the ground continued to shake and Mount Vada bled lava and vomited smoke, he stepped closer to Utho. "You broke your vows, trampled on your honor. You killed Conndur the Brave. What are you now, Utho? What is left? Are you a Brava—or not?"

"I am loyal to . . . to . . ." Utho's face contorted, and his voice was raw.

"You are loyal to your konag! Loyal to me—not your delusions!" Adan shouted. "You see now that I was right, and Kollanan was right. Wreths and dragons! Look around you at what is happening to the world." He swept a hand up as the enormous beasts swooped through the skies.

Adan could have seized his sword from Mandan's body so he was at least able to defend himself, but he was no match for even an injured Brava.

"I demand your loyalty!" He pressed closer, well within reach of Utho's sword. "You can see the terror ready destroy us all."

The Brava was tangled in his own conflicting drives. He could not tear his eyes from the dead body, and his face registered shock, even despair.

Adan knew there was no time to delay. Dragons crashed down upon the extended army, shrieking and hissing. The legends said that if Ossus were killed, Kur would remake the world. But surely letting these great dragons wreak their destruction would be just as lethal for humans.

He stepped so close that his hot breath struck Utho as he issued his order. "I am the konag, and I *command* you to fight against those dragons. With every last fiber of your being, I demand that you defend the Commonwealth. Try to save us."

As the monsters fell upon the battlefield, crushing entire regiments and ripping them apart, Utho screamed with inner turmoil—then bounded away without a word.

Adan found himself shuddering.

The loss of his ramer was a more grievous wound to Utho than losing his arm. He staggered away carrying only his steel sword, and struck at anyone who got in his way. He was lost, unanchored.

I am the konag . . . and I command you!

He groaned an animalistic sound deep in his throat, and anguish roiled up from the center of his chest.

The konag . . . the konag . . . the konag . . .

It was not possible! There was no justice. Utho had made the hard decisions and taken the necessary actions. He had done the most difficult, most terrible thing in his life, sacrificing Conndur—his friend!—before the man could lead the three kingdoms to complete ruin.

And still they had lost, failed. Fulcor Island was no longer in the hands of the Isharan animals, but it was a ruin. His vengewar had never even reached the shores of Ishara to burn their cities and kill their hated people. Now, here, Utho faced the utter destruction of everything he knew. He had not even been able to protect Mandan, his ward. All his hopes for the human race and his fellow Bravas crumbled in the face of the impossible wreths.

And these even more impossible dragons.

And his own utter failure.

I am the konag . . . and I command you.

The pain of his severed arm was nothing compared to that. He had discarded so much of what made him the man he was, for good or ill, but Mandan was dead. Utho could not dispute that. Next in the line of succession for the konag's crown was Adan Starfall. No convolutions of logic or revenge could change that fact.

A Brava must be loyal to the konag, and Adan had made his demands. The *konag* had made his demands.

Utho of the Reef had to prove his worth as a Brava by fighting the dragons.

The nine monsters that had emerged from the mountains continued to wreak havoc on the battlefield. He could see the bright slashes of fiery blades on the chaotic battlefield—more ramers . . . more Bravas. At least three of them.

Even without his ramer, Utho still had his sword.

After the quake and eruption, only one of the wreths' large machines remained functional. Four shaken mages, two sandwreths and two frost-wreths, worked together, entirely united now as they struggled to shift the sandstone armature, turn the broad, pale-blue ice lens.

A terrifying dragon pounded its wings and dove toward them, but the mages managed to throw their magic into the apparatus, concentrating the blow through the rotating frozen disk. A spasming lance of deadly magic launched out of the lens and struck the dragon overhead. The scaled monster shrieked and recoiled, as if it had been doused with acid. Its wings flapped and shredded; its bones broke apart, and the dragon dissolved into slime and debris, falling into its own diseased components.

The mages ducked, shielding themselves from the awful rain that tumbled out of the sky. The huge dead hulk, still falling apart, crashed down upon them, flattening the apparatus and crushing the mages.

Intent on his own target, Utho bounded toward where two other Bravas fought a landed dragon that was ravaging the Commonwealth army. The human forces regrouped and tried to fight, but they were like ants against the monster. Many of them were torn apart. Suderran soldiers fought the beast with shadowglass-enhanced weapons. Wreth fighters also raced in, bristling with spears and swords.

Two Bravas attacked the dragon, hacking into the scaly side with their ramers. Utho recognized them—King Kollanan's man Lasis . . . and Onder, with the rune of forgetting still plain on his face. But he had ignited a ramer! Had he broken the memory block, like Elliel, or had he just rediscovered the magic in his blood?

The dragon lashed sideways with a huge claw, and Lasis met it with his fiery sword. The blazing ramer amputated two of the curled talons. Nearby, Onder joined in, hacking at the monster's forelimb, cutting deep into the scales. The dragon hissed and lurched backward with a flap of giant wings. The gust of wind knocked the Bravas back, but they stood their ground, ready to keep fighting.

Onder seemed fearless, risking injury or death—so unlike when he had faced the godling that struck Mirrabay. This dragon was many times more fearsome, but the disgraced Brava seemed elated as he threw himself against the monster.

Then Utho was there among them, shouting. "We fight together! We kill the dragons." He growled. "It is the konag's command."

Whirling, Lasis raised his ramer, ready to strike Utho down. His face was filled with disgust. "We know what you did."

Onder shook with anger. "You killed Gant in the camp! You killed Konag Conndur—I brought the message from Master Onzu!"

"And I killed Onzu as well." Utho watched as the tattooed young Brava reeled at the news. "I stand by my choices. Right now, I swore to kill dragons . . . or do you just want to talk?" He lifted his sword and charged at the dragon as it continued to thrash. Its barbed tail smashed down like a club and bowled over five wreths who attacked from the flank. "I am still a Brava—and we fight."

Lasis said, "You lost the right to be a Brava the moment you decided to kill Conndur the Brave."

Onder wrestled with rage and grief, but when the dragon roared, he steeled himself. He lifted his crackling ramer. "My heart is Brava, and this is my fight. What will you do, Utho?" He turned away and attacked the reptilian monster.

More wreths hurled their spears, and one split the stretched membrane of the dragon's left wing, crippling it. The monster writhed, and nearly a hundred frostwreth and sandwreth warriors swarmed onto its muscular body with sharp axes and long swords. When they hacked off part of the wing, the severed chunk broke apart and dissolved into shadows.

Lasis also ignored him, as if Utho were beneath his contempt. The two Bravas fought side by side as they drove toward the wounded dragon. The monster collapsed, hissing and struggling, overwhelmed by wreths. The Bravas reached its sinuous neck and struck and struck with their ramers.

Mortally injured now, the dragon sagged, rotted, broke apart. It collapsed into a myriad of black stains that roiled across the ground, mixing with the blood of the fallen, while other fragments of the dragon rose up, borne on the anger in the air, and dissipated.

Utho grasped his sword and ran off to find another dragon.

Leaving Queen Koru with her wreths to relish the emergence of the dragons, Kollanan galloped across the unsteady ground, clinging to Birch.

He felt sick inside as he watched the armies tear each other apart and the mountain split open. He was the king of Norterra. He had failed his beloved Tafira. He was unable to save the people at Lake Bakal. He could not end this war, nor bring together these armies.

But he could save his grandson. He could do that one thing.

He rode away looking for a safe haven where he could keep his grandson away from the mayhem of the battlefield. Storm dodged two wreth warriors who haphazardly struck at them, but the bulk of the wreth armies were charging toward the dragons, and they didn't bother with a man and a boy on horseback.

"Keep an eye out for shelter," Koll said.

Suddenly, shapes flitted around them, small-statured figures that skittered out of the trees and rock outcroppings. The gray-skinned creatures waved and chittered. Birch brightened, and he pointed urgently. "The drones! They'll help."

Pulling Storm to a halt, Kollanan sat back, grasping the reins. As the drones came closer, Birch spoke to them in their strange language, which Koll didn't understand.

The drones began gesturing, running ahead. Koll trusted them without hesitation; they had helped him plan the attack on the Lake Bakal fortress, helped keep Lasis alive after Queen Onn left him for dead, and they had helped Birch.

"They'll take us someplace we can hide," the boy said. "It's sheltered." He listened, frowned, and looked back at his grandfather. "They say some of our people are already there."

Koll looked at the turbulent battlefield, the wreths throwing themselves upon the dragons, and the human armies caught between them. He held Birch in front of him in the saddle. "Then we'll follow."

Many of the small creatures rushed along with them, keeping to the shadows of the trees and rocks, safe on the fringes of the battlefield. They had accompanied the wreth army on its long journey, but they had distanced themselves more and more from the wreths.

Birch seemed excited. "They followed me from Queen Koru's palace. I made her promise to keep them safe, and now they'll keep us safe." He looked back, grinning. "I told them to stay well away from the fighting if they could."

At the end of the hills where the Norterran and Suderran armies had built their sprawling camp, huge talus boulders formed buttresses. The rocks had shaken in the quakes, but they remained as sturdy as fortress walls. To Kollanan, they looked to be the most stable place among the mayhem.

Scampering ahead, the drones guided Storm, and Koll thought he saw a natural shelter where he could hide his grandson, a cave overhang. The drones ran forward, pointing and celebrating. Kollanan spotted another horse and some tents in the shadow of the giant rocks, and he recognized Shadri and Pokle huddled among the talus.

Pokle's eyes were wide with terror, his hair sticking out in all directions as if he had just wrestled an enemy warrior. The scholar girl seemed full of consternation. She made noises, speaking a few words in the drones' language. The small-statured creatures hurried around, protective and excited.

"Is it safe?" Koll called as he dismounted.

Shadri paced in front of the rocks, as if she had already spent a good deal of time considering the question. "The area seems stable enough, but if the world cracks open, who knows? At least we're upslope from where the boulders will fall if the ground keeps shifting."

Birch ran forward with a group of drones, and they huddled in the shadow of the rock. Kollanan joined them, sitting on a boulder where he could watch the terrible battle. He could see the bright flares of several ramers, Bravas fighting the dragons. One of the monsters was struck down, and the great hulk dissolved into a mass of dark, roiling fragments.

"The mages used the last one of their magical machines to kill another one," Shadri said. "The dragon died, but it crashed into them and killed the mages, too."

Queen Koru had rallied her wreths to focus on a third dragon, as if she considered no enemy invincible. He saw her hurl the legendary spear to pierce the monster's eye. Human soldiers were fighting the same dragon, hacking great wounds into its scaly side, and bringing it down.

Koll held Birch's shoulder. The drones looked rapt as the third dragon died and broke down into a miasma of evil and scattered fragments.

After three of the nine dragons were slain, though, the other six seemed to be joined by a common purpose. They pounded their great wings and flew up above the battlefield. Wreth warriors hurled countless spears into the sky, inflicting more and more damage. Human archers showered countless shadowglass-tipped shafts into the air. The six huge dragons swirled in the plume of smoke and ashes from Mount Vada, flying closer together, tightening their spirals.

Then the dragons slammed together, grappling with clawed talons and still flapping. They circled with such speed that they became a blur of scales, barbed tails, sharp claws, and fangs until the entire mass shimmered, shifted, blurred. . . .

From six individual dragons, a single tremendous monster emerged from the whirlwind, a dragon larger than all the others combined—so enormous that it drew upon all the evil in the world, all the hatred and violence, all the darkness that had come from the heart of a god.

The unspeakably huge dragon, the size of a city, burst forth and let out a roar that shook the sky and the mountains.

Ossus had awakened and emerged at last.

101

⚥

A T the haunted wreckage of the Plain of Black Glass, Penda and Glik
screamed in unison. Together, they felt a sudden inexpressible dread
that resounded through the ground and echoed off of the shimmering oil-
black pools.

As if buffeted by unfelt winds, Ari and Xar swirled around in panic and
made sounds unlike anything Penda had ever heard. Baby Oak wailed out
loud, sensing the same dread.

Off on the blasted plain, Mage Horava collapsed face-first onto one of the
obsidian pools, cutting herself. The two sandwreth warriors hesitated, then
bounded away as the ground began to tremble.

Penda couldn't concentrate with the buzzing roar in her head. She could
neither express nor understand the hammering sensations. A shuddering
premonition hurtled toward them like a slavering monster.

Shouting in alarm, Cheth ignited her ramer and stood prepared to face
any enemy, but as she turned about in a wary, defensive stance she could see
nothing. Seenan and the escort soldiers closed in around the queen, ready.

"*Cra*, it's what I saw in my visions!" Glik shouted, partly in awe, partly in
terror. She scrambled backward, grabbing Penda's arm. "We've got to run far
from the shadowglass."

Penda didn't argue. The silent incomprehensible roar kept growing louder,
and the ground emitted a dark and ominous sound. Her teeth chattered, and
her long, dark hair crackled as if a lightning storm were imminent.

The ground lurched, as if a deep storm built far beneath the surface of the
world. Something terrible was on its way.

Cheth raised her ramer like a beacon and led the escape, and Xar and Ari
swooped overhead, urging them on. The Banner guards drew their swords,
looking for an enemy.

They ran to the top of a rise on the perimeter of the plain, fleeing the ancient devastation, and Penda finally turned, heaving great breaths. She held
baby Oak against her. Cheth stood close enough that Penda could feel the
heat and angry buzz of her ramer. Tears ran down Glik's face.

Seenan came running to join them, leading two horses. "For you, my
queen!" His face was flushed. Young Hom trotted beside him, tugging on a
halter rope, though the mounts were skittish in the rumbling wasteland.

Glik pushed Penda toward the horses as she scrambled to mount one herself. "Ride, Sister!"

Then Penda saw something shift and shimmer among the petrified ponds of sinister material. Glowing cracks rippled through the smooth shadowglass, and the obsidian pools became liquid again, like quicksilver.

Far away, the small figure of Mage Horava climbed to her feet, shouting something incomprehensible in the distance. She stared down at the shadowglass and screamed.

The black glass mirrors churned, their edges blurred, and the smaller ponds flowed together like blood droplets forming a much larger pool. The shadowglass material seemed to come alive, flowing in an oily midnight film over the boulders and broken debris, swelling until it engulfed and erased the remnants of the wreth camp.

Penda's horse whinnied in terror. "Retreat! Farther!" The mounted soldiers ran toward the line of hills that bounded the rocking plain, unable to guess how much distance would be enough. Hom opened and closed his mouth like a fish thrown up on the dry shore.

"We'll never outrun it," Glik said. Penda turned to look.

The distant mage stumbled, then her body swirled in the air like a feather caught in a whirlwind. She dropped down, flailing, and vanished inside the shifting obsidian, as if a bottomless midnight had swallowed her up.

Behind them, the Plain of Black Glass transformed again. The empty blackness glowed with a shadow darker than black that greedily sucked any light from the air.

This ancient battlefield had been the site of countless thousands of deaths, both wreth and human. Immeasurable magic had infused the blasted landscape, leaving black mirrors and crystal fragments of unforgotten pain. The shadowglass awakened in a new way into an expansive empty void.

"The shadowglass screams," Glik cried out, as if in a trance. "It is carving a hole in the world. A . . . passageway!" She gasped. "This is what I saw in my visions. It's coming. Something terrible is coming."

"Is it Ossus? Did we somehow awaken Ossus?" Penda asked.

"Not the dragon—something different. And . . . just as dangerous."

The combined shadowglass pools bubbled and roiled, and then all the black glass evaporated into an open pit that did not remain empty, but rather became an immense portal.

Penda shielded her eyes and ducked behind the questionable shelter of a large rock. A shrieking, explosive turbulence belched from the shadowglass portal. What followed was an entity like none she had ever seen or imagined, a thunderhead filled with anger, roiling eyes and screaming faces, lightning and wind. The thing roared and flashed until it had emerged completely.

Penda covered her eyes and her ears. The baby wailed. Glik just stood staring.

Penda had heard of such unusual forces before, entities created by the magic of Ishara, by blood sacrifices and constant prayers. But the three kingdoms had no such magic, and no one here had ever created godlings. She knew about them only from tales her father had told about his trading journeys to the new world.

But this was so much more powerful, a being impossible to behold and understand. The godling continued to flow out of the black glass like a never-ending plume of harsh smoke. The godling's gigantic incorporeal tentacles stretched out, studded with thousands of golden eyes that flashed in all directions and saw everything, yet somehow did not notice, or care about, the handful of humans.

Cheth raised her ramer in defiance. "I will defend the queen of Suderra!"

"No, Cheth," Penda said. "You'd be no more than a gnat against an enraged bull." The boiling monstrosity made all of them feel completely insignificant.

"It's the most powerful force in the universe," Glik said. "I don't know why I'm afraid. I . . . I don't understand it."

The astonishing bulk hovered above the shadowglass portal, circled above the ancient battlefield, as if searching for something. Then the deity gathered itself, tumbling, expanding, and swirling in a dizzying mass of power, smoke, lightning.

With a clap of thunder, the godling swept away and headed due east, toward the Dragonspine Mountains.

102

~∅~

ALL her life Shadri had sought out new experiences, interesting information, and answers to her questions, but now her mind simply could not grasp what she was seeing. "Ossus!"

The six reptilian beasts had merged to create one enormous dragon, the totality of all dragons. That's when Shadri stopped watching and dashed back into the shelter. But she couldn't ignore the dragon so easily. When Ossus roared, the sound made Mount Vada's eruption seem like it had been a mere whisper.

"I don't want to know this," she muttered to herself, hiding in among the giant talus boulders. "I don't want to see this." She pressed her back against the comforting surface of the rock, but she could not close her eyes. As she kept staring, she only gradually realized that Pokle had wrapped his arms around her, shuddering, squeezing her tight—seeking comfort, giving it, and too terrified to know what he was doing.

Kollanan's grandson stood with a few drones away from the slanted rocks, gazing at the wreth armies that raised all their weapons in a united front to face this opponent that destiny had delivered to them. The bearded king placed himself in front of Birch. "Take shelter in the boulders."

But the boy shook his head. "It won't matter. I want to see."

Kollanan's expression fell as he, too, realized that hiding in the rocks would not protect them from whatever was about to happen. "This is . . . beyond me. Beyond all of us."

Quiet, nervous drones clustered around them, also staring.

On the battlefield, the thousands of wreths formed ranks, and Queen Koru screamed as she looked up at the spectacular dragon. "This is Ossus! Kur has commanded us to destroy the great dragon." She brandished her spear, as if Ossus might remember being wounded by the same weapon long ago. "To make a new world!"

Peering back out, Shadri wondered if the great dragon had been smaller, weaker in ancient days when Dar's original attack had driven it beneath the mountains. Perhaps all these armies, all the treachery, hatred, and violence, had made the monster's evil grow more powerful.

Ossus crashed among the wreths, killing hundreds in a single blow. Koru hurled the spear, and the legendary weapon broke through a line of shimmering scales. The shaft plunged into the monster's flesh, but it looked like no more than a fleck of straw.

Ossus flinched as if the pain were a mere annoyance rather than a mortal wound. With the sweep of a sharp black wing, the dragon mowed down the front ranks of wreths like a great scythe, sending dozens more victims flying, broken and bloody. The monster careened forward, crushing others with huge taloned claws, smashing an entire line with its barbed tail. With a cavernous mouth, it devoured dozens of wreths who stood to fight.

Birch gasped with dismay as the monster targeted the frostwreth queen, but Koru danced aside, raised her shield, and pulled out her sword. She stood defiant and still alive, challenging the monstrous dragon that could snap her up in an instant. Ossus reared back.

Then something strange happened. The milling wreth armies parted as if shoved apart by an invisible hand to create a pathway. A lone figure strode forward—a wreth, but a strange one.

Thousands of skas circled in the sky like multicolored sparks, shrieking and clicking. Behind the lone man came the flash of a ramer, as a black-clad woman ran after him. Shadri knew exactly who it was.

Needing to see better, she emerged farther from her hiding place to stand next to Kollanan and his grandson. Together, in silence, they all watched the fate of the world unfold.

Thon came forward to face the dragon.

Even as Elliel ran after him, Thon seemed unaware of anything but his determination. He used magic to drive the wreths apart and create a path for himself.

She called after him, raising her bright ramer. "Thon, let me help you fight."

The skas flurried about like an honor guard, flecks that had once been part of the greater dragon but were now transformed into a part of the evolving world. The reptile birds showed no fear of Ossus, and swarmed around the monster like gnats, as if their own redemptive presence could somehow diminish the darkness embodied in the giant creature.

When Thon turned to her, Elliel flinched at seeing the side of his face stripped of skin. With the rune of forgetting gone, he had a different presence about him. He embodied the mission for which he had been created. "I love you, Elliel, but you cannot help me. I am here to balance the evil and control the destruction."

"No, I fight with you," she shouted.

"You can't." With his good eye, Thon held her gaze for as long as he could. "This is my purpose and mine alone. I know now. I am the fulcrum between good and evil. The darkness must be used to strengthen instead of destroy."

As Ossus raised its jagged wings and let out a roar loud enough to crack mountains, Thon spoke softly to her. "You taught me love. You made me understand that the good and the faith of humanity can control the evil left behind by a god. The only way to destroy the evil is from within." He drew a breath. "Please go. To fight this battle, I need to know you are safe."

She remained defiant, determined. "My place is by your—"

He flicked his other hand, catching Elliel in a swift yet gentle push. A wind flung her away to safety as if she were nothing more than a dried leaf. She cried out, but could not fight it. She tumbled on the ground, keeping her ramer extended as she rolled, then sprang back to her feet. Wreths stood all around her, transfixed by Thon and the dragon.

He seemed tiny and insignificant as the titanic creature loomed over him, its enormous scarlet eyes blazing down at the single dark-haired wreth.

Elliel felt her heart breaking. Ossus was so much more tremendous than she had imagined. She could well believe that over the centuries humanity had spawned its own evil, fed the presence of the dragon beneath the world— Utho murdering Konag Conndur, Mandan ordering his own troops to attack an innocent Norterran town, what Cade and Utho had done to her, countless more injustices and indignities.

The dragon must be stronger now than when Kur had extracted it from himself. In the time since, human hatreds had strengthened it.

Ossus flapped its black wings, creating a windstorm, then thrust a serpentine neck forward to strike. But Thon raised a hand and slapped at the air. The resounding force sent the great dragon staggering back.

Thon spoke in a normal voice, which somehow resounded everywhere. "I have come for you, Ossus." With another invisible blow of his unbridled and incomprehensible magic, he made the great dragon reel.

The monster recovered, flapped its huge wings, and threw itself forward.

Thon stood unmoving, either confident or uncaring.

Ossus lunged down and snatched him up in its jaws. The great world dragon devoured Thon in front of all the stunned armies.

Elliel screamed.

103

WITH a ravening shock wave, the godling rolled across the land. It tore up the landscape and shot forward with all the force of a meteor. Composed of smoke and lightning, terror and destruction, it ripped its way through the air and sent out a resounding boom of challenge.

The thunder of its approach drew the attention of the armies facing Ossus.

Elliel stood shaking from what she had witnessed. Thon had flung her to safety, and she still felt as if she were spinning. He was gone—the great hope that Kur had left behind to save the world. The secret weapon. The fulcrum! She had believed that Thon was the only force that might possibly defeat the dragon.

Yet he had been snapped up as no more than a tiny morsel. He had seemed to *let* himself be devoured.

Elliel dropped to her knees. Had he finally understood something in all the enigmatic discoveries Shadri had brought? With his rune tattoo gone, what had he learned? Or had he just made a terrible mistake? Now he was gone.

Ossus let out a deafening bellow and rose up in all its reptilian immensity. Then the dragon trumpeted a challenge.

Across the open landscape to the west, the godling roared forward like a horrific storm. The sight of the two opposing forces stunned Elliel with disbelief. Even the wreth armies were cowed into silence.

With Thon already forgotten, Ossus drew back its wings and heaved itself up, roaring with fang-filled jaws as it faced its gigantic enemy. The godling hurtled in, and the two collided.

Utho found another mangled Brava body on the battlefield, a woman—Jennae. Her face had been crushed, but her eyes were open. Inside her black finemail, her bones were pulverized to jelly. He stared down at her, trying to imagine what could have done such damage, but then he saw the golden ramer cuff on her limp arm, and that was the only thing that mattered.

Utho examined the stump of his arm. The cauterized skin and bone still leaked blood, and the pain throbbed brighter than ramer fire, but he dispensed with that pain and drove away the distraction.

His sword was a good blade, given to him by Konag Conndur as a reward for flawless service. But it was an inadequate weapon now, especially for a Brava . . . especially for what might be the world's last battle. He cast the sword aside and knelt beside Jennae's body. He fumbled with one hand, released the golden band, and took her ramer as his own. Propping his good arm against his knee, he folded the cuff in place and pressed until the golden fangs drew blood. He drove back a wave of dizziness, focusing only ahead. The konag, his konag . . . Konag *Adan* had issued commands, had bound him with Brava loyalty.

Utho expected to die, but he would do so remembering exactly who he was. He would regain honor and perhaps inflict some kind of wound on the titanic dragon. He had nothing to atone for, no regrets, but he would die as a Brava following his konag's orders.

He felt the weapon ignite. The fiery blade grew from his half-breed blood, though its color seemed diminished. He was weak, crippled, but not insignificant.

He turned toward the battlefield where Ossus had just devoured Thon—and to his horror watched something more terrible approach, an atavistic force composed of elemental power, screaming winds, and his greatest fears.

A godling! Here in the Commonwealth! Crossing from the west like a nightmare of hateful emotions and beliefs, a manifestation of Isharan practices, of Isharan vengeance.

He let out a howl of rage and indignation. He hated the primal entities as much as he loathed the Isharan animals. But this godling was ten times the size of what he had seen before. And it had come here, into the heart of the three kingdoms! This evil Isharan stain violated the entire land.

Raising his new ramer, Utho felt the energy of vengeance surge through him, and he bounded toward the monstrous conflict.

Suddenly, Elliel was there in front of him blocking his way, her eyes red, her face drawn. "If nothing else, I will see you dead before the end of this day, Utho. I can't defeat Ossus, but I can rid the world of your evil!" Her body shuddered with grief and rage. She approached him, drawing back her fiery sword for battle. "I have lost so much—but I will gain this."

Utho held up his own ramer, frustrated that she would block his final moment of glory. The rune of forgetting on her face was like an insult. "You waste your energies. I have the konag's orders."

The godling and Ossus slammed into each other, tearing and fighting, throwing hurricanes of energy into the air, ripping up the land. Even with his ramer and all his Brava fury, Utho was no more than a dust mote in that hurricane.

But he was Utho of the Reef, and he refused to be insignificant. "This will be my last battle—get out of my way!"

Elliel blocked him. Her ramer flared and thrummed. "You will pay for all your atrocities."

"I have many debts to pay." Utho looked past her to the black-scaled dragon the size of a mountain. He knew the foolish impossibility of his task, but everyone on the battlefield would see how he, Utho, threw himself against the greatest forces the world had ever seen.

The konag had ordered him. Ordered him! And he was a Brava.

Elliel swung her ramer at him, and he barely raised his own fiery blade in time to block it. She attacked him again, her lips drawn back in revulsion. "You stole my life, my legacy."

Utho's own anger dulled the pain in his severed arm. He parried her slash. "You keep making the same mistake. It was never personal, never about you. You were just a convenient solution." Beyond them, the dragon and godling were locked in mortal combat. Her interference galled him. He should be fighting them, inflicting damage, hurting them somehow. But instead he fought Elliel. "You never mattered to me at all."

Elliel flinched as if she had been struck a physical blow. In that moment, he kicked her hard in the middle of her chest and knocked her out of his way. "This is my moment. This is my legacy and how I will be remembered!" He dismissed her, raised his ramer, and turned to face the dragon and the godling.

Elliel struck him down before he could bound away. Her fiery blade cleaved all the way through his chest, nearly cutting him in two. As he collapsed, she said, "You don't deserve an honorable death."

He fell to the ground, and Elliel stood over him. "One moment does not redefine an entire life." As the two omnipotent monsters battled behind them, she thrust her ramer again and burned a hole through his heart.

King Adan rode to his Suderran troops and called them into a defensive line. The soldiers held up their shields and swords, but even with shadowglass weapons, the Commonwealth armies could be no more than bystanders.

Onder and Lasis had joined him. The two Bravas were scuffed, exhausted, and spattered with blood. "What do we do, Sire?" Lasis said. A gash ran along his left cheek and blood trickled down his neck.

Adan could not fathom what Thon's purpose had been. Created by Kur to help them somehow? With all his demonstrated powers, how could Thon have been so . . . useless? Had he truly been their last hope?

In the battle, Ossus seemed to grow even more enormous, roaring, biting, and slashing at the amorphous churning form of the godling. The battle was like a hurricane crashing into a mountain.

However, as the world dragon pounded its wings and drew back, Adan saw its scales rippling. The dragon's sheen became tarnished like bruised fruit or rotting skin. The monster twisted, spasmed.

"It looks like Ossus is sick," Onder said. "Something is happening inside the beast."

Growling and struggling, Ossus broke away as the godling tried to engulf it again, to embrace and crush it with arms of clouds and lightning.

A chill ran down Adan's spine as he remembered what Shadri had said . . . what *Kur* had said. "The only way to destroy the evil is from within."

The huge dragon began to change color all over, shifting, convulsing. Lines and cracks appeared through its black-scaled body, like the flawed glaze of pottery misfired in a kiln.

"Thon . . ." Adan said.

The godling took advantage of the dragon's weakness and disorientation, battering with cloudy limbs and bursts of electricity. The Isharan entity became a smothering shroud that sapped the dragon's energy and drained itself with the effort. But even as the godling weakened visibly, it did not relent.

Ossus tried to flap its wings and the thin extended bones snapped, as if the whole body was crumbling. The fleshy wing membranes folded, then tore. Widening cracks shuddered through the dragon's chest, as if it were being eaten from the inside, burning and breaking.

As he watched, Adan was convinced that this had something to do with Thon—unlocking his own destiny, destroying the world dragon's huge black heart, splitting its ribs.

Ossus craned back its serpentine neck, and its jaws split open wide as it trumpeted in agony. The innate catalyst of Thon did its work. The godling kept pressing as well, pouring its elemental power into the battle . . . and Ossus *shattered,* breaking apart into six smaller dragons—which in turn crumbled into hundreds of much smaller dragons.

Though clearly weakened from the combat, the godling spread itself out like a net, extending its powers. Misty, smoky tentacles snatched the countless small dragons out of the air, crushing them. Some of the reptilian fragments kept breaking up, smaller and smaller, until all that remained of Ossus was thousands upon thousands of new-made skas.

Afterward, the godling was reduced to little more than a sparkling mist that settled over a stunned and silent battlefield, a rain of leftover magic returning to the world.

Silence fell like an eclipse.

104

As the monstrous dragon broke apart and faded away, Kollanan felt a trembling in the air. The ground still rumbled, though it seemed like a sigh of relief, shaking with exhaustion rather than preparing for the end of the world. The air smelled like the aftermath of a great thunderstorm.

Fearless, Birch tugged on his hand and pulled him farther from the talus shelter. He was eager and amazed to see what had happened. Somehow, despite all the horrors he had been through, the boy retained an optimism that Koll had not let himself feel for a very long time.

"I think it's all right now," he said. "Look at what's happening."

Shadri joined them, her skirts tattered and her hair in tangles. Pokle continued to hide in a shadowed cleft of rock, but the scholar girl dragged him out. "You should see this." Then she set her jaw firmly. "You *have* to see this! I won't allow you to miss something so important. You can tell your children someday."

"What children?"

Though Ossus had been destroyed, faint remnants of the Isharan godling still throbbed in the air. Flickers of blue-white lightning laced through its smoky tendrils and the unwinding cyclone at its core. The tremendous deity was a shadow of what it had once been, a squall instead of a hurricane. Because the thing was not exactly alive, Kollanan couldn't understand what was happening to it, but the expended deity seemed to be dying, torn to shreds in its final battle against Ossus.

It paled, fading to gray and then misty white, infused with sparkles of rainbows, glimmering colors that flared and dissipated. The godling's remnants spread out like prayers spilled across the landscape.

The Dragonspine foothills as well as the broken peaks themselves were battered and damaged, devastated from Mount Vada's eruption and now torn apart by thousands of soldiers marching across the ground. The godling spangled and stretched outward like a faint but comforting blanket. It infused the old world, bringing a warm flush of green and fresh growth to the burned volcanic landscape.

With wonder, Kollanan watched the unnatural change on the bleak wasteland, the shift in colors from stark blacks and browns to a wash of verdant plants. The godling's last vestiges seeped into the old world.

As a side effect, Koll felt his own heart healing as well, his aching and exhausted muscles, the heaviness inside himself. His grief contracted from an open wound to a hard, pale scar.

Next to him, Birch was filled with energy. He hugged his grandfather, looking up at him. The boy's eyes were brighter, the shadows on his face faded away as sunlight broke through the sky and washed over them.

Kollanan the Hammer felt strong again, reminded at last of what it was to be a king. He even experienced a hint of hope.

Storm pawed at the ground, and Koll reached over to take the warhorse's reins. He hoisted Birch into the saddle. "Come, let's go find Adan."

The kings of Norterra and Suderra rode through the stunned armies, trying to offer strength and reassurance. Battlefield surgeons tended the wounded, while other soldiers wrote down notes and stories to record the legacies of the fallen.

Adan was glad to find his uncle still alive and Birch unharmed. So many human soldiers lay fallen—many of them killed by their comrades, who had followed corrupt Mandan. Adan felt a cloud on his own heart. "I killed my brother. Utho forced the two of us to fight."

"Utho killed my brother too," Kollanan said. "It would be too easy to blame all this pain and death on one Brava. Maybe that is how I should ask Shadri to write the histories. It's what Utho deserves."

Adan pressed his lips together and shook his head. "The people need to know what truly happened. Utho was a great manipulator, but Mandan was not free of blame. Legaciers must remember it and retell it for whatever future we are going to have."

Frowning, Kollanan nodded. "Whatever that future may be."

Adan, Koll, and Birch found the wreth queen among the remnants of her fighters, victorious, yet somewhat confused. Koru was wounded, but even with a battered face she gave a twisted smile of triumph. Miraculously, she had retrieved the ancient spear of Dar. It was even more splintered now, its leaf-shaped point chipped and stained with blood. Her wreths had been massacred, more than half of her warriors and nearly all of the mages wiped out. Still, no matter the cost, she crowed with victory. "Ossus is destroyed! We succeeded in what our god commanded us to do!"

Kollanan gestured around at the remnants of the wreth army. "And what exactly did you achieve with all this?" Although the land itself had become green and healthy, thousands of bodies lay strewn about on the bloodstained battlefield.

Koru's exuberant look was tinged with obsession. "We will be rewarded. The world will be remade!" She looked around, as if she expected everything around her to suddenly sparkle with newfound glory. Her gaze locked on Birch, sitting in the saddle in front of Kollanan. The boy smiled at her.

"The godling already did some of that," Adan pointed out. "This could be a new world, if that is what we make of it."

"That was not the legend!" the wreth queen said. A few surviving wreths dredged up a few more threads of excitement to let out a cheer.

From the hills, a figure began walking toward them, someone so incongruous that Kollanan didn't understand what he was seeing—an old man frail and bent, drawing no attention to himself, yet all eyes turned toward him as if he were a lodestone.

Kollanan hadn't seen where the man came from or how he had appeared. He walked on bare feet over the newly green landscape, stepping around boulders strewn about by the eruptions, avoiding dead horses and the corpses of soldiers. His pace was slow and painstaking, and he ignored the staring sandwreths and frostwreths, the human soldiers, as if he were merely on a stroll through a meadow.

Koll sensed something odd about the man, and a chill went down his spine.

"Who's that?" Birch asked. "He looks very old."

Holding her legendary spear, Queen Koru stepped up to stare at the stranger. The old man's features made him look like a wreth, or something similar. He was ancient, but his skin was unwrinkled. His hair was pure white, the white of age, not the paleness of a frostwreth. He seemed somehow perfect, yet weak.

Never deviating from his slow, determined course, the old man approached the wreth queen and the two human kings. He looked at each one, assessing, then he nodded with a calm smile. "I am Kur."

Kollanan blinked.

Adan gasped, "But . . . how?"

Queen Koru's pale eyes flew wide, and she dropped to her knees, unable to speak. "You are here to obliterate the world and create it anew."

The strange old man frowned at her and said, "I see what you all have done." He sighed. "I could not have accomplished it myself, and all of you . . ." He looked at Koll and Adan, then back at the wreth armies. "I am proud of my creations—and, in turn, I am proud of *their* creations, the humans. I learned so much from watching you! You accomplished what I did not dream possible . . . what I found impossible in myself."

"You returned, as was promised," Queen Koru finally said, bowing deeply. A humming murmur rippled through the gathered wreths. "Take us away. Reshape the world, and make it perfect for us."

"Ah, but I cannot do that," Kur sighed. "Not exactly. I made myself weak long ago by denying half of what made me strong enough to create. Peace becomes malaise if we cannot resolve conflict. Ripping out all of my hardness, dulling all of my sharp edges was a mistake. If you removed all of your bones, would you be stronger? No. I should have corrected my wreth children's mistakes, but I was a coward. So I released my own evil into the world, and it contaminated them. I wanted to help them overcome the evil, but I could no longer defeat it."

The ancient man hung his head.

Elliel, weeping, openly approached him. "You have more power than you're admitting. You created Thon. How could you let the dragon devour him?"

A smile broke across the old man's face. "Ah, Thon was perfect! He was the balance I no longer had. Balance revealed the precise weak spot inside the dragon. He destroyed the evil from within."

Elliel remained distraught. "You let an innocent wander through life completely lost. You didn't tell him his purpose. You didn't let him be . . . alive! I loved him."

Kur gave her a somber nod. "Yes, and that love gave him more power than even I imagined. Just when Ossus was stronger than ever, Thon was able to fight him, thanks to you. And his innocence was part of his strength." He paused, gathering his thoughts. "It seemed . . . the best decision at the time. After I had purged myself of so many negative qualities, what else could I do? I had to let you win the battles and solve the problem."

His smile was incredibly weary but sincere. "And you have done so, you and these remarkable humans. In addition to Thon, it was humanity's beliefs, their own powers, that created the godling, which was also necessary to destroy Ossus. You achieved victory, together." He looked at them all. "Not I. And now you have a better world. As I promised."

Koru seemed miffed. "But this is our old world. You are Kur, our god. You can build us a perfect world."

"The world was badly wounded. Evil roamed free, and I could not restore myself." He took a step toward her, but his knee buckled. He swayed, nearly fell, but caught his balance.

As Kollanan watched, the ancient man seemed to lose his strength. "I could never remake the world as I promised, so you have done it for me. With Ossus gone, you already have a new world. What will you do with it?"

A gruff anger rose within Kollanan. "You released evil into the world, and wreths nearly destroyed it. It was humans who saved everything, nursed the land back to health. We built all this ourselves."

The ancient god extended his hands. His fingers trembled, his arms shook, and his voice had a watery quality, as if the words themselves had become thinner. "Well done. And this is your remade world, your new world. I give it to you, to the wreths and to all of humanity. But in truth it is already yours. Make of it what you can."

His rattling laugh became a sigh, which turned into his last words. "Thank you. You have given me hope. Alas, I have nothing more to give you, but myself."

Then Kur swayed and crumpled to the ground, like a pile of delicately balanced sticks knocked over by a puff of wind. He evaporated into a sparkling mist that settled over the ground and gradually faded as he poured himself back into the land.

105

A FTER the old man's essence soaked into the damaged land, the opposing forces fell into a hush of both contemplation and confusion.

Elliel's heart felt as empty as her memories had been from the rune of forgetting. Her salty tears, mingled with blood and dust, dried into streaks of pain on her cheeks. She tried to wipe them away, but they stayed on her face, seeming as indelible as the tattoo.

"Thon . . ." she whispered, still angry at Kur for his blithe abdication of responsibility. He had simply left pawns to repair the damage he had done. Thon hadn't even known his purpose, until the very end.

Right now she wanted to hold him, to celebrate this great victory together, but since he was gone forever, she felt no triumph. Elliel had always known the mysterious man was unique—something apart. She remembered when she first saw him preserved beneath Mount Vada, sealed away in his crystal-lined prison. He should have awakened by himself when his time came; he should have found any instructions Kur had left for him. Perhaps Elliel should have noticed them. But when she rescued him there was no time as the mountain shook and tunnels collapsed. She had barely escaped with her own life and Thon's.

She had realized that he was no normal man, that he had a mysterious, terrible destiny. And Thon had indeed served his purpose as a catalyst, destroying the black heart of Ossus from within. Without Thon's sacrifice, the horrific dragon would even now be obliterating the world and everyone in it.

But how she missed him! It felt achingly wrong to be in a new, growing world without him.

In the sky she heard a buzz building to a crescendo in an odd kind of music— the shrieking of innumerable skas flying about. Thousands of colors circled in an incomprehensible storm. The winged creatures clustered together, flying closer and closer, their cries rising with joy.

All around Elliel the soldiers on the battlefield looked up, watching without comprehending. The incredible flock of skas grew denser, swirling together until they formed a definable shape. Countless small reptile birds assembled a new flying thing out of tiny fragments, colorful and exuberant.

The skas coalesced into a grand, beautiful dragon. This one was not evil and black as midnight, but a rainbow of colors, as if composed of gold and every imaginable gem. The majestic creature beat perfectly formed wings and soared above the battlefield, riding on updrafts from the rejuvenated magic that Kur and the godling had infused into the world.

The wreths looked upward, and a resounding ripple of awe stirred the air. Every person on the battlefield fell silent, holding their breath.

From within, Elliel felt her heart uplifted, her spirits brightening. The new iridescent dragon flapped its wide wings and came down to a gentle landing as the surviving fighters drew away to give it room. Hundreds of leftover skas still circled in the air, glittering like sparks from a grinding wheel, but the shining golden dragon was whole and strong.

The beast was so rich with colors that Elliel's eyes ached. Its head was plated with precious metals and stones. Its jaws were as large as a wagon and filled with teeth, but the creature made no threatening moves. Instead, the new dragon's eyes widened, sparkling, to look at them all.

When the rainbow dragon's gaze fell upon Elliel she was nearly bowled over with the force and intensity in its eyes, which were blue like crushed sapphires. "Elliel," it said in a voice that contained the boom of thunder, the roar of ocean waves, and the rushing sound of summer rain. "Elliel . . ."

The dragon turned its gaze to the others there. "King Kollanan of Norterra, King Adan of Suderra." Then it regarded the wreths. "Queen Koru of the wreths."

Elliel walked forward, not understanding . . . or unwilling to understand. Then she gasped and ran toward the dragon. "Thon!"

The creature flicked its long iridescent tail. "Part of me is Thon. Part of me is what Kur left in the world."

Heat, crackling static electricity, and incomprehensible benevolence radiated from this new manifestation. Elliel touched the scales on the dragon's neck, felt energy and love flowing into her.

Adan and Kollanan joined her in front of the huge shimmering creature. Clearly not sure how they should react, they each gave a formal bow.

Queen Koru came to stand by the kings, her long pale hair flowing behind her. Her skin was marked with numerous wounds, and she wore a perplexed expression. "What are you, dragon?"

The iridescent creature lifted its head, and a rumble came from within its scaled chest. "Indeed, what am I? There is magic in the world again. It formed me. It holds me together." The dragon swung its head back to Elliel. "*You* are what holds me together."

"Where did you come from?" Adan asked.

The dragon answered, "I am . . . everything else. I am here."

Elliel caressed its scales one more time and stepped back.

The rainbow dragon flapped its huge wings. "I was always here." The iridescent creature raised itself from the ground, and a heavy wind buffeted the soldiers who watched it take flight. "I will always be here."

Elliel raised her hands and shaded her eyes as she followed the dragon's path through the sky. Amid all the bloodshed and pain on the great battle-field, after all the generations of growing evil and darkness, she felt hope.

"You will always be here," she whispered.

The dragon flew up and away, circling once more over the battlefield as countless playful skas joined it, skirling around. The dragon beat its wings, rose higher, and then soared off into the blinding sun.

Even though it was gone along with whatever part of Thon it still carried, Elliel's heart was happy. He was alive. She knew she could find him again if she needed to, but for now this was enough.

106

⁊⁊

THE frail old man, the last remnant of an ancient and powerful god, had walked among the wreths and spoken to Queen Koru. Warriors and mages, workers and nobles, had all heard Kur's words and seen the newly formed iridescent dragon that was a fresh manifestation of magic in the world.

Previously, the poison of Ossus had twisted them, inflamed their jealousies and anger, provoked them into bloody conflict. Now, the saddened and weary wreths were united by what their departing god had told them to do. Just as Kur had given their race a mission thousands of years before, now he had given them a new reality to hold on to, a better world that belonged to them . . . and to the humans.

On the vast battlefield in the foothills, some wreths brooded and remained in their camps, feeling cast adrift. But the rejuvenated landscape felt like the release of a long-held breath. Queen Koru walked among her people, letting sandwreths and frostwreths see her. "We lived with hatred for so long, are we strong enough to live without it? We must learn to be strong enough for peace." The queen raised her voice, and her pale hair flowed behind her. "Kur gave us another difficult task. Let us see what we can make of it."

The human armies had a different kind of response. They had faced two grim fates: to be destroyed by the dragon and the uncaring wreths, or to simply be erased from the world. The soldiers of the three kingdoms had fought against one another, but they eventually found a solution they had not thought possible. Kollanan still had a hard time accepting the idea of peace and harmony with *wreths,* after all the horrific things they had done. Now, though, even the wreths had been cowed, brought to their knees.

Maybe there would be peace. The old world had healed after thousands of years of human nurturing and tending, and was now rejuvenated with the extra life force from the godling and from Kur. The Commonwealth would be lush and fertile again, given time.

Kollanan was reminded of when he had returned from the old Isharan war, exhausted and heart weary from all that useless fighting. He had gone to Norterra with the intent of becoming a gentleman farmer and letting everyone have a peaceful life. Now, maybe he could do that.

For Adan, the new konag of the three kingdoms, life would be very different. After the death of Mandan, he had feared a continued civil war, that the Convera armies had been so poisoned with hatred that the three king-doms would never unite again. But many of Mandan's recruits had expressed doubts from the beginning. They knew the young man had issued unwise and vindictive orders, and they now knew that Utho had driven them into a reckless frenzy. Brother had fought against brother, bound by conflicting obligations and loyalties.

But Mandan was dead now, as was Utho.

Taking the mantle, Adan sent riders throughout the hills to announce that he was now the rightful konag, and the armies of the three kingdoms raised their swords in a resounding cheer. They acknowledged Adan Starfall as the leader of the Commonwealth—even those who had ridden from Convera un-der Mandan's banner.

As their cheers echoed around him, Adan felt a flush rise to his face. The lively voices grew louder, and he raised his shadowglass-inlaid sword in sa-lute to them all. He raised his other hand and splayed his fingers in the open-hand symbol of the Commonwealth.

As the cheers rose louder and louder, Koll watched him and nodded. Adan said to his uncle in a quiet voice, "I suppose I need to tell Penda that we're moving to Convera Castle."

"And I plan to return to Norterra with my grandson," Koll said. "We'll try to rebuild whatever quiet peace I can find. I suppose Shadri will pester me with questions so she can write her history of this war." He squeezed Birch's shoulder and chuckled. "But Norterra is no longer threatened, and I have my grandson back. That is enough for me."

A few remaining skas flew around, taunting the soldiers, mischievously steal-ing shreds of meat from the cookfires and racing away with a series of whis-tling clicks. With the flurry of colorful scales and feathers, Adan didn't at first notice Xar.

The green reptile bird circled over his head as he sat outside his command tent with his vassal lords, discussing how to disperse the armies and send the soldiers home. Lord Ogno tried to shoo the ska away, but Adan recognized the collar around the scaly green neck. "Xar! You came from Penda."

With a burbling sound, the ska landed on his shoulder, incensed that Adan had taken so long to acknowledge him. A tiny slip of paper was tied to the taloned leg, and Adan fumbled at the thread, then finally cut it with the sharp tip of his dagger. Xar scolded him as he unrolled the message.

Penda told him she and Oak were safe, and Bannriya was safe. She de-scribed the emergence of the godling, and explained that she was hurrying home to Suderra. She longed to see him again.

Adan couldn't stop grinning as he looked around at his advisors. Lord

Ogno let out a loud deep-throated laugh. "I know that expression. I miss my wife, too!"

Since he could not work the magic of the mothertear, Adan called for paper, ink, and a freshly sharpened quill. He wrote a note describing as much as he could on a tiny scrap, telling her the war was over. After Adan secured the note, he set the ska free. "Go find Penda. Tell her I will see her soon."

Xar took flight again and gulped two large moths flitting around the campfires as he flew off. Adan watched reptile bird disappear into the night, and he felt as if a great weight had gone with it.

107

THE fire had caused significant damage to the empra's palace, even though the new godling had extinguished it. Iluris's tower chambers had been gutted as flames roared through rooms and narrow passages. The tapestries and bedding were charred. When Cemi climbed the damaged stairs to stare at the ruined chamber, she felt a lump in her throat, remembering just how many days she had spent here at the empra's side. She could barely breathe with so much smell of smoke lingering in the air.

"Everything can be repaired," said Captani Vos. "Bring in fresh curtains and bedding. Replace essential furnishings. We will repaint walls and fixtures. We'll—"

"I don't need to sleep here. Not now." Cemi remembered some of the terrible places she had bedded down when she was younger. She squared her shoulders, considered what Iluris would do. She had to think like that now. "We have higher priorities in Ishara."

Her new role still hadn't sunk in, although Iluris had assured her she was ready . . . ready enough. "A good leader is in the heart as much as in the mind," the old woman had once told her. "You can find advisors to give you the knowledge you need, but a person's heart is who she *is*, what she has made herself, what she believes—and I trust your heart, Cemi."

Empra Cemi.

"My bedchambers are not the thing that Ishara needs most. Restore the throne room as soon as possible. Serepol and Ishara need to know that their empra is back after such a long and dark time."

The repaired portions of the empra's palace were obvious—clean white stone, fresh woodwork, and tinted glass windows. Black smears of soot still ran up the outer walls, but intrepid young workers dangled in rope harnesses to scrub away stains high above the plaza.

Vos and his hawk guards boldly wore their scarlet capes and polished gold armor. Cemi promoted all guards who had protected them down in the hidden chamber, and with many new recruits, the guard ranks had swelled back to normal levels.

"I am Ishara," she muttered to herself, and Vos glanced over at her. She smiled at him. Despite his slightly bent nose, Captani Vos looked special to her—brave, loyal, resplendent in his new uniform, and proud of his position.

Work crews scoured the throne room clean, replaced the damaged tapestries and hangings, polished or repaired the gold ornamentation. A dedicated carpenter rebuilt and restored the empra's throne. He was considered the most skilled craftsman in the land, even though he was missing three fingers from a woodcutting accident. When Cemi finally sat in the new throne and leaned back into the velvet-covered cushions, she knew his reputation was well deserved.

Still, she felt out of place. She closed her eyes and concentrated. *Empra Cemi.* She was intimidated to follow in the footsteps of Iluris. She would do what was right, make decisions not for herself, but for the people—for *her* people.

She felt naked without the invisible force of the new godling that had helped protect and guide them, but it was gone. They had heard nothing since the combined godling had plunged through the shadowglass portal to fight the distant growing evil.

But that did not mean all godlings had left Ishara. Magic still resounded in the land, and it was hers to do with as she needed. Through prayer and sacrifice, the people strengthened all of the other godlings across Ishara, and their faith soon sparked a new Serepol godling.

From the restored throne, she could feel a new power building—the faith of the people, their willingness to let her rule them. That sensation confirmed in her heart that she was a real empra. She recalled with a smile when she had been a scrawny but bold girl climbing vines outside the Prirari governor's mansion because she wanted to speak with Empra Iluris. She had never expected to get far.

Now this . . . She had never believed such things could happen.

"Captani Vos," she said from the high seat. "I want reports from every neighborhood in Serepol. Find the reliable people who supported us during our time of hiding, the merchants, tradesmen, farmers, and smiths. And Saruna, of course. I want them as part of my council to organize the rebuilding efforts around the city. We have only begun to repair all that the godling destroyed when Klovus unleashed it."

Vos agreed, issued orders to his hawk guards.

Cemi reached a decision. "Right now, I want to see all of the district priestlords, since Klovus summoned them to the capital. Some fundamental changes need to be made in Ishara, and I must have the support of the priestlords."

"Be cautious, Excellency," Vos said. The term of address startled her, but she would have to get used to it. "They were not the empra's allies when it was most important."

"I will not begin my reign by starting a war with the priestlords. Klovus was an anomaly—I hope—and these others did not know what he did to Iluris. The people of Ishara need their godlings, and they create their godlings. It is the wisest, most meaningful way to heal this rift and heal the land."

Klovus had been subsumed into the unified godling, and Priestlord Erical was gone from Prirari, having traveled with the barbarians to the Commonwealth, but the other eleven priestlords responded to her summons. Standing before her, some of them looked intimidated, some were awed in her presence, some even ashamed. She knew few of them by sight, but she had learned their names and all about their districts in her study sessions with Chamberlain Nerev.

A thin woman with braided hair from Tamburdin District was the first to bow. "Excellency." She bent her entire body. "My empra."

Three more district priestlords bowed, then all eleven gave their respect and fealty to the empra. Cemi sensed no undercurrents of hatred or resentment. For effect, she held the silence for a long moment as she considered her decision, but she knew the right thing to say, the best approach for making them into allies.

She spoke with greater formality. "Our city was wounded, but my people are united. Ishara must heal and grow strong again, and for that I need your help. After we bury our dead and remember them, we will rebuild the damaged structures, clean up from the fires." She hardened her voice. "We must punish those who took advantage of our weakness and distraction."

Some of the priestlords flinched.

"We must never forget that we are Ishara. We know what Ishara is meant to be. We understand Ishara's needs, weaknesses, strengths, and aspirations. We know our people's faith." She paused, then added, "And I intend to rebuild the Magnifica temple."

She heard Vos's indrawn breath. Even the district priestlords seemed surprised.

"But we will do so only when it is appropriate and in a proper, cautious manner. Empra Iluris stopped the construction because she feared that a too-powerful godling could be abused by an ambitious priestlord. That is exactly what happened. The wreckage in our city shows the folly of a key priestlord who considered himself superior to the faith of our people."

The Tamburdin priestlord bowed her head again, her braids swinging forward like pendulums. "A godling can slip out of a priestlord's control. When the people are angry and afraid, then the godling is angry and afraid. Sometimes it is . . . beyond us."

"Our primary godling is gone now, but the faith of our people is not," Cemi said. "Countless local entities still reside in their temples, strengthened by prayers and sacrifices. Soon enough, the beliefs of Serepol and the magic of the land will create a new godling for us. The spark is already there." She leaned forward on her throne, facing the line of priestlords. "Our new Magnifica above all will be a place for people to gather and worship. It will be a great temple, yes, but not the monstrosity Klovus tried to build. Our new godling will reside in Serepol, but as a *guardian,* not a destroyer."

The hawk guards and the district priestlords all muttered. Dovic, the priestlord from Sistralta District, said, "But we are at war. We must bring our godlings together to fight against the old world. Priestlord Erical is already with our fleet, and we know that is where the great Magnifica godling went. There is so much evil there! Right now we should press our victory and eradicate the godless."

"We should press for peace!" Cemi snapped. "We have a chance to defeat hatred. Have you not sensed it? The darkness has been extinguished. There is no reason the old world and the new must be mortal enemies. They are our distant family. We come from the same ancestors." She let out a sigh, thinking of Fulcor Island. "Konag Conndur realized this before anyone did. He wanted us to be his allies against a tremendous growing evil. Now we know that he was right."

Cemi rose from her throne and raised her voice. "*He was right!* I know what was in Conndur's heart, and I know what was in Iluris's heart. They both wanted peace, but treachery from our own key priestlord, as well as traitors among the konag's men, ruined it. It is time to do the right thing."

She crossed her arms over her chest and regarded them all. "This is what I've decided. Captani Vos and his hawk guards will accompany me on an expedition to the Commonwealth. We will take one of our remaining ships, but not a warship. I will meet with the konag of the three kingdoms and work to change the course of our two lands."

108

WHEN he saw the ancient walls of Bannriya again, King Adan—*Konag* Adan—felt as weary as this legendary city. After his long ride from the mountains, Adan was dizzied by his new responsibilities, as well as rejuvenated by thoughts of the new Commonwealth . . . the new world.

Most of all, he was excited at the prospect of being with Penda and their baby again.

After dispatching Xar with the message to his wife, he had worked with Kollanan and even the wreth queen to disperse their armies in an orderly fashion. The vassal lords of all three kingdoms had come together to proclaim their loyalty, but with the Commonwealth so strained and torn, Adan needed to take up residence in Convera Castle as soon as possible. Everything would change.

Now, as he looked ahead of him and saw flags flying on the high points of the wall, the old city truly looked like home. How could he leave here?

Queen Penda rushed to greet him as he rode through the gates. He swept her into his arms and kissed her. "I'm home for now, but you know we have to go soon." He stroked her long, dark hair. "Time presses on us."

After days of countless meetings and celebratory feasts, Adan took his wife up to the tower observation platform. The sun was low on the horizon, coppery orange against the rugged mountains and the desert beyond. He drank in the sight of Bannriya's market districts with vendor stalls like cells in a beehive, spice merchants and leatherworkers showing their wares on tables under awnings.

Xar flew lazy circles overhead. Adan heard a family singing together in a cul-de-sac of old dwellings. The sights, sounds, and memories left him with a bittersweet taste. He still couldn't believe Hale Orr was gone, even if Queen Voo had paid dearly for it.

Cheth climbed the tower stairs to deliver even more reports to the king and queen, with Glik trotting close beside her. Ari immediately took flight from Glik's shoulder and flew with Xar.

Cheth had made preparations for the new konag's procession to Convera, rounding up carts of supplies, travel tents, and wardrobes with garments that Adan and Penda would need when they reached their new castle.

Adan glanced up at the sky, which was painted with deepening colors. Already, a few of the brightest stars had appeared. He thought of the many times he had stared into the dark vastness, thinking of the universe and of his legacy. Mapping out constellations in great detail had told him nothing. He had fought his own battles and made his own destiny, no matter what the stars said. The world had shaped him as much as he tried to shape the world. He had been a good king to Suderra and hoped he would be a good konag to the whole Commonwealth.

Glancing at the tangled streets below as lanterns and cookfires were lit, Adan spotted many colorful tents set up in open areas as two more Utauk caravans entered through the eastern gate and found places to bed down.

"*Cra,* we will be fine." Penda wrapped her arms around Adan's waist. "The Utauks will escort us to our new home. And my home is in your presence, wherever we are."

109

Eᴌᴌɪᴇʟ and Onder rode together over the mountains, seeking out Master Onzu's training camp. They made an odd pair, both with Brava features, both with tattooed faces, both with ramers on their belts. Elliel wore her black finemail, body armor, and cape, though it had seen better days. Onder wore a brown jerkin and rough-spun breeches, but his entire attitude was different now, strong, humble, and determined rather than crushed by questions and shame.

The long overland journey from the battlefield made Elliel recall her days as a young paladin roaming the land to protect the people, and she told Onder stories. He listened to her like a starving man offered a feast. She reminisced about those innocent days, before she had offered her service to Lord Cade, before he had drugged her, before . . .

Now she had a different mission.

After the war, Elliel had intended to stay with Kollanan as his bonded Brava, but the Norterran king had rested the blunt end of his war hammer against the ground, as if he hoped he would never have to lift it again. "A time of peace and calm has come to the three kingdoms, and Lasis will be more than adequate to protect me in Fellstaff." His eyes were earnest. "Our new konag is the one who needs the services of as many Bravas as we can find. Go there with him."

Onder had joined them in the battlefield camp. He had not recovered his past, but he established a new honor, if not his memories, and he ignited the ramer. "That is good enough for me," Lasis explained, speaking on the formerly disgraced man's behalf. "I consider him a Brava again."

Elliel thought of the vicious accusations she had endured after receiving the tattoo on her face, remembered how the Scrabbleton miners had stared awkwardly at her, believing the stories that she had slaughtered children in her blood rage. She nodded to the young man. "We will serve as Bravas to the konag."

"The world needs more Bravas," Lasis said. "We must value every one."

The two rode off, heading over the Dragonspine Mountains toward the capital. But first, Onder would lead Elliel to the training village, where Master Onzu had taught his students. "Utho disgraced us all, and the people of the Commonwealth need to see what a Brava truly is." He brushed the tattooed side of his face. "I have seen both sides of it, and will tell them my story."

Elliel was up to the task of training, but not at an isolated village. "After Utho's atrocities, those students need to be reminded of genuine Brava honor. We can instruct them, not just in fighting, but in all that underlies it." She smiled as they rode along. "I don't think many have forgotten."

Onder remembered the secret paths through the forests, and he brought Elliel to the site of the training village, where they found the wooden buildings abandoned, no horses in the stable. The two uncovered stored food, some sacks of oats, and a barrel with a few old apples. They drank from the stream, slept in empty bunks, and the next day they made their way to the nearest human village to inquire about Onzu's wards.

"My father went to confront Utho, and he died." Onder hung his head. "But he left many students behind. We can create a legacy from them."

They found the Brava children living among the townspeople. Some of them were in their early teens and full of imagined adulthood, while the younger ones were brash and energetic. They did their chores and sparred in mock battles, just as Master Onzu had taught them to do. Looking at the group of eager young people, Elliel could see the half-wreth heritage in their features. She could also see that they would all become real Bravas.

In the village, Elliel called out to the young trainees. "There is a new konag in Convera. Onder and I will be his bonded Bravas, and we will want many apprentices. The Commonwealth needs as many Bravas as we can train—if you are up to the task. Will you come with us?"

She swept her gaze across the eager young men and women. With shining eyes, they all agreed. "Follow us to Convera, and we'll make real Bravas of you all."

Elliel glanced up into the clear sky, blinking in the bright sunlight, and thought she saw a flash of golden wings.

110

⤫

Back home in Fellstaff, King Kollanan looked at his city with new wonder and appreciation. The walls, sturdy and solid, had withstood the test of time. He saw the busy streets, the shops and markets, neighborhoods with people crowded in clusters of homes, extended families working and living together. Farmers brought in their late-autumn harvests as the people prepared for what might not be such a terrible winter after all.

From outside the castle, Koll had looked at the great keep, the new shingles he had helped install on the sloped roof not so long ago . . . yet an entire era in the past.

The air was colder now and had a deep bite. The first light snows were dancing through the skies on the day he and his army returned to Norterra. Now he realized the winter was not a thing to dread, but the natural order, a cold season that would then lead to spring.

The castle halls still held shadows, gloom, and a lonely chill that even fires in every hearth could not dispel, but Fellstaff Castle was not quite so empty, now that Birch was back with him.

The king sat in his big reception hall, the throne room where so many consequential events had begun—wars decided, armies launched, terrible news received. It was his castle, his kingdom, and his responsibility. Kollanan loved his people, and they all hurt along with him.

On the wall behind his sturdy, dark wood throne, he had mounted his war hammer, still inlaid with shadowglass. This time he would not hide it away in a reading room for no other purpose than nostalgia. He still hoped never to use the weapon again, but it hung in plain view as a reminder never to let his guard down.

Koll didn't merely brood, as he had since losing so many family members. Instead, he actually smiled, letting his thoughts be diverted as he observed the tussle in front of him with joy. In the open area before the throne dais, Birch held a short sword, which was just his size, and his gaze was intent, focused. The boy still had a wiry look, but he would put meat on his bones now that he was eating regularly again.

Birch faced Lasis on the open floor. The blond Brava wore a blank expression as he raised his sword, then drew it down to parry as the boy swung his small blade. A metal clang rang out as the short sword struck the Brava's steel.

"You should use a dagger against me," Birch said, "so it'll be a fair fight."

"It will never be a fair fight, boy, because I am a Brava," Lasis replied. "Besides, truly fair fights occur only in stories. You have to be prepared to fight any opponent you face—even me."

Birch swung his short sword, knocked the tip of the Brava's blade away, and then ducked under the reach of the steel. Kollanan laughed out loud as the boy moved with amazing speed, darting beneath his opponent's defenses. He got close enough to poke Lasis in the vulnerable abdomen. Lasis managed to snatch the boy by the collar and yank him up in the air. Dangling, Birch slashed with the flat of his blade and managed to brush the Brava's chest armor.

"It seems you're the one who expected a fair fight, Lasis," Koll said.

Squirming in the air, Birch tried to score points. Looking up at the throne, Lasis set the boy back on the ground. "Your grandson will make a fine warrior someday, so long as I continue training him."

With pride, Birch stepped back and held up his short sword, ready to keep fighting.

"Maybe by the time he is ten," Lasis said, and Kollanan chuckled again.

Queen Tafira's throne was empty beside him—a heartache and another reminder, like the war hammer. She was always there in spirit, and he remembered how she would counsel him to keep his thoughts and emotions in check.

On the far side of the room, Pokle tended the fire in the hearth, adding more logs. He used tongs to arrange the split pine so that orange flames danced higher and warmth spread out, even if it didn't manage to reach the corners. He brushed splinters and bark chips off his loose gray jerkin.

In a quiet, busy rush, five drones hurried into the throne room, each one carrying a chunk of split wood to place in a pile beside the fireplace. Pokle's hair was a mess, and he seemed confused by the drones. "That's my job," he said. "I can do it myself." But the drones stacked the wood and turned from the roaring fire to look toward the throne.

"They need something to do," Birch said.

"There's plenty of work in Fellstaff," Koll said. "They just need to be guided." He knew the old city needed countless repairs, walls and roofs to be mended, drainage gutters to be cleaned, hay to be piled, food stores distributed, roads cleared, cobblestones patched. His people had been too busy preparing for winter and shoring up for war, but now the capital of Norterra could reach its potential.

"The drones don't mind, really," Birch said. "And they're very glad to stay here. They love their new home."

The creatures chittered and nodded their understanding of the boy's words. Forty of the small creatures had accompanied the Norterran army from the great battlefield, and Kollanan had cleared one of the barracks for them to live in. The drones reveled in their new dwellings as if they had been given mansions, which, compared to their previous squalid hovels at the ice palace, did seem to be the case.

Shadri hurried into the room with a flush on her face, trudging with great determination. Pokle grinned up at her, but her sole focus was the king. "Sire, it's important!"

Koll straightened in his throne. From her alarmed expression, he thought the scholar girl might have discovered some other revelation in the wreth records.

But she surprised him. "Visitors at the northern wall—frostwreths! Queen Koru is here."

Birch turned to his grandfather, actually smiling, and Koll rose to his feet. "Then we had best go meet her."

They swiftly reached the lookout point on the thick stone walls, where the guards fidgeted, uncertain, and the people muttered in the streets.

Outside the barred northern gate, the frostwreth queen sat in her battle sleigh, which was drawn by a pair of muscular oonuks. Five wreth warriors served as an escort guard, riding their own shaggy wolf-steeds and holding sharp ice pikes—ceremonial weapons, he hoped.

"King Kollanan of Norterra," Koru shouted up when she saw him. She spotted Birch at his side. "Will you receive me?"

Looking down, Kollanan recalled Adan's description of how the sand-wreths came to Bannriya demanding entrance, threatening to flatten the city into rubble. But the world was different now. *A better world,* according to what ancient Kur had told them.

He placed a hand on his grandson's shoulder. "Yes, come inside. I invite you to our castle."

❧

Although he doubted anything from his kitchens would be seen as a feast for the great queen of the north, Koll ordered his staff to do their best. They brought out platters of steaming food prepared with the exotic spices that Tafira had enjoyed. As the smells wafted to him, he felt a pang of longing for his lost wife. So many reminders everywhere, with every sense. His chefs had Tafira's Isharan recipes, and he had ordered more spices and instructed them to keep preparing the food exactly as their queen would have wanted.

Cold, regal, and beautiful, Koru sat in the guest chair with Birch beside her. She ate the food without a flicker of insulting arrogance—which, in itself, Koll considered a victory.

He slurped a spoonful of warm lentil stew liberally spiced with cumin seeds. "The wars are over, and the world will grow stronger," he said. "The people of the Commonwealth have learned their lesson."

"As Kur meant it to be," the queen said, and Kollanan did not argue the point. She still had not explained the reason for her visit.

He made a decision. "Konag Adan has united the three kingdoms. His coronation is in two weeks, and Birch and I will soon journey overland to Convera." He paused, not sure whether he was overstepping his authority by extending the invitation. "Our konag would consider it an honor if the wreth queen were to come. It would demonstrate a change in the relationship between wreths and humans."

Birch looked at her with hopeful eyes.

Koru considered for a long time and frowned. "I think not. I would be a distraction and a disruption. My wreths have too much of our own building and healing to do."

Although the boy seemed disappointed, Koll felt a flush of relief at her answer. Still, he was glad to have made the gesture.

She continued, "Frostwreths and sandwreths, the descendants of Suth and Raan, have been separate for far too long. That division goes back to the darkest bloodshed in our history." Her pale lips formed a hard line. "But we must remember that Raan and Suth were also sisters, and from the same family. All wreths are from the same family."

Koru looked up at the king and appeared uncertain for the first time that he could recall. "That golden iridescent dragon has been seen flying overhead, catching the sunlight. It is blinding when you try to look at it, but it is a reminder. There has been a greening. The devastated deserts and the frozen wastelands are beginning to change."

The queen seemed filled with wonder. "I have seen it myself, and we are all reminded of how the world was before our wars devastated it. We wreths destroyed so much." She sat up straighter. "We know what we have to do. Kur gave us this world back with a new command to make it better. If we can restore those lands, then my people will have more territory than we can imagine. And this time we are mandated to make it thrive." She swallowed hard. "Rather than make it burn."

Kollanan was glad to see her change of heart.

She gestured with a pale hand to the walls of the castle, but indicating much more. "These lands are yours, King Kollanan. The humans have reclaimed them, and we hope you can thrive as well. Now it is the wreths' turn to do that work."

As a strange emotion filled him, Kollanan realized it was relief. He had wondered if he would ever feel safe again, if his people could go about their own lives as they had before. Now, maybe that would happen.

After the frostwreth queen finished part of her meal, the Fellstaff servants hurried in with crystallized honey candies for dessert. Koru ate one, perplexed by the taste, and then not-so-subtly gave the rest to Birch.

She looked up again, tossed her pale hair. "I came to you with an offer, King Kollanan of Norterra. My mother and her warriors destroyed your town of Lake Bakal with a winter wave. Thanks to this boy, I have come to understand what that meant to you."

Koll didn't know how to answer, and a familiar pain shot through his heart at the reminder.

"My frostwreths would offer to rebuild. Our workers and mages can easily clear away the ice, restore the lake, rebuild your town, though you will have to help us to understand your dwellings."

Koll had not expected this. "Lake Bakal is a wound that needs healing if we are ever to be at peace with the wreths."

"Good, it is settled then." The queen was clearly pleased, and added, "The drones were very insistent. They wished to go there and work."

Birch perked up. "The drones?"

"Many of them escaped from the north and are living in the forests around Lake Bakal. They will help rebuild." She seemed impatient. "They always want something to do."

"It will be a new world," Kollanan said. "A better world."

"The north is changing, and so are the deserts," Koru said. "Your people can inhabit the town at Lake Bakal again, and we swear never to allow harm to come to them." She paused, not just gathering her thoughts but wrestling with a decision. She looked first at Koll, then down at Birch. "And perhaps the boy can come visit?"

111

∽

A FTER so many bad memories, Adan wanted to ensure that his coronation ceremony was a more vibrant and joyous occasion than when
his brother became konag. Mandan had been so wounded and broken after
seeing their murdered father—never suspecting that Utho had done it—that
he'd simply held a rushed event. But this time, Adan and Penda would allow
Convera to prepare.

The ceremony itself would be four weeks hence, to give the people time
to come from across the three kingdoms, including as many Utauk tribes as
could make it. It would be a heartfelt celebration.

The new konag had much work to do first, to heal some of the major
wounds in the land and the people.

The vassal lords and military commanders had watched over the capital
city in case of unrest after Mandan's overthrow, but the citizens welcomed
the news. From Donnan Rah's widely distributed message, they already knew
what the konag and Utho had done, and they accepted Adan with relief. Across
the three kingdoms he was known as a wise and benevolent ruler of Suderra,
and he would bring that experience to the Commonwealth as a whole.

In Convera Castle, his new home, Adan held court, meeting with numerous nobles and trade ministers. So much to do, clearing the roads over the
mountains, reestablishing regular commerce, communicating with each of
his vassal lords—fifteen from Suderra, most of whom he knew well, eight from
Norterra, and twenty-one from Osterra's smaller, more populous counties.

Trying to get the world back to normal, and at peace.

In the throne room, he wore fine garments for all his meetings, including
a blue fur-lined cape that had belonged to his father. He would not actually
wear the crown until the coronation ceremony, but he was the konag, and no
one doubted it.

In the queen's throne beside him, Penda wore a colorful gown sewn out of
fabrics from all three kingdoms and then embroidered with Utauk designs.
She complemented her clothing with a bright mothertear and a delicate saltpearl necklace, despite the sinister origin of the pearls. Penda had agreed to
wear saltpearls only on the condition that the Isharan captives be freed from
Cade's holdings and allowed to make their own lives, given a choice between

going home to Ishara, or accepting a parcel of farmland in Osterra. In either case, each former slave was given a small chest of saltpearls as reparations.

Mandan's disturbing painting of the Battle of Yanton had been taken down and burned in the courtyard. The more Adan learned about what had been going on in the Commonwealth over the past few years—much of which even Conndur must not have known about—the more he vowed to rule the three kingdoms better.

This was a new world, as Kur had said, and the people of the three kingdoms would make the best of their second chance. The dragon Ossus was truly destroyed, and his insidious influence no longer permeated the land. Adan would help his people work together.

The Utauks had been welcomed back into society after going into hiding from Mandan's harsh crackdown. With the daughter of Hale Orr now on the throne beside the konag, the tribes had much more confidence. The people grieved for their murdered matriarch along with so many others in the heart camp and were angry at the injustice Konag Mandan had heaped on them.

In the wreckage of the tents and overturned carts, someone had found Shella din Orr's intricate rug with its countless threads denoting family lines. Penda had the rug cleaned and repaired, then hung on the wall of their throne room, where the bloody painting had once been. For the time being, Penda Orr spoke for the combined tribes, but the Utauks would hold their own large convocation when all representatives could travel together before winter set in. They would choose a leader for their own people, and one to speak with the three kingdoms on their behalf. Inside the circle, outside the circle.

Glik entered the throne room, carrying baby Oak in her arms. The girl had been cleaned up—under protest—and given acceptable court clothes, marked with the colors of many Utauk tribes, since she belonged to all of them.

She had recently become inseparable from their infant daughter, and insisted on caring for Oak, shooing away Hom and any other members of the castle staff who tried to share in the work. Her blue ska flew around the halls and into the throne room, often accompanied by Xar. Glik paid no attention to courtly expectations or rules, much to the consternation of ministers, vassal lords, or trade representatives. Adan found it amusing.

As Konag Adan and Queen Penda held court, a man entered the throne room and presented himself as Mak Dur, a former voyagier whose trading ship had been seized and conscripted into the Commonwealth navy. He was a dark-haired, confident man who showed deference and respect, but with a hint of swagger.

"My beloved *Glissand* was damaged in the recent battle at Fulcor Island," he said. "And then ruined when we came back to Rivermouth Harbor. She was a beautiful trading ship, neutral, and served Konag Conndur and Hale

Orr several times, before Mandan's navy seized her, forced her to war." His voice caught. "And Utho wrecked her."

Both Penda and Adan winced. Adan said, "This is only one of countless similar stories we have heard. Mandan was only konag for a short while, but in that time . . . ah, so much damage."

Mak Dur straightened, found more strength, and continued. "For weeks, I've made my home on land among other Utauks, but my heart is at sea. My heart was with the *Glissand*. What's left of her is still scuttled at the docks in Rivermouth. If at some point you could find a way to grant me the means to repair and rebuild my ship, I would be happy to serve as your swift and reliable messenger, whenever and wherever you need me. And these days, you will need my services a great deal, all up and down the coast and even to Ishara. The whole world needs to know what has happened." The voyagier raised his chin. "So long as I'm allowed to trade cargo as well."

Penda smiled. "The *Glissand* . . . my father sailed with him."

Mak Dur bowed. "Yes, Hale Orr led us to great adventure and profit."

"It will take decades to make all the reparations necessary after this war," Adan said with a sigh, "but it is a debt the Commonwealth owes you. Yes, we will surely need your services."

112

֍

A STEADY breeze pressed against the striped sails, driving the Isharan flagship across the water. Cemi stood at the bow with Vos at her side, as always. She inhaled the fresh air, remembering when she and Empra Iluris had sailed to Fulcor Island. The garrison there had been a bleak and ugly place, a barren rock in a strategic position. And what had happened there . . .

Her first glimpse of the Osterran coastline, though, was green and beautiful, not at all like the drained wasteland that Key Priestlord Klovus had claimed the old world must be. This continent looked different from home, yes, but alive. Fishing villages surrounded small harbors, boats bobbed on the water, and gentle hills rose up from the shoreline covered with a patchwork of crops, vineyards, and orchards.

"Their main harbor is a place called Rivermouth," Vos said. "We have charts that Klovus took from that Utauk trading ship."

"Assume the entrance will be guarded by the Commonwealth navy," Cemi said, unable to cover her concern. "We must fly a peace flag. They have no idea we're coming. Or why."

"Very well." Vos hoped they would not encounter the navy. Cemi faced forward, silently promising to bring her message to the konag.

The prow had once carried an iron-fist battering ram, but Cemi had replaced it with a polished figurehead of Empra Iluris in a flowing gown, created by a Serepol woodcarver. An Isharan banner fluttered from the foremast—definitely not a flag of war.

During the voyage from Serepol Harbor, Cemi had had plenty of time to think, but no chance to reconsider. The flagship was guided by adept navigation and a little bit of magic from two priestlords who joined the diplomatic mission. Cemi hadn't allowed them to bring a godling, however. She was confident in her wisdom.

She smiled at Vos as the coastline grew nearer. "It's good that I'm a new empra and not set in my ways. I can be nimble, open to new possibilities." Her voice became quieter. "And I hope their new konag is, as well."

They approached the wide harbor formed by the mouth of the river. Numerous ships were tied up to docks, while others sailed in the open water, some of them heading down the coast. Trading ships, fishing vessels, not warships.

Vos said, "We don't know what our great godling did when it journeyed here, or even what happened there after . . . after Fulcor, when Konag Conndur was murdered."

"Murdered by his own man," Cemi pointed out, "from what we know of that night."

Vos's brow furrowed. "But surely they blamed us, just as Key Priestlord Klovus attacked Iluris and blamed the konag's man. There are people who want war and destruction."

"Well, I am not one of them." Cemi gripped the rail and looked ahead. "I will talk with them, and I will hope."

A lookout from the mainmast shouted that ships were approaching.

Cemi glanced up at the distinctive red and white stripes on their sails. "I knew we'd be seen before long." She whispered under her breath. "Hear us, save us."

"I have a hundred hawk guards aboard, Excellency," Vos said. "We will protect you, no matter what."

"I don't want it to come to that," she said. "Head to the harbor. I make no secret of our intentions. Fly the truce flag."

"Hear us, save us," said one of the priestlords on deck.

The lookout called down. "I see a circle! A circle on their sails."

Cemi felt a quick flood of relief. "Utauks."

Vos nodded slowly. "That may be a good thing, Excellency."

The two Utauk ships came close enough so their crew could shout across the water. The merchant captain bellowed, "We are not military ships. We were just curious."

"We are not a military ship either," Cemi said. "I'm the empra of Ishara on a mission of peace to see your konag. It's time we resolved our differences."

The second Utauk vessel stayed farther away, letting the first captain speak for both of them. He shouted, "Konag Adan will be glad to hear that. We are all weary of war."

Cemi allowed herself a moment of optimism.

The Utauk captain called, "Let us guide you through Rivermouth and up to the confluence." He added, as an afterthought, "We'd like nothing more than to restore routine trade with Ishara."

The empra's flagship followed the two Utauk vessels into the large harbor.

113

⁓

ᴀ ᴍᴇꜱꜱᴇɴɢᴇʀ raced up the river road with an urgent report: An Isharan
ship had arrived at Rivermouth—a diplomatic vessel, not a warship—
and Utauk traders were guiding it up the Joined River. "The Isharan empra
herself is aboard!" the messenger said. "She says she wants to forge a peace."

Adan was shocked, but pleased. "I did not expect this, did not expect her."
He glanced over at Penda.

"But of course we will listen, won't we?" she asked.

He breathed faster, trying to believe what he had heard. "My father spoke
with the empra on Fulcor, made overtures of peace, until it all went badly. I
don't know why she would be willing to try again."

"Oh, this isn't the old empra," the messenger said. "It's a young woman, a
new empra named Cemi. I doubt she's even twenty years old."

Adan called up a welcoming escort to guide the empra and her party as
soon as the Isharan ship pulled up to one of the intact docks on the river
below the castle, while his ministers rushed about the castle, preparing to
receive the leader of Ishara.

Adan held out hope. This might be one of his most important meetings as
konag. Conndur had already made peace overtures—with Utho and Mandan
present—which had gone disastrously wrong. Would Ishara demand revenge
and restitution, or would the empra be willing to listen?

But this was a new empra, as he was a new konag . . . and this was a new
world.

He and Penda sat on their thrones as the great chamber filled with vassal
lords, advisors, functionaries, all of them curious. Glik joined them, having
begrudgingly washed again and donned clean clothes.

Two days earlier, Elliel and Onder had arrived with a group of Brava children, asking for them to be quartered and given assignments at the castle so
she and Onder could set up a training school for them. Now, while Onder
worked with the trainees in one of the open yards, Elliel came to stand by
Adan in the throne room as the konag's bonded Brava, and Cheth stood at
the queen's side. They made impressive guardians.

Empra Cemi was escorted into the castle with a contingent of her hawk
guards in vibrant red and gold uniforms. The young woman was petite,
pretty, and tough. Adan wondered if she had been thrust into this position

unexpectedly, under dramatic circumstances, just as he had found himself with the crown. They probably both had many stories to share, answers to give, legacies to record. Cemi looked young and fresh, but her eyes held a deep wisdom, and she walked with confidence. This was not a fragile little girl but someone who understood that she ruled an entire continent.

Unexpectedly, breaking protocol, Adan rose from his throne as she approached, giving respect to the empra of Ishara. Penda stood as well, and the two of them extended hands in greeting.

Standing before the two thrones, Cemi gave a formal bow of acknowledgment. "We are strangers to each other, Konag Adan. I do not know Commonwealth politics or your background, but I'm given to understand that neither of us expected to rule our respective lands."

Adan smiled. "You're right. This is not where I expected to be. My father . . ."

"Your father was Conndur the Brave," Cemi said. "I was at Fulcor Island myself, and I heard him speak. I heard him make his offer to Empra Iluris, and I know what he wanted for our lands. My predecessor . . . my mentor wanted the same. I was with her there. I heard her talk. Iluris believed we could end the division between our two continents, but she . . . she was attacked and nearly killed in an act of heinous treachery."

"We did not have anything to do with that," Adan said quickly. "It was—"

The young empra looked up. "I know. Konag Conndur was also killed that night. Ishara was meant to take the blame, but it was not us."

Adan nodded. "We know that now. Every person responsible has met the proper justice." He glanced at Elliel, who had paled, but remained motionless and implacable.

"Too many people have died for those misunderstandings," Penda said.

"We wanted Ishara's help," Adan continued. "There was a terrible threat from the past—the wreths meant to wake the dragon and destroy the world. They nearly succeeded."

"Even from Ishara, we sensed the evil here," Cemi said. "Our most powerful godling . . ."

Whispers rippled among the audience in the throne room. Adan nodded. "Your godling helped to destroy Ossus, the dragon at the heart of the world. Our combined armies with all their strength and weapons could not defeat Ossus alone. Your godling used itself up and brought new life to our tired and damaged lands. It helped save all of us."

Empra Cemi bowed. "My . . . Empra Iluris was part of the godling."

Penda reached over and took her husband's hand. "We have a baby daughter, and now it seems that we all have a future."

"If we don't destroy it," Adan said. "I'm glad you came to us. I hope you'll stay long enough for us to talk and build a new foundation for our two lands."

Empra Cemi smiled. "I have no hatred for your people—I do not know you, Konag Adan and Queen Penda, but I would like to start afresh. Perhaps we can open trade between the Commonwealth and Ishara."

Elliel glanced at Adan. At his slight nod, she spoke up, looking over at Cheth. "Our race held an ancient grievance with Ishara because our colony was massacred. Some Bravas have long called for a vengewar, but . . ."

Cheth interrupted, "But that was long ago."

The young empra clearly knew what they were talking about, and she looked ashamed. "I learned the history because Key Priestlord Klovus wanted to know. I found the records he discovered, and we located the site of your long-lost colony."

"Valaera," Elliel said. "Every Brava knows that legend and feels the pain. It . . . it drove Utho mad."

"I can't erase the pain," Cemi said, "but I can acknowledge the injustice that was done, so long ago. We know the exact place, and if . . ." She paused and drew a deep breath. Her hawk guards stiffened, coming to attention. "If some of your people would like to visit the site of Valaera . . . I am willing to discuss it."

Still holding hands, Adan and Penda stepped down from the raised platform to meet the Isharan empra. "Your words gladden our hearts, Empra Cemi. Shall we begin with a provisional truce while we develop an official treaty?"

"I agree on that, if you'll set aside time for some trade negotiations," the empra said.

With a warm smile, Queen Penda said, "You arrived at an auspicious time. We hope you will all stay to be our guests for the coronation of Konag Adan Starfall."

114

ے

R IDING on the buckboard of a rickety wagon beside the windcaster, Priestlord Erical—or perhaps he was just Erical now—thought of when he had walked from Prirari District to reach the capital city, expecting to attend the consecration of the Magnifica. He had admired the varied landscapes of Ishara as he made his way, and the rejuvenating energy of his godling helped carry him along.

Now he sat on a rough wooden seat as the old nag pulled them forward. His body was sore—especially the part he sat on—from the wheels rattling over the rocks and ruts.

Old Mystia also ached, but she was happy to join him on this long journey. "We made you welcome enough in our village," she said. "Don't know why you'd want to look for a ship and sail across the sea just to get back to the land that sent you away in the first place." She snorted. "If the new konag even allows it."

"He's said that Isharans can go home," Erical said. "There were prisoners held in one of the counties up north, and they'll want to be reunited with their families." He heaved a hopeful sigh. "I do miss my temple and the people. The godling is always with them. If they kept making sacrifices and maintained their prayers, then part of her is still there. I need to lead them as their priestlord."

"I suppose that's more important than helping me around the cottage," the windcaster grumbled.

Erical extended his thoughts into the air and tried to find any glimmers of his godling, any colorful residue. When he caught a stray glint of light, a momentary shimmer from the corner of his eye, he wanted to believe, but he decided it was just a false hope.

The road swung inland, heading westward toward the confluence. Over the next day, they made their way toward Convera, picking up news and gossip along the way. Erical was pleased to learn that Isharan ships had come to the Commonwealth, bringing the empra and her hawk guards on a mission of peace. Erical could hardly believe what he was hearing.

"The empra is alive then?" he asked the farmer who had passed along the gossip. When he set sail with the Isharan navy, Iluris had been missing for a long time.

"Why wouldn't she be?" asked the farmer. "It'd be a foolish thing to sail across the sea with a dead empra, wouldn't it?"

Mystia nodded, agreeing that was true.

After more confused and awkward conversation, Erical learned that the empra was not Iluris, but a young woman, barely more than a girl. Erical was amazed. "And does Key Priestlord Klovus still serve the Magnifica temple in Serepol?"

The farmer looked at him as if he'd spoken a different language. "How would I know any of that?"

The old windcaster nudged Erical in annoyance. She set the old nag into motion again, pulling the wagon, and said to the farmer, "We wouldn't expect you to. We'll learn more in Convera." She cracked the reins, although the plodding horse didn't seem to manage any more speed.

The capital city was crowded and colorful in preparation for the upcoming coronation ceremony. Konag Adan's vassal lords had come from all across Osterra, Suderra, and Norterra.

As they entered the outskirts of the sprawling city, Erical was astonished, never having seen anything like this before. The culture of the Commonwealth was quite different from Ishara's, from the smells of foods to the banners, the architecture, the music played on street corners, the clothing of the families who worked in shops and their customers. Special coronation markets had sprung up, selling all forms of souvenirs and trinkets that commemorated the crowning of Adan Starfall.

Mystia was just as amazed, because Convera was so unlike her tiny village of Windy Head. The wagon horse was more intimidated than impressed, and they had to halt for the old woman to mount blinders so it wouldn't get spooked.

Erical looked ahead up to the castle on the bluff, where numerous supplicants pushed toward the open gates, waving and shouting greetings up toward the towers. Joining the press of people, Erical screwed up his courage and explained that he was Isharan and needed to see the empra.

Those words earned him many stares, but because his request was so bold and because his features did have a foreign look to them, Erical made his way through the outer guards to another ring of guards. A stable handler promised to take care of the horse and their battered old cart.

It took him several hours, but he did catch the attention of those he needed to ask. Finally, he and Mystia made their way to one of the wings of the castle, where the young empra and her entourage were staying as they awaited the coronation ceremony.

The hawk guards, resplendent in gold armor and red capes, regarded Erical with skepticism and surprise. The captani asked, "Were you one of the captives being held up north? A saltpearl diver?"

Erical shook his head. "No, not at all. I came here with the Isharan navy and was shipwrecked on the coast. I . . . Not many of us survived. I may be the only one."

He glanced up as a young woman approached from a back room. She wore colorful Isharan gowns with her head wrapped in scarves, just as Empra Iluris had dressed. But this empra was much younger, just in her teens. She was—

"You're the street girl in Prirari!" Erical gasped. "You offered a rat to my godling!"

The young woman turned toward him, and her eyes flashed with recognition. "You look different—well worn, but not quite used up yet. You're the Prirari priestlord."

"I'm Erical," he said. The captani glanced at the empra and she nodded. Erical stood before her, bowing, unable to believe what he was seeing. "You're the empra now? The girl Iluris took under her wing!"

"Yes, I'm Empra Cemi." As soon as she spoke, colored lights appeared in the corner of his eye. The priestlord shook his head, trying to clear the distraction. Again, the sparkles appeared, but closer, with a flash of barely visible rainbow hues.

Empra Cemi glanced around, noticing them as well.

Erical caught his breath and began searching, but the glimmers swirled to one side, dancing just out of his line of sight.

He felt a warmth in his heart, though. "Excellency, I am Priestlord Erical." With those words, the faint vestiges of the godling grew brighter and stronger.

115

❧

HUGE crowds gathered in front of Convera's main remembrance shrine. Adan was glad for everyone who attended: faithful bodyguards—including his bonded Bravas—advisors, appreciative subjects, and friends, but he could never forget the cost of what they had all been through. Thankfully, he did see a brighter path ahead, for the three kingdoms and for Ishara.

Two days earlier, King Kollanan had arrived with Birch in Convera, accompanied by his own Brava Lasis, as well as the scholar girl Shadri. Kollanan brought word from the wreth queen, which also pleased Adan and gave him confidence. He was relieved, however, that a party of sandwreths and frostwreths had not come to the coronation. . . .

Countless Utauks flashed their clan colors, whistling and shouting as they lined the main street leading to the large square where the coronation would take place. They led the crowd in a cheering welcome as the new konag and his queen glided along on the procession. Adan knew they were celebrating Penda at least as much as they celebrated him, and he couldn't have been happier. He would need the Utauk tribes, their trade, and their information to knit the three kingdoms back together into one strong Commonwealth.

He looked up, following Penda's gaze. In the sky, hundreds of colorful skas circled, Xar among them. Much higher, he saw a flash of gold, maybe just a glint of bright sun in his eye . . . or maybe an iridescent dragon flying just out of sight.

Xar swooped down, a flash of green feathers and emerald scales, teasing Adan—just as when the reptile bird had stolen his pendant in Bannriya, long ago . . . and that had led to him meeting his beloved Penda in the first place. Adan felt warm inside as he remembered. Xar burbled and flew up into the air again.

A blue ska flitted in, chasing Xar away. Glik laughed as she rode beside Konag Adan and Queen Penda, holding baby Oak against her. The Utauk girl turned the child, showing her all the colorful distractions of the celebration. "Inside the circle," she said. "All of us inside the circle, now."

They reached the remembrance shrine, and a hush fell over the crowd. King Kollanan was already there, standing proud in plush Norterran furs and an embroidered tunic, next to the chief legacier. The scholar girl was at the front of the crowd, looking up with starry eyes at the remembrance shrine.

The implacable stone lions stared out at the sea of people as Adan and Penda ascended the platform, holding hands. Together they turned to Chief Legacier Vicolia. The tall, thin woman wore brown robes trimmed in gold, and she looked supremely important. A polished marble slab had been raised behind her, showing Adan's name deeply engraved in the stone, beside Penda's.

By special arrangement, Empra Cemi and her hawk guard entourage waited in a section to the left, honored as important dignitaries. News of the Isharan peace overtures had swept through the capital, and although many people were skeptical of the age-old enemies, others were relieved that another bloody war was not looming.

Adan felt light-headed and happy.

The chief legacier spoke on and on, reciting the words she had written for the momentous occasion. Finally, King Kollanan stepped forward and cut her off. "Thank you. A remarkable speech, Legacier. But it's time to let Konag Adan get on with his rule!"

The king of Norterra extended the konag's crown, and Adan bowed as his uncle reverently placed it on his head. The crown felt heavy, too ornate, filled with jewels, but as the plaza resounded with a welcoming cheer, Adan felt stronger.

Konag Adan.

The chief legacier bowed and spread her hands. "Long life and a great legacy, Konag Adan."

The crowd shouted, "Long life and great legacy!"

"It must all be written down," said Vicolia. "We have teams of legaciers who will chronicle all the events in your life, Sire."

Adan regarded the stern, self-important woman for a moment, then gestured toward the eager face at the front of the crowd. "Thank you, but I've already chosen a legacier. I will tell her all the details I can remember, and she will record them."

Vicolia was taken aback, but Adan continued, "Shadri is the konag's legacier." He beckoned to her. "Come forward so that everyone can see you and know that they should cooperate and help you in any manner." Raising his eyebrows, he gave the chief legacier a pointed look.

The scholar girl bounded up onto the platform, and Kollanan surprised them all by embracing her as she passed him. Shadri's eyes were sparkling.

Adan said, "I am trusting you to write my legacy. Do you feel up to it?"

Shadri said, "I do. I'll write every bit of it! It will be a great story."

Penda smiled and glanced at Adan. Together, they traced a circle around their hearts. "The beginning is the end is the beginning."

ACKNOWLEDGMENTS

Special thanks to all those who helped with the heavy lifting on this trilogy, especially Tom Doherty, Christopher Morgan, Beth Meacham, John Silbersack, Diane Jones, and, as always, Rebecca Moesta.